1914

A NOVEL

Charles B. Smith

1914 is a work of fiction. Though it is set within an historical framework, the characters, places, entities, institutions and events depicted herein are either fictional, or are portrayed in a fictitious manner. Interactions with historical figures are likewise fictitious.

ISBN-13: 978-1494236007
ISBN-10: 1494236001

www.charles-b-smith.com

For those who served

PROLOGUE

It took time for his eyes to adjust to the change. Transitioning from the warm, bright morning sun into the low, incandescent light in the pit made the lengthy and gloomy descent seem that much gloomier. The faint, yellow-orange glow from the light bulbs strung along the wall illuminated what would have otherwise been a pitch-black tunnel, and they were spaced just far enough apart so that each bulb's light barely overlapped with the next.

Eerie silhouettes and shadows danced across the walls as the lights slowly pulsated from the current flowing through them. Were the electric lights replaced by torches, he and his coworkers could just as easily have been entering a subterranean dungeon, pulled straight from the pages of a medieval legend. Actually, from what he'd read of medieval dungeons as a child, some sounded downright quaint in comparison to where he was headed.

As he walked, his eyes followed the insulated wires and cables which ran along the sides of the floor and the walls—umbilical cords for the machines waiting idly at the end of the shaft. Two sets of parallel steel tracks ran along the center of the floor, and would soon have coal carts rumbling along them as they guided full carts to the surface and brought the empty ones back. The heavy wooden beams set into the shaft's walls and low ceiling held at bay millions of cubic feet of earth, and were all that separated the men moving down the tunnel from entombment and untimely death.

He scrutinized every beam as he walked underneath, and silently prayed that each squared arch would continue to successfully do the

5

one thing it was supposed to do. That was his ritual every time he traveled beneath the surface; cringing on the inside each time he passed a beam. Mining was a grown man's job, and though he was tall and strong he was still young—a boy of just seventeen. His eighteenth birthday would arrive in a week, but that made him feel no older or safer. It also made him no less apprehensive about descending ever deeper underground. He didn't want the other men to know, but even after three years, the descent into the pit still bothered him.

The change in scenery was one thing, but the change in atmosphere was another. He'd worked at the Wharncliffe-Silkestone Colliery since the age of thirteen, first as an errand boy, performing assorted tasks for the foreman, all aboveground. His father got him the job after he'd quit school and refused to go back. Working aboveground at a coal mine was dirty enough, but when he turned fifteen, he started working underground and was exposed to the true meaning of filthiness. Three years later, he still felt unaccustomed to moving from the fresh air at the surface to the musty, choking air of the underground shafts.

Coal dust covered everything down there. When moving feet kicked it up, the fine dust lingered in the air, suspended like fog. He could smell it, even *taste* it, bitter and noxious. If a man (or a boy) planned on breathing in the pit, then he was forced to inhale air saturated with the microscopic black granules. At shift's end, it always jarred him to sneeze or spit and see dark grey mucus ejected from his nose or mouth. That stuff did not belong inside anyone's body.

Further down the shaft, the air density and temperature changed considerably. At first, it grew cooler, but past a certain point in the descent the temperature began to increase. Each step brought him closer to the fires of Hell. If the miners kept digging deeper, he thought, then one day somebody would eventually knock through the wrong wall and come face to face with Satan himself. The devil had to be down there somewhere, for why else would the conditions be so hot and miserable?

The warm, stifling, oxygen-depleted air made normal breathing much more difficult. When the sweating started, as it inevitably would, the soot clung to moist skin, staining it a greasy black. The other men moving down the tunnel had all worked there longer. He always wondered if they were still disgusted by the grime that came along with the job. He knew his father didn't much care for it, and the old man had been doing it for more than twenty years. Most days, father and son walked down the shaft together to start their shift, but his dad had the day off, a rarity to say the least.

6

Some conversed and joked on their trip down, but the boy wasn't paying attention to their banter. He just wanted to get to work. The quicker they got to it, the quicker the day would go by and he could wash up and go home. His best friend would return from his first year of university later that day, and the two hadn't seen each other for several weeks. It'd be nice to catch up, and he looked forward to it.

When they reached the end of the shaft, the walls fanned out, revealing the machinery, empty carts and equipment they'd use to break up and remove the coal deposits in the low-ceilinged cavern. The electric coal cutter helped expedite the work, but every man carried his own pickaxe as well. It was darker in there; the coal embedded in the walls seemed to gobble up the light. For additional lighting, some of the miners carried safety lamps. The handheld lamps were a convenient, mobile and safe way to more brightly light a specific area. In the past, lamps with open flames were the standard, but as mining grew more complex and reached deeper into Earth, the risk of gas explosions grew, rendering such primitive contrivances dangerous and obsolete.

The miners took their places to commence chopping, cutting, lifting and moving. The boy's primary job was shoveling the piles of busted up coal onto an electric conveyor belt, which then deposited the coal into a waiting cart. He worked hard, straining his back all morning. Noon came and went, and then it was time for lunch, and not a moment too soon; he'd worked up quite the appetite. The group returned to the surface, and he retrieved his old, tarnished and dented tin lunch pail. His mother had put a hefty roast beef sandwich inside, and he was grateful she still made him a lunch before every shift. He devoured the tasty sandwich, drank a cup of tea, and prepared to head back into the shaft to finish out the day.

Less than two hundred feet inside the tunnel, the foreman caught up to the group. "Hold on, lad," he said, "I need you to move these empty crates out of here." The man pointed to three sizeable, heavy wooden boxes set against the wall. They were empty, having once contained coils of cable or something of that sort. It was partly that the foreman still sometimes viewed him as an errand boy, but also because the foreman was small and skinny and the boy was big and strong, that the man asked specifically for his help.

The boy watched the rest of the men disappear down the tunnel and the foreman exit to the surface, and then he placed his large hands on either side of the first crate. He let out a grunt before lifting it off the floor. Even empty, the crate was substantial, and carrying it two hundred feet out of the shaft was not an easy thing to do. By the

7

time he'd made it to the surface, his whole body shook from the expenditure. His fingers throbbed from pressing them into the wood to maintain his grip. And he still had two more crates to go.

Trudging back down, he shook his hands to wiggle away the ache in his fingers. He placed his hands atop the second crate to gather himself, but before he could lift, the light bulbs along the wall in front of him flashed considerably brighter. They made an audible hum. They flickered. A rush of air move past him down the tunnel, and then *BOOM!* The noise and tremors from a large explosion emanated from further within the shaft. The sound reverberated through his entire body. The entire world shook. There weren't many earthquakes in England, not major ones at least, but that must have been what they were like.

"Oh no..." he said, just as a strange blackness began crawling up the shaft toward him. The boy turned to run, but the creeping dark mass was much faster. It caught up quickly, and enveloped him in a cloud of rushing air, dirt and coal dust. It knocked him forward, but the boy caught himself with his hands and continued to scramble from the tunnel, blinded by the suffocating black haze. When he stumbled into the afternoon sunlight and the black dust cloud billowing out of the shaft entrance dissipated, a flurry of activity began. The workers on the surface reacted quickly. They moved with intense, concerned purpose. The boy did not.

From head to toe, every inch of his body was covered in a thick, black layer of dust. Barely able to breathe and mentally jarred by the darkness that had chased after him, the boy walked around dazed and aimless. In shock, he stumbled about while the running and shouting men moved past him and into the shaft.

"Hey, kid! What in the hell just happened?!" the foreman hollered. "What did you see?!" He grabbed the boy by his arms.

"I...don't...I don't know," the boy mumbled back, unable to assemble any coherent thoughts. He obviously couldn't tell *exactly* what happened, how could he, but judging from the noise and the rumbling, there had either been a gas explosion or a tunnel collapse, maybe both. Whatever it was, it had most likely killed some of his coworkers, of that he was almost certain.

He was a big lad, working a man's job, and men weren't supposed to be afraid, they weren't supposed to cry, but his close call had frightened him greatly and he fought back tears as the foreman looked him in the eyes.

"All right, young lad," the foreman said, letting go of the boy's arms to give him a firm hug, "you're all right."

Sometimes, men took a risk when they took a job. That was their choice. The boy had made that same choice at a very young age, one at which such choices should not even have been an option. He was *still* young, in fact, maybe too young to be there, but he was there, because he was allowed to be. And now he had to deal with the ramifications.

He couldn't help it; he'd just received the scare of his life. Men he knew personally had just died in an accident that easily could have claimed him too. The reservoirs behind his eyes, which he battled to keep from overflowing, had already reached capacity. An invisible hand clutched at his throat, choking him. Had a simple twist of fate not intervened, he'd have been standing right alongside those men. Worse, on any other day his father would have been there as well. It was too much.

Cognizant that simple chance had spared his family, guilt overcame him. The other miners had families, too, but they'd benefited from no such luck. As the foreman patted his upper back, the boy slumped forward and rested his head on the man's shoulder, and he cried.

GORDON

Gordon Graham stood back and proudly marveled at his work, the culmination of an obsession which began fifteen years earlier, when he was just six years old. Fully assembled, his creation never would have fit inside the barn, so he'd finished the assembly outside. It had been a long journey to get to this point. In minutes, he'd find out if the time spent had been worth it.

In the summer of 1899, while walking home from a friend's house on the outskirts of Dayton, Ohio, Gordon happened upon two men in a large field. The two gentlemen were flying an enormous double-decker kite, performing their first experiments testing wing warping as a means for controlling heavier-than-air flying machines. Gordon watched in awe as the men manipulated different wires, moving the kite back and forth across the sky. Enraptured, he resolved in that moment, as a little boy, that he would learn everything he could about the forces that kept the kite airborne. He went back to the field every day that summer, patiently watching from afar, hoping to see those two men testing their prototypes. Some days his patience was rewarded, some days not.

Gordon began his first year of school at the end of that same summer. He was a smart little boy, and school was easy for him. He achieved top marks in his classes and did all the work, but he did it all as fast as possible so every day he could get back to the field and spy, at least until winter began and the kite experiments halted. Dur-

10

ing free time in class, he made tiny kites with paper and string, and would run across the schoolyard trailing his miniature creations behind him as soon as the bell sounded.

When winter ended and the weather warmed, Gordon returned to the field with the brave intention of asking the two men some questions, but they didn't come back. As it turned out, they had moved their experiments to the sandy beaches of Kitty Hawk, North Carolina, where higher winds and smoother terrain promised them added freedom and safety to begin their experiments with manned gliders.

For the next three years, little Gordon paid close attention to the careers of Orville and Wilbur Wright. He also sought, at all corners, to improve his understanding of kite-making and beyond that, aerodynamics. He read what he could find, read books that were vastly beyond the comprehension level of other children his age, but it was sometimes difficult to get his hands on the most up-to-date material. His father, Anson, bought him a number of books and journals, but could offer little help beyond that, because he owned his own fledgling bricklaying company and worked long hours. Gordon's mother Virginia ran the Graham household, and while she encouraged him to pursue whatever piqued his interest, she wasn't much help either. Nor did Gordon's older siblings have much to offer him; they didn't share in his passion.

On December 17, 1903, at Kitty Hawk, the Wrights became the first men credited with flying a piloted, heavier-than-air machine when Orville made a short hop of 120 feet in their *Wright Flyer I.* The flight lasted just twelve seconds. An historic precedent was set, and a ten-year-old Gordon proudly displayed the December 18 issue of *The Dayton Herald* with the headline "Dayton Boys Solve Problem" in a frame on his bedroom wall.

As Gordon grew older, his understanding of aeronautical principles ballooned. He was able to procure ever more books and journals pertaining to aeroplanes, as they had come to be known. His favorites were *Progress in Flying Machines* by Octave Chanute, and *Artificial and Natural Flight*, by Hiram Maxim, the inventor of the machine gun. He also read his copies of *The Aeronautical Journal*, a publication from England, until they were worn to tatters.

In 1910, at the age of seventeen, with a firm knowledge base and the confidence that he had what it took to do it, Gordon decided it was time to try and build his own flying machine. The sport of flying was catching on across the civilized world, and many amateur fliers had begun purchasing or building their own aeroplanes. Although he could not possibly have afforded to buy one outright, building his own alleviated some of the costs, allowed him to spread those costs over time, and additionally allowed him the freedom to employ some of his own ideas in design.

The most interesting things in aviation at that time were happening in Europe, particularly France, but Gordon would not be headed there any time soon, he thought, so he made do with what he could in Dayton. He worked on his project piecemeal. First, he spent weeks drawing up precise plans. Then he began purchasing spruce wood, piano wire, fabric and plywood whenever he could afford it. Provided he had the requisite supplies, he spent every second of his spare time assembling his design elements.

Like his three older brothers, he worked for his father laying bricks, but unlike them, all of Gordon's money went into his passion for flight. He toiled for two years that way, slowly putting his machine together, reading of the advances in the science of flight, expanding upon his considerable intellect in a great many subjects, while simultaneously getting bigger and stronger helping his old man.

At the end of May in 1912, right about the midpoint of his project, Gordon learned that Wilbur Wright had died of typhoid fever. That, coupled with further news that the *Wright Flyers* purchased for testing by the U.S. Army were having their safety called into question following a series of fatal crashes, was disheartening and nearly made Gordon give up the entire venture. In the end, though, he could not abandon his project and resumed his work after a three week hiatus.

During the final six months of the assembly, he saved every cent he could scrounge to purchase a small motor, which would power his two hand-made propellers and take him aloft for the first time. He'd spent weeks measuring, carving, sanding and finishing his hardwood propeller blades. Such precision was essential, as even the slightest inconsistency or imbalance could cause dangerous reverberations capable of shaking his machine to pieces.

The motor was used, and fairly similar to the one the Wrights utilized eleven years earlier. Though aviation had only been around for a decade, the engine was underpowered and outdated, only able to make twenty horsepower. In spite of its age, Gordon had faith it could get the job done. The instant he got the motor home and into the barn, he dismantled it, and took the time to learn the intricacies of a basic internal combustion engine. He'd enjoyed every aspect of the four year project, absorbed every bit of knowledge he could and now, on that early summer day in 1914, he hoped all his hard work would bear fruit.

"Gordy are you sure this thing will fly?" asked his younger sister Liza. Her eyebrows were furled with concern for her brother's safety. She was a cute little thing, overdressed for the occasion in a dark blue, short-sleeved dress with a big white bow dangling from the collar. Her frizzy hair was gathered in a bunch atop her head and, as she often did in the summertime, she wore no shoes. The Grahams had long since abandoned asking her to wear them; Liza claimed her feet just needed to breathe.

"Absolutely not," Gordon answered her, with his golden-boy smile. "But it certainly won't if I don't try." He was as good-looking as they came—a strong jaw, a great smile, chiseled features and a chiseled frame, made sturdy by hard work. His eyes were grey, but not grey in the conventional sense. Grey, so often associated with drab, did not do them justice. They were bright. They shone. Like him, they were strong, at least as eyes went. Stronger than anything else, though, was his mind. His parents and his siblings were smart, or smart enough, but he was far more than that. Whatever intellectual capacities were engrained in Anson and Virginia Graham's blood, their son Gordon had inherited all of it, and then some.

Dressed far more appropriately for the task at hand than was his little sister, Gordon wore dirty grey coveralls, the same pair he'd bought at Woolworth's four years prior and worn every day since when working on his aeroplane. Brother and sister stood next to Gordon's machine in the large field behind their house. He'd spent eight hours the previous day cutting the high golden grass in a forty foot wide strip down the middle of the field, the same strip that now stretched out for hundreds of yards ahead of him. Today was the day, no question about it. A light breeze drifted directly toward him; it would provide an optimal amount of added lift. The conditions were perfect.

"Do you have the camera ready?" he asked.

"Yup."

"Okay. Take some shots of me standing beside the machine, then run down the field and take more when I'm off the ground."

"You got it. Don't forget to smile."

Liza was thirteen years old, and Gordon's favorite sibling. She also just so happened to love photography, and owned a No. 1A Kodak Junior camera, one of the first cameras to use film. Gordon wanted pictures, to prove to his peers that he'd taken to the air in a machine of his own design. He posed proudly, chin held high, for three photographs in front of his biplane, which wasn't entirely dissimilar in appearance from the *Wright Flyer*. Then he took a deep breath and climbed aboard the flimsy wood and fabric craft.

The machine was mostly open space, with just a small seat in the center of the craft, situated between the lower and upper planes. The planes were made of plywood skin bent over thin, spruce-wood ribs, and were joined together by thin spruce struts which ran vertically from the upper surface of the lower plane to the underside of the top plane. The struts were spaced evenly apart near the wings' leading and trailing edges. Piano wires, strung diagonally from the top of each strut to the bottom of the one next to it (and vice versa), criss-crossed each other in an X between each set of struts for further bracing support.

Rather than placing the elevator (which moved up and down) in front of the craft and the rudder (which moved left to right) in back as in the *Wright Flyer*, Gordon chose to combine them at the tail of his craft, as he had seen photographs of the aeroplanes in Europe using such a configuration (it became the standard for virtually all aeroplanes).

In the *Wright Flyer*, the pilot laid on his stomach to more evenly balance his weight in the craft. Because he'd moved the elevator, thus changing the machine's weight distribution, Gordon knew that sitting in a seat, thus centralizing his weight, would make up for his moving the elevator to the tail section. He'd spent considerable time working the numbers and was certain he'd gotten the seat placement right.

The pilot of the Wright's machine also lay in a hip-cradle, which was attached to the wires that warped the wings (for banking the craft left and right) when the pilot moved his body side to side. Gordon dispensed with the hip cradle and instead opted to attach the warping wires to one of two control levers that he positioned in front of his seat. The wing-warping lever could move left and right to bank the craft, and pulling that same lever backward would raise the lower plane just high enough to create lift beneath it. Gordon designed the second lever using a wire configuration which allowed him to move the elevator by pushing the stick forward and backward, and the rudder by moving the stick side to side.

Gordon hunched over the back of his seat to fire up the motor, which he'd mounted behind it. When it chugged to a start, he watched excitedly as the counter-rotating, chain-driven propellers started spinning. The counter-rotation canceled out the propellers' torque, balancing the aircraft. If they'd rotated in the same direction as one another the craft would have had the tendency to fall in the opposite direction of their spin.

Like the *Wright Flyers*, Gordon's machine used a "pusher" configuration where the propellers, set behind the engine, faced the opposite direction in which the craft would travel, thus *pushing* it through the air ("tractor" configured craft placed the propellers in front of the engine, *pulling* it). To roll the craft down the field, Gordon mounted two children's bicycle wheels on a bracket underneath the lower plane beneath his seat, and a small metal skid beneath the short tail section, to prevent the machine's tail from dragging along the ground.

Liza tip-toed away, protecting her camera, and got into a favorable position downrange. She waved to let him know she was ready. She was cheering or something to that effect, but he could not hear her.

All right Gordon, this is it. Make Wilbur and Orville proud. He opened the throttle on the motor. Soon the airscrews were spinning fast enough to edge the craft forward. Within a few seconds, the machine had picked up speed and it rumbled sluggishly across the meadow, away from the Graham household. Gordon didn't know it at the time, but his mother, who claimed she was too afraid to watch her boy "fall from the sky like a rock," gazed out the back window, her curiosity overcoming her fear. Scared as she may have been, she was proud of her son's passion, determination and hard work.

The ground was much bumpier than it looked and as *The Hawk*—Gordon's name for his machine (for Kitty Hawk)—rolled faster and faster, he jostled back and forth in his seat. He'd pondered utilizing shock absorbers for the wheels, and they would have helped, but he couldn't spare the added weight. The engine was not powerful enough. The jolts and bumps the craft was taking made Gordon fear his machine might break apart before it had a chance to lift off. When he'd reached what he thought was sufficient speed, he gently pulled back on the wing-warping control stick and the elevator control and suddenly the bumping and jostling stopped. He got a tingle in his stomach as his craft left the field and then—weightlessness.

Son of a bitch it works! Gordon had done it! He howled in triumph. He'd become a man turned bird. He wasn't simply flying *The Hawk*, no, he <u>was</u> *The Hawk.* No longer was he the twenty-one year old man of mere seconds before, he now soared among the gods, an immortal, the master of a domain that but few others could ever say they'd braved. How could he possibly return to Earth an unchanged man after such an experience? Could he not just stay airborne forever? Gordon knew in that instant, from that point forth he *needed* aviation, every bit as much as a garden did water.

The wind rushed over his skin, a strong, soothing breeze, while the engine puttered away behind him. The machine inched higher, and in seconds, he'd reached a height taller than the weathervane atop the Graham's house. He passed over Liza, who had her camera aimed at him the whole way.

I'm high enough now. I should try a turn.

He pushed the warping control stick to the right, attempting a light bank. In his exhilaration, the push on the stick was too great, the left wing lifted too much, and twenty seconds after *The Hawk* took flight it fell hard to the right and crashed to the ground, crunching and splintering into a thousand pieces. In an instant, four years of hard work was now a pile of broken wood, twisted wire and torn fabric, and its builder lay right in the middle of it.

Gordon, dazed, but so far as he could tell, surprisingly unhurt, could hear his mother screaming his name off in the distance as she ran out the back door of the house. Closer to him Liza shrieked, "Gordy are you all right?!"

He climbed gingerly from the wreckage, unsure of the damage the crash had caused. He took a few steps back to get a better picture, his hope being he might salvage some of the materials and repair the machine within a matter of weeks. With his hands on his hips, Gordon stared at the remains of *The Hawk*. He shook his head and summed up exactly what the crash had left him to work with by mumbling just one word.

"Shit."

ARTHUR & PERCY

"I don't see how a dead Archduke should have anything to do with me," Percy shrugged, indifferent to what he'd just been told. He kept his eyes affixed to the glass of cheap, bottom-shelf scotch on the bar in front of him, only half paying attention.

"I know it seems like it shouldn't," Arthur answered, "but hear me out." Arthur was a good looking young man, with smooth features, soft blue eyes, and light brown hair, always parted left to right.

"Well why are you so wound up about it?" Percy asked. He turned his head to face his friend. A cursory look into Arthur's eyes revealed icy, unfamiliar blues staring back. They burned with rare intensity, a sure sign that he meant business.

"Let me talk for a spot and I'll get to that," Arthur said.

Percy blew a long breath out of the corner of his mouth. He had his suspicions his ear was about to be talked off.

It was Monday, June 29. An excited Arthur Ellis had just stormed into the pub to speak to his best friend Percy Ward, sidling up next to him and slapping a newspaper onto the bar. The front-page headline announced the previous day's assassination of Franz Ferdinand, Archduke of Austria and heir to the Austro-Hungarian throne. Ferdinand's wife Sophie, Duchess of Hohenburg, was also killed.

The Archduke was observing military exercises for the Austro-Hungarian army in the empire's southern province of Bosnia and Herzegovina, on orders from his father, Emperor Franz Joseph. Upon conclusion of the exercises, Ferdinand took Sophie on a tour of Bosnia's capital, Sarajevo, to attend a museum opening and to celebrate their upcoming anniversary. Shortly after their arrival in the city, while being chauffeured in an open-topped car, would-be assassin Nedeljko Čabrinović threw a bomb at the Archduke, which Ferdinand deflected away from his vehicle. The bomb detonated beneath a trailing car and injured several people. Čabrinović then swallowed a cyanide pill and jumped into a nearby river. The cyanide, not potent enough to kill him, only made him sick and he was promptly arrested.

After essentially brushing off the attempted assassination and continuing on to attend a reception in spite of very obvious danger, Ferdinand and Sophie then insisted on visiting those injured by the bomb in the hospital. In one of the more unfortunate navigational errors in human history, on the way to Sarajevo Hospital the driver of Ferdinand's car mistakenly turned onto a crowded side-street (coincidentally named Franz Joseph Street). After briefly coming to a stop before attempting to back out, the car stalled. A young Bosnian Serb named Gavrilo Princip emerged from the crowd and approached the Archduke's vehicle. He fired two shots from a small caliber pistol, striking Ferdinand in the neck and Sophie in the abdomen. Princip also took cyanide. Like Čabrinović, his suicide attempt failed, resulting in his arrest and subsequent imprisonment. Ferdinand and Sophie died before their wounds could be treated.

To emphasize the potential significance of what the assassination meant, Arthur pushed the newspaper forcefully into Percy's hands, bumping his glass and spilling some of the cheap scotch.

"Hey, what gives?" Percy said.

"Percy, the heir to the Austrian throne can't be murdered in a place like Bosnia without there being serious consequences!"

"Sure, I bet the chap what shot him is in heaps of trouble."

"No it's more than that!" Arthur said, striking the bar with his fist. "I just know it."

Some of the patrons in the dimly lit pub looked up from their drinks. Percy nodded to them and picked up his glass, raising what was left of it, before turning his attention back to his friend. He leaned toward Arthur and whispered, not wanting to cause another outburst. "All right, Art, I'm listening," Percy sighed. "But I know far less about this rubbish than you, and care even less than that, so if you've got some sort of point to make, go on and make it."

Arthur could smell the drink on Percy's breath. *Mid-afternoon and he's already pissed*, he thought. "Okay Percy, I'll try to explain as simply as I can." Arthur cleared his throat, indicating that he planned on speaking quite extensively. "The Balkans have been a sticky wick-et ever since Austria-Hungary annexed Bosnia from the Ottomans six years ago."

The "Balkans" are the states of the south-easternmost peninsula of Europe, across the Adriatic Sea from Italy (Greece is on the southern tip of the Balkan Peninsula). Because of the wide diversity of races, cultures, religions and languages which converged there, the Balkans were a highly tumultuous region.

Percy fought an internal battle to absorb what Arthur would say to him. A pub was no place for a history lesson, yet it sounded as if one was coming.

"Because Bosnia's population is Slavic, the Serbians believe it should belong to a Slavic state. They almost went to war with the Austrians over that very belief. Russia backed the Serbs, what with Slavs looking out for one another, so Serbia might have been able to make a strong case. Ultimately war was avoided because Germany is allied with Austria, meaning war with Austria meant war with Germany as well, and both we and France refused to offer Russia support, so they backed off."

Arthur took a deep breath to try and slow his heart rate; the anticipation of what he had to say was getting to him. He truly was wound up. He liked talking about this sort of thing anyway, but with an additional motive, it was even more exciting. Percy raised his eyebrows, still bewildered by that excitement.

"The Serbs still went to war, though," Arthur continued. "Do you remember when the Balkan states joined together and fought against the Ottomans, defeated them, but then couldn't decide how to divvy the territory they'd won so they fought each other?"

Percy remembered next to nothing about the First and Second Balkan Wars, fought from October 1912 to August 1913, and the tiny snippets he did all came from when Arthur tried to discuss the subject with him once before. He retained very little of it. Percy nodded solemnly; he didn't care much for learning, and yet there Arthur was, trying to teach him something before getting to his point.

"Serbia gained southern territory after the wars, but Bosnia is to their north, and they still have designs for it. There's strong anti-Austrian sentiment in Serbia because of that, and I think you can probably understand how the Austrians feel about a small country like Serbia challenging the authority of their almighty empire."

Percy was growing bored. He knew his friend was excited, but that didn't mean he had to feel the same. "I suppose it pisses the Austrians right off," he said, disinterested. "Probably got them so mad they can't finish their strudel. Still not sure where this is going."

"Hold on, Percy, I'm getting to that."

Arthur delved deeper, trying his best to describe a complex political situation in the most simple and straightforward manner possible. Percy sat at the bar, staring at the newspaper but not reading it, still struggling to comprehend his friend's enthusiastic and long-winded rant. He listened as Arthur went on to cover the so-called "Triple Entente," which began with the *Entente Cordiale*, French for "cordial agreement." Signed in 1904 between Britain and France, it was a series of accords resolving a slew of territorial conflicts between the two formerly bitter rivals. The *Entente Cordiale* and subsequent pacts between Britain, France and Russia brought the three great nations into a loose defensive alliance. The Triple Entente was viewed as a means of curbing a threat, both perceived and real, from the German Empire, with its powerful military, expanding navy, and increasing territorial ambitions.

By the time Arthur had finished laying it all out, Percy was all but asleep on his barstool. "If you're quite finished, Art," he yawned, "I think I've had enough. Unless you get to it right this second." He tapped his index finger against the bar.

"I'm there, I'm there," Arthur said. "The Austrians will use the assassination as an excuse, Percy." He spread his arms in front of him and turned up his palms, indicating he was making his point. "They're going to invade Serbia. They're going to go to war."

"Who gives a shit?" Percy replied.

Arthur's shoulders slumped. *You'll just have to tell him straight out.*

Percy didn't understand how any of what he'd just heard could possibly impact his life. Why should he care about some Archduke, dead or alive, from a country not his own? *The Slavs are savages; let the Austrians deal with them if they want to.* His was a sentiment shared by millions of men and women the world over. Austria and Serbia had nothing to do with him, so how could the death of one Austrian man and his wife be of any significance? *Why* should it be?

Arthur did not share in that sentiment. Something loomed on the horizon, something big, and Arthur had studied the political situation in Europe enough to know that even in Lymington, England, a dead Austrian Archduke could potentially impact lives. Acknowledging the potential did not mean anything would actually happen—he was no clairvoyant—but Arthur was confident some changes were in store for the continent. If those changes were to involve England, he wanted to get in on the ground floor. And he wanted Percy to go with him.

Lymington, a port town in Hampshire on the southern coast of England, sits on the Solent, the narrow strait between the Isle of Wight and the English mainland. Arthur and Percy grew up in Lymington, and had been best friends for as long as either could remember.

As a child, Arthur was undersized and scrawny, so the much larger Percy became his protector, a role he'd never really relinquished. He scrapped with anyone who picked on his friend, even if Arthur may have run his mouth from time to time. It didn't help the young Arthur's cause in that he scored better marks than nearly everyone else in school—a smartass who was smart to boot. Percy, on the other hand, never enjoyed school. He quit going when they were thirteen. From that point forth, at least on the schoolyard, Arthur had to learn to fend for himself.

Their lives took different paths in the intervening years after Percy left school, but their friendship never faltered. Arthur pursued a scholarly course; he'd just finished his first year at University College, in Southampton. Percy spent the five years since leaving school working at the Wharncliffe-Silkestone Colliery in the town of Pilley, a few miles from Lymington. In spite of the stark contrast between student and miner, the two boys saw each other whenever they could and spent as much time together as possible.

Both boys turned eighteen years old a short time before Ferdinand's assassination; Arthur on April 1, Percy on June 6. Arthur, no longer the undersized whelp he once was, had filled out his frame and grown to just over five foot eight. Percy, however, towered over him. He was beefy, and a hair's breadth short of six foot four.

While life had gone well for most of that time, on May 30 of that fateful year of 1914, things had changed drastically and abruptly for Percy. He narrowly escaped death when sparks from a malfunctioning coal cutter caused a gas explosion which rocked the colliery, killing eleven men and injuring four. Percy only survived because a short while before the explosion, his foreman asked him to stay behind, to move some heavy crates. The task delayed his entering the pit, and kept him away from the deadly blast. Before the explosion his job had always worried him, but in the month after the disaster, it terrified him. After every shift he headed straight to the pub, in a vain attempt to alleviate the fear he dealt with every time he set foot in the pit.

That was the sad state in which Arthur found his friend that Monday in late June. He knew his pal was suffering, he knew he felt trapped, but he had a plan to get Percy out of there—out of that pub, and out of that goddamned mine.

"Percy, we're joining the army."

Percy nearly reeled from his barstool. "What the fuck are you talking about, Art?" He looked at Arthur as if he'd lost his mind.

"I know how much you hate the colliery. You're wasting away in this shithole pub every day," Arthur chided him, louder than he intended to. He glanced at the scowling barkeep, who'd heard him, and said, "I meant no offense, it's a fine establishment," before focusing on Percy again. "You're eighteen years old, for Christ sake, not some sad old Lushington."

Percy looked to his left and right at the other men nursing their drinks at the bar. Arthur was right about the pub and its sad clientele, and he was right about the soul-sucking colliery. Percy hated mining and there weren't many alternatives for a kid like him. He wasn't particularly bright and had limited education, so the military did not sound like such a bad alternative. But why would Arthur, well-educated, well-read and much smarter, want to join the army? He could do just about anything he chose. What the hell was he thinking?

Arthur didn't feel the need to say so, but he'd simply grown tired of school. He wanted a reason, a justifiable reason, to take a break. Once he'd learned that Percy had nearly died on the job, he'd begun brainstorming ways to get his friend away from the colliery. When he saw the newspaper headline that Monday morning, everything came together in his head. The military was something for which they were both eligible, and volunteering for service to one's country was the finest of reasons for leaving a job, or school, or anything for that matter. As soon as Arthur had finished reading the article detailing the assassination, he grasped the significance and immediately made his way to the pub to sell the idea to Percy.

"Art, are you sure your mum and dad will let you leave university?" asked Percy. He doubted they would. Arthur was an only child.

"We'll find out today," Arthur answered. "Come on." He stood up to leave, but Percy still had misgivings.

"Arthur what if there's a war?"

"That's what I've been trying to tell you, Percy!" Arthur said, slapping him on the shoulder. "I think there *is* going to be a war."

"Then why in bloody hell would you want to sign up for that?" Percy exclaimed. He clamped his meaty right hand on his friend's upper arm to stop him from walking away.

"I think going to war sounds like fine sport!" the blue-eyed loon replied. "Just picture it. Fighting for Merrie Olde England in the name of the king, marching forth to a fife and snare tune with your regimental colors flying proudly. Haven't you ever wondered what it might be like?"

"Maybe when I was little."

"Then let's go."

From an early age children from all countries, especially young boys, were regaled with tales of war and heroism. Stories of knights, of fair maidens, of powerful conquerors and mighty kings, of noble and glorious victory, all painted a muddied image of the nature of conflict. Arthur was intelligent and perceptive, but like most boys, he bought into the delusion. So did Percy. While joining the army had not crossed his mind to that point the military, war or not, suddenly did sound like the better choice. He was in.

The two left the dank and dreary pub and stepped out into the warm summer afternoon. Dim pub to bright sun hurt their eyes and they held their hands in front of their faces and squinted. Arthur drew a long, deep breath through his nostrils, to rid himself of the smell of spilled liquor and stale smoke. Chirping birds replaced clinking glasses.

Arthur and Percy were closer to the Ward residence, and so went there first. There they found Percy's mother and father seated at the kitchen table having a cup of tea. Upon joining them at the table, Arthur coyly looked around for Percy's oldest sister, but she wasn't there.

Martin and Maggie Ward, aware that for the last month their son hated every second he spent at work, listened as Arthur did most of the talking. He detailed the assassination, the politics, and the potential conflict looming in the distance. The Wards were attentive, knowing full well their son's limited prospects beyond mining. Arthur detected a gleam in Martin's eyes as he outlined his reasoning. He was confident the Wards would have no problem with Percy joining up.

Martin Ward stood six foot three. With broad shoulders and a thick black beard that hid a square jaw beneath it, he looked like the miner prototype—the kind a foreman would design if that were possible. Percy looked just like his father, minus twenty years, right down to their beards and beady hazel eyes. Both men weighed nearly two hundred and thirty pounds and had monstrous hands, strong and callused by hard labor. If Arthur hadn't known the two men his entire life, they would have been intimidating to say the least.

Maggie Ward was a full foot shorter than her husband. A small and attractive woman, her lack of size belied her disciplinary bent. Martin let his children get away with a lot and balked when it came to punishing them, so he left the discipline to Maggie. Her sandy blonde hair stayed in a near perpetual bun atop her head. She was always doing some sort of work around the house and never allowed her locks to get in the way. She had deep, dark brown eyes, which Percy swore could turn black if he or his sisters pissed her off enough, though he and his siblings had little desire to give their mother that much trouble.

Martin had spent his entire adult life mining and while it provided for the Ward family, Percy knew his father would have preferred he not do the same thing. The old man viewed it as the type of job in which a fellow just got stuck—the longer you stayed, the harder it was to get out. Percy remembered his father telling him as much when he was a young boy, an attempt to instill that idea at an early age, to inspire him to stick with school. But he felt the way he felt about school and never planned on staying, despite his father's wishes. Growing up, knowing he just didn't have the smarts that other kids had, Percy always believed he'd end up mining one way or another, so that was what he did.

Even after the Wharncliffe-Silkestone disaster, Percy could have toughed it out and continued to go to work indefinitely, swallowing his anxieties each and every morning, and drinking them down every afternoon. He was just made of that kind of stuff. Mr. Ward probably knew as much, but the army might be his boy's way out. Martin had read the stories too, and while he'd never want to lose his son to a battle, he never wanted his son to lose his soul to mining either.

"Are you sure this is what you want, Percy?" Maggie asked. She was typically a stern woman, but the way she asked revealed her uncertainty and concern.

"Well, it's a different way for me to make a living, isn't it?" Percy answered. "I hate the pit."

"I know dear, but what happened at the colliery was an accident." She reached across the table and grasped his hands. "If you join up and war ever comes, in battle soldiers are killed on purpose. How can you fear one and not the other?"

His mother had a point. Percy ran his hand through his beard, formulating a response. "I never said it wouldn't be scary, mum, but at least soldiers die in service to king and country," he answered, parroting Arthur's earlier statement in the pub. "It's a more noble death than going out unexpectedly in a dirty hole for a few quid." The second part was his argument, though he wasn't entirely sold on it. Death, after all, was death. However, Percy *was* certain that soldiering was better for him than mining.

"Son, if you feel this is your way out of the colliery then by all means do it," Martin said. He then turned to Arthur. "Will your mother and father allow you to follow through with this?"

24

"If Percy's going, then so am I," Arthur replied without hesitation. "Besides, I don't need their permission to volunteer." He had already made up his mind, and would be damned if anyone was going to tell him otherwise.

"Well my boy," smiled Mr. Ward, "I think they may disagree with you."

Andrew Ellis ran his own ferry boat company, shuttling passengers to and from Lymington across the Solent to the city of Yarmington on the Isle of Wight. He and Arthur's mother Cassandra had both attended University College, though back then it was called Hartley College, where they met for the first time. They married after graduation, and had Arthur two years after that. Andrew founded A.C.E Ferries a short while later, with Cassandra working as the company's accountant.

Mr. and Mrs. Ellis intended for Arthur to graduate from University College, work for, and then eventually assume control of the family business. Andrew made it clear when Arthur was still in secondary school, though, that while he preferred his son join the business it was not the only option. Arthur wasn't totally opposed to the path laid out for him; he just wasn't particularly intrigued by it. To his great benefit, the Ellises gave their only child more freedom than other parents of an only child might have. They loved him enough to know that stifling his interests and narrowing his path through life would be of no service to him. They rarely discouraged him from trying new things, but then again, Arthur joining the army had never come up before. They might be a harder sell than were the Wards.

The boys passed through the quaint streets, past the neighbors' houses, 'round the hedgerow at the corner, and approached Arthur's house, not far from the Cricket Field and the water tower. The top of the tower could be seen from the back yard. A plump woman with shoulder length reddish-brown hair was picking flowers in the front yard. She wore a grey house dress with a white apron. She waved as they approached.

"Hey mum," Arthur greeted her, "is dad home? We have something to tell you two."

Mrs. Ellis stepped out of her garden as the boys walked around the hedges and into the yard. "He's not home from work yet, dear," she said, wiping her hands on her apron. She was already suspicious. "Would you boys like to wait for him inside?"

"Yes, I suppose I'd prefer you be seated," Arthur answered.

"Oh my, what is it Arthur?" She held her hand to her mouth. "Are you boys in trouble?"

Arthur laughed. "No, mum, nothing like that. Let's just wait for dad."

Cassandra let the boys in, and the three sat down at the dining room table. She offered to serve tea, which they both refused, Arthur because he was anxious, and Percy because that cheap scotch, in tandem with what had since become an out-of-the-ordinary day, had turned his belly to rot. They had only been seated for a minute or two when Mr. Ellis walked through the front door and Arthur, unable to contain himself, blurted it out.

"Percy and I are joining the army!"

His mother gasped. He expected a long, heated argument to follow. He'd geared himself up for it. So when his father walked into the room, smiled and said, "All right, Art," it caught everyone by surprise. No one more so than Arthur's mother.

"Andy!" she gasped again. "You can't be so cavalier about him leaving school!"

"Sure I can." Arthur's father walked around the table and positioned himself behind her chair. For his age, he was still a lively fellow, though the strain of owning a business left permanent bags under his blue eyes. Father and son looked alike, but father was considerably thinner. Mr. Ellis placed his hands on his wife's shoulders and said, "Cassie, these boys are young. They could use some adventure! I mean, my goodness, Percy, the poor chap..." Mr. Ellis nodded in Percy's direction, "he's been at the colliery since he was thirteen! And UC will surely still be there when Arthur comes back. Soldiers travel the world! How many Lymington boys would be able to say the same thing?"

Mrs. Ellis scowled. "And what if they're sent off to some faraway, bug-infested colony to quell the uprisings of savages?"

"They'll be all right, Cassie," he assured her. "And anyway, who are we to stand in the way of our boy's desire to serve the crown?"

"What if there's a war?!" Mrs. Ellis squeaked. "The Austrian Archduke was killed yesterday, you know."

"Yes I've heard. But there is a wide chasm between a dead Austrian and a British war. *If* there is a war, and I've got my doubts about that, then these two will simply be doing their part. Just as many other boys their age would be expected to do."

"I can't believe I'm the only one who considers this a foolish proposal," Cassandra said. "Percy, did Arthur talk you into this?"

"He did," Percy replied, "but I agree with him."

"Oh Arthur..." she said, and she made a long, disappointed face.

Arthur had seen his mother cry before, but when her blue eyes began to glisten during the conversation, he could not help but feel guilty. While Mrs. Ellis persisted in her argument for a time, the matter was settled without Arthur having to make his third sales pitch of the day. The fact that he'd grown tired of school didn't even need bringing up. He wondered whether his father saw right through him.

VERNON

Sally was baking bread. There was just something about the smell of warm, fresh bread, a food so simple, yet so deliciously aromatic, that Vernon wished the house could always smell that way. Sally's auburn hair dangled in a ponytail that stretched to the mid-back on her old brown house dress. She had such beautiful hair. He stood in the doorway of the little stone, wood and thatch cottage where she stayed, just watching her back while she worked.

Some wives stayed with their husbands in the barracks, but after faithfully accompanying Vernon and his battalion to India, Morocco *and* Egypt, in Ireland she'd decided it was best for her to live *near* the barracks, rather than *in* them. Vernon's wages covered most of her added living costs; Sally worked part-time to cover the rest. He didn't like the thought of her sleeping alone at night, but she insisted on it, and woe be the brigand who dared trespass in Sally's abode. She was far tougher than she looked.

"Have you heard the news of the Archduke of Austria?" Sally asked, her back still turned.

Vernon thought his presence had gone undetected. He could tell she'd been waiting all day to share the news with him. He pretended he hadn't already heard.

"No, what happened to good old Franz?" he answered. "His pop finally snuff it and pass him the crown?"

"Heavens, no, the poor man's been assassinated!" Sally replied. She turned to face him. Her pretty face, with her adorably distinct

28

pouty upper lip, was wrought with sad sympathy. "His wife was killed, too."

Vernon did not particularly care about Ferdinand, but when he saw Sally's face and the look in her olive eyes, it cajoled him into at least some semblance of sympathy. Her eyes—a smooth, solid, milky green, like manzanillas stuffed with black pimento—could do that, could make him empathize with her, over almost anything. She was one of the strongest women he'd ever met, yet with all her toughness, she was, above all else, extraordinarily kind-hearted and gentle. In India, she'd spent nearly everything she had on supplies and clothing for the children of a village near the British garrison. In Morocco and Egypt, she did much of the same. She rarely complained, never yelled, and in twelve years of marriage, he'd seen her cry but once.

"That's a shame…" Vernon said. He tried to sound reflective.

There were times, many times, he wished himself able to provide his wife with a better life. And he knew that she knew it. Sally assured him time and again that he was exactly what she signed up for; it was just hard for him to get beyond his belief that someone as special as her deserved more.

While only thirty years old, Vernon Hayes had a craggy, weathered face with deep set, blue-green eyes. Sally, or Sal as he often called her, was thirty as well, but each passing year was much kinder to her comely complexion.

Vernon had that tough guy type of face, the type other tough guys might try to test themselves against, though he no longer placed much stock in tough guys. Slim, almost gaunt and standing five foot eleven, he was deceptively strong. His bony knuckles might do serious damage to a cheek, chin or nose if the need ever facilitated itself, and they certainly had done so in his adolescence, but marrying Sally when he was eighteen had calmed the brawler in him long ago.

They met as seventeen-year-olds in Chester, the county town of Cheshire, near England's border with Wales. Vernon, a scrappy but decent man on the verge of finishing primary school (per his mother's wishes) and preparing to enter service in the British army, had lived in Chester since his mother moved him there as a child. When he was still very young, too young to remember, his father, a soldier in Her Majesty's forces, was killed fighting the native resistance in Burma. That was when Vernon's mother made the move to Chester.

Felicia Hayes was a good woman, though sad, and she never married again. She did her best in raising Vernon on her own, and never gave in to pitying herself. She died of cancer during his first year in the army, the unjust reward for a respectable and honest push through a difficult life, the final sixteen years of which she spent struggling to give her son the best life she was able. She did live long enough to see her son both finish school and marry, however, and that meant a lot, to her, to Vernon, and to Sally. She and Sally hadn't gotten the chance to know one another for long, but she loved her daughter-in-law, and died proud of what her son had become.

Sally's parents were still alive. Her family, the Blythes, were originally from Chester, but after giving their daughter away, they'd since moved to London. She'd leave Vernon to visit them from time to time, but was never away for long—she disliked being apart from him just as much as he did her. Despite his belief that Sally deserved more, Vernon had an amiable relationship with Mr. and Mrs. Blythe. They were much more well-to-do than his mother had ever been, but they never once passed judgment on her, or her son.

When Vernon was in India, he learned that nearly all Indian marriages were arranged, that mother and father would attempt to give their daughter to the wealthiest man who would have her. The daughter, for her part, was often given no say in the matter. Vernon was glad the Blythes did not share in such a philosophy. Marrying for love, he believed, was much more sincere.

"Is that all you'll say on the issue?" Sally asked, clearly expecting more. She changed the tone of her voice to sound gruff and mocked, "That's a shame..."

"Well, the silly bloke shouldn't have been parading around Sarajevo in the first bloody place," Vernon replied.

"Liar!" Sally laughed. She pointed an accusing finger at him. "You already knew!"

"Aye," Vernon conceded, holding his hands up. "I think just about everyone knows by now."

"You needn't have played dumb."

"I know, but you seemed so very excited to share the gossip. I didn't want to spoil it for you."

"Oh, Vernon," she scowled, waving a dismissive hand, "I'm not one of those hens, clucking every chance I get about this or that."

"That you are not," he agreed. "Yet another of your many redeeming qualities."

"And don't forget it."

"I won't."

"What do you think will come of it all?" she asked.

"Of the assassination?"

"No, of the many other topics we've covered since you walked through the door," she teased.

"Of course," Vernon grinned sheepishly. "It's hard to say, but if I had to venture a guess, I would expect no small amount of political posturing, perhaps an idle threat or two, and then a month or so from now, no one will remember or care."

"Ferdinand's children will certainly still care," she scowled.

"You know what I meant."

"What did Llewelyn have to say when he found out?"

"He mumbled something to the effect of 'at least husband and wife went out together.'"

"I still worry about him," Sally said. She wiped the flour from her hands on her apron and sat down at the kitchen table.

"I do too, sometimes," Vernon said, and he joined her.

"Is your captain still singling him out?" she asked.

"When he gets a chance, yes," said Vernon.

"Gosh...Ever since Egypt. And still no one knows why?"

"No one. Bannister is just a hard old cad. Whatever reason he has for hounding Llewelyn, and I doubt there is one, he's never revealed it."

Sally frowned. "That's just rotten," she said. "Llewelyn is such a sweet fellow. The last thing he needs is some bully holding a foolish, unjustifiable grudge against him. Especially a superior officer."

"It's true. But there's very little anyone can do."

"What rubbish," Sally declared. "Maybe I'll just go slap some sense into that captain of yours." She raised her had to Vernon's face and patted him on the cheek. "That might set the old codger straight."

"I'm sure that would work out well for all parties concerned," replied Vernon. He took hold of her hand and kissed her palm. She still had bits of dough encrusted on her fingers. He stared at them and pretended to take a bite.

"I suppose you'll be wanting a slice of bread," she said, stating the obvious.

"If you could spare it, mum," Vernon answered, in what was his best beggar's voice. He meekly clasped his hands together.

"All right, all right, Oliver Twist. Just make sure you bring some to Llewelyn."

"I will."

Sally got up, kissed him on the cheek, found her bread knife, and cut four big slices from the loaf that had been cooling on the countertop. She brought him his slice, placing it on a plate in front of him, and sat back down. "Are you sure everyone will forget about the Archduke in a month?" she asked.

"No," Vernon said, "but I will."

31

ARTHUR & PERCY

It took two days to get their affairs in order. Two days they likewise had to reconsider. Alas, two days later their suitcases were packed, Percy had quit his job at the colliery, and now Arthur stood in the doorway of his childhood home, saying his goodbyes. After shaking hands with his proud father, he turned to face his mother. She may have been proud underneath, but outside, she was all worry. With tears in her eyes for the second time in three days, Cassandra Ellis hugged her only child.

"Make sure to write us, Arthur," she said. There was an obvious lump in her throat. She barely croaked out her words.

Arthur laughed and replied, "Mum we'll be training in England. I'll be able to visit you!" He gave her a kiss on the cheek, picked up his suitcase and headed off down the street to his friend's house.

"We love you, Arthur!" she called out as he walked away.

He turned around to wave. "Love you too. Don't worry about me."

"I'm supposed to, it's my job!" she cried.

On his walk to Percy's, Arthur grew nervous. *What if we do end up going to war and I get Percy killed?* Were the two boys making a rash decision? Well, it was a rash decision. Was it too rash? *How could I confront his family if he died and I came home? What would I say to them?* It may not have been too late to say the hell with it, but Arthur's mind was made up. He'd already committed himself to the idea and that was that. Besides, it was his argument that convinced

Percy to quit his job. There was no way he'd let his best friend down by backing out at the last second.

The entire Ward family stood in their front yard waiting for Arthur. Next to Martin and Maggie stood Percy's three sisters—Elizabeth, age seventeen, Winifred, age eleven and Julia, just five years old. Each girl wore a different colored flowery dress, the oldest in blue, the middle in green, and the youngest in yellow.

Percy held little Julia's hand. Her skinny arm was stretched above her head so she could reach. She squeezed the ends of his fingers as hard as she could, unable to wrap her miniature hand around his giant palm. Julia didn't want her big brother to go. Percy felt a twinge of guilt as his baby sister clutched his fingers.

"Hullo everyone," Arthur greeted the family, and then he met eyes with Elizabeth. She smiled at him. He quickly looked away. *Gosh, Ellie looks lovely.* It was almost automatic that he looked at Elizabeth first, but when he averted his gaze to Percy, specifically his chin, he grinned. It was something he should have noticed right away, even from a distance.

"Percy, where's your beard?!"

"Fell off last night, Art."

"How many razors did you go through?"

"Razors? I had to use the fucking lawnmower!"

Martin chuckled, Julia gasped, and Maggie slapped her son on the arm. "Language, Percy!" his mother said.

"I'm sorry mum."

Percy had shaved to look more presentable for the recruiter. Arthur hadn't seen his best friend without hair on his face for more than two years, and almost forgot what he looked like underneath. Percy may have been a big boy, but without his beard he was just that—a large, smooth-faced boy, barely eighteen years old. Arthur's face required no shaving whatsoever; he'd never been able to grow facial hair.

Stepping forward, Percy turned to his family. "I guess it's that time," he said. "Got a train to catch."

Having already spent the morning saying goodbye, he shook hands with his father, then hugged his mother and each sister one last time. He had to kneel to hug Julia. Her yellow dress was splotched with tears. Placing his hands on her tiny shoulders, Percy looked her in her watery hazel eyes and said, "I'll be back before you know it, little nipper."

She sobbed.

He stood up and moved back so his friend could say goodbye as well. Martin and Maggie were like second parents to Arthur, and had been for most of his life.

Arthur shook Mr. Ward's formidable hand. It was like shaking hands with a granite statue.

"Good luck to you, Art," Martin said.

"Thank you, sir."

Mrs. Ward gave Arthur a loving hug, and then placed her firm but warm little hands on the side of his face, fixing her dark eyes on his. "Make sure you help Percy keep his spirits up, dear," she said. "I think you're the only reason he's smiled at all this past month."

"I won't let him sulk, ma'am. I promise."

She patted his right cheek softly and removed her hands from his face. "Thank you for being such a good friend to him, Arthur," she said.

"All the schoolyard drubbings he rescued me from?" replied Arthur. "I owe him much more than just unwavering friendship."

Percy's mother smiled.

Arthur again glanced at Elizabeth, in her sleeveless blue dress dotted with little white flowers. She held her smooth, fair-skinned arms against her lower abdomen, resting her left hand atop her right wrist. *You look beautiful, Ellie. Just tell her!* As Arthur moved toward her and extended his arms for a goodbye hug, Elizabeth lunged at him, wrapping her arms around his neck and pressing her cheek against his. When she did, he caught the faintest whiff of her lilac perfume; she never wore too much, always the perfect amount. When she hugged him her hair grazed his nose—it too smelled of lilac. *Well Arthur, this is new,* he thought.

She squeezed him much harder than he expected and whispered softly into his ear, "Goodbye, Artie."

Artie. She always called him that. He hated being called Artie by anyone else, despised it in fact, but the way she said it was just different.

When they were younger, Elizabeth was pesky, and incessantly demanded she be allowed to spend time with Percy and Arthur, but they rarely let her. As a boy Arthur considered her a nuisance, and even picked on her from time to time for that very reason. Even then, she never relented in her seeking permission to join in their adventures, no matter what they were doing or how filthy they'd get when doing it. Eventually her tagalong demands relented, and Arthur relented in his picking on her, and for the past three years he had begun to view her much differently. It was impossible not to. She was gorgeous.

34

Elizabeth had wavy brown hair that hung past her shoulders and a wide, bright smile she'd gladly share with anyone. A tiny scattering of light-colored freckles across the bridge of her nose added a measure of cuteness to what were exquisite features. At five foot six, she stood two inches shorter than Arthur, and though her father and brother were just short of gigantic, she was thin and elegant, with long, smooth legs Arthur had seen only once, while swimming in the Solent the previous summer. Luckily for Elizabeth and her two sisters, they'd inherited their physical characteristics from their mother.

Most captivating of all were Elizabeth's big, sparkling amber eyes. In a certain light they took on a glow like orange topaz, fiery and intense, yet within that intensity dwelled an innocent, gentle and kind soul. Arthur never spoke to anyone about it, but he viewed Elizabeth's eyes as the single most beautiful thing he'd ever seen, or would ever see, in his entire life. They were utterly mesmerizing—at least on those rare occasions when he actually found the courage to peer into them.

Arthur had eyes for her and only her. He never paid much attention to other girls. But he couldn't tell whether Elizabeth saw him the same way, and he lacked the courage and confidence to tell her his feelings. Arthur was a smart, handsome young man but his self-doubt ran deep and always got in the way. It clouded his ability to see the way she looked at him. It was as if he knew, yet could not permit himself to believe it.

Because she was his best friend's sister he was around her frequently, and he tried to exercise subtlety when glancing her way. Sometimes, though, he couldn't help but stare. On days when Arthur ate dinner with the Ward family, or when he happened to cross paths with Elizabeth in town, he often thought she caught him staring—that brief moment of eye contact and the awkward feeling of knowing he'd been spotted. It never occurred to him that he may have been catching her instead.

Now, with her arms squeezing his neck, her body pressed against his for the first time, he allowed himself to believe that maybe, just maybe, she felt something for him. His heart thudded in his chest. He worried that she might feel its thudding too; then she'd realize just how nervous he was in being so close to her. The sensation of having her smooth, warm cheek pressed against his was almost intoxicating. In all his years of knowing her, they'd never once hugged. Was that odd? To know someone so long yet never have hugged them?

He hoped that even though he and Percy were leaving, he wasn't losing the opportunity to hug her that way in the future. On his first leave, whenever that might be, he resolved to return, to find out her true feelings, and perhaps summon the courage to tell her his.

The hug lasted longer than a normal hug. He wanted it to go on longer, but it had to conclude at some point. With his lips close to her ear, the hug nearing its conclusion, he was compelled to whisper something impressive, something eloquent and emotive. *Say something she'll remember!*

"Bye Ellie."

Come on, Arthur.

When she relaxed her grip on his neck, Elizabeth turned her head ever so slightly to nuzzle her cheek against his, just enough for him to notice. His hands slid from her lower back to her hips; her arms slipped from around his neck. As they separated and the space between them slowly widened, she rested the weight of her arms on his shoulders, maintaining contact from her elbows all the way through to the tips of her fingers, until they finally slipped from his shirt. Arthur didn't want the hug to end, and was pretty sure she didn't either. Had the rest of the Wards not been standing there, he might have tried to kiss her.

Arthur gave Winifred a short hug, then put his palm on little Julia's head, tussling her hair. She grabbed his hand with both of hers, to stop him from messing her blonde curls.

"Stay out of trouble, nipper," he told her. It was the only name he and Percy ever called her.

"I will," Julia said, and she sniffled.

As he and Percy began their walk to Lymington Town station, Arthur turned back to look at Elizabeth once more. He waved. *You should've told her how you felt a long time ago. What if you missed your chance?* She fixed her beautiful, captivating eyes on his, a sadness on her face that even Arthur could read, and waved back.

SLEEPWALKERS

As bad news tended to when it took place somewhere else, Franz Ferdinand's assassination faded from the minds of most Europeans within mere days of its happening. In Austria-Hungary, however, the politicians and military planners began igniting the first sparks in the geopolitical tinderbox that was 1914 Europe.

When Čabrinović and Princip were arrested, it became clear that the two young men were part of a larger group of conspirators with at least some backing from Serbia itself, including help from military officers and Serbia's Chief of Military Intelligence. The two Serbs were part of a group of six assassins, all Serbian, all young, and all trained by Serbian officers, sent to Sarajevo that day. Their bombs and guns were likewise supplied by officials. All six assassins were eventually caught.

Although a general consensus existed in most countries that Serbia was at least in part to blame and thusly in part culpable, there was no such consensus on how to levy an appropriate punishment. Many Austro-Hungarian politicians favored immediately going to war. Their desire for war was matched or exceeded by some—but definitely not all—officials in Germany, who whispered their urgings into any Germanic ears willing to listen. Itching to demonstrate to both Europe and to the world at large just how powerful and mighty their empire had become, those German officials, of both high-ranking military and political status, pressed their Kaiser and the Austrians to stoke the fires.

One notable exception to the war fever was Count István Tisza, the Prime Minister of Hungary. He rightly understood that due to the alliances between Serbia, Russia and her allies, an invasion of Serbia would ultimately lead to a massive conflagration involving all the major powers of Europe. Tisza made his opinion known but on July 7, at a meeting of the Austro-Hungarian Crown Council it was decided, over Tisza's objections, that an ultimatum to Serbia should be drafted.

The ten point ultimatum, intentionally written so as to provoke its rejection by Serbia, sought to emasculate the Serbian nation. Several tenets involved the quelling of any and all anti-Austro-Hungarian sentiment, of which there was plenty. Curtailing free speech was nothing new. The most unacceptable demand, however, involved Serbia allowing Austrian officials (police) into their country to take part in the investigation of the assassination plot. Such a demand was a clear and insulting violation of Serbia's sovereignty. The ultimatum, delivered on July 23, came with a forty-eight hour deadline given for a response.

Serbia, embarrassingly willing to accept nine of the ten demands, refused to allow foreign investigators into their country. Leaders and diplomats from Russia, Britain, France and even Germany all attempted to mediate what had become a highly contentious situation, but in the end diplomacy failed and Austria-Hungary got exactly what it wanted. With Serbia's rejection of only the single most ludicrous of Austria-Hungary's demands, war was declared on July 28, exactly one month after Franz Ferdinand's death.

Though the die had been cast for Austria-Hungary and Serbia, the great powers of Europe had the chance, even the incentive, to avoid any conflict. But on the news of Austria's declaration, Tsar Nicholas II of Russia ordered a partial mobilization of the Russian army in those districts which bordered the Austro-Hungarian Empire. The partial mobilization upset many of his advisors, who insisted that only a general mobilization was appropriate. On July 30 Nicholas, in direct communication by telegraph with Kaiser Wilhelm II of Germany, informed him that he had ordered a partial mobilization, but only against Austria-Hungary.

The Tsar and the Kaiser (both words translated to Caesar in their respective languages, read: emperor), were great-great-grandsons of Paul I of Russia, making them third cousins by bloodline. They were also first cousins through marriage. They corresponded with one another in English, calling each other "Willy" and "Nicky". Both men additionally shared King George V of England ("Georgie") as a first cousin (Wilhelm and George were grandsons of Queen Victoria, while George and Nicholas's mothers were sisters).

Despite the fact that Nicholas informed Wilhelm that Russian forces were *only* mobilizing against Austria-Hungary, Wilhelm stubbornly ordered his forces to mobilize anyway, offering to stand down only if Russia demobilized immediately. Nicholas, in a gesture of good faith, called off his mobilization. Facing mounting pressure from his foreign minister, war minister and top generals, who all argued that a response to Germany's aggression was necessary, Nicholas ultimately showed his true ineptitude as a world leader and decision maker, reversing his decision once again and ordering full mobilization. In response, on August 1 Germany declared war on Russia.

Even still, France and Britain had the power to remain free from the conflict. However, Germany's mobilization was set to a strict timetable of operations called the Schlieffen Plan. The plan, designed nine years earlier by then German Chief of Staff Count Alfred von Schlieffen, and slightly modified later by his replacement Helmuth von Moltke, detailed the operations for fighting a two-front war against the armies of France and Russia. It assumed, because of Russia's immense size and poor railway system, that a full mobilization of Russian forces would take considerable time. Thus it called for over ninety percent of German forces, divided into three separate arms, to advance through Belgium, Luxembourg, and Alsace-Lorraine into northern and eastern France, respectively.

The intention of the three-pronged attack was for the larger northern arm (First, Second and Third armies) advancing through Belgium, and the eastern armies (Fourth and Fifth through Luxembourg, Sixth and Seventh through Alsace-Lorraine) to encircle the armies of France in a massive pincer attack. The thinking was that the pincer, its northern claw passing to the west of Paris, could surround the French army, who would already be occupied by an engagement against the German center. The move would outflank the French and ultimately crush the entirety of the French forces.

If their armies were outflanked and crushed or captured, the French government would then have no choice but to surrender. The entire first phase of the plan, from mobilization to destruction of the French army and surrender of France, was supposed to take just forty-two days. After completing phase one, a sizable portion of the forces in France would then rapidly deploy eastward by rail, before the "Russian steamroller" initiated its invasion of East Prussia, the easternmost province of the German Empire.

Strictly speaking, Germany did not *have* to deploy its armies in accordance with the Schlieffen Plan, but for essentially an entire decade, the plan had been *the* order of operations. It was dogma, and firmly engrained in the psyches of Germany's military commanders.

And so, on August 2, in spite of assurances from Britain that it could keep France out of the war provided Germany did not mobilize any forces westward, Germany initiated its occupation of Luxembourg. The same day, another ultimatum was issued, this time from Germany to Belgium, asking for free passage for German forces on their way into northern France. Unsurprisingly, King Albert of Belgium refused to allow any violation of Belgian sovereignty. On August 3, Germany declared war on France, and a day later, on Belgium. Immediately following Germany's declaration of war with Belgium, Great Britain made good on her pledge to protect her Belgian ally, and declared war on Germany.

An entirely avoidable conflict was about to engulf the major powers of Europe. A Great War had begun.

HENTSCH

"Hentsch! Get the hell over—"

Thwack!

The leutnant's sentence ended with an odd and sickening sound as a bullet burst through his forehead. Hentsch, lying on his stomach and taking cover in a shallow ditch just ten feet away, flinched at the noise. He watched, wide-eyed, as the officer collapsed, killed instantly. He'd never seen a bullet kill a person before, never saw a person die from anything as a matter of fact. Five seconds prior, Leutnant Kimmell was issuing an order, now Kimmell was dead. The way he'd fallen, his head turned sideways, he appeared to be staring in Hentsch's direction, an almost surprised look on his dead face. It was decidedly unnerving.

Hentsch rolled over, putting the dead man to his back. The hostile machine gun emplacement chattered a hundred yards in the distance, as bullets snapped inches above him and spat up dirt along the lip of the ditch in front of him. He tapped Decker on the shoulder. Decker was face-down, hands clasping the back of his helmet. He didn't respond to the first tap, so Hentsch grabbed him by the wrist and tried to turn him over. Decker had taken a bullet directly into the top of his skull, punched straight through the top of his helmet. He was gone too. Two men, one on either side of him, dead within minutes of the opening shots. It was not a good start to the war.

Gefreiter (lance-corporal) Augustus Hentsch crossed the Belgian border a day earlier on August 4 as part of General Alexander von

Kluck's First Army. General von Kluck's Army was the northernmost force of the Schlieffen Plan's northern wing, which consisted of Kluck's First Army, General Karl von Bülow's Second Army, and General Max von Hausen's Third Army. The northern wing's objective was to sweep through Belgium and into northern France, with First Army ultimately passing west of Paris.

Hentsch was an infantryman serving in 13th Kompagnie, III Bataillon, of the Mecklenburgisches Fusilier Regiment Kaiser Wilhelm Nr. 90 (FR90 for short). Mecklenburg, a province on Germany's Baltic coast, was the regiment's major recruiting area, and most of the Mecklenburg Fusiliers hailed from that province's cities.

Fusil, the French word for musket, was the root of *fusilier* (musketeer), a term historically used in the names of a number of regiments in the German, French and English armies to denote different roles throughout the centuries, but by the turn of the twentieth century it had become more of a traditional remnant than anything else. It basically just meant *rifleman*, which most infantrymen were. Hentsch's regiment was part of the 34th Brigade der Infanterie, of the 17th Division der Infanterie. The 17th and 18th Divisions comprised IX Korps, commanded by General Ferdinand von Quast.

The basic structure of most armies followed similar hierarchical formats, breaking down into smaller and smaller units, each with their own command structures. Even the words for most of those units were similar in the respective languages. A German army group was highly complex, but as far as the infantry was concerned, an army was composed of at least two corps (korps) plus any reserves (Kluck's First Army had four korps, plus three more in reserve). Each corps employed anywhere from twenty thousand to over forty thousand men. Corps were made up of two divisions, each of which typically contained between ten and fifteen thousand men. Each division had three brigades of around five thousand men each, and each brigade was composed of two regiments, of two to three thousand soldiers.

Regiments broke down further into three battalions (bataillon), battalions into four companies (kompagnie) plus one machine gun company. Companies were comprised of three platoons (zug), and platoons of four sections (korporalschaft). A section contained two squads (gruppe), the smallest unit. A German gruppe entailed one gefreiter commanding eight basic soldiers given the rank of gemeine ("common," equivalent to private). Each smaller unit was subordinate to the larger. Other armies varied slightly in the names and numbers, but were similar nonetheless.

Hentsch received his promotion from gemeine to gefreiter just before the mobilization. His promotion meant he took command of a gruppe, making him responsible for the eight men of 2 Gruppe, in 1 Korporalschaft, 1 Zug of 13th Kompagnie.

He hadn't had time to learn all their names, and Decker's was one of the few he knew. In just twenty minutes of fighting, Hentsch already saw his zug commander killed and lost one of his own men. At that moment the entire 34th Brigade was heavily engaged with the Belgians around the city of Visé, on the banks of the River Meuse. Visé was the first objective of the invasion, followed shortly thereafter by the fortress city of Liège, also on the Meuse, about ten miles to the southwest.

Hentsch could stay in the ditch no longer. He intended to carry out the order he knew the dead officer was about to give—find a way to silence the machine gun. There were many thousands of men fighting the battle for thousands of yards on either side of him, but the deadly machine gun lay directly ahead. It was Hentsch and his gruppe's sole concern. Other men down the line had other objectives.

With great caution, he peeked his head just high enough out of the ditch to see the Belgians operating the gun. It was probably the same move that had gotten Decker killed. So far as he could tell, the weapon was manned by a crew of two. One man was the gunner and the other helped him reload. The gunner was barely visible behind the weapon, but during reloads Hentsch was able to see the second man from the shoulders up. He figured if he could kill him, then the gunner might struggle to reload fast enough. With one man out of the picture, a small team might be able to storm the gun and knock it out of commission.

"Hey, get over here!" Hentsch shouted, waving to the five men closest to him. Each scrambled over on all fours and made it to him safely, though one stout little fellow held his head too high and got his pickelhaube shot off. The pickelhaube (literally "point bonnet") was a boiled leather helmet with brass fittings and a brass spike on top. The spiked helmet was standard issue for German infantry. While it was technically a helmet and not a hat, its leather shell offered little to no protection from bullets or shrapnel. Decker could attest to that.

Hentsch eyed each of the five men, sizing them up. They, like him, wore the standard infantryman's uniform. Their wool tunics were almost entirely grey, save for thin red piping down the front opening, around the collars and sleeve cuffs and a red crown and W (for Wilhelm) monogrammed on their shoulder straps. The shoulder straps had white piping, and fastened to the tunic with a button numbered

13, for 13th Kompagnie. Their tunics fastened with one row of eight nickel buttons down the center, and the sleeve cuffs fastened with three. Two sealable pockets, one on each tunic skirt, sat below the leather waist belt of their equipment packs, near their hips.

Their trousers, also grey, had red piping down the outer seam. They wore tall, brown leather jackboots over their lower pant legs, the tops of which reached to just below their knees. Because pickel-haubes were made of shiny blackened leather, men in the field wore fabric covers over them, which hooked onto the front and back of the helmet. Despite the vast majority of their uniforms being grey, the fabric covers on their pickelhaubes were a light tan color, with a large, red embroidered *90* on the front to indicate their regiment.

Hentsch knew the name of the stout man with the hole in his pickelhaube. He was called Ackerman. The names of the others elud-ed him. Neither he nor they had ever seen real combat before and though Hentsch was afraid, the others looked scared beyond their wits.

"All right listen! We won't get anywhere unless we rid ourselves of that machine gun," Hentsch announced to his wide-eyed com-rades.

Ackerman, obviously terrified from his close call shrieked, "We can't get to it! It'll cut us to pieces!"

"We can," Hentsch replied. "We must wait for them to reload. As soon as the loader shows himself, I'll shoot him in the head and we'll charge. Now fix your bayonets."

The men reluctantly complied, reaching to their hip scabbards and drawing their fourteen inch Seitengewehr 98/05 bayonets. Hentsch did the same, sliding the machete-like bayonet onto the lug beneath the end of his rifle barrel, and then snapping it into place. The blade had deep grooves on either side that glinted in the sun-light. It was a fearsome looking accessory, and it added an extra foot to the end of his rifle.

Another soldier sporting a bushy moustache—Hentsch thought his name was Beckenbauer—got antsy and shouted, "You can't hit his head at a hundred yards, you asshole! You'll miss and get us killed!" he punched the dirt next to his knee, emphasizing his point.

Ignoring the man, Hentsch slid his bolt-action Mauser Gewehr 98 (Mauser Rifle Model 1898) over the lip of the ditch, waiting for the rattling of the enemy gun to stop. He'd honed his skills as a marks-man during training, but long before his conscription into the army he was a fine shot with a hunting rifle. As soon as the chattering ceased, he slinked high enough to get his sights on the man holding the fresh ammo drum. *It's simple. Either kill him, or he kills more*

Germans. He'd trained for it. Now it was time for the real thing. Aiming the slenderest fraction high and to the left to allow for a slight wind and an incremental drop, Hentsch squeezed the trigger.

POW! The rifle kicked into his shoulder and a less than half a second later the Belgian fell from view. A spritz of light crimson mist puffed into the air, and lingered briefly where he'd stood. *Got him.* Hentsch had just killed the first man at whom he'd ever pointed a rifle, but there was no time to think about what that meant.

"Let's move!" he shouted. He was concerned as to how quickly he and the others could run with their heavy packs strapped on, but that was just one of many concerns.

The six men sprang to their feet and initiated their hundred-yard charge as the Belgian machine gunner, now alone, scrambled for his ammo drum. Hentsch and his men made it to within fifty yards before the gun was reloaded and resumed its rattling fire. They couldn't turn back now. Beckenbauer took a round to the kneecap in mid-stride, which collapsed his leg backward and sent him sprawling into the dirt, screaming in pain. His war was over, but he'd probably survive.

Though one bullet had hit home, the panicked machine gunner must have been too terrified to shoot straight. He sprayed his fire wildly in uncontrolled bursts. Hentsch, standing a slim and athletic six foot four, led the charge with his bayonet-tipped rifle pointed forward and his mouth held open in a roaring battle cry. His pack was indeed slowing him down, but that was of no consolation to the Belgian watching him approach. Upon seeing the tall, sharp featured and fast-moving German leading four other men trailing closely behind, the gunner abandoned his weapon and fled.

Seeing the gunner give up the fight, Hentsch slowed down.

"Let him go!" he shouted.

The man to Hentsch's right ignored the instruction, raised his Mauser to his shoulder, took aim and shot the retreating Belgian in the back. The Belgian's arms flailed upward when the bullet struck him, and he fell flat on his face.

"God dammit, man!" Hentsch shouted. "He'd given up his weapon!" He shoved the soldier who fired the shot.

"Fuck him," was the soldier's only reply.

The men had captured an intact Lewis gun, easily distinguishable by the circular ammunition drum mounted above the breech and the large cooling shroud around its barrel. The barrel, still smoking, pointed skyward on its tripod. Hentsch surveyed the scene, unable to resist looking at the young man he'd killed. For a moment, the clatters and screams of the battle around him faded away. It was just him and the poor fellow lying there next to the gun.

A member of the Garde Civique (Civic Guard), the man did not have much of a uniform, just a dark blue overcoat over what looked like street clothes. A short, blood smattered top hat with the brim turned up on one side lay next to the body. The shot struck him in the left cheek bone, distorting the shape of his face. His eyes and mouth were open. As Hentsch gazed into that set of dead eyes, with absolutely nothing resembling life behind them, taking in what he had just done to another human being, the vomit briefly rose into his throat. There was only one way for him to justify his action. *He would have killed me just the same.*

First Army successfully pushed the Belgians back at Visé, suffering heavy casualties in the process. A casualty is any solder removed from combat by being killed or wounded. Some casualty figures also include men who are captured, as they are likewise removed from the combat equation. In the fighting at Visé, the 34th Brigade der Infanterie alone suffered thirty casualties among its officers, and an additional 1,130 among its enlisted men, a loss of more than twenty percent of its fighting strength in just one battle.

Liège, because of its proximity to Belgium's frontier with Germany, was the most heavily fortified city in the country. Surrounded by a ring of twelve fortresses spaced approximately two and a half miles apart from one another and at a radius of just over four miles from the city center, Liège was a formidable obstacle to the Schlieffen Plan's timetable. Capturing the city was essential, as Germany's massive northern armies required use of the railways which ran through the city in order to move the colossal amount of supplies necessary for arming, clothing and feeding hundreds of thousands of troops and pack animals.

Each of Liège's forts was constructed entirely of thick concrete and encircled by ditches and barbed wire entanglements. As a further protective measure, every fort shared intersecting lines of artillery fire with its neighbor on either side. To augment the effectiveness of the artillery, each fort was constructed atop a high elevation point, with the earth sloping away to allow greater visibility. The artillery pieces themselves were housed in retractable, rotating steel cupolas, and ranged in size from the largest 21cm howitzers, to 12cm and 15cm cannons, to smaller rapid-firing 57mm field guns.

Howitzers, specialized cannons which fire projectiles on a high-arching trajectory, made them effective weapons for siege-style warfare. The high trajectory enabled long-range firing and allowed a howitzer to lob rounds over the walls of fortifications, over hills, into entrenched positions, etc. Field guns and cannons are those weapons which fire projectiles in a relatively straight line. A third type, mortars, fire at the steepest trajectories, making them effective for combat in closer-quarters, allowing gunners to drop rounds directly on top of intended targets.

Construction of the fortresses at Liège was finished in 1891 and upon their completion, the fortresses were state-of-the-art. Their walls could withstand fire from artillery pieces up to and including 21cm howitzers, at the time assumed to be the largest piece of artillery that could readily be moved across land. The intervening twenty years saw significant advances in siege weaponry, however, with no additional upgrades being made to the Liège fortifications.

To prepare for the coming German onslaught, King Albert of Belgium ordered Lieutenant General Gerard Leman, commander of the fortresses, to "hold to the end with your division the position which you have been entrusted to defend." The fortresses were held by five hundred men each for a total of six thousand troops, while Leman commanded an additional thirty thousand men of the Belgian 3rd Division. They were tasked with holding the intervals between each fortress, to block any incursions into the city.

Hentsch and the entirety of the 34th Brigade were temporarily withdrawn from Kluck's First Army and reassigned to German Second Army in the attack against Liège as part of General Otto von Emmich's Army of the Meuse, a mixed group of brigades pulled from six other korps (III, IV, VII, X, XI, and II Kavallerie Korps). The remainder of First Army would bypass the city to the northwest.

The Belgian artillery, already ranged on specific zones of the surrounding countryside, inflicted harsh casualties on the advancing columns of German soldiers as they approached the forts, marching in strict formation. Machine gun fire cut down entire squads as they crossed the rolling fields, unable to reach proper cover.

On the march toward Fort Evegnée east of the city, Hentsch watched in horror as a gruppe from 13th Kompagnie a hundred feet in front of him took a direct hit from a 21cm shell. They disappeared in a gigantic brown fountain of uplifted dirt, and when the smoke and dust cleared there was nothing left of them but an eight foot deep crater. The blast wave knocked Hentsch and a few men near him on their rear ends. A wall of air pressure from the explosion temporarily disabled his hearing, save for a tremendous ringing in his head so high-pitched it made him clench his eyes shut. Dazed from the blast and with his heavy pack keeping him off-balance, Hentsch found himself unable to stand. Under increasingly heavy fire, the German columns were beginning to scatter.

A man from Hentsch's gruppe by the name of Engel grabbed him by the back of his collar and began dragging him across the ground toward the safety of a nearby shell hole, freshly made just minutes earlier. Machine gun and rifle fire kicked up dirt all around them. As Hentsch began to recover from the immediate effects of what was the first concussion in his life, certain images caught his attention and were seared into his memory, frames, like ghastly works of art in a gallery of horrors. The first was a severed hand, coated with dust, its fingers curled toward the palm. Engel stepped on it without so much as noticing. The hand didn't notice, either.

Within yards of the hand Hentsch saw a soldier, or at least *some* of a soldier, more just a set of legs and part of a torso with a pile of guts spilled from the end. *Where is the rest of him?* Engel dragged him straight through the dead man's entrails, smearing blood, shit and other vile juices onto his uniform. Another soldier, shot in the chest and drowning in his own blood, reached out a hand as Engel passed by. Hentsch briefly made eye contact with the terrified young fellow. He'd be dead soon, having survived less than two days of battle.

Reaching the shell hole safely, the grip on Hentsch's collar relaxed and both men tumbled into the crater, unsure of what to do next. It was just deep enough to accommodate them, and they cowered to avoid the bullets and shrapnel. Hentsch removed his pickelhaube and rubbed his hands on his head to try and ease the pain of his pounding concussion headache. His crew-cut brown hair was damp with sweat. After massaging his temples, he ran his index finger and thumb over his thin moustache and around the corner of his mouth before holding his chin to contemplate his situation. He couldn't think straight. The stink of acrid powder smoke hung heavy in the air. It worsened his headache.

He looked at Engel, who rested on one knee. Still short of breath from dragging Hentsch to the shell hole, Engel's face contorted as he sucked in air. His pupils were dilated so large that Hentsch could barely see the hazel of Engel's irises. Engel had a large nose, and his nostrils flared wide with each heavy breath. The exhausted face he made while breathing open-mouthed pulled back his lips, revealing a mouthful of crooked teeth. He was not a good-looking fellow. While he'd spoken to Engel once, maybe twice before mobilization, Hentsch did not know him well. Unfamiliarity didn't change the fact that Engel had probably just saved his life. He owed him for that.

"Are you hurt?" Engel shouted over the continuous bursting shells, prattling machine guns and snapping bullets.

"I'm fine!" Hentsch shouted back. "My head is throbbing, that's—"

CRUMP! Another 21cm shell burrowed into the ground and burst nearby. The ground shook, showering them with clumps of grass, dirt and rocks, but the walls of the shell hole protected them from the shrapnel and blast wave. *Jesus Christ!* Hentsch yanked his pickel-haube from the ground and slapped it back onto his head, then clapped his hands over his ears. He struggled to gather his wits.

"Can we make it to the fort?!" Engel asked.

"Not if this fire keeps up!"

A number of soldiers scurried past, the tops of their spiked helmets just visible from inside the crater. They were running away! One of them, an unteroffizier (corporal), stopped and peered over the edge, wild-eyed and frantically beckoning to Hentsch and Engel. It wasn't Unteroffizier Strauss, their commander in 1 Korporalschaft, but the man's order sounded as good as anyone else's.

"Get out of there, you two!" he shouted. "We're falling back!"

With that, the man turned to run. Hentsch and Engel scrambled out close behind him, dashing back across the rolling landscape they'd already traversed, hurdling shell holes, bodies and bodily fractions. Close by, Hentsch spotted the other five men under his command making their retreat amongst the swarm of retreating Germans. *Thank God they're still alive.* With every step, the disconcerting tickling sensation of bullets zipping by within inches made Hentsch almost certain he'd take one to the back of the head at any second.

They'd run a quarter mile or so when Engel stepped on a patch of dirt so slick with blood that his feet slipped from beneath him. He sprawled onto his back. Hentsch skidded to a stop in order to pull his new friend onto his feet, partially returning Engel's earlier favor. *Maybe I should drag him through a pile of shit and guts, too.*

The unteroffizier who'd called them out of the shell hole was about fifty yards ahead, moving at a strong clip. He was making for a small gulley a short way in front of him. The gulley wasn't saving anyone from the arching, heavy shellfire, but it offered protection from rifles and machine guns. Hentsch watched the man intently as he and Engel sprinted behind. *Hurry, friend. Just a few more steps and you'll make it!*

Before the unteroffizier reached the gulley, a jet of earth rose up mere inches to his right. A small caliber shell had found its mark. Upon its detonation, the man lifted off the ground. His right leg came apart and its disintegrated bits jettisoned away from the rest of him at high speed. His body floated two or three feet upward and away from the explosion, limbs flailing, and then flopped to the ground as if he were made of sausage links. His body contorted into a position no living person could handle. Hentsch and Engel didn't bother stopping to help him. He was most certainly dead. Engel jumped over the man's folded corpse while Hentsch strode over the shell hole that killed him. They slid into the gulley and continued their retreat.

Hentsch, Engel and the five other men of 2 Gruppe eventually reached the fallback positions safely. The initial infantry attack on Fort Evegnée was a disaster, with high casualties and nothing to show for the trouble. An attack on Fort Barchon, the next fort to the north, by the 53rd Regiment fared even worse. Infantry alone could not usurp the fortress city. Liège would have to be taken another way.

After falling back, Hentsch and his men were exhausted. He and Engel collapsed in the long afternoon shadow cast by a supply wagon, and used its front wheel as a backrest. Their faces were covered in grimy sweat and their uniforms soiled with dirt and the blood of the dead and wounded. They glanced at one another and Engel gave Hentsch a nod, then a crooked-toothed smile. He had flecks of dirt in his teeth. Hentsch hadn't noticed before, but Engel's big ears stuck out like fins below the rim of his pickelhaube.

It was uncomfortable sitting down with his heavy pack on; he couldn't lean back as far as he would have liked, but Hentsch didn't care. He was too tired to take it off. Apart from the six leather cartridge pouches at the junction of his leather waist belt and pack straps (three pouches on either side), most of an infantryman's equipment was kept on his back. Extra clothes, boots, food, a blanket and tent cloth were carried in a large cowhide knapsack on his upper back, with a greatcoat rolled up and strapped atop the pack. An aluminum mess tin was held against the knapsack's exterior by two leather straps. His brown cloth haversack hung from the waist belt behind his right hip and contained rations, personal effects and eating utensils. An aluminum water bottle covered in cloth clipped onto the haversack, and the bayonet scabbard and an entrenching tool hung next to it as well.

"Hentsch, you smell like shit," Engel informed him.

"I suppose I should. You dragged me through someone's guts."

Engel laughed and replied, "I should have left you there. I won't be able to take a nap with your stink sitting next to me."

Hentsch punched him on the shoulder. They barely knew one another, but in a very short time they'd been through quite an ordeal. He knew how bad he smelled, but his exhaustion outweighed his will to remove his knapsack and sift through it for a change of clothes. That would have to wait, disgusting as he felt.

Scores of weary soldiers trudged by. Many limped, their pant legs stained red from fresh bullet wounds, while others walked arm in arm with friends too wounded to stand on their own. Hentsch stared as one boy, his face totally expressionless and his right arm missing from the elbow, stumbled toward a regimental aid post, clutching the bloody stump with his other hand. The tattered remnants of his tunic's right sleeve swayed back and forth beneath his fingers, heavy from blood soaked into the fabric. *How in the hell is he still on his feet?* If the boy managed to not bleed to death, he'd go home, but his brief war experience had already taken something from both his body and his mind that he'd never get back.

As Hentsch began to nod off, he tilted his head back against the rolled greatcoat atop his pack. Staring skyward, he was surprised to see an enormous silver zeppelin almost directly overhead. There was a large, black Iron Cross on the airship's side. The zeppelin was on its way to bomb Liège. Unable to see the city directly, he followed the airship with his eyes as it floated toward its objective. After perhaps fifteen minutes he heard the bombs detonate, bearing distant witness to one of the first air raids in history.

From his headquarters inside the city, General Leman ordered the withdrawal of the Belgian 3rd Division, sending them to join the rest of the Belgian army mobilizing to the west.

The next day, August 6, Hentsch and his regiment rested. But elsewhere, Generalmajor Erich Ludendorff, acting as an observer for Second Army headquarters, learned that the commander of the 14th Brigade had been killed during a brutal frontal assault against one of the forts. The brigade lost nearly half its men in the attack. Ludendorff personally assumed command of 14th Brigade, ordered up supporting artillery and captured a piece of high ground overlooking Liège. He then sent a party forward under the flag of truce to demand General Leman's surrender. Leman refused, and afterward left his headquarters to take shelter in Fort Loncin, on the city's western side.

When Leman withdrew the 3rd Division, German infantry was able to bypass the fortresses and infiltrate the city. The fortresses, however, still held out. On the 8th, Fort Barchon was overwhelmed by a German infantry assault from within the city, after most of its artillery pieces had been damaged by German shellfire. It would be the only fort to fall to an infantry charge.

Hentsch began steeling himself for another harrowing attack. He wouldn't have to just yet. The German field artillery pounded the forts continuously, attempting to pummel them into submission, but the thick concrete structures refused to buckle. Inside the forts, though, built-in shortcomings were making themselves highly apparent to the Belgian defenders more or less trapped inside.

The fortresses did not have forced-air ventilation, which meant the concrete dust from numerous shell impacts, along with the powder smoke from both the firing Belgian guns and the exploding German shells hung in the air with no fans to dissipate it. At different points during the siege, some forts experienced well over a hundred shell impacts every hour. While the strongholds were supposedly equipped and supplied to hold out for a month during a siege, their construction had placed many essential facilities (including the barracks and sanitary facilities) facing the city near the forts' outer areas, making them untenable during the German assault. The continuous shelling and the threat from German infantry now inside the city (and thus behind the forts), pushed the Belgian defenders into the deep recesses of the concrete structures. The forts' interiors alone were unable to facilitate five hundred men. Sanitation and air quality rapidly eroded.

Four days passed with no major calls upon the infantry, and by August 12 Hentsch was beyond anxious. An assault against the fortresses had to come soon, and with the days of unrelenting bombardment, the defenders inside had to be pissed off and ready to take it out on someone. At lunch that day, Engel was asked by Unteroffizier Strauss to visit a supply dump close to the rear positions. After being gone for what must have been two hours he suddenly came back, out of breath and very obviously excited.

"You must come and see this!" he gasped. "They're bringing up the siege guns!"

A small band of soldiers from 13th Kompagnie, Hentsch's gruppe among them, followed Engel as he walked rather briskly back to the rear positions a mile and a half away. Hundreds of soldiers, motor cars and lorries and horse-drawn wagons traveled the road in both directions, on their way to destinations along or behind the miles of battlefront.

"Hey Hentsch, how old are you?" a skinny gemeine asked on the way. He had a higher-pitched voice that wasn't quite high enough to be comical. It was one of 2 Gruppe's men, the quietest one. Hentsch felt bad for not remembering his name. It was the only one he still didn't know. He'd heard it a number of times over the preceding days, it was just that the shy little fellow was somewhat forgettable.

"Twenty-four," Hentsch replied.

"Where are you from?"

"Schwerin."

"Me too!" the young man said, bringing his hand to his chest. "I had a gymnasium teacher that looked just like you, blue eyes, light brown hair and everything! He even had the same trimmed moustache. And wouldn't you know it, his name was Hentsch!"

In Germany, gymnasium was essentially the equivalent of high school.

"Some coincidence," Hentsch smiled. "That's my father."

"You don't say! He was a good teacher. My name is Simon, by the way." The gemeine extended his arm for an introductory hand shake.

"Simon. Right." *This time, I'll remember.* Hentsch reached out his hand to the pale, skinny young man. Simon's uniform hung from his shoulders as though it were a size too large. His hand was soft and small. *He doesn't look like a soldier in any sense of the word.*

Simon had light blonde hair, pale blue eyes and stood just five foot seven. He informed Hentsch, seemingly without taking a breath, that he was twenty years old, had two younger sisters, his dad worked at a power station, his mom baked the best cakes he'd ever eaten, and his dog was named Betty. Judging from his rapid-fire conversational manner, Hentsch also inferred that Simon loved to talk, provided he had someone to listen.

The little fellow was open and friendly, and went on to quietly reveal that, so far, he'd yet to fire a shot at any Belgians. It was something he didn't want the other men walking with them to overhear, though why he thought it okay to tell his gefreiter was anyone's guess. *What is a boy this gentle doing in the infantry? He should be an orderly, or a cook.* Hentsch, of course, had fired his weapon, but he understood where Simon was coming from and refused to pass judgment. The dead eyes of that Belgian soldier weren't something he'd soon forget.

"Hentsch, have you heard the rumors?" Simon asked, leaning toward him, as if he intended to pass a secret.

"About what?" Hentsch answered, with just a hint of sarcasm. He was curious as to the sort of crazy stories his fellow soldiers were already starting to concoct.

"I heard civilians have fired on our men, and we've retaliated by rounding up suspects to make examples of them. I've even heard of some troops robbing houses and raping women."

"Where would you have heard such things?"

"If you keep your ears open and stay quiet, you hear many things."

"A lie is a thing."

"So is a truth."

"Indeed," Hentsch said. "I think we could agree that what went on in those towns dwells somewhere in between."

Hentsch hadn't heard any such rumors, let alone witnessed such acts. He hoped it wasn't true. On the way to Visé, the 90th Regiment had passed through a small village and experienced nothing of the sort.

Simon was clearly mortified by the rumor and said, "I won't hurt any civilians, even if they do fire at me. We invaded their country, you know." He nodded at Hentsch as if he were unaware they stood on foreign soil.

"Yes, Simon," Hentsch said, eyebrows raised. "I know we did."

"Holy shit!" a soldier ahead of them gasped.

The men approached a wide clearing in which there was great commotion. Hundreds of men and three immense horse teams were moving the three pieces of a disassembled Krupp 42cm siege howitzer into place. For two hours Simon, Hentsch and Engel made small talk with the other soldiers, watching as the crew assembled the huge, black steel weapon. The "Big Bertha," as it came to be known, was built by Friedrich Krupp AG, a steel and weapons manufacturer based in Essen, Germany. The forty-three ton weapon, with its 42cm (16.5 inch) internal barrel diameter, was operated by a crew of 285 men and fired a projectile weighing in excess of 1,800 pounds at a sluggish, but devastating rate of eight rounds per hour.

Apart from the guns mounted on heavy naval battleships, the Krupp 42cm was the largest and most destructive weapon on the planet. From the ground to the tip of its high-angled barrel, a Bertha stood nearly twenty feet tall. The two wheels of its massive carriage were as tall as a man, weighed thousands of pounds each, and in place of tires were ringed with metal "feet," which were a series of thick steel plates used for traction and to prevent the gun from bogging down. Owing to the cost of production and maintenance, just twelve Big Berthas were ever built.

The crew finished the assembly, and the first gigantic shell was loaded into the breech. Hentsch's group gained permission to watch the weapon fire, but they had to move almost five hundred yards away to do it safely. The gun was fired electronically by its crew, all wearing protective headgear, from a distance of three hundred yards. A person standing next to the gun as it fired could be killed by the percussion alone. Even from hundreds of feet away, the pressure wave from the launching shell could burst unprotected eardrums. Hentsch and the others held their hands over their ears, waiting in excitement for the gun to fire.

Seconds ticked by, and the anticipation grew. Hentsch had never seen such an impressive weapon in operation before. Without warning, the distant barrel recoiled, smoke bellowed from the end, the carriage lurched, and a second later *whoosh!* A shockwave blew past them. The ground trembled beneath their feet as the tremendous *BOOM* echoed across the countryside. Hentsch was amazed. *I bet you could hear that thing from twenty miles away.*

He put himself in the shoes of a Belgian, stuck inside a fortress with the nearly one ton shell, packed with a high-explosive (HE) payload, dropping onto the roof above his head. The thought of being anywhere underneath that detonating shell was horrific. He glanced over at Simon, who looked upset. His face somehow became even paler—his sympathy for the Belgians was unmistakable. On the walk back, everyone was silent. Seeing the Bertha fire was impressive, but in a way, sickening at the same time.

For four more days four Big Berthas, along with several slightly smaller and more versatile Škoda 30.5cm howitzers on loan from Austria-Hungary, pulverized the Belgian fortresses. The Škodas, manufactured by the Austro-Hungarian firm Škoda Works, were also transported in three sections. A specially-fitted fifteen ton tractor pulled each section on its own separate trailer. The fifty thousand pound guns were operated by a crew of about fifteen, assembled in just fifty minutes, and could fire two different projectiles at a rate of ten rounds per hour—one was a delayed-action fuse shell weighing 850 pounds, the other a lighter, 630 pound impact-fuse shell.

One by one each fortress fell, pulverized into surrender by the monstrous guns. Great plumes of smoke and dust rose thousands of feet into the air, blanketing the fortresses, the city, and the surrounding countryside. Hentsch grew ill at the thought of what the poor men in the fortresses suffered through. *No sleep. No reinforcements. No retreating. They're completely helpless.* There was no way for them to retaliate against the massive guns firing from several miles away. While staying inside the forts and refusing to surrender took tremendous courage, the suffering of the men inside was truly a fruitless endeavor.

On what would prove to be the siege's last day, August 16, Fort Loncin took a direct hit to its ammunition magazine, exploding the walls and collapsing the entire structure in on itself. When the Germans approached they found General Leman, wounded and unconscious, lying in the rubble. Upon capturing the commander, he was brought before General von Emmich, where Leman formally surrendered, requesting it be a matter of record that he was unconscious when the Germans found him. After surrendering the city, Leman attempted to offer his sword to the German general.

Out of respect, and in an act of true chivalry, von Emmich said to Leman, "No, keep your sword. To have crossed swords with you has been an honor."

The Belgians suffered twenty thousand casualties in their valiant defense of Liège.

DENIS

Général Charles Lanrezac's French Fifth Army was on the march, heading northeast toward the Belgian frontier. To join up with Fifth Army, Denis Roux and the men of 2nd Bataillon, 144th Régiment d'Infanterie had spent the last two weeks of mobilization crossing the French countryside first by train, then on foot. Garrisoned at Bordeaux in southeastern France prior to the declaration of war, the regiment had been closer to Spain than they were to Paris. After crossing the country, the 144th joined Fifth Army as part of the 70th Brigade d'Infanterie, of the 35th Division d'Infanterie of XVIII Corps. XVIII Corps was commanded by Général Jacques de Mas-Latrie. Fifth Army had orders to guard the River Meuse, which ran through northeastern France and across southern Belgium.

Chef d'État-Major de l'Armée (Army Chief of Staff) Général Joseph Joffre issued Fifth Army's orders as part of Plan XVII, the battle strategy he helped design in the event of war with Germany. Much like Germany's Schlieffen Plan, it was the only plan the French had, but unlike Schlieffen, Plan XVII allowed for more flexibility concerning the deployment of French forces.

Joffre opted to send the majority of his troops on an eastward offensive into Alsace and Lorraine, the territory south of Luxembourg, a large portion of which Germany had annexed from France after France's humiliating surrender during the Franco-Prussian War of 1870-71. Joffre fought in the siege of Paris during the Franco-Prussian War, and his decision to launch an assault into the very territory that became Germany's spoil of war greatly informed that decision. Losing Alsace-Lorraine had been a tremendous blow to French pride, and the political consequences of not launching an assault to retake those territories were far-reaching.

Another lingering effect of the French defeat during that war was a rigid belief in the power of the all-out offensive. Put simply, strategic retreat was the absolute last option. Any territory lost to the enemy needed immediate retaking via counterattack. The bayonet charge, while still a potentially effective tool when used in opportune moments, was overemphasized greatly in the training of French infantry. Rapid and coordinated marching was the standard, as it was viewed as having contributed to France's defeat in 1871. Indoctrinating the infantry in such tactics would have been fine in the decade or so following the Franco-Prussian War but firepower, both individual and massed, had increased exponentially in the forty years since the conflict ended.

The invention of the machine gun by Hiram Maxim in 1884 had revolutionized warfare. With the Maxim Gun, a crew of three to four men could pour five hundred rounds per minute toward the enemy's lines, equaling the firepower of thirty men armed with bolt-action repeating rifles. In terms of individual firepower, not even the bolt-action repeating rifle had been in wide use during the Franco-Prussian War. While the weapon's concept had been invented several decades earlier, it took many years to develop and was not adopted by most of Europe's armies until the 1880s or later.

The French had themselves spurred the advance of artillery, introducing a type of rapid-firing cannon in 1896 that quickly led other nations to do the same. Yet even after their own military had introduced a groundbreaking and highly destructive new weapon, *still* the French did not greatly alter their training protocols. The offensive mindset of the French commanders, combined with the infantry and cavalry's dated training philosophies in the face of modern weaponry, spelled disaster in the conflict to come.

Joffre's initial deployment of his forces indicated a near total disregard of Belgian reports that a sizeable German force had crossed the River Meuse and advanced into Belgium. He viewed the Germans' northern advance as being limited in scope, and thus sent only Fifth Army and the much smaller British Expeditionary Force, recently arrived in France, to oppose it.

In the event, the execution of Plan XVII began with an incursion into lower Alsace on August 7, by Général Yvon Dubail's French First Army. The Battle of Mulhouse was the first engagement fought between the French and Germans in the war, and took place just miles from the border with neutral Switzerland. Initially, the French pushed the Germans back, but the arrival of German reinforcements on August 10 swung the momentum and the French were forced to withdraw to their initial jumping-off points.

Joffre next ordered Général Paul Pau's Army of Alsace, and the newly-formed Army of Lorraine, comprised of the last of the French reserve forces and commanded by Général Michel Maunoury, to join an all-out offensive with the First (Dubail) and Second (Général Edouard de Castelnau) Armies along the entire Alsace-Lorraine front. Beginning on the 14th, the French clashed with German Sixth and Seventh Armies, commanded by Crown Prince Rupprecht of Bavaria. The ensuing fight involved hundreds of thousands of soldiers, spread along a forty mile battlefront, marching in formation straight into heavy machine gun, rifle and artillery fire. The French offensive was a total failure and resulted in appalling casualties on both sides, culminating in a disastrous French retreat.

Aspirant Denis Roux, more than a hundred and fifty miles away from the Battle of Lorraine, was unaware of the death and destruction then occurring in the southeast. All he could think of was the blazing sunlight beating down on him. Fifth Army had already marched twenty miles in ninety-degree heat, and his canteen was bone-dry.

"Dammit," he said, shaking the empty canteen above his open mouth. He ran his tongue along his pallet and across his lips, trying to moisten them. He'd not anticipated such heat, and was upset with himself for not sipping his water more sparingly.

Denis removed his dark blue wool kepi, a type of cap with a circular top, vertical walls and a small visor. He ran his hands through his black hair, slicking it back. His head was drenched with sweat. He flicked his hand toward the ground to wick the moisture from his palm, before wiping the remainder on the leg of his bright red wool trousers. He glanced up at the sun, focusing his dark blue eyes directly on the shining disk for a fraction of a second. When he looked away, fuzzy dots lingered in front of his eyes, making it difficult to see the long, dark blue coats of the men marching in line ahead of him.

"Hey Denis, have a sip."

Denis's best friend Patrice held out his canteen. It was still half-full.

"Thanks Pat," Denis said as he took the canteen. He took a small swig and handed the canteen back to Patrice, swishing the water in his mouth as they walked. He wiped the back of his hand across his mouth to free the droplets trapped in his trimmed black moustache.

The stubble on his cheeks and chin had already grown back; it scraped against his hand when he wiped his mouth. He'd last shaved back in Bordeaux.

"I miss her already," Patrice complained.

"Come now, Patrice, we left but two weeks ago."

"Yes, but things were going so well. And you've seen her. Tell me I can find a better looking girl than her, and I'll tell you you're full of shit."

Denis looked at him and smirked. Patrice was the type who became overly excited about all manner of things, women especially. When he spoke of them, his green eyes lit up. Denis sometimes thought that Patrice's green eyes would have been better suited on a girl, rather than on a man who loved to talk about them. Every so often, he made fun of his friend by telling him to grow his hair longer and shave his pencil moustache so as to become the female God had always intended him to be.

While Patrice was fairly handsome, he had shiny brown hair and soft, slightly effeminate facial features. That, coupled with his green eyes and the fact that he stood just five foot six, led to Denis teasing that Patrice was girly enough to be his own sister. He'd say that the only thing keeping Patty, the sister, at bay was the moustache and the occasional haircut. Patrice hated that joke.

Patrice had less of a military bearing than Denis. He was conscripted into the army as an ordinary soldat ("soldier" or private). Denis, on the other hand, was a graduate of the prestigious École Spéciale Militaire de Saint-Cyr (literally the "Special Military School of Saint-Cyr," or Saint-Cyr for short). He attained the rank of aspirant upon his graduation. His next step would have been to attend infantry school, to further his rank to sous-lieutenant (second lieutenant). The war may have interrupted his infantry school plans, but it did not disrupt his chance for promotion. On the battlefield, in fact, he might have a chance to ascend the ranks even faster, a fact of which he was keenly aware.

At his request, he was given command of a squad, usually a job reserved for a caporal (corporal). While technically a demotion of sorts, he preferred to have immediate responsibility to a group of men under his command, to demonstrate his ability to lead. As luck (or special request) would have it, he took command of 2 Escouade, of the 1st Half of 2 Section, in F Compagnie, 2nd Bataillon. The lowest levels of the French infantry's hierarchy consisted of sections (platoons), split into two half-sections, with two escouades (squads) in each half-section. His squad just so happened to included Patrice, making Denis his immediate superior. In Denis's mind their friendship superseded rank and, generally speaking, he acted the same with Patrice in uniform as well as out. He made a point of treating the other twelve men under his command with the same respect he gave his friend, viewing them as his equals rather than subordinates.

"When do you suppose this thing will be over?" asked Patrice.

"I don't know, Pat, how can I? Hopefully we'll have won before Christmas."

"Damn. That's a long time," he scowled. "What if Cécile won't wait for me?"

"Well then hell, Patrice!" laughed Denis. "If she can't wait a few months, then she wasn't worth the trouble!"

"Oh, she's worth it," Patrice said. "Her tits alone are worth it." He held his hands out in front of his chest, mimicking the sizeable bust of which he spoke.

"I bet she'd love to hear that," Denis scoffed. "Such a romantic."

"What girl wouldn't want to be told she has nice tits?"

"The Kaiser's wife."

Patrice laughed. He had only met his girl about two months before the mobilization, but Denis was happy his friend had someone specific to think about and fight for. During the month in which he'd known her (Patrice held off introduction the first month), Denis had gotten a kick out of seeing the two lovers together. Cécile was indeed a busty and shapely young woman. She also stood the same height as Patrice. While she was very cute, Denis was certain that due to her bust size and curves she and Patrice shared a similar bodyweight.

Cécile was safe back in Bordeaux, a long way from any fighting. Denis, however, had interests much closer to danger. He grew up in Cambrai, in northeastern France, just twenty-five miles from the Belgian border. His parents and his sister Louise still lived in Cambrai, where his father worked as a carpenter, his sister, a nurse at a local hospital. Mrs. Roux stayed at home, where she managed the household and tended the family's substantial garden. They'd be safe so long as Fifth Army prevented the Germans from crossing the border.

On August 14, the news began to filter out of Belgium that Liège was on the verge of surrender. On the 15th, the most forward elements on the right flank of Lanrezac's Fifth Army—Général Franchet d'Esperey's I Corps and Colonel Henri-Philippe Pétain's 4th Brigade—clashed with and subsequently pushed back General Manfred von Richthofen's I Kavallerie Korps near the Belgian city of Dinant, on the River Meuse. General von Richthofen was the great uncle of a young man who would rise high in prominence (quite literally) during the coming few years...

New orders came from Joffre at le Grand Quartier Général (General Headquarters, or GQG for short) in Vitry-le-François. Fifth Army was to halt their eastward march toward the German center in the Ardennes, and instead proceed northeast into Belgium toward the fortified city of Namur, at the intersection of two major rivers, the Sambre and the Meuse. The River Sambre was a tributary of the Meuse, and flowed generally east northeast from the French border city of Maubeuge to Namur. The Meuse flowed out of France from almost due south, running northward to its intersection with the Sambre at Namur, before turning east across Belgium and flowing past Liège.

It had still not dawned on Joffre that the strength of Germany's northern army group was radically underestimated. Even after learning of the fall of Liège, and of Lanrezac's report that German Third Army was currently attacking his forces near the Belgian city of Dinant, Joffre insisted on taking the offensive. Dinant rested on the eastern bank of the River Meuse, mere miles from another fortified French border city at Givet. In sending Fifth Army to the inverted V of the two rivers, Joffre had ordered them into a wedge, with General Max von Hausen's German Third Army to the east, presently engaged at Dinant, and General Karl von Bülow's Second Army approaching from the north.

Fifth Army began arriving at the Sambre on the 20th. They were spread across a twenty-five mile front from Charleroi in the west to the fortress at Namur in the east. They awaited the arrival of the British Expeditionary Force (BEF) then advancing toward the city of Mons further to the west. The two armies were to be linked together by Général Jean-François Sordet's Cavalerie Corps. Even with the strength of their combined forces, French Fifth Army and the BEF were vastly outnumbered by the three German armies.

Fifth Army's right flank began heavily engaging Max von Hausen's Third Army along the Meuse on the 21st. Elements of von Bülow's Second Army had also successfully crossed the Sambre in two places, establishing bridgeheads the French could not push back across the river. It was now morning on August 22. The 144th Regiment was positioned near the center of XVIII Corps' line on Fifth Army's left flank, advancing due north toward Charleroi. They had yet to meet the Germans.

Denis wiped the sweat from beneath his cap once again. Wearing a heavy blue greatcoat and weighty pack in such sweltering weather would have been torturous enough were it his only concern. Alas, he and his fellow soldiers wore their greatcoats and packs in addition to the concern of hostile Germans marching their way. The country was essentially treeless for miles around, with undulating farm fields and simple wooden fences forming odd geometries that stretched in all directions. Only the occasional tree was scattered along the road-sides, offering next to no shade to keep the sun from pounding against the marching men. Some units had already engaged the ene-my further east. Denis heard the faint rumble of the German artillery firing at his countrymen off in the distance.

F Compagnie's advance paralleled a road. They marched abreast one another rather than in a column. A long line of soldiers in red kepis, dark blue coats and red trousers stretched for hundreds of yards on either side of the narrow dirt road. Denis and his squad were about a hundred feet from the road's left shoulder, moving through the grass next to the wooden fence of a large barley field. The soldiers marching on the opposite side of the fence moved knee-deep through the golden barley plants, *whooshing* through them with each step. Due to the land's undulations and the scattered farmhous-es and barns, Denis was unable to see much more than the two hun-dred thirty men from F Compagnie on either side of him, before an obstacle or the landscape concealed the rest of the bataillon.

The other compagnies were close, but Denis couldn't shake a feel-ing of isolation in his being unable to see them. Regardless, out of his line of sight the sections and compagnies of 2nd Bataillon, and tens of thousands more men from hundreds of compagnies in a multitude of bataillons would all soon lock horns with the Germans.

As the line moved forward, men stepped slower and more delib-erately as the distant battles intensified. An increasing number of units collided with the Germans further down the line. The din from those collisions drew closer by the minute. The men planted their feet carefully, as if navigating bare-foot through a field of broken glass. They slinked and crouched lower every few yards.

Denis had never experienced such a heightened level of alertness, not in his entire life. He heard individual blades of grass crunch be-neath his feet. When someone nearby stepped on a twig, Denis snapped his head in that direction fearing it was the first gunshot. Those next to him may have breathed normally, but to Denis their inhalations and exhalations were the pumping of bellows. His own breath roared inside his head, loud as a rushing waterfall. Only punching himself in the chest could have matched the intensity at which his heart thumped inside his ribs.

"Denis," Patrice whispered between shaky breaths, "I see them." He nodded ahead. Others had seen them too, and they pointed. Some gasped.

Approximately half a mile away, an unbroken line of tan helmets began to sprout from the fields, emerging from behind the top of a wide knoll. The heads blended well with the golden brown crops, but when their grey shoulders rose into view, they were much easier to spot. Denis shifted his eyes from left to right, examining the width of the grey mass creeping over the knoll. The line was several heads deep. *There are thousands of them.* He could only see the long line directly ahead of him—it was daunting enough. He was unaware that General von Bülow had ordered three entire corps—over a hundred thousand men—to launch a frontal assault against the full length of Fifth Army's line.

Without a word, Lieutenant Armistead, 2 Section's commander, ran a few steps in front of the French line, about twenty yards to Denis's right. The lieutenant wore battle dress similar to that of his men, his only obvious visual distinction being the sword on his left hip, and less so, the two gold bars on his greatcoat's sleeve cuffs. He held up his hands and the line stopped. Reaching to his belt, the lieutenant flipped open the binocular case on his right hip and brought the field glasses to his eyes.

After ten seconds, Armistead put the binoculars down and signaled to the men by lowering his hands. The men smoothly and silently dropped down to one knee, raising their rifles to their shoulders while the lieutenant moved back behind them. Fifty hands released the locking lugs on their rifle bolts all at once, making fifty audible clicks.

"I wish we were in that barley field," Denis whispered to Patrice. In a crouched position, the plants would hide his red trousers and a significant portion of his coat. Patrice nodded to Denis to acknowledge him. He was so nervous the nod was more of a spasm.

"Shhh!" someone nearby hissed. Some were more high-strung than others. Denis was somewhere in the middle.

Snap! The first supersonic 7.92mm Mauser round whizzed by somewhere to Denis's right, startling him and everyone who'd heard it. Just over two seconds later, the distant shot echoed across the expanse. No one was hit. *Pop!* Someone in the barley field could hold their fire no longer, and answered the first German shot. All at once the silence vanished in an uproar of French rifles. The Germans, still almost eight hundred yards away, continued marching forth.

Choosing an individual target and aiming carefully at that distance, while possible, was only reserved for the most supremely talented and steady marksmen. At a half mile's range, most simply took an educated guess as to where their shot would go, and then pulled the trigger.

Denis aimed above the tan helmet of an individual he'd singled out. Nothing particular about the German had prompted his selection; it was just the luck of the draw. He couldn't make out any facial features, couldn't tell if the man was young or old, couldn't read his insignia to learn his rank, he just knew his duty was to kill him. His hands trembled and his sights swayed, as subconsciously his humanity shuddered at his murderous intentions. His soul screamed at him to remove his finger from the trigger, but he squeezed it anyway. Compassion had no place where he found himself, and would only serve in getting him killed.

Pow! The rifle recoiled into his shoulder and sent its deadly 8mm round zipping downrange at over two thousand feet per second. For the first time in his life, Denis had fired a shot at another human being. The bullet took less than a second to travel the eight hundred yards. He watched for his target to fall, but the man kept walking. He'd missed.

"Shit!" Denis quietly chided himself.

"Are you hit?" Patrice asked with concern, loud enough to be heard over the gunfire. He squeezed off a shot.

"What? No. I missed."

"You must be ashamed, missing such an easy one."

"Right. Where'd your last shot end up?"

"Who knows?"

Denis aimed at the same man again. He waited several seconds, steadying his hand, letting the distance close up a bit more. In the corner of his eye he saw Germans dropping elsewhere down the line; at least some French shooters were hitting their mark. He fired again, and again the man did not fall.

He was mad at himself, but he was also mad at his target. As he took aim for the third time, the Germans—closed to within six hundred yards—disappeared. They'd taken up a firing line and would soon return heavy fire. The Battle of Charleroi was fully underway.

Over the shooting, Denis heard a soldier in the barley field scream. He turned his head to look left in time to see the man fall forward, blood spurting from his chest, before vanishing into the plants. Two men next to him sprang into action to aid him. From the shoulders up, those in the field were dark blue and red against a golden backdrop. It wasn't any safer for them, not unless they were to lay prone. They could if they wanted to, making themselves virtually invisible, but in so doing would surrender their ability to effectively return fire. Shrinking into the barley would diminish the section's effective firepower and weaken the line, betraying the men with little to no cover. Hiding was not the courageous option.

A man to Denis's right, ten feet off the side of the road, yelped and fell backward, clutching at his thigh. A soldier next to him shouldered his rifle and dragged the man away from the line for treatment. If two men within a hundred feet had already been hit, Denis wondered how many across the miles of battlefront had become casualties in the past several hours. The artillery he'd heard rumbling further east must have been wreaking havoc.

FOOM! The first shell sailed over the French line a hundred yards to Denis's left. It detonated at the far edge of the barley field, hundreds of yards behind the nearest men. At the sound of the explosion, most of the line dove to their stomachs to lay prone. Lying prone made them far less likely to be hit by flying shrapnel when the German gunners found their range. Even as the artillery opened up, the French soldiers kept their eyes focused on the German infantry ahead, firing at any targets of opportunity while the shellfire increased around them.

F Compagnie held their part of the line for the whole day, keeping the Germans pinned. The opposing sides bit off small chunks of the ground which separated them, waiting for the chance to breach and then exploit any weaknesses in the other's line. Denis fought hard, praying in silence that a bullet or shrapnel ball wouldn't find him. Many prayers went unanswered that day, and several men within a hundred yards of him were killed or wounded throughout the encounter.

He had some close calls himself, hearing more than one searing hot shrapnel ball or bullet zip by, but as dusk fell it appeared the French positions would hold. He had no idea how many Germans there were to the north and east, but in Denis's mind his squad, section and so far as he could tell the entire bataillon had made a fine account of themselves.

GORDON

Gordon dropped an armful of bricks on top of the pile with a familiar *clink* that he'd heard so many times before. He wiped the sweat from his forehead and brought his hands to his lower back, pushing out his chest to stretch. Since crashing his aeroplane almost two months earlier, he could think of nothing but getting airborne again. The thought was all-consuming. At work, he slogged through his days, pissing them away in a haze of boredom, frustrated with the monotony.

He couldn't tolerate waiting another few years of saving money just to start a second project from scratch. It was too long to wait. Materials were too expensive, and he'd been able to salvage almost nothing from the wreck. The way he saw it, he had only one chance to fly in the near future. At the dinner table that night, he planned to bring it up.

The evening's dinner was a rare occasion. The entire family, including his older twin brothers Jonathan and Ezra, their wives and children, and his sister Luanne and her new husband were there. Jon and Ezra were twenty-four. Jon married his wife Anna when he was just eighteen, and they had their first boy, Anson, two years after that. Ezra and his wife Lottie had been married for just over a year; their baby girl Flora was two months old. Luanne was only eighteen; so was her husband Jerome. They'd gotten married three weeks before Gordon finished building his machine. David, a year and half older than Gordon, had moved out on his own that summer; he brought his girlfriend Cleo. Like Gordon, his younger brother Thomas, age nineteen, and Liza, the youngest, still lived at home.

Everyone was in a good mood, chatting loudly as the smell of Virginia Graham's cooking wafted from the kitchen and spread throughout the house. Gordon kept to himself while dinner was prepared. He sat outside on the front step in silent contemplation, playing out the potential scenarios as to how his family, mainly his mother and father, would react to what he had planned. The scent of his mother's delicious meal trickled through the open windows and onto the front steps, and his nostrils and belly informed his brain there was more than just one objective that night. He was hungry.

With everyone gathered at the table, Anson clasped his hands together to say grace. Gordon wasn't interested in praying—he was famished and the food spread out before him looked heavenly. His mother made a big turkey, mashed potatoes, sweet corn, green beans and Gordon's favorite, cornbread. Steam rose from every dish and the aroma made the empty pit in his stomach feel as though it might turn him inside out. Everyone folded their hands and bowed their heads, while Gordon reluctantly participated, subtly rolling his eyes.

"Dear Lord," his father began, and Gordon's mind instantly wandered. *What bullshit. God didn't put the food on this table. Our family's hard work did. We've done our part and earned everything we have. I've worked hard, too, much harder than many people my age, and I deserve a chance to do what I love, same as anybody else.* He didn't place much value in prayer, or in God for that matter. It didn't escape him that a lot of people who prayed still had things pretty rough. Heck, half the hard working, God fearing families in the neighborhood had trouble putting enough food on the table. Murder, rape, hatred, childhood disease, the war in Europe he'd begun reading about in the papers. Where was the Lord in all of that?

"Amen."

Anson finished his prayer, and the family (minus Gordon) parroted him in unison. Gordon would make his announcement soon, but he'd let everyone eat first; let them get full and contented. He worried what he had to say might lead to an argument. He looked around the table at all the faces. One of his eldest brothers was smirking at him. *What the hell are you looking at, Ezra?*

"So Gordon, I heard you crashed your flying machine," Ezra taunted, as he scooped mashed potatoes onto his plate. His bald head glistened from the light hanging over the table. He had a small gap between his front teeth; Gordon had hated that gap-toothed smirk for as long as he could remember.

Ezra's wife jabbed him in the ribs. He knew about the crash two days after it happened, the whole family did, so well past a month later it needed no bringing up. It was obvious to Gordon his brother just wanted to get under his skin.

"You're right, Ez," Gordon replied, "I crashed. Right after the machine *I* built flew over five hundred feet across the field back there." He pointed his finger toward the window before reaching for the cornbread. "What was the last thing you built?"

"A wall."

"That must have been difficult."

"So what? At least mine is still standing. You crashed. Your little experiment's over. It's time to stop sulking at work like a child."

The mocking tone his oldest brother took made Gordon clench his fist under the table. "Eat shit, Ezra..." he muttered.

"Gordon!" his mother hissed. "There are children present!"

"Sorry ma," Gordon said. "Sorry Liza. Sorry Anson." Jonathan's little boy was hardly paying attention.

"You're the one who ate shit, Gordon, when your flying toy hit the ground."

"Ezra Graham, that's enough out of you!" Virginia said. She knew full well just how much Gordon's aeroplane meant to him.

Jonathan, the mirror image of his twin, with a mouthful of turkey and needing to add his two cents said, "Ma, Gordon wasted almost four years on that stupid project, and look where it got him. He spent everything he had."

Jon's wife shot him a dirty look.

Anson Graham was used to the older brothers picking on Gordon. For most of their lives he let it happen, just as long as it didn't get out of hand. He figured it would toughen Gordon up, and he was right. This time, though, he took a side. "Hey Jon, Ezra, what sort of grades did you boys get in school?" he asked.

The two men stopped chewing their food and looked at each other before Jonathan answered humbly, "We did okay, pa."

"Did you? See I remember otherwise," Anson grinned. "What sort of grades did you get, Gordon?"

Gordon smiled at his father before taking an enthusiastic bite of his cornbread. Anson kept track of all his children's grades, start to finish. Gordon had never once missed a day of school, and maintained a perfect average from the day he began kindergarten to the day he graduated high school. Jon and Ezra couldn't say the same for themselves, not even close.

"You two dummies have no business diminishing anything Gordon has ever done," Anson said, a hint of anger in his voice, "let alone calling his doings stupid. When he sneezes he shoots out more brains than you boys ever had. Let's see you two build an aeroplane. Dang, let's see you bricklaying fools even draw a picture of one! You know what the difference is between you boys? Gordon lays bricks for extra money, you two do it because it's all you're good for!"

During the argument, Liza had quietly excused herself from the table. She came back with four photographs in her hand. "Fetch a look at these, you ugly, bald shitheads."

"Liza!" Virginia snapped. "Do I have to get the soap for this whole family?! What's gotten into all of you?"

"Give her a pass just this once, Ginny," their smiling father urged his appalled wife.

Gordon tried not to laugh as his little sister slapped the pictures down in front of the twins. When he was her age, he'd never have mouthed off to Jon and Ezra like that.

In addition to three shots of Gordon standing by his machine, there was one more. During his short flight, Liza was able to snap just one picture, and she'd made the most of it. In the fourth photo, Gordon could clearly be seen sitting in his pilot's seat, an ear to ear smile spread across his face, conveying the overwhelming joy he'd felt in getting airborne. In the background, a distant tree line visible beneath the aeroplane demonstrated irrefutably that he and his craft had achieved proper flight. Jonathan and Ezra didn't say another word, put in their place by a twelve-year-old girl.

When everyone had finished eating, it was time for Gordon to announce his plan. He looked around the table again, cleared his throat and said, "While you're all here, there's something I want to share." He didn't wait for every eye to look up at him. "I'm going to join the Army Signal Corps."

The table fell silent. Virginia opened her mouth to speak, but Gordon interrupted her to say more.

"Back in July, Congress voted to create an aviation section in the Signal Corps. I'm joining the army, and I'm going to fly aeroplanes."

His mother frowned and said, "Gordon, I don't think the army has a place for—"

This time Anson interrupted her. "Ginny, the boy knows more about aeroplanes than just about every man in the army, I wager. Why shouldn't he be given a chance to show it?"

"But Anson!" she protested. "We're—"

"No one at this table needs a refresher on that, Virginia, we're all aware. Gordon just wants a chance to serve his country and it's just as much his country as anyone's," Anson said, wagging his finger at each family member. "The Constitution says so. He's got the most brains of anyone you or I have ever met, and we both know he's got a lot to offer. No matter what he chooses to do."

"Daddy," Luanne said, "the men who wrote the Constitution weren't really thinking about us when they wrote it."

The older brothers simply shook their heads.

Thomas and Liza were huddled together at the end of the table, whispering back and forth. Anson noticed and asked, "Do you two have something you want to say?"

"We think Gordy can do it," said Liza.

Ezra rolled his eyes and mumbled, "What do they know? Stupid asses..." The remark prompted another jab from his wife.

Anson ended the discussion by saying, "We won't speak any more on this. Gordon, tomorrow you'll put on your nice suit and I'll drive you to speak to the army recruiter in town. You'll bring those photographs to show him, too."

"That was my plan."

Gordon was so nervous and excited that night he could hardly sleep. He stared at his bedroom ceiling for hours, and finally dozed off unsure of the time.

The drive to town the next morning was even worse. Gordon wracked his brain, rehearsing what he planned to say over and over. He fidgeted in his seat, adjusted his blue silk tie a hundred times, and smoothed out the lapel on his grey suit to look as crisp as possible. *No other men volunteering for the Signal Corps have built their own aeroplane. Only me. They'll have to understand that.* Based on merit, intellect, hard work and knowledge of the subject at hand, Gordon had to be considered a viable candidate.

He took a long, deep breath, and let it out slowly as his father pulled his new Ford Model T up to the curb at the recruiter's office. It was a small brick building, on a dingy side street, lodged between a tailor and a barber shop. Some people across the street stared, likely surprised that Anson owned an automobile.

"Good luck, Gordon," Anson said. "I'll be waiting right here."

Gordon paused outside the building for a moment, adjusting the knot on his tie one last time. He tugged on the quarters of his coat to straighten them, and then gently turned the brass knob on the office's green wooden door. The knob was loose, and the door creaked when he opened it. He peeked his head into the small room first.

The recruiter sat at his desk, head pointed down, writing something on a sheet of paper. He ignored the first creak. When Gordon pushed open the door, it creaked even louder and he flinched, not wanting to annoy the man at the desk. He stepped inside and said,

"Hello, sir, my name is Gordon," and the man looked up from his paperwork.

The office's interior was unremarkable. The floor, unvarnished wooden plank, was dirty, and creaked almost as loud as the door had. There were only two windows. Both were shuttered. A stack of wood chairs sat in an empty corner. A small electric table fan hummed on the recruiter's desk. The room was incredibly stuffy.

"What can I do for you, boy?" the man said, with a pronounced southern drawl.

Boy, Gordon thought. *Damn.*

"Well, sir, I'd like to join up," Gordon said, "I'm interested in flying aeroplanes for the Signal Corps."

The man made an *are you kidding me* face before saying, "Now, son, we—"

"Please sir, just hear me out." Gordon cut him off before anything dismissive could be said. He stepped forward, holding the four photographs in his hand. "Please just take a look at these." He held out the three pictures of him standing in front of *The Hawk.*

Reluctant, the recruiter reached across the desk and took the photos.

"Those first three are me, standing next to an aeroplane that I designed myself and built from scratch."

The man shuffled through the pictures, looking at each one briefly. He then raised his eyebrows and looked back at Gordon.

"And this last one is me, mid-flight, in that same machine," Gordon said, and he handed him the fourth photograph. "Sir, aviation is the most fantastic thing I have ever experienced in my life. I love everything about it. I understand the principles, the science; I can fix engines and solve mechanical problems. I belong in the air, and with proper training I would be a valuable addition to the Army Signal Corps."

The recruiter held the picture with two hands, staring at it. Then he sighed. Gordon smiled at him, waiting for the man to speak. Deep down inside, for whatever reason, he thought the recruiter would be impressed enough to give him a chance.

Gordon and his siblings had been given many advantages in life that scores of children like them never got. Their father had worked extremely hard to build a successful business, overcoming obstacles that might have held other people in his situation back. Anson provided a great example that taught his kids to persevere in order to overcome obstacles of their own. Virginia and Anson Graham loved all their children dearly, raised them right, taught them the value of hard work, and never discouraged them. The Grahams were a special family, Gordon most of all, and could make it through just about anything.

The recruiter cleared his throat and slid the picture back across the desk.

"Son, the army is never going to let a nigger fly aeroplanes."

It seemed there was one disadvantage Gordon could not overcome.

VERNON

The British Expeditionary Force began landing at Le Havre, France on August 9. Vernon's ship arrived on the 16th. The declaration of war and call for mobilization had come like a whirlwind. It was as if one day Vernon and Sally were sitting at her kitchen table in Londonderry and the next, he was on a troop ship in Belfast harbor.

Following a tearful goodbye, Sally had packed her things and headed to London to stay with her parents. It was the first time in all Vernon's deployments that Sally was unable to go with him. It was a strange feeling, leaving her like that. In his twelve years of service as a professional soldier he'd been garrisoned in India, Morocco and Egypt, but she'd always been nearby. She'd been with him, faithfully, every step of the way. To France, she could not follow.

Vernon and the 1st Battalion of the Cheshire Regiment left Ireland for France with sealed orders. By the end of the day on August 16, their orders were apparent. They, along with the 1st Battalions of the Norfolk, Bedfordshire and Dorsetshire Regiments concentrated in the Le Havre area. They formed the 15th Infantry Brigade of the 5th Division in II Corps. While the British no longer used regiments in their command hierarchies, regiments were still responsible for raising and training battalions which would then be dispersed to different brigades, for service throughout the empire. Most often, battalions of the same regiment would not serve together in the same brigade.

The British, unlike France, Germany, Austria-Hungary and Russia, did not use conscription in order to field their army. Instead, they relied entirely on volunteers. As such, the BEF, while composed entirely of professional, well-trained soldiers, was significantly smaller. The disparity of available troops at the opening of hostilities permitted the British to send to France just two corps, with a combined total of less than one hundred thousand men.

I Corps and II Corps were commanded by General Sir Douglas Haig and Lieutenant General Sir James Grierson respectively, and comprised the British Expeditionary Force, or BEF. The commander-in-chief of the BEF was Field Marshal Sir John French. In addition to the BEF, the British Territorials were also called to France. They numbered about another two hundred thousand men, but were scattered in colonies throughout the empire. Their arrival would take considerable time.

The British Empire's total military strength at the beginning of August was less than one million men. Many of those men were forced to remain in place, be it for home defense or to protect Britain's multitudinous interests overseas. The strength of Europe's other major powers dwarfed that of Britain, with Austria-Hungary fielding over three million men, France and Germany over four million apiece and Russia, with its tremendous land mass and huge population, nearly six million.

"All right you fucking ninnyhammers!" Captain Bannister shouted, "Move your arses, on the double!" Apparently, he did not approve of the pace at which the men of E Company marched. He stomped up and down the column shouting obscenities.

"Looks like the stick up his arse hasn't fallen out yet, aye Vernon?" Pritchard whispered. He leaned in close so the captain would not hear him.

"No, Lew," Vernon answered, "I think it's gone up further. And swelled."

"Pritchard!" the captain barked, "you Welsh sack of shit! Shut your mouth before I make an example of you!"

Bannister was on edge. The six foot tall captain charged to within inches of Vernon and Pritchard, matching their strides as they marched. His thick grey moustache, which bracketed his mouth and connected to his mutton chops, nearly touched Vernon's cheeks as the red-faced man yelled at him, showering him with spittle. Vernon turned his head to look into the captain's eyes.

"Hayes!" Bannister roared, his pinprick black eyes burning holes into Vernon's. "Keep your bloody imbecile Welshman quiet!"

"Yes sir." *You belligerent cunt.* Vernon wiped the spit from his cheek when the captain stomped away. He would never admit to fearing any man, but when Bannister got in his face, even Vernon was a little intimidated.

Private Llewelyn Pritchard was Vernon's best friend. They first became acquainted in India, not long after Pritchard joined the battalion. Bannister was posted to E Company much later, in Egypt, and the trouble with him began not long after that. At first it was just spiteful glares, the occasional barb, the sort of stuff that might just be shrugged off—it wasn't as if the captain was jovial with any of the others. Later, and sporadically it seemed, it turned into additional and heavy individual scrutiny and loud, exaggerated berating, directed solely at Pritchard. Vernon and others suspected the captain had issues with drink, and his leaning on Pritchard coincided with his overconsumption of spirits. So far as anyone knew, Pritchard had never done anything that should have made Captain Bannister despise him as much as he apparently did.

Vernon hated the way the captain talked to Pritchard. Some of the things Bannister said and did had a profoundly negative impact on his state of mind. Since they'd arrived in France, Bannister had even upped the intensity some. In a way, Vernon viewed the captain as a sort of predator, singling out those whom he might consider weak. Pritchard was a sweet man, quiet and shy, which might be perceived as weakness by someone who didn't know him better. But Vernon *did* know him better. He knew his story.

Pritchard had a rough life. He grew up in Buckley, Wales, the only child of poor parents. His father was a violent and abusive drunkard, his mother, a pitiful enabler. Because he was lower class, Pritchard was harassed in school and had to scrap a lot as a kid. He didn't like to fight, but sometimes a kid just didn't get a choice and had to deal. Scrapping with the other boys, and then going home to get his ass kicked by his father taught him how to win those scraps, too.

Apart from a childhood of painful memories, the only thing Pritchard had to remember his father by was a permanent bend in the upper part of his nose—a lifelong gift from a knockout punch his dad gave him when he was thirteen. Pritchard returned that favor in spades after he turned sixteen. One day, when he came home, his father tried to rough him up for the first time in a while. Pritchard was finished with that, and damn near beat his father to death with his bare hands. He spent a short time in jail afterwards. That was when he left Wales and made his way to Ellesmere Port, in Cheshire.

A life such as his could have turned any young man sour, but Pritchard, through it all, remained decent. When he turned eighteen, he joined the army. On leave one day, he met Daisy, the woman who would become his wife, and things truly began to turn around for him. That was nine years earlier, and for the first eight of those nine years Pritchard was happy. He went from a young man in Wales with nothing, to a professional soldier with what he felt was everything. He loved the army for that.

Two weeks before the battalion was to leave Egypt for Ireland, Daisy contracted malaria. She died just one day before their ship departed Alexandria Harbor. Darling Daisy, as Vernon called her, was just as sweet as her husband and stood less than five feet tall. Once she contracted the disease, there was no way her petite little body could have beaten it.

Daisy's sudden passing was the only time Vernon had ever seen Sally cry, as the two women became close friends during their time as military wives. Sally managed her sorrow well, but Pritchard struggled. Vernon did what he could to help his friend pull through, but losing Daisy had taken some of the life out of Pritchard and it had yet to come back. Bannister's persistent, unwarranted prods were pinches, or sometimes fistfuls of salt on lost love's gaping wound.

Vernon glanced at his friend. After being bawled out yet again by Bannister, Pritchard hung his head, ashamed. He stood just an inch or so shorter than Vernon and was thin like him, too. Pritchard was an average looking twenty-seven year old, apart from the bent nose. Like most men who could grow one, he had a moustache. His large, brown eyes were like a puppy's, and may have been one of the reasons the captain singled him out. Even when Pritchard was smiling, even when he was angry, his eyes had an unmistakable sadness behind them.

Pritchard wasn't small and he wasn't weak. He was tough. But there was something about Bannister that just broke him down. Sweet and quiet though he may have been, Pritchard was still a good soldier. Every bit of training he'd ever received had taken and held, and he did not deserve to be treated the way the captain treated him. For an officer to behave toward Pritchard the way Bannister did could only be described with one word, in Vernon's opinion: *cowardly.*

Though they had yet to meet the Germans in battle, II Corps had already suffered one major casualty. On the train east from Le Havre to Amiens, II Corps' commander, Lieutenant General Grierson suffered a heart aneurysm and died at 7 a.m. on August 17. Grierson was replaced by General Horace Smith-Dorrien, formerly in charge of the Home Defence Army. While Vernon was saddened by the sudden death of a high-ranking commander, he was thrilled that the man chosen as Grierson's replacement was General Smith-Dorrien. The new commander was one of Vernon's heroes.

Smith-Dorrien was chosen personally by Secretary of State for War Horatio Herbert Kitchener, as Kitchener knew that Smith-Dorrien would have the courage to stand up to Field Marshal French if the need ever arose. John French did not like Smith-Dorrien and had wanted General Sir Herbert Plumer to replace Grierson instead. Ultimately, French's feelings were ignored and Smith-Dorrien arrived at General Headquarters (GHQ) on August 21.

It was now late in the evening of the 21st and 1st Battalion prepared to halt their march until first daylight.

"Vernon, do you know where we are, exactly?" asked Pritchard.

"We crossed the Belgian border earlier today."

"So where the hell is Fritz?"

Fritz was a popular slang the British used for Germans. It was a common name in Germany.

"I don't know," Vernon replied. "Maybe they saw Bannister coming and turned tail."

Minor engagements had already taken place ahead of them between British and German reconnaissance units, and a Private John Parr became the first British soldier killed in combat during the Great War, but neither Vernon nor Pritchard were aware of that.

Pritchard snickered at Vernon's joke as he unclipped the fastener of his equipment belt. He slid the straps off his shoulders, dropping his kit on the ground next to him. The front of his khaki serge (light greenish-brown) tunic was stained dark with sweat where the belt and straps had been. He unbuttoned his thin, black leather chin strap and removed his khaki cap, the same color as his uniform, revealing wet brown hair pasted to his head.

The British wore a traditional peaked cap, a style common in the military and in law enforcement. The cap had a small, hardened leather peak (or visor) covered in khaki cloth and a flat, circular top from which the sides tapered in to the band.

A red line ran above Pritchard's eyebrows where the edge of the cap's band had dug into his skin. They'd marched the entire day without stopping, and he hadn't removed it once.

"Goodness me it's hot carrying all this rubbish," Pritchard complained. "I'm knackered. It's as hot here as any desert or jungle!"

He was right. The weather was uncharacteristically warm. In full uniform with full packs, they might as well have been in Egypt.

The standard equipment kit for a British infantryman was substantial, but manageable. It contained eating utensils, rations, and personal effects kept in a haversack on the left hip. A bayonet and its scabbard, along with the helve of the soldier's entrenching tool sat beneath the haversack, and 150 rounds of ammunition, in charger clips of five rounds each, were stored in ten separate pouches, five on each side of the body, at the junction of the shoulder straps and waist belt. The entrenching tool's spade head, its holder, and a khaki-covered steel water bottle hung from the right hip and a greatcoat, extra clothing and an extra pair of boots were kept in a pack on the upper back.

The pouches and packs were held together by an interconnected system of thick, webbed cotton straps, and could be removed quickly by unfastening a single front buckle and then slipping off the two shoulder straps. The webbed straps were an innovation for their time, as most armies still used leather. While it was a lot to carry, careful attention had been paid in the equipment's design and development process to make it as convenient as possible for a soldier to fight effectively in full gear. The combination of the soldier's khaki serge uniform, which offered some camouflage, along with his well-designed and high-quality equipment system, made the British infantryman the best equipped infantryman on the battlefield.

In addition to the gear, the soldier carried a Short Magazine Lee-Enfield Mark III .303 caliber bolt-action rifle, the life blood of the infantry. The Lee-Enfield was extremely reliable, and the best rifle of any of the belligerent armies of Europe. Its bolt was positioned nearer the trigger than other rifles, allowing for faster cocking and firing. The gun also incorporated a detachable, spring loaded ten-round box magazine, double the capacity of the German Mauser.

The Lee-Enfield had a very distinct look, as nearly its entire barrel was shrouded in wood. The nose cap and small bayonet boss were the only metal visible at the gun's firing end. Because the British rifle was shorter than the German Mauser, the British adopted a longer, sword style bayonet, similar in design to the bayonet used by the Germans, but a full three inches longer.

Vernon shed his kit as well. He pulled his greatcoat from his backpack, unclipped his water bottle, and retrieved a journal from his haversack. He unbuttoned and flipped open the right front breast pocket of his thick wool tunic and fished out a short pencil, one of the two he kept in each front pocket. Doffing his cap revealed his light brown hair, tinted a shade darker by a copious amount of sweat. He had a high widow's peak, and his forehead glistened until he wiped it with his sleeve. His cap had also left a red ring around his head. It itched. He rubbed his head with the back of his hand.

His scalp free to breathe, Vernon turned his cap around in his hand to look at it. He stared contemplatively at the regimental badge above the visor. *The Old Two-Twos will be in it soon,* he thought. The Cheshire Regiment's badge featured a white metal eight-point starburst, with a brass acorn and oak leaves set in the center of the starburst. White metal, or pot metal, was a combination of any of several light-colored, inexpensive alloys and was commonly used in the crafting of British badges. Beneath the starburst and attached to its bottom three points was a flowing ribbon, again in white metal, with *CHESHIRE* embossed in its center.

Vernon, like every man who served in the 1st Battalion, was extremely proud to be a Cheshire. The regiment's history extended back to the year 1689, when it was called the Duke of Norfolk's Regiment. In 1771 it became the 22nd Cheshire Regiment of Foot, before obtaining its final title of the Cheshire Regiment in 1881.

He set his cap atop his pack and then unfastened the hook to loosen his tunic collar. It had been making his neck itch all day. Apart from the hook and eye on the collar, the tunic fastened with five brass buttons down the center. Each button had an emblem similar in style to his cap badge, but instead of having *CHESHIRE* embossed on a ribbon beneath the starburst, *THE CHESHIRE REGIMENT* was embossed in a ring around the acorn and oak leaves inside the star. The same style button was used to fasten the tunic's shoulder straps, which featured a two-inch wide brass *CHESHIRE* shoulder badge. Along with the two breast pockets, the tunic also had two hip pockets with flaps. Those pockets fastened with brass buttons as well.

Vernon reached into his greatcoat's front pocket and withdrew a small, red silk handkerchief. Sally had given it to him before he left, *for luck,* she told him. He wasn't superstitious, not usually, but since she'd said so, he took it to heart. He brought the handkerchief to his face, smelled it briefly, and then tied it around the waist belt of his pack, above the haversack, so he could look down to it whenever he needed a reminder of her. Best to display a talisman rather than hide it. After tying the knot, Vernon set his greatcoat on the ground, sat down, took a sip from the water bottle, and penned the first letter he'd send to Sally as soon as he was able.

Dearest Sal,

How I miss you already. We've yet to meet the Germans, but it shan't be much longer now. General Grierson died four days ago. You'll

likely have read that in the newspaper long before I've sent this. Need-
less to say I'm rather pleased that General Smith-Dorrien has been ap-
pointed to replace Grierson, as you know my opinion of him.

We've marched some forty miles in the past two days. I cannot re-
call a time when my feet have gone that far in such a brief span, and
they're letting me know about it. Bannister is still harsh with Llewelyn,
perhaps harsher still. Why he feels the need I'll never fully understand.
Maybe one day Lew will end up saving the old cad's life, and then per-
chance he'll finally come around to him. I doubt Lew would save him
anyway. I need to rest. We've had a long march and it's been positively
scorching. All my love.

During the day on August 22, the BEF's forward elements engaged those of the Germans, mostly in cavalry skirmishes. Some units of II Corps had reached the Mons-Condé Canal, while I Corps moved to link up with the French Fifth Army to the east. The French were already widely engaged in heavy fighting with German Second and Third Armies. While II Corps began to disperse along the canal on a west to east line, I Corps attached itself to their right flank at an odd, almost ninety degree angle, aligning nearly north to south.

Another day of marching brought 1st Battalion to within just a few miles of Mons. After he received reports that Liège had fallen and that Brussels had declared itself an open city in order to avoid destruction, Field Marshal French began to understand that the German forces rolling through Belgium were much greater than he and Joffre had originally anticipated. Général Lanrezac of French Fifth Army was already aware of the scope of the German advance, as his forces were being pushed back at Charleroi and Dinant. The fortress at Namur was on the verge of surrender, and Fifth Army was in trouble.

Lanrezac contacted Field Marshal French, requesting that the BEF hold the line at Mons for a period of twenty-four hours, to protect Fifth Army's left flank from German First Army. Thus, John French ordered II Corps to form an outpost line along the southern bank of the Mons-Condé Canal, to await the arrival of the Germans. II Corps' orders were to hold the line as long as possible, in order to allow Fifth Army to move to safer positions.

As 1st Battalion marched through the early morning haze, tensions mounted. Somewhere ahead, the Germans were advancing. The serene chirping of songbirds caught Vernon's ear; they were a bizarre contrast to the hundreds of marching soldiers. Belgian civilians seemingly ignorant of what was about to happen went about their daily lives, either unwilling to believe that war truly was at their doorstep, or unwilling to leave their homes in spite of it.

On either side of the road life went on as usual. Nature was being nature, ordinary people being ordinary people, indifferent to the herds, the long lines of marching men with their boots *clump-clumping* in monotonous synchronization. A herd of wild animals moving over a landscape might have been something to behold—a natural marvel. When uniformed men herded together, however, rare good could come of it. The men stomping down the road were headed toward an objective that was anything but natural.

Vernon was unsure whether nerves were making him so sweaty or if it really was as hot as the Egyptian desert, but it felt far too hot and humid for so early in the morning. He brought his left hand to his neck, tugging at his collar to loosen it. Beneath his backpack, the moisture had soaked through his uniform. The same was true of the haversack on his hip—the sweat collecting under it was rolling down his leg. Able to feel his pulse in both calf muscles, he worried he'd wrapped his puttees too tightly. The puttees were long, narrow strips of cloth wound around the lower leg for additional protection against water and dirt, to prevent foreign substances from getting inside the soldier's ankle boots.

Why does everything feel like it's strangling me?

Pritchard tapped Vernon on the shoulder.

"What is it, Pritch?"

"Do you hear that?" Pritchard said. He held his hand to his ear. "I hear gunfire."

Captain Bannister, on horseback a way down the column, ordered the men to halt. He held his arm in the air and hundreds of men fell silent all at once. Sure enough, they could hear the popping of rifles far off in the distance to the east. A few Cheshire boys rattled their proverbial sabers.

"Sounds like old Tommy Atkins is giving it to 'em!"

Tommy Atkins was a popular slang term for a British infantry-man. The origin of the term, while unclear, had certainly been around since the mid-1800s and perhaps as far back as the 1700s.

"Let's get up there before Fritz pisses himself and goes home!"

"We'll chase them all the way back to Berlin!"

Most of the "Tommies" chomping at the bit to get at the Germans had never had a rifle, let alone a machine gun or artillery round fired at them. Vernon hadn't either. While the men of the BEF were pro-fessional, well-trained and well-equipped, the British had not partic-ipated in a major conflict since the Second Boer War, fought against the Dutch in South Africa from 1899 to 1902. Most of the current infantrymen were not in the service at that time, or were just starting out when the war ended. Vernon joined up after his eighteenth birthday in 1902, missing the end of the South African conflict by mere months.

Many of the BEF's commanders *had* fought in Africa, whether in the Boer Wars or even earlier engagements. II Corps' newly appointed commander, Horace Smith-Dorrien, served in Africa during the Anglo-Zulu War in 1879. The story of what happened to him there was the very reason why Vernon idolized him.

Smith-Dorrien was one of just four officers and less than fifty British soldiers to survive the massacre at Isandlwana, where twenty thousand Zulu tribesmen armed with spears and leather shields overwhelmed the firing lines of a British contingent equipped with the most modern weapons of the time. Of the approximately 1,800 soldiers in the contingent, around 1,300 were British, and they suffered the harshest fate. The remaining five hundred soldiers were colonials and natives, many of whom survived. Smith-Dorrien narrowly escaped on his pack pony and was nominated to receive the Victoria Cross, Britain's highest military honor, for his efforts in helping others escape the massacre. Ultimately the award was never bestowed upon him due to a bureaucratic technicality.

As a boy, Vernon read accounts of Smith-Dorrien's dashing escape. Along with the father he never knew, he viewed the general as his main inspiration for joining the army. Now Smith-Dorrien was responsible for forty thousand soldiers, Vernon and the 1st Cheshire among them. Where Smith-Dorrien had once escaped twenty thousand Zulus as one of less than two thousand standing in opposition, he now led his forty thousand soldiers toward a much larger German force, which was vastly better trained and equipped than African tribesmen. Every man in the BEF knew there were Germans ahead, a more obvious point there could not be, but unbeknownst to anyone in II Corps at that time, they were on course for a head-on collision with the two hundred thousand men of Alexander von Kluck's First Army.

"Hope you brought a sharp eye and a steady hand today, chaps," Lieutenant Hood said sternly as he addressed the marching platoon. "The captain's just received word from a runner at battalion HQ that we're to assist in holding along a canal."

Hood was the officer in charge of E Company's Fourth Platoon. The lieutenant was a good-looking young man, just over six feet tall with dark blonde hair and a prominent chin. He was five years younger than Vernon, but he had his respect. He had the entire platoon's respect.

As an officer, Hood's uniform was different than the enlisted men. He wore brown riding breeches, with a flared upper leg. He was not on horseback, but in wars past most officers traditionally rode, and many British officers still retained the look. From just below his knees to his ankles, his pants and the tops of his black leather ankle boots were wrapped in khaki-colored puttees, like the enlisted men.

Rather than a heavy wool tunic, Hood wore a tailored jacket made of higher quality wool. Because it was custom made by a tailor of his choosing, the color did not quite match the standard tunic, and so was a shade greener. Many officers' tunics shared a similar degree of variation. The jacket had an open collar with a thin lapel, exposing the tan shirt and tie worn underneath. A small regimental badge was fastened to each lapel. There were shoulder straps for epaulettes, but he didn't wear any. Instead, his rank was indicated by two diamond pips on the three-pointed cuff flaps of his jacket sleeves, and the single chevron stripe around the cuff which extended from the cuff flap's middle point. His peaked cap, of the same color as his jacket, was also made from finer wool and of better quality construction than the enlisted men's. It retained the same regimental badge.

Vernon was in Fourth Platoon's 3 Section. Each platoon had four such sections, or squads. Vernon's section leader, Corporal Spurling, spoke to Vernon and the other eleven men of 3 Section after Hood jogged ahead.

"All right, then," Spurling said, "this is what we've come for. Time to go and shake hands with Fritz."

"What if they're not interested in shaking hands?" asked Private Lockwood.

"Then I guess we'll have to shove a bayonet up their collective bums!" Spurling replied.

Corporal Spurling was twenty-four, and like Hood, had the respect of his charges. He stood on the shorter side, about five foot seven, and was spindly. His high, sharp cheekbones and pointy chin perpetually appeared as if they might shred through his skin to reveal his skull. As a non-commissioned officer (NCO), Spurling wore the same uniform and cap as did each private, the only difference being the two off-white chevrons sewn, point-down, onto the upper sleeves of his tunic.

At the behest of Bannister and Company Sergeant Major Cortland, the men of E Company hastened their pace. Two hundred pairs of boots thumped at increased speed down the road. Spirits were high. Somewhere within the column ahead, one man began to sing. Vernon barely heard the first words over the footsteps, but the fellow started strong, and he was just able to pick them out.

Up to mighty London,
Came an Irishman one day.

A few men near the songster joined in straight away, still barely audible over the stepping boots.

As the streets are paved with gold,

When the voices of several more men close to them merged in, the volume grew and the words became clearer. Vernon's heart jumped when he recognized the song. It was a good one. A chill ran down his spine, sending electricity into his legs and adding spring to his step.

Sure, everyone was gay,

The excitement welled inside him. The energy began to resonate through the column as each man started to sing. The popular tune, about a man longing for home, was upbeat and great for quick-marching. It seemed tailor-suited to their present situation. While they'd nearly all left loved ones behind and longed to see them again, the anticipation of marching into battle in the name of Britain was a great honor, and depending on how one looked at it, cause for merriment.

Singing songs of Piccadilly, Strand and Leicester Square,

Smiling while he looked around at the eager faces bursting with pride for their regiment and country, Vernon met eyes with Pritchard, who winked at him and joined in the song.

Till Paddy got excited, then he shouted to them there,

Unable to resist any longer, Vernon and the entirety of E Company, save for probably Captain Bannister and maybe his officers, joined in all at once for the chorus.

"It's a long way, to Tipperary! It's a long way to go!"

E Company, energized, all but skipped in formation as they sang "It's a Long Way to Tipperary," written in 1912 by Jack Judge and co-credited to Henry James Williams. For scared, or at the very least nervous men headed toward their first battle, singing an upbeat song was a fine way to temper that fear. The raucous singing persisted all the way to the canal, over the rumble of a heavy fight going on further to the east, toward Mons itself. Vernon heard the battle rumbling over the joyous music and thumping boots, but at the water ahead, the shooting had yet to start.

Upon reaching the shallow entrenchments dug along the Mons-Condé canal by II Corps' earliest arrivals the previous day, the men of E Company took up their positions to bolster the line, about two hundred yards from the nearest bridge. The canal's bridges were the choke points at which German opposition would be heaviest and thus needed the strongest defense. Capturing an intact bridge would be a boon for any units looking to rapidly advance beyond the water.

Vernon and Pritchard lay prone alongside each other, their Lee-Enfields pointed across the water, past the opposing bank. The land beyond the canal's northern bank stretched flat for a hundred yards before reaching a long row of fir trees running parallel to the water. Past the trees was another clearing which then morphed into a veritable wasteland of slag heaps and small, dirty wooden homes strewn amongst a sea of mills and sheds.

The weather was incredibly hot and muggy, the sky overcast, and Vernon could tell the heat and anticipation were making his friend twitchy. Pritchard breathed heavily. His cap was spotted through with sweat. The marching of the past few days had left white salt stains zigzagging around his cap's band. Dirt and black dust clung to Pritchard's face and to the wet spots on his uniform. *This place is disgusting,* Vernon thought.

Vernon's heart pounded. It tried to climb right out of his throat. He swallowed it back down with a pronounced gulp. Over the battle to the east, he heard the Germans coming before he could see them. An individual's footsteps might be audible from a few feet away, but when hundreds, perhaps thousands of footsteps joined as one, that made real noise. And that noise was frightening. There was an occasional shout, probably an officer calling out orders. Soon the Germans would be firing their rifles. Their cannons. Soon they'd be trying to kill him.

A bead of sweat rolled from beneath Vernon's cap, down his forehead and into the corner of his eye. He blinked hard to wash away the sting. Sweat in the eye was not a good thing to have while shooting. The first *pop* from a Lee-Enfield came from fifty yards further down the canal, to the east. Hundreds of heads along the water's edge turned in unison in that direction. Vernon and Pritchard looked as well, before turning their attention back across the water. Well beyond the fir trees, a number of Germans came into view from behind the slag heaps. The men lying in wait on the canal's bank opened fire.

The British put great stock in training their soldiers in the art of musketry. Through frequent practice, soldiers' shooting skills were precisely honed to allow them to place rapid and accurate rifle fire down range. Tommies were run through a drill called the "mad minute," which required them to put fifteen rounds into a twelve inch target, placed three hundred yards away, in a minute or less. Many British soldiers then in service could exceed that score, which by any barometer was an impressive act of marksmanship.

In the opening moments of the Battle of Mons, as more and more Germans emerged from behind obstructions, Tommy Atkins ran the mad minute, and he ran it for much longer than that.

Vernon rested his sights on his first target, close to four hundred yards away, framed between two fir trees. The man's grey uniform set against the drab grey slag heaps blended him almost seamlessly into the backdrop. The only part of him which stood out was the light brown of his spiked helmet. Vernon held his rifle steady, squeezed the trigger and *POW!* His rifle punched him in his right shoulder. The soldier dropped, clutching his abdomen.

There it is, Vernon. You've just killed a man. It was his first. New to killing, but an old hand when it came to firing his rifle, he cocked the bolt in the blink of an eye, turning the four-step cocking cycle into one quick, metallic *snap*.

There were different methods in which Tommies were trained to cock and fire their rifles. Because the bolt was close to the trigger, Vernon had adopted the unorthodox but faster method of constantly maintaining contact on the bolt with his thumb and index finger, and pulling the trigger with his middle finger. The style allowed for faster firing than the more traditional method of triggering with the index finger, then completely removing the shooting hand from the gun to grasp the bolt with either an upturned palm or the thumb and index finger, cocking, and then releasing the bolt to place the index finger back on the trigger. To truly attain the highest rate of fire, Vernon's method was the only way.

He aimed again, but before he could fire at his man the stocky German's head whipped backwards and he fell, shot through the helmet. It happened a few hundred yards away, but it was close enough that Vernon spotted the puff of blood from the soldier's head as his helmet flipped into the air.

"I got him!" shouted Pritchard, racking his bolt in a flash.

That was probably his head shot. "Nice shot, Lew! Keep firing!" Vernon shouted back. The act of shooting a man in the head was not cause for celebration, even if it was a good shot (and his first kill).

A short time later, during which Vernon had dropped two more men, a bullet smacked into the dirt a foot in front of Pritchard. It must have startled him, and he pulled back from his firing position to get his upper body behind the embankment. Unfortunately, Captain Bannister was observing the line from a covered position about thirty feet directly behind him. Bannister noticed immediately and charged forward, ignoring the German fire from across the canal. He kicked Pritchard's feet hard and startled both he and Vernon, neither of whom saw the captain coming.

"Pritchard you fucking coward!" the captain screamed. "Get your worthless arse back in position!"

Vernon glared over his shoulder for just a moment to try and make eye contact with Bannister. He was furious the man had called his friend a coward for shifting his body a mere foot. *Shut your mouth you son of a bitch*, he wanted to shout. He hoped a Mauser round might clip the captain and quiet him down.

"Spurling! Keep your goddamn men firing!" Bannister shouted at 3 Section's corporal, five men further down the line. He was busy shooting, and hardly acknowledged him. The captain stomped back to his position, unharmed. Vernon resumed firing.

Pritchard returned to his prone position to continue the fight. Over the constant popping and echoing of British and German rifles and the sporadic screams of the first wounded Tommies, Vernon yelled to him in the hopes of keeping his spirits up. The last thing he wanted was for that bastard Bannister to get inside his friend's head during an engagement. Maintaining Pritchard's strict focus on the attacking men ahead could mean the difference between Vernon going home to Sally, or going home to Sally in a pine box.

"Forget what he says, Pritch!" he shouted, while still aiming and firing. *Pow!* "Piss on him!"

"He's got no reason!" Pritchard answered.

Pow!

"So forget it!"

It was not the time to carry on a conversation. The two refocused on the task at hand. Vernon ejected the last smoking shell from the breech, his tenth shot, and reached for the ammo pouch on his right side, fishing out two five-round charger clips. The chargers were small, black metal brackets which allowed the soldier to load his magazine five bullets at a time.

He snapped the first clip into the breech, dropping the charger on the ground after the bullets had slid into the magazine. He snapped in the second clip and cocked the bolt, knocking the second charger onto the ground. Before he could choose a new target, he heard the whistle of the first artillery shell. It was about to land somewhere nearby. *Bugger. Fritz got his cannons here first.* The fight had just started, but an artillery salvo was already on its way.

FOOM! The shell landed just twenty feet short, and splashed into the canal before detonating. It sent an enormous column of water into the air which soaked Vernon, Pritchard and several men on either side of them. Nearly the entire platoon ducked behind the embankment when the shell burst. In the sweltering heat, dressed in wool, with full kit and under fire, only one thought ran through Vernon's head following the explosion, proving the mind—even with the heart racing—could certainly go to odd places when under duress.

Christ that water was refreshing.

HENTSCH

The battle raged approximately a mile ahead, but there were far too many obstacles in the way to see the action. Mons was in Belgium's industrial heartland, and as such the land was littered with mills and all manner of outbuildings. Large slag heaps, a by-product of the iron ore smelting process, dotted the countryside. The smell of burning coal hung in the air and amplified the already stifling heat. The ground was filthy with coal dust. The dust coated the men's boots and uniforms as they stomped through it.

Hentsch's uniform clung to his body. He had already discarded his last one, too soiled and reeking to keep. Now his only remaining clothes were soaked with sweat and collecting millions of grimy black coal particles. The dust adhered to the moisture on his exposed skin. It itched.

The cluttered landscape made it nearly impossible for 1 Zug, let alone the entire 13th Kompagnie, to march in formation. Hauptmann (Captain) Fleischer ordered his three zug commanders to separate and make their way to the canal in order to strike at different points. To affect a crossing, the canal's bridges needed capturing. To prevent the British from concentrating their defenses near those bridges, their attention had to be held at every point along the canal.

Oberleutnant ("above" Leutnant, akin to full lieutenant) Richter, commander of 1 Zug, subsequently ordered his four korporalschaft commanders to disperse and remain in visual contact with one another. Unteroffizier (Corporal) Strauss, Hentsch's leader in 1 Korporalschaft, led his two units toward the area around a small mill. He ordered Hentsch and 2 Gruppe to a position behind a distant slag heap, to then await further orders.

Reaching the canal meant working their way around slag heaps, storage shacks and a pair of small houses, all of which were situated in an entirely random fashion, with seemingly no regard as to convenience of location. The houses, which were ramshackle and dirty, and the land they were on, stood as a testament to the cost of industrialization. It could not have been healthy to live there.

Hentsch steered 2 Gruppe through the back yard of a little white house, the paint of which had morphed less from a white and more toward a light grey from the particulate residue of coal smoke.

While crossing the yard, the last such before 2 Gruppe reached their position, someone behind Hentsch commented, "Why does anyone defend a place like this? They ought to surrender this shit pile and save everyone the trouble."

Hentsch knew who said it. It was the same man who shot the Belgian machine gunner in the back at Visé. His name was Michael. He was a cocky twenty-year-old, with a near permanent scowl on his face. He had black hair and a slightly darker tone to his skin, and his eyes were a very dark brown, capped with heavy black eyebrows. Hentsch was certain Michael had at least some Eastern Slavic lineage.

"You must be joking," Engel answered testily. "This is where their mining and ore production takes place. It's crucial for their industry. And it's crucial we take it. That's why they defend it, you dolt. "

Michael rolled his eyes.

"It's their home, Michael," Simon added. "You know the whole country is not this way. We've marched across it for days. A home needs a basement. This is Belgium's."

"Yes, Simon," Hentsch agreed. "You're right." He looked back at Michael. "You'd fight to protect the least pleasant lands in Germany, wouldn't you?"

Michael rolled his eyes again and made a sickening, know-it-all face before grumbling, "But the Fatherland isn't this dirty."

As if you've traveled every square mile of the Empire to know such a thing. "Is that so?" Hentsch said. "Where do you suppose our artillery comes from? How about the steel in our rifles? The lead in our bullets? It's all mined, milled, and manufactured. And where that happens? It looks just like this."

Michael had nothing more to say.

The soldiers of First Army had indeed seen much of the Belgian countryside. After Liège fell, the 34th Brigade rejoined von Quast's IX Korps on its march west to the city of Tirlemont, where they clashed with the left wing of the retreating Belgian army then on its way to the fortress of Antwerp. The Battle of Tirlemont resulted in heavy casualties for the Belgians, though the Mecklenburg Regiment missed most of the fighting. Further north, elements of First Army had faced Belgian rearguard actions at Diest and Aarschot. There they inflicted still more casualties on the retreating enemy. In the aftermath of the fighting at Tirlemont, Hentsch witnessed confirmation of some of the rumors Simon had heard at Liège.

German commanders, who suspected Belgian civilians of firing at their marching columns from windows, cellars and alleyways, ordered the systematic arrests of alleged perpetrators. The francs-tireurs, literally "free shooters," were used as justification for the horrors which followed. Homes of suspected shooters were looted and set ablaze, men were rounded up and shot in the street, and some women suffered awful brutalization. Many innocent civilians were forced from their homes.

No city suffered such fate worse than Louvain, northwest of Tirlemont. In spite of having declared itself, like Brussels, to be an open city, with von Kluck having even established his headquarters there for a short time, the German paranoia and agitation fell out of proportion with reality. In what could only be described as an orgy of destruction, hundreds of civilians were killed, tens of thousands more were displaced, and thousands of buildings burned to the ground as retribution for the actions of francs-tireurs who may or may not have even been there.

While Hentsch witnessed nothing as outrageous as what occurred at Louvain, at Tirlemont he saw more than enough. The looting of abandoned houses quickly became a common sight, and the breaking into and emptying of wine cellars even more common than that. During a halt, Hentsch had come upon a fellow German forcing himself on a young Belgian girl in an alley. Without so much as a noise, Hentsch snuck up behind the man, grabbed him by the scruff of his neck and his belt, and smashed him head first into the wall next to the frightened girl. Not knowing what else to do, or what to say to the girl, he walked away and left the unconscious man lying on the ground, leaving him to whatever fate might befall him. He told no one of the incident.

Engel had liberated a single bottle of wine from an already broken-into cellar, and while Hentsch did not approve, the two drank it while resting on a hay bale. The wine was the only spoil of war

Hentsch resolved ever to allow himself to imbibe. Simon, horrified by the looting and mistreatment of non-combatants, refused to take a sip when it was offered.

Much of Belgium was ruined. Because of the rapidity of the German advance after Liège, and the Belgian Army's vain attempts to slow that advance, many of Belgium's bridges and railroad lines had been demolished by their engineers during the retreat. The Germans cut phone and telegraph lines to interrupt Belgian communications and burned entire villages in reprisal for the francs-tireurs. Thousands upon thousands of acres of crops, abandoned by evacuating farmers, baked and rotted in the broiling sun.

The corpses of men, pack horses and livestock, bloated and stinking from the heat, littered the countryside. With no one to bury the dead and dispose of the animal carcasses, the decaying flesh attracted rats, giving them their first taste of human flesh, along with hundreds of millions of bluebottle flies. Sheets of maggots writhed as they feasted on an almost unlimited bounty of rotting flesh.

During the German march across Belgium, stories of the utter destruction and the atrocities committed there soon reached the newspapers in other countries. The articles painted the Germans as Huns and Vandals, as barbarians with no regard for the rules of war. Though some men *were* guilty of such abhorrent behavior, many more thousands, an incredibly vast majority in fact, were not. As was typically the case with wartime propaganda, no inconvenient attempts at distinction were made, however, and "Huns" soon became a popular slang word used to describe Germans, especially among the British. The term had originally reared its head fifteen years prior, during the Boxer Rebellion in China, when the Kaiser had *once* compared his German forces—then being dispatched to help quell the rebellion—to the ancient armies of Attila the Hun.

Hentsch, and so far as he knew, his charges, were no Huns. They did not burn any houses, nor destroy any property. If they were anything like him, they would never have dreamed of harming a civilian either. He would rather have faced a court-martial before obeying an order to shoot a civilian, had he been given such an order. Seeing other men his age and younger doing some of the terrible things they'd done, though, added a new wrinkle to his opinion what war was, and what it made men do.

He had his nationalistic sentiments like anyone else, but even strong sentiments could be persuaded. After shooting his first man and looking into his dead eyes, then seeing the utter destruction rained down on Liège, not to mention the harsh and undeserved retribution paid to the Belgian civilians, the glorious tales he'd read of war and patriotism began to fissure. Revelations came quickly in such extreme circumstances.

After Tirlemont, IX Korps and the rest of First Army had marched westward in accordance with the Schlieffen Plan's timetable, save for a detachment sent to besiege Antwerp. On the 21st General von Bülow sent orders to von Kluck, requesting he halt his march west and instead turn south toward Maubeuge, France, right on the border. That southward turn had brought First Army to Mons, to their current and somewhat unexpected collision with the British Expeditionary Force.

Hentsch's battalion, not in the vanguard, had been closer to the artillery being brought up and positioned in the rear areas. The rumbling artillery had started up more than an hour earlier. With each hurried step he and his men took toward the fight, the noise of exploding shells and gunfire intensified. The fight was so close, and it was ferocious. When 2 Gruppe reached the slag heap, Hentsch stepped out from behind the obstructing grey mass and the canal finally came into view.

The water was roughly five hundred yards away. A long row of fir trees ran parallel to it, perhaps a hundred yards or so from the bank. The trees offered some protection from gunfire, but crossing the four hundred yards of flat ground to get to them presented a significant hazard. There were a number of German casualties lying out in the open, both leading to the trees and beyond them. Brave medics and stretcher bearers tended to some of the wounded, exposing themselves to murderous fire. Through the space between the firs Hentsch could just barely make out the khaki caps and rifles peeking over the opposite bank.

The echoing staccato *pop-pop-pop* of British rifles rolled across the canal, bouncing off every impediment and amplifying the din. Many German units had established themselves in workable positions, and were returning fire. The slag heap, however, did not offer a good angle from which to safely fire.

Hentsch gawked in fear and disgust at the scattering of wounded Germans writhing on the ground out in the clearing. The blood from their wounds mixed with the soot and dirt they lay in, turning the injuries greasy and black. They fell where they were hit, in the open and exposed to further enemy fire. Some could crawl to help or to cover, but many could not. They cried for aid, but the medical personnel were preoccupied. Hentsch felt sorry for them, but he wasn't a medic. There wasn't much he could do. At least that was what he told himself. *If you're wounded in this fight it will be covered with filth in an instant. God dammit Augustus, don't get shot here.*

"The British must have a whole battery of machine guns!" Simon cried, drawing Hentsch's attention away from the wounded. There certainly was a concentrated amount of fire coming from the four hundred yards of canal frontage visible from his position. The casualties lying in the clearing were a testament to that.

"There's no way we can get across," Engel added.

Hentsch did not disagree. The fire was heavy. What he and his men did not know was that there were no British machine gun batteries. In fact there were only two machine guns assigned to each battalion in the BEF, roughly one for every five hundred British soldiers. The massed Lee-Enfield fire coming from the canal was simply that rapid, intense and accurate. Whatever their firepower, the Tommies offered stiff resistance, of that there was no doubt.

The men from 1 Gruppe had taken shelter behind a pair of overturned coal carts and piles of railroad ties about twenty yards away. They were among the units returning fire. Hentsch ordered 2 Gruppe to remain behind the slag heap in order to wait for the artillery to take greater effect. The German shells whistled overhead, fired from high ground overlooking the canal to the north. Hentsch, leaning against the heap, tried to watch the shells land, without catching a bullet for his curiosity.

As the minutes passed, one of those shells fell decidedly short of the British positions, and landed on the wrong side of the fir trees, only three hundred yards beyond where Hentsch stood. It detonated next to a cluster of German corpses who'd fallen near one another, sending exploded body parts swinging and twisting into the air. Although the dead could not die twice, the spectacle of launched limbs was a chilling one.

"That sounded close!" Simon shouted. "Are we hitting them?"

"That one didn't," Hentsch answered. "But some are. It may take time for our gunners to get a strong fix on their positions."

"Are those 7.7 rounds we're firing?"

"How the fuck should I know?! Probably!"

Though they *were* 7.7cm cannon rounds, Hentsch had yet to learn the sounds made by different shell calibers.

"Yeah Simon!" Engel yelled. "Who gives a shit as long as they land where they're supposed to?" He didn't know either.

Simon made a face at Engel and shrugged. "I was just asking."

Eventually the artillery began to hit the British hard. Small segments of the enemy's line fell silent from the occasional direct hit, diminishing the effectiveness of the rifle fire from across the canal.

The German rifles were likewise able to strengthen their response. After more than two hours, the popping of Lee-Enfields had slowed considerably. German units were edging closer to the water. Hentsch was comfortable enough to step around the slag heap and perhaps lead his gruppe toward the fir trees. Clutching his rifle to his chest, he crept around the edge.

"Hentsch don't get shot in the bloody head!" Engel warned.

"Thank you, Engel, that's sound advice. I'll try not to."

The British had begun abandoning their positions. There was still shooting—covering fire for those with their backs already to the canal. They were retreating, having had no answer for the German artillery on the high ground. As Hentsch prepared to react to the Tommies fleeing the canal, he became distracted momentarily by a break in the hazy cloud overhead. Sunbeams shone through, illuminating the battlefield. The beauty of seeing the sun above, shining bright over the filthy, casualty-laden field momentarily transfixed him. Then a rifle round snapped past his left ear and smacked into the slag heap. *Holy shit that was close!* He was no longer distracted.

"Simon! Engel!" he shouted. "Come on you men they're running away!"

Hentsch spotted two British soldiers leap up from their prone positions and turn to retreat. The man on the left had some sort of short red streamer dangling from the pack on his hip. Hentsch wondered what it was for. The man with the streamer grabbed the other man, and pushed him away from the bank, then shielded him from fire with his own body.

Maybe he's an officer, protecting his man. The two Brits ran toward the safety of the slag heaps behind them. In a moment they'd vanish from view. Hentsch quickly raised his Mauser, with no time to take proper aim, and fired one shot at the Tommy he thought might be an officer. The soldier kept running and was gone.

"Dammit..." Hentsch said, lowering his rifle. He'd expected the man to fall. Then he could have crossed the canal at a nearby bridge and ascertained what the red streamer was for.

"Hentsch did you get him?" asked Engel.

Simon stood behind Engel, unable to see through the trees. "Who'd you shoot at?" he asked.

"Jesus Christ Simon, who do you think?"

When it became evident that the entire BEF had fallen back, First Army began the hasty recovery of its multitudinous wounded. There was no time for the advancing army to stop and bury the thousands of dead bodies scattered for miles along the canal—chasing the British was imperative. Because of the rapidity of their retreat, the BEF's

Royal Engineers were not given the chance to demolish many of the canal's bridges so crossing, at least in Hentsch's sector, was easy.

Upon reaching the opposite bank, Hentsch was able to see the effects of the 7.7cm artillery fire up close and personal. British dead lay along the water's edge, and more lay scattered on the flat ground further away. The dead men lying there, because politics and geography had decreed it so, were his enemies, whatever that meant. While their artillery and rifles would have done the same thing to him if given the chance, it was still a terrible sight. Knowing that was what men did to one another, simply because the men in power ordered them to, crushed a part of Hentsch's soul. He grappled with the entire concept, but there he was in the midst of it, doing it too. *The men who sent us here sit in comfort, miles behind the lines, moving their chess pieces.* He stepped over a tattered body. *But men are not chess pieces.*

After stepping around or over several more very dead men, Hentsch paused next to one British corpse and shook his head.

"Poor bastard took a direct hit."

The man lay on his back, nearly cut in half by an exploded shell. A narrow strip of flesh connected his torso to his legs, and his shredded guts hung from the open chasm in his abdomen. One broken, white rib, smeared with blood, jutted out from beneath the man's tattered, crimson-stained tunic. The smell was horrible. He'd shit and pissed his pants, and more runny shit leaked from his torn intestines. Death took everything, even a man's dignity.

Hentsch knelt next to the body, resting a hand on the corpse's shoulder. He was appalled, yet something compelled him to move closer to that one specific casualty. He didn't know why. Perhaps it was the look on the dead man's face, particularly in his eyes. *My God, his expression...* It was ghastly. He'd spent the last seconds of his life in sheer terror. The fear was frozen into his features. Despite his look, his eyes were somehow not as dead as that first Belgian's.

Hentsch said, "I'm sorry, friend," and softly patted the man's shoulder before standing up. They weren't friends, but what could he say to a dead man? When a hand unexpectedly touched Hentsch's leg, startling him beyond reason, he stumbled and fell on his backside. *Christ almighty he's still alive!* The dead man wasn't dead.

With his last ounces of strength, the delirious Briton reached for his haversack. His weak, shaky hand slowly patted the canvas bag. His blood-filled mouth opened and closed, but no words came out. Hentsch rose cautiously and knelt next to the man once again. His heart pounded so hard he thought he'd throw up.

Before him lay someone who had, at least to that point, survived one of the most horrific wounds imaginable. That he'd die was a forgone conclusion; that it hadn't happened yet was mystifying. He should have died within seconds, minutes at the most. It was not a kind death. The last thing he would ever feel in life was the most intense pain and suffering that any person could possibly experience, and he'd had to feel it for longer than he should have.

"My...wife..." the soldier whispered. It was barely audible through the blood gurgling in his throat. The man whispered it again, still slowly fumbling at his haversack with his left hand.

Hentsch moved the trembling hand aside and reached into the pack. His fingers probed for, and then found, what the soldier wanteded—a photograph of him with his wife. The picture was warped, yellow on the edges, as if it had been moist. It was obvious to Hentsch that the fellow must have held it with sweaty hands, for minutes at a time, missing the love he'd left back home. The couple in the picture looked happy, and the woman was pretty.

She'll never see him again, Hentsch thought, and he felt terrible. *There's no way she deserves that.*

The dying man was far too weak to raise his hand high enough to grasp the picture, let alone hold it in front of his face, so Hentsch held it there for him, allowing him to look at his wife one last time.

"Help..." another whisper.

"I...I don't know what else to do for you," Hentsch whispered back. "I'm so sorry." He realized then that there were tears in his eyes. *What can I do? Shoot him in the head? Is that the humane thing?* There was no way he could shoot the poor man, even though he knew it would end the horrific pain and more quickly bring about the inevitable. *The bayonet?* Slashing his throat with a bayonet was too gruesome. Too savage.

"Wa...ter."

A mangled, bloody right hand, missing the thumb and index finger, rested on the man's water bottle. Hentsch pulled the bottle from the belt, opened it, and gingerly placed it against the man's bloody lips. He only poured out a little. The gesture was pointless, symbolic. What good would water do him? Tears streamed down the dying man's cheeks, and Hentsch began to sob as he stared into the fading eyes.

He hadn't shot that particular person, an artillery crew had, but kneeling there with him as he died was too disheartening to not affect Hentsch on a visceral level. The Tommy took one last breath before gradually exhaling. Hentsch saw the exact moment in which the last spark of life disappeared. Dead, lifeless eyes stared back at him.

Hentsch tucked the picture of husband and wife into the dead soldier's hand, and moved the hand to rest it near the man's heart.

"What are you doing, Hentsch?" Engel's concerned voice asked from behind him.

"Nothing," Hentsch said. He stood and quickly wiped the tears from his eyes.

"Did you take something from that body?"

"No, dammit. He was still alive."

"With that wound? Bullshit."

Hentsch turned around. He wasn't going to squabble over it. In avoiding eye contact with Engel, he noticed something over Engel's shoulder, in the direction of the canal. "What's he doing?" he asked, nodding toward the water's edge.

Engel turned to look. "I don't know," he said. "Why don't you ask him?"

Michael was crouched over a dead body, cutting the buttons from the deceased man's tunic. Hentsch clenched his fists and shouted, "What the fuck are you doing, Michael?!" It was a rhetorical question. He was looting.

No one else was looting corpses. Engel was right next to Hentsch and Kirsch, Ackerman and Nussbaum were all within twenty-five feet of him. Units were reassembling. The march would soon resume. There was no time to trophy hunt. As far as Hentsch was concerned, there was no place for it anyway.

"Michael, get your ass over here and leave the bodies alone!" he bellowed.

Michael stood up slower than he should have when ordered. Hentsch watched, angry, as Michael rested his boot on the chest of the corpse he'd just robbed and shoved the dead body into the water, before calmly strutting closer to the group. Hentsch glowered at him, trying his best to avoid slugging the cocky young man in the mouth. Out of the six men left under Hentsch's command, he trusted Michael the least. When they'd passed through Tirlemont, Michael had disappeared for a short while during a break, and though Hentsch had nothing but assumption to go by, he was fairly sure Michael had been looting or worse. Seeing him rob the British corpse bolstered that suspicion.

Simon moved slowly along the canal's bank about fifty feet away from what Michael had just done. He'd witnessed the entire episode and seemed to be hesitant in joining his comrades. After another minute he finally sulked over to where 2 Gruppe stood. The redness in his eyes and the smudged dirt beneath them was a dead giveaway. The aftermath of the Battle of Mons had, at least briefly, proven too much for Simon to maintain his composure. Like Hentsch, his emotions had gotten the best of him.

"You all right, Simon?" asked Hentsch. He wasn't going to admit that he'd just been crying as well, but it probably showed on his face either way.

"This is just..." the ghost-faced young man drifted off. "...I don't know."

Hundreds of dead Germans lay on one bank, and hundreds of dead Tommies lay on the other. The same was repeated for miles down the line in either direction. Each side suffered casualties in the thousands. Hentsch stood with his hands clasped behind his lower back, struggling to comprehend the carnage. *What is this really for?*

Whether following orders from generals, kings, emperors or God himself, the man tasked with the fighting and killing paid the true price. Hentsch was starting to appreciate just how extraordinarily high that price could become. The things he'd seen and done in just three weeks of war began to pile a burden upon his conscience, and he repeated just one thought in his mind as First Army marched after the retreating British. The thought scared him, but he believed it to be true.

Some day we will all have to answer for the role we played in this war.

DENIS

By the time Lanrezac called for retreat, Fifth Army's left flank and center had fought von Bülow's Second Army for three days, on a twenty-five mile front from Charleroi to Namur. The right flank fought von Hausen's Third Army from Namur to Dinant. While Joffre insisted that Lanrezac continue to push Fifth Army on the offensive, Lanrezac recognized the futility of attempting to attack the massive German forces opposing his own. His request that the BEF hold the canal for twenty-four hours, and his subsequent decision to call for Fifth Army's retreat had most likely saved his army from destruction.

While the BEF's defense at Mons may have resulted in their falling back, and Fifth Army had technically been defeated at the Battle of Charleroi, those retreats were essential. Had the two divisions of Smith-Dorrien's II Corps remained on the canal, the six divisions of von Kluck's Army sent to attack them would have overwhelmed and crushed the much smaller British force. The destruction of II Corps would have exposed the rear flank of Haig's awkwardly positioned I Corps further to the east, allowing von Kluck's forces to roll over the remainder of the BEF, completely eliminating them from the battle as an effective fighting force.

Had Lanrezac then continued to push his attack, German First Army would subsequently have found nothing but Sordet's Cavalerie screen preventing them from advancing straight into French Fifth Army's left flank. If events had played out that way, Lanrezac's forces would have been surrounded on three sides with a massive unwinnable numerical and strategic disadvantage. Luckily for the French and British, that did not happen.

Général Lanrezac and Field Marshal French ordering their forces to fall back may not have seemed like success, but it was much better than the alternative. At 9:30 p.m. on August 23, earlier than was expected by the British, Lanrezac ordered a retreat to a line extending from Maubeuge in the west to Givet in the east. While both cities were in France, due to the shape of the border in that region most of Fifth Army still remained on Belgian soil.

In assisting Fifth Army, the BEF had defended Mons at great cost to itself. Lanrezac's retreat order on the evening of the 23rd was not properly communicated to Field Marshal French, and the essentially unannounced withdrawal of Fifth Army left the British right flank dangerously exposed, forcing the British to hasten their withdrawal out of sheer necessity. With hordes of Germans in extremely close pursuit, the BEF's retreat fell into disorder, forcing some units to fight deadly rearguard actions to allow the majority of the BEF to escape.

Earlier in the day on the 23rd, as French Third and Fourth Army engaged German Fourth and Fifth Army further east in the Ardennes, an entire French division was crushed at Rossignol, Belgium. The 3rd Colonial Division literally ceased to exist after suffering eleven thousand casualties out of its original strength of fifteen thousand. Its commander, Général Léon Raffenel was shot, and the remaining survivors symbolically buried their colors. Of all the fighting in the month of August, which would become known collectively as the Battle of the Frontiers, the waves of Frenchmen ordered into frontal bayonet charges on the relatively small (six hundred yard) battlefront at Rossignol was the single deadliest individual engagement for the French.

From the Belgians to the BEF, across the French Armies to the border with Switzerland, the Germans routed every force opposing them. Tens of thousands died along the hundreds of miles of battlefront. Denis, his squad and the four sections of F Compagnie had come under intense and prolonged fire during the Battle of Charleroi, and many soldiers within a hundred yards of him were killed or wounded. Luckily, no one from his squad had been hit. The same could not be said for Fifth Army as a whole. In the Battle of Charleroi, French Fifth Army suffered approximately thirty thousand casualties.

As the French columns marched south, Denis was bitter about his first engagement ending in retreat. True, the Germans had pushed hard. Their artillery came to their aid more quickly. Apparently, they had even opened small breaches elsewhere in the French lines, forcing hasty withdrawals. But the line hadn't broken where Denis fought. He recognized that if command had decreed it so, then falling back was necessary. It just left a sour taste in his mouth. He had no way of knowing how close he'd come to destruction.

Patrice had other concerns. "You know, it must be easy for the boche to shoot our men when we're wearing these gaudy uniforms," he whined. "A canary would find our colors too bright. I should know, I've asked one."

"You did?" Denis said. "What'd he say?"

"He chirped something or other, a real wise-ass. I'm sure it had to do with my colors."

"We stand out to be sure," Denis replied. "But tell your canary friend these are all we've got for now."

"It's harder for us to see the boche than it is for them to see us."

"I know it is. We'll just have to outshoot them. Besides, their grey is only marginally less obvious."

"Than red and blue?" Patrice replied with indignation. He pointed to his kepi, and then tugged a fistful of cloth on his red trousers to demonstrate. "I'd hardly consider this marginal. It's unfair, our having to compensate for this circus garb, while we clowns defend our homes from the boche's grey scourge."

Boche, a derogatory French slang term for Germans, was the shortened version of a combination of two French words: *Allemande* (German), and *caboche* (cabbage). They were combined to form *alboche*, which literally meant "German cabbage head." A better translation, though, was "block head," an ethnic stereotyping of the shape of a Prussian's head.

"There, there, Patrice," Denis mocked soothingly, "I'm sure our fellow poilus will manage fine dressed as clowns." He smiled. "Perhaps the boche will show mercy! After all, it cannot be easy to shoot a clown."

"I'd happily shoot a boche clown," Patrice said. "Hell, I'd happily shoot a French one if we weren't at war."

"Perhaps you are less compassionate than the boche."

"Ah yes, the ever so compassionate boche, always a friend to the poilu! How could I forget?" Patrice smacked himself on the side of the head.

Poilu, literally "hairy one," was an affectionate slang term for a French infantryman from the days of Napoleon Bonaparte.

"I will tell you this," said Patrice. "Win or lose, this poilu will not look upon this outfit with affection when the war is over. That is, if it does not get me killed before then."

Patrice's dislike of his uniform was not misplaced, nor was it uncommon. The French had not made significant changes to their uniform design in decades. In some sense, they still clung to the dated concept of armies marching shoulder to shoulder, clashing on open plains. War in years past required that armies wear colors which allowed soldiers fighting with bayonets and swords in close quarters to easily distinguish friend from foe. Traditionally, those colors were some representation of the national colors. When wielding firearms that were both slow to load and inaccurate at long distances, it mattered little what colors a man wore, no matter how bright and garish. Modern war, however, was different. Rifles were accurate at ranges of many hundreds of yards, and were deadly from much further still.

A prime example of an army dispensing with tradition in favor of a modernized uniform was that of the British. For hundreds of years, the British infantry wore the classic red coat and a white equipment pack with white straps. The pack straps, which ran diagonally from each shoulder across the chest and to the opposite hip, formed a large white X across the soldier's red torso. In the days of musket volleys, that was acceptable. With the accuracy of modern rifles, however, the British realized that placing a white X on an infantryman's chest turned a man into a walking target, inviting a kill shot. The British had adopted the drab khaki serge uniform for that exact reason—the more and brighter colors a man wore, the easier he was to hit.

Denis scanned Patrice head to toe. The uniform subject had come up before, but now, in the midst of war, the French Army's clinging to old tradition would come with consequences.

Patrice's cloth kepi had a bright red crown and a dark blue band. It might as well have been a bullseye. The kepi had their regimental number *144* embroidered in red lettering in the center of the blue band above the visor. The kepi was held fast on his head by a thin leather chin strap which buttoned above the visor when not in use.

He wore a large, double-breasted, dark blue greatcoat with another *144* embroidered in red on its collar. The coat had two rows of six brass buttons that each bore a flaming grenade. The front quarters of the greatcoat, which hung past his knees, folded and buttoned back to allow more freedom for his legs to move.

His pants were every bit as absurd as the hat. Bright red and baggy, they puffed out over the tops of the black leather gaiters laced around his calf and over the tops of his leather boots. Denis wore a nearly identical uniform, except for his kepi, which had a dark blue cloth cover. He had a broken gold bar on his greatcoat's lower sleeve to indicate his aspirant rank, whereas Patrice, a soldat, had one diagonal black bar on his sleeve.

Their equipment was also substandard. The infantryman's black leather haversack, which required constant maintenance (including waterproofing), was worn on the back, and very difficult to put on without assistance. Patrice couldn't do it without help, and there wasn't a soldier alive who could put his on quickly in an emergency. Attached to the pack's leather waist belt were three leather ammo pouches, two in the front on either side and one on the back. The rear ammo pouch was hard to reach as it sat beneath the haversack.

The haversack was large and heavy. It weighed over sixty pounds when fully loaded, and foolishly had a wooden frame and dividers inside for separating the items it held. The frame and dividers added significant and unnecessary extra weight. The pack only came in one size, which meant that smaller men like Patrice, adjustable shoulder straps not being available, suffered great discomfort on long marches due to their packs not fitting properly. A rolled up blanket and a mess tin were strapped atop the pack, along with an entrenching tool on the pack's left hand side.

Inside the pack were extra clothes, a second pair of boots, shaving kit, personal effects and, because of the rarity of field kitchens, cookware and extra food. The cookware included bowls and assorted cooking implements. Extra food came in the form of items such as biscuits, tins of beef, salt and pepper and bags of coffee. Some men were made responsible for carrying the coffee grinder belonging to their section, while others were assigned different essentials like a frying pan or cooking pot. In addition to the haversack, a second bag made of canvas was worn on the hip and contained a day's rations, eating utensils, a steel canteen covered in blue fabric and a steel drinking cup.

Even a Frenchman's primary weapon could at times be cumbersome. The bolt-action Fusil Modèle 1886 M93 (Rifle Model 1886 Modified 1893), also known as the Lebel, had a spring-loaded, eight-round capacity tube magazine. The rifle was about on par with the German Mauser where accuracy and velocity were concerned, but its shortcomings were that its tube magazine was slower to load, and its sights were not particularly robust—they could be knocked out of alignment if bumped too hard.

The full metal jacket Lebel 8mm round was the first bullet ever to be given a pointed tip (a.k.a. a spitzer round), and a boat-tail (tapered rear end). Those features in tandem greatly improved the bullet's ballistic performance. The introduction of the revolutionary spitzer round led to its adoption by other nations shortly thereafter, making rifle fire much more accurate and deadly from longer ranges.

The major drawback for the Lebel came when its bayonet was attached. The French used the Épée-Baïonnette Modèle 1886, another relic from a different type of war. The needle-like bayonet, nicknamed *Rosalie* by the troops, was more like a small sword at twenty inches in length, and possessed an X-shaped cross section. Purposed for stabbing, the quadrangular blade could open a gruesome puncture wound and was designed to penetrate thick clothing. Because of the bayonet's length, a poilu's rifle from the stock to the tip of the bayonet stood as tall as the man himself (or taller, if he was a short man), making it unwieldy in extreme close quarters.

All things considered, only fleeting concern was paid to convenience in equipping the modern French soldier with the best available gear. Denis could do nothing about it, except play it off casually. "Patrice, I agree, you do look much like an asshole in that uniform." He winked.

"Let's not pretend you pull it off any better, Aspirant Roux," Patrice snarked. "In fact you may be worse, armed with two blades and two firearms." He pointed his index finger toward Denis's belt, waggling it back and forth at the assortment of weapons. "I can't tell if you're a poilu or a pirate. All you've forgotten is your peg leg."

"Very funny," Denis scoffed. "Perhaps I'd be better off a pirate," he said, placing one hand on his pistol holster and the other on the hilt of his sword. "I'd probably last longer than I will here!"

"You might."

"I'd prefer to keep both legs, though."

"Sorry, that's not optional."

Another mistake, born from tradition, was distinguishing French officers from the rank-and-file by equipping them with swords. Technically, as an aspirant, Denis was not yet a true officer, but he was still issued a sword and a pistol. He wore the sword and scabbard on his left hip, the pistol and holster near his right, and because he commanded an infantry squad, he also carried a rifle, and wore the accompanying bayonet and sheath on his belt as well.

While the garish braids, epaulettes and insignia worn by officers had been reduced over the decades since the Franco-Prussian War, an officer's sword, with its long braided knot and tassel suspended from the pommel, made him easy to spot and identify in battle. The visible distinction would lead to a high casualty rate among officers in the field. During the withdrawal at Charleroi, when he was on his feet, Denis had heard what he thought were an inordinate number of bullets snapping close by.

After disengaging at Charleroi, Fifth Army marched almost due south toward Lanrezac's proposed line of retreat. In XVIII Corps, Denis moved southwest in the direction of Guise, approximately forty miles from Charleroi. Many viewed the retreat as only being essential for reestablishing the offensive. They were still unaware of just how greatly the three German armies outnumbered them. Spirits stayed relatively high for the first day of the retreat, but in the afternoon of the 24th a sobering sight would change the tone abruptly.

The column approached a T-shaped intersection of two dirt roads. Up and down the intersecting road, as far as the eye could see, were French families, mostly peasants, evacuated from their homes ahead of the German advance. The poor, sad souls, pulling what little possessions they had behind them in rickety handcarts or mule-drawn wagons, were a depressing lot. The dust kicked up from their dragging feet hung over them, a brown pall, and epitomized their collective spirit. Old couples, women and children, hanging their heads as they trudged down the dirt road in the choking heat, brought home the reality that it wasn't just the fighting men who were affected by war.

The 2nd Bataillon marched alongside the peasants, and the healthy young French soldiers steadily outpaced the slower civilians. It was odd, being an army in retreat, leaving in the dust those they were sworn to defend. Denis pitied the little children dragged from their homes; they weren't old enough to fully understand what was happening. It was hard to look at them. He stopped to pick a blue and yellow flower on the side of the road, and presented it to an adorable little girl who had fixed her teary eyes on him as he walked by.

"For you, mademoiselle," Denis said. He lifted his cap and bowed, handing her the flower. She bashfully took it then leaned into her mother, who smiled wearily.

"You mustn't cry, my dear," said Denis, "surely your tears will break we men's hearts, and our hearts are difficult to break."

The corners of the child's mouth curled, and her cheeks dimpled. Her tears had left dirt smudges across her cheeks. *Look what grief the boche have brought this poor child.* While shaken by the sight of the refugees, the only thing Denis could do for them was to push on and continue the fight when the orders came. He walked backward as his squad moved past the little girl and her family, and brought his right hand to his heart and raised his left hand in the air to say, "Fear not, m'lady, we shall yet force the barbarian horde back from whence they came. You have my word as a man of honor."

He hoped his gesture brightened the little girl's day. Clutching the flower, her gift from the valiant, unnamed knight passing by, the little girl waved goodbye. Denis, still walking backward, bowed and tipped his cap once more before about-facing to continue his southward march.

VERNON

The fighting never stopped after the sun went down at Mons on the 23rd. Upon falling back from the canal that afternoon, the assumption was that 5th Division would make a defensive stand, as a line of hastily fortified positions had been prepared a few miles to the south by the engineers and reserves. Instead, at 2:30 in the morning of the 24th word began to spread that the French had abandoned the BEF's right flank, the Germans were closing in, and that an immediate retreat was necessary. The lack of coordination between French Fifth Army and the British forces would cost the 1st Cheshire Battalion dearly.

As frightening as fighting the Germans during the day had been, falling back in the middle of the night with the Germans in hot pursuit was terrifying. The troops communicated very little and moved hastily. They ignored the fatigue, thirst and hunger from having spent nearly the entire day before either marching or pitched in battle. With their senses distorted by anxiety and darkness, gunfire seemed to break out from all directions as different units, from sections up to entire platoons, were forced to turn and face the Germans.

Dreadful, incalculable increments in time passed with just the sounds of nervous footsteps and clattering rifle slings swaying to and fro, and then a shot would ring out in the distance, echoing through the darkness. Shouts followed shots, spoken in German and English, calls for surrender met with colorfully worded refusals, then exchanges of gunfire barked and ripped until one side fell silent.

The men of 3 Section kept close together. Corporal Spurling led the way. They'd lost the road a while back, and were navigating through a fairly sparse maple forest. In the darkness and confusion, Fourth Platoon had begun to scatter. A cloudy sky blotted out most of the moonlight and the undulating ground pushed E Company's platoons out of line of sight from one another. Vernon took up the rear of 3 Section's group. Pritchard was on his right, Private Willoughby on his left. Willoughby whimpered with fear, unable to keep calm.

"Willoughby shut the hell up!" Vernon whispered forcefully. "They're going to hear your bumbling." It probably wasn't true, but the whimpering was getting on his nerves and adding to his jitters. The private sniffled, trying his best to get a grip. A breeze rustled the leaves overhead, and in his heightened sensory state Vernon shot a glance past Willoughby, just as the whimpering private brought a forearm to his nose to wipe the snot away.

Thwack! Blood splattered in Vernon's face, and a shot echoed through the darkness. Willoughby yelped. He'd been hit in the shoulder and he fell forward. He screamed in pain.

"3 Section, MOVE!" Corporal Spurling shouted. Vernon slung his rifle and reached for Willoughby's shoulder strap while the men of 3 Section, minus Pritchard, dashed away into the black. Pritchard moved to grab the wounded man as well.

"Get the fuck out of here, Pritch!" Vernon shouted.

"Like hell, Vernon! You'll need my help getting him on his feet!"

"No, goddammit!" Vernon cried. He shoved his friend forcefully. "I'll get him moving, he doesn't need two of us!"

Pritchard still hesitated, even after another shot rang out closer to them. It missed, and Vernon screamed, "NOW!" just as the distinct *clop-clop* of horse hooves approached from somewhere behind. Reluctant, Pritchard ran. He looked back at Vernon, who'd just succeeded in pulling Willoughby to his feet.

"All right, Willoughby, we've got to go," Vernon said.

When his friend had disappeared from view, Vernon grabbed the wounded man around the waist and commenced walking with him, expecting the urgency to quickly turn their walk to a run. The almost dead weight of Willoughby's body was surprising. It was as if the man was unwilling to help himself.

Clop-clop.

"Come on, Willoughby," Vernon urged, "you can move faster than this. I saw where you were hit. Don't get me killed trying to save you."

Clop-clop. They were close.

Vernon was shocked at how little effort the man made in trying to walk with him. He was hit in the shoulder, not the legs, he should have been able to run, yet Vernon was practically dragging Willoughby along the ground. *Has he fainted?* He wished he hadn't been so quick to dismiss Pritchard.

"Let's move you bastard!" he shouted, desperately tugging at his section mate's waist.

Clop-clop. Closer.

"Willoughby you son of a bitch!" Vernon strained his legs and arms pulling nearly the full weight of another man.

Clop-clop. The hooves were upon him.

"Halt!" A deep German voice shouted from horseback, just feet behind them. Vernon stopped. He clenched his eyes shut in frustration.

Shit. I'm either dead or a prisoner.

With his arm still around Willoughby, Vernon struggled with the ragdoll of a man to turn and face the German cavalryman. The mounted rider trotted his muscular, black horse to within feet of the two men. A thin beam of moonlight found its way through the clouds above, and glinted off the horse's shiny coat.

"Name, rank and unit," the German said.

"Private Thomas Atkins, sir," Vernon lied.

The cavalryman immediately drew his pistol and aimed it at Vernon. "Cheeky, Private Atkins. But you are in no position for jokes, and I haven't the appetite for British cheek. Name, rank and unit."

Vernon might be a smartass once, but he wasn't about to do it with a pistol aimed at his head. "Private Vernon Hayes 6823, E Company, 1st Cheshire Battalion."

"Ah, another Cheshire. Very good. Put that man down," the German said, waving his pistol as he dismounted. Four more men on horseback had arrived behind him. Vernon debated unslinging his rifle and shooting it out, but there was no way he'd be able to kill all five men before one of them got him first. Better a prisoner than a dead man. Another rider dismounted. He took Vernon's weapon, and then stepped back beside his horse.

Not wanting to drop Willoughby, Vernon said, "This man is wounded, sir. I'd rather not let go of him."

"I said put him down," the German responded sternly, stepping closer. His uniform had braided boards on the shoulders. He was an officer. Of what rank Vernon was unsure.

"But sir..." Vernon began to protest. At the same time, the officer raised his pistol. Without so much as flinching, he shot Willoughby in the head. Bits and pieces of skull and brain splashed into Vernon's face. He tasted the metallic zing of blood on his lips.

"Jesus Christ!" Vernon shouted, dropping Willoughby with a thud. "I've given up my weapon. We're your prisoners!"

"Who has taken you prisoner?" the German asked, looking over his shoulder at the men behind him. "I'm not taking any island apes as my prisoner. Clearly I haven't taken him prisoner," he said, pointing his pistol at the body lying next to Vernon's boots.

The officer pointed the pistol in his direction yet again, and Vernon lowered his head. He took his last breath. Sally was his only thought. He was sorry that he'd never see her again. There was nothing else for him to say or do. He was dead.

POW! The pistol sounded more like a rifle. Blood spattered Vernon's face for the third time in as many minutes, but only a light spritz. He waited a full second for the burn to take hold somewhere in his body, but it didn't. He opened his eyes to look at the cavalry officer. The German dropped his pistol, staring blankly at a wound directly above his heart. He fell to his knees.

TAC-TAC-TAC! A startlingly loud but familiar sound ripped through the air, chattering nearby, as the four remaining German cavalrymen and their horses were riddled with bullets.

That's a Vickers!

"Hurry up, Vernon!" Pritchard said, and he slapped him on the shoulder. He'd come out of nowhere. "I found those boys and told them my friend needed help." He nodded in the direction from which the machine gun fire came. Pritchard had just saved Vernon's life.

"You arsehole Pritch! I told you to run!"

"I did run! And then I came back. And now we'll both run, right after this." Pritchard quickly hopped next to and knelt alongside the dead cavalry officer. He picked up the pistol. "Luger makes for a nice gun," he grinned, tucking the pistol in his haversack. "It's quite a prize. Might come in handy later. Thank you kindly mister..." he leaned over the body to search for the dead man's name on his uniform. He grabbed one of the braided silver shoulder boards and exclaimed, "Vernon, this bloke is a major!" Apparently he knew more about German rank insignia than did Vernon.

"I'd be rude not to thank you for the Luger, Major...Kastner," Pritchard said irreverently, "so thank you." He smacked the dead officer on the cheek, took the spare pistol magazines from the leather pouch on his belt, and tucked them in his haversack.

A larger group of shouting German infantry was within earshot. Vernon and Pritchard had to get out of there, and soon. The Vickers crew emerged from the trees and trotted over to them. One man carried the gun, another the tripod, and the third had several fabric ammunition belts slung around his neck. Their footsteps thudded from the extra weight they carried, and the ammo carrier jingled as his ammo belts swayed back and forth.

"You chaps clear on out," said the man holding the gun. "We'll set up shop here and give these fuckers what-for." He affectionately slapped the fluted cooling shroud around the gun's barrel. The shroud was basically just a tubular water tank with a series of grooves running along its length. It covered the entire barrel, save for the muzzle booster emerging from the end of the shroud.

"No," Vernon said, "you need to come with us."

"No can do, old boy," the man with the tripod replied as he dropped it to the ground. "You Cheshires are scattered all through these woods and we need to buy you some time. Don't let this go to waste."

Vernon looked to their cap badges. The crew wasn't from his battalion. At the top of their badge was a white metal sphinx, sitting atop the word *MARABOUT*. Beneath that, in the center of the badge was a white metal castle, with the words *PRIMUS IN INDIS* embossed below it. Encircling the castle were two brass olive branches. They extended from either end of a banner, set at the bottom of the badge, which was embossed with *DORSETSHIRE*.

Though the 1st Dorsetshires were in 15th Brigade, Vernon had no idea how the crew had ended up so far astray from their battalion. They must have just fallen behind the rest of the Dorsetshires in the confusion.

"What are your names?" Vernon asked. He wished to learn the identities of the three men who were likely about to die for the sake of their fellow British.

"What the fuck does that matter?!" the gunner said as he set the weapon atop the tripod. "Just get out of here before Fritz catches up!"

"Thank you chaps," Vernon said. "Good luck." He and Pritchard ran. They weren't about to let the brave men sacrifice themselves in vain. They made it about two hundred yards before the Vickers crew opened fire, a heroic attempt to take as many Germans with them as possible before being overwhelmed. Rushing into the darkness in search of any signs of E Company, Vernon regretted that he'd not gotten the names of those three valiant men.

The retreat went poorly. Entire sections and platoons were essentially wiped out after being forced to turn and fight in the darkness. Those men who weren't killed in their delaying actions were wounded, captured or both. The individuals, sections, and platoons that sacrificed themselves allowed the disorganized retreat of the larger forces to continue. A multitude of unnamed heroes died during the night and the following morning so that their countrymen might live.

From the canal to the nighttime retreat, E Company lost thirty-six men, dropping its strength to well under two hundred. They managed to escape total destruction, and rejoined the battalion at sunrise. Fourth Platoon had lost nine men, though Willoughby was the only 3 Section man killed. The retreat continued south throughout the morning of the 24th. The space bought by the rearguard actions of their fellow soldiers was limited, and as clashes echoed throughout the countryside behind them, there was no time to stop and rest.

At about noon, just after E Company had marched past the small village of Elouges, a runner arrived to speak with Lieutenant Hood. When the runner departed Hood looked shaken. He brought his right hand to his forehead and placed it over his eyes.

This will not be good news, Vernon thought.

After gathering himself, Hood addressed Fourth Platoon. "Listen up, men," he said, "Bannister's just gotten word from Lieutenant Colonel Boger at Battalion HQ. The retreat is going to pot, and the whole of the division is in trouble. We're to halt and delay Fritz here for as long as it takes."

Vernon and Pritchard looked at one another with long faces as Hood explained the situation. Brigadier General Gleichen, 15th Infantry Brigade's commander, was asking the 1st Cheshires, along with the 1st Norfolk Battalion and 3rd Cavalry Brigade, to fight a holding action for the sake of 5th Division and indeed the entire BEF. The retreat had fallen into disarray, and was coming unhinged. Someone had to buy them some time.

When Hood finished speaking, Pritchard turned to Vernon. "Well..." he began, "you dodged it last night, mate, but it looks like you'll be coming to a sticky one anyway." He laughed nervously. There was a large German force close behind them, and the odds were stacked against the Cheshires and Norfolks making it out of there at all.

E Company marched for fifteen minutes further south, toward the village of Audregnies, and took a position near the end of 1st Battalion's line, between A Company to its north and B Company to its south. The Cheshires deployed along a road running roughly north-south, oddly enough at what was almost a right angle to the Germans advancing from the north. There was no time to dig proper cover. Their location along the road offered slight concealment, but the flat country provided little to no protection, whilst in the distance, where the Germans would arrive, the landscape was obscured by corn stooks and—just as at the canal the day before—more slag heaps. The stooks, large piles of grain stacked head to head, formed tall, teepee-like structures. There must have been hundreds in the acres of field ahead.

The 1st Norfolks were about a mile further north, near a colliery that stood roughly a quarter mile from a set of railroad tracks that ran east to west. The 3rd Cavalry Brigade made up the extreme left flank, taking their position southwest of the 1st Cheshire's line. Two artillery batteries established themselves about a half mile behind the line, one battery east of the Norfolks and one battery east of the Cheshires.

To the last, all those lying along the road were visibly afraid, and Vernon was no exception. He was unsure which affected him more, the dusty thirst in his mouth, the churning emptiness in his stomach, or the horrible butterflies swirling around inside the cavern in his belly.

"Hey Pritch," Vernon said between fast, shallow breaths, "how are you holding up?"

Pritchard looked at him and said, "I'll probably be with Daisy soon, and I'm all right with that." He reached over and grabbed Vernon's arm. "If it comes down that, though, I swear to you I'll do what I can to make sure you get out of here and home to Sal."

Vernon smiled, but he had his doubts he'd be going home. "If the 1st Cheshire is to be stricken from the rolls," he whispered, "I hope Bannister goes with it."

After a short chuckle Pritchard answered, "We should be so lucky. He'll probably be the only one that makes it out of here. He'll be hailed as a hero, just like Smith-Dorrien with the Zulus."

"Sickening. A merciful God would never let that happen."

Poom! Poom! Poom! The artillery a mile northeast of their position opened up all at once, before Vernon could even see the Germans. Pritchard flinched at the sudden roar shattering the uneasy stillness. The booming rolled over the countryside, and Vernon prayed the British gunners might send the Germans running.

One artillery battery could not chase away the entirety of General Friedrich Sixt von Arnim's German IV Korps, advancing toward the two British battalions. The Germans outnumbered them ten to one. The guns behind the Cheshire's line opened up minutes later, and still the Germans had not come into view. The artillery hit the enemy columns marching in close formation with great ferocity, but it wasn't long before the German field artillery batteries were in position and responding to the British with counter-battery fire.

"There they are!" Vernon shouted as he caught a glimpse of the advancing enemy infantry in the distance. He marveled at their number. The grey wave was more than a thousand yards away when the first Lee-Enfields opened fire, running the mad minute at thrice the range. After a time, during which the approaching Germans gradually closed the distance, a British cavalry charge cut across 1st Battalion's line of fire and toward the furthest advanced Germans. The charge, while brave, accomplished little and was harshly repulsed, sending the surviving riders retreating past the British infantry.

Despite the failure of the cavalry's almost suicidal charge, it, along with accurate shooting by the artillery, the rapid and skilled firing of the British rifles, and a small number of machine guns countable with one hand, worked synergistically to slow the German advance. The enemy commanders believed they were faced with a much larger British force, equipped with more machine guns than were actually present. The leading German columns deployed defensively, and IV Korps halted.

FOOM! The counter-battery fire of the German cannons sailed a shell much closer to E Company than to the British cannons behind them. As more German guns were brought into position, the shellfire directed at the Norfolks and Cheshires increased, as did rifle and machine gun fire.

Private Rhodes, situated on Vernon's right, took a round to the forehead. Out the corner of his eye, Vernon saw Rhodes's rifle drop and his head slump forward onto it. *God dammit, another Cheshire shot in the head right in front of me.*

FOOM! A shrapnel round landed close, and detonated on the road in front of Third Platoon about forty yards away. The explosion obliterated at least four men and wounded several more. A tiny, sizzling bit of shrapnel bounced into the dirt in front of Vernon; he shuddered at the thought of just how much the hissing pellet would hurt were it lodged somewhere inside his body. Medics, ducked low to avoid the lead storm, scrambled to help the soldiers wounded by the blast. Unwounded men frantically dragged the mutilated wounded away from the road.

"How bloody long do they expect us to stay here?!" Pritchard shouted during a reload.

"Long as it takes!" Vernon yelled back. Deep down, he struggled to come to terms with dying along that road. So long as it meant the escape of the division, maybe it was all right. That, however, had not yet been decided. He had plenty of fighting left to do.

Thwack! Private Trask, positioned on Pritchard's left, was mortally wounded by a rifle round to the lower half of his face. He dropped his weapon and rolled about on the ground, screaming in fear and agony, clutching at his mangled face. The screams chilled Vernon to the bone, and continued for more than a minute before Trask mercifully expired just as a medic arrived to try and help him. Sprawled on his back when he succumbed, he'd spread blood all over himself, his equipment and the grass around him. Three men down. *Is my turn coming soon?*

By approximately 2:30 p.m., the Norfolks were under threat from a German advance on their rear flank. Their battalion commander sent two runners to Lieutenant Colonel Boger's headquarters to communicate the 1st Norfolk's intention to withdraw. Fire was so heavy, though, that both runners were killed before they made it to the 1st Cheshire's commander. Thus, the Norfolks began their retreat while the Cheshires remained in place, unaware.

The Germans were getting uncomfortably close. Squads and individuals ducked behind and scurried between the corn stooks, inching ever closer to the British defenders. While they presented better targets at close range, there were far too many of them to fend off for much longer. Ammunition on the British side began to run catastrophically low. When Vernon realized he'd used all but a few of the charger clips in his ammo pouches, he rolled over to Rhodes's body. Flipping his dead section mate over, he looted the remaining clips from the deceased man's belt.

"Sorry Rhodesey, but Fritz needs these far more than you," Vernon politely informed the corpse. He rolled back to his spot next to Pritchard and handed him roughly half the clips.

Casualties climbed up and down the Cheshire's line. The Norfolk's un-communicated withdrawal made the situation even direr. The line managed to hold for a further hour and a half. Men dropped by the minute. Vernon made every trigger pull count. He fired only when he was certain not to miss. The longer he had bullets, the more separation 5th Division could gain, but again, he was running low.

"Lew! You need to grab the rest of Trask's clips!" Vernon urged; he had just two chargers left.

"He's got his fucking blood everywhere!" cried Pritchard.

"Just grab them!"

"Aw, shit!"

Pritchard rolled next to Trask. He dug his hands into the blood-stained ammo pouches. It took him just seconds to get the clips, but when he rolled back to Vernon to pass him a share, his hands and the bullets were soaked in blood. The elbows, sleeves and stomach of his tunic were smeared a sticky, coagulated dark red.

"At least it's not mine!" Pritchard shouted, wiping his crimson hands in a patch of unsoiled grass. He popped two chargers into his magazine, and aimed toward the Germans once again. Vernon had no time to count the clips his friend had grabbed, but there weren't many. If the others had a similar number of rounds left, he estimated the firing line might be able to hold for perhaps forty-five more minutes. And that was without taking into account the chance of the Germans pushing forward with a bayonet charge. Still conserving his fire, Vernon had given up counting how many men he'd shot.

After somehow stretching out another hour of fighting, killing, and witnessing more men of Fourth Platoon dying, Vernon noticed Lieutenant Hood kneeling down and speaking to a runner further down the line. *Good to see the lieutenant is still alive,* he thought. The time was approximately 5:00 p.m. Hood had a hand on the runner's shoulder, and was leaned in close to hear what the messenger had to say. Suddenly the runner stood and scampered away from the line, headed east.

Hood rushed from section to section, speaking to his surviving corporals for mere seconds per man. *What the hell is he saying to them?* Corporal Spurling remained among the survivors, and when Hood said whatever it was that he'd said, Spurling jumped into action.

"We've been given the order to withdraw!" he shouted, waving his right arm to signal his men to move back. "Let's get the hell out of here!"

Why didn't the runner move toward B Company?

Vernon could ponder that later. He might just survive the day, after all. He and Pritchard sprang to their feet, and 3 Section commenced its mad dash away from annihilation. Before he joined them, though, Vernon reached for Rhodes's water bottle. He could ignore his thirst no longer. He'd found a bullet hole through his own bottle after fleeing the canal the day before. A certain amount of guilt came with looting his dead mate, but as with the bullets, the dead man no longer needed water.

"Thanks again Rhodesey." Vernon said. "I'm sorry." He clipped the bottle to his waist belt and dashed away.

The remnants of E Company's four platoons ran for dear life, in total disorder, spread out over hundreds of yards. While their charge was chaotic, there was only one general direction in which they could possibly head, and that was southeast. The Germans had advanced behind the British line during the battle, and nearly had them surrounded. Those Cheshires who managed to escape did so by the skin of their teeth.

It sounded like there were still hundreds of British rifles that remained in place, firing away, holding along the line. More men should have been making it away from the road. As far as Vernon knew, the other companies had not been overwhelmed. It was as if the entire group of Cheshires retreating southeast was from E Company, and only E Company. "Hey Spurling!" he shouted on the run.

Corporal Spurling, ten yards ahead, glanced back to indicate he'd heard.

"Where are the other companies?!"

"How should I know?!" Spurling called back to him. "Why don't you go back and check?"

"But they should be right behind us!"

"Hood got Bannister's order and we cleared out! End of story!"

They ran for miles. Vernon's lungs burned and his feet felt like they shattered with every step. He hadn't eaten in nearly a day, and the water bottle he took from Rhodes was already empty. His head ached from the noise of hours of relentless battle and the smoke from hundreds of discharging rifles and exploded shells.

The stand taken by the 1st Cheshire and 1st Norfolk Battalions delayed the advance of German IV Korps for six hours. Incredibly, four of those six hours were shouldered by the 1st Cheshire Battalion alone. The 5th Division was able to escape, but the escape came at a dear price to the two battalions tasked with enabling it.

When E Company and the shredded remnants of 1st Battalion finally rejoined the retreating 5th Division, Vernon knew something was wrong. A number of men from E Company were dead, that was indisputable, but there were disproportionately more present from his company as compared to the others. Those from the other companies who did escape had arrived nearly an hour later than E Company. It was soon apparent that virtually the entire battalion had been wiped out. Even Lieutenant Colonel Boger had vanished, presumed killed or captured by the Germans.

After catching up to the tail end of 5th Division, the battered battalion was not given the option to sit and rest. They joined in the forced march, a tattered column, less than half what it was at sunrise. Vernon was so tired he could hardly lift his head to see the man ahead of him, but when he did, he saw someone nearby who might have some answers.

"How did we get out of there?" he quietly asked Lieutenant Hood. "Where are the other companies?"

"They're gone," Hood answered solemnly. "We've got but a few hundred men left in the entire battalion. Bannister must have learned of the retreat before the other commanders and pulled us out in the nick of time."

Vernon doubted the veracity of Hood's response. E Company was smack in between two others. There was no way their captain had the scoop on any information that wouldn't have found its way to the captains on either side of him. Vernon had a pretty good idea of the truth as to how E Company escaped. *Bannister called the retreat before he'd been given the order from HQ.* He wouldn't say as much to his platoon leader, not without more evidence, but it was the only sensible conclusion. To be sure, the order had saved him and nearly a hundred of E Company's men. Vernon was torn over whether or not one might consider their early departure an abandonment of their Cheshire comrades.

Had there been more time to prepare before they'd made their stand, the Royal Engineers and Signal Corps could have installed field telephones, placing each headquarters in direct contact with the others. Because the entire BEF was in full retreat, however, the use of telephones was impossible. Wireless telegraph might also have been an option, but the hectic retreat prevented any technical troops from contributing in their areas of expertise. During the fighting at Audregnies, all messages were dispatched by runner, and most of those runners were killed or captured before reaching their intended destinations.

The vast majority of A, B, C and D Companies received their fallback orders much too late, if even at all. They remained in their positions until 6:00 p.m., performing well above and beyond any call of duty. They'd even attempted a bayonet charge after exhausting the last of their ammunition. Lieutenant Colonel Boger was wounded and captured when he left his headquarters to try and establish contact with his company commanders. When the Germans finally surrounded the surviving Cheshires, they had no choice but to lay down their weapons and surrender. There was no other option, save for needlessly dying. They'd done what was asked of them, and more.

Though 5th Division had escaped, the BEF's retreat was still in disorder. As the forced march extended into August 25, the Germans caught up to Haig's I Corps near the city of Landecries. General

Smith-Dorrien decided the retreat was coming unraveled too greatly to continue. He ordered II Corps to halt their retreat near the town of Caudry, west of the larger city of Le Cateau. II Corps would stand and fight, to hold off General von Kluck's First Army and allow the safe retreat of Haig's I Corps further east. Because 1st Battalion had fought so ferociously and sustained such immense casualties, losing almost seventy-five percent of its fighting strength, they were kept in the reserves and would not play a large part in the upcoming Battle of Le Cateau.

DENIS

On August 26, the dry, baking heat briefly turned into a muggy, torrential downpour. Because of the holding actions fought by the BEF, Fifth Army fought no major engagements that day. In the falling rain, a gift delivered straight from the heavens, each man rushed to fill his canteen without having to resort to wringing out the water from a drenched greatcoat. Water was water in a pinch, but water laced with blue dye and a week's worth of dust and salty sweat was hardly refreshing. When the rain subsided and sundown approached, Capitaine Bex, F Compagnie's commander, approached the men during a brief rest. He walked with his right hand behind his back, and rested his left hand on the hilt of the sword hanging from his left hip.

Bex was in his forties, and had a thick moustache, twisted to a point at both ends, which obscured his upper lip. The moustache was far and away the most prominent feature of his slim visage. His face matched his wiry body type; at just under six feet tall, he could not have weighed more than a hundred fifty pounds. Like Denis, he wore a blue cover over his kepi, the brim of which shadowed his brown eyes.

Rather than a greatcoat, Bex wore a dark blue officer's tunic, with three gold chevron stripes around the sleeve cuffs. Instead of red, the *144* embroidered on his collar was gold. He wore a small, black leather satchel on one hip and his black leather binocular case on the other, and their black shoulder straps crisscrossed his chest. A silver whistle hung from his breast pocket, and his trousers, the same

122

bright red, additionally had black piping on the outer seams. His tall, black leather riding boots reached to just below his knees, and their spurs jingled as he walked.

"The British have been defeated at Le Cateau and Landecries and are in full retreat," Bex said. "The boche are in close pursuit."

The news wasn't particularly shocking to anyone else, but for Denis, it meant something different. He realized it immediately. In having fought his first engagement and enduring what had been an exhausting retreat thereafter, the fact that the Germans had crossed onto French soil hadn't registered until then. In retreating, Fifth Army hadn't done what he'd initially hoped they might do. *My God, the British have retreated past Cambrai!* He gasped audibly when the revelation struck him. Depending on the width and troop dispersal of the German advance, the boche could very well sweep straight through his home town.

Upon hearing him gasp, the capitaine glared at Denis. Though the kepi riding low on Bex's forehead and his heavy moustache veiled any readable expression, he may have been frowning underneath them. "Have you something to say, Aspirant?" He sounded annoyed.

"I...ah...no sir," Denis stammered. Bex spoke no further, and moved down the column to personally apprise the remaining sections of the current situation. He may have held it in while the capitaine stood near him, but as soon as the officer walked away, Denis turned, desperately, to his best friend.

"Patrice!" he cried, "my family!"

Denis was an aspiring officer and led by example, but in that moment he lost his composure and panicked. His breathing rate increased, the moisture evaporated from his mouth and his vision blurred. He grew dizzy. He was still drenched from the rain and sweat from marching in the muggy, late-summer heat, but suddenly the sweat poured from beneath his kepi. He thought he might faint.

"Denis you must breathe, my friend," Patrice said softly. "Calm yourself. I'm sure everyone is safe. Your father would never put your mother and Louise in danger!"

"What if..." Denis gasped, "...they weren't..." *gasp* "...fast enough?"

"It could be the boche will not move so far west," said Patrice. "Perhaps they will have passed east of Cambrai."

It made sense, as Cambrai was roughly fifteen miles north and west of Le Cateau, and the battle there had involved the BEF's left flank versus German First Army's right flank. Still, it wasn't easy to accept Patrice's logic in his present state, and Denis's racing mind persisted. *What if the boche captured them? What would they do to mother and Louise? Would they arrest father?* His head was spinning. Patrice squeezed Denis's shoulder so hard it started to hurt.

"Sir, are you all right?" asked Isaac, his forehead wrinkled with concern. He clutched his kepi in front of his chest with both hands.

"He's fine!" snapped Patrice, "it's merely the heat."

"Okay, Christ I was just asking," Isaac replied, raising his hands in submission. He was a younger soldat, just nineteen. His smooth, boyish face had only a trace of wispy brown hair, mostly on his chin. It was so scraggly and sparse he should have just shaved it off while they were still in Bordeaux.

The poilus resumed their march, and Patrice's calming influence slowly brought Denis's nerves back to a manageable level. *Of course they're safe. Father would never put them in harm's way.* He had never fallen under such an acute panic, and he repeated positive thoughts over and over in his head to stifle the worrisome ones. The rain had stopped and the clouds vanished from the sky as night fell, and while thoughts of his family consumed him internally, externally Denis had responsibilities to his men.

The British defeat at the Battle of Le Cateau by von Kluck's First Army had allowed Fifth Army to continue their southward retreat unmolested. Bülow's Second Army was forced to halt while Kluck's forces dealt with the British, and was unable to close the resulted distance between them for more than a day. The French marched onward for hours, a seemingly continuous mass of blue, exhaustedly stomping down the road in the moonlight. There was no time for sleep.

At command's highest level, Joffre frantically traveled back and forth to the headquarters of his generals facing the Germans' northern advance. He was still convinced that if all the forces opposing the Germans could launch one coordinated offensive, a breakthrough might be achieved. Tense meetings took place between Joffre and Lanrezac after the Battle of Charleroi, as Lanrezac strongly disagreed with Joffre's assessment of the potential for a successful offensive.

From the outset of the war, in fact, Lanrezac disagreed with the entire premise of Joffre's plan XVII, which adhered strictly to the principle of the all-out offensive. Lanrezac knew the German advance through Belgium was the most threatening aspect, while Joffre clung to the idea that victory would be achieved via breakthrough in Alsace-Lorraine.

While the meetings after Charleroi between Lanrezac and Joffre had been heated, an even tenser meeting took place between Joffre, Lanrezac and Field Marshal French as the Battle of Le Cateau raged on. Sir French was probably a difficult man for Lanrezac and Joffre to communicate with, owing both to a language barrier and to French's bitterness over Fifth Army leaving his flank unannounced during the Battle of Mons. He complained openly of Lanrezac's behavior, and refused any requests to halt the British retreat.

The BEF had come to France with less than a hundred thousand men, and at Mons and Le Cateau those numbers had been diminished by no insignificant amount. The potential for destruction of the BEF on French soil was real, and the field marshal had specific orders from Lord Kitchener forbidding him from allowing such an unacceptable thing to occur.

French's reluctance to further assist Fifth Army infuriated both Lanrezac and Joffre, but because the BEF operated as an independent entity, Joffre could issue no orders forcing Sir French to cooperate, and as a field marshal, French outranked Joffre anyway. The atmosphere grew increasingly hostile, and Lanrezac reached a point where he refused even to eat lunch with the British commander. He could not stay in the same room with him and so left the conference. Following Lanrezac's abrupt departure, the atmosphere calmed when Joffre also expressed to French his discontent with the Fifth Army commander. Regardless of the two leaders' shared sentiments, the British would continue their retreat.

Before Denis knew it, his uniform had dried. Only the insides of his boots were damp and his feet squeaked inside them as he walked. He needed a sip of water; his mouth had been dry ever since his panic attack. Still very worried, his pulse pounded in his neck and temples. His throat was so parched it tasted of dust. He reached to his knapsack and grabbed his canteen; it was far too light. When he jiggled it back and forth and nothing sloshed within, he knew what was coming, but he unscrewed the cap anyway. When he brought the canteen to his mouth, he let out a slow, exasperated sigh. *Fucking empty. Again.*

"Does anyone have any water?" he asked. He had a guess as to what the answer would be.

"No sir."

"Sorry sir."

"I've been empty for hours, sir."

None of his men had water, either. Denis rolled his tongue back and forth and pursed his lips, but everything was dry. He might as well have been chewing gauze all day.

After the one, splendid rainstorm on the 26th, the weather turned hot and humid again. The first men began to collapse from exhaustion and dehydration mid-day on the 27th. Men wept at their thirst out of sheer frustration, then wept harder when they realized the cruel truth that they lacked the tears with which to cry. Lips split, then bled, and mouths became as sandpaper. Even saliva was a luxury. A man could go without food for weeks if he had to, but marching in heavy gear in scorching heat with no water could kill that same man in just a few days.

"Denis, do you think if I cut my finger and drank my blood that it might quench my thirst?" Patrice asked. It was an absurd thing to ask, but he didn't sound like he was joking.

"I'm not sure, Pat, but I doubt it. If I were you I'd drink my piss before I resorted to blood."

"If I could piss I'd happily drink it. I haven't had a piss since early yesterday. If I don't get water soon the next piss I take I'll probably have to squeeze out by hand. Like a lemon candy."

Denis laughed. It conjured a gross mental image. "Maybe after you push out your dick candy you can suck on that. A tasty treat to moisten your mouth."

"You're right," Patrice grinned, "I'll save some for you, too."

"I'm honored that you'd share, but I'll pass, thank you." Having a sense of humor about their increasingly dangerous dehydration was the only way to avoid it consuming their minds.

On August 28, Joffre issued orders to Lanrezac to halt Fifth Army's retreat, and to launch a counterattack against von Bülow's Second Army. At that time Fifth Army was near the town of Guise on the banks of the River Oise, less than twenty miles east of St. Quentin.

The countryside around Guise was heavily wooded, with small streams and ravines which cut across the land. No matter how dirty the stream or river that lay before them, the men made sure to drink at least one canteen full and top off another before marching to face the Germans. Partially rehydrating before launching their counterattack likely saved many lives later on.

At six o'clock in the morning on the 29th, in heavy mist, Fifth Army launched their attack against the pursuing Germans. XVIII Corps was northwest of Guise, near Fifth Army's left flank, and ran face-first into a well-positioned onslaught from German field artillery. The German artillery fire, mostly in the form of field howitzers launching their shells over the treetops, killed scores as the two forces approached one another.

Marching just to the east of Denis and his men in F Compagnie, D Compagnie was partly visible through the trees, owing to gaps in the forest and a gradual downward slope to the land. The poilus on the adjoining company's left flank were decimated when two shrapnel shells landed directly on top of them in short succession. The carnage left by the two impacts made Patrice particularly antsy, as that end of D Compagnie's line was suddenly flattened and remained that way. Luckily for 2 Escouade, they were unable to see the brutality up close.

Eventually the advancing belligerents made visual contact, and the German artillery ceased its fire. The popping of Lebels and Mausers began in its place. The trees and uneven ground provided plenty of cover, but they also made it difficult to shoot one's target at a distance. The void separating the two forces shortened by the minute as men leapt from one covered position to another. Some French squads outdistanced others in their haste to both meet the enemy and find new cover, and F Compagnie's sections began to fragment. As more men were hit, their screams mixed with the gunfire.

A young soldat from 1 Escouade fell dead just twelve feet in front of Denis, hit in the heart while attempting to move between two trees. It was such an odd thing—Denis had seen the young man's face many times before, saw his smile, heard him laugh at a joke and converse with a buddy, and now the boy lay there, dead. One shot to the chest, a flop to the ground, a few short gasps, and then he was nothing. He'd never do anything ever again, because a tiny piece of metal had struck him in a critical spot.

Denis had killed his first man on the second day of the Battle of Charleroi. It was from hundreds of yards away, and he did not see his face. While killing a boche wasn't something he relished, the previous week's experience had made it easier to aim and fire. They were on French soil, after all, and he could not recall hearing anything about the Germans being invited.

Denis leaned against a large oak tree to steady his aim. Though he was scared, his hands did not tremble and his rifle did not sway. *Pow!* The boche on the receiving end spun like a top and fell to the ground.

Ceding no ground to the enemy, the men of F Compagnie fought on for close to an hour. The distance between the closest opponents shrunk to within less than fifty yards. When ammunition began to run low, the German commanders must have deemed a breakthrough possible. Thus, the combat in many areas of the battlefield devolved from covered rifle fire into a German bayonet charge. When the German whistles blew and hundreds of shouting Germans suddenly leapt from their covered positions and charged, Denis knew some of his men were about to die.

"Patrice!" he shouted, as he stared at the oncoming attackers. With their spiked helmets, they were a stampede of murderous rhinoceros-men. "You stay right fucking next to me, you understand?"

"Yea!" Patrice yelped nervously.

"Men!" Denis cried, steeling himself. "Keep in tight as you can! Protect yourselves and those near you!"

Most had already fixed their bayonets, but as the rest frantically attached theirs, Denis did not. Instead, he rested his empty Lebel against a tree and drew his sidearm, a Pistole Revolveur Modele 1892. With the pistol in his left hand, he drew his sword with his right. "Attack!" he screamed, and he led 2 Escouade's charge into the approaching Germans. He'd ordered them to keep tight, but when the collision came, that was impossible.

There should have been no place for a sword on the battlefield, but when the bullets ran dry and rifles turned to spears, the man with the sword might have an advantage, provided he had the skill to wield it. A rifle with bayonet had longer reach, that was its purpose, but Denis's sword was lighter, faster and easier to attack with than was a ten pound rifle with a long knife at the end.

The sword was something he'd practiced with during peacetime. It being a one-handed weapon, he also had the six shots from his revolver working in his favor. In a hand to hand fight, his sidearm had the potential to save his or someone else's life six times over. It was a massively advantageous card to hold.

The first man who charged him swung his Mauser like a club, and Denis dove to the dirt to avoid being struck. The German's forward momentum carried him past Denis, and by the time the man stopped and turned to face him Denis had already aimed his pistol. It was strange to look a man in the eye while pulling the trigger. *Bang!* He fired his first bullet, hitting the man underneath the Adam's apple. The boche's eyes widened as blood began to spurt from the wound. *Shot number one.*

Denis had no time to feel remorse as the German dropped to his knees, hands wrapped futilely around the spurting neck wound. He ran past him, around the trunk of a nearby tree, and drew back his sword to swing at a boche who hovered over Clemence, about to bayonet him.

Clemence, who'd somehow lost his rifle and lost it quickly, was lying on his back. He held his hands up as if to urge the German to rethink, but the blade was already on its downward trajectory. The doomed Frenchman was one of Denis's men. He desperately wanted to save him, but his sword strike arrived too late. The German's bayonet plunged into Clemence's chest just as Denis's sword cleaved deep into the German's neck. The force of the sword strike knocked the man out cold and he collapsed to the ground in a heap. He'd die from blood loss while unconscious, and not feel a thing.

When the German fell, he let go of his rifle, and as its weight tipped to one side the bayonet, still stuck in Clemence's chest, acted as a lever on his ribs. He screamed in pain, and he wailed when his ribs gave way and broke under the strain. He began to choke on the blood in his lungs and throat. Mortally wounded but fully conscious, Clemence looked Denis straight in the face and cried for help. "Sir, please help me!" he coughed, spraying blood onto his coat. Blood spurted from his chest. His teeth were red.

He is killed. You have to leave him here. "Clemence I can't!" Denis shouted, "I'm sorry!"

"No! No! Please sir I want to go home!" the dying man screamed.

"There's nothing I can do!" Denis yelled. It hurt him to speak so callously to the young man, but it was true. What was he supposed to do? He had two options. One was to hold Clemence's hand as he died and die with him, and the other? Be realistic.

"DENIS! PLEASE!" Clemence wailed.

Denis left the sobbing, wheezing, dying Clemence and fired a shot at a boche from ten feet away. He hit the fellow in the head and killed him instantly, knocking the spiked helmet from his head. *Shot number two.* He turned to look for Patrice, and found him just in time to see his friend stove a German's helmeted head in with the butt of his Lebel. *That was disgusting*, he thought. For a split second Patrice met his gaze, and winked before moving to attack another boche. *What the hell, Patrice?*

An unexpected force suddenly struck Denis in the back and lifted his feet from the ground. A charging rhinoceros had tackled him from behind, knocking the sword from his hand and nearly making him drop his revolver. The sword clanged off an exposed tree root several feet away. The German's helmet landed next to it. Denis fell on his stomach and got a face full of dirt and leaves. He expected to feel the searing pain of a stab wound, but didn't. The big boche must have lost his rifle or gotten it stuck in a rib cage and figured he'd give it a go bare-handed.

Denis spun his body to get onto his back before the German could pin him to the ground. He wrapped his right arm firmly around boche's neck and wrenched it hard, making his opponent grunt and scream and throw wild, uncoordinated punches. The man must have never seen the gun in his hand. Denis pressed the revolver's barrel directly against the top of the man's head, leaned away, and pulled the trigger.

Bang! The top of the German's head split open and Denis was sprayed by a burst of things he'd rather not have been sprayed with. *Shot number three.* For the briefest moment he laid there, the dead boche on top of him, the gun barrel pushed into the man's liquefied brain.

Surveying the butchery around him and still pinned under the heavy corpse, Denis was forced to act when another man charged. He yanked the pistol out of the skull. Slimy strings of red and greyish goo flung into the air, and he promptly shot the charging man in the chest. When the bullet struck the boche he tripped over his own feet, and fell forward so hard his body tumbled over itself. *Shot number four.*

Denis then spotted something strange through a gap between two nearby trees. He saw Reynard, another soldat from 2 Escouade, standing upright with his back against a tree. He was standing, but he was dead. His arms dangled at his sides, and his head hung lifeless, chin rested on his chest. A Mauser and bayonet protruded straight out from his stomach. Reynard was tacked to the tree trunk by the weapon that killed him. *Son of a bitch,* Denis thought. *That's two of my men gone at least.*

Over the desperate cries of fighting and dying men, Denis thought he heard the bugles sound, but he wasn't certain. Bugles meant retreat. His suspicion was confirmed when Lieutenant Armistead blew into his shrill whistle from somewhere much closer by. It was time to go.

He shoved the dead German away and hurriedly wiped the blood, brain and bits of skull from his face with his sleeve. He spat once to get the nauseating taste of blood and tiny bone shards from his lips. Patrice dashed over to him, carrying his rifle in his right hand. He bent over mid-stride to pick up Denis's sword with his left hand as Denis also began to run.

"Come on men!" Denis shouted. "They've sounded the retreat!"

Most in the section had already heard the bugles or Armistead's whistle and were in the process of disengaging. Some turned to run too quickly, and were bayoneted in their backs before they'd gained enough space in which to flee. As F Compagnie extricated itself from the fight, the Mausers behind them were hastily reloaded and the fleeing Frenchmen had to contend with the threat of taking a bullet in the back.

Denis and Patrice ran side by side amidst a gaggle of French troops, jumping over roots and stumps and splashing through narrow creeks as rifle rounds snapped past their ears and smacked into the trees around them. Sprinting for dear life, in what was an extremely stressful situation to say the least, Patrice smirked and passed Denis his sword like it was the baton in a relay race. "You dropped this!" he yelled. "Lose it again and you're not getting it back!" His face and uniform were flecked in blood, dripping with sweat, and covered in dirt. He had killed at least one man in gruesome fashion and probably killed more, had likely just missed being killed several times himself, they were running for their lives and still in mortal danger, and he was *joking* with Denis.

Snatching the sword from Patrice, Denis shouted over the chaos around him, "Are you fucking losing your head, Patrice?!"

"I don't think so!"

"Then stop acting like it!"

During the French retreat from Guise, General von Bülow saw an opportunity to land a decisive blow against Fifth Army's left flank. Bülow ordered his right flank to give chase in order to destroy the fleeing XVIII Corps. If their left flank were destroyed, Fifth Army would be in serious peril. Denis and the entirety of XVIII Corps were on the verge of being crushed. They continued to fall back as the day progressed, with the trailing Germans not far behind.

The sun had long since passed overhead, and soon began to set. The men were on their last legs after an entire day of extreme duress. Just when it seemed as though the finishing stroke might come, however, the German advance was halted dead in its tracks. Général Franchet d'Esperey's I Corps had come to the rescue!

Général d'Esperey and his men had previously been on Fifth Army's far right flank, having engaged Max von Hausen's Third Army at Dinant just days earlier. During the retreat, I Corps had wheeled all the way around from the right flank to the left, and in the late afternoon the men of I Corps smashed into the German right flank, allowing XVIII Corps to limp away and make their escape. The dramatic sunset charge by d'Esperey's and his men saved the day for Fifth Army and gained d'Esperey many accolades as a commander, raising his reputation with Général Joffre at the GQG.

Shockingly, even with the disastrous campaigns fought by the French to that point, Général Joffre refused to accept the reality of just what had happened to his armies in the Battle of the Frontiers. In less than one month of fighting between the million-man armies, the French had suffered approximately 200,000 casualties, 75,000 of which were fatalities—a ghastly and appalling rate of attrition. On top of the loss of life, the industry-heavy territory abandoned to the Germans during the retreat included significant percentages of France's iron ore, cast iron, and steel production.

With the German northern wing having routed Joffre's proposed counterattack, all hope of an immediate Entente breakthrough had evaporated. No British or French troops were poised to strike. All forces were pulling away from the Germans.

The Great Retreat was in full swing.

BERTHOLD

"Isn't von Rennenkampf a German?" asked Ostermann.

"Well if he ever was, he's not anymore," Berthold answered.

"With a name like that, someone in his family sure as hell was German," Lang added. "How could a German with any measure of self-respect fall in with the Ivans?"

"Clearly Rennenkampf has no respect for himself, his namesake, or the fatherland," sniped Hertz.

"He'll be wishing he was still German soon I can tell you that," Lang said.

It was somewhat odd for the men of Eighth Army to face a Russian commander with a German patent of nobility, but there they were, with General Pavel von Rennenkampf's Russian First Army opposing them to the east.

When a German family received a patent of nobility, the "von" was affixed to their last name. The men of a family with such a distinction were given the title of *Freiherr* (free lord), while the women were titled *Freifrau* (free lady). The designations were a standing relic from the Holy Roman Empire, and represented the second lowest rank of nobility. Baron and Baroness were roughly the English equivalent. The titles were permanent and passed down through generations, which explained why Pavel von Rennenkampf still possessed his title even as a Russian commander.

The Russians had mobilized two armies for the invasion of East Prussia, and they'd done it faster than the Germans expected. The first clash between the opposing forces occurred at Stallupönen, East Prussia, just miles from the Russian border.

Gefreiter Berthold Kastner was the gun layer in his artillery crew, Gun Number 6 of the 7th Batterie, III Abteilung (Detachment) of the 16th Feldartillerie-Regiment, 1st Feldartillerie-Brigade. The 1st F.A. Brigade was attached to the 1st Division der Infanterie of General Hermann von François's I Korps.

Berthold and his five fellow crew members had seen limited action in the Battle of Stallupönen. That was nearly two weeks earlier, and since then I Korps had withdrawn twenty miles west to Gumbinnen, where they, but more so the infantry, subsequently endured fairly severe Russian artillery attacks. On August 20, after the Russians had expended most of their ammunition, I Korps counterattacked, pushing the Russians back about five miles. The arrival of the Russian 29th Division then halted the progress of the German counterattack.

South of I Korps, General August von Mackensen's VII Korps and General Otto von Below's I Reserves had initiated a retreat, panicked by the presence of General Alexander Samsonov's Russian Second Army advancing from the southeast. Because of I Korps' halted progress and the retreat of both Mackensen and Below, German Eighth Army's commander, General Maximilian von Prittwitz, feared Samsonov's Army might launch an attack into Eighth Army's rear flank. He ordered a full retreat behind the River Vistula, more than a hundred miles to the west. The retreat, a radical overreaction on von Prittwitz's part, began a chain of events that would drastically alter the course of the war on the Eastern Front.

Chief of the Oberste Heeresleitung (Army Supreme Command, or OHL for short) Helmuth von Moltke, upon hearing the news that von Prittwitz planned to entirely abandon East Prussia, immediately removed the general from command of Eighth Army. In his stead General Paul von Hindenburg, called out of retirement, was quickly dispatched to the Eastern Front. Chosen as Hindenburg's Chief of Staff was Erich Ludendorff, the victor of Liège and a recent recipient of the *Pour le Mérite*, Prussia's highest military honor.

L'Ordre Pour le Mérite, while a Prussian award, was a French phrase which meant "The Order for Merit." It was created in 1740 by King Frederick II of Prussia (a.k.a. Frederick the Great), who spoke mostly French. A recipient of the award received an elaborate and handsome medal, and bestowment of the honor meant the recipient was inducted as a member of lifelong order, alongside all who had ever received it. The medal was a symbol of their induction. The *Pour le Mérite* and the glory that came with it became *the* coveted prize for German soldiers during the Great War.

Upon assuming command, Hindenburg and Ludendorff immediately halted Eighth Army's retreat, which had already fallen back fifty or more miles in some places. No force traveled further than General Hermann von François's I Korps. After retreating from Gumbinnen, I Korps ended up back at the fortified city of Königsberg in northern East Prussia, where they'd been garrisoned before the mobilization began.

When I Korps retreated, Rennenkampf chose to halt his advance in order to regroup, while Samsonov continued advancing his forces westward. When Hindenburg learned the positions of Russian First and Second Armies, understanding that the gap between them continued to widen, he ordered I Korps to leave Königsberg to travel more than a hundred miles south by rail. The move positioned them on Samsonov's Second Army's southern flank.

One of Hindenburg's staff officers, Max Hoffman, was aware of a personal rift between Rennenkampf and Samsonov. He made an assumption that because of the wide gap between the two Russian armies and the animosity between the two Russian commanders, the communication and cooperation between Rennenkampf and Samsonov would be insufficient, with neither general truly willing to be subordinate to the other. Hoffman devised a risky battle plan, based purely on assumption, and presented it to Hindenburg and Ludendorff.

Hindenburg proved willing to take the risk. The Russian armies at that point were separated by more than forty miles, with a forested and swampy region called the Masurian Lakes between them (Rennenkampf to the north and Samsonov to the southwest). The region was dotted with nearly two thousand lakes, large and small, hence the name. Hoffman's plan called for Eighth Army to encircle and destroy one army before turning their attention to the other. By ordering I Korps to travel south, the German commanders had moved nearly all of Eighth Army in the direction of Samsonov's forces, essentially leaving Rennenkampf's Army unopposed in its westward march.

Samsonov, not wanting von Rennenkampf to share in any victory, attempted to defeat Eighth Army on his own. He advanced the majority of his forces, three separate corps, into the German center near the city of Orlau. To bait the Russian commander into moving further west, Hindenburg ordered the German center, XX Korps, to fall back. Samsonov took the bait.

On August 26, after leaving Rennenkampf free to advance, German XVII and I Reserve Korps marched south and destroyed Russian VI Corps, the only force protecting Samsonov's northern flank. Ignoring any situation that might be developing against Samsonov, Rennenkampf did not alter his course and marched First Army due west. German XVII and I Reserve Korps were free to advance to the rear of Samsonov's main forces then chasing the retreating German XX Korps. Russian Second Army, unaware of the presence of German I Korps to its south, was marching straight toward a total envelopment.

It was now the 27th, and von François's I Korps was about to strike Samsonov's southern flank.

"Push, goddammit!" Obergefreiter Lang shouted. "We should be firing within the next few minutes!"

His rank of obergefreiter (acting corporal) was one peg higher than the other five men, as he was the crew's gun commander. He was also the oldest, at twenty-five. He grew up in Bischofstein, East Prussia, about twenty miles west of Berthold's home town of Rastenburg. When not on duty, Lang lived a rough and tumble lifestyle—his face belonged on a forty-year-old, with deep grooves and sunken features. He had a thing for prostitutes, and spent most of his free time either screwing whores or stumbling drunk. In combat, with alcohol rationed, however, he reined in whatever issues he may have had, and provided a strong voice for the crew to follow.

Berthold, Ostermann, Roth and Hertz were hand-pushing the 2,200 pound gun carriage into place. The horses had done most of the work getting the dark grey beast where it needed to be, but the men had to finish setting it in position. The wheels had to move just a few more feet; then the crew could prep the gun for firing.

"PUSH!"

"I'm pushing as hard as I can, Lang!" Berthold shouted. "Any harder and I'll shit my pants!" He had a stocky build, and the heat wasn't making his job any easier. Because he kept his blonde hair short, there wasn't much of it to soak up the sweat from his scalp. It trickled from beneath his pickelhaube, down his forehead and the sides of his face, obnoxiously tickling him. As an artilleryman he, like his five comrades, was issued the same boiled leather pickelhaube as worn by the infantry, but rather than a brass spike atop the helmet, artillerymen had a brass ball. Their pickelhaubes also had tan cloth covers, with an embroidered red *16* on the front for their regiment.

They wore the same grey wool tunics as the infantry, except their collars and sleeve cuffs were piped in black instead of red. Artillery tunics retained the red piping down the front closure. The tunic fastened with eight yellow metal buttons instead of nickel, and the same went for the buttons on the pockets, sleeve cuffs, and shoulder straps. Their shoulder straps were piped in white, and featured another embroidered red *16* beneath a flaming grenade.

Their grey trousers were piped in red down the outer seam, and they wore knee-high leather jackboots. Where they differed greatly from the infantry was in standard issue weapons and equipment. In place of a large haversack and knapsack, they had a single backpack, and rather than a rifle, each man wore a pistol in a leather holster on his belt. The load artillerymen carried on their person may have been lighter, but then again, infantrymen did not have to hand-push a one ton cannon anywhere. The gun carriage was one whole hell of a lot heavier than a haversack and rifle.

Berthold wanted to let go of the carriage and wipe away his sweat with his hands. Still straining against the gun, he leaned his head into his right shoulder to try and wipe his face where a bead of sweat had just made him itch. Tilting his head made a droplet of stinging sweat fall into the corner of his left eye. He let go of the gun with his left hand and furiously rubbed his scratchy wool sleeve across his face and head. The itch was maddening. He was beyond annoyed.

"Dammit Kastner!" Lang shouted. "Get your hands back on the gun! The rest of the battery is already in position!"

"I've got sweat in my eye, you asshole!"

"Just push the fucking thing!"

"I'm pushing!" Berthold snapped, throwing his shoulder into it. He squeezed his blue-green eyes shut to force down and internalize his frustration. It tended to boil over sometimes. He bit his lip and strained some more.

Gun Number 6 was a 7.7cm Feldkanone 96 n.a. (Field Cannon Model 1896. n.a. stood for neuer art, or "new type,"). The cannon, a modified version of an outdated 1896 design, incorporated a new breech, carriage, and barrel recoil system, a design feature unavailable when the weapon was first produced. The "new type" was a direct response to the revolutionary French 75mm cannon nicknamed the *Soixante-Quinze* (literally "sixty-fifteen," or seventy-five). Before barrel recoil, the force from a fired projectile leaving a stationary barrel would knock the gun carriage out of position after every shot, requiring that it be re-positioned before resuming fire.

With the introduction of the French 75mm and its hydropneumatic recoil system, the barrel, mounted on a slide, was able to absorb the recoil, meaning the carriage stayed in place during operation. The new feature allowed for a much more rapid rate of fire, and was quickly adopted by other armies, making artillery exponentially deadlier. Germany had to modify many of its existing "old type" 7.7cm cannons to incorporate the new design, as entirely scrapping them from the arsenal would have been costly and impractical.

The men got the gun into place and began to prep it for firing. They were the last crew from 7th Batterie to do so. The battery was positioned atop a low ridge, overlooking the advance of the infantry approximately a mile ahead. During their prep, Weber returned, having just finished tying up the horses a safe distance behind the gun. Of the six men in the crew, he was the only one who wore grey riding breeches rather than infantry trousers. Weber was the artillery driver, so he spent far more time on horseback than the others.

"The horses are situated," Weber declared. At nineteen, he was the youngest of the bunch. He grew up in Zinten, about twenty miles south of Königsberg, and had been assigned to the crew just weeks before mobilization. Despite his newcomer status, the men treated him fairly, as he knew a great deal about horses and seemed to put the animals at ease. The other crewmen did not have as much experience with horses so they left the driving and most horse-related tasks to Weber. He was a skinny kid, and at five foot seven was also the shortest in the group.

Berthold was only an inch taller, but his stocky build made him much heavier and more robust than Weber. It was strange that the smallest man in stature held the most sway over the big, strong horses, but the crew didn't mind leaving it to him. Weber was strong for his size and could handle it.

"All right Weber," Lang said, "Why don't you start stacking the shells on that flat spot over there." He pointed to a spot in the grass about six feet behind and to the right of the gun.

The gun's shells came in tubular wicker baskets, lashed together in threes, which acted as shock absorbers during transport and muffled the noise of steel shells clanging together. Weber began pulling the baskets from the artillery trailer, and stacked them closer to the gun. The artillery trailer was a small, two-wheeled wagon with a chest for transporting shells and supplies. During a shoot, Weber shuttled the shells to Hertz, the breech operator.

Ostermann stood to the left of the gun, holding a pair of field glasses to his eyes to observe the battlefield ahead. "Kastner you want to take a look?" he asked. Ostermann had excellent eyesight, which was why he was the spotter and carried the field glasses. He was twenty, and had been married to his wife Minna for just over a year. Both he and his wife were from Elbing, which lay just south of the Gulf of Danzig and about twenty miles east of the River Vistula.

Their one year anniversary was ruined by the declaration of war and the subsequent mobilization. He spoke of her frequently, and the men knew he hoped the war would end soon that he might celebrate his first year with her.

Berthold moved to join Ostermann, and stepped around Roth, who was pushing the spade at the end of the gun carriage's trail into the ground. The trail was the long, heavy metal counterbalance which extended behind the gun and rested on the ground, acting as an anchor to keep the weapon in place. While firing, Roth exerted pressure on the handspike, a lever attached to the end of the trail above the spade, which pushed it into the ground and further prevented the carriage from moving.

Roth was Jewish and grew up in Soltmahnen, about twenty miles east of Rastenburg, and twenty-five miles from the Russian border. Next to Lang he was the oldest, at twenty-three. By far the crew's strongest man, he had a strongman's physique, stood five foot eleven and weighed over two hundred pounds. He might well have been the strongest man in the entire detachment. He had dark eyes, greasy black hair and a thick, black handlebar moustache. While the crew occasionally ribbed him over his heritage, the ribbing never went too far. He could have kicked any of their asses if he chose to, and they knew it.

Berthold took the glasses from Ostermann and peered across the battlefield just as the men of the 1st and 2nd Infantry Brigades opened fire at the Russians barely visible in the distance. Through the glasses, the warring infantrymen were small as tin soldiers. The muffled popping of rifles echoed over the distant field. The opposing forces were still more than half a mile apart, and were firing in volleys. Berthold handed the glasses back to Ostermann, and they met eyes. Ostermann had bizarre, yellow-green eyes with a sort of golden luster to them. Berthold wondered if their strange, almost animal-like coloration had anything to do with his exceptional vision.

BOOM! The battery fired its first ranging shot sooner than Berthold had expected, and he jumped. Forty yards away Wachtmeister Trommler, the commander of 7th Batterie, hovered over the shoulder of Gun Number 1's gun layer, personally assisting in registering the Russian targets.

"Missed them long," Ostermann said quietly, speaking more to himself than anyone in particular.

The wachtmeister (artillery sergeant, but literally "watch master") shouted instructions that Berthold couldn't quite hear, and the gun fired again. After another shot, Gun Number 2 also opened fire and soon the two cannons were on target. Ranging a visible target was extraordinarily simple, and did not require much in the way of complex calculations, just basic estimates of distance followed by a consultation with the gun's range table, a preset chart of firing distances and barrel angles. Based on the range table's information, test shots were fired, and necessary corrections were made based on the results.

To effectively attack the Russian line, 7th Batterie's gun barrels were aligned roughly parallel to one another, which would allow them, after each gun was ranged, to hit the line at different points. Since each of the six guns sat on what was basically a level surface, upon aligning the guns the crews needed only match the barrel elevation of Gun Numbers 1 and 2, then make any slight adjustments to compensate for their own overshoots or undershoots.

"Elevation, four thousand!" Trommler hollered, revealing the range, in yards, from the battery line to the target. "Fire at will!"

The commanders of the other cannons repeated the wachtmeister's figures, and the gun layers got to work dialing in their respective weapons.

"Kastner get back here!" yelled Lang. Two additional guns had already opened fire.

Berthold ran to the gun and sat in his small seat behind the weapon's protective splinter shield. Four feet of the gun's seven foot barrel protruded through an opening in the shield's center. The gun layer's seat, sighting mechanisms, and hand wheels were to the left of the breech, where the shells were loaded. Hertz, the breech operator, sat to the right.

"Did you catch what Trommler said?" asked Lang.

Berthold nodded and got to work. He turned the small hand wheel of the gun's elevating mechanism, raising the barrel's angle toward Trommler's prescribed range setting. He dialed in the proper range, and also made a slight adjustment to the barrel's traverse (the direction in which the barrel pointed on the horizontal plane), by twisting its hand wheel a half turn. "Ready," he said.

Hertz pulled the operating handle atop the end of the gun toward him, sliding open the horizontal breech, and Weber loaded the first shell, a FeldKanoneGeschoss 11 (Field Cannon Projectile 11), or FKG11 for short. The round, a mix of HE and shrapnel, weighed fifteen pounds, and was packed with nearly three hundred lead pellets. The combination shell was effective against massed infantry formations moving in the open—exactly the type of Russian force at which they were about to open fire. Hertz pushed the operating handle forward, sliding the breech block into place. The gun was ready.

"Here it comes, Ivan," Hertz said. He was twenty-one and like Weber, hailed from Zinten. In his spare time, he caroused nearly as much as Lang, only Hertz didn't like paying for it. He preferred the chase as opposed to the transaction, and strove to meet normal girls rather than hookers. Hertz had just two problems with the ladies. The first was that he was not handsome, and the second, he lacked the finesse and charm to persuade them. He often regaled the crew with tales of his exploits, though Berthold was certain the majority of those tales were complete hogwash.

"Fire!" hollered Lang.

Hertz pulled the firing mechanism, and *BOOM!* The barrel slid back, gobbled the recoil, and the carriage rocked but remained in position. The shell hurtled toward the approaching Russians more than two miles away. Berthold leaned away as the barrel recoiled so as to avoid being struck by the heavy breech. His ears rung.

Hertz slid open the breech to eject the hot and smoking empty shell casing with a hollow *thunk*. Weber, standing at the ready with another shell, pushed it into the back of the smoking barrel. Hertz closed the breech block again, and awaited the order. The noxious smoke rising from the ejected shell case burned inside Berthold's nostrils. It was not a good smell, but in a way he enjoyed it. It was the smell of purpose.

"Long, one hundred yards!" yelled Ostermann.

"Just missed them, Kastner," Lang said. "Minus one-zero minutes." He peered over Berthold's shoulder at the direct-fire sight. Berthold lowered the barrel angle incrementally and Lang issued the order to fire once more. The men repeated the process, awaiting Ostermann's observation.

"Long! Fifty yards!"

"Dammit!" Berthold shouted. He was impatient. He wanted each and every shell to land on Russian heads. He wanted the 7th Batterie, and his gun especially, to eradicate as many of them as quickly as possible. He hated the thought of Russian boots on the soil of his home province.

Russian Second Army, in reaching the Orlau area, had already advanced beyond Rastenburg, his home town, which lay about sixty miles southeast of Königsberg and right in the path of the advancing Russian First Army's southern flank. There was a chance that Rennenkampf's unopposed army might even occupy his home city. Whether or not they'd done so, Berthold was unsure. The thought worried him, but he kept it to himself, though he was certain Lang and Roth harbored the same concerns for Bischofstein and Soltmahnen.

Despite East Prussia's proximity to Russia, and the inevitable mixing of ethnicities which that lead to, Berthold did not particularly care for the Russians as a people. He considered them inferior, both in culture and breed, something his father instilled in him early on, and so it was impossible not to be impatient with Russian armies on Prussian soil. His mother Frieda and his sister Yvonne were still, at least as far as he knew, home in Rastenburg. Berthold's father Mathias was a career soldier, a cavalry major, and had been dispatched with Kluck's First Army to the Western Front. The two Kastner men were forced to leave the two women of the family by themselves.

With the barrel angle lowered another fraction, the third shell was launched and Ostermann excitedly shouted, "We hit an entire group of the bastards! Put some more on them!"

The men moved like lethal clockwork then. The six cannons of 7th Batterie joined one another in an almost unending chain of gun blasts. With each gun able to fire eight to ten rounds per minute, a destructive shell sailed toward the enemy every one and a half seconds or less. Weber scuttled back and forth delivering fresh shells to Hertz, who promptly delivered them to the Russians. Berthold savored the action. His gun was saving German lives, and ending Russian ones.

Ten minutes into the bombardment, with acrid smoke hanging thick in the air, a random rifle round pinged off of Gun 6's splinter shield. It startled Berthold so much he jerked back and fell from his seat. The crew laughed at him.

"My goodess, Kastner!" Roth shouted over the ongoing blasts, "You'd think a Russian shell had fallen! Don't piss yourself over one bullet!"

"Fuck you, Roth!" Berthold shouted. "You Hebe cocksucker!" He picked himself up and wiped the dirt from his uniform.

"Fuck *you*, cabbage head," Roth replied.

Berthold glared at him for a moment, and Roth winked at him. He sat back in his seat and the crew resumed firing. Minutes later, several more rounds hit the shield in quick succession, *ping-ping-ping!* They were probably from an errant and extremely lucky machine gun burst. No one flinched.

From that distance, even Ostermann looking through his field glasses could not truly ascertain what the shrapnel rounds from 7th Batterie's cannons did to the Russians.

Upon detonation, the hundreds of searing-hot, ten gram pellets sprayed outward in every direction, like an oversized shotgun blast. Due to the high explosive charge, men closest to the blast were blown to bits. Men further away suffered gruesome shrapnel wounds. Limbs were taken apart. Shattered lead sprayed into faces and eyes, and miniature bits of toxic metal indiscriminately buried themselves throughout men's bodies. Surviving serious shrapnel wounds, which happened with great frequency, often meant a lifetime of pain and suffering thereafter. But it was war, and in war that was what men did to one another. Had he seen it up close, Berthold Kastner would have had no problem with that whatsoever.

Gun Number 6 sat in relative safety and launched shell after shell into the doomed Russians two and a half miles distant. The Russians had artillery as well, but their ammunition had run low, and orchestrating effective counter-battery fire was impossible with German artillery surrounding them. Berthold's gun was but one of hundreds of artillery pieces spread along the miles which surrounded Russian Second Army.

The German field cannons and howitzers rained continuous shrapnel and HE upon the soon to be defeated Russians. The hundreds of thousands of men in Samsonov's Army could do little but hope the next shell did not bare their name, whilst waiting for their corps, brigade or regimental commanders' inevitable surrender.

The Battle of Tannenberg, as it came to be known, resulted in the annihilation of Samsonov's Second Army. Although the majority of the fighting took place almost twenty miles east of Tannenberg, near Orlau and Allenstein, Max Hoffman thought it befitting to name the conflict after a centuries-old battle of the same name. In the first Battle of Tannenberg, fought in the year 1410, the Teutonic Knights (a Germanic military order) suffered a crushing defeat at the hands of a combined force of Slavic Poles, Lithuanians and Tatars (ancestral Turks). Hindenburg, likely believing he played an avenging role in the battle of Teuton versus Slav, agreed with Hoffman, and thus chose the name to commemorate his great victory, a stunning reversal of the outcome of five hundred years earlier.

German Eighth Army had succeeded in the total envelopment of Samsonov's forces. When von François's I Korps smashed into Second Army's southern flank, the Russians were doomed. Rennenkampf, still miles to the north, finally realized the gravity of what was about to happen. He turned his march southward, but it was too late. Russian First Army was too far away. For an entire day, the German artillery rained death onto the Russians from three directions.

At the Battle of Tannenberg the Germans achieved one of the most spectacular military successes in modern history. Out of its original force of over 180,000 troops, Samsonov's Second Army suffered 78,000 men killed or wounded and 92,000 more taken prisoner. Just ten thousand men were able to successfully retreat. The Germans suffered less than twenty thousand casualties. Additionally, they'd seized five hundred Russian artillery pieces. It took sixty trains to move the captured Russian equipment and prisoners out of East Prussia to camps further in German territory.

On August 29, too terrified to face Tsar Nicholas II to tell him he'd lost an entire army, Alexander Samsonov killed himself.

ARTHUR & PERCY

Pow!

"Thirteen!"

It was coming down to the wire. Arthur had a chance, but he couldn't miss again.

Pow! Bullseye.

"Fourteen! Come on Ellis! Five, four, three—"

His hands wanted to tremble. Nerves urged him to sway the sights off the target. He wouldn't oblige them.

Pow!

"Fifteen! Well done, Ellis! And in the nick of time!"

Arthur racked the empty shell from the breech of his Lee-Enfield and remained in his prone firing position, staring at the target three hundred yards downrange. He had just scored fifteen hits in the mad minute for the first time. Smiling to himself, he clicked his rifle's safety catch to the on position, and looked over his right shoulder to smile at his musketry instructor.

"Good show," the instructor said.

"That was fine sport, sir!" Arthur exclaimed.

"Good to see you getting a strong feel for that Enfield, Ellis," the man replied.

"Yes sir."

Percy, who scored his first fifteen a day earlier, congratulated Arthur with a slap on the arm when he'd stood. Both boys had caught on to soldiering quite well, and right on schedule. The news filtering back from France over the past two weeks did not, overall, paint the prettiest of pictures. The BEF was retreating behind Paris, and the French were falling back everywhere.

After they joined up in London on July 1, the boys were sent to Yorkshire County, in northern England, where they'd spent the next eight weeks training. In late July, when it became obvious to British planners that there was something serious brewing on the European mainland, Arthur, Percy and the other recruits then in training began to receive accelerated instruction. Between marching, inspections, drilling, classroom instruction, and a heavy emphasis on musketry, the boys were kept extremely busy.

As it turned out, they'd not been given the chance to visit home, and it appeared as though they wouldn't be doing so any time soon. Troops were desperately needed in France to bolster the strength of the struggling BEF, and Lord Kitchener did not place much faith in the Territorials then on their way—he considered them next to useless in combat.

Arthur had penned a handful of short letters home, informing his mother and father how busy he'd been, to let them know that he was all right, and that he'd write again after arriving in France. He hoped the brevity of his half-page notes was not received with too much disappointment. He'd also toyed with the notion of writing to Elizabeth; since he'd left she'd occupied much of his thoughts. The goodbye hug they shared, the passion he'd felt, he wanted to delve deeper, but so far he hadn't the time. Or the courage.

Because they had signed up nearly two months earlier, the boys were much further along in their training than was the first wave of over one hundred thousand wartime recruits. Parliament had issued the first call for volunteers immediately upon the declaration of war, and some of those boys had begun arriving in Yorkshire in mid-August, almost five weeks after Arthur and Percy. It was now September 2, and several hundred thousand additional volunteers of Kitchener's New Army, commissioned by Parliament on August 21, were on the way. Arthur and Percy would be gone before the bulk of those recruits arrived.

When news of the Battle of Mons reached England, the British Army experienced a boom in recruitment. An iconic image from the period was a recruiting poster with the huge caption *BRITONS*, printed across the top, and underneath that a picture of the mustachioed Lord Kitchener pointing directly at the reader, followed by the text *Wants You, Join Your Country's Army! God Save the King*. The poster, designed by Alfred Leete, was a powerful motivator that inspired many to join. Others joined out of national pride, were lured by the prospect of steady pay, or had read the stories as children and just signed up for the adventure. Another enticement for some young men was the formation of so-called "Pals Battalions," where friends, co-workers and neighbors could join up together with the promise of training, deploying and fighting alongside one another. The first such battalions were assembled shortly after Mons, and the concept began to gather steam after that.

"Did you see those chaps drilling in red tunics?" laughed Percy. He and Arthur walked across the training ground toward their barracks, and took in the spectacle of what were rather shoddy-looking new recruits. One was a group of redcoats, donning uniforms the regulars hadn't worn in battle since 1885. Before the mobilization, troops had retained the aesthetic, but only out of respect for tradition, and *only* as a dress item, nothing more. Seeing trainees drilling in red coats was far from normal.

"The blokes in the old uniforms look more dignified than those sorry saps who've been training in civilian clothes," Arthur commented. "Don't they?"

"I guess. I hope for their sake they're not sent across the Channel to fight as lobsterbacks."

"They won't be."

As a nation which had begun to curtail its reputation as a militaristic conqueror, Britain was not prepared to properly equip, train, or lodge a large wave of recruits. Though the volunteers were essential for raising the sizeable army which Kitchener believed was necessary to win the war, a multitude of logistical problems quickly arose when the first waves arrived for training. Owing to shortages, some were forced to train in their civilian clothes, while others were issued all manner of outdated uniforms taken from storage. Percy had gotten quite the kick upon seeing the redcoats drilling in the field, but for planners and those recruits affected by the shortages, it was anything but funny.

While Percy and Arthur stayed in proper barracks, many of the new men stayed in tents, as the military frantically constructed marginally better accommodations. In the warmer summer and fall weather, the tents were acceptable. When winter came, tents would not suffice.

The British even had difficulty obtaining enough drill instructors. Hundreds of thousands of new troops needed officers to train them, and since the professionals of the BEF were otherwise occupied in France, many retired officers were called back into service. Most of

Arthur and Percy's instructors had been doing so before hostilities began, so their preparation was top-notch. The dip in the quality of training for Kitchener's New Armies, though, potentially meant trouble for the British as the war progressed.

Arthur and Percy were deploying to France earlier than they'd originally expected, but they believed they were ready. Because the BEF had experienced such a high casualty rate in August, it needed as many full strength units ready for front-line service as could be mustered, and it needed them forthwith. The boys were to be assigned as reserves to the 2nd Battalion of the York and Lancaster Regiment. The 2nd York and Lancaster were currently in Ireland, and would cross the English Channel to become part of the 16th Infantry Brigade. The 16th through the 19th Infantry Brigades would comprise the 6th Division, commanded by Lieutenant General Sir John Keir. The 6th Division was to ultimately join the 4th Division (which was already in France) as part of Lieutenant General Sir William Pulteney's III Corps.

In just three days, Arthur and Percy would travel by train to the Channel coast, before boarding a troop transport and departing for Le Havre. As they made their way across the parade ground and back to the barracks, Arthur had something he needed to get off his chest.

"Percy, I have to ask you something, all right?" He stopped walking.

Because of the tone in which he'd asked, Percy instantly focused on Arthur's eyes. Sure enough, the icy resolve was there. Whatever Arthur planned to say, it was important to him.

"All right then, Art," Percy said. "What is it?"

Arthur took a breath. "I'd like to write to Elizabeth before we leave. If you don't mind." He waited for a response, worried he was about to be told off.

"Well it's about bloody time," Percy answered with an exasperated look. "Wouldn't you say?"

"Huh? What are you talking about?" Arthur asked, confused.

Percy thought his pal might have been playing dumb, but just in case he wasn't, he said, "Listen, Art. I've lived with my sister for seventeen years. And for thirteen of them, she's thought the world of you. I've grown tired of answering questions about 'Artie' over the years, especially during these last two."

What? Arthur's jaw dropped.

Percy wasn't finished. "I mean Christ in Heaven, Arthur; I've overheard her asking my mum about things she might say to you. Winnie knows, Julia knows, my dad knows. Don't look me in the face and tell me you didn't know I could tell how you looked at her." He remembered a veritable catalogue of instances when he'd been conversing with Arthur, only to realize that his friend was distracted. Elizabeth's mere presence, be it in another room, through a window, in the yard, or in town somewhere, invariably resulted in Arthur phasing himself out of a conversation as he furtively, or not so furtively, cast glances her way. "And that goodbye hug of yours? Before we left? You should have seen the smile on my mother's face."

"You arsehole, Percy!" Arthur shouted. "Why haven't you told me this before?"

"'Cos I thought you already knew, and why should I have to tell you something you already knew?"

"Well I didn't know! If you could tell how I felt, then why didn't you tell her?"

"Oh, bugger off! I'm not your middleman."

"If she's asked about me, as you say, what did you say to her?"

Percy shrugged. "I told her she'd better go and ask Arthur, not me. And let's not pretend you ever ventured to talk to me about it. For all I knew, you were trying to keep it secret."

While he understood Percy's viewpoint, Arthur had to justify his side and said, "I didn't think you'd want to talk about your sister with me." *And I was afraid you'd tell her if I did.*

"I don't want to!" Percy agreed. "Not one bit. I want *you* to talk to my sister about my sister, leave *me* out of it. You're a good chap, Art, and a good chap is what Ell deserves. Write the letter. I'm sure she'd love to hear from you. And stop being such a bloody pest while you're at it."

"I'll write her tonight!" Arthur exclaimed.

"Hurrah," Percy replied dryly, shaking his head.

Arthur, inspired, resumed walking, and at a faster pace. As they drew nearer the barracks, his walk ramped up to a slow jog. Percy increased his stride to keep abreast. Soon their strides lengthened into a run. They smiled at one another. Arthur shoved Percy to give himself a head start and began to sprint.

Percy chased close behind, intent on beating his friend to the barracks. Arthur turned the final corner, hugging the edge of the last building. Percy was right on his tail, his heavy feet thumping the ground. When they got to the door of their barracks, Percy pushed Arthur past and charged inside first. He made his way to Arthur's bunk and snatched his notebook.

"You knobhead, Percy!" Arthur cried. "Give me that!" He jokingly slugged his much larger friend in the chest.

"I'll tell you what. If you can kick my arse," Percy said, dangling the notebook in front of him, "then I'll hand it over."

"If I kick your arse, I'll just take it!"

"Good luck," Percy laughed. They'd never actually have fought one another, not over anything. He didn't want to say as much, but he was elated that Arthur planned to write his oldest sister. He'd been waiting for something in that vein to come to fruition for some time, before some other prick came along and ruined it. He loved his three sisters very much, and had the same protective urges for them that he did for his best friend. Arthur was a good person, he had what it took to go places, and he was a good match for Elizabeth. Percy handed over the notebook. "I don't know what it is she sees in you," he joked. "I'd prefer if she found someone smarter. And handsomer. And taller."

"I will not accept judgment from you where looks or brains are concerned, thank you kindly!" Arthur retorted, snatching the notebook from Percy's hand. "And I'm not that short." He stood on the tips of his toes and craned his neck, but Arthur only met eyes with Percy's chin. "And I'm certainly not as short as you are dumb."

"Piss off," the larger boy sniggered, and he pushed the top of Arthur's head down with his index finger, returning his heels to the floor. "Or I'll write Ell myself and tell her you've been disfigured in an incident. She'll lose interest if she thinks you've grown any uglier."

"Wait, you can write?"

Both boys chuckled. Percy knew of other girls back home who'd showed interest in Arthur over the years, and he was glad Elizabeth was the only one who had his attention. Arthur was kind, and smart, and—though Percy would never admit it—a nice-looking young man. He loved him, the same way he would have were they brothers.

"What should I say to her?" asked Arthur. He sat down on his bunk.

Percy gave him an incredulous look. "Now I know you're joking," he said. "I will not play a part in anyone's writing a love letter to my own sister. Have you gone mad?"

"I'm not writing a bloody love letter."

"Whatever it is you want to call it, count me out. I'd tell Prince Edward himself to shove it up his arse if he asked for help with such a thing. You're on your own." With that, Percy walked outside to allow Arthur some privacy. He stood guard by the door, blocking any residents from entry.

Arthur tapped his pencil on the paper repeatedly, debating what he should and should not say to her. Should he reveal to her his feelings in a letter rather than in person? Would she even want to receive letters from him? *What if she's not really interested?* His self-doubt descended upon him like a tidal wave. *What if Percy misunder-*

150

stood and she never actually had feelings for me? The memory of their goodbye hug stood front and center in his mind. *What if I misread our goodbye? Was I just seeing what I wanted to see even if it wasn't there?* Suddenly, he was embarrassed. *Arthur, you idiot. She's probably been courted by now.*

Still, deep down in his psyche, buried beneath the doubt, Arthur knew that to go without telling her—feeling the way he did—was just impossible. She had to know. But would she care to? What if she threw it back in his face? Nothing would feel worse than Elizabeth's rejecting him. *Oh the hell with it.* He didn't care if she'd been courted in the two months since he'd last seen her. He knew her first. He brought pencil to paper and began.

Dear Ellie,

Soon we will pack our kit and board a train to the coast. We've trained hard here in Yorkshire, and our presence is requested in France. It seems our help is much needed, as you may have read in the papers. Percy and I are doing well. Our shooting, if you care to know, improves day by day. That should please you, as, if one chap can outshoot the chap who is shooting at him, there is a good chance that first chap will pull through just fine. We'll put it to the Germans when given the chance, but we'll spend time in the reserves in France before we're sent in to the fight.

I've thought about you often, and perhaps when the war is finished and we've done our bit, you'll let me call on you, with your permission. If not, I'll understand. It would be nice to see you when I come home, and the thought of you will stay with me as we march across France. Don't worry about Percy, I'll protect the big oaf. Please send my regards to your family.

Sincerely yours,
Arthur

Satisfied with what he'd written, hinting at his feelings yet not revealing too much, Arthur mailed his letter the next morning. She'd get the letter in a few days, but there would be no way for her to respond as Arthur would be on the move. He'd write her again after becoming situated in France, just in case she was interested in writing back.

Two days later the boys were on a train, southbound through the English countryside. They were dressed in their khaki serge service uniforms, and had been issued their full complement of equipment, and peaked caps with York and Lancaster regimental badges.

The badge featured a white metal crown, set atop a Union Rose of the same metal with a bronze center. Beneath the crown and rose in the center of the badge was a tiger, also in bronze. A banner with an olive branch on either end, again in bronze, encircled the tiger and rose, and attached to each side of the crown. YORK AND LANCASTER was embossed on the banner. Both boys had stared long and hard at the front of their caps upon receiving them. It was a proud moment.

With their train about twenty miles from the coast, Percy sat quietly in his seat, breathing through his nose, as he had for almost the entire trip. Arthur nervously bounced his knee up and down while he gazed out the window at the rolling yellows, greens and browns of the English farmlands. His stomach fluttered with anticipation, and maybe just a little trepidation. A bullet could kill anyone, after all, and what he'd read in the papers made it abundantly clear there were a hell of a lot of bullets flying around in France.

"Percy, what do you think being shot feels like?" Arthur asked. He imagined the sensation of a bullet striking him in the leg, like being hit with the edge of a cricket bat, swung by a very strong man.

"I suppose it bloody well hurts," Percy answered, his voice hushed. It wasn't something he wanted to think about.

"Are you afraid?"

"I'm not sure how I feel just this second."

"I'm nervous, if I'm being honest," Arthur said, ignoring Percy's reticence. He continued speaking out of anxiety. "A lot of blokes are dying over there, and they were soldiers for a lot longer than we've been." He wasn't trying to sound fatalistic, but he came off that way. "I mean, are we even soldiers yet?"

"Got the uniforms and the guns," Percy said, fixing his worried eyes on Arthur. "I don't know what else you'd call us." He did not want to share how he actually felt—he was frightened, and greatly so. Frightened for himself, and frightened that a situation might arise where he failed to protect his best friend. He saw fear in Arthur's eyes too. Rather than icy blue resolve staring back at him, he saw only timorousness—a kid on his way to a place that was no place for kids.

In his mind he looked to the future, to the day when they'd be thrown into the fray. What if he had just one shot at a German, with the accuracy of that single shot determining whether or not the German killed Arthur? Would his hands remain steady enough to aim as others aimed at him? Training did much for a soldier, but no one tried to kill you or your best friend in training. There was no preparation for something like that. For the remainder of the train ride, the boys were introverted.

When their train chugged to a stop at the station, what greeted them put a much welcome damper on their fears. From the train station to the harbor, the port bustled with energy. The two thousand reserves making their way to the waiting troop ship were nervous, but the throngs of people there to see them off helped to alleviate the anxiety. Parents, grandparents, siblings, well-wishers and scores of pretty young women in their finest dresses lined the streets all the way to the docks.

The throngs waved miniature Union Jacks, they cheered as the uniformed boys marched by, and the girls blew kisses. Many in the crowd handed out flower bouquets or small care packages to soldiers, filled with treats and other conveniences. The boys on their way to France were given a hero's send-off. Arthur wondered if his parents might be somewhere in the crowd, even though he'd neglected to inform them from where he'd depart.

Arthur and Percy beamed with pride as they walked up the ramp to board the transport. It was nice to have so many people cheering for them. How often in life did that happen to ordinary boys? When they reached the deck Arthur walked along the starboard railing, running his hand over the cold steel while he moved toward the bow. When the troops had boarded, the ramps were lowered, and the ship blew its whistles and began to move. Arthur stared down at the noisy crowd, taking in the smiling and shouting faces. For a second, he thought he heard someone call his name. He took a few more steps toward the bow, and then he faintly heard it again.

"Artie!"

Must be another Arthur somewhere behind me.

"Artie!"

He scanned the crowd. His eyes darted back and forth. *What if...*

"Arthur Ellis, I'm over here!" a pretty young girl yelled. She waved to him frantically, with both hands over her head.

Oh my God it's Ellie! She's waving to me!

There she was, pushing her way through the crowd, struggling to stay parallel with Arthur as the hundreds of men on deck forced him toward the bow while the ship crept forward. He grabbed the railing with both hands and planted himself firmly in place, forcing his fellow soldiers to move around him. He waved back girlishly, unable to mask his excitement.

I swear she gets lovelier every time I see her. Elizabeth looked absolutely elegant. She wore a small black hat with a wavy brim, topped with pink flowers and tilted onto her forehead. Her hair was in a bun tucked underneath the hat, and her graceful, slender neck was fetching and sultry, even from afar. Her short-sleeved dress was light pink and flowed to her ankles, and she had a black sash wrapped around her waist. *How did I miss her to begin with?* Her beauty stood out starkly in the crowd.

"Ellie what are you doing here?!" he shouted, smiling ear to ear.

"I came to see you!" she yelled back. "I'm so sorry I missed you!"

"You're here now!"

"I tried to be here sooner!" She sounded disappointed.

Oh no, she's crying. He saw the expression on her face, and could just barely make out the glisten of tears streaming down her cheeks. It crushed him to see tears in her beautiful eyes, having no idea what he could do to assuage them. He wanted to leap into the water and scale the dock. Had he lost his mind and done it, he most certainly would have kissed her then. The harsh discipline meted out afterward might have been worth it.

They continued shouting to one another as the ship slowly picked up speed. Arthur pushed his way past his fellow soldiers, heading back down the deck toward the stern.

"Please don't cry, Ellie!" he called to her. "I'm glad I got to see you at all!" *That gorgeous girl is crying because of you, Arthur. For you.*

"Artie I wanted to give this to you!" cried Elizabeth. She held up a small brown package. There was no way she'd be able to throw it up and onto the deck at that point. The ship was too tall. The distance between them increased. The boat was nearing the end of the dock. Arthur was already near the railing at the stern. Elizabeth was having more and more difficulty pushing through the crowd.

"Artie please be careful!" she cried. "I'll miss you!"

The open water was mere feet away.

"Artie!"

She was so clearly distressed that Arthur had developed a knot in his throat. It was agonizing seeing such a sweet girl cry. He frenetically thought of what he could do that might make her feel better. Drawing a blank, he ran his hands over the abdomen of his tunic, touching his waist belt, pockets and ammo pouches. There had to be something meaningful he could do. Something he could give to her.

Your cap Arthur! Throw her your cap!

Eureka! He yanked the cap he'd been so proud to receive from atop his head, and motioned to her his intention to throw it. It was a standard part of his uniform, he might be reprimanded for losing it, but there'd be more caps in France. There was only one Elizabeth Ward. Her glistening eyes widened and she rapidly nodded her head up and down several times. A beaming smile spread over her teary face. She held her hands at the ready.

Arthur took one last look at his York and Lanc badge and wound up by bringing his arm across his body. *One shot Arthur, you'd better not miss.* He flung the hat like he was throwing a playing card, sending it spinning over the water and toward Elizabeth's waiting hands. Arthur clenched his fists and leaned back, steering the hat with his eyes. His heart stopped. It was going to fall short!

Arthur you idiot! Now she'll feel worse!

The whirling cap was on its way into the water. Elizabeth leaned into the railing and hung her upper body over the edge. She reached out with one hand, and snatched the cap with her fingertips. Arthur breathed a tremendous sigh of relief, thrilled that his gesture had succeeded.

"Nice catch, Ellie! I'll be back soon! I'll miss you!"

He waved to Elizabeth, who clutched the cap with both hands, hugging it to her chest above her heart. Arthur leaned against the railing at the stern, watching the lovely girl in the pink dress shrink off in the distance as the troop ship made its way across the Channel.

I hope I live long enough to come back to her.

VOGEL

Vogel's observer was visibly outraged as he climbed from the forward cockpit. Holding his cap in his right hand, he angrily grasped a bracing wire with his left and stepped onto the lower starboard wing. He jumped to the ground. Fuming, he glared at Vogel and said, "Those assholes were shooting at us, you know."

"I'm sure our men shoot at their machines too, sir," Vogel replied.

"I'm talking about our men, Vogel! Our own fucking men were firing at our machine!"

"What? Are you sure, Oberleutnant Adler?"

"I'm an observer, *Flieger* Vogel," Adler snarled. "Do not question my observations."

"Yes sir," Vogel answered. "Sorry sir."

Adler tucked his cap under his left arm, then reached up and brushed his right hand across his left shoulder, drawing unnecessary attention to his shoulder boards. As an aviation officer, his boards were embroidered with rows of silver bullion wool which formed a series of elongated, U-shaped arches, one inside the other, the largest around the edge and the innermost compressed together in the center. His boards had one gold-plated brass diamond pip designating his rank, and a gold-plated brass winged propeller which signified his status as an officer in the flying service.

Adler sometimes treated Vogel as if he were nothing more than a glorified taxicab driver. He often made it a point to emphasize the word *flieger* when he said it. Flieger (flyer) was Vogel's rank, typical for a pilot, which essentially meant he was a gemeine who flew aeroplanes. The role of observer was more important, at least according to command, and so the observer was almost always an officer, the pilot, his subordinate. It begged the question, though—how would the observer get in the air to do his job without a pilot to take him there?

The oberleutnant tugged his peaked cap from beneath his arm and placed it atop his head. The cap's flat, round top was grey wool with a band of red piping around its edge, and the grey walls tapered in to a wide, red wool band. Two small, metal cockades were centered above its shiny, black leather visor, one in the grey fabric and one in the red. In the grey was the national cockade, a circular red center ringed in white, surrounded by a black ring with a serrated outer edge. Beneath it, on the band, was the Prussian state cockade of the same design and dimensions, with a black center instead of red.

Oberleutnant Heinrich Adler was the stereotypical Prussian officer—arrogant, judgmental, and rigid. He seemed to hold it against those who didn't come from a Prussian family with a strong military background. Always proper, always formal, his tunic stayed perpetually crisp and clean, his jackboots polished, his riding breeches pressed.

Vogel could nary remember a time when he'd seen Adler out of uniform. The oberleutnant seemingly only ever removed his peaked cap, which he did during flight, as it would not stay on his head in the rushing air. For whatever reason, though, he always saw fit to bring the cap with him. The six-foot Adler even *looked* like the stereotypical Prussian, with a strong, stocky build, a square jaw, close-cropped blonde hair and blue eyes. Vogel didn't much like the oberleutnant, but it was their duty to cooperate with one another.

Adler's uniform was similar to that of an infantry officer. He wore a grey officer's tunic, with the collar and cuffs piped in black and the shoulder straps in light grey. The front closure was piped in red, and fastened with eight gold buttons. His collar was embroidered with gold lace, and on his left breast was a brass flying badge—a biplane in mid-flight, surrounded by a wreath and crown. He wore riding breeches with knee-high black leather jackboots, and a brown leather belt with a pistol holster, ammo pouch, and binocular case.

Vogel's uniform, on the other hand, was a step down in quality. He wore the basic infantryman's tunic, piped the same as Adler's. His shoulder boards were grey wool felt, with a red embroidered winged propeller in the center. His buttons were nickel, and rather than gold lace on his collar he had a simple gold bar. He too wore the flying badge on his left breast. He was issued a shako, a tall, decorative stovepipe hat with a small visor, but shakos were impractical, and he wouldn't have been caught dead wearing it unless he faced an inspection. Vogel shunned riding breeches in favor of regular grey trousers piped in red, and his boots were the same knee-high style as Adler's, but brown.

Adler looked down on Vogel; that was made clear during training, long before the war began. Vogel just wasn't the Prussian type. He graduated from a gymnasium in his hometown of Krefeld, not a military academy. Krefeld, a large city in the Prussian Rhine Province, was one of the empire's westernmost cities, only miles from the provincial border with the Netherlands and Belgium. Adler was from Essen, another of the Rhine Province's large cities, about thirty-five miles northeast of Krefeld.

Unlike the solidly-built oberleutnant, Vogel stood just five foot six, with narrow shoulders and longer brown hair, which he parted down the middle. His face, hands and uniform were frequently dirty from working on his aeroplane with the mechanics, and since he wasn't much for wearing caps, his hair was usually a mess. He was soft-spoken, and possessed few leadership qualities.

When they first met more than a year prior, the very first thing that Adler ever said to him—with the restraint of rabid hound and the subtlety of a dreadnought—was, "What happened to your face?" because Vogel had a large scar that ran from his lower lip to the underside of his chin. As a child, he'd fallen from horseback and injured his face quite severely. He'd been apprehensive around horses ever since. He didn't trust them.

Though his scarred chin may have been the focal point of his visage by default, his eyes came in a close second. His bluish-grey irises were ringed with a markedly darker blue, and while not noticeable from afar, at conversational distances they often earned him complements. The girls seemed to like them.

Flieger Johann Vogel joined Die Fliegertruppen des Deutschen Kaiserreiches (The Imperial German Flying Corps) in the spring of 1913. He and Adler had trained together as a pilot/observer team when they entered the service, and happened to be paired up once again when the two were assigned to the same reconnaissance unit. That unit, Feldflieger Abteilung 12 (Field Flying Detachment 12) or FFA 12, was attached to Alexander von Kluck's First Army.

Their machine was a Luft-Verkehrs-Gesellschaft (Air Motoring Company) B.I biplane, or LVG for short. The LVG B.I was the aircraft firm's original design, and was the most common German machine then in use. It was relatively stable and easy to fly, which made it a good observation platform. Powered by a liquid-cooled, inline six-cylinder 100 horsepower Mercedes D.I engine set high behind the propeller, the plane could reach a top speed of sixty-five miles per hour, but its typical cruising speed was around fifty-five miles per hour. Its biplane was of unequal span, meaning the lower plane was slightly shorter than the upper.

They had just returned from flying over the lines, observing the French and BEF formations retreating ahead of First Army. Something was brewing. For the last few days the only thing they'd had to report was the enemy's constant retreat, but that retreat had slowed. Judging by the movement of both the trains and what was apparently a new French force massing near Paris, a counterattack was imminent.

Adler stomped off, still angry, to inform Hauptmann Günther von Detten, FFA 12's commander, of what he'd observed. Vogel stayed with the aircraft, to speak with the mechanics walking across the aerodrome's grassy field. They were coming to collect the machine.

Leon arrived first. The twenty-five year old had the most skill of any of FFA 12's mechanics, a veritable maestro with an aircraft engine. His talented hands turned repair work into less a trade, and more an art form. Vogel regarded Leon as an absolute genius, and it was that genius which kept him safe from equipment failure while he soared two thousand or more feet above the land.

The small, dark haired mechanic's gentle, light brown eyes did not belong with the rest of his features, which were, generally speaking, always twisted in one way or another in deep concentration. His pale skin was often obscured by a layer of dirt, oil and grease, so much so that even with the beating sun of the past month, the semi-permanent grime on his skin had shielded him from its rays. Most in the detachment, pilots, observers, and ground personnel alike, were sunburned. Leon was not.

He kept a thin, wispy moustache, but the smears and smudges on his face made it difficult to discern where the moustache ended and the dirt began. Like he did from dawn until dusk, and sometimes longer, Leon was dressed in filthy coveralls. His filthy grey coveralls were his calling card. With the amount of grunge associated with his job, the wearing of finer garments would have been unreasonable.

"Afternoon, sir," Leon greeted Vogel. "Did she fly well?"

"She flew just fine, Leon. What did you say to her to get her to behave?"

On their last flight, the engine had run poorly enough that Vogel considered bringing the machine down just beyond the German lines rather than risking the longer flight back to the aerodrome.

"A whisper here, a minor tweak there, sir," answered the mechanic. He'd been very upset with himself when he heard the engine had been slightly problematic.

"Come now, Leon, enough with the sir rubbish. I'm no officer. My name is Johann."

He could tell Leon was uncomfortable with his encouraging informality. When FFA 12 and First Army were still in Belgium, Adler had harshly rebuked Leon for no other reason than to make it clear just where the mechanic stood in the order of things. Vogel decided to change the subject rather than press it.

"Adler says our own men fired on us as we flew over them."

Leon raised an eyebrow. "Is that so?" The white of his eye beneath his raised brow was extra bright against his grease-darkened skin.

"That's what he said. Too bad they didn't hit him, yeah?" joked Vogel.

"Sir," Leon replied, not amused. He was too afraid of Adler to joke about something like that. He began to walk around the machine, running his hand along the side of the fuselage. The plywood fuselage had flat sides, covered with fabric skin. When he reached the starboard wing section he tugged on several bracing wires, making sure they were still tight, then moved on to the wooden wing struts.

Vogel walked around the tail section, to check the machine's port side. The tail had a small skid mounted beneath, and rose just inches from the ground. The LVG had a triangular tailfin, like a shark's dorsal fin, and triangular horizontal stabilizers. Vogel gave the tail a once-over as he passed around it, and then he ran his fingers over the fuselage's stiff fabric skin. It was doped with nitrocellulose to make it rigid and waterproof. After doping, the fabric had been painted a very light brown, with a black Iron Cross within a white stripe on the side of the fuselage, just behind his cockpit. He reached the port wings and just as he was about to check them, Leon shouted.

"My God!" he exclaimed. "Sir! Come and look at this!"

Vogel vaulted over the tail section and ran to where Leon stood at the end of the starboard wings. The mechanic was resting his elbow on top of the lower plane, staring at the upper plane's underside.

"What is it, Leon?"

"There's a bullet hole right there, sir!" Leon yelped as he pointed to the upper plane.

Vogel rested his hands on the lower plane and examined the spot where Leon pointed. Sure enough, about eight inches from the wingtip was a single circular puncture, half an inch across. A blue dot of sky was visible through it.

"That is one lucky shot..." Vogel said incredulously. "Can you imagine how difficult it would be, hitting a target at almost sixty miles per hour at two thousand feet?"

"Impossible," Leon answered. "Do you think it was from our troops as you descended?"

"I suppose that's a possibility," Vogel replied, "Maybe Adler was right after all. Although I don't appreciate our being fair game to anyone who feels like taking a crack."

"I would hope the infantry possessed more discretion than that," Leon said.

"I would too..." Vogel shrugged, still staring up at the hole. "Let's hope Adler informs Hauptmann von Detten. Maybe he can persuade General von Kluck or his staff to issue orders for his men to show restraint."

"Will you show Oberleutnant Adler the bullet hole, sir?"

"No. Go ahead and patch it."

"Yes sir."

It mattered little whether a German, a Frenchman or an Englishman had fired the lucky shot. What mattered was the bullet had come close enough to make Vogel nervous. He wasn't foolish; it was war, and warring men shot at one another. Large numbers of men were dying on the ground, but he sincerely believed airborne reconnaissance should not be subject to hostility. Apparently, at least one man on the ground saw it differently.

With weather not playing any significant role over the first weeks of First Army's advance, he and Adler had flown at least one operation, or sortie, almost every day. Even from two thousand feet up a man could process the difference between dead bodies lying flat and scattered randomly, as opposed to living bodies still on their feet. Uniform colors weren't hard to distinguish either, especially those of the French, and the color-coded corpses left in the wake of the rolling masses of men were all the verification he needed that a job in the military was dangerous. The bullet in the LVG's wingtip brought home the reality that in war, the odds of death rose for all participants, even those not directly involved in the shooting. He wasn't immune to gunfire simply because of his unconventional branch of service.

Bullets might have made him nervous, but they could never frighten him from the air. Vogel loved to fly. It offered almost total freedom, and a view of the battlefield unheard of in wars past. When men by the hundreds of thousands squared off with modern firepower, the immense destruction could only be truly appreciated from the air. During the fighting at Liège, when the heavy siege guns began their bombardment of the fortresses, Vogel flew over the city and could, faintly, feel the percussion from the exploding shells, even from two thousand feet up. As the fortresses crumbled under the heavy shelling, a hazy, rolling grey smoke blanketed the Belgian countryside for miles in every direction. Without a bird's eye view, the notion of an artillery attack affecting the air over nearly a hundred square miles would have seemed preposterous.

After Liège fell, he and Adler witnessed the destruction at Louvain. There, the smoke blanket was black, and the sooty clouds rose high into the air, pushed skyward by the fires raging beneath. Vogel didn't know why the city burned; he just knew that viewed from above, the damage was widespread and catastrophic. Until he saw such things for himself, he never would have imagined the scope of genuine devastation wrought by war.

With one lucky shot, an unknown man had sent Vogel notice that he was susceptible. He tried not to think about it, but the revelation heightened his fear for his younger brother Frederick's safety.

Frederick was a pilot with Eighth Army, on the Eastern Front. He joined the air service earlier that year, and had obtained his wings in April. It was a proud moment for the two brothers and their parents, and on the day of Frederick's certification, their mother Ingrid snapped a photograph of the boys, both dressed in their Imperial Air Service uniforms. Johann kept a copy of the picture in his breast pocket, and as far as he knew, Fred did the same.

DENIS

On August 31, after learning of the surrender at Givet, and fearing a pincer attack from German First and Third Armies, Général Lanrezac ordered Fifth Army to fall back another twenty-five miles, behind a line which extended west to east from Compiègne, to Soissons, to the fortifications at Reims. General von Bülow opted not to pursue the French for a period of twenty-four hours, in order to rest his troops.

On September 1 the fortress at La Fère, about twenty miles southwest of Guise, was occupied by the Germans. On the 2nd, Lanrezac ordered his men to fall back an additional *sixty* miles south to the River Seine, in an attempt to remain alongside the still retreating BEF. That same day, the French government left Paris for Bordeaux, and Général Joffre appointed Général Joseph-Simon Galliéni as military governor of Paris.

Immediately upon his appointment, Galliéni began lobbying Joffre and Field Marshal French, urging the commanders to launch a counterattack across a huge swath of the Western Front, from Paris to Verdun. The situation was not so simple, though. After learning of the French government's evacuation, the British commander had seriously entertained the notion of withdrawing the BEF back to the Channel, to evacuate them from France. If the French were to press the attack, they needed British help. Persistent in his urging French to halt the BEF's retreat, Joffre eventually convinced the British commander to remain in the fight.

During Fifth Army's southward exodus, further to the east in Lorraine, French First and Second Army squared off yet again against Crown Prince Rupprecht of Bavaria's Sixth Army, near the fortified city of Nancy. The French inflicted enormous casualties on the Germans, pushing casualty figures as high as seventy percent in some regiments. After regrouping his forces, Rupprecht ordered a frontal infantry assault on Nancy itself. The attack against the heavily fortified and well-defended city failed, and the battlefront in Lorraine fell into stalemate. Both sides temporarily dug in.

The petty bickering at command's highest levels and the death and destruction in Alsace-Lorraine would have been little more than a footnote to Denis and those around him, had they known about it. They'd been taxed as hard as any of France's armies, and without question had force-marched considerably further than any of their fellow countrymen.

The men of F Compagnie slowly, miserably, and silently shambled south in retreat. The weather was so very hot, and every ounce of the troops' energy had been expended in harrowing combat and frantic retreat. The clink of buckles and clasps, long, exasperated sighs, and the thumping and dragging of hundreds of tired boots spoke louder than words. Men breathed heavily, occasionally someone vomited, and as the march continued more and more soldiers began to fall out of line, too weak to continue.

The unprecedented heat often lingered above ninety degrees. Exhaustion, coupled with a lack of food and water, made increasing numbers sick. Thousands of horse hooves, wagon wheels and boots marching on dirt roads kicked up enormous dust clouds, which coated the men's uniforms and choked their already dry lungs. Opening one's mouth meant tasting the grit of fine dust between clenched teeth, with no water to wash it out and no saliva to spit.

Because men drank what water they could find when they could find it, many resorted to drinking from filthy pools of standing water or small streams polluted by industrial runoff. Dysentery began to run rampant, and pushed some to the brink of death. Denis had already lost Clemence and Reynard in the fighting at Guise, and Maurice collapsed from exhaustion on September 2. He was thrown in the back of a horse cart and rushed to a field hospital.

Denis had never been so depleted, so weak, not in his entire life. He glanced worriedly over his shoulder at Patrice, but had nothing to say. He hadn't the energy to speak. *Patrice looks like hell,* he thought, *but I suppose I look the same.*

Everyone looked terrible, and Denis was no exception. His black hair was disheveled and greasy. Dust from the roads coated his skin. The whites of his eyes were pink and irritated. His black moustache, normally trim and clean, was unkempt, and still encrusted with blood flecks from the German he'd wrestled and shot. He had no water to wash it out, and he sure as hell wasn't going to lick it away. It stunk beneath his nose. The arid conditions had turned his lips a crusty white; they cracked and bled, driving him mad with frustration. Unshaven for weeks, his stubble was now a beard.

He'd lost his kepi at Guise, and his blue greatcoat had faded from wear and constant exposure to beating sunlight. Large swaths of the coat's fabric were stained brown from caked on dirt and dried blood. White stains beneath the armpits divulged just how much sweat he'd lost—it was not easy to sweat through a tunic and greatcoat. His red trousers were torn at both knees and were grass-stained and dirty. Somewhere along the line, the gaiter on his left calf had come unlaced and gone missing. He couldn't remember when.

The unrelenting dry heat and nearly endless marching had torn the leather in his boots, exposing his toes. The soles were starting to pull apart. His feet and legs throbbed, a persistent, maddening pain, and he had to constantly center himself to prevent his frustration from bubbling over. Others showed no such self-control, and they tearlessly wept as the column slogged on.

Denis's appearance was the standard, and many looked worse than he. Thousands suffered from heat exhaustion and dysentery, and the stress of combat and ceaseless forced marching had pushed some in Fifth Army to suicide, though the problem was limited to just a handful of cases. The unavailability of water and food infuriated some, and morale was flagging.

The stench of thousands of soiled uniforms infested the air around them. It turned Denis's stomach. Even though he'd smelled and lived it for days, there was no adapting to such foulness.

"Denis, your pack is torn," Patrice rasped, breaking the silence. He barely managed a whisper. "I'm sorry I did not notice until now."

Oh no. Denis's hair stood on end. His heart dropped into his empty gut. *When did it tear?* He didn't want to speak, but he had to find out what he'd lost.

"Would you look inside and tell me what's missing?" he croaked.

Patrice begrudgingly approached. Denis swayed back and forth, barely able to keep his balance as his friend sifted through his pack.

"Your boots are gone," said Patrice. "And if you had any food left, that's gone too."

Denis's anger erupted. "GOD DAMMIT!" he roared, startling the weary marchers around him. He immediately regretted it. The tired eyes that turned toward him in the wake of his outburst embarrassed him. His throat and chest were far too dry to be shouting, and a sharp pain in his lungs made him clutch his chest. He gritted his teeth and squeezed his eyes shut, his face crinkled in pain.

He'd planned on changing his boots the next time they stopped to rest. He could have sworn he'd saved a few biscuits and a tin of beef as well. *Now I'll starve while I die of thirst. Maybe I can get an infection in my feet too.*

He could not fathom when or how the pack had torn. It wasn't at Guise; he'd taken food from the pack after the battle. He shuddered as the march continued, furious that he'd lost his things. He fought the urge to hit, kick, or throw something in anger. His men did not need such a poor example.

On September 3, Général Joffre removed Charles Lanrezac from command of Fifth Army. Joffre claimed Lanrezac "lacked fighting spirit," even though Lanrezac's calling for Fifth Army's retreat from the River Sambre had likely saved them from destruction. To replace him, Joffre appointed Général Franchet d'Esperey, the former commander of I Corps and the savior of XVIII Corps at Guise. That night, the French troops holding the fortress of Reims—approximately halfway between and slightly north of Paris and Verdun—chose to abandon the city rather than die inside it. Reims was subsequently occupied by General Hans von Kirchbach's Saxon XII Reserve Korps. The next day, Général Louis Ernest de Maud'huy replaced de Mas-Latrie as commander of XVIII Corps.

The miserable retreat finally ended at the River Seine, southeast of Paris. Fifth Army was given a brief opportunity to regroup and receive reinforcements. Denis joined a wall of men on the Seine's northern bank, desperate to put an end to his maddening thirst. The more uninhibited shed their soiled clothing and leapt into the river nude, splashing, and frolicking, and drinking, young men freed, briefly, from the sun's oppression and dehydration's merciless clutch.

Denis guzzled gulp after gulp of cool water from his canteen, nearly emptying it for the second time in just over a minute. His stomach was so thoroughly void that he felt the cool liquid course through his belly. It gave him a welcome chill. Water spilled from the corners of his mouth and dripped onto his filthy clothes.

He'd not eaten in close to four days, save for a few biscuits shared amongst his squad. He drank as if he'd never see water again. In the haste to quench his agonizing thirst, he drank too much too quickly, and he became nauseated. Lowering the canteen from his lips, Denis bent at the waist and put his hands on his knees. The water rushed back up from his stomach, still cold, and splashed onto the ground in front of his feet.

"Goodness me, Denis," Patrice cried, "take your time!"

More water sprayed from Denis's mouth. "Son of a bitch," he gurgled. Then he vomited again. Out of breath from chugging, then vomiting, he gasped for air.

When he'd finished, he flung away his greatcoat for the first time in what felt like months, revealing his dark blue officer's tunic beneath. The tunic was much cleaner than his greatcoat, but had white sweat rings around the collar and armpits. He unbuttoned the tunic and removed it as well, then pulled off his blue wool undershirt and sat in a patch of dried grass. He lay down. His face and hands were darkened from sunburn, but his arms and torso were pale, buried beneath heavy clothing for days on end. The sun, so treacherous to a man in heavy gear, was magnificent on his bare skin. It was soothing, almost therapeutic.

Hundreds of pallid, shirtless poilus wandered about. They were hairy ones indeed. Denis was certain if the same scene had played out just three weeks earlier, there would not have been nearly as many ribcages jutting through their pasty skin. If bodies deteriorated that quickly in harsh conditions, what might a prolonged war bring?

His mind began to wander. He fell into a haze as he pondered what Fifth Army had gone through over the past week. He wondered about his family. He'd almost forgotten about them over the last several days as thoughts of water, food and rest were all-consuming—survival trumped all other considerations. Now that he could sit, eat and drink, the Roux family again became his central focus.

Having thrown up his first attempt at rehydration, Denis paced himself the second time around. He sipped small mouthfuls rather than drinking a canteen at a time.

"Are you better now, Denis?"

"Yes Pat, thank you."

"We must get to the supply depot," Patrice gently urged. "They may be able to give you new boots. You'll have priority for boots. You should ask for a new haversack as well."

"I know Patrice," Denis mumbled, "just let me rest a minute."

"All right, but the longer you wait, the lesser your chances of refitting."

Denis gingerly removed his worthless boots. He tossed them in the grass a few feet away. His socks were shredded, and blisters on his heels had opened up, drenching the fabric with blood. He held his right foot above the ground with his left hand, and with his canteen in his right, poured water back and forth across the bloody, dirty foot. When the liquid touched the open sores, he winced in pain, and sucked a gasp through his clenched teeth. *Shit. This hurts. Even with new boots, marching will be painful.*

After washing both feet, Denis lay on his back atop his greatcoat. He stared at the sky as tiny white puffs of cloud passed overhead. With heavy eyelids and the warm sun blanketing his skin, it became harder and harder to keep his eyes open. He dozed off, and fell into an almost catatonic sleep.

"Here."

The brand new boots and haversack thumped in the grass next to Denis, startling him from his slumber. Patrice had walked to the supply depot and gotten them while Denis slept. He eyed Patrice's boots. They were the same pair he'd worn for the past month. *Son of a bitch got boots for me instead of himself.* Patrice pulled a new pair of socks from his greatcoat pocket and threw them at Denis.

"Come on, wake up," said Patrice. "We'll be moving soon."

"When did you hear this?" Denis asked. "And where?"

"At the supply depot. I overheard some officers. Sixth Army has engaged the Germans near Meaux along the River Ourcq. We're heading back north."

"Are you sure?"

"That's what I heard."

"When?"

"From the sound of it, very soon."

Denis tried to mask his disappointment. Patrice had heard correctly, which they learned a short time later when their commanders ordered them to form up.

Upon Galliéni's appointment as military governor of Paris, he initiated feverish defensive preparations around the city in case of a German siege. When Joffre and Field Marshal French agreed to launch a counterattack, Galliéni sent Général Michel-Joseph Maunoury's Sixth Army to engage the right flank of von Kluck's First Army. Maunoury's Sixth Army had previously been in Lorraine, but were redeployed to Paris by rail on Joffre's orders when he finally realized the imminent German threat came from the north, not the east. The battle began to unfold on the banks of the River Ourcq, approximately twenty-five miles east and slightly north of Paris.

Galliéni moving Sixth Army to attack the German right flank would prove crucial in the upcoming Battle of the Marne.

SEBASTIAN

He'd spent his entire life near the Königsberg docks and had sailed on all manner of vessels, but Sebastian was still a touch wary. The docks at Heligoland, where he now stood, were far less familiar, and he was soon to depart on a voyage the likes of which he'd never experienced before. They'd run exercises before the war, of course, but this was the real thing.

Heligoland, a small, two island archipelago thirty miles off Germany's North Sea coast, was the fleet's forward base of operations. The main island, Hauptinsel, had a surface area of less than half a square mile, with the harbor located on the island's northern end. The other island, Düne, was hardly used, and was even smaller than Hauptinsel. The archipelago lay on the northwestern boundary of the Heligoland Bight, which was the southern portion of the German Bight, a large bay formed by Germany's northern coast and the western coast of the Jutland Peninsula.

Sebastian would soon set foot on a boat that had not participated in the first patrol, which took to the sea in early August. That first patrol, while historic, had shown very little promise. Out of the ten vessels which departed, one turned back with engine trouble, and two were lost—one vanished without a trace, and the other sank after being rammed by a British light cruiser.

Following the first patrol's lack of success, more bad news had come on August 28 after the British Navy's one-sided victory at the Battle of Heligoland Bight. It was the first major naval engagement of the Great War, and resulted in the sinking of three German light cruisers, one destroyer and two torpedo boats. Six more vessels suffered damage, some severely. Over seven hundred German sailors were killed, more than five hundred wounded, and an additional three hundred taken prisoner. In total, the British suffered less than one hundred casualties, and only one light cruiser took significant damage. Sebastian could only pray that when this patrol set out, the tide would shift in Germany's favor.

Sebastian Eberhardt's father Viktor had worked the docks at Königsberg since before Sebastian was born. A large port city on the Baltic Sea, Königsberg was the regional capital of East Prussia and the easternmost of the German Empire's major cities. The Eberhardt family had lived there Sebastian's entire life. Viktor met his wife Oksana while working at the docks as a young man. She was Russian, from St. Petersburg. They met by chance, when her ship landed at Königsberg while she vacationed with her parents.

The eldest of three brothers and four sisters, Sebastian was twenty-one, born almost nine months to the day after his parents were married. Before he turned eighteen, he spent his summers working on or near the waters of his hometown, like his father. He'd graduated from gymnasium, but ended his schooling there. The sea was his passion, and it promised steady work and a decent living. Within days of his eighteenth birthday, he joined the Kaiserliche Marine (Imperial Navy), and became a matrose 1.klasse (seaman 1st class) after just over a year of service.

At six foot one, Sebastian was taller than most. He was of average build, enhanced some by four summers of physical labor. His mother, being of Eastern Slavic descent, had passed some of her physical traits on to him and half his siblings. He and his youngest brother received her dark hair and eye color, and their skin had a moderately darker hue.

His other brother, Uri, looked more like his father—Prussian through and through. All the Eberhardt children had thick hair, slightly larger foreheads than might be considered average, and wide faces. Two of Sebastian's sisters—Beatrix, seventeen, and Wendelin, thirteen—had also inherited their mother's darker features. The other two sisters—Ilyana, nineteen and Florentina, sixteen—had the blonde hair and blue eyes of their father.

The life of a dockworker and sailor had hardened the skin of Sebastian's hands. He had permanent calluses on his palms and fingers, like tiny, protective patches of rock. Sailing had also hardened his lifestyle; working every summer kept him from spending significant time with girls his age. He'd never experienced falling in love, and had no point of reference as to whether he'd missed out on anything. He rarely paid it much thought.

His virginity was no concern—a pretty, big-breasted whore had taken care of that back when he was sixteen. He did not frequent the brothels, but he didn't shun them, either, and would visit on those occasions when he had the urge, most often when he was with his shipmates. In his three years of service in the Imperial Navy, when granted leave Sebastian always made a point to visit his family first, before joining his mates at whatever bar, dance hall or whore house they might patronize that evening.

"Hey Eberhardt, how about you help us carry this stuff, yeah?" Jollenbeck gibed him, "Quit thumbing your ass." He shuffled past with a large wicker basket full of elongated loaves of bread. The fresh bread looked delicious, but there was no way the crew would finish eating it all before the ship's moist environment turned it moldy. Sebastian imagined what the fuzzy bread might look like in two weeks. It wasn't appetizing.

Jollenbeck was a friend from back home. He was the same age as Sebastian, about two inches shorter, and rail-thin. He had light brown hair, and a pointy nose that turned up at the end. As appearances went, he was average. Average, that was, until he opened his eyes—they were heterochromic, and strikingly so.

His right eye was normal, just a dark shade of blue, but the left, that eye told the story of a close call he had as a nineteen-year-old matrose 3.klasse. Less than a year into his service in the Imperial Navy, in a dockside accident, a stack of oil drums broke from their lashings and crashed around and onto him. One drum struck him in the head. Fortune smiled on Jollenbeck in that he wasn't killed by the drum that struck him, but it still saw to it that the incident affected him for the rest of his life.

When the heavy drum smashed into the left side of his face, it swept him off the dock and plunged him, unconscious, into the cold winter water of the harbor. An alert dockworker saved him from drowning, but the impact nearly broke Jollenbeck's neck. It shattered his cheekbone and severely damaged his left eye, turning the iris black and staining the white red, blinding him for months afterward and almost ending his short naval career.

It took time, but his vision, though diminished, returned. The blue in his left iris did not. It remained black, at least upon a casual glance. Up-close and in bright light, it was actually a deep, dark red. Had both his eyes been colored in such a way, women and children might have run from him in the street.

Sebastian watched his friend step off the dock and onto the narrow deck of the light-grey ship. Jollenbeck knelt alongside the open foredeck hatch and passed the bread basket into a pair of hands waiting beneath. On his return trip down the dock, Jollenbeck put his lanky arm around Sebastian's shoulder and guided him toward the stacks of supplies still waiting to be brought aboard. When it came to dockside labor, Sebastian typically required no prodding, but the prospect of the war patrol had clouded his focus.

The two uniformed young men stood beside one another for a moment as the flurry of dockworkers and their fellow shipmates swirled purposefully around them. The enlisted men all wore their basic onshore service uniform, which consisted of a navy blue wool pullover, with a traditional cornflower blue sailor's collar with three white stripes around its outer edge. Beneath the collar was a black silk neckerchief, knotted in front at mid-chest and tied with a white string.

Their caps were navy blue wool, of the traditional sailor style, with round tops which tapered into the band and no peak. Only officers wore peaked caps. Around the sailor cap's band was tied the cap tally—a long, thin ribbon, knotted in the back, the tails of which hung loosely. *Kaiserliche Marine* was embroidered on the tally in gold bullion thread and displayed in front. Above the cap tally was the red, white and black national cockade.

They wore long, loose-fitting navy blue trousers, which most men cuffed at the ankle to prevent any chance of tripping in the cramped environment of the ship's deck and interior. Simple lace-up, black leather sea-boots were the standard issue.

"Here, Eberhardt," said Jollenbeck. He thrust a heavy box full of tinned beef into Sebastian's chest. "Take this onto the boat. And wake your ass up while you're at it."

His mind still cloudy, Sebastian hauled the box toward the ship, joining the rest of his shipmates in lugging provisions aboard. The tins stacked inside the box rattled against one another. They were heavy. He imagined how quickly their weight would sink to the bottom of the harbor were they thrown into the water.

The hefty box, an anchor in the sea and a burden to carry on land, was a miniscule fraction of a fraction of the weight being placed inside the ship. The two hundred and ten foot long vessel would carry within its narrow pressure hull the extra fuel, drinking water and supplies necessary for its thirty-five man crew to embark on an extended operation, in which they might not see land for weeks.

He stepped onto the crowded foredeck, ahead of the ten foot tall conning tower, which was located amidships. The men moving back and forth across the narrow deck had to step carefully, lest they stumble into a shipmate or catch their foot on one of many low-lying obstacles. Only twenty feet wide at the beam (the ship's widest point), most of the deck's navigable space was even narrower.

The deck had two levels. The raised portion ran down the middle of the ship for the full length of the outer hull, and had safety railings lining its outer edges. The port and starboard sections of the deck were a foot lower, surfaced with wooden plank, and began twenty feet back of the prow (the bow's leading edge), and gradually widened out to the beam before tapering again toward the stern. The shorter side sections of decking more closely approximated the length of the pressure hull contained within the significantly longer outer hull.

Sebastian ducked underneath an antenna cable, one of two which ran from bow to stern. The antennae started low on the ship's deck and passed over the conning tower on either side, like a pair of hundred and fifty foot clotheslines. After ducking the cable, he stepped around the foredeck's large wireless telegraph mast, used for long-distance communication. The nearly thirty-foot-tall mast was one of two such masts, one each on the fore and aft deck. They were set off-center, and could be folded downward if necessary, but at that moment stood upright.

Sebastian made his way to the open foredeck hatch, and handed the heavy box of tinned beef to the hands inside. The crewmen within the vessel were putting every ounce of their organizational skills to the test, as storing the large amount of supplies inside the cramped hull took considerable effort. Earlier that day they'd brought aboard the ship's six torpedoes, a monumental task in and of itself. Each torpedo was eighteen feet long and weighed well over a ton.

Following a number of trips back and forth down the dock, the last of the supplies were tucked into the remaining nooks and crannies in the pressure hull. All hands boarded the vessel. More than half the crew remained above deck as the ship's two 850 horsepower diesel engines fired.

A large puff of black smoke belched from the exhaust vents on the conning tower when the twin beasts rumbled to life. Sebastian and Jollenbeck were among those still outside; they'd have plenty of time to spend crammed inside the narrow sardine can with their thirty-three fellow crewmates. The weather was calm and sunny, and the two wanted to enjoy their last few minutes in port.

The excitement of the moment was undeniable; they were headed on their first war patrol, but Sebastian could not help but feel a nagging anxiety. One-fifth of the first patrol had not returned, and no matter how he spun it, that was a scary number. Still, the crew was optimistic, and as the ship crept out of the relative safety of the harbor and into the vastness of the North Sea, the men remaining above deck waved goodbye to the dockworkers. When the vessel cleared the harbor, the engines were brought to full throttle, and the tiny Heligoland archipelago gradually shrunk away.

U-20 was on the hunt for the capital ships of the British Grand Fleet.

HENTSCH

Engel lifted his rifle to fire at the aeroplane overhead. Hentsch had seen men do it before, but he saw no point in shooting indiscriminately at any and all flying machines. The aeroplane, still a thousand or more feet up, might well have had a black Iron Cross on its side, but even with his sharp eyesight it was hard to tell for sure.

"Engel, I think that might be one of ours," Hentsch said. He put his hand on the barrel of Engel's Mauser and gently pushed it down. "Best not to chance it." Several men nearby started firing their rifles skyward, and Hentsch rolled his eyes. One of the shooters was from 2 Gruppe.

"Michael!" Hentsch shouted. "Cease your fire!"

The young man made a face, and then flicked his safety catch. He swung his rifle down and slung the strap over his shoulder. Every motion was exaggerated, performed with attitude.

Hentsch wanted to snatch the rifle from Michael's hands and jab him in the gut with the stock. The days of marching on the heels of the retreating French and British had not been pleasant, and with each step the Germans took they extended the length of their supply lines and upped the mileage on their boots.

They may have been winning to that point, but the Germans suffered the same problems as their enemies. Heat exhaustion, dysentery and thirst had taken their toll on many men of First Army, but to that point most of 13th Kompagnie's men were holding up all right. Feet had begun to drag after the Battle of Mons, but the loudest whining and complaining came from Michael, which Hentsch found embarrassing but not totally unexpected.

The column had stopped along a dirt road to wait for word from brigade headquarters as to the location of the French. The men ate some of what little rations they had left and took a few sips of water. Another fight was coming soon. Unteroffizier Strauss, the leader of 1 Korporalschaft, approached Hentsch and 2 Gruppe with the latest information.

"Oberleutnant Richter says the French and British have launched a counterattack along the entire front. Hauptmann Fleischer wishes us to disperse from this road in ten minutes." There was a detectable quiver in Strauss's voice. He sounded nervous, and he looked rough. There were large, puffy bags under his bloodshot hazel eyes, and his unkempt facial hair was blotchy and scraggly.

His uniform was the same as the enlisted men, save for the golden thread embellishment on his collar and sleeve cuffs, and the larger button on his collar bearing a royal crown. He'd obviously had a close call in an earlier engagement—the fabric cover on his pickelhaube had a long tear on the left side, and there was a gouge in the black leather beneath it. Just inches to the right and he'd have had a bullet hole in his head rather than a scratch on his helmet.

While the expectation that another fight loomed was anything but reassuring, Hentsch remained cautiously optimistic. If the French and British were turning to fight, perhaps defeating their counterattack might end the war within the week. Surely the attack had to be the Entente's last gasp. On the other hand, what if the French and the BEF successfully broke through? How much of a setback would that be?

"All right, sir," Hentsch answered after a brief hesitation. "We'll be ready." Strauss moved on to speak to the men of 1 Gruppe, as 2 Gruppe packed their mess tins and rations, threw their haversacks onto their backs and took up their rifles.

Michael frowned and shook his head, as if the order for him not to fire on the aeroplane had somehow deeply offended him, so much so that the offense still lingered.

"Do you have something to say?" Hentsch asked.

Michael grinned smugly. "No *sir*," he replied.

Again with the attitude. A chill ran up Hentsch's spine. His body urged him to lunge at the young man. To hit him. To strangle him. *I hate this fucker. Why did I have to end up in charge of him?* With his mouth closed so no one could see, Hentsch squeezed his tongue with his teeth, trying to get the tingle in his spine to go away. He glared at Michael, who glared right back at him.

Hentsch's blue eyes might have burned with rage as he glowered at him, but the soul behind his blue eyes was still decent. He felt remorse, empathy and sadness for what was happening to the world around him. He worried for his men, respected and cared about their well-being. Despite the lives he'd taken in the name of duty, he still had kindness in his heart. But when Hentsch stared into the darkness of Michael's eyes, he saw nothing—just a young, spoiled, arrogant shit of a man, who probably enjoyed the trigger pull so long as there was a human being on the receiving end. There wasn't a single redeeming quality about Michael, not as far as Hentsch could tell. *What is it that makes a man this way?*

"Hentsch, how do you know that was a German aeroplane and not a French one?" asked Engel. He was still watching the machine above as it crept out of view.

Breaking his stare-down with Michael, Hentsch answered, "I don't, not really, but what if it *was* a German and you shot him right in the ass?"

Michael scoffed audibly so that every man heard him. Hentsch glared at him again. *I'll shut you up one of these days.* He envisioned a day coming when the two of them might square off physically. While Hentsch was taller, a lean six-foot-four, Michael stood just over six feet tall and had a sturdy build. Judging from the whining he did while on the march, though, Hentsch figured the young gemeine was not as tough as he looked or acted.

"What's the point of their buzzing around up there anyway?" asked Simon. His skinny white neck was bent back as he looked toward the sky. The oversized pickelhaube on his head made him appear as if he might fall backward.

The aircraft's humming engine was fading as the machine traveled out of sight at more than a mile per minute.

"They're doing reconnaissance, like the cavalry in the air," Hentsch explained. "Think about it. They fly well over the lines, and do not have to worry about meeting an enemy patrol. From up there they can observe the size of enemy forces, and from what I hear, they travel at almost seventy miles per hour. No horse in the world can come close to that." Hentsch had once met a German pilot in a pub before the war began, who sold him on the merits of air reconnaissance.

"How about we stop worrying about what's over our heads and start worrying about the Franzmenn in front of us?" Nussbaum commented. A smooth-faced, handsome young gemeine, he hailed from Wismar, less than twenty miles north of Schwerin on Germany's Baltic coast. He was normally quiet, following orders without asking questions. Hentsch didn't know much about him other than that he didn't cause problems. The young man had a point.

"You got it, Nussbaum," Hentsch said, nodding to the others. "He's right, men. Never mind the damned aeroplanes. Leave them alone."

The group finished packing their gear, and an eerie silence swept over the area. Conversations had halted after the announcement of the French and British counterattack. No one knew much about it, but after routing, then chasing them for the past two weeks, most were led to believe that the enemy's morale had been broken, and that the French and British were all but defeated.

While up to that point the Germans were the resounding victors, it hadn't come without great cost. Command had pushed them hard in their pursuit of the Entente forces.

In the month of August, Kluck's First Army suffered 7,869 men wounded and 2,863 killed or missing. A further eight thousand were rendered combat ineffective due to illness. Bülow's Second Army fared even worse, with 12,151 wounded, 5,061 killed or missing, and over nine thousand sick. Hausen's Third Army suffered as well, especially during the fight for Dinant, but he'd lost nowhere near as many men as First or Second Army. Many tens of thousands more Germans were killed and wounded in the brutal fighting further to the east.

During his pursuit of the BEF, General von Kluck had ordered his forces to shift southeast, effectively ignoring his directive under the Schlieffen Plan. He was supposed to have moved south and slightly west, to sweep around the western end of Paris. First Army's abrupt and unexpected turn forced General von Bülow to alter Second Army's course, so as to avoid a collision with First Army and the confusion that would have caused. Those course-corrections, while not devastating, potentially altered the sequence of events that followed, though any speculation as to how much was purely hypothetical.

The pursuit of the retreating French and British had pushed a hundred and fifty mile salient into a line which spanned from Paris in the west to the fortress city of Verdun in the east. A salient, formed when the advance of one army forces its opponent's line to bend, is like a peninsula, in that the army which pushed itself into the salient has enemy forces on three sides.

German First through Fourth Armies stood inside the Paris-Verdun Salient. Elements of First Army and the majority of Second Army had crossed the River Marne, which meandered across the countryside away from Paris in a generally easterly direction before turning south approximately ninety miles east of Paris. Third and Fourth Army stood east of the Marne's southward bend, while German Fifth Army was northeast of Verdun. German Sixth and Seventh Army remained in Alsace-Lorraine, aligned diagonally with German Fifth Army, and opposed by French First and Second Army.

While the French and BEF retreated into the salient, Général Joffre recognized the necessity of eventually halting that retreat to mount the counteroffensive. As such, he had smartly shuffled forces from Alsace-Lorraine to reinforce his outnumbered and beleaguered forces retreating from the north. By the time the allies halted their retreat and began their advance, their numerical disadvantage had turned into a sizable advantage. At the start of the Battle of the Marne 980,000 French troops alongside 100,000 British, with a combined total of three thousand artillery pieces, squared off against 750,000 Germans with 3,300 artillery pieces, spread along the entire line of the Paris-Verdun Salient.

Though Hentsch and his German comrades were unaware the tables had turned as greatly as they had, the prospect of facing a renewed attack was daunting, even without the facts. In silence while they waited to deploy, Hentsch heard a faint breeze whispering through the trees beside the road. It was a rare moment of quiet in a month of noise. He envisioned the trees' whispers as coming from the thousands upon thousands of dead men scattered, after just one month, in the Great War's wake. Each voice implored him not to leave the road, not to march south toward more killing. He would have loved to obey the voices, but as a duty-bound soldier, he could not. Soldiers obeyed the orders of their commanders, not the voices of the dead, even though the dead had learned better.

"All right, let's move," said Unteroffizier Strauss, and the tired men sluggishly followed his order.

They walked side by side into the forest, leaving the road behind. The whole of 13th Kompagnie deployed the same way. They formed a long, unbroken line through the woods, linked with the other kompagnies of III Bataillon. Hundreds of men marching through the forest made a lot of noise. Leaves and twigs crunched beneath their feet. An occasional boot thumped against a tree root obscured by leaves. More wind swept through the leaves overhead. The whispers grew louder.

Hentsch's ears perked when a distant firefight erupted somewhere ahead, against 34th Brigade's leading edge. The wooded terrain made it difficult to determine exactly how far away the shots were, or even the exact direction from which they came. There was artillery fire as well, but those explosions sounded even more distant and were probably closer to another bataillon further west.

It didn't matter how far off the fighting was. It would only get closer. The bulk of General von Quast's IX Korps was about to clash, along with General Ewald von Lochow's III Korps, with French XVIII, III and I Corps near the River Grand Morin.

Heavy fire soon opened up, closer than before. Having left the road more than an hour earlier, 13th Kompagnie continued to travel abreast one another through the woods. Other units near them, but out of view, were already engaged. Hentsch could no longer hear the trees whispering. Machine gun and rifle fire dominated the air. That there was no artillery yet was fine by him. Bullets were bad enough without artillery support. He hoped the French cannons stayed well clear, bogged down or broken and unable to assist.

There was a clearing through the trees ahead. It might make for a hard crossing if the French were waiting on the other side. As they neared the forest's edge, the line moved with increasing deliberation. Hentsch couldn't see anyone in the tree line beyond the clearing, but that didn't mean the enemy wasn't there.

Crack! A bullet missed Michael by inches and snapped through the trees behind them. He dove to the forest floor. *Pop,* the accompanying shot rang out. The French were just a few hundred yards ahead, firing from the woods beyond the clearing. More bullets cracked by, and soon hundreds of French rifles began to pour fire toward 13th Kompagnie.

"Get down!" Hentsch yelled as the battle erupted. Two men from 1 Gruppe were hit immediately. They dropped to the ground just feet from Hentsch and 2 Gruppe. One man was hit in the chest and died quickly. The other was wounded in his right hip. He shouted for help, and held his hands atop the spurting wound. Another from 1 Gruppe ran to him, grabbed hold of one of his bloody hands, and dragged him away from the line. It took a fine amount of bravery for a man to expose himself to enemy fire for the sake of a wounded companion. Hentsch prayed a French bullet wouldn't find either of them before they found a medic or an aid station.

Hentsch, Simon and Engel took cover behind the fallen trunk of a large, mossy tree, with the other four men of 2 Gruppe on either side of them. Simon was finally firing his rifle, at least in the enemy's general direction. Positioned as he was, with a stable platform from which to fire, Hentsch was able to use his marksmanship skill to a decided advantage. Any Frenchman in his line of sight was a dead man walking.

He shot two in quick succession, when a squad-sized team emerged from the tree line. Seeing two of their own fall so quickly, the remaining poilus dove for cover behind a small rise of earth that just barely concealed them. Their red and blue hats peeked over the top. They were stuck. Hentsch glimpsed enough of one soldier's head to zero in and fire.

DENIS

Thwack! Blood splattered in Denis's face. Patrice was likewise spritzed. They both flinched, surprised. Marcel had just taken a round to the head. He collapsed face down, lifeless, right between them.

Denis reached a hand to Marcel's shoulder. He turned him over to see if there was a chance he'd just been wounded. Marcel was dead. The bullet struck the right side of his forehead, about an inch from his temple. His eyes were rolled back and his tongue protruded from his mouth. Blood poured from the hole in his head and from his nostrils, and trickled through the grass and pooled on the flat ground by his boots.

The men of 2 Escouade were ducked behind a tiny, grassy earthen mound which Denis had considered just tall enough to provide defilade, though he hadn't much time to think about it before diving behind. Marcel must have held his head up a few inches too high.

"God dammit, Marcel!" Patrice shouted. "It's these fucking caps!" He tore his kepi from his head and flung it over the other side of the mound. He was done wearing a bullseye-red cap. Denis knew he'd rid himself of the kepi at some point, and seeing a man killed right in front of him because of said cap was a plenty good enough reason.

"One of the boche over there is a crack shot!" cried Denis. "Keep your heads down and don't try to spot him!" *I've already lost three of you boys. I can't lose any more.* He had already witnessed his share of death at Charleroi and Guise, having lost two of his own. He'd even dealt a fair amount of death himself. But a comrade having his brains shot out just inches away was even more shaking than seeing Clemence and Reynard killed by bayonets.

One shot, whether it was a well-placed one or a lucky one, was all it took. In a bayonet fight, a man might decide his fate with his own skill and ferocity, but a single rifle round fired from a thousand yards away could kill him before he'd ever known his time was up.

The French rifles had opened fire first, but the Germans were sending it back with equal fervor. Denis and his squad had been caught out in the open not long after the firing began, and having seen two of 1 Escouade's men immediately go down, were forced to dash behind the small, grassy earthen shield behind which they now cowered. The mound was only about three feet high and fifteen feet long, and tapered to flat ground on either end. They were pinned behind it, and the deadeye firing on them from the trees beyond the clearing was not about to let them out of there. What they needed was machine gun or artillery support.

"Where are the fucking Soixante-Quinzes?" one of the men yelled. It was Isaac, and he was failing to grasp the difficulty of moving heavy gun carriages through a wooded area. In flatter sectors, or those accessed by roads, the artillery had already been positioned. They could hear those 75mm cannons booming away in the distance.

"They'll have a tough time getting them in place," Denis replied, "the ground here is rough and the forest is thick. We may be stuck for a while."

They lay there for several minutes, unable to peek high enough over the mound to aim and fire. Bullets thudded against the opposite side of the embankment. More snapped inches overhead. Despite Marcel's grisly example, Vincent must have likewise held his head too high. A bullet tore through his kepi, sending it flying from his head. He'd escaped death by no more than an inch. His eyes went so wide they took up half his face.

Denis lay with his back against the mound and saw his man's cap leap skyward and roll across the ground. *You lucky bastard, Vincent,* he thought, glaring at him for his carelessness. *God, that boche can shoot.* Vincent did not bother to retrieve his cap; like Patrice, he was finished with it.

A French Mitrailleuse (machine gun) Saint Étienne Modèle 1907, which had been rattling from the tree line approximately a hundred yards east of Denis's position and holding the Germans at bay, had since fallen silent, its crew of three killed. The crew had yet to be replaced, leaving potentially hundreds of rounds sitting idly instead of flying toward the Germans. Because Denis knew roughly the German

183

marksman's position, he wagered that if he could get to the machine gun and place concentrated fire on the boche shooter, it might allow his men to either escape or advance. If they remained pinned in that spot, eventually other Germans would descend on their position and they'd be killed or captured.

"Patrice!" Denis shouted. "I'm going to try and get to that Saint Étienne! Stay with the men, and all of you, keep your fucking heads down!"

He slid on his back to the level ground behind the embankment, assuming a low crouching stance, like a sprinter waiting in the blocks. He eyed a cluster of trees about forty feet away. *If I can make it to the trees, I'll have enough cover to get away from the sniper and to that gun.*

If Denis stood too high while running, the German deadeye would kill him. If he crawled to stay low, he'd never make it to cover in time. *I need to move as fast as possible. No extra weight.* He unbuckled his haversack, dropping it to the ground, and then shrugged away his greatcoat. When he rested his Lebel in the dirt, Patrice grew upset.

"Denis what are you doing?!" he shouted. "What if you can't make it back and you need your things?"

Ignoring Patrice, Denis dug the tips of his boots into the ground, turning his heels back and forth to push his toes deeper. The cuts and blisters on his feet stung inside his boots, but he pushed the pain to the back of his mind. Aching feet were a trifling consideration.

"Denis!"

"Shut up Patrice!"

Visualizing his path to the machine gun, Denis reached his hands to the grass in front of him and squeezed large clumps between his fingers. He needed every bit of leverage to propel his body forward, and pulling the grass was just one more way of gaining an advantage. He drew in long, deep breaths, and tried to zone the cacophonous gunfire out of his mind.

All right Denis, MOVE! He drove hard with his legs and tugged the grass with his arms, launching himself ahead using every ounce of stored energy in his legs. Shot from an invisible cannon he leapt forward, his body as low as possible.

"Denis, wait! God dammit!" Patrice shouted.

Dirt flung from beneath his feet as Denis took long and powerful strides. He reached deep within, tapping into his primeval, animalistic reserves, churning his legs faster than would have ever been possible under lesser circumstances. He *had* to make it to those trees. He *had* to protect his men.

HENTSCH

Caught by slight surprise, Hentsch saw the black-haired Frenchman spring forth and start to run. He'd been waiting for heads to pop up and was not prepared for someone to dash away. With just seconds to react before the man made it to cover, Hentsch trained his rifle on the cluster of trees he thought the soldier was running toward and *pow!* Hentsch took his shot and waited for the man to fall.

"Shit!"

"You missed that Franzmann, didn't you?" asked Engel.

"He made it to the trees. Keep your eyes on the others and hold them there. I'll try and keep my sights on him."

He could just barely see the Frenchman's red pants moving through the opposing tree line. The man was in an all-out sprint, moving parallel to the clearing with enough cover to prevent a clean shot. Following the man, rifle trained on him, Hentsch sought another opportunity to fire. He debated taking a shot through the trees. He should have. Suddenly the Frenchman dove forward and Hentsch lost sight of him.

"Where did he go?"

Thwack-thwack-thwack! Several bullets struck the tree trunk directly in front of Hentsch, kicking up splinters just inches from his face. They were accompanied a half-second later by the echoing *tac-tac-tac* of a chattering French machine gun. The Frenchman was placing accurate fire directly against Hentsch's position. He and 2 Gruppe might have had the French squad pinned down before, but the escaped Frenchman now knew exactly where they were. He had the upper hand. Simon and Engel grabbed Hentsch by the shoulders, pulling him completely behind the tree. Now *they* were in severe danger. They'd have to rely on someone else to put the French gun out of commission.

"Son of a bitch Franzmann!" screamed Engel. "Fuck you!"

"What do we do now?!" Simon shouted, over the cracking wood and echoing machine gun fire. His high voice grew shriller the louder it got.

"I don't know I didn't see the gun!" Hentsch yelled back.

"Maybe if you'd shot straight he wouldn't have gotten there in the first fucking place!" Michael hollered. He was lying on his back, tightly clutching his pickelhaube to his head.

"Then why didn't you shoot him, you dick head?!" Simon yelped. Before Michael could respond, the situation worsened.

KABOOM! A French 75mm shell exploded in the treetops about fifty yards above and behind them, sending the top twenty feet of a tree snapping and crashing through the lower branches to the ground below.

"God dammit a cannon!" Hentsch screamed, stating the obvious as he stared at the falling tree. Thousands of yellow and green leaves fluttered to the ground and the nearby treetops swayed from the shell burst. Were he not surrounded by explosions and bullets, staring death in the face, the cascading leaves would have been serene.

BOOM! BOOM! BOOM! The French had managed to get at least one of their rapid-firing 75s close enough to the clearing and with enough room to fire through the trees. As if a machine gun trained directly on their position wasn't enough, 2 Gruppe, along with many others near them, now had to contend with being blown to smithereens. The entire forest canopy seemed about to give way. Trees shattered and splinters rained. Large limbs and treetops exploded and fell. Showering leaves nearly obscured the men's visibility.

Hentsch scanned the panicked faces of 2 Gruppe and shouted, "We have to get out of here!" It was hard to see, but other units nearby were pulling back as well. He led the way as he and his charges began belly-crawling away from the fallen tree. They shuffled across the ground while murderous fire passed above.

With hundreds of thousands of leaves, twigs and wood splinters raining down, scattered by shell bursts, 2 Gruppe were nearly buried by debris. Hissing shrapnel from nearby bursts pelted the ground, missing Hentsch and his men by inches. On watch for larger falling debris, he navigated the forest floor, slithering between and around obstacles, his men in tow.

"Come on Engel! Come on Simon! Let's go you men!" Hentsch urged them. "Crawl faster! Faster!"

"We are, you asshole!"

They made it out of the woods and away from the cannons, but barely. What was worse, their close call had meant nothing. Soon after their forces had regrouped, they learned that General von Kluck had issued orders for IX Korps to disengage the French in front of them, to instead join in the attack against French Sixth Army almost forty miles to the west. Even if 13th Kompagnie, or perhaps even the entire bataillon, regiment or brigade had captured any appreciable amount of ground, they would have immediately surrendered it back to the French in order to move west.

Having marched so far already, the news came as a slap in the face.

"So we're to march another thirty miles to attack the French, when there were French directly in front of us?! How does that make sense?" Michael snarled, his dissatisfaction clear.

For once, Hentsch reluctantly agreed with him. If IX Korps simply pulled back from the French, what was to prevent the French from filing into the gap which IX Korps would obviously leave? Hentsch saw no reserves moving forward to take the place of the units leaving the front line. Would command really just leave an open space?

They were all sick of marching. Command had asked much of them, and enlisted men did not have the luxury of horses or staff cars. While not every mile of their march across Belgium and northern France was on foot—troop trains played an integral role, especially in Belgium—they had without a doubt put mileage in the triple digits on their boots. Hentsch's feet throbbed, and with the heat, his lower legs were constantly moist and itchy from his tall black jackboots. His first pair, the brown ones, had already worn out; he hoped another long-distance trek would be kind to his replacement pair.

Though 2 Gruppe had escaped the French cannons, the experience had been harrowing. Simon and Engel seemed okay to Hentsch, as did Kirsch and Nussbaum. But Michael was agitated; the scowl on his face and the lines in his forehead deepened with every mile of their westward march. Ackerman took the close call the worst. He was fidgety, twitchy, as if he feared a Frenchman with a bayonet were sneaking up right behind him. Ackerman's pupils were so widely dilated, and stayed so, that his eyes were black. The skin of his round face was flushed a rosy red.

"Ackerman," Hentsch said quietly, "are you doing all right?"

"Huh?" Ackerman said. His head snapped around like Hentsch had startled him. He spoke rapidly, and his whole body was trembling. "Uh...wh...what?" he stammered, "um...what do you want Hentsch? Just leave me alone."

"Hey, take it easy Ack," Hentsch said. He raised his palms. "We're okay now." He wasn't sure what else to say, and that was the best he could come up with. Fearing he might have made it worse, Hentsch decided to leave him alone.

Following their brief exchange, Ackerman's trembling intensified. His legs wobbled as he walked and his heavy, rapid breathing made the others glance surreptitiously in his direction. The French artillery had done a number on him.

"He's lost it," Michael mumbled. "Cracked up. Haven't you Ackerman?"

"Shut the hell up Michael!" Engel growled. "Leave him alone."

"Yeah just leave him be, you prick!" Kirsch added.

"Kiss my ass Engel," Michael replied. "You too, Kirsch."

"You know what, Michael?" Engel said. "You're a piece of shit." He took a step toward him, a scowl plastered across his face the intensity of which Hentsch had before never seen from him.

"Oh yeah? Well fuck you!" Michael countered.

"That mouth will get you killed one of these days, you arrogant bastard," Kirsch growled. He threw a hard shoulder into Michael's chest and knocked him back a step.

It was looking like the three men might get into a scrape. Everyone had grown tired of Michael and his lousy attitude, but outwardly, Kirsch and Engel disliked him the most, and they were about to do something about it. Even by himself, barrel-chested Kirsch was no pushover; he stood a solid five foot ten. He'd obviously been a scrapper before the war, and had a number of small facial scars and a missing upper front tooth. The twenty-six year old man from Güstrow probably could have thumped Michael on his own, without Engel's help. With his help, they'd beat him senseless.

"How rotten must your parents have been for you to end up this way?" Engel inquired. No one in 2 Gruppe knew where Michael was from, let alone ever spoke to him about his upbringing.

"Leave my parents out of it, you son of a bitch!" Michael snarled. He reached his hand behind his back.

He's going for his bayonet.

Nothing would look worse to a commander than three of his men in a physical altercation. Hentsch stepped in before the confrontation escalated any further. Placing himself between the three would-be belligerents, he shoved each of them and prevented anyone from lunging. By that point, most men from 1 Korporalschaft had taken notice. It would only be a matter of seconds before Unteroffizier Strauss intervened.

"Why don't you three just shut the fuck up?" Hentsch snapped. "Keep your mouths closed for the next hour and calm your stupid asses down."

"You'd never take my side anyway, Hentsch," Michael whined. "You can kiss my ass too."

Rubbing his hands over his face in exasperation, Hentsch did not bother acknowledging Michael. The march west continued, the tension amongst 2 Gruppe's men palpable.

VERNON

The British Expeditionary Force had suffered terribly in August. Marching even further than the French armies, they had, by the skin of their teeth, escaped total defeat more than once. Like the French, the BEF lacked adequate water, food and supplies. Along with the stress of long forced marches, illness, thirst and lack of food, the BEF's men had also fought each engagement knowing full well the German armies opposing them were radically greater in number. Had the tide of battle gone any less in their favor, they could have been completely crushed and every man killed or captured.

When the BEF's retreat from Mons fell into disorder, General Smith-Dorrien ordered II Corps to stand their ground and fight, knowing the retreat could not continue in its chaotic state. In the early morning of August 26, II Corps squared off against the Germans for the second time.

Because the 1st Cheshire Battalion had nearly been destroyed at Audregnies, they did not see much action in the Battle of Le Cateau, though they faced a light artillery bombardment during the fight. At Le Cateau, the Tommies' accurate rifle fire and, more significantly, air-bursting shrapnel fired by the Royal Artillery in extremely close quarters, wreaked havoc against the pursuing Germans.

The fighting delayed the German advance long enough to allow the BEF to escape. In the Battle of Le Cateau the outnumbered British suffered 7,812 casualties and lost thirty-eight artillery pieces. Again, entire units were decimated by the Germans, and while technically viewed as a defeat, the holding action ordered by General Smith-Dorrien halted the advance of Alexander von Kluck's entire army and allowed the BEF to further its retreat in relative safety. Even in that relative safety, however, trailing units were forced into smaller rearguard actions.

It was a testament to the resilience of Tommy Atkins that upon receiving orders to halt the retreat at the River Seine and launch a counterattack, the BEF did so without fail. They had marched over two hundred miles in just two weeks, and were now asked to do an about face and march north once again. At different points during their retreat, Vernon and the 15th Brigade had marched, in full gear and roasting heat, more than twenty miles in a single day.

The poor conditions during the retreat had taken a sharp toll on every man, Vernon included. Beating sunlight hadn't done anything for his already weathered face, which was covered by that point with two weeks' worth of stubble, dirt and what was just short of first degree burns. His eyes were dry and itchy, and though he'd drank as much water as possible when finally given the chance, his lips were split so severely it would take days of adequate hydration before they had even a remote chance to heal.

Vernon looked and felt miserable, and was compelled to keep a close watch on his friend. The days of marching mile after mile in extreme heat, and the maddening frustration of being unable to quench his thirst for several days during that retreat had pushed Llewelyn Pritchard to his breaking point. His sad, brown eyes were surrounded by red, and had large, dark bags underneath them. At different junctures during the exodus he had pulled his water bottle from his hip, knowing it was empty yet checking it anyway. On one such occasion Pritchard's frustration overtook logic, and he foolishly threw his bottle into the woods.

Captain Bannister had prodded him repeatedly, taking out his own frustrations on the poor man who'd long been his punching bag. It was mind-boggling that the captain would waste his time harassing one individual during such a strenuous ordeal. Vernon had at one point considered slugging Bannister in the mouth, or perhaps even challenging him over E Company's questionable escape from the Germans at Audregnies, but thought better of it. Bannister would have probably had him shot and then treated Pritchard even more harshly.

With Pritchard's having saved him from the German cavalry major on August 24, Vernon made sure to let both Corporal Spurling and Lieutenant Hood know about it. They congratulated Pritchard for his bravery, but neither the corporal nor the lieutenant had much say in how Bannister treated him. He was their captain, too. How they viewed him personally was rendered irrelevant by duty.

After reaching the Seine, II Corps were given just a short while to rehydrate, eat and re-equip with what little extra supplies were available. Vernon and Pritchard had taken the time to walk more than a mile to the battalion supply depot in the hopes of getting new tunics, as theirs were soiled in blood. Pritchard also needed a new water bottle. The tired men walked the extra distance only to be handed two pairs of socks and a set of puttees upon their arrival—it was all the battalion's quartermaster sergeant had allocated them.

The disappointing lack of supplies and the news of Field Marshal French's ordering them to march back north toward the Germans had shocked Pritchard into near-panic. That march had since commenced, and he'd yet to calm down.

"So we head into a gap between two entire Hun armies?!" Pritchard asked, indignant. He'd heard the latest scuttlebutt of what lay in front of the BEF, and he clearly did not relish the thought of hundreds of thousands of Germans on either side of him.

"That's what it sounds like, Lew," Vernon said calmly.

"Christ almighty, what if they collapse on us?" he said, his reddened eyes gaping and his jaw dumbly slackened. "We'll be annihilated!"

"Maybe so," replied Vernon. He feared the same thing, but wasn't going to be as vocal about it. "Or maybe we'll roll Fritz's flank and send him running. We've got our orders. Command knows what they're doing. Keep in mind, old boy, we've also got protection on either side of us for the first time."

General William Pulteney's III Corps, which then consisted of the 4th Division and the 19th Brigade, had joined the BEF at the Seine. The new arrivals advanced on II Corps' left, while Douglas Haig's I Corps was on II Corps' right.

When von Kluck responded to French Sixth Army's attack to the west, he ordered von Quast's IX and Ewald von Lochow's III Korps (the two corps of First Army's left flank) to leave German Second Army's right flank. When Quast and Lochow disengaged French Fifth Army's left flank and moved west, it opened a thirty-mile gap between Kluck's and Bülow's forces. That was the gap into which the BEF advanced. Since Quast and Lochow had disengaged French XVIII and III Corps, those forces also advanced into the gap alongside and ahead of the BEF.

While exploiting the fissure between the German armies was crucial, Field Marshal French and his subordinate generals believed their comparatively small force had been stressed and battered enough. As such, the BEF's march into the gap proceeded excruciatingly slowly, at least from the point of view of the French commanders. The BEF cooperated with Joffre's forces, but at their own pace. As the survivors of the tattered 1st Battalion marched toward another potential confrontation, Pritchard grew increasingly uneasy. They'd lost so many men, and the odds of escaping death in such trying situations decreased with each engagement.

"Dammit Vernon, we'll be cut off!" Pritchard said. "I know it!" He couldn't keep his thoughts to himself. With his rifle slung over his shoulder, he alternated his hands from squeezing the back of his neck, to wringing them together in front of his stomach.

"Come on Pritch you've got to cool off," Vernon replied. "If Bannister hears you talking like this—"

"I don't care about that pugnacious cunt!" snapped Pritchard, his voice low but strained. "We're going to die here and he'll die with us!"

"You were okay with that before!"

"Well I'm not fucking okay with it now!"

Vernon grabbed him by the arm and squeezed hard, pulling the panicked man close to him to speak through gritted teeth. "Llewelyn Pritchard, you need to pucker your arse! Tough it out!" He tugged Pritchard's arm again. "I need you to fight alongside me, understand? Keep your bloody wits!"

The man had saved his life and shown great courage in so doing, but the stress was hitting Vernon's friend harder than it was hitting him.

On cue, Captain Bannister stomped toward them. He'd spotted Vernon clutching Pritchard's arm from a distance. He must have been watching the two of them from the get-go.

Corporal Spurling saw him coming first, and tried to warn them. "Psst!" he whispered, "heads up!"

Vernon turned his head left to look at the corporal, and judged by the look on the young man's bony face that he was about to get an earful. Turning to the right, he knew why, but by then it was too late. The fire-breathing, walrus-moustached Bannister, in his tall, brown leather butcher boots, riding breeches and tailored jacket, had already moved to within a few yards.

The captain's jacket, unblemished despite the conditions, had three diamond pips on its three-point chevron lace sleeve cuff, and around the cuff were two chevron stripes. On each of his lapels was a brass Cheshire acorn and oak leaves badge. As Bannister approached, Vernon could not help but wonder how such an asshole was ever given command of a company. It shouldn't have been that way. The captain was boorish, sadistic and crass. Officers were supposed to be gentlemen. Hood was a gentleman.

"What in the fuck are you two poofs doing?" Bannister roared. "Is there a problem back here?"

"No sir, no problem at all," answered Vernon. Pritchard stared at the ground. He refused even to look at Bannister anymore.

"I thought so," said the captain. "Just remember, Hayes, you keep that bloody Welshman in line or I'll have the lot of you court-martialed. And Pritchard, you little dandiprat weasel, if you go yellow next time we see Huns I'll shoot you myself." He patted the holster of his Webley revolver. "Spurling!" he shouted, and the corporal flinched. "Am I going to have to find a more competent section leader, or can you manage these two shitheads from this point forth?"

"No sir, Captain Bannister sir, they'll behave themselves." Spurling turned to the two friends. "Right gentlemen?"

"Yes sir," Vernon replied, not wanting to compound the situation. He stared at the captain, and the two met eyes. His hatred for E Company's commander grew each and every day. His cheeks warmed as they flushed with anger while Bannister sneered back at him. The captain's eyes had as much personality behind them as a shark's, and were every bit as black. He was worse than any Hun.

What a nasty son of a bitch. What is wrong with him? I hope one of these days a Fritz bullet plugs Bannister square in his bonce.

Still glowering at Vernon, Bannister suddenly shouted, "Hood!" before turning away, heavily clomping his boots on the ground. He was off to berate Fourth Platoon's lieutenant for whatever it was that had just happened.

"Sorry about that, Spurling," Vernon apologized. It hadn't been his intention to stir up any trouble, and the corporal did not deserve Bannister's threat. While Pritchard bore the brunt of the captain's ire, those on his periphery were inevitably caught up in it, and Spurling had dealt with it since his elevation to corporal back in Londonderry.

"I'm sorry too…" Pritchard muttered.

"Never mind that," Spurling replied nonchalantly. "We both know the captain has it out for you two, and it's unwarranted. Lieutenant Hood knows it, too."

By mid-day on September 7, II Corps had advanced only a few miles into the gap. They were still several miles away from the River Petit Morin, the last known position of German Second Army. Command decided to halt their march again, before proceeding toward the Petit Morin the next day.

"Looks like we'll halt here for the night," Captain Bannister said. "You boys aren't cut out for marching the way men are supposed to." He condescended to the whole company, but as was his custom, directed it at Vernon and Pritchard when he said it. "We marched twice this far against the Boers, in hotter weather to boot."

Atwater, a soldier from 1 Section, nudged Vernon with his shoulder as Bannister walked away and asked, "That's some story. I bet he won the war single-handedly."

Vernon turned to him and said, "If you asked him, that's likely what he'd tell you."

"Funny I don't see the VC pinned to his chest," Atwater said.

"Didn't you hear? Bannister's won ten of them. One for every thousand Boers he killed with his bare hands."

"With one hand tied behind his back."

"If he took a cannon shell to the arse I bet no one would miss him."

"I'm with you, Hayes," Atwater agreed.

Nightfall approached, and the bright, waning moon shone in the cloudless sky. Vernon sat with Pritchard and tried not to think about what the next day might have in store for them. Pritchard was quiet. He sat on his pack, picking the dirt beneath his fingernails with the tip of his bayonet. He grasped the weapon by the blade, which glinted in the moonlight. The others conversed softly, about what Vernon could not tell. He had only one concern.

"Hey Pritch, are you holding up?" he asked.

"Just a bit edgy, is all," Pritchard replied. He lowered his bayonet and made eye contact. "I'm sorry again about earlier."

"Eh..." Vernon said, and he waved his hand. That was over and done with.

"It's been a rough few weeks, aye?"

"Aye Pritch. Never been so thirsty in my life. Nearly drove me mad, that."

"You saw what it did to me," Pritchard said, shaking his head shamefully. "Tossed my fucking bottle in the trees..."

"We all get frustrated."

"But I got stupid."

"Semantics."

They sat quietly for about thirty seconds, before Pritchard asked, "Do you miss Sal?"

"You know I do, mate," Vernon said. "That's why I must keep steadfast, my head on straight, so I can get back to her when this rubbish is done." He rested his hand on his haversack, and wrapped the red handkerchief around his palm. He pictured the day he'd return and his wife would run into his arms, showering him with kisses. "You've got to help me get there, yeah? I need you to stay with me and we'll both make it out alive." *You've already saved me once. I owe it to you to get you home safely.*

"Sure, Vernon," Pritchard said. "But when we get there, what have I to go back to? When I lost Daisy..." his voice wavered and he looked at his feet. "...Something in me went missing, and it's not come back. I've got nothing and no one to go home to. Hell, I've got no home at all."

"You'll always have a home with Sal and me..."

"I'd never wish to burden you..."

"You'd be no burden."

"You know, Daisy and I were going to buy a little house in Ellesmere Port, once I'd left the service. She wanted a family..." a solitary tear trickled down Pritchard's cheek. He sniffled and then shook it off. "Fucking Egypt..."

Having known personally the sweet woman of whom his best friend spoke was heartbreaking for Vernon. He sniffled too, and swallowed a knot in his throat. He did not want to tear up while attempting to comfort Pritchard—that would not have been very comforting at all. "I can't pretend to know how much it hurts, Pritch," he said. "I know how much you love and miss her. Sal and I loved her, too. But you and I both know that Darling Daisy Pritchard would never have let her husband crack up, not over anything. So don't bloody crack up on me."

"Vernon, what in the world will I do if you're killed?" Pritchard said. "Bannister will probably order me on some damn suicide charge, and then shoot me if I refuse."

"I guess I just won't get killed."

Pritchard rolled his yes. "I'm not joking, Vernon."

"Llewelyn, listen to me. You've already saved my life once, and I will not leave you alone in this war. We're going to win. And we're going back to England together. Understand?"

"I hope you're right."

"I know I'm right."

They sat quietly again. Pritchard resumed picking at his fingernails with his bayonet. Later on, Corporal Spurling and Lieutenant Hood approached them. Spurling had been spending a little more time with Hood since the platoon's sergeant had been killed the week before, and his elevation to sergeant seemed imminent. They'd been making the rounds that night, speaking with the men.

"Do you chaps mind if Spurling and I join you?" the lieutenant asked politely. He was always a gentleman.

"Of course not, sir," Vernon replied. "Please." It was refreshing to hear an officer address him with respect and dignity. Spurling and Hood both took a knee. They glanced at one another for a moment before the lieutenant nodded assuredly to the corporal.

"Llewelyn," Spurling began, "we've had discussions with lads from the other sections, along with a few blokes from Second and Third Platoon, including their officers. They're all sick and tired of listening to Bannister lay into you. He's not much better to any of them, either, and it's wearing on them. On all of us."

Pritchard shrugged his shoulders and continued to fidget with his bayonet. He didn't have to tell anyone he'd grown tired of it a long time ago.

"So we're going to try and do something about it," Spurling said. "Lieutenant Hood and I, along with three others, will speak with battalion headquarters as soon as we're given the chance."

Hood shifted forward on his knee and removed his cap. He held it with both hands and leaned toward Pritchard. "I know this Bannister situation has dragged on you, Private. A lesser man might have buckled by now. So, you see, Corporal Spurling and I just want to thank you for your outstanding service thus far."

Spurling nodded in agreement then added, "Your actions during the retreat are of the sort that wins a man a commendation. Bagging a cavalry major *and* rescuing your friend? That's bloody brilliant soldiering."

"Absolutely," Hood agreed, "and I will make certain battalion hears about it as soon as I'm able."

Both the corporal and the lieutenant were younger than either he or Pritchard, but Vernon could not help but feel a profound respect and admiration for the two men as he listened to them intently.

Hood, a dashing young officer, could have been much more interested in furthering his career, but there he was, discussing his intention to circumvent Bannister in the name of a solitary private. Spurling, meanwhile, constantly drew Bannister's ire simply because Pritchard was in his section, but he never resented him for it. He absorbed the captain's persistent barking, and continued to give Pritchard the respect he deserved. It was leadership like that which inspired men to fight.

"What about the machine gunners?" asked Pritchard. "I want credit for nothing unless those Dorsetshire chaps are given the lion's share of it. Who knows how many they saved that night?"

"I understand, Llewelyn," answered Hood. "Maybe when we've gained more ground against Fritz I can spare a runner or send a rider to Dorsetshire HQ and find out which gunners they're missing. As of right now I have no way of knowing the identity of those men."

"Either way, Pritchard," said Spurling, "you saved Hayes, and the Hun cavalry has one less officer. That's a fine feather to stick in your cap."

"It should have been enough to get Bannister off your back in and of itself," Hood added. "It would likely have won the favor of any sane officer. It's just another reason we must go to HQ."

"The captain won't care even if you do," Pritchard said quietly.

Hood rose to his feet, placing his cap back on his head. He stepped closer to Pritchard and rested a hand on his shoulder. "Well, we're still going to try. You're a fine soldier, Llewelyn Pritchard, and I'm proud to have you in Fourth Platoon. Carry on, gentlemen."

Spurling stood up with the lieutenant, but before they could leave Vernon spoke up. He wasn't sure that he should, but the sincerity of the past few minutes led him to feel as though he might get a straight answer.

"Sir?"

"Yes, Hayes?" said Hood.

He tried to resist, but the lingering, nagging question scratched and clawed its way out of Vernon's mouth. "What is the real reason so many from our company made it out of there?"

The lieutenant smiled half-heartedly, with closed lips. "I think you already know, Hayes, or why else would you ask?" He and Spurling started to walk away, but after a few steps Hood stopped and spoke again. "There is another side to that. What do you suppose would have happened to you, to us, had we not received Bannister's order?"

"Well, Lieutenant, I suppose not much good at all would have come from it," Vernon answered. There was no denying a basic truth—Bannister's decision to pull E Company from Audregnies had saved the lives of over a hundred men, or at the very least kept them from capture.

Hood nodded subtly and said, "Maybe it *was* to save his own arse. But it saved our arses as well. Good night, chaps." The lieutenant tipped his cap, and he and Spurling continued their rounds.

DENIS

XVIII Corps forced their way into the gap between the German First and Second Armies, right alongside the BEF. After Denis's escapade with the boche deadeye and the machine gun, the German forces opposing them had surprisingly pulled back, leaving the gap into which XVIII Corps currently advanced. With renewed purpose, the tired and achy poilus ignored the wear and tear on their bodies and instead focused on taking back as much French ground as possible.

"Denis, do you think you'll win a decoration for what you did yesterday?" Patrice asked as the column pushed north. He was still excited over what Denis had done to save 2 Escouade.

"I don't care, Pat. I just wanted to protect my squad."

"That boche could have killed you, though," Patrice needlessly reminded him. "Then what would we have done?" He shuffled in front of Denis, walking backward to converse with him face to face.

"If I'd been killed, the artillery would have bailed you out, and command would have found you a new squad leader," Denis replied nonchalantly. "There may well come a day when I am killed, probably sooner than later. We've already lost many officers who were far better soldiers than I."

Patrice furrowed his eyebrows. Denis realized his friend did not take the prospect of him being killed so matter-of-factly. He wouldn't have wanted Patrice to have such a casual attitude toward death either.

"I don't know about that, sir," replied Nicolas, who must have been eavesdropping. "You'd not be so easy to replace."

"Sir, I don't believe that either," added Thierry. He and Nicolas were close friends, much like Denis and Patrice, a tighter pair within the larger tight-knit squad. They were both from Bordeaux and went to school with Cécile, Patrice's love interest. Though Nicolas and Thierry weren't related, they were often mistaken for brothers, even out of uniform. Both stood a similar height, about average, and wore thick moustaches, which homogenized their faces to a degree. In uniform, their matching greatcoats and kepis made them as twins.

The men all agreed, one by one. Patrice gave Denis an I-told-you-so smile and said, "You see, neither they nor I want another squad leader. So don't take any more unnecessary risks. Send one of us like you're damned well supposed to."

Denis was moved by the men's respect. As a squad leader and aspiring officer, it was his duty to issue orders, but that did not make it any easier. Ordering men to do what might get them killed was not a particularly desirable responsibility, and came much easier for some than for others. It was far easier to study for it in school than it was to put into practice.

Those under Denis's command were his friends and brothers. It hurt him to the core when he saw Clemence and Reynard die at Guise. He still had Marcel's blood on his clothes. The guilt of leaving Clemence to die had eaten at him ever since. Denis grappled with the shame that the last moments of Clemence's life were spent alone, with the knowledge that his squad leader had left him lying in the dirt.

The northward advance continued in the general direction of the village of Montmirail. While they were headed toward a clash with General Karl von Einem's VII Korps, the right flank of Bülow's Second Army, Denis knew no such specifics, he just knew another fight would come, probably in the next day or so.

A further two hours into the march, having only heard the faintest rumble of artillery far to the east, the men began to wonder exactly where the Germans were. At least *some* boche had to be close. Denis jogged ahead to speak with Sergent Chouinard, his half-section commander, after seeing the man unfold a small map.

"Excuse me, sir?" Denis said as he approached the NCO.

Chouinard was a big man, about five inches taller than Denis and nearly half his weight over again. A large head sat atop his large body, and his kepi rested high on his forehead, making him even taller. Luckily for the sergent, he had a dark blue cover for his cap—his head was exposed enough already and did not need a red bullseye.

His kepi's leather chin strap was stretched to the limit beneath his jowls, and was the only thing keeping the cap in position. His round cheeks and heavy jaw were covered in thick stubble, and as it was with most of the men, his grey eyes were bloodshot and distant. The skin of the sergent's doughy neck bulged over the high red collar of his dark blue tunic.

Chouinard's eschewing a greatcoat in favor of the tunic was probably a prudent one, as the heat likely would have killed him otherwise. His was the newer 1914 model tunic, different from those worn by Denis, Lieutenant Armistead and Capitaine Bex. The high collar was red, rather than blue, with black collar patches bearing a red *144*. The tunic closed with seven gold, flaming-grenade buttons, and had no breast pockets, just two slit pockets on the hip. Chouinard's rank insignia was a thick, gold bullion chevron stripe running diagonally around his lower sleeve at about mid-forearm, just above the cuff flap, which was red with gold buttons.

He wore the heavy infantryman's haversack, but on his larger back it looked much smaller and more manageable. Because he had thick legs, Chouinard opted to wrap his calves with dark blue puttees—he probably could not find gaiters large enough to fit over his red trousers. With feet as large as his, the standard sizes likely proved inadequate. His black leather boots were very obviously custom made, sturdily reinforced, and of much higher quality than those issued to the enlisted men. Denis pitied any boche who had the misfortune of suffering a stomp from the sergent's heavy boot.

"What is it, Aspirant Roux?" Chouinard said. He took his sweaty left hand off the map, leaving dirty smudges where his fingers had been.

Every man in the column smelled bad, but the heavyset sergent smelled worse. He probably hadn't, but he smelled liked he'd shit his pants. The stench of his soiled uniform made Denis wince, and he nearly gagged.

Up close, it was clear the man's tunic had gotten more than just sweat and body odor caked into its dark fabric—he'd also been splattered with a copious amount of blood. Sergent Chouinard wasn't afraid to mix it up with the enemy, and cuts on his knuckles indicated that point even further than did the bloody tunic.

"Sergent, I do not mean to pry, but have you broken your hand?" Denis asked, upon catching a glimpse of Chouinard's right hand.

A bony lump jutted from the outer edge of the sergent's palm, and his last knuckle had shifted noticeably downward. Close to half of the skin on the top of his hand was a mottled, purple, blue and yellow mess. He kept his pinky pointed straight, and held the map with his thumb and three fingers. The little finger quivered uncontrollably. Denis knew the sergent must have been in a considerable pain.

"Yes, I believe so," Chouinard answered. "I cracked it against a boche's jaw last week. It hurts, I must say."

A week. My God. I wonder if the punch killed the man who suffered it. Denis could not take his eyes off the deformed hand. He marveled at the sergent's toughness. "Sergent," he winced, "Should you not wrap it at least?"

"I've tried wrapping it in puttee cloth, but the pressure makes it worse. And I cannot go to the aid station, as I fear I may be withdrawn. A broken hand is not sufficient cause to abandon F Compagnie."

"You cannot continue neglecting it, Sergent, it may heal improperly."

"So be it," Chouinard said, and he tugged on his right sleeve, moving the cuff further down his hand to cover the injury. The move drew Denis's attention to the diagonal golden chevron stripe above the sergent's cuff. It, too, was splattered with blood.

The bloody, broken gold bar on Denis's greatcoat sleeve indicated his slightly higher status than that of the NCO. Denis cared little about their respective ranks. The man standing before him had already proven his mettle on the field of battle. He was suffering, yet still pushing on. Their blood-stained insignia were the true indication of rank. No high-ranking commanders had blood on their chevrons, bars, or their fancy golden braids.

Denis and Chouinard were about the same age, but Chouinard had been an infantryman longer. He'd obviously earned his promotions, as well as his posting to half-section leader. Realizing that his pressing the sergent about his hand was making the man uncomfortable, Denis averted his gaze and changed the subject. "I was wondering if you might let me look at that with you, sir," he said, nodding toward the map. "If you wouldn't mind."

"Of course not," Chouinard answered. He held the smudged, sweat-dampened map in front and to his left while they walked, so Denis could get a better look. The map was badly worn, with hand-drawn symbols indicating the presence of forests and small villages. The rivers were represented by single lines, and their depths and widths were not listed. Bridges were indicated by two short, parallel lines intersecting the line of a river. While basic topography was given, Denis doubted its accuracy. He hoped headquarters had better maps to go by. They likely did.

"Lieutenant Armistead says the boche have halted somewhere around here," the sergent said, pointing toward the line of the River

Petit Morin, indicating the Germans had withdrawn across the river to its northern bank. They'd pulled back almost fifteen miles. "Air reconnaissance has placed massed formations here," he pointed to a spot, "and here," he pointed to another. "We're roughly right here," he pointed again, "Probably about five miles away."

"Have we any indication of their strength?"

"Only spotty reports from the airmen, so far as I know, but we may have numerical superiority."

"And artillery? Where are the boche cannons?"

"Of that, I am unsure." Chouinard sighed, probably at the thought of facing more shellfire. Denis understood the sentiment well.

So much death flew through the air when the fighting started, but the prospect of an exploding shell was so much more daunting. Whereas a bullet had to hit a man directly, cannons need only land their projectiles somewhere in his vicinity. A surgeon could extract a bullet and stitch a man up, but when a shell took a man's arm or leg, he wasn't getting it back, no matter how skilled the surgeon.

"What of our cavalry?" Denis asked. He didn't want to focus on cannons until he had to stand before them.

"Conneau's Cavalerie has outpaced us and pushed further north. Whatever their objective, it will not be alongside the infantry."

"Understood. Thank you for the insight, Sergent," Denis said.

"You're welcome, sir," replied Chouinard, folding up the dirty map.

The two men saluted, and Denis turned to make his way back to 2 Escouade. Still shaken by the sergent's broken hand, he nevertheless walked away from the conversation impressed. The exchange was by far the longest they'd had since mobilization, and it was reassuring to know the next man up the chain was such a tough son of a bitch. Seeing a man in such obvious pain made Denis's battered, aching feet insignificant in comparison.

"So where are the boche, Denis?" asked Patrice, "What did the sergent have to say?" He and the other eight men waited for Denis to answer, and stared at him expectantly.

"They're about five miles ahead, across the Petit Morin. We'll probably meet them west of Montmirail. Are you men up for another fight?"

"Yes sir!" they replied in unison.

"Good to know," Denis responded with a grin. He was proud of their spirit, and thankful to have such fine men under his command. When the squad resumed talking amongst themselves, trying their best to take their minds off the looming battle, Denis could not resist telling Patrice about Chouinard's hand.

"Did you know that the sergent has broken his hand?"

"What do you mean?"

"I mean he's got a damned bone jutting out of his right hand!" Denis said, slapping the outer edge of his right palm with his left. "Broken and bruised. Plain as day."

"How'd that happen?"

"Punched a boche in the face."

"Wow. I wonder if the punch killed him."

"That's what I thought!"

To the east of d'Esperey's Fifth Army, the German Third Army under General Max von Hausen had already run headlong into Général Ferdinand Foch's French Ninth Army near the St. Gond marshes. Ninth Army hit the Germans hard, and von Hausen's attack began to flounder after incurring heavy losses. Had Foch's Ninth Army broken, Fifth Army's rear flank would have been completely exposed and open to attack, as their advance into the German gap had already pushed them well to the north and west of the marshes.

Further east, Général Fernand de Langle de Cary's French Fourth Army squared off against Duke Albrecht of Württemberg's German Fourth Army between Vitry Le Francois and Revigny, near the River Ornain. That battle was east of the bend in the River Marne.

Even further east, Kaiser Wilhelm's son, Crown Prince Wilhelm's German Fifth Army had bypassed Verdun. They moved through the Argonne Forest, east of the fortress city and into the Paris-Verdun salient. Attacking the heavily fortified city would have been a massive undertaking, requiring a prolonged bombardment from Germany's heaviest siege guns. Wilhelm's forces were, like all the belligerent armies, already exhausted from their participation in the Battle of the Frontiers, and simply could not have sustained such an attack against Verdun. Wilhelm's army was faced by Général Maurice Sarrail's French Third Army. The two forces clashed violently, but neither would make any significant progress, even after the crown prince's army circumvented Verdun.

In Alsace-Lorraine, French First and Second Armies, commanded by Générals Dubail and Castelnau respectively, still faced the German Sixth and Seventh Armies, under Crown Prince Rupprecht of Bavaria. Those armies had been relentlessly throwing themselves at one another, churning their men into the meat grinder and gaining almost nothing. Despite the losses, the lines there remained nearly static.

VOGEL

The LVG, with Vogel in the rear cockpit and Adler in the forward, flew east through the cool, late summer air, two thousand feet above the British and French forces then advancing into a widening gap between First and Second Army. Only sparse wisps of cloud dotted an otherwise soft blue sky. The golden, blinding disk of the afternoon sun had begun its slow descent toward the western horizon. Vogel couldn't think of a finer way to spend the afternoon, for it was September 8, his twenty-second birthday. With three hours in the air under their belts, having also reconnoitered the area behind French Sixth Army, Adler finally finished his observations. With his hand, he signaled to Vogel that he should turn the machine north, to return to the aerodrome.

Vogel gently toed the rudder bar and feathered the control stick, banking the aircraft to port. The wind whipped against his face and the rushing air tugged at his hair. With ground temperatures still above eighty degrees, the only respite from the heat came in the form of a sortie. It was just another reason, amongst many others, why he loved to fly.

Reorienting the machine to a northerly heading, Vogel noticed something out of place against the blue backdrop. Ahead, off the LVG's starboard side, a small black dot, increasing in size every few seconds, indicated the presence of another machine. It approached from the northeast, very near the LVG's level.

Vogel and Adler had seen a handful of British and French reconnaissance machines in the sky before, and had even passed close enough to some to greet them with a wave or salute. In spite of the evidence he and Leon had discovered to the contrary, Vogel still preferred to view air reconnaissance as a non-combative facet of warfare. Adler, he knew, saw it very much the same. Neither man saw any point in showing hostility to fellow airmen, regardless of nationality.

At a half mile's range, Vogel began to pick up details of the oncoming machine's silhouette. Compared to the LVG, the aeroplane moving toward them looked quite different, incomplete in a sense. He knew the type—it was a two-seater Blériot XI. Rather than a biplane configuration, the craft utilized a monoplane, meaning it had just one set of wings.

Whereas the LVG had one plane suspended above the fuselage and attached by struts and a second set mounted flush with the bottom of the fuselage, the monoplane's wings were flush with the top of its fuselage. In the LVG, additional wing support was achieved by attaching the upper and lower planes firmly together with struts and bracing wires. For wing support in the monoplane, bracing wires ran from different points on both the bottom and top of the wings and were attached to two triangular steel brackets, mounted behind the engine, one on the top side and one on the underside of the machine.

Because the Blériot had only one set of wings, both pilot and observer protruded—from the shoulders up—out of the fuselage, with no structure above them, whilst the biplane's upper wings sat above its occupant's heads. From behind the pilot's cockpit, the Blériot's fuselage had no fabric covering, revealing the latticework frame construction of its tail section along with its rudder and elevator control wires.

From a distance, Vogel could not tell whether its occupants were British or French, as both countries utilized the Blériot XI design. As they drew nearer, he began to feel an uneasiness he could not quite put his finger on. When the Blériot had approached to within two hundred yards, Adler turned to Vogel and shouted something to him over the roar of the LVG's engine. There was no way Vogel could hear him, but he thought he saw Adler's lips mouth the word *rifle.*

The distance closed in an instant. The observer in the Blériot was holding a rifle, and he was aiming it. With just hundreds of feet separating them, the Union Jack painted on the side of the Blériot's fuselage came into view. The airmen were British, and they were hostile! Through wide and panicked eyes, Vogel watched the muzzle flashes as the observer fired three shots in rapid succession, and then the machines were past one another. It was over quickly.

As far as Vogel could tell, the man had missed. Adler very obviously was not hit; he shook his fist at the British machine and shouted something, most likely profanity, which neither Vogel nor the British men could possibly hear. The flying rifleman condescendingly saluted Vogel and Adler as the British pilot pulled the Blériot away and headed for the British lines.

Being fired upon by another aircraft was something Vogel and Adler had never experienced before. As far as Vogel knew, in point of fact, no German airmen had *ever* been fired upon by another aircraft. Having a rifle aimed in his direction and lacking any means with which to defend himself had thrust him into a heightened state of alertness, and it was not the birthday present he had envisioned getting when he woke up that morning. In the minutes that followed, he was paranoid. He scanned the sky, head on a swivel, to make certain another hostile machine did not get the drop on him.

With a racing mind, his thoughts turned to his brother Frederick on the Eastern Front. He wondered if the Russians were putting aeroplanes of their own into the sky. If so, were those pilots taking shots as well? Fred was a kind young man and a wonderful brother, and the thought of him being subjected to such hostility was a dreadful one.

Air to air shooting may have been a new and harrowing paradigm shift, but as he flew the LVG back to the aerodrome, Vogel began to calm down. The Brit *had* missed, after all. The shocking experience left its psychological mark, sure, but he was still where he wanted to be, doing what he loved doing. It would take a lot more than a few bullets to change that.

For the remainder of their return northward, to ease his mind, he reveled in just what it meant to take to the sky. Soaring over the land at two thousand feet, he could see the horizon in all four directions. He gazed into the sun, which had begun its shift from noontime yellow to sunset orange. The rays warmed his face, even with the wind of the roaring propeller blasting against his skin. He blinked hard to rid his eyes of sunspots.

If he squinted, he could just make out the city of Paris, approximately thirty miles to the west. The shimmering blue-green of the River Marne slithered away from Paris like a colossal snake, and separated the advancing British from Vogel's countrymen in Kluck's First Army. The French countryside, with its abundance of small farms and their sundry crops, formed a colorful patchwork quilt which spread over the surface of France for hundreds of square miles. That millions of men stood in opposition below, fighting and dying on top of that magnificent quilt, was the most bizarre of dichotomies. *How can something so beautiful be populated by creatures so intent on destroying one another?*

The sun had dipped halfway behind the trees when Vogel touched the LVG's wheels back onto the grass field of their aerodrome at Troësnes, about forty miles northeast of Paris and well behind the front lines. Adler was even more upset than the last time he'd been shot at. He cursed to himself as he leapt from his cockpit, his cap held in a white-knuckled grip. Vogel had calmed down during the flight, but his observer clearly had not.

"What in the fuck was that, Vogel?" Adler said, with Prussian-blue fire in his eyes. "Is that what we're doing up there now? Shooting at one another?!" His cheeks were rose-red. His jaw muscles pulsated. The furious oberleutnant, so mad he was grinding his teeth, forcefully slapped his peaked cap back atop his head.

"I don't know sir," Vogel answered quietly. "It didn't seem sportsmanlike. We weren't armed."

Adler threw his hand in the air. "Well that's the last time we go up without some sort of armament. I'll get you a Luger before we fly again."

"Yes sir," Vogel replied. He doubted the man would actually get him a pistol.

Adler stood motionless, his hands on his hips, silently teeming with rage, for a further thirty seconds—an angry Prussian statue, a monument to vexation. The last time he'd been shot at by ground forces he'd stayed mad for hours, but following his statuesque pose, his anger subsided comparatively quickly. The oberleutnant had another issue he wanted to address.

"Vogel, when we flew over the Ourcq did you happen to notice the activity on the roads leading to the front?"

"No sir."

"They were clogged with automobiles. It looked to be a complete mess. But it was odd. Most were heading toward the front lines rather than away, I'm sure of it."

"I wonder what that means," Vogel pondered.

"I don't know, but the frogs were definitely up to something."

What Adler had seen were the infamous "Taxis of the Marne". During French Sixth Army's attack on von Kluck's right flank, Général Galliéni, fearing railroad breakdowns might hamper the success of Sixth Army's attack, ordered French police to commandeer more than a thousand of Paris's black Renault taxicabs. Galliéni used the taxis, which carried four or five men per vehicle, to transport the men of the 140th Infantry Division, along with the 103rd Infantry Regiment, thirty miles northeast of Paris to the battlefront near Nanteuil.

The decision to dispatch reinforcements by taxi, while interesting, would not play a significant role in the outcome of the larger Battle of the Marne. The clogged roads Adler witnessed were the result of the taxicab plan's poor execution. While the first cabs arriving at the front dropped their charges off successfully, those empty cabs then turned around to take the very same roads back to Paris.

The narrow roads were unable to accommodate such an increase in traffic, and that led to collisions, break downs, and jam-ups. Many cars veered from the shoulders and into side ditches. Nightfall made the logistical problems even worse. Some troops were forced to walk several miles to the front after being dropped off early due to the congestion. The "Taxis of the Marne" would eventually become a legendary facet of the battle, but the reality was much less legendary.

Adler walked away, and then Vogel heard the unmistakable sound of approaching automobiles. He looked toward the road at the northern end of the aerodrome. Soon, a line of fancy cars came into view. The cars had grey bodies, with black tops, fenders and side skirts. Shiny chrome covered their trim, radiators, headlight bodies and hood ornaments. The vehicles were far nicer than the old, brown, motorized turnip cart of a car the officers of FFA 12 shared. Vogel wondered who might be inside of them. He stood next to his machine, arms folded, waiting for the cars to pull up and the occupants to step out. At the same time, Leon approached from the sheds on the eastern side of the aerodrome; he was also staring at the vehicles.

When the cars stopped and the men inside began opening their doors, the *pop* of a rifle echoed from the woods at the western edge of the field. Leon froze in his tracks. Vogel snapped his head around. Past his idle machine, a group of men on horseback emerged from the trees. For a second he thought they might be retreating German cavalrymen and that one had accidentally discharged his weapon. Shadowed by the trees, it was just too hard to tell. Strangely, though, the profile of their helmets was wrong—they were too tall for German cavalry. They almost looked like the decorative helmets worn by the Dragoons and Cuirassiers of the French cavalry.

But Troësnes was miles back of the lines. French cavalry had no business being anywhere near there. When a narrow beam of orange sunlight cut through the trees, illuminating the shoulder of one of the riders, it hit Vogel like a punch in the mouth.

Holy shit those uniforms are blue!

"Leon, RUN!" he shouted.

Vogel finished his warning just as the French cavalry patrol opened fire. Bullets ripped through the LVG, which sat between Vogel and the men out to kill him. He hurried toward the parked cars to take cover, and watched in absolute shock as General von Kluck and his staff members emerged from the vehicles. The commanders of First Army had driven their staff cars directly into the advance of a French cavalry division.

The French patrol was raiding well behind the German lines, and by sheer accident had stumbled upon a potentially huge prize. The German officers who wore them drew their pistols. Those that did not had no choice but to hide.

Vogel ducked behind one of the cars. For the second time that day, he had no weapon with which to defend himself. He debated making a run for the woods on the aerodrome's eastern side, but the fear of catching a bullet in the back glued him in place. Adler, who could have escaped, instead dashed toward the line of automobiles. He slid on his knees, and ended up right alongside Vogel.

"Here," the oberleutnant said. He tossed Vogel a brand new Pistole Parabellum 1908 (or P.08) 9mm semiautomatic pistol, which was colloquially known as a Luger, the name of its designer. "It's already loaded," Adler said, "safety's on. Make sure you flick the catch off before you try and shoot someone. You've got one in the chamber and seven more in the magazine."

"Thank you, sir," Vogel replied. *Why in the hell would you charge in this direction Adler? You could have made it out of here.* He might have thought the oberleutnant a fool for returning, but was sure glad the man came bearing gifts.

The shiny black Luger, with its distinctive angled grip, thin barrel and jointed cocking arm, was the first of its type Vogel had ever held. Grasping the brown walnut grip with his right hand, he manipulated the weapon, getting a feel for its weight. As an airman, he'd never envisioned himself having to fight for his life, yet there he was, holding a firearm and about to use it. He slid his thumb above the grip, and flicked the safety switch to the off position.

The men from the staff cars formed a firing line, attempting to keep the French cavalry at a distance. It was a unique sight to behold. First Army's commanders, unexpectedly locked in a life or death fight, knelt in the grass and dirt behind their fancy automobiles. Their elaborate uniforms, with heavy braiding, medals and ribbons on the chest and tasseled epaulettes on the shoulders, were utterly impractical in every regard. Their garb represented the epitome of form over function, and now the gaudy and expensive costumes were getting dirty. Vogel hoped the dirt would not soon turn to blood.

Leon had run to FFA 12's small weapons cache when he saw the horsemen emerge from the tree line. Like Adler, he also bravely returned, and was carrying an armful of rifles. Other mechanics joined him, and brought more rifles. They dispersed the weapons amongst the men of Kluck's staff. Each mechanic kept one for himself. They joined the fight, side by side with obersts and generals.

On an ordinary day, such a thing would have been unheard of. The lowly mechanics rested their greasy elbows on the expensive cars and took aim. The lowest ranking men in the army stood side by side with the highest, their lives fully dependent on their cooperation with one another. Formality went out the door with death on the line.

Other pilots and observers from FFA 12 who'd been on the aerodrome also joined the fight. Vogel and Adler both began discharging their Lugers at the French. Adler yanked several extra magazines from his coat pocket and slapped them onto the hood of the car. A rifle round zipped between the two men and a hail of bullets pinged into the car's opposite side.

The fancy automobiles, worth more money than Vogel wanted to know, had already been shot full of holes. The men ducked behind those cars were in quite the jam, highly outnumbered by mounted troops. Vogel feared he was about to die, having failed to protect General von Kluck from the enemy. *I will go down in history as one of the idiots who got Alexander von Kluck killed or captured. If we lose the war, the men of Feldflieger Abteilung 12 will be the scapegoats.*

Vogel fired the last of his magazine, and slid the empty clip from the pistol butt, quickly jamming in a fresh one. As he reloaded, the six foot tall Adler clamped a heavy hand on his shoulder and shoved him into a crouching position behind the front tire of the staff car.

"Get your ass down, Vogel!" the oberleutnant shouted.

Adler crouched beside him just as a machine gun burst riddled the car. Shattered window glass sprinkled around them, jettisoned away from the bullet impacts like crystalline shrapnel. *I didn't see that gun at all. Adler just saved my life.* The French machine gunner sprayed his fire indiscriminately, peppering the line of cars and the dirt in front of them. A mechanic behind the next car over was hit in the shoulder. He dropped his rifle and fell onto his back, shouting in pain.

Bullets shredded Vogel's LVG, caught in the open with no one to protect her. He was more concerned for his life, but he hadn't forgotten about his machine. "Stop shooting my aeroplane you hairy cocksuckers!" he screamed in anger, as he cowered behind the automobile, shielding himself from the pelting glass. He raised the pistol over his head and blindly fired over the hood of the car.

"Don't waste your bullets, for fuck's sake!" Adler scolded him.

With such paltry numbers, they would not be able to hold off the French for much longer. Soon they'd be overrun, the general and his officers, captured. A vision flashed into Vogel's mind of a French Dragoon, still on horseback, running him down and cleaving his head from his body with one saber stroke. But just as the French cavalry had benefited from sheer luck in catching First Army's staff off-guard, so would First Army's staff, and by extension the men of FFA 12, benefit from a spot of luck as well.

Vogel and Adler had their backs against the car. They faced the forest at the eastern edge of the aerodrome. Both were surprised to see a small group of German infantrymen emerge from the tree line. The men moved with purpose. The two airmen glanced at one another curiously for only a second, before turning their attention back eastward. Vogel's jaw dropped at what came next. He watched in shock as the small group of infantrymen grew into a grey tidal wave of charging German soldiers, pouring out of the woods in a steady stream.

The men of Arnold von Bauer's 17th Infantry Division stormed out of the forest and headed straight for the French cavalrymen. General von Bauer's troops dashed across the aerodrome with fixed bayonets, and their furious charge pushed the French cavalry back. The arrival of the 17th Division saved the day for von Kluck, his staff, and those on the aerodrome, and hit the French cavalry patrol so hard that by the time it finally made its escape, it had lost close to half its men.

After about an hour, the German division had chased the French far enough westward that the atmosphere on the aerodrome began to calm. One of von Kluck's staff officers asked Hauptmann von Detten to assemble the pilots, observers and mechanics of FFA 12 near Vogel's tattered aeroplane, which still sat in the middle of the field. Detten ordered the mechanics to line up near the machine's tail, and the pilot-observer teams to stand together near the LVG's nose. A few minutes later, General Alexander von Kluck himself made his way toward the waiting personnel.

The general was of average height. At sixty-eight years old, he'd lost most of his hair. The hair he had left was short, white and confined to the sides and back of his round head. His moustache was a darker grey, and was trimmed at the edges of his mouth.

Though he'd just been in a firefight, his uniform was immaculate. His shoulder boards, two thick gold cords braided around one silver, had two diamond pips. The golden tassels dangling from the bullion fringes of his shoulder boards were crammed so tightly together they resembled armor, though they were anything but. The front sides of the collar on his dark grey tunic had decorative red patches with golden embroidering, and his chest was adorned with a menagerie of ribbons and medals.

His sleeve cuffs were equally fancy, with golden buttons emerging through red and gold embroidered patches similar to his collar. Like all officers, he wore riding breeches, and his black, knee high leather boots had not a scuff on them. His sword, in an elaborate scabbard, hung from his hip. Vogel shuddered on the inside to think how much money the general wore on his body. His sword alone was probably worth more than every article of clothing the men of FFA 12 owned.

Kluck personally thanked each of the men for their bravery in holding off the French assault. One mechanic had been killed, and several more wounded in their defense of von Kluck and his staff. Vogel's LVG, its fabric riddled with holes and its engine and controls shot to pieces, would have to be written off and replaced, as it was far too damaged to repair. Until a replacement could be sent, Vogel and Adler would remain grounded. After General von Kluck addressed the group, he turned his attention to the damaged aeroplane.

"And whose flying machine do we stand next to?" asked the general.

"Ours, sir," Vogel and Adler answered in unison.

The general stepped toward them, resting his right hand on the hilt of his sword. "The rest of you may disperse, thank you," Kluck said to the others.

They all clicked their heels and saluted, then began to wander away, exhausted. Hauptmann von Detten likewise saluted the general and made his way toward a group of staff officers gathered near the vehicles. Members of FFA 12's support staff were cleaning the broken glass from the insides of the cars.

"I recognize you two," von Kluck said to Vogel and Adler. "You were positioned three cars away from me. You're a fine pair in a fight."

Adler and I, a fine pair? Whatever you say, sir.

The general looked directly at Vogel, eyeing him briefly from head to toe before fixating on his chin. "Where did you get that scar, young flieger?"

Adler lowered his head, probably trying his best not to laugh.

What is it with Prussians and my chin?

"A fall while horseback riding, sir," Vogel answered. "When I was a boy."

"Ah, I see," the general said. "No cavalry for you then, I suppose." He had an almost boyish grin on his face. The aeroplane had only just been invented when von Kluck was fifty-seven years old. Vogel was certain the old general did not place as much stock in air reconnaissance as he did in the cavalry.

"No sir," Vogel replied. "Not unless horses learn to fly."

"And stop bucking young riders," Kluck said.

"Yes sir."

The general smiled. "Well, gentlemen," he said, "Thank you again for your service. We'll be sure to get you a new flying machine in short order."

"Thank you, sir," they both replied.

"Sir, if I may?" Adler said, before Kluck walked away. "There is a large gap between First and Second Army, and the British and French have advanced into it. They are driving a wedge between yours and General von Bülow's forces, sir."

Kluck nodded once. "I'm aware, oberleutnant. Our attack west of the Ourcq is forcing the French back on Paris, and their threat to our flank is diminishing. As soon as we've pushed them back far enough we'll respond to the British and French there. Thank you for addressing the matter."

"Yes sir," Adler said. He and Vogel saluted, and General Alexander von Kluck left them, to converse with his staff.

DENIS

Denis woke early on the morning of September 9 to the sound of whispers. His men were already awake and wearing their gear, conversing with one another and laughing quietly. He smelled coffee. It pleased him to know their morale was holding up so well. Not all squad leaders were as fortunate, or even had as many of their men left. He yawned and rubbed the crusted sleep from his itchy eyes. Dew had accumulated on the ground and dampened his clothes, yet did not trouble itself to moisten his eyes.

"Ah, Denis!" Patrice exclaimed, raising his arms in the air. "You're up!"

"I am," Denis replied, spitting a foul taste from his mouth. "How long have you men been awake?"

"Thirty minutes or so. Since we're about to grab the boche by their scrotums and give them a twist, we wanted to be ready for it." Patrice picked up his Lebel, grasping the stock with his right hand and the barrel with his left. He brought the gun to his lips and gave it a smooch.

"That's fine fighting spirit," Denis commented proudly. "Thank you, gentlemen."

"No thanks are necessary sir," Thierry replied, "we're fine fighting men!"

"Hear! Hear!" said the others, and they raised their drinking cups.

"Indeed you are," Denis said.

They'd already eaten, but Denis was hungry. Nicolas made the coffee, which he'd burned. Denis ate a biscuit and drank what was left of the coffee. It was bitter, but it woke him up and made his damp uniform feel less uncomfortable. After he'd packed his gear and thrown on his haversack with an assist from Patrice, Denis and 2 Escouade were ready to march.

While the other sections gathered themselves, Capitaine Bex moved from squad to squad, making sure the men of F Compagnie were aware of just what was at stake. When Bex reached the squads of 2 Section, he first spoke with Lieutenant Armistead, nearer to where the men of 1 Escouade sat. Denis could not hear what they said to one another, but when Armistead looked down at his feet and Bex patted him on the shoulder, Denis knew whatever it was the capitaine said, it had not been taken as good news. Sergent Chouinard, seated with 1 Escouade and most likely eavesdropping, also appeared dejected after Bex spoke, though the conversation was not intended for his consumption.

Armistead collected himself and tugged on the front skirts of his tunic. He raised his chin. Following their exchange, the two officers stood with 1 Escouade for a short period, with Bex doing the talking. Denis watched Chouinard to gauge any reaction the sergent might have, but as soon as the capitaine and lieutenant finished their conversation and turned to speak to the squad, the big sergent perked up and pretended he hadn't heard whatever it was he'd gleaned. The telling moment came when the officers moved in the direction of 2 Escouade. As soon as their backs were turned, Chouinard shook his head and brought his hands to his face.

What in the world did he hear?

"Good morning Aspirant Roux," the capitaine said. He nodded to the rest of the squad, who stood at attention. "Gentlemen."

"Good morning, Capitaine," they answered as one.

"As you were," Bex said.

Armistead stood mute alongside Bex. The strain of the first three weeks of war had already reaped most of what it could from the twenty-six year old lieutenant. He was not a high-ranking officer—lieutenants fought right in the thick of things. They saw the death up close, and dished it out when they had to. Responsibility to a section meant its commander knew each and every man beneath him, and Armistead was no exception. He'd suffered the loss of far more men than Denis had, and it showed on his gaunt, sunburned face.

"Men," Capitaine Bex said, looking into the eyes of each man, "You're all fully aware of the significance of our actions this day. GQG has asked much of you already, but today you must give them, give

216

me, that much more. You are tired, but so is the enemy, and unlike you, he does not fight for his very home. Should we strike with enough ferocity today, we may just break his desire to continue the fight. Steel yourselves gentlemen, we march in fifteen minutes."

"Yes sir," 2 Escouade answered softly. When Bex and Armistead had moved far enough away, the men looked at one another concernedly.

Denis did not envy the capitaine; at the company level an officer bore responsibility for more than two hundred men. F Compagnie had sixteen squads. Sixteen different groups which Bex would address individually. He had to look into the faces of that many men, knowing they would not all be there when the battle was finished.

Denis was still curious about the capitaine's exchange with Armistead. He sauntered over to Sergent Chouinard, to find out what he'd heard. The big man sat on his haversack, resting his arms on his knees, his head slumped forward, gingerly cradling his busted hand.

"Sergent, what did Bex say?"

Chouinard lifted his head. "What? Oh, nothing. Probably the same thing he said to you and your men."

"No, I mean what did you hear him say to the lieutenant? I saw your reaction."

"Shit..." the sergent mumbled.

He leaned toward Denis and beckoned him closer. Whatever he had to say, he didn't want 1 Escouade to hear it. Denis crouched in close to Chouinard. He still stunk like shit.

"An airman reported the boche ahead of us have artillery batteries in place, and in a strong position. Whatever ground we've taken back thus far, they're not going to give us any more. We're about to walk straight into cannon fire."

"Oh..." Denis replied, and he looked down to his feet just as Armistead and Chouinard had done. "I guess I understand why he didn't share that with us. I'd rather not have known."

"Yes..." Chouinard trailed off, disinterested in saying any more.

Shortly thereafter, the bulk of XVIII Corps began an advance toward the Petit Morin, southwest of Montmirail. General von Bülow had pulled his forces behind the river, and General Karl von Einem's VII Korps waited at the ready, prepared for battle with Général d'Esperey's troops.

The shelling from the German artillery began with a round which overshot Denis's squad by several hundred yards. They heard it sail well overhead, and seconds later the battlefield erupted with the rumbling cacophony of field cannons and howitzers, firing from well beyond the river's northern bank. The Petit Morin had yet to come into view. It would only be a matter of minutes before the boche gunners found their range.

It didn't matter that the first shells were overshoots; the psychological effect of whistling howitzer shells and booming explosions made all but the hardest men tense, no matter where each round fell. The act of marching toward such destructive power flew in the very face of rationality, yet millions of Europe's finest soldiers, from all sides, continued to do it time and again. It was unsustainable.

National pride meant something, orders did too, but pride and duty alone could not hold a man's mind together indefinitely. Sooner or later the shock of watching friends losing limbs or getting blown to smithereens would lead any man to think the next shell had chosen him. Denis wasn't there yet, but a glance down the line at his men revealed a group of soldiers fraught with anxiety. Vincent mumbled to himself, Paul appeared to be praying, and Thierry and Nicolas briefly grasped one another's hands. They may have kept their spirits high leading up to it, but they were afraid, and rightly so.

"Denis, tell me we'll make it out of this one," Patrice said, just loud enough for him to hear.

"I can't make any prom—"

Whistle blows shrieked over the shell explosions, interrupting Denis before he could answer. Sergent Chouinard shouted the order to fix bayonets and then he cried, "FORWARD!"

Frightened or not, the duty-bound men obeyed. They drew their twenty-inch *Rosalies*, and snapped them to the ends of their rifles.

The four squads of 2 Section began to move with added vigor, and soon all men within Denis's field of vision had likewise hastened their step at the behest of their section commanders. The faster they moved, the harder it was for the German guns to hit them. The line of advancing Frenchmen rumbled forth, and within thirty seconds their advance turned into a furious charge. The men roared, convincing themselves to follow through, despite the insanity. Denis clutched his Lebel tightly to his chest. The poilus streaked ahead, rifles ready to fire as soon as the boche came into view.

The whistling shells and explosions were getting closer, spraying dirt, grass, bits of rock and shrapnel at the charging Frenchmen. As Denis rushed across the open, grassy expanse toward the banks of the Petit Morin, the shockwaves from bursting shells *whooshed* by him. The pressure waves from nearer blasts hurt his eardrums. He flinched when the air thumped against his body, drumming inside his hollow belly. Running hard, shielding their faces from flying debris, 2 Escouade pushed on, keeping abreast with the other squads.

Then it happened. It came in an instant, but to Denis, the moment took place in distinct frames, like separate flashes within a tiny increment of time, captured and frozen by his senses in living photographs.

FOOM! A shell sailed directly at his squad. It was much too fast for any of them to react, or to even conceive of reacting.

CRUMP! The shell buried itself in the dirt twenty feet to Denis's right and exploded just inches from Isaac's feet. There was a bright but extraordinarily brief burst of light. The earth erupted.

The blast wave felt like a giant hand, which swatted the entire right side of Denis's body. The pressure made his right ear feel as if his brain had sprayed through his ear canal. When the blast wave hit him, his feet left the ground and his body was lifted unevenly into the air and pushed away from the explosion. His momentum carried him forward. He crashed back to the ground. His left shoulder and head landed first. The ground was hard, dried out from the baking sun. It offered no cushion. Everything went black.

Denis opened his eyes after an indeterminate amount of time. He was dizzy and disoriented, and lying on his stomach. The world swirled around him and a painful whirring noise in his head drowned out the sounds of the raging battle, wherever it was. His left cheek itched from the crinkly dead grass beneath it, and one of the blades poked into his left eye.

Breathing was extremely difficult, as if someone had kicked him in the ribs. His head pulsed with every rapid beat of his heart. Subconsciously, he knew what happened, but outwardly, he struggled to come to grips with it. *Why am I lying in this crusty grass? How long have I been here? Am I hurt? Have I lost any limbs? Where are my men? Where's Patrice?*

"Patrice..." he groaned.

Patrice had been on Denis's left side, which placed him a few feet further away from the explosion. The blast wave had knocked him off his feet as well, and had turned him sideways, causing him to land on his back and skid to a stop. The back of his head had bounced off the ground; he'd been unconscious, too. Only slightly less shocked and disoriented, he sat up and crawled to where Denis lay.

"Are you hurt, Denis? You must get up!"

"How long have I been lying here?"

"I don't know!"

"Where...Where are the rest of the men?"

"They're fucking dead, Denis!"

"Who's dead?!"

"Everyone!"

219

With blurred vision, and unaware he'd been unconscious for minutes, Denis scanned the area toward the river, where he thought his advancing men should be. No one was there, save for scattered wounded. In making an effort to sit up, he looked at the ground next to him. There, lying right next to his leg, was an arm, still wrapped in a blue coat sleeve, its detached end a stringy mess of skin and bloody flesh. He didn't know whose arm it was.

Patrice helped him to his knees. When he spotted a crater thirty-five feet away, with slain men in blue and red scattered around it, Denis began to grasp exactly how devastating the shell had been to his squad.

Isaac was just gone. Disappeared. If anything was left of him, it was little more than shredded bits of cloth, tattered canvas, and indiscernible globs of skin, guts and bone. Thierry's legs were missing—his right from the hip and his left from the knee. He'd already bled out. Paul's head had been blown almost clean off, along with his left arm and shoulder. Denis did not want to know or see where Paul's head, or what remained of it, had landed.

Vincent was also missing his legs. He'd lived for a few moments after the blast, confused and afraid, but too shocked by the impact to fully grasp he was dying. Denis could tell that, because Vincent had tried to drag himself away, and his exploded legs left two trails of blood in the yellow grass. Nicolas and Richard were so riddled with shrapnel the sides of their bodies that faced the blast were just ragged cloth and mangled, dark red mush. Emery and Gustav were nowhere to be found, but since they'd been on Patrice's left, Denis assumed in the heat of battle they'd continued their charge along with the rest of the line.

In pain, Denis and Patrice stood. The confusion and delirium from their severe concussions began wearing off, though their pulsing headaches and body aches lingered. They were scraped and bruised, covered in dirt, and unable to hear with their right ears, both of which had a small trickle of blood encrusted on the earlobe. They limped toward the Petit Morin, arms wrapped around one another. Thousands of popping rifles and machine guns chattered in the distance, beyond the river. They were now well behind the 2nd Bataillon's advance, which had just made contact with the German infantry. In that moment, Denis and Patrice were in no condition to take up rifles and participate.

The dead and wounded were scattered for hundreds of yards across the field, leading right up to the Petit Morin's southern bank. Medical personnel tended to some, but the casualties were overwhelming. When the dizziness and ringing in their ears died down, the two friends came to terms that they would not play a part in the combat that day. Instead, they would try to help those whose wounds were much worse than their own. If there was time later, they might assist in the burial of their 2 Escouade brothers, but only after helping those who could still be helped.

The Great War was taking friends from everyone, on all sides. Accepting loss was essential for the psyches of all who were involved. Those who could not cope with loss fell apart. Those who could cope remembered those they lost, and fought on for those still with them. For Denis and Patrice, the shock of knowing that their friends had just died a gruesome death rapidly began to subside, not because they were callous, but because it had to. Others needed their help. Denis knew he must push on, but as he limped across the field a thought nagged at him. Apart from Patrice, and hopefully Emery and Gustav, his entire squad had been destroyed in less than a month. *What sort of leader is the soldier who sees all but three of his men killed? How will anyone trust me to lead them now?*

"Denis! Come and help me carry this man!" Patrice called out from a short distance away. His voice sounded muffled and quiet. Denis's ears still suffered from the blast. He limped over as quickly as his roughed-up body would go.

The poilu lying at Patrice's feet groaned. He was a 4 Section man, wounded in the stomach, and he couldn't move his legs. They'd have to carry him to the aid post the medical troops would have established somewhere behind the advance. Like so many terrified and gravely wounded men, he'd pissed himself.

"What's your name, friend?" asked Denis.

"Em...manuel," whispered the man. "They got me..."

"Yes, they got you," Denis said, "But now we've got you, and we'll get you some help."

The front of Emmanuel's tunic and his face were smeared with bloody vomit. He smelled terrible—a mix of piss, sweat, shit and puke, and Denis gagged. He felt guilty for gagging, but the combination of his pounding headache, the fear, the adrenaline, the shock, so much gore and death and the sour smell of bloody throw up had conspired to churn the contents of his stomach. He quit breathing through his nose, to dampen the stench.

"All right Emmanuel," Denis said, "we must pick you up and carry you to a surgeon." In pain himself, he dreaded having to carry the man, but he had to do his part for a fallen countryman. "You'll be just fine. Ready Patrice? One, two, lift!"

Denis grabbed Emmanuel underneath the armpits and Patrice held him by the ankles. There was no movement whatsoever in his legs and they were wet with piss, making them heavy and difficult to hold onto as they carried him. At one point Patrice's hands slipped, and he dropped the poor soldier's legs. Denis maintained his grip on the man's armpits, but the extra weight caused him to fall backwards, jarring the injured poilu and furthering his agony. He groaned and vomited more blood.

With great effort, they eventually got Emmanuel to the aid post. Many wounded had already been brought back by stretcher bearers and other infantrymen with minor injuries. Hundreds of casualties, mostly shrapnel wounds of a wide range of severity, stood, sat or lay scattered about in no discernible order, awaiting their turn.

"Can we get some help, please?!" Denis cried, out of both concern for the young man, and because his leg and back muscles were on fire.

"They got me..." Emmanuel mumbled again.

"I know they did, Emmanuel..."

An older man in his mid-fifties reached them first. A medical officer, he wore the dark blue officer's tunic and red trousers—both stained with fresh blood. A white brassard with a red cross was wrapped around his upper left arm. "I see he's wounded in the abdomen," he said. "Was it a bullet or shrapnel?"

"We're not sure," replied Denis, "but he can't move his legs."

"Has he an exit wound on his back?"

"I don't know, sir."

"You," the officer pointed a finger at Patrice, "place your hand on the skin of his lower back and feel for an exit wound. Please continue to prop him up, Aspirant."

Patrice reluctantly let go of Emmanuel's legs and reached his hand behind the man's back. Twisting his neck to look away as he concentrated on his blind search, Patrice bit his top teeth over his bottom lip. His contorted face was the picture of grossed-out focus.

"They got me...they got me..."

"Well?" the officer asked impatiently.

"I can't find anything," Patrice answered, pulling his arm back. There was no more blood on his hand than before.

"Then whatever hit him is still inside his abdomen. We'll need to get him further back to the brigade station. The facilities here are not well-suited for this type of surgery."

"Where should we put him, sir?" asked Denis.

"See that wagon over there?" the officer pointed to an empty wagon with a beautiful brown and white filly waiting patiently in front. "Place him in the wagon bed and he'll be carried away to surgery shortly." With that, the medical officer walked away with businesslike determination.

Emmanuel had faded in and out of consciousness all the way to the aid post, but his wheezing breaths let Denis know that carrying him was still worth the effort. They lugged him to the wagon and gently lay him flat on his back. The last vestiges of color had drained from his face and the young soldier, in shock and delirious, raised two clumsy hands in the air and weakly swung them at Denis and Patrice.

"Hey, take it easy Emmanuel," Denis said, dodging the slow hands. "This wagon will take you to surgery, all right?"

"They got me….they got me…"

"He's not going to answer you," Patrice murmured. "We've done our part. We can do no more for him."

"You're right," agreed Denis. He firmly grabbed the wounded man's hand, squeezing it tight. "Good luck to you, Emmanuel."

"They…got…"

"I know they did. But we'll get them back."

Denis walked to the front of the wagon, and ran his hand across the big horse's shoulder, neck and muzzle. The animal leaned her head forward and snorted once, wiggling her head left and right.

"That's a good girl," he said, stroking her muzzle. He had trained with horses at Saint-Cyr, but as an infantryman on the front lines he had much less contact with them. He saw plenty of the majestic animals between battles, though; they were used for just about everything. Capitaine Bex occasionally rode, but Denis had not been close enough to a horse to touch one in a while. He loved horses, and it relaxed him to be near the animal. The creature had no murderous intent, just a willingness to do what was asked of her, and she'd do it whether the environment was dead calm or she was surrounded by bullets and explosions. That day, her task would be to play her part in saving Emmanuel's life.

She made Denis wonder. Was bravery a purely human construct? What about valiance? Animals did not wage war, yet horses were forced by their masters to play an integral role, and they never complained. Knowing how hard life was for the horses and other pack animals, Denis pitied the large, healthy filly. Unless the war came to an abrupt halt, she probably would not look that way in a few months, if she was still around then.

"All right, sweetheart, my friend and I must be going," Denis said, and he patted her muzzle one last time. He rejoined Patrice at the back of the wagon.

"My God, Denis, look at these men." Patrice pointed to a jumble of corpses, piled atop one another. Each body was missing at least one limb. None of their uniforms had a square inch of fabric that wasn't drenched in blood. Even the grass surrounding the bodies was saturated. They'd been carried there alive, but died before anything could be done. The cadavers' gaping eyes and mouths were an open invitation for flies, and the obnoxious little bugs had already started to collect and feast. Pests wasted no time.

Another poor boy lay in a stretcher on the ground beside a second wagon, only about ten feet from the pile of corpses. He held his bloody hands over his stomach. Denis saw the pinkish intestines sticking out between the boy's fingers—he was trying to hold his own guts inside his belly. The boy stared at the sky, too afraid to look at the viscera protruding out of him.

I bet he turned eighteen years old within the last six months. Now he'll probably die. Thinking he might comfort the younger soldier, Denis approached him, while Patrice aimlessly wandered off, stunned by the day's carnage.

"Hello friend, what's your name?" Denis asked the young soldier.

The boy's eyes remained fixed skyward, and he did not answer. He breathed slow and shallow, probably fearing that breathing too hard might push his guts out further. It very well could have. Tears trickled from the corners of his eyes and fell into his ears.

Denis had never met him before, did not even recall seeing him previously, but the boy's insignia showed he was from 2nd Bataillon's D Compagnie, and he could not have been more than a few hundred yards away during most of their skirmishes. The age gap between them was only five years at the most—Denis was just twenty-three—but the teary young soldier made Denis want to kneel down and hug him, as a father would his child. That was a human being laying there, someone's child, young and frightened, swept up in a conflict he played no part in bringing about.

"Has anyone tried to help you?" Denis asked.

No answer.

"I'll go find someone."

There were many others who needed caring for, and only so many medics and surgeons, but a boy with his intestines hanging out should have had priority. Denis walked away, unsure whether or not the boy had heard him.

He again passed Emmanuel, still lying in the wagon but now accompanied by a medic. The shock of being badly wounded had begun to wear off, and Emmanuel screamed at the top of his lungs, maddened by the pain and the inability to move his legs. His wagon companion held his arms down and begged him to calm down. Even if he survived surgery, the high potential for infection, and months upon months of recuperation, he'd still be crippled until the day he died.

It took almost five minutes to find a medic who wasn't already in the middle of tending a severe casualty. Said man had just finished wrapping a bandage around a sergent's eyes when Denis spotted him. If the blood on the exposed part of the sergent's face was any indication, there probably were no eyes left beneath the bandages.

"Excuse me, but I've found a man who is in serious need of attention," Denis said to the medic. He gestured for him to follow. The medic wore the same infantryman's greatcoat and trousers as Denis, but had the white medical brassard wrapped around his left arm.

"Yes sir," the medic answered. He wiped the blood from his hands on the skirts of his greatcoat. He followed Denis back to the injured boy. They passed the spot where Emmanuel's wagon had been—it was gone. The big filly had finally received her task. Fifty yards away, Denis saw her head and neck over the top of the wagon and driver as she trotted away, her brown mane swaying to and fro.

The boy still lay in the stretcher next to the wagon; he hadn't moved an inch and continued clutching his belly. "There he is," Denis said, pointing at him. The medic pushed past, and took a knee next to the stretcher. He reached for and held the young man's wrist for several seconds, then let go of the wrist and placed his middle and index fingers against the boy's neck. He waited another ten seconds, then the medic turned to Denis and said, "This boy is dead, sir. I'm sorry."

Dammit.

He didn't reply, not with words, but Denis's face said everything. The medic stood up, to find someone else to help. He patted Denis once on the shoulder as he walked past.

Patrice eventually found his way back. Having seen far too much, he teetered on the edge of tears. He and Denis meandered away from the aid post, not entirely sure what they needed to do next. At the most, 2 Escouade had just five men left counting the absent Maurice, and Emery and Gustav could very well have been killed after crossing the Petit Morin.

"Will everyone eventually die in this war?" Patrice asked quietly. His voice still sounded muffled.

"I don't know Pat, but if it continues at this pace for much longer, I don't like our chances." There was no need to mince words. In such large-scale engagements, thousands of men died each day. Percentages caught up. Charging into artillery and machine guns was a game of chance, and nothing more. "Someone will have to be left standing at the end."

"The last man left, king of Europe," Patrice mused. "With a hundred million women in his harem."

"Won't he be lucky..."

"Christ in Heaven, I've not even sent any letters to Cécile," Patrice complained, shaking his head. "The boche will do me in long before I ever see her again."

"Why don't you write to her?" Denis said. "At least you know where she is. I've no idea where my parents and sister are, or whether or not they're even safe." He didn't necessarily want to downplay his friend's concern, but felt justified in offering perspective.

"Actually I've been...Ah...You're right, Denis," Patrice replied. "I shouldn't complain when your situation is much more difficult. Besides..." he hinted at a smile, though his eyes were still glossy. "I don't know Cécile's address!"

Denis stared at him blankly, astounded. "Are you joking?"

"No."

"So you find a girl, a nice one, you go off to war, and you don't bother to get her address before you leave?"

A hangdog grin spread across the green-eyed man's scratched and dirty face. The tears seemed ready to fall from his eyes, but they didn't. He hadn't done anything wrong in the conventional sense; he'd just proven himself flippant as ever. "I just forgot..." he said.

"You went to her house once, did you not?"

"Yes. I walked there with her."

"And you saw no street signs? Landmarks?"

Patrice puffed his cheeks and blew out a long breath of air. His eyes rolled up and to the left. "The...cemetery...maybe?"

"Maybe?"

"Is that what you'd be paying attention to if you were walking alongside her?"

"I certainly think I could maintain my focus on her and still know where I was."

"Well good for you. I was busy staring at her tits, and wondering what they looked like underneath her dress."

"You know she probably thinks you're dead," Denis admonished him. "I bet the poor girl checks the papers every day, hoping to find out what happened to her precious Patty." He had to throw the nickname in, to rib him a little.

Patrice frowned. "If she ever calls me Patty, that'll be the last time she hears of me."

Denis snorted. That he could muster even that after such a day was a positive sign.

VERNON

Dearest Sal,

I miss you so very much. It has been difficult to find time to write, as battle and endless marching in miserable heat has us all positively knackered. I feel my love for you may be the only thing keeping me alive. That, and protecting poor old Llewelyn. I'm worried about him. He's bringing up Daisy with some frequency. I fear the strain of battle and the sight of death serves as a constant reminder of losing her. His wits are still with him, though, so perhaps I look too deeply into it.

I hesitate to tell you, but I'd be remiss were I to keep anything from you. You will surely have read of our battle near Mons. What you will not have read concerns a close call I had during our retreat. It seems Fritz took a fancy to me and decided he preferred I not leave. As Lew and I made our escape I felt a knock by my hip. When we'd gotten away I found a proper bullet hole, straight through the middle of my water bottle. Not a day later, I had yet another close call, and who came to my rescue but Llewelyn Pritchard himself! Retreat was the story after that, no doubt you've read that too, and thirst nearly drove us all mad. I tell you, I've been thirsty before, but never have I been so parched as to think it might kill me.

Our boys are gritty beyond words. The battalion has lost many killed, wounded and captured, and our feet throb and bleed, but we march on. More and more suffer from illness, or collapse in the heat. We've marched from Belgium to the Seine, and have now turned right *back around to face Fritz again, yet our spirits remain high. We've proceeded slowly into a gap between two German armies, and are now poised smack between them. I think our cavalry boys had one or two dustups ahead of us and have captured bridges for their trouble, but we've yet to do more shooting just yet. I've heard whispers that Fritz has begun a retreat, but I can't say for sure whether that's true. Maybe they'll run all the way home.*

We've lost a lot of good chaps, but don't worry about your dearest Vernon. Pritchard watches out for me the same as I for him. It gets more difficult, seeing young boys die, but alas, it does not stop there. The horses suffer every strain we men do, and on top of it they've got no option to fight back. The poor creatures carry and pull so much of what we need, and all they'll get in return is a bullet to the head when they've finally broken down. I've seen hundreds blown to bits by artillery, and hundreds more lay dead on the sides of the roads, felled by thirst or exhaustion.

Horses with men on their backs are covered in open sores, and I find myself wondering why the riders cannot walk out of mercy for the animal. You can have one guess as to which officer treats his mount the worst. I've pondered sneaking away in the middle of the night just to let the captain's horse free. I apologize for painting such grim pictures for my beautiful wife, but such is my reality. All in all, this is a treacherous war we've gotten ourselves into. All my love.

A number of things converged to keep British casualties during the Battle of the Marne comparatively low. Field Marshal French's hesitance to thrust his troops into the fray certainly prevented what could have been larger-scale encounters. Additionally, the gap between German First and Second Army had opened because General von Kluck shifted forces from the south to the west. Those shifted troops were generally moving away from the British as they exploited the gap, so the slow pursuit allowed the Germans to outpace them. Location was probably the most significant limiter. The French Sixth Army's attack on von Kluck's right flank and French Fifth Army's attack on von Bülow's right flank were the two greatest threats in the Paris-Verdun Salient, and thus were the most hotly contested by the Germans.

The heaviest fighting between the British and Germans during the Marne campaign occurred at or near the river's bridges. German engineers managed to destroy upwards of ten bridges, but several more were seized by both the British 3rd and Sir Edmund Allenby's Cavalry Divisions, enabling river crossings at different points. Because General Pulteney's III Corps was on the BEF's left flank, they were the closest infantry to von Kluck's forces. They faced heavy fighting at La Ferté Sous Jouarre, but it paled in comparison to the massive collisions which took place between the French and Germans elsewhere.

Vernon and 1st Battalion did not fire a shot, nor did they have shots fired at them. That was not due to a lack of spirit on their part, as they and the rest of the BEF were ready to do what was asked of them. Indeed, the very act of transitioning from the chased to the chaser lifted their morale near to where it had been upon their arrival in France. Had a fight presented itself during the Marne campaign, they would have accepted the challenge and risen to face it.

That challenge would come within the week.

HENTSCH

General von Quast's IX Korps had reached the Ourcq on September 8 and taken position as the northernmost flank of Kluck's First Army. The next morning they advanced against the French 1st and 3rd Cavalry Divisions, forcing them back in the direction of Paris. After an artillery bombardment pushed back French IV Corps, Quast's IX Korps then fought the French 61st Reserve Division, which was compelled to fall back as well. During the French retreat, Hentsch found a good firing position and by his count scored four long-range kills, against the backs of retreating men. His ability to hold his hand steady under pressure made him an effective asset in combat, but with each pull of the trigger, the weight on his conscience grew.

September 10 arrived, and the prospects looked good. Even as he soured on the act of sanctioned murder, it occurred to Hentsch that if the French could just be forced into one final, major retreat, they might surrender, and the killing would stop. First Army stood within just twenty-five miles of Paris. They had their boot heel on France's throat. They were so close. It was unthinkable that the war might end in anything but French defeat. They needed to continue pushing Maunoury's Sixth Army back toward Paris, right onto the city's doorstep, and then bust down the door. They had the French on the run. So many of their countrymen had died to get them to where they stood. Paris was almost close enough to touch. Victory lay within reach.

"Attention men, we've been ordered to withdraw, forthwith!" Hauptmann Fleischer shouted. He sat atop his white and brown horse, in a half-gallop, having approached from the direction of III Bataillon headquarters. From the sound of Fleischer's voice, he was clearly dissatisfied.

Engel and Hentsch stood beside one another, and looked at each other quizzically as the hauptmann and his horse passed by. Officers and enlisted alike were confused by the hauptmann's words. In the back of his mind, Hentsch thought it might be some sort of bizarre joke, although Fleischer was not the humorous sort. *This cannot be. What is he talking about?*

"Why would we withdraw?" Simon inquired softly. "Did the French break through further south?" His voice cracked.

Simon's confusion was shared by everyone. Hands were placed on hips, arms folded across chests, and shoulders shrugged. Poor Simon wanted the fighting to end more than anyone. He absolutely hated the war. He missed his home, his family, his dog, and he was sick and tired of seeing lives end on both sides. Every man who died was somebody's loved one. The fighting had already taken thousands of husbands and sons. Children lost their fathers, older brothers and uncles.

Belgium and northeastern France had been destroyed, everyone knew that, and (almost) no one liked it, but all that sacrifice had to mean *something*—even Simon accepted that. The French *had* to surrender soon, or what was the point of all the killing and dying? Why else would von Kluck have marched them hundreds of miles through Belgium and France in the sweltering August heat, with everdwindling water and food supplies? Were they really about to concede even one more inch of hard-won territory?

"We must have been pushed back in the south," Kirsch mumbled. "It's the only plausible explanation." He and the rest of 2 Gruppe seemed too dumbfounded to grasp Fleischer's order, and did not make much of a ruckus. Other men in 1 Zug, though, did.

"We're not fucking retreating!" a man from 1 Gruppe bellowed.

"We're so close to Paris!" cried another. "This is bullshit!"

"What in the hell even happened?"

More 1 Zug voices joined the aggravated chorus, and soon the shouting grew so discordant that Oberleutnant Richter was forced into action just to quiet them down. "Quiet!" he barked. "You know nothing of the greater situation!"

Hentsch gritted his teeth. He had an idea what the greater situation was. Their westward shift from First Army's left flank to the right to face the French threat from Paris had done exactly what he feared. The BEF and French had exploited the very positions which IX Korps had vacated. He knew it would happen, command must have known it too, but what he could not know was how the situation had actually played out on the ground. He listened to Richter intently.

"Our orders are direct from Chief of Staff Moltke at the OHL," Richter said. "We are to retreat at once and reestablish contact with Second Army."

Engel slowly, dejectedly removed his pickelhaube from atop his head, a blank expression on his face. He held his battered and dirty helmet against his hip. His expression became yet another image that would stay with Hentsch for the rest of his days.

Engel appeared to age a decade in those few seconds. He was only twenty-eight, but had already lost a significant amount of hair, and had a pronounced widow's peak. Upon hearing the word *retreat*, every muscle in his face died all at once as a look of complete disappointment and total incomprehension overtook him. Even the hazel in his eyes faded and turned grey. His features sagged, his eyes drooped and his mouth fell open. Even his big ears drooped. He was at his ends.

"It's not true. Someone misunderstood an order," Engel murmured almost inaudibly. "We need to hold our positions until someone comes back with confirmation."

Hentsch didn't say anything. Direct orders from OHL were all the confirmation anyone was going to get. He shouldered his Mauser and turned his back to Paris and the retreating French. To the last, no infantryman in First Army could fathom what had happened. The threat to their right flank had been answered. They were poised to deal the finishing strike. What could possibly have gone wrong?

As it turned out, when General von Bülow realized the BEF and the left flank of French Fifth Army had exploited the gap between his and Kluck's Army, a lack of communication between the two generals caused Bülow to overreact. His fear of being completely cut off from First Army became one of a series of unfortunate circumstances which conspired to snatch victory from Germany's grasp.

For reasons unknown, when the war began, the decision was made to move Helmuth von Moltke and the OHL to Luxembourg, which kept them far from the front lines as the war progressed into September. Communication between the armies and OHL was pathetic—the cramped, unaccommodating headquarters at *Army Supreme Command* had just *one* telephone. One. The notion that one telephone was adequate for communication with the commanders of seven different army groups—spread over hundreds of miles, with literally millions of men relying on adequate coordination—was utterly preposterous. During the Battle of the Marne, proper communication might have led to a much different outcome.

Because of the lack of communication von Moltke—sickly, panicked and nearing total mental breakdown—sent one of his staff officers, Oberstleutnant (Lieutenant Colonel) Richard Hentsch (no relation to Augustus), on a tour of the battlefront on September 8, in order to ascertain how the war situation was unfolding directly from the mouths of his generals.

The oberstleutnant's tour brought him to the headquarters of Fifth, Fourth, and Third Armies, and eventually to General von Bülow's headquarters on the 9th. There, Bülow's assessment of the threat both to his army, and also to the threat posed by French Sixth Army engaging von Kluck's forces further west, convinced the oberstleutnant that immediate and drastic action was necessary. The fear was that the BEF might strike the rear flank of Kluck's army, thus crushing them between two allied forces. However, Kluck's maneuvering had already answered that threat (from Pulteney's III Corps). Any further attack from the BEF against First Army would have been met with a firm response.

While the gap between the two armies was dangerous, there existed a strong possibility that von Kluck's army could have defeated French Sixth Army in the west before turning more of its forces against the BEF and French armies to the east. In the event, after leaving Second Army, Richard Hentsch next traveled to First Army headquarters. Because of what he'd heard from Bülow, his mind had essentially been made up. Without bothering to speak to General von Kluck, instead opting to briefly speak to Kluck's chief of staff, Oberstleutnant Hentsch's appraisal of the situation upon his return to the OHL was dire.

And so, on September 10, Helmuth von Moltke and the OHL ordered all armies within the Paris-Verdun Salient to initiate a general retreat northward, to more strategically favorable positions. That was the order which the men of 1 Zug were so shocked to hear. They did not know the specifics, how could they? All they knew was that they were about to win the war, and that high command had suddenly told them to tuck their tails between their legs and run away.

"Why would General von Kluck obey this fucking order?!" shrieked Simon. "Does he not understand how close we are?!" The skinny, pale little soldier was not threatening when angry, and had the news not been so excruciatingly depressing, his reaction might have been funny. Hentsch understood how disappointed the poor young man must have been, and he shared in it. Wars did not end in victorious retreat. Simon would not be going home to his family within the next few weeks, as he likely had sincerely believed.

Engel was still dumbfounded. His head was hung low, but his frustration began to trickle out. "We should send a rider to brigade, or to General von Quast's headquarters, to tell them we're still prepared to attack," he said, looking up at Hentsch. "Maybe someone will listen. Maybe they'll contact General von Kluck and talk some sense into him. Maybe von Kluck can convince OHL to let us press on. Or maybe these generals are just too fucking far from the battlefield to make level-headed decisions! I hate this fucking war!" Engel whipped his arm back to throw his pickelhaube, but Hentsch grabbed his hand before he could. He had to say something before Engel completely lost his head. Luckily, the oberleutnant had walked away, or they would have already been getting an earful.

"The oberleutnant was right, we know nothing but what's in front of us. It could be far different elsewhere," Hentsch said, playing the voice of reason. "You've seen the aeroplanes above. They may have spotted things we'd never see from down here. What if the French moved reinforcements against us? Or the British sent more troops? Who knows, gentlemen? Maybe falling back saved our lives and we just don't know it yet."

"Yeah..." Michael said, speaking for the first time. "Or maybe falling back just won the war for the French." His dark eyes were black and menacing. Michael was an asshole, but even he could not have been anxious for the war to drag on any further, whether he enjoyed killing French and British or not.

"Honestly, I don't know," Hentsch said calmly. Deep down he was sickened by the news and every bit as furious as anyone else, but rage would not change their situation. "Perhaps we'll counterattack as soon as we've regrouped."

"No, now we'll just keep getting shot up and bled away by the fucking frogs and lords," Michael said. He snarled and his forehead crinkled. His eyes became narrow, black slits and he muttered, "If I ever meet the men responsible for this retreat..." He reached for his bayonet. "...I'll run a knife right through them." Michael slapped the flat side of the blade against his palm.

Now he threatens high-ranking commanders. He's out of his mind. "Don't speak of such foolishness out loud, Michael," Hentsch scolded. "If the wrong ears were to hear, you'd be court-martialed for sure." *Though that might not be such a bad thing.*

First Army fell back, albeit unwillingly. Exhausted and still reeling from the Battle of the Frontiers, the French and British did not enthusiastically pursue. Stalling just short of Paris, and ending in retreat at the Battle of the Marne, Germany's Schlieffen Plan had failed. If the Great War was to be won by Germany, it would have to be won another way.

At the Marne, the German armies inflicted shocking casualties against the French, who suffered close to a hundred thousand sick, wounded, dead or missing. The British, even in their lesser role, still lost 1,700 men. German casualties were just over 99,000, with many thousands captured.

The "Miracle of the Marne" halted the German momentum and saved France from defeat. Less a miracle and more the confluence of renewed Entente spirit in the face of an exhausted and uncoordinated German defense, the allied victory at the Battle of the Marne ensured the Great War would not be resolved by any plans conceived beforehand. To consider the outcome of the battle a miracle, which implied the involvement of divinity, detracted from the monstrous effort and strength of will put forth by the French, British and German forces alike. There was no divinity in the killing or wounding of hundreds of thousands, and the prolonging of an already devastating war.

BERTHOLD

"Hey gents, I just spoke with men from the supply column," Weber said, as he trotted on horseback toward Gun Number 6 and the crew. "They told me they heard the Russians are kicking the shit out of the Austrians." Weber had just returned from the supply column, further back in the line. He'd taken the horse to pick up an extra bag of oats, in order to feed the horse team.

"What do you mean?" asked Berthold. "How bad is it in the south?"

"Apparently over the past two weeks, the fighting has been severe, and the Russians have captured many prisoners," Weber answered. He dismounted the scruffy, reddish-brown horse, and then tugged the heavy burlap bag of oats from the animal's back, dropping it to the ground. A puff of white dust rose from the bag when it landed.

"How do you know the supply guys aren't full of it?" Roth asked, probably viewing Weber's revelation as little more than worthless gossip.

"I don't know, Roth," Weber shot back. "But why would they want to lie about something like that? What's the point?"

Berthold turned his head from one man to the other during the exchange. Weber continued the discussion while guiding the horse by its reins toward the other animals.

"Who knows?" replied Roth, "maybe they're just assholes." The rest of the crew listened, half-amused, but also half-concerned that Weber spoke the truth.

"Oh yes, that makes perfect sense, Roth," Weber derided, "they've got nothing better to do than conjure stories about our staunchest ally. And such funny stories to spin, they are, considering it's taking place just a few hundred miles south of here."

Lang jumped in to interrupt them. "We've got more important things to worry about than the Austrians, gentlemen. We may be in our pal Rennenkampf's path again very soon. You can worry about what's going on in the south later."

"You're right, Lang," Weber agreed, "So fuck off, Roth!"

The men laughed at the youngest, skinniest crewman running his mouth to his polar opposite. Roth did not trouble himself to retort. Weber removed the horses' feeder bags from the trailer and poured some oats into each bag. He then strapped the bags onto the horses' muzzles. The column would move again soon, and the animals needed their energy.

After destroying Samsonov's Second Army, Hindenburg had immediately moved Eighth Army northeast, in the direction of Rennenkampf's First Army, which had withdrawn further east to a line extending from Königsberg in the north to the area around Angerburg and the Masurian Lakes to the south. Hindenburg ordered I Korps and XVII Korps to advance into the middle of the Masurian Lakes. He sent the 3rd Reserve Division south of the lakes to the city of Lyck, thirty miles south of Rennenkampf's left flank. The newly arrived Guards Reserve Korps and XI Korps, sent by Moltke from the Western Front (possibly to the detriment of the Schlieffen Plan), were sent north against Russian First Army's right flank, closer to Königsberg. XX Korps advanced against the center of Rennenkampf's lines.

The first attacks began on September 5, and were intended to hold the Russians' attention as Hindenburg moved his southern forces into position behind Rennenkampf's army. In the south, on the 7th, XVII Korps collided with Russian II Corps. After a day of clashes, the Russians positioned themselves to turn XVII Korps' left flank, but I Korps arrived from further south the next day and outflanked the Russians, pushing them back. Berthold and his crew did not factor in the battle, as advancing the artillery through the region fast enough to play a role proved difficult.

Rennenkampf simultaneously ordered a counteroffensive in the north, centered on German XX Korps, which subsequently retreated, attempting to draw the Russians further west just as they had done to Samsonov at Tannenberg. When news of the German forces advancing from the south reached Rennenkampf, he had no choice but to order a retreat to the east or face the same fate as his deceased counterpart.

That was where Berthold, his crew, and the 16th Feldartillerie-Regiment found themselves, trailing the advancing German infantry as they attempted to position their forces between the Russians and the Russian border. With the march resumed, the men of III Abteilung were struggling to help their horse teams pull the heavy gun carriages and equipment up a long, muddy hill. A heavy rain the day before had turned the roads into a soggy, slippery mess. The rain had since passed, and the weather turned hot and muggy. Tempers began to flare as the men inched their equipment up the hill.

"Come on you men!" Lang shouted. "Push!"

"We're pushing as hard as we can, Lang!" Hertz snapped back.

"Yeah, you loudmouthed dick!" cried Ostermann. "Back off!"

Berthold pushed with everything he had, digging his right shoulder and collarbone into the left corner of the gun's splinter shield. When the horses hauled the two-wheeled artillery trailer and gun, they were harnessed to the trailer, which subsequently had the gun carriage's trail hitched to it. During transport, the barrel aimed away from the direction of travel, thus Berthold pushed against the shield's face as it moved up the hill. Lang did the same, but on the right side, while Ostermann and Hertz pushed against the trailer. Roth Stood ahead of the horses, tugging on their reins, while Weber, as usual, sat in the driver's seat.

Tensing every muscle in his body, the pressure welled in Berthold's head as he strained against two tons of steel. For a moment he thought he felt his eyes bulge from their sockets. His boots slipped with every push. The gun moved just inches at a time. Due to the precarious position in which he stood, if the horses were to slip and the gun somehow came loose and rolled down the hill, he'd have been crushed beneath the carriage's heavy wheel. The Feldkanone 96 n.a. might have been one of the smallest, most maneuverable cannons in the arsenal, but the wheels of its carriage still stood as tall as Berthold's ribs and could turn him to mincemeat were he caught beneath one.

"Push, you dandies!" Lang groaned. "Ten more feet!"

"Lang I swear to Christ I'm going to draw my pistol and shoot you if you don't shut your fucking mouth!" Hertz warned him.

With his legs on fire and about to give, Berthold found one last burst of energy and expended it all as Gun Number 6 rolled onto the top of the hill. He was unprepared for what lay on the other side.

The hill was much taller than he'd realized, and overlooked a deep depression into which the landscape gradually sloped away for miles, revealing dark green stands of forest, tiny, snaking blue streams and an enormous, rolling yellow field which stretched to the northeast horizon. There were a number of small lakes in the distance, twinkling in the afternoon sun. Rastenburg was not so far away, yet he'd never seen anything quite as majestic as the land laid out before him. The road ahead turned slightly north and west as it descended into the depression, and for as far as Berthold could see, an unbroken line of soldiers, horses, wagons, guns and motor lorries stretched along its every inch.

When the trailer and gun rolled onto the hill's flat top and the horses were able to pull the equipment themselves, Berthold let go of the shield. His legs were tingly, and they shook and wobbled. He sat to prevent them from giving out. He rubbed his throbbing right shoulder and collarbone, certain they'd be covered by bruises within the hour. A hundred and fifty feet down the road, a wheel on Gun Number 3's artillery trailer had snapped from its axle, spilling cannon shells and supplies across the narrow road. While that crew cleaned the mess and repaired their wagon, the column ground to a stop.

"At least we've stopped on top and not in the middle!" laughed Roth.

Ostermann was already surveying the open countryside ahead. Something in the field to the northeast must have caught his attention. He brought his field glasses to his eyes and gazed for about thirty seconds, then turned to Lang.

"There's a group of Cossacks over there," he said, pointing northeast. "About three miles."

The Cossacks, a race of East Slavic peoples, hailed from many regions of southeastern Russia. Militarily speaking, Cossacks were renowned horsemen and were most often grouped together in their own fighting units, used almost exclusively as mounted troops for scouting and reconnaissance. While fierce fighters, they generally lacked in tactics and sophistication as compared with regular Russian units. The stereotypical image of a Cossack typically entailed the placement of an oversized cylindrical fur hat atop his head.

"Let me see!" Lang said. He snatched the glasses from Ostermann and brought them to his eyes. Staring for a time, Lang then lowered the glasses and snorted. "There's no one else around but them. Even from up here I see no other Russians, not anywhere. What are they doing down there?"

"Deserters?" said Ostermann.

"Maybe," Lang replied. He handed the field glasses to Berthold. "Kastner, take a look."

He could just barely make out the small band of men and horses through the lenses. The Cossacks appeared to have just set up a camp. It was odd that they remained where they were, despite the thousands of Germans who they no doubt could see coming over the hill. Then again, who was going to waste time going after such a tiny band? Berthold wondered to himself what those men would do if his crew sailed a cannon shell their way. He'd heard whispers that the Cossacks were savages, that they murdered prisoners of war. They probably deserved a cannon shell.

Just as he was about to suggest they ask permission to turn their gun around and take aim, Hertz pointed a finger to the southern sky, interrupting Berthold's train of thought. There he saw a low-flying aeroplane, coming from the south but heading north and slightly west.

"That's one of our observation machines," Hertz said. "It's having engine trouble. Can you hear it?"

The men fell quiet, to listen for the engine trouble of which Hertz spoke. Berthold cupped a hand behind his ear. Sure enough, he heard a faint *brrrp...brr...b....brrrrrr*—the sound of a choking, sputtering engine, stopping and starting. The aeroplane was losing altitude, and was headed toward the same field as the Cossack campsite. The men on the hill's forward slope pointed at the troubled machine as well. The German machine's engine cut out completely soon after.

"They're going to crash in the field!" shouted Hertz.

"What will the Cossacks do if they see them?" asked Roth.

"They're going to see them if they haven't already, I assure you," Ostermann said.

Berthold knew what they'd do. "They'll probably kill them," he said. "And there's no way the airmen are running away from men on horseback. Not on foot."

"Then we've got to do something!" cried Weber.

"I agree," said Lang. "Unhook the horses and turn the gun around! Quickly! I'll obtain permission to fire on them!" He ran halfway down the hill's rear slope, slipping in the muck and almost losing his balance. "Wachtmeister Trommler!" he shouted, "I urgently request your permission to open fire!"

Trommler sat on horseback near the bottom of the hill. The 7th Batterie commander spurred his horse, and the heavy black draft horse, a beautiful Percheron, galloped to the top of the hill. Its thick muscles rippled beneath its glistening coat as it high stepped through the mud. Though the horse's feathered feet were once a bright white, their large tufts of fur had been stained brown by the muddy road. Berthold questioned why the gigantic beast was not being utilized to pull something heavy, but then remembered some- one mentioning Trommler had owned the horse since it was a colt.

"What's going on up here?" the wachtmeister asked.

"Look, sir!" Lang shouted frantically.

Trommler removed the field glasses from the case on his hip and peered across the expanse. With the glasses held to his eyes and the aeroplane fluttering silently just a few hundred feet above the ground, he spoke tersely to the men of Gun Number 6. "Do what you can to help those airmen, but in your haste *do not* hit them or it will be my ass and yours."

"Yes sir," Lang said. "Hurry up boys!"

The men were still scrambling to situate the gun. Theirs was the only cannon atop the hill and the only one in any sort of position to fire. The aeroplane would crash within the minute, and depending on the proximity of the crash to the Cossacks there would be another few minutes, maybe four or five at the most, before the horsemen reached the crashed machine.

Weber had already released the gun from the artillery trailer and guided the horses into the grass on the side of the road. He tugged one case of cannon shells from the chest and lugged them to the gun. He set the wicker-encased missiles in a patch of grass a few feet away, and then took his place alongside the others, to push. The six tired men struggled to spin the gun around, and got it turned toward the field just as the reconnaissance machine crashed. The aeroplane upturned in the tall yellow grass approximately two miles distant. That left the machine's occupants with about a mile between them- selves and the Cossacks.

"They saw the crash and are mounting their horses!" shouted Os- termann as he watched through his field glasses.

"Wachtmeister Trommler, shouldn't you send a group of men on horseback to try and chase the Cossacks away?!" Weber yelped.

"They'd never close the distance in time," Trommler replied. "The Cossacks are at least a mile closer."

"Shit!" exclaimed Lang. "Then we'll just have to aim true."

"I must let the other crews know your gun will open fire soon, so as not to incite a panic," Trommler said. He spurred his horse again. As animal and rider moved away he shouted, "Remember! If you're going to miss, make sure it's an overshoot!" The wachtmeister and his heavy steed rumbled down the forward slope, loudly informing the other crews as to Gun Number 6's intentions.

Berthold hopped into his seat behind the splinter shield and began frantically adjusting the direct fire sight, though he was sure it would not matter owing to the awkward angle at which they'd be firing. Hertz flopped into the other seat and slid open the breech block. Lang placed a hand on Berthold's back and looked over his shoulder into the sight. He let out an almost undetectable sigh, and whispered "damn" under his breath. The gun commander knew the ordeal would not end well. Berthold had the same feeling, but they had to try and do *something.*

"All right Kastner we're firing on targets three miles away at a significantly downward angle," Lang said sternly. "There's nothing on the range table to go by. I think if we aim the barrel straight ahead there's a chance the shell may drop far enough."

Berthold rapidly turned the elevation hand wheel, lowering the barrel almost as far as it would go. The Cossacks were on the move, and headed directly for the crashed machine. Ostermann continued to watch them through the glasses. The men of the other crews on the forward slope un-holstered their Lugers and began firing in the direction of the advancing horsemen.

Hitting the Cossacks with pistol fire at that distance was mind-bogglingly unlikely and just short of impossible. Even if a bullet did happen to hit one of the riders it would probably have been tumbling by that point, and would have lost every ounce of its lethality and stopping power. That didn't prevent close to a hundred men from trying, though, and a hailstorm of 9mm bullets were sent toward the field, useless an endeavor as it was. The best the men could hope for was that the Cossacks' knowing they were being fired upon might discourage them from approaching the downed machine.

"The pilot and observer just crawled out!" Ostermann hollered. "They're all right!"

Weber pulled a shell from the basket and shoved it into the breech. Hertz quickly slid the block shut and rested his hand on the firing mechanism.

"Fire!" shouted Lang.

BOOM!

Berthold stood from his seat, just able to make out the position of the Cossack riders leaving a wake of swaying grass in their trail. The shell burst well behind them. The barrel was angled too high. He turned the hand wheel as far as it would go, dropping the barrel another half-inch. That was it.

"I don't think it's low enough!" he shouted.

Hertz had just closed the breech after Weber loaded the second shell.

"Fire anyway, Hertz!" Lang cried.

BOOM!

Again the shell traveled too far. The riders were getting closer.

"Roth! Kastner! Weber and Ostermann! Help me lift the trail!" Lang shouted. "We'll aim the gun downward ourselves!"

"Lang I think that might be too risky!" Berthold said.

"Do it!"

"But it's dangerously inaccurate!"

"JUST FUCKING DO IT!"

Berthold sprung from his seat and practically leapt into position next to Roth. Weber handed the third shell to Hertz, and then joined the four men standing at the back of the gun's trail. They crouched to grasp the heavy trail and lifted it approximately a foot above the ground, lowering the gun's firing angle.

"Fire the shell, Hertz!"

BOOM! A fair amount of recoil lurched the unanchored carriage's wheels. The force knocked the trail from the men's hands and it thudded to the ground. Lang stumbled backward and fell in the mud, while Berthold just missed having his fingers crushed. The men shouted one or two choice words before turning their attention to the breech operator.

"Did we get them, Hertz?!" Weber shouted.

"No! And the Cossacks are only about five hundred yards away!"

"GOD DAMMIT!" Lang screamed. He kicked a clump of mud.

The men dropped their heads. They could not fire un-ranged artillery at targets so close to men they were attempting to save, let alone do it by aiming in such a ridiculous fashion. Even doing it once had been extremely unsafe. They drew their Lugers and ran in front of the gun, joining in the frivolous waste of pistol ammunition. Wasting pistol rounds mattered little; it was the first time most of them had fired their handguns since the war began. Firing at least let them feel as if they weren't just sitting idly by as the scene unfolded.

"Can the airmen see the Cossacks coming?!" Roth asked, with an emotional intensity in his voice that Berthold had never heard from him before, not even in the thick of an artillery battle.

"I don't know!" Ostermann answered. He had the only semi-detailed view through his field glasses; the rest of the crew could not see much with the naked eye. "They're just sitting there with their backs against the machine!"

The overturned aeroplane was situated at an angle to the Cossacks, and the airmen had crawled out from the side opposite the approaching horsemen. There was a good chance they'd not seen the oncoming riders, but they had to be wondering what the German column was firing at. Those crews in 7th Batterie and the others of III Abteilung able to see the crash had begun yelling at the top of their lungs to try and warn the airmen to get out of there.

"Why the hell aren't you moving, you stupid sons of bitches?!" Berthold screamed. He turned to his comrades. "They heard our cannon and small arms fire, why do they not react?"

"I don't know," said Ostermann. "Maybe one of them is wounded. Maybe both are. It's too hard to tell from this far away."

When the Cossacks were within about three hundred feet, the airmen finally began to run.

"Jesus, now they're running!" Ostermann exclaimed, "It looks like the man on the left is hobbled."

Berthold and the others lowered their weapons. The pistols further down the hill ceased their fire at the same time. The riders were too close to the airmen for it to matter anymore. Every man in the column fell silent, and watched as the Cossacks caught up to the two airmen. The lead rider ran his horse between the two men, knocking them to the ground. The riders then formed a circle around the two Germans. The artillerymen watched in horror as the Cossacks dismounted. The circle closed in on the airmen, and obstructed them from view.

"What are those animals doing?!" asked Lang.

Ostermann watched through his glasses for a moment longer, then shook his head and pushed them into Berthold's chest and said, "I can't tell what they're doing, but I can't watch this anymore." He turned his back to the field and walked about ten feet away, cupping his hands over his face.

Berthold raised the glasses. He hoped the things he'd heard about Cossacks weren't true. Maybe there was a chance they'd just take the two Germans prisoner. He was to be sorely disappointed.

With shaky hands, he had a difficult time keeping the lenses trained on the right spot. From what he could tell, the riders were crouched low over the airmen, beating them, but he wasn't certain. Then he saw the first article of clothing fly out of the small circle. Several more were thrown out in quick succession. Less than a minute later the Cossacks stepped back, mounted their horses, and rode east. Berthold could just barely make out the naked, bloody bodies of the two airmen lying in the trampled grass.

"My God, they beat them to death..." he mumbled.

"Those fucking savages! YOU FUCKING SAVAGES!" Lang screamed at the Cossacks as if they'd hear him.

The men in the column needlessly opened fire with their pistols once again. Wachtmeister Trommler and his black horse galloped back up the hill. The commander repeatedly shouted the order for them to cease their fire. By the time the horse had traversed the hill the pistols, save for a solitary few, had been holstered.

"Sir, should we try and hit them again?" Lang asked Trommler softly.

"No. You'll just be wasting a shell. You tried, gentlemen, it was all you could do."

"Will you permit us to give chase?" Berthold inquired, though he already knew the wachtmeister's answer.

"Absolutely not, Kastner. You'd never catch them. However, Hauptmann Schäfer has requested I send a small party to check the airmen's identities, bury them, and burn the machine."

"Why do we have to burn it?" Weber asked naively. Everyone looked at him with raised brows.

Trommler scoffed and said, "Well we're certainly not taking it with us, and there's no need to risk it falling into Russian hands, no matter how damaged it might be."

"All right sir," Berthold answered, "Ostermann, Weber and I will do it."

"Very good. Make it quick, though. The hauptmann would like it done within the hour."

Five minutes later, the three volunteers were on horseback, leaving the road and making their way into the high yellow grass. It wasn't often Berthold rode the horses individually; most of the time only one crewman ever needed to ride a horse by itself. Since mobilization, that had almost exclusively been Weber's domain. During transport, the men would often jump on the horses' backs while they were hitched together, but that was typically the only riding they did. On Weber's advice, Berthold chose to ride the scruffy, reddish brown Hanoverian that he'd used to fetch the oats earlier in the morning. She had an even temperament, and though they were not in the habit of officially naming the horses, Weber always called her Ginger.

Ostermann picked the dark brown male Estonian with a streak of white on its muzzle. An older horse, he was the smallest of the six, but was still strong. Because of his age, the horse would probably not survive the war. Ostermann had taken a liking to him, and called him Old Timer. Berthold didn't quite share in his fellow crewman's sympathy for the horse. The animal would give everything it had and that would be that, but without the horses the guns didn't move, and without the guns, the Russians would sweep through and raze East Prussia. Better the horse than Rastenburg.

The slightly more fidgety filly, a light-grey Zweibrücker with darker grey legs was Weber's choice. When he spoke his nickname for her, he spoke it softly. Why Weber chose to call her Princess Victoria was beyond Berthold's comprehension, as nothing good could possibly come from naming the horse after the Kaiser's mother.

The crash site was easy to spot from atop the hill, but at the lower elevation they could not see it through the high grass, not even from atop the horses. Maintaining a general heading, the upturned machine's wheels eventually came into view.

"There it is," yelled Weber, leading the way.

"You don't think they left any traps, do you?" asked Ostermann.

"Do you honestly believe those savages are clever enough to set a trap, let alone do it in the short time they were here?" Berthold answered testily. "I doubt it."

There wasn't a man from their crew or any who witnessed it that wasn't appalled by what had happened to the two airmen, but Berthold and Ostermann had taken the deepest of offense. It saddened Ostermann, and infuriated Berthold. What those Cossacks had done was criminal, pure and simple. He'd heard bad things about them before, sure, but to see it unfold right before his eyes? The fury burned hotter and hotter inside him as the horses brought them closer to the bodies.

Dismounted, the three artillerymen, spades in hand, approached the corpses of the poor airmen. Their naked bodies were covered in purple splotches—bruises from a storm of punches and kicks. Worse, each man was smeared with blood from violent stab wounds, including many to their hands and forearms from vain attempts to shield themselves. One of the fellows was a skinny young man with long brown hair. He was much smaller than the other. Both airmen's eyes were stabbed out.

Most shocking of all, and so far beyond the scope of comprehension as to render the act quite literally inhuman, both men's genitals had been cut away. Berthold shuddered and angry tears stung his eyes. He wished he could chain the Cossacks together in a line, stand them in front of the cannon, and blow them to Hell with a high explosive shell. He wished he could do the same to their families.

"I cannot believe those animals will get away with this," he said, gripping his shovel with white knuckles. "Mark my words. If we're ever in a situation where it's up to us to take Russian prisoners, I'll kill the lot of them myself." He stood, seething, contemplating the emptiness it must have taken to inflict such brutality on unarmed men.

246

"Hey," Ostermann said, slapping Berthold on the shoulder. "It sickens me too, but we have less than an hour to give these two some semblance of a proper burial. Let's not waste it. We can be angry later."

Snapping from his enraged trance, Berthold agreed without speaking and lifted his shovel. He plunged the spade into the ground a few feet from the bodies.

"I'll gather their things and try to find some identification," declared Weber.

"That's fine. We'll dig," Ostermann answered. He stomped his spade into the ground as well.

The three went about their business, with the two diggers moving hastily. A shallow grave shared by two was better than no grave at all, and with the narrow time frame allotted there was absolutely no chance to dig proper, separate graves. Perhaps later on, their bodies might be dug up and reburied by rear-echelon troops.

"The bigger one is an officer," Weber said, a bundle of grey clothes in his arms. "Oberleutnant Fenstermacher. He was in uniform, but this other fellow was not. So far, I haven't found his identification." He continued to shuffle through pockets to find the second man's identity.

"I don't think we have to know their names," Ostermann said. "Their commanding officer will know who is missing."

"I would like to know," Berthold said. "Maybe we could carve their names on a makeshift cross before we leave, you know, for a headstone. There's plenty of scrap wood from their machine."

"We'd be cutting it close on time," said Ostermann.

"It's the least we could do for them."

"There's a photograph in this coat pocket," Weber said, having gathered the scattered clothes together and sifted through them. "It looks like the pilot has a brother." He pointed at the skinny man with the stabbed out eyes and handed Berthold the picture. "See?"

Stomping his shovel into the ground so it stood vertically, Berthold examined the photo. In it, two young men, similar in appearance, stood together, an arm around the other's shoulder. Both men were short and skinny, and dressed in their service tunics and shakos. The man pictured on the left was the dead body lying in the grass.

He brought the picture closer to his eyes, and was just able to make out a large scar on the chin of the other fellow. He flipped the photograph over to see if anything was written on the back and found just four words, printed in sloppy cursive. The words, beyond helping establish the pilot's identity, meant little else to Berthold—

the pilot was just another of his countrymen lost to the savagery of war—but to someone else, a mother, a father, or a brother, they meant everything.

Vogel brothers April 1914.

GORDON

Gordon stood on deck, at the ship's stern, breathing in the ocean mist. In twenty-one years he'd never seen the ocean before, and now he was a passenger on a boat in the middle of the Atlantic. The vessel, bound for Cherbourg, France, would reach its destination in less than two days. In his childhood, the Graham family traveled to Lake Erie once every summer, so he *had* seen a large body of water before, but the vastness of the Atlantic astonished him. Lake Erie was a drop in the bucket.

An older couple shuffled past behind him. They appeared surprised—perhaps offended—by the sight of a young, well-dressed black man, leaning on the railing, cheerily smelling the air. Gordon nodded to them and smiled, but they looked away and kept moving. *They probably think I belong in the boiler room, shoveling coal.* His cabin was in steerage, but he hated being below deck and spent most of his time outside. He only returned to the cramped cabin to sleep a few hours per night. His mere presence likely miffed many passengers, but he kept to himself and avoided them.

With evening approaching, in Gordon's opinion the stern was the place to be. He'd made it a point from the very beginning of his trip to be on deck for every sunset, and that late afternoon was shaping up to be the best sunset yet. He watched the giant orange fireball slowly descend, and he reflected upon the turn of events that brought him there...

After leaving the recruiter that day, insulted to his very foundation, his head hung lower than it ever had in his life, Gordon sat in silence, fuming, as his father drove him home. He had no delusions about the world in which he lived—it was fraught with injustice, but for whatever reason, he thought that day would end up different. He'd later look back upon that moment embarrassed, not only at what had been said to him, but at his own naïveté.

He'd been called a nigger before, many times, but to hear it in that moment—with his hopes set so high—obliterated the belief he once held in the phrase "All men are created equal." They *weren't* created equal, in point of fact. Some were better. *He* was better. He was smarter. He was tougher. He had more to offer. But based on ridiculous and misplaced ideology, his country spat in his face and told him he was *lesser*. Once, when he was a boy, the assholes in white hoods came to Dayton and paraded through the streets, preaching their particularly disgusting brand of ignorance. It was one thing for them to say so, but for his *country* to say it? That was another thing altogether. Offering prejudice in response to a young man's offer to serve had no place in a society which had the gall to consider itself civilized.

Knowing well his family's history, Gordon could not stand for what he'd heard at the recruiter. His grandfather was born a free man, the son of a freed slave. Even as a free man, free to make his own choices, he volunteered for service in a colored regiment of the Union Army during the Civil War. Gordon never met his grandfather; he survived the war only to receive a knife in the belly a few years after Lincoln's assassination, courtesy of a former Confederate. The crime went unprosecuted. That the man could serve in the war that ended slavery, yet fifty years later have his grandson called *nigger* for offering to serve the same nation's army in a different capacity was downright appalling.

When they arrived home and Anson pulled the Ford up to the Graham house, he looked at his son and asked but one question. "What is your next step, Gordon?"

His mind having raced through option after option and scenario after scenario for the entire drive, with no hesitation Gordon replied, "I'll go to France, to join the French Foreign Legion. I'll fly aeroplanes there if they won't let me here." It was the only thing that made sense to him, if it even made sense at all.

"Son," Mr. Graham sighed, "I know you're frustrated. Your thoughts right now are reactionary. Not the best ones to go by."

"No. My thoughts are what they need to be," Gordon said, shaking his head. "I know what I must do."

"Who is to say the French would let you fly aeroplanes? What if you were to go and they said the same thing?"

"They won't. I'll convince them."

"You didn't do much to convince anyone here."

"Don't pretend you still believe our die here isn't already cast, father. Believing in something doesn't make it true."

"Isn't there more you can do here?" asked Anson. "Aren't there other paths to get you where you want to be?"

"Not for me. Not for...a nigger."

"We don't use that word, Gordon. And you'll not start now."

"Yes sir."

Anson rubbed his forehead, contemplating. "There must be another avenue to pursue. Europe is not the place to be right now!"

"An avenue like what, the courts?" Gordon folded his arms and shook his head. "Why don't I file suit at the courthouse downtown? And when the judge, wearing a black robe in place of the white one he'll probably put on later, dismisses the case? I'll run my appeal to the state supreme court, if they'll even hear it. Same result. Maybe then, years from now, I could march my appeal right up the steps of the U.S. Supreme Court, so nine eighty-year-old white men can wipe their asses with the Constitution and call me a fool for even trying."

"Some changes do take time."

"Not for me. Not this. I need this now."

"What now, Gordon? You won't be in France tomorrow."

"I can be there sooner than I'll ever find fair treatment here."

Anson breathed, long and deep, through his nose. "This Foreign Legion," he said, "do you know enough about it?"

"Dad," Gordon said, "it's me."

"You're so damned hard-headed," Anson said. He reached over and rapped the top of Gordon's head. "I don't understand how God crammed such a big brain into such a thick skull."

Gordon's father understood his determination. Anson did not fight with him, nor try to dissuade him after they exited the car. If Gordon wanted to try, even something foolish, there was no sense in trying to stop him.

Virginia Graham put up a fight. A spirited one. She had watched her son fall from the sky once before, and the thought of him falling from the sky again, over a warzone no less, terrified her. She was mad at first, and then she battled tears, but she too came to grips with Gordon's determination, but only after he promised he'd come out clean on the other side.

It took weeks for Gordon to save enough money for the train ticket to New York and the boat to Cherbourg. Even with what he'd read of the conflict in the papers during that span, he was not dissuaded. Anson helped with funds, and gave Gordon about half of what he needed. Liza gave him every cent she had. She loved reading about Paris, and the thought of her brother actually going to France on an adventure was the most fantastic and exciting thing she'd ever heard.

Gordon arrived in New York City late in the afternoon, the day before his ship's departure. He hadn't slept on the train ride from Dayton, nor did he when he got to New York. The thought of boarding the ship to France was far too exciting.

"It's beautiful, isn't it?"

A girl in a light-green dress stood at the railing on his right. Gordon had been deep in thought while gazing west at the sun, and failed to notice her move next to him. He looked to his left, then over his shoulder to make certain she was speaking to him and not someone else.

"Um, yes, yes it is, ma'am."

She smiled and said, "My name is Amy. What's yours?" She reached out her hand.

Gordon hesitated briefly. He did not feel up to the task of having someone put him in his place for displaying the audacity to touch a white girl's hand. Then again, she was the one initiating the handshake. *Ah, the hell with it.*

"My name's Gordon Graham, miss."

He clasped her hand, which, while soft, was much firmer than he expected. *She's got worker's hands. Probably not high-society. That's good.* She was fairly pretty, with straight red hair and smooth, creamy skin. Her eye color matched her dress. Tall and thin, she stood about eye to eye with the five foot ten Gordon, an inch shorter at most. She held a little white parasol against her shoulder, and twirled it back and forth every so often. Gordon assumed it was to shade her fair skin from the sun, as there wasn't a cloud in the sky.

"Are you a steerage passenger, Gordon Graham?"

Is that a serious question? No, I'm first class. Captain, in fact.

"Yes, ma'am."

"Well ain't that so. Me too."

She had the slightest twang in her voice. Gordon didn't much like when a person had a deep southern twang (for obvious reasons), but her voice was soft and her accent so mild as to be almost imperceptible. She sounded pleasant.

"So Gordon, why are you headed to Cherbourg?"

"I'm on my way to Paris. To join the French Foreign Legion."

"What's that?"

Gordon had studied the French Foreign Legion long before he'd ever considered joining—he studied a great many things—so he told her a little something about it.

"It was founded in 1831 by King Louis Philippe. It is unique in the world because it allows men of all nationalities to volunteer for the French military. Men who join don't swear allegiance to France herself, as that would violate international law, but pledge to obey the orders of their French officers."

"Why didn't you just join the army back home? Are you so anxious to be in the midst of war?"

"No, ma'am it's not that. I want to fly aeroplanes, and our country doesn't want boys like me to fly them."

"And you think since this French Legion accepts everyone, that they're going to let you, is that it? What if you sign up, they hand you a gun, and that's that?"

"No," Gordon shook his head. "That can't happen. I won't let it. I'm different than the average volunteer. And if any man can volunteer and fight alongside men of different skin color, to me it says that in France, all men are given a chance to prove themselves, be that on the ground, or in the air."

"You might find things different when you get there."

"Even still, I have to try."

"How hard did you try back home?"

"You sound like my father."

"Well he sounds delightful."

Gordon smiled.

"So what makes you different than other volunteers?" she asked, with growing interest. She edged closer to him, closer than he was comfortable with while on a tin can in the middle of the ocean, surrounded by whites. Still separated by a foot of railing, he didn't want to offend her by backing away.

"I've spent years studying aeroplanes. Put everything I had into it. I even built my own," Gordon replied. "I'm smarter, and more qualified than other men. Flying is what I'm meant to do, I know it, and I have to get back in the air. No matter what."

Placing a hand on her hip, Amy said rather sassily, "Well aren't you just the picture of confidence?"

"Yes ma'am," he answered, with a touch of cockiness. "Sometimes you have to be."

"Please stop calling me ma'am, Gordon. I'm twenty-two and not one for honorifics. My name should suit just fine."

"All right, Amy. So, why are you headed to France?"

"I'm joining the French Foreign Legion, too."

Gordon's gave her a look.

"No I'm kidding!" she laughed. "I can't believe you fell for that!"

"Funny," Gordon said. He rolled his eyes, feigning embarrassment.

Amy continued, "Actually, I have relatives in Pau, and since they're nowhere near the fighting I figured now would be as good a time as any to visit them. I've always wanted to go to Paris, too, it sounds so beautiful, but right now that's probably not such a good idea."

Pau. Gordon recognized the name. Pau was where the Wright brothers demonstrated their *Wright Flyer* in 1909. They subsequently established a flying school there. In the intervening five years, Pau had become one of the centers of French aviation. A number of training schools operated in the fields around the city, and French aircraft manufacturers had moved production facilities to the area. Gordon envied Amy for being able to go there, but to keep the conversation flowing he pretended not to know where she was headed.

"I'm not familiar with Pau," he lied. "Where is it?"

"It's only about fifty miles or so from the border with Spain. And it's next to the Pyrenees Mountains, so I'll bet the scenery is something else. I really can't wait to see it."

"That sounds nice."

"It gets better. They've promised to take me to the mountains!"

For several minutes, Gordon had felt the eyes of other passengers on his back. His discomfort was growing. *She's friendly, but the white folks are starting to stare.* "That really does sound nice, Amy," he said, "I hope you enjoy yourself, but I must be getting back to my cabin."

He thought it best to walk away, so as not to inflame any tensions. He lifted his hands from the railing and was about to make his exit when Amy reached over and grabbed his wrist. She returned his palm to the railing, then let go of his wrist and gently patted the back of his hand.

"You're not going to leave me here by myself, are you Gordon?" she asked, tilting her head toward him as if to scold.

"I..."

"Never you mind what the peanut gallery thinks," she said, subtly nodding that she knew the gawkers were there, but never looking away from him. "If they want to be sour pusses, they should go suck a lemon."

Gordon had to smile.

"Now," Amy said, "I was hoping you'd let me watch the sunset with you. I've spotted you here every evening thus far, and you're the only nice boy I've met on this entire boat."

What's she trying to do, get me thrown overboard?

Torn between what he was expected to do—conform to a meaningless racial status quo—or the polite, friendly thing which he preferred, the young man contemplated his two options. But why even contemplate? *You know what Gordon, forget these people! Be kind to her, and don't mind them, like she said.* He'd spent twenty-one years minding his "manners" around white people, in even the most routine and inoffensive scenarios imaginable. Why should their glares and false superiority dictate his actions? That evening, on a trip he'd worked hard to take, he would not be rude to one nice white girl just to mindlessly placate others who'd never debase themselves to give him the time of day.

"Well then, I suppose I'll stay," Gordon said. "You expressed a disinterest in formality but, Miss Amy, would you please do me the honor of enjoying an Atlantic sunset with me?"

With a sweet smile she replied, "Why yes, Mister Graham, I'd love to."

They sat at the railing, discussing where they came from, what their families were like, and how they'd done in school. Amy was from Richmond, Virginia. Her firm handshake came from working in a textile mill, which she'd done since graduating from high school, with honors, four years earlier. She, like Gordon, could not afford college, but continued educating herself after leaving school. It didn't take Gordon long to recognize she was bright, and an adept conversationalist. In twenty-one years, he hadn't partaken in many exchanges with white girls his age, or any age, but he doubted most white girls were like Amy. They conversed until the orange sun melted into the water, and vanished beyond the horizon.

While the sky darkened, Gordon and Amy gazed above as tiny flecks of starlight began to dot the cloudless evening. A half-moon rose over the sea and the water reflected its white light in a large, shimmering strip along the surface, trailing in the ship's churning wake. The day had been warm, and when the sun went down, the temperature dipped just ten degrees. It was balmy, and a gentle, soothing breeze perfectly complemented the night's serenity.

A soft gust flowed across the deck, and lightly fluttered Amy's hair as she stargazed. Gordon glanced at her just in time to notice. There was something about that one instant, something mysterious buried within that one particular increment, that hair flutter revealing her neck, but he couldn't quite pinpoint what that something was. A feeling, maybe. About her, or about the moment, or maybe about where he was going. When he glanced at her, she looked at him too, and the corners of her lips curled shyly. He hadn't been as comfortable with anyone as he was then, not for quite some time.

That evening, the all-consuming thought of flight and the anticipation of what he was about to try to do faded into the back of Gordon's mind, if for only just an hour or two. He had the pleasantest of nights speaking with the friendly young woman. By the time the moon had passed high overhead, the two decided to part ways and get some rest.

"It was a pleasure meeting you, Gordon Graham," Amy said. She placed her hand tenderly on his forearm. "Maybe we'll cross paths again at some point."

"I hope so, ma'am." *But I doubt it.*

Amy winked and strolled away, twirling the parasol on her shoulder.

Gordon watched her until she was gone, and then remained at the railing. Never in his life, not once, had a white girl touched him like that. It was such a simple gesture, mundane even, but it jolted through his blood like a lightning strike. There were probably millions of white people throughout America who embraced colored people the way Amy just had, but in a segregated country, he'd never had the pleasure of meeting one until then. It wasn't that there was some sort of additional allure—forbidden fruit—because she was an attractive white girl. In a sense, that was irrelevant. It was the interaction, and that had nothing to do with skin tone.

He'd had colored girlfriends who were every bit as pretty, if not more so, in the past. What warmed him so overwhelmingly about his interaction with Amy, if color played a part at all, was her complete disregard of what his skin color meant to *others*, bigots and their scowls be damned. Did she see the color of his skin? Of course she did. Different people had different colored skin, but so what? It was such a basic concept, yet so many people bungled it so spectacularly and maliciously without ever examining the irrationality of it all.

It was late, but Gordon wanted to prolong what had ended up being a splendid night. He stood at the railing for a time, watching the stars reflecting on the water. He could not help but feel excited about his meeting Amy. In some ways, she was a revelation, and a fantastic one, a reaffirming of the decency of some, in a world poisoned by the awfulness of others. Heavy eyelids were tough to fend off, however, and Gordon soon felt himself succumbing to their weight. The bed in his cramped cabin beckoned, and the more tired he grew, the further away it became.

He walked to the nearest stairwell which led below deck, but before he could get there a man stepped in front of him, exuding an aura that was Amy's polar opposite. A fat and sweaty man, his mouth was obscured by a dirty brown walrus moustache, stained yellow on the bottom from excesses in food and tobacco. He stunk.

Here it comes. This is where I'm expected to apologize for having a nice evening with a nice girl. Someone had to balance the equation.

"Where ya headed, boy?"

Boy. That fucking word again.

Gordon winced, and almost flashed his gritted teeth in anger. There weren't many words he hated, they were just words, but there were a few. "Just below deck, mister," he replied, "To my cabin."

He tried to walk past the man, who reeked of booze, sweat and smoke. The drunk lifted a hand and slapped it against Gordon's chest, leaning into him, preventing him from moving by. He'd been touched by white men that way plenty of times. It was the touch of belittlement, and it came as no surprise that it should follow so closely on the heels of a more genial and contradictory experience. *Please, don't let this happen, not now.* Gordon surveyed the environment around him. Most of the passengers had left the deck; no one was paying attention.

"Not so fast, darkie. I saw you with that pretty little girl back there."

"Is that so? Then you saw that all we did was talk. If you'll excuse me."

Five meaty fingers pushed more firmly into his chest, and Gordon felt the man's fingertips contract—he was digging them in. Pestilent breath crawled up Gordon's nostrils, a potpourri of snuff, cigar, whiskey and rot. It was the foulest mix he'd ever had the displeasure to inhale.

Trying his best not to react, but still standing his ground, Gordon shifted his weight against the rigid hand as the man squeezed harder. It hurt, but there was no way the young black man was going to give the pathetic, bigoted drunk the smug satisfaction of intimidating yet another in what was probably a long line of undeserving colored people. With fingers still dug into his chest, Gordon leaned further forward and the man's hand trembled. What sort of sick game had he gotten caught up in? What was the man trying to prove? Something in Gordon gave way as he realized the worthlessness of minding his actions around people as awful as the one standing in his path.

I'm not putting up with this shit. Not tonight.

With a swipe quick as a hummingbird's wing, he slapped the hand away from his chest. The man lurched forward as Gordon squeezed by to make his way down the stairs, but the drunkard would not let it go. He lunged after Gordon, and grabbed him by the shoulder. That was it. Gordon had had more than enough. He spun around, too fast for the drunk to react, and threw a granite-fisted punch directly into the man's nose, which crunched as the bone shattered.

The man's eyes rolled back in his head. Felled like a tree by a knockout blow, he toppled backward and thumped his head against the stairs. Looking both ways once more to make sure no one had witnessed, Gordon couldn't help but snicker in satisfaction when he heard gurgling snores rattle out of the broken nose. Blood was already trickling from the nostrils. *He came at you, Gordon. Got what he deserved. Now get out of here before somebody sees you!*

Leaving the unconscious man lying in the stairwell, he ran to his cabin and locked the door behind him. When he'd caught his breath, he became upset with himself. *I should not have done that. What a foolish thing to derail my plans over.* With any luck, the guy would wake up with an enormous headache, not remember what happened, and assume he'd broken his nose falling down the stairs. No matter how that situation had been presented, there weren't many people on the ship, besides Amy perhaps, who would have taken Gordon's side were he found out. He understood that, but sometimes it was worth taking a risk to stand up for oneself.

He remained hidden in his cabin for the last day of the trip, just in case trouble had been brewing outside, and managed to avoid any further situations. The boat landed at Cherbourg, and Gordon did not see Amy again. He had hoped they'd run into one another as they left the ship, but he never spotted her. He had other business to attend to in Paris. Wasting no time, Gordon made his way to the train station and boarded the next locomotive bound for the capital.

DENIS

Denis and Patrice sat on their haversacks, completely exhausted. When the Germans fell back on September 10, the two stayed behind the lines to recuperate. The shell had roughed them up, but after they'd gotten light treatment, a medical officer had since cleared them to return to the front lines.

In August, many thousands of men had received no burial at all, Clemence and Reynard included, but at least the squad's two known survivors were present to assure the rest of their mates weren't left aboveground to rot. No words were spoken nor funeral services performed; each man was laid into his own four foot deep hole and unceremoniously covered with dirt. A small, wooden marker bearing their relevant information was driven into the ground where they lay, alongside the markers for many others killed during the Marne, and the two exhausted men who put them there walked away, too worn out and battered to shed any tears.

It was dark, and the half-moon provided just enough light for them to see one another. Patrice calmly and methodically ran a small whetstone along the edges of his *Rosalie*, while Denis leaned forward, elbows on his knees, hands holding the sides of his head. His life in the Great War to then was a living nightmare—dead friends, close calls, punishing heat and thirst and perhaps worst of all, total uncertainty as to his family's fate. He could not assemble a coherent train of thought. All the negativities trapped within his skull were jockeying for position and swirling together.

"Denis, do you hate the boche?"

The question penetrated his eardrums, but failed to register in Denis's overloaded brain. "What?" he asked, discreetly grabbing handfuls of hair and tugging on them to try and focus.

His friend looked at him cockeyed, and repeated the question.

"I don't know, Patrice. Do I hate that they've invaded? Obviously. But at the same time, their men are following orders the same as we are, and I bet most of them didn't ask for this."

"I hate them..." Patrice replied. He tapped his finger on the end of his bayonet to check its point. "They killed our friends."

"That they did. But how many friends do you suppose you and I have killed? Right this second, there are men having this exact same conversation over there." Denis pointed north, in the direction of the new German lines, miles away, across the River Aisne.

"I don't care about their fucking friends, Denis," Patrice said sharply. "I'll kill more as soon as I get the chance!" He thrust his *Rosalie* into the soil next to him.

"I have no doubt you will. But you must keep a clear head. Blind rage can do to a man exactly that, and that won't help you at all in a fight."

While he was bitter and saddened over losing his squad, Denis struggled with the notion of hating men for doing what they were required to do. He didn't like the Germans, how could he, and he hated that virtually the entire German army stood on French soil, but *hating* the men across the river was different. Politicians and emperors had started the war, and young men on both sides were being forced to determine the outcome.

"Why did you go to Saint-Cyr?" Patrice asked. "I don't think we've ever talked about it. Not really." He pulled his bayonet from the ground and wiped the dirt from the blade, before sliding it back into the sheath.

"You never asked me," Denis replied, wondering where that had come from, and why then. "Did you know my grandfather died fighting the Prussians?"

"No...Why didn't I know that?"

"Again, you never asked. He was a Saint-Cyr graduate, and had reached the rank of capitaine by the time he was killed in the Siege of Paris. When he died, my father was a little boy..."

Patrice listened, his face attentive.

Denis continued, "...Losing his father devastated him, as it would any young boy, but my grandmother's reaction when she heard the news hurt him far worse. She nearly lost her mind, and was never the same after my grandfather died. Eventually, it became too much for her. She killed herself four years after the war ended."

"Jesus Christ, Denis. I'm sorry."

"It's all right. I never knew them."

"Even still, that's horrible."

Patrice shifted forward on his haversack, intrigued by the story he should have already known. Denis realized then that he'd not shared his family's history with many people at all.

"What happened when your grandmother died?"

"My father was still young, and he'd lost both parents to war, or because of war. His older sister, my aunt Rosa, still young herself, was forced to raise him. When he got older he grew increasingly critical of politicians and militarism. When he turned eighteen, he refused conscription, not just for what the military had done to his family, but because he could not stand the thought of being forced to cause such grief to another family, or of leaving a family of his own behind."

His features wrinkled in deep, contemplative silence, Patrice seemed unable to grasp why Denis chose the path he did. It took a moment for him to ask, "What in the world made you want to join, then? To throw it in your father's face?"

"No, no, absolutely not," Denis replied, hurt that his friend would misperceive his intentions in such a way. "I love my father and respect very much the decisions he made. But my mother and father were not destroyed by war. I never met my grandparents, and in the stories I heard of my grandfather he sounded like a hero. He attended Saint-Cyr and fought for France, so that's what I wanted to do."

"How did your father react when you told him?"

Denis's head dipped when he thought back to that moment. "He wept, as did my mother and Louise. It pained me to see, but I would not have refused conscription anyway. If I was to be in the military one way or the other, why not attend a great school as well?"

"That makes sense," Patrice agreed. "And you'd still be caught up in this war regardless. Without Saint-Cyr, you would never have ended up in the 144th Regiment, in command of yours truly." He brought his hands to his collar and pushed out his chest.

"True. I'd still have been in Fifth Army," Denis stated, "just not with you." He thought it an obvious point, but gaging his friend's confused expression, he realized the point wasn't so obvious. *He has no idea what I'm talking about.* "Do you mean to tell me you don't know the constituents of the very army in which you fight?"

"Well..." his friend stretched his retort, "...I guess I don't know *all* of them."

"You're hopeless!" Denis exclaimed. He threw a handful of dirt and grass in Patrice's direction. "Had I been conscripted, I more than likely would have ended up in the 1st Regiment, since they were garrisoned at Cambrai."

"So?"

"So? They're in the 2nd Brigade."

"And?"

Denis sighed. "I have a hard time believing you're this dense, Pat, even you."

"Hey, who am I, Patrice Joffre? I do not study this shit, nor am I required to."

"The 2nd Brigade is in I Corps. I recall I Corps saving our asses no more than two weeks ago."

"Oh. Well I know of I Corps," Patrice shrugged, "just not who's in it. And sure, they might have saved our asses, but only because we softened the boche up for them first." He reached over and poked Denis in the upper arm. "Either way, you finagled yourself into a much finer regiment, I must say."

"It took no small amount of ass kissing on my part," Denis replied with a grin.

"Well however many asses you kissed, I'm glad you kissed them. I'd probably have been court-martialed or killed by now were I not serving with my best friend as squad leader."

Denis's face and heart sunk together. "I can be no squad leader when I've no squad left to lead."

Patrice lifted himself from his seat. He took a knee in front of Denis and grasped both of his hands. "I am truly sorry for what has happened. But no decision you could have made would have saved them. They did not die on your orders. You did not send them somewhere you should not have. It's not your fault. The boche killed them, so we'll kill the boche."

"But they died so quickly," Denis replied shamefully, "nearly my whole squad in less than a month."

"Yes, but better a quick death than a slow one," Patrice answered. "And what of those many squads who lost every man?" He squeezed his hands harder. "What of entire sections or companies laid to waste? You've lost men, yes, but everyone has. For all we know, Emery and Gustav are still alive, and don't forget about Maurice! He's probably recovered by now and could be on his way back to us very soon, unless of course he was reassigned. Have we lost more of our brothers than we have left? Yes. But it could be worse."

"I know," Denis replied, still picturing the mangled bodies of his men strewn around the shell hole. He'd had a nightmare about it the night before and hardly slept. "Let's just get some rest. We must catch up with and rejoin the bataillon. They'll probably cross the Aisne within a day or so."

"The Aisne, the Oise, the Meuse, and all the way to the Rhine, until all of Germany is ablaze," Patrice said quietly

"With any luck. But one river at a time, yes?"

"Yes. Good night, my friend."

"Good night, Patrice."

VERNON

After their retreat from the Marne, German First and Second Armies took up defensive positions near the River Aisne, which crossed roughly east to west through the region. It passed about ten miles north of Reims, then snaked west past Soissons before meeting with the River Oise near Compiègne, fifty miles northeast of Paris. In trail behind the Germans were the BEF and French Fifth and Sixth Armies. The contested area from Reims to Compiègne encompassed just over fifty miles of front, with the BEF sandwiched between the two French armies. The Entente forces approaching the river from the south faced spirited opposition from the retreating Germans.

Beginning later in the day of September 12, the BEF began leaving their positions south of the Aisne, advancing closer to the river against the Germans. Their advance followed a heavy exchange of artillery fire, particularly between German First Army and French Sixth Army, on the front extending from Compiègne to Soissons. Unable to see the fighting there, Vernon certainly heard it—a constant, unending rumble, echoing through the Aisne river valley. After the artillery battle, the Germans withdrew their guns north of the river and their engineers demolished nearly all the Aisne's bridges.

The BEF took up the line on French Sixth Army's right, southeast of Soissons to Bourg further east, with the French manning the line thereafter. In all, the front occupied by the British encompassed eleven bridges, each of which had been demolished, though some still partly stood. As they had at the Marne, Smith-Dorrien's II Corps was situated between Haig's I Corps on the right and Pulteney's III Corps on the left. The French XVIII Corps represented French Fifth Army's left flank and marched alongside Haig on the BEF's right flank.

The terrain posed challenges, to say the least. The Aisne traversed the countryside through a wide, flat-bottomed valley, with bluffs and ridges to its north and south rising as high as three to four hundred feet in elevation. Atop the ridges on both sides, the land leveled into a plateau. Though the high ground followed the Aisne's general contour, the heights varied greatly in their distance from the riverbanks, with numerous spurs—some being hundreds or thousands of yards in length—projecting away from the main ridge line, often perpendicularly, and reentrants, or draws, which were smaller ravines either between two spurs or carved into the main ridgeline.

Large swaths of the valley walls were wooded, and often those forested areas stretched over the top of the ridge and beyond, shielding and obscuring what lay behind. The valley's width varied from as narrow as half a mile to as wide as two miles. In some spots, the river snaked closer to the northern slopes and in others, closer to the southern, and all configurations in between. Where the Aisne moved away from the northern slopes, the intervening ground there was particularly flat, and offered little to no cover. The southern banks were forested and hilly, and in many places rocky. Small towns and villages sat along the slopes on either side, as did the larger cities of Soissons and Compiègne.

By day's end on September 13, units from Pulteney's and Haig's Corps had managed to effect river crossings in the face of strong German machine gun and artillery fire. After falling back further, the Germans halted their advance on the high ground north of the river, and thus commanded generally far superior positions. Haig's I Corps was successful in pursuing the Germans onto the plateau, and pushed well past the Aisne to as far as two miles north of the river, though they were forced back to within a mile of the northern bank after a German counterattack.

To move onto the plateau, the BEF's remaining forces needed to cross the Aisne and scale the northern slopes, most of which were grassy, forested, rocky, or some combination of all three. Where the ridge was rocky, men would be forced to utilize narrow footpaths which cut through the cliffs and led to the top of the ridge.

By nightfall, the British troops still south of the river had established outposts all along the southern bank in preparation for the crossing. Because the Aisne was up to fifteen feet deep in places, fording it was out of the question. With the bridges demolished either partly or fully, the Royal Engineers would have to improvise a solution while they attempted to erect temporary bridges. The German guns, now atop and aback the ridge, could deliver indirect howitzer fire upon any troops endeavoring to cross or any engineers attempting to build temporary structures. The German defenders also had the luxury of positioning machine guns and field cannons on the heights, giving them wide zones of fire.

Whereas some German units had withdrawn a significant distance from the riverbanks, those opposing the 5th Division on a stretch of front between Bucy-le-Long and Condé held their ground on the lower elevations for almost a full day longer. The resistance offered by the Germans there centered mostly on the exchange of machine gun and artillery fire. On the 14th, they finally pulled their defenses north. Their withdrawal gave them the advantage in elevation already obtained by other German units, including indirect fire capability. Because of that capability, the 5th Division's night crossing of the Aisne was crucial.

Cramped into a makeshift pontoon boat—a wagon body wrapped in tarpaulins—Vernon and the nine men of 3 Section clung to the sides as the wobbly craft inched across the River Aisne. The sky was dark. It was late in the evening of September 14, and a steady rain had fallen for more than an hour. A thick, soupy fog had rolled in, and it obscured the opposite bank from view. The pontoons had already shuttled most of the 14th Brigade and 15th Brigade's men to multiple bridgeheads on the river's northern bank. A sizable force began to gather in waiting along the water's edge.

"Hey Spurling, what exactly is our objective?" asked Private Lockwood in a low whisper.

Vernon didn't expect to hear anyone speak during the crossing; he'd been listening to the raindrops tinkling against the water's surface and the sloshing of the oars, and Lockwood's breaking the silence startled him enough to make him jump. Pritchard was the only one who noticed, and gently nudged Vernon with his forearm to let him know his nervous flinch had not gone completely undetected.

Nine sets of worried eyes fixed on Corporal Spurling. They'd all had the chance during the day before to gaze across the valley at their destination. Whatever was coming, it would not be easy.

Whispering himself, Spurling replied, "Lieutenant Hood said the 14th Brigade will advance ahead of us, to seize the villages of Sainte-Marguerite and Missy. When they're secure, 15th Brigade is to assist in the capture of the Chivres Spur. We'll make our approach southeast of the spur while the 14th attacks from the front."

The Chivres Spur was the most important tactical feature of the landscape facing the 5th Division. Sharing its name with a village which lay deep within a smaller ravine along the foot of its western slope, it projected outward at a southwestward angle from the main ridge, and was shaped like a gigantic spear head aimed directly at the village of Missy-sur-Aisne. The spur's steep, sloping sides led to a plateau at its top, almost half a mile wide at its widest point. Any German defenders situated atop the spur could rain murderous fire on the Tommies in the valley below. The 14th Brigade's other objective, the village of Sainte-Marguerite-sur-Aisne, lay just over a mile to the west of Missy.

"What sort of artillery support can we expect for our assault?" Vernon queried in hushed urgency.

"Nothing tonight, Hayes, you know that. But I'm a corporal not a bloody general," Spurling answered. "I don't know what the bloody artillery is doing. For all I know they're staying south of the river and sipping fucking Earl Gray."

"South of the river?!" Pritchard squeaked, prompting a slap on the arm from Private Granville.

"Shut up!" Granville chided him. "You want Fritz to hear us?"

"Come on, Granny," Vernon said quietly. "With the rain and the distance between us and them, they wouldn't hear us if we shouted. Our men on the banks probably can't hear us."

"Or see us," Lockwood added. "Even if Fritz did by some magic hear us, how in the hell would they spot us through this fog? If it were daylight we wouldn't be able to see Missy from here, let alone the top of the spur."

"Well go on and shout then," Granville said, "test your luck."

When the pontoon bumped against the northern bank, its occupants hopped out one by one. Vernon's feet splashed into sloppy mud that sucked at his boots. He didn't sweat the muck. The rain had already soaked through his tunic and trousers, and his feet were bound to get wet and muddy anyway. The wetness weighed him down. His equipment felt as though he lugged boulders on his back and hips. He dreaded the idea of dragging himself and his drenched gear up a hill, especially in the face of opposition.

In the foggy darkness, the officers and NCOs struggled to organize their forces in preparation for the assault. The four battalions of 15th Brigade separated and moved east, whilst the 14th Brigade moved north toward the villages.

Vernon was nervous. As bad as combat was at any time, at night it was worse. Everything was more stressful. He'd learned that firsthand, the night after Mons. He'd thrown up once from the stress

267

already, because he knew how difficult and dangerous their advance might be. No one was sure as to the strength of the German force before them. The prevailing thought, though unsubstantiated, was that the enemy had fallen further back on the plateau. With any luck, that was the case.

Because of the fog, Vernon could not see the terrain ahead, but he and the others knew full well what they advanced against. If there *was* a strong German opposition waiting for them, then climbing the Chivres Spur in their waterlogged clothes and gear would be anything but a walk in the park.

"Maybe the fog will hold thick and we'll run right over the Huns before they know what hit them," whispered Pritchard.

"Aye...maybe," Vernon answered. He could tell from his friend's shaky whisper that he was frightened, but at least he was talking. Most men kept their mouths shut. Their boots clunked and squished against the damp ground, their equipment rattled and they breathed deeply, but their mouths stayed shut. Wrestling with his own anxiety, Vernon squeezed his hands around his Lee-Enfield, to release the tension building inside him. *At any minute, the first shot will ring out and Fritz will know we're here.*

1st Battalion cautiously moved through the fog, away from the river and toward the southeastern slope. They and the three other battalions of 15th Brigade separated in order to attack different points on the hillside. The diminished Cheshire force crept forward, with their ragged companies grouped loosely together. With the minutes ticking away and the assault yet to commence, Vernon feared the rain would cease and the fog shroud would vanish.

The pattering rain, dark, and fog were a double-edged sword of sorts—the Germans could not see or hear their approach, but those same issues also made it easier for companies and platoons to lose track of one another, inhibiting coordination efforts considerably. The 1st Cheshire Battalion could ill-afford another fight even remotely resembling the fighting at Mons and Audregnies.

Vernon's hands hurt from clutching the rifle so tightly, and despite the rain his mouth was dry. He reached for his water bottle, unhooked it from his right hip and opened it to take a small sip. Dry mouth had become psychologically intolerable over the last month. He raised the bottle to his mouth the same instant that muffled shots echoed from the direction of Missy. Startled, he spilled some of the precious water. The 14th Brigade had reached its first objective.

E Company fanned out, and Fourth Platoon skirted along the edge of a wood. The other platoons drifted out of sight and vanished into the fog and darkness. They should have maintained visual contact with one another. Judging strictly from the sound, the opposition being offered to the 14th Brigade at Missy seemed to Vernon to be relatively light. Still, he couldn't shake the stomach-churning nervousness.

Lieutenant Hood stood at the head of the platoon. He was barely more than a silhouette through the fog. As soon as he trotted back alongside his four sections with his pistol drawn, Vernon almost threw up a second time.

"All right, chaps," the lieutenant said. "It's time to head up."

"Sir?" Pritchard said faintly, sounding unsure.

"Yes, Pritchard?" Hood replied.

"Where is everyone going to be? How can we advance up the hill when we can't see anyone or anything?"

"Well..." the lieutenant paused and looked down. "We've little choice. If there are any defenses positioned up there, attacking at night is our best hope of overwhelming them."

"*Do* they have defenses positioned up there?" Vernon asked. He clung to the hope that Hood knew more than what Spurling had already told 3 Section's men on the pontoon crossing.

"I don't know, Hayes. Last word from command was that they believed they'd pulled back another few miles, but they could not say for certain. Either way, we need to try and establish a foothold on the high ground."

"Yes sir."

Hood jogged ahead to lead the platoon. His thirty-odd men followed, Sections 1 through 4 trailing him roughly in order but far from single-file, their heavy footsteps splashing on the sodden terrain. They crossed a small gravel road and a set of railroad tracks, then their boots squished into a muddy wheat field which had been harvested sometime in the last month. Vernon didn't know exactly where they were, as there was more than one wheat field in the area, but he specifically remembered seeing one during the previous day which ran along the spur and ended just short of the tree line, approximately a quarter of the way up the hill. If they were in that field, the platoon's climb would begin shortly.

Sure enough, after trudging a hundred yards or so through the mucky, rutted soil, the gradient began to increase. Fifty yards and a twenty degree incline later, the field came to a stop and the first trees emerged from the fog.

"Do they know we're coming?" asked a voice from 2 Section.

"Someone was shooting, so someone knows," one of his mates answered. Another shushed them.

The ascent grew steeper and the advance more difficult. Feet slipped on mossy rocks or slick mud and a veritable dictionary of curse words were quietly spat from aggravated mouths. Vernon had no idea where the other platoons of E Company were, let alone the other companies or battalions of 15th Brigade. They could have been at the top of the spur, or yet to begin their climb. It was not a good time for things to feel so disordered.

Following what must have been ten minutes of stopping, starting, and struggling up the slippery hill, Vernon happened to glance forward in time to see Lieutenant Hood stumble hard and land on his stomach. Oddly, when he fell, one of the lieutenant's feet remained suspended above the ground, held by an invisible force. The platoon halted immediately, and two men from 1 Section sprung forward to help the lieutenant to his feet. Vernon was surprised when Hood spun over and sat up quickly, shoving the two men backward.

"TRIPWIRE!" Hood shouted. "DOWN!"

Oh, shit.

Crack! A bullet snapped past the group, accompanied a fraction later by the *pop* of a rifle. The Germans were somewhere ahead, and not far off. The platoon flopped to their stomachs. Vernon's eyes darted back and forth to the men around him; no one had been hit by the first shot, but everyone grabbed their heads and pressed their cheeks against the ground in preparation for what was to come. The tripwire was there for only one reason—slowing an advance and mowing it down with bullets.

TAC-TAC-TAC! The German machine gun chattered through the mist. The muzzle flashes were coming from a thicket ahead. In the dark and haze, they looked like soft pulses of harmless light, but rain and fog served little to stifle the gun's terrifying clatter. Foolishly, insanely, belly-crawling toward the pulses, 3 and 4 Sections moved up and alongside 1 and 2, and the platoon formed a firing line. Apart from trees, they hadn't much cover to speak of, and they hugged flat against the wet soil like ticks. When the machine gun commenced its fire, the German infantry who'd been lying in wait to spring their trap began firing their rifles in earnest. The Tommies shouted back and forth to one another over the heavy gunfire, bravely lifting their heads to aim and return fire.

"How the fuck do we advance against this?!"

"We can't!"

"Maybe another platoon will break through!"

Vernon and 3 Section had crawled near to where Lieutenant Hood tripped. The wire that caught him was strung low to the ground between two trees. Where there was one, there would be more. Most in the platoon were panicked over the German defenses ahead, but the young officer kept his cool and started hatching a plan with Corporals Spurling and Tickner. Vernon barely overheard it above the shooting.

"Spurling! You and your men move along the hill to your left!" Hood shouted, clasping his hands over his head and laying on his side. "The rest of us will lay down a suppressive fire until you're clear. We'll hold their attention while you outflank that bloody gun!"

Corporal Spurling nodded, and Hood slapped him firmly on the upper arm. When the corporal attempted to roll away, though, the lieutenant grabbed hold of his sleeve. "Wait!" he said, "I've changed my mind! I'm coming with you. Corporal Tickner!" he hollered at the man from 1 Section, then turned over to face him. "Tickner you're in charge. Hold here until we return."

"Aye, sir!" Tickner replied.

"All right men!" Hood screamed at the top of his lungs, loud enough for the entire platoon to hear. "Suppressing fire on the machine gun! Aim for the muzzle flash!"

Twenty-four Lee-Enfields aimed at a single point ahead and opened fire. The German machine gun ceased its rattle and 3 Section, along with their officer tag-along, scrambled to their feet and ran laterally across the slope. German rifles were still popping away, biting and snapping into the trees so close to Vernon he could not believe they'd missed. It wasn't more than ten or fifteen seconds before the machine gun was chattering again.

The further from Fourth Platoon the men moved, the less the untargeted rifle rounds threatened them. Moving speedily along the side of the wet hill was treacherous, and they struggled to keep their footing. An awkward or careless step could break an ankle or leg in the blink of an eye, and it was difficult to step carefully when running in the dark on such unfamiliar and uneven ground.

Pritchard slipped in front of Vernon, who stopped to help him. Spurling crashed into his back. Unhurt, the three men disentangled themselves, with help from Lieutenant Hood.

"Hold here!" he shouted to the others. "We've gone far enough. Let's go up."

Fourth Platoon's gunfight had blended in with others breaking out elsewhere on the spur. With pattering rain and echoes, it was hard to tell where all the shooting came from. Between Vernon's tension, fear and windedness, the battle seemed to surround him. He wasn't even entirely sure there weren't Germans somewhere behind them, but one thing was certain. The enemy's defenses were there, and they were there in force.

The lactic acid built up in his legs, and a deep burn and tightness harassed each labored step he took up the slope. Burning legs were fine; at least no one was shooting at them yet. The way it was going, Vernon thought they might actually be able to sneak up on and out-flank the machine gunners and riflemen targeting the rest of Fourth Platoon. Pushing through the pain in his legs, he and the others slow-ly scaled the heights. With no visual cues as to how far they'd gone or how much further they needed to go, the journey up the hill lasted an eternity.

A reinforced wire fence ahead abruptly impeded their progress. It had a line of barbed wire across the top. The German engineers must have been busy during the previous day.

"Damn!" Hood whispered angrily, kicking one of the posts. "We'll have to try and find a weak spot further along. Everyone stay low and be quiet."

Rather than running as they had before, they now crept along the edge of the fence, hoping there wasn't an enemy machine gun or pla-toon waiting in ambush and listening for movement.

"Shh! Do you hear that?" whispered Private Dawson, who hap-pened to be at the front of their eleven man line. Everyone halted in their tracks. Disembodied voices drifted through the fog ahead. To hear the voices over the fighting, they had to be close. Hood and Spurling slinked quietly ahead of Dawson. For a handful of tense sec-onds, Vernon heard each man subtly click off his rifle's safety catch in preparation for a shootout. He and Pritchard clicked theirs off at the same time.

"Why in God's name are they speaking so loudly?" Pritchard asked much quieter.

"I don't know, Pritch, but I think those are our boys," Vernon re-plied. He thought he heard a few curse words spoken in English, but he didn't want to hop to his feet and say hullo just yet.

The voices grew louder, but still no men had come into view. *If Fritz is anywhere near us, they'll know we're here now.*

"Vernon, I think I just heard one of them say—"

TAC-TAC-TAC! A German gun opened fire much closer than Vernon would have expected. Rounds spattered into the mud and leaves on the other side of the fence and clipped the fence's wires as they zipped through it.

"Get down!" Hood cried out, so quickly it almost sounded like he beat the machine gun to the punch. Every man flopped stomach-first to the ground for the second time, and 3 Section was soon returning fire. German rifles also joined in the fracas.

Vernon slid the end of his rifle through the fence and aimed to take a shot at the flickering muzzle flash. As soon as he placed his finger on the trigger and his eye on the sights, a burst hit the ground directly in front of him and sent a blinding spray of gritty mud into his open eye.

"Fucking hell!" Vernon yelped in pain. He tried to wipe the stinging away, but his hands and sleeves were dirty and offered no relief.

"*GHAAA!*"

One of the men near Vernon suddenly screamed. It was Lieutenant Hood. Through his clean eye, Vernon saw that a bullet had struck the lieutenant in the shoulder near his right collarbone. Hood rolled onto his back, clutching near his neck as blood started pouring out.

"Jesus Christ I'm hit!" Hood shouted. He picked up his revolver with his bloody left hand. When the bullet struck him, he'd dropped the gun from his right. "Fuck you, Fritz!" the stricken man cried. Still on his back, he angrily emptied his weapon, upside-down, in the direction of the enemy gunfire.

"Son of a bitch!" Spurling yelled, after seeing the amount of blood emanating from Hood's injury. "Sir, we need to get you out of here! Someone get Lieutenant Hood out of here!" he roared, over the lieutenant's salty objections.

Though the wound was bad, Vernon believed there was a slim chance Hood could be saved were he to reach treatment fast enough. Any man who saved an officer would gain praise from higher command—something his best friend sorely needed. Fearing the present situation may go poorly, he wanted Pritchard to get the hell out of there anyway. He reached over and punched Pritchard in the shoulder to grab his attention.

"Pritch!" Vernon yelled, pointing at the injured Hood. "You should drag him out of here and to the river! Spurling!" he called to the corporal, who turned quickly. "Llewelyn will take him!"

"Fine! Go!" Spurling answered.

Pritchard vacillated between pulling his rifle back and going for Hood, or keeping his sights pointed up the hill. "What about you, Vernon?!"

"Either we'll break through or fall back! We'll be fine!"

"What if Bannister sees me running away?!"

"Running away?! What?! If Hood makes it and Bannister does anything but recommend you for a medal I'll kill him myself! Now go!"

"Ah shit!" Pritchard barked. "You'd better make it out of here, you bastard!" He slung his rifle, rolled over to the wounded officer and grabbed him by the shoulder straps, before assuming a low crouch. He commenced dragging the fallen lieutenant away from the fence and the German machine guns and rifles beyond. In daylight, he'd have been dead to rights, but in the darkness and mist, only bad luck would prevent him from making it to the bottom of the Chivres Spur.

Come on Lew, you can make it! Vernon watched over his shoulder as his friend dragged Hood, squirming in pain, down the hill. The two disappeared into the mist after about fifty yards. He hadn't noticed it until then, but the fog had thinned. If that continued, it would soon offer no protection at all.

DENIS

Though 2 Escouade had been destroyed, it was only a matter of time before more men would be placed under Denis's command. Until then, he and Patrice were absorbed into 1 Escouade, after rejoining F Compagnie in the afternoon of September 13. Sergent Chouinard had survived the assault across the Petit Morin, and when Denis and Patrice found him he informed them that both Emery and Gustav had been wounded, neither man fatally, before the German retreat to the Aisne. Though Denis was relieved they were not killed, he still believed his apparent curse had played a part in their fate. Patrice did not hesitate in reminding him that the two were safe behind the lines and would no longer be forced to fight, which could not possibly be a bad thing.

Casualties had taken their toll on F Compagnie, reducing its strength to just over sixty percent of what it was upon mobilization. Less than a hundred and fifty men remained from the two hundred and thirty who first marched on Charleroi less than a month before. As such, 1 Escouade became an amalgamated unit, larger than a squad but smaller than two, with Sergent Chouinard in command, Caporal Gerard his number two, and the still-shaken Denis, an officer candidate who outranked them both, a subordinate.

Lieutenant Armistead, who'd also survived the battle, had looked Denis square in the eye as soon as he and Patrice made it back. Based solely on what he'd seen (or hadn't seen) looking back at him, the lieutenant made the decision—much to Denis's unspoken relief—to temporarily place him among the rank-and-file, to rediscover his ability to lead.

With XVIII Corps representing French Fifth Army's left flank and the force nearest the BEF's right, their advance moved at a pace relative to that of their British allies in Haig's I Corps. That advance pushed them further north of the line held by French Sixth Army and the BEF's other corps. Where the British II and III Corps faced stiff German resistance relatively close to the Aisne, ahead of XVIII Corps and Haig's troops, the right flank of Bülow's Second Army had positioned themselves more than two miles or more beyond the river. The Germans there commanded another high ridgeline, the Chemin des Dames.

The Chemin des Dames (Ladies' Path) was actually a road, named in the 18th century after King Louis XV's two daughters, known together as the *Ladies of France*—as it was a route they frequently traveled. The road with which the ridge shared its name ran parallel to it from east to west for over eighteen miles, starting on the heights about a mile northeast of the village of Craonne and continuing west. A plateau stretched north beyond the heights of the Chemin des Dames. The high ground provided the Germans with a clear view of the land to the south, which consisted of low, undulating fields providing sparse cover for the French troops. There were forested areas south of Craonne which masked the French advance to a point, but the forests stopped well short of the heights and also provided perfect targets against which the Germans could range their artillery.

XVIII Corps advanced toward German Second Army's far right flank in the area around Craonne after a largely uncontested crossing of the Aisne, while the rest of Fifth Army moved against the main body of German Second Army's lines in the direction of Reims to the east. Ferdinand Foch's Ninth Army stood next in line, and attacked Bülow's left flank east of Reims.

Though not as pronounced as it had been at the Marne, a soft spot still existed between German First and Second Armies. Between Haig's I Corps and Maud'huy's XVIII Corps, the combined Entente force was poised to exploit that vulnerable area. On September 13, XVIII Corps took Craonne and gained a foothold on the eastern tip of the Chemin des Dames. Their grip on the important piece of ground was tenuous at best, and the full strength of the corps would be needed to hold it.

Denis's pulse thumped as he passed through the thick forest. It was well before dawn on September 15. The 144th Regiment had not factored in the initial fighting for and capture of the ridge, but they were about to move from the protection and concealment of the woods to cross the thousands of yards of open field leading up to the Chemin des Dames. Général Maud'huy needed every last man to withstand the inevitable German counterattack. The rain from the night before had mostly let up, but the fog bank still held, though not as thick as it had been earlier. The sun was still at least an hour away.

In the moist air, it would be a long while before Denis's clothes and equipment dried. The squishiness inside his boots was unpleasant and the persistent dampness chilled him to the bone. Sleep hadn't come easy over the past two days, and with his constant shivering during the previous night it hadn't come at all. His mind was hazy and unfocused from the lack of rest, but his body felt much better moving than it had just sitting on the ground being cold.

The shivering continued even after he got his blood flowing. Patrice must have heard his teeth chattering, and attempted to place an arm around Denis's shoulder while they moved about the trees. Because Denis was a few inches taller and his haversack sat fairly high on his back, Patrice had to sling the arm around his neck. Denis leaned into his friend to walk with him.

"I never thought I would miss it, but I would sure like to feel the sun right now," Patrice said.

"Doesn't take much to make you realize which of the two is better," Denis replied, "though during our retreat I recall praying more than once for a torrential downpour."

"Well my friend, here is your wish, belated though it may be," Patrice said, raising a hand to the sky. "The Lord, in all his infinite power and wisdom, must have gotten your message a touch later than any of us would have liked."

"So it would seem."

"Perhaps you might pray for him to strike the boche dead with one fell swoop. He may answer by year's end."

"I think we all pray for that. Something tells me we'll have to decide the outcome ourselves."

"I think you're right."

When they emerged from the tree line and into an open field, the company commanders of 2nd Bataillon organized their men and the push toward the Chemin des Dames began. The 144th Regiment's other bataillons did the same. It was unlikely they'd come under any artillery fire so long as the sun was down and the fog was up, but with more than a mile of flat land to cross, there was still a chance they'd be caught in the open. The last thing on Earth Denis wanted to hear was the whistle of a shell speeding toward him and Patrice as they passed over open terrain.

He had but one friend left, his best friend, a friend he could not fathom losing. If the sun rose and the shooting began, there was nowhere for them to take cover. All it took was one shot, and Denis would be alone. That he could feel alone while surrounded by a veritable sea of men in blue and red hardly made sense to him, but that served little to alter the truth of it. They were all brothers in arms, but the term *brother* was supposed to be more intimate than that.

Maybe it really was possible to be alone, even amongst them. He didn't want to find out if it was. Patrice was alive and well, and Denis was willing to give his life to keep it that way. As 2nd Bataillon's column marched north, he clamped a hand on his dear friend's shoulder, squeezing hard as he struggled to suppress a nagging image of Patrice lying dead in the mud. He wanted to hug him, to tell him that he'd do anything to save him, but they were on the move.

His friend seemed to get the message anyway, and he brought his hand up to rest it on top of Denis's. "Are you all right?" he asked, with a look of utmost concern. His gentle, green eyes pierced through the dark and fog, and peered directly into Denis's soul.

"I don't know," Denis said. "I fear what this day may bring."

"I do too," Patrice replied, affectionately grasping the hand still clutching his shoulder. "We're all afraid. Anyone who's not is either lying or mad."

"Even if I make it through the next day or week, I'm not sure I can take responsibility for men's lives anymore," Denis muttered. His voice wavered.

"You don't have a choice. *Honneur et Patrie.* Is that not the motto of Saint-Cyr?"

"Yes. How did you know that?"

"It's no secret, is it? Honor and Fatherland is a straightforward and simple mantra that anyone can get behind, even a shit soldier like me."

"You're not a shit soldier, Patrice. You're anything but."

"Well...No matter. If I can buy into Saint-Cyr's motto, then Aspirant Denis Roux, a distinguished graduate, can hold true those principles as well. When we've made it through this day and beyond, when next you're offered a command, you will accept it and do what is asked of you. Maintain your honor for you, for me, for 2 Escouade, your family and especially your grandfather. We'll fight for our fatherland until we've knocked the boche into the Rhine."

Denis was impressed by his friend's encouragement. To hear Patrice espouse the merits of upholding honor and duty was something he never would have expected to hear from a man who only donned a uniform in the first place because he'd been conscripted.

278

"You know, Pat, you have become a changed man these last weeks."

"Maybe. I think it more a side effect of a desire to kill as many boche as I can. Plus, I can't stand the thought of you blaming yourself for what they've done to our friends. I want revenge, as much of it as I can get, before they get me."

Vengeance still did not seem the proper motivation to Denis. He didn't want to discourage Patrice's fighting spirit, though, so he left it alone. He did, however, want to address one thing.

"They're not going to get you, Patrice."

"We'll see," Patrice replied. "We'll just see..."

VERNON

How do they keep missing? Vernon could have sworn a hundred bullets per second cracked all around him as he lay next to the fence. He and the others were returning fire, but still had only muzzle flashes at which to aim. Jones had caught one in the head; they left him lying right where the bullet struck him. No use moving him. The voices that had stopped 3 Section in their tracks had turned to shouts as soon as the Germans opened fire, and Vernon could now see the men to whom those voices belonged. They were running along the fence in his direction. Their peaked caps and khaki serge dress were a far more welcome sight than pickelhaubes and grey tunics would have been.

"Who the fuck are you boys?!" yelled one of the approaching men. He had three chevrons on his upper sleeve. *A platoon sergeant. He doesn't look familiar.* Behind the sergeant, a man yelped and tumbled down the hill, shot and probably dead.

"1st Cheshire Battalion!" Spurling answered, "Who are you?!"

The sergeant, an older man with grey stubble on his face, dove to the ground next to Spurling. The platoon—or what was left of it—behind him followed suit, and aimed their rifles uphill.

Vernon was close enough to glimpse the man's cap badge, which was one of the more intricate badges he'd seen. A brass banner at its bottom embossed with *MANCHESTER* revealed the sergeant's regiment. The rest of the badge was all white metal, and was an emblem Vernon knew well. It was the city of Manchester's coat of arms. Manchester was about forty miles from where he grew up. Just above the badge's brass banner was a smaller one which read *CONCILIO ET LABORE*. Above that was a shield with three diagonal stripes and a ship in full sail embossed on its surface. Standing on their hind legs on either side of the shield were a mythical dragon-like antelope on the left, and a lion wearing a crown on the right. Atop the badge was a strange symbol—a globe covered in bees.

"2nd Manchester!" the sergeant answered. "You 15th Brigade lads must be lost!"

"No sir!" the corporal replied. "I think you and your boys might have wandered too far east!"

"No point in arguing, lad! What we need to do is find a way around this fence and up the hill!"

"I don't think that's going to happen, sir! We couldn't find any gaps. The whole bloody thing's been reinforced!"

"Aye, we couldn't find any either!"

A bullet must have zipped within a hair's breadth of Spurling's head. He flinched and brought both hands to his head. "Christ!" he shouted. "Well I'm not asking anyone to climb over this fucking thing, are you?!"

Another yelp and a stream of curses signified the death of another 2nd Manchester boy and the panic and aggravation of his mates. The sergeant rolled over to see who had just bought it, then turned back toward Spurling.

"No!" he said. "No I'm not!"

"Then we've not much choice!" Spurling cried, still bending his hat against his head. "We need to fall back!"

"Where is the rest of your platoon?!"

"Further east and lower! Our lieutenant was with us but he's been shot! They're pinned down and waiting for us!"

"Well those boys will have to figure it out on their own! We spend any more time here and these Huns will eventually find their aim!"

Spurling nodded in concurrence.

His mind made up, the old sergeant reached over and grabbed the corporal by the collar, tugging him closer. "You and your boys watch your step on the way down! Those bastards set trip wires all through these woods!"

"We know!"

The man let go of Spurling's collar and said, "Good luck to you, corporal!" He thrust out his hand.

"And to you, sir!" Spurling replied, accepting the brief handshake.

"ALL RIGHT SECOND PLATOON!" the sergeant roared, "DOWN THE HILL ON THE DOUBLE!"

The entire platoon of 2nd Manchester boys sprang to their feet at once and in a flash headed down the slope. A few were hit almost instantly and tumbled head over heels. If the bullet didn't kill those who fell, the tumble might have. Vernon and 3 Section hadn't the time to waste watching the Manchesters leave them in the dust.

"Come on then!" Spurling bawled, "Let's move!"

Vernon sucked in two quick breaths, and then shoved against the fence to propel himself away. A shower of lead chased him as he rapidly gathered momentum just steps into his bounding descent. Any number of dangerous obstacles could have been waiting for him and his 3 Section mates. At that speed, a collision with a tripwire would snap a leg bone in two.

"Somebody help!"

King had taken a round to the middle of the thigh and could no longer run on his own. Vernon would have stopped, but Dawson and Hawkes had already rushed to King's aid and stood on either side of him. They draped his arms around their necks. The two would attempt to carry him out of harm's way at great peril to themselves.

Through the thinning fog, Vernon spotted a rocky outcropping ahead. If he could get beyond that, the rocks would help to shield him from the lead storm ripping through the forest. Were Dawson and Hawkes to make it there as well, there was a much better chance of their getting King to safety.

"This way!" Vernon yelled, waving his arm wildly at them while he ran. He made it to the outcropping, and then stopped and turned to wait for the group of three in case they needed help. *Hurry up, chaps. You can make it!* They didn't have much further to go.

He heard the individual burst that got them. The German machine gunner had called their number, and called it loudly. A well-placed (or ill-placed) burst caught all three men numerous times in their legs and backs. They crumpled limply into a tangled pile.

"Bloody hell!" Vernon cried. He slugged the rock next to him with the side of his fist. The machine gunner had found his mark with precision, and Vernon watched helplessly as two men died trying to save a third. He turned angrily away and charged down the rocks on the heels of several other fleeing Tommies as round after round shattered the stone surfaces around him. Specks of exploding debris whipped against his skin and stung his face, and pebble-sized chunks of freshly chipped stone made finding proper footing more and more difficult.

Adrenaline propelled him faster, but the strenuous dash down the outcropping proved too much for his agility. Vernon planted his leading foot atop loose gravel and his foot slid forward, throwing him off balance. He kicked himself in the heel. His momentum kept his body moving forward, and carried him past his center of gravity. He sprawled face first onto the rocky ground and skidded on the jagged surface. His rifle tumbled from his hands, flipped end-over-end, and clattered to a stop fifteen feet in front of him. He bashed the left side of his face hard against the rock, and the jarring impact nearly knocked him unconscious.

It probably seemed far longer than it actually lasted, but he lay there for a time, analyzing which areas of his body he may have injured. His face and head were the worst, and a sting deep in his nasal cavity made his eyes water. Throbbing ribs were trivial, but the pain in his knees left him all but certain the skin had been raked clean off his kneecaps. His lower right thigh was tingly, numb, and worse off than the left. Second to his face, his right knee must have hit the rock the hardest.

Get your arse up and move! He didn't have time to fully comprehend just how much the fall had hurt. He thrust his hands against the ground and pushed himself to his feet, picked up his rifle on the run and continued his mad dash down the slope and toward the Aisne, limping the whole way. When he emerged from the trees and into a small grassy field, he knew he'd made it to relative safety. Relative, at least, to where he'd come from.

Because he'd fallen, the surviving men of 3 Section had already beaten him to the foot of the Chivres Spur. Private Granville was the first man he spotted. Granville was kneeling in the middle of the field, doubled over and gasping for air. Of all the men in Fourth Platoon, he was the only one with whom Vernon had gone to school when they were boys, though the two barely remembered one another from back then.

"Granny, are you hurt?" Vernon asked. He limped over and crouched beside him. The pain from his fall was setting in.

"No," Granville gasped. "I'm just bloody well winded!"

"Where are the others?"

Falling to one knee, Granville pulled in a deep breath and began to sob. "King, Dawson and—"

"I saw," Vernon interrupted him. "Where is everyone else?"

"How the fuck do I know?!"

"Hey, come now Granny...Let's see if we can't find them, all right?"

"All right."

Vernon helped the shaken and winded man to his feet and they moved across the field away from the spur. He had no idea at which point they'd emerged from, but as they came to a small wooden fence at the field's edge, he realized they'd moved further west on the spur than he'd thought. A little red house emerged through the fog. They were in someone's back yard.

"We must be in Missy, right?" Vernon asked rhetorically.

"Looks that way."

Movement near the edge of the house made the two men instinctively raise their rifles. Three shadowy figures were moving toward them.

"Stop right there!" shouted Vernon, flicking his safety catch off and applying nervous pressure to the trigger.

"Whoa! Whoa!" a startled but familiar voice answered. "Don't tell me I got away from Fritz only to be shot by Thomas!" It was Corporal Spurling, accompanied by Lance-Corporal Milburn and Private Lockwood. As a lance-corporal, Milburn was Spurling's second in command. Four of their men had fallen in the dustup, but at least the rest of 3 Section made it down unharmed, though Pritchard's fate was still up in the air. Both rifles were lowered simultaneously, and five sighs of relief issued from the mouths of the on-edge men.

"King, Hawkes and Dawson are dead," Vernon informed them.

"Son of a bitch…" Spurling murmured, lowering his head.

Lockwood buried his face in his hands, while Milburn stared at the sky. Neither said a word. The five of them stood in silence, while the gunshots and machine gun bursts of varying pitch and volume echoed through the forest and into the valley from the German defensive positions scattered along the heights. Confused shouts and whistle blows drifted down too—vain attempts to coordinate a floundering assault. British units were still stuck up there, struggling to maintain order amongst the chaotic tangle of trees, fences, trip wires, fog and dark.

"What do we do about the platoon?" Vernon asked, breaking 3 Section's stillness.

"They'll have to find their way down, same as us," replied Spurling. "Right now we should head into the village and wait for daylight. We don't need to be running around in the dark shouting for one another. Come on." Placing a hand on the two men beside him, the corporal guided them back toward the house. "Let's go Hayes, Granny. You too."

Unable to convince himself that heading back up the spur was of any value, Vernon complied without objection. *Maybe we'll find Llewelyn while we're here.*

Five wet, battered and exhausted men moved through the yards and gardens and onto the streets of the village of Missy, searching for other British soldiers. They did not have to search long. Hundreds of men from the battalions of both the 14th and 15th Brigades were gathering within the village, and the further 3 Section traveled into the heart of the town, the more men they saw. Small groups of Norfolks, Bedfordshires, Suffolks, East Surreys, and others stood or sat about, smoking cigarettes and quietly conversing, many of them in various states of injury and all of them weary.

Another group, the sergeant of which had a newly familiar face, loitered in front of a small general store. They were the men of the 2nd Manchester whom 3 Section had run into on the hill. Most of them had made it down unhurt, save for the sergeant. He sat on a small bench on the store's front porch, while two of his men tended to a bloody wound in his right shoulder. When he spotted Corporal Spurling heading down the street toward him, he called to him right away.

"Hey, it's the Cheshire boys!" the sergeant waved with his good arm, beckoning Spurling and the men to join him.

Vernon wasn't interested in chatting; he just wanted to find his friend. But he didn't want to be rude, either. He kept his head on a swivel while they joined the 2nd Manchesters, hoping he might see Pritchard wandering through the streets looking for others from 1st Battalion.

"I see you caught a good one, aye Sergeant?" Spurling said to the wounded NCO.

"Fucker passed right through the meat. No broken bones as far as I know. Just getting it patched up so I can go and pay it back double to the Huns."

The two men working on him glanced at one another briefly. They weren't as optimistic. There was no way the old sergeant would stay on the front lines, not with the amount of blood he'd lost. The point at which the bullet had exited appeared to indicate he'd suffered severe muscle damage. He'd likely be unable to move his arm for some time.

While Spurling carried on a conversation with the sergeant, Vernon paid little attention. The fog which had been so thick earlier was fading by the minute, and the inky black of the predawn morning was just beginning to lighten as the sun crawled out of the east. Soon it would break the horizon, and the thinning grey fog would turn a soft yellow.

"Vernon! Hey Vernon!" an excited voice squawked from directly behind him. It was a relief to hear.

"Pritch!" he shouted, spinning to face his friend. "You made it! And you're all right!"

"Not a scratch!" Pritchard beamed. He and Vernon hugged, firmly and reassuringly, while the others smiled and looked on. They all knew the strong bond the two friends shared. After breaking their grip around one another, Vernon took hold of Pritchard's upper sleeves and looked him in the eyes.

"How's Hood?" he asked.

"I think he'll make it. They've already taken him across the river."

"Well then congratulations, old boy! You just saved a man's life. Again."

Spurling, Granville, Milburn and Lockwood each patted him on the back for saving the lieutenant, but Pritchard quickly changed the subject.

"My God Vernon you look horrendous. Did we lose anyone else?"

He didn't want to sully Hood's rescue, but the truth was the truth. Vernon answered honestly. "Yes. Four for certain. And the rest of the platoon could still be up there."

"Ah..." Pritchard trailed off, shaking his head. "God dammit."

"I know..." Vernon said, rubbing his eyes. "...it's horrid."

"Speaking of horrid, Vernon. You've really been dusted up."

He most certainly had been. His soaking wet uniform was covered in all manner of dirt, mud and forest detritus. His tumble on the rocks had ripped holes in his tunic, and the knees of his trousers were torn wide, as was the skin underneath. There were dark, oozing gashes above his kneecaps, with dirt and tiny rocks mixed into the sticky blood. When he hit the ground, the left side of his face had made hard contact. His entire cheek was scraped along the rocks. Blood trickled from gashes on the left half of his face and dripped onto his tunic. His palms were scraped and bloody from a vain attempt to break his fall.

Pritchard looked better, though he had blood on the skirts and sleeves of his tunic. It was Hood's blood, but it was still gruesome.

"Which four died up there, Vernon?"

"Um...Jones, Hawkes, Dawson and King."

"Ahh," Pritchard said, grabbing the back of his neck. "They were good chaps. Dawson and Hawkes had little ones."

"A lot of good chaps are getting killed up there."

"You look like you nearly joined them. Come on, you've got to clean up."

The two found a spot to sit in front of the store, and Pritchard helped Vernon begin the process of cleaning and dressing the deep gashes on his kneecaps. The men around them mingled, smoked, conversed and ate, while others managed to sneak a nap, tired enough to sleep despite the shooting above Missy. Pritchard used water from his own bottle to rinse away the dirt and coagulated blood coating Vernon's knees.

"Lew don't waste your water!"

"I can get more from the river," smiled Pritchard. "But you'll have a hell of a time doing much of anything if we don't get these wounds cleaned and bandaged."

"I'll give you some from my canteen if you need it later," Vernon said.

"It's quite all right."

"WHAT IN THE HELL DO YOU CALL THIS?!" a devilish voice suddenly roared, materializing out of the foggy abyss.

Pritchard jumped and dropped his canteen.

Christ, not now. The captain came out of nowhere, and was right on top of them. E Company's brawny commander leered, seemingly on the verge of breathing fire.

"Vernon's wounds need cleaning, sir. I was just help—"

"I don't give a shit about Hayes and his pathetic scratches! Do you want to be a nurse, Pritchard? Is that what you're here for?"

"No, Captain Bannister, sir, I—"

"Shut your mouth, nurse Pritchard! Why are you men down here? Why are you not on the ridge?!"

Vernon was briefly left speechless, but found his words and said, "Captain Bannister, sir. We were up there. We've been pushed back under heavy fire. Lieutenant Hood was wounded. Llewelyn here saved his life! Dragged him all the way back."

"Hood should have had the courage to die up there, for the sake of the attack! Instead he left his platoon and they fled with their tails between their legs, much like you. Pritchard only brought Hood back to extricate himself from the fight even earlier, the coward! I ought to shoot him right now."

At least Fourth Platoon got away. It was welcome news, despite its source.

"Sir, may I speak?" Spurling interjected. The skinny young man held his bony chin high, and stood at attention behind and to the captain's right. His pointy face was defiant and confident.

Bannister turned to face the corporal. "I see Hayes and Pritchard's cowardice has rubbed off on you as well!" he growled, blind with fury.

"Sir!" Spurling snapped sternly. "I lost four men up there! DEAD!"

"And you failed to accomplish your objective, Corporal! They died for nothing!"

Vernon's jaw dropped. *This bastard. Why do men like Bannister survive, while good men fall in their place?* Pritchard's smile from knowing he'd done well melted from his face. He hung his head. Spurling, on the other hand, glowered. The much smaller man, highly agitated, appeared ready to lunge forth and strike, like a venomous snake with aims for larger prey. Smartly, the corporal held still, stifling whatever irrational urges he must have had in that moment.

"I can attest to their situation, sir," said the sergeant from the 2nd Manchesters. "My platoon and I were right alongside them, and they held for as long as I or anyone else would consider reasonable." The man was clearly woozy from blood loss, but he stood with one soldier's help. He held his wounded arm against his stomach. If ever there was a man who Bannister should listen to, it was the old sergeant. Wounded and bloody, his face etched with deep lines, his stubble white and grey, he was much nearer Bannister's age, if not older. He removed his cap. His hair was short and white. The stately NCO deserved respect from any man, regardless of rank.

Captain Bannister turned to the sergeant, looked him head to toe and snarled, "I did not ask you. Nor I do care what some dumb Manc cunt has to say about it. Fuck off, *Sergeant.*"

"Yes sir," the man replied, plainly offended. He sat back down, next to his shocked men, who were left just as offended as he.

"So..." the captain said after rudely dismissing the 2nd Manchester NCO, "...Nurse Pritchard...How did you manage to infect an entire platoon from a battalion not your own? I knew you were toxic, but Mancs too? Incredible..."

They weren't even up there at the same time, you damned bloody moron.

"Captain. Sir," Vernon said, rising to his feet. He winced in pain. "In the name of all that is decent, please. Men who help their fellow soldiers in trying situations are the ones who win decorations. You're berating a hero. For God's sake, leave him alone."

Bannister's hand moved toward his holster. He popped the button and gripped the butt of his Webley. He drew his firearm, aimed it at Vernon, and clicked back the hammer. The Mancs and Cheshires gasped.

Go ahead and shoot. Show everyone here the kind of man you are.

"I'm in no mood for defiance," the captain said. "I'll kill you where you stand, Hayes."

Do it then.

"Please, sir," Pritchard said softly, "I'm sorry for...running. It won't happen again, I swear it. Vernon is just upset that four didn't make it back."

Lew, no! Don't apologize!

"That's right, Nurse," Bannister sneered. "A Welsh coward. Flee one more time and this pistol will be aimed at you."

The captain waved his weapon at Pritchard, then lowered it and slid it into its holster. He turned abruptly and walked away. *What in the world just happened?* Vernon looked at Pritchard, who had tears in his eyes.

"Lew, you can't possibly let that rotter's head games get to you. You saved Hood's life! Bannister is the coward; he hasn't a speck on his uniform. He's got no idea where we've been."

"I don't know, Vernon, I was glad to get out of there when I did. I was terrified."

"And you think the rest of us weren't? I assure you, so was everyone else."

"But you stayed."

"Jesus, man, I'm down here now, aren't I? Hood is alive because of you, and don't ever forget it. I didn't carry anyone else out of there, and Dawson and Hawkes both died trying to do the same thing you did." Vernon gingerly sat back down as he spoke. "You made it out, you saved Hood, and Bannister is the biggest fucking cunt we'll ever meet in our entire lives. He's worse than any Hun."

Pritchard shrugged, his eyes still glossy, and knelt once again to finish cleaning Vernon's wounds. Vernon had nothing more to say. He rested his hand on the side of Pritchard's face, wrapped his fingers around to the back of his neck and squeezed gently to let his friend know he appreciated his help.

They had been in the first wave, which the Germans beat back harshly. Command was still compelled to push for a breakthrough, though, so more waves would come. It wasn't long before the next columns were marching past the general store, on the way to test their luck against the massive obstacle that was the Chivres Spur. Far too beaten to join in the action, the men of 3 Section watched the columns march by.

"Good luck chaps. Give them hell up there," Vernon encouraged the boys as they moved past, knowing many marched toward their death. While his words were meant to encourage, he could not help but notice that as the columns filed past, the fear in their eyes grew when they saw him. *My look must not be inspiring.*

The sun finally crested over the horizon beyond the river valley, and shortly thereafter heavier shooting commenced on the heights above Missy. The six survivors of 3 Section stayed at the store for another hour, and then left to search for signs of 1st Battalion within the village. When the captain left, he hadn't even bothered to let them know Fourth Platoon's or the rest of E Company's whereabouts. Because of the confusion of the earlier fighting, the entire village remained a mishmash of units, the officers and NCOs of which were still working to reorganize. Some were further along than others, and those that had collected their men were forming up in the yards, or moving into the fields on the outskirts of the small town.

"Vernon," Pritchard said, nudging him with an elbow, "I hear an aeroplane."

"And?"

"What if it's one of theirs?"

"I don't care. Hopefully it crashes."

Many of Missy's villagers had not evacuated, and some slowly began to peek out of windows and doors, having spent most of the previous few days hiding beneath beds or in cellars. Chimneys started smoking, as some residents began cooking meals for the hungry soldiers. Soon, a menagerie of delicious smells wafted through the streets. The scent of baking bread and boiling soups made Vernon's mouth water and his belly rumble.

The fog continued to lift and the fighting on the spur continued to chatter, but in the village, even with its close proximity to the shooting, Vernon felt oddly safe. Another hour passed, and their search still had not produced any sign of 1st Battalion.

"Bonjour," Spurling said to an old Frenchwoman standing in the front yard of her tiny yellow house. She waved. Vernon glanced at her as they walked by, and her eyes followed him. *Tough-looking old bird,* he thought.

FOOM! A horrible and familiar sound, different in pitch but familiar nonetheless, smacked Vernon in the ears. The air rushed from his lungs and his eyes flared wide as saucers. Something heavy crashed through the roof of the old lady's house, and an instant later the walls bulged outward and exploded when a massive shockwave decimated the entire structure. It almost didn't register, but when the house blew apart Vernon saw the front door fly from its hinges and strike the old lady's back. It cut her in half. Instinctively, the men of 3 Section hit the ground the second they'd heard the whistle. Debris scattered in every direction, showering them with wood splinters, nails and shattered brick. Because they reacted so quickly, no one else was injured. A thick, billowing black cloud was all that remained where the little yellow house once stood.

"What was that?!" Pritchard shouted. He coughed from the dust and smoke.

"Sounded like a howitzer!" answered Spurling.

"They killed that woman!" Vernon cried, sickened at seeing her grisly death. His ears rung from the huge blast. Everyone sounded like they spoke through a pillow.

"It was that bloody aeroplane! He told the artillery there were troops concentrated in the village!" Pritchard noted.

"We might be in trouble then!" said Granville.

Another explosion within the village was all confirmation they needed that the Germans were about to clear Missy with an artillery bombardment. A third explosion shook the ground three streets away; the blast thumped beneath Vernon's feet and inside his abdomen. Another black cloud rose over the tops of the houses. The men picked themselves up and ran for the village outskirts.

Screams from soldiers and civilians wounded by the exploding howitzer shells rolled through the streets. Confusion reigned supreme. Those civilians who hadn't fled were now caught in the line of fire, strewn about the soldiers fighting to protect them. Women and children ran from their homes and into the arms of the fighting men, most of whom did not speak their language.

A young mother cradling a wailing baby in one arm and dragging a teary-eyed little boy in tow with the other approached Vernon and cried, "Aidez-moi! Aidez-moi!" He didn't speak a word of French, but it didn't take much thought to put her cries into context.

"All right! Come with us!" he said, waving to her. He snatched the weeping boy into his arms, and 3 Section, with three helpless civilians under their protection, hurried through the streets of Missy toward the flat farmland south of the town. Vernon hadn't eaten much that day and lugging the boy, small as he was, in addition to his gear and rifle, was incredibly taxing.

Passing through the streets of the panicking village with high explosive shells falling haphazardly every thirty seconds was a strange, alien aspect of warfare. Shells didn't discern innocent from combatant. At least a man firing a rifle or machine gun chose his target most of the time. The artillerymen were operating their weapon from a mile, or two, or three or more away, and their shells didn't care whether they blew up fighting men or innocent children.

On their hasty journey through Missy, two more shells detonated close enough to Vernon's group for them to feel the percussion and see the smoke, but they made it to the village outskirts and into a turnip field.

"Where's the fucking river?!" Lockwood shouted, ignoring that he was in the company of a lady and small children. They might not have spoken English, but Vernon was pretty sure the woman knew that *fuck* was a curse word.

"We're further west, there's more ground to cross," Vernon answered with a scowl. "Let's get these three to a boat and we'll go back and try to help others."

When 1ˢᵗ Battalion first crossed the Aisne, their landing point was to the east of Missy, where the distance between the riverbank and the spur was much shorter. However, the river bent southwestward at a dramatic angle about five hundred yards before it reached the village, so the flat ground between the town and the Aisne was considerably wider, and grew more so the further west one traveled. From the point at which they emerged from Missy, the river lay more than half a mile due south.

Panting, they hurried away from the devastation raining upon the once quaint little town. They passed over roads and the railroad tracks, and across hundreds of yards of field. Luckily at the water's edge, a group of engineers from the 14ᵗʰ Brigade was just about to shove off in one of their makeshift pontoon boats, and 3 Section caught them in the nick of time.

"Wait!" Spurling shouted to the engineers. "We need you to take these civilians across."

"What's going on back there?" asked one of the engineers, staring north.

"Howitzers," Spurling answered, "heavy ones too."

"Well come on then, let's get them in the boat," said another engineer. "I get a feeling we'll be doing this a lot today."

"I get a feeling you're right," replied a third.

Vernon hoisted the little boy into one of the men's hands, and then gently eased the baby out of the mother's arms. She was reluctant to let the infant go, but eventually did. After he handed over the baby, Vernon motioned for her to climb aboard as well. Before she climbed into the pontoon, she looked back with glistening eyes at the men who, for the time being, would stay behind. "Merci," she said, holding her hand over her heart.

"Keep moving south," Vernon said to her, pointing across the river. "South...Don't stop."

She nodded and climbed in, and with one last wave goodbye, the pontoon headed across the Aisne, and the six soldiers were running back toward the inferno.

DENIS

The Entente troops didn't know it, but as Maud'huy's XVIII Corps, Haig's I Corps and Général Louis Conneau's Cavalerie Corps slowly advanced onto the heights of the Chemin des Dames, they were exploiting another gap between German First and Second Army. Over the course of September 15-16, the German cavalry divisions weakly linking Kluck's and Bülow's forces had pulled back on the plateau, opening a brief window ripe for exploitation. Unfortunately, the French left and British right were advancing too sluggishly to take full advantage, their commanders unaware of the prize in front of them.

Denis wasn't sure how long 2nd Bataillon had been pushing onto the plateau, but their columns, flanked on either side by the rest of the 144th, had put close to a mile between themselves and the ridgeline north of the tiny village of Craonnelle, a mile southwest of Craonne. Their advance to the heights had brought them through another forest, and then to the farmlands beyond. Nearly the full strength of the 70th Brigade, and most of the 35th Division would participate in the advance, with a small contingent remaining behind to hold a defensive line in case of retreat.

The time was approaching noon, the day, September 17. The air remained warm, but a gloomy and ominous grey hung in the sky overhead. A storm was coming. Denis smelled a mild, damp sweetness in the charged atmosphere. The static zinged inside his nostrils and the pressure welled in his sinuses. The world was a shade yellower. Conneau's Cavalerie had pushed close to two miles ahead, and the slower infantry no longer had sight of the mounted troops.

"Shouldn't the cavalry have met them by now?" asked Patrice.

"Yes…" Denis answered distractedly. He was lost in contemplation as to why there was no shooting ahead. "You would think…"

There was fighting further east and west, but why the boche offered little to no resistance from due north was baffling.

"It's probably a trap…" said Patrice.

"Shit, Pat, use your head. Where are the boche hiding?"

"I don't know, dammit. They're boche. It would be just like them to employ dirty tricks."

"Let's not pretend we wouldn't use dirty tricks against them, given the option. That's beside the point. This is no ambush."

"What is it, then, retreat?"

"Maybe."

"Then I hope Conneau's men catch them and shoot them in their backs."

Gunfire erupted from the north, and although it was distant, it prompted Denis to glance sarcastically at Patrice and lift an exaggerated eyebrow. "Perhaps that is precisely what we hear. We'll soon find out. The cavalry has either met a rearguard action, or it's counterattack."

It was the latter. The German cavalry screen had pulled back to allow General Josias von Heeringen's German Seventh Army and the German VIII Reserve Korps to advance from the north and reinforce the line between Kluck and Bülow. Seventh Army had been pulled from lower Alsace after the fighting there fell into stalemate. To the east, near Reims, the German units that had earlier fallen back also initiated their counterattack. The French and British on the plateau were advancing against what was about to become a fully reinforced and unbroken German line.

The bulk of Kluck's First Army to the west and Bülow's Second Army to the east were already dug in, and their artillery positioned. Much of French Fifth Army remained all but stationary in front of Bülow's army, and was unable to advance against the heavy German fire. The same was true for French Ninth Army on their right, and for French Sixth Army on the BEF's left. The only segment of the front in which the Entente forces had any chance of making significant headway was the five mile stretch of the Chemin des Dames held by Maud'huy, Conneau and Haig's men.

Conneau's Cavalerie fought the battle they could, but their retreat was imminent. Their withdrawal was initiated before the infantry could charge forth to assist them. Faced with annihilation from a superior German force, Conneau's troops bolted south. A disorganized and battered squadron of mounted riders rumbled past 2nd Bataillon and back toward the ridgeline, but the infantrymen maintained their northern course. They would not surrender what they'd retaken without first making their case.

A week earlier, after burying his men, Denis had considered symbolically throwing his sword in the Petit Morin, in the belief that he was undeserving of wearing it. But symbolism would have proven nothing. He kept it instead, and now it was coming in handy. When Conneau's Cavalerie pulled back, the Germans advanced more quickly than expected. Their leading edge caught the advanced forces of XVIII Corps, Denis, Patrice and 2nd Bataillon among them, in a frontal attack. There was a light exchange of artillery fire, and when the cannons stopped, both sides scratched and clawed for ground. Neither side would surrender an inch. Distances closed, as they did when both sides fixated on the advance. The fighting fell to hand to hand combat when the French commanders called for a bayonet charge. Denis found himself caught in yet another horrific and savage close-quarters fight.

He'd already thrice fired his revolver, and missed once. He tried to stay close to Patrice, but his friend was a madman, unleashing his rage and frustration on the men in grey he hated so much. Patrice wildly swung his rifle back and forth at the heads of any nearby boche, screaming curses and all but frothing at the mouth. He was possessed by the blind rage of which Denis had warned him.

Bang! Denis shot a man who'd rushed him, bayonet outstretched. *Shot number four.* He surveyed his space then looked for Patrice again, and found him just as a German moved to thrust a bayonet into his friend's back. Clemence's death flashed through his mind. *Hurry! One shot!* He'd never forgive himself if he was a second too late to save Patrice. He raised his pistol in a blink. He had no time to aim. If he missed, the shot might hit Patrice. And if a miss didn't hit him, it still meant Patrice got a bayonet in his back.

Bang! The German fell dead, shot in the back of his head. What a surprise that must have been for him, expecting to put an end to a Frenchmen and then briefly feeling that firm punch to his head. His helmet rolled away and his rifle fell to the ground, and its bayonet came so close to Patrice that it landed between his legs. He'd heard the shot and must have felt the rifle hit the dirt behind him, and he spun to face Denis, pointed at him in appreciation, and continued the fight.

One more shot, Denis. Better make it count.

Locked in a struggle to the death, the killed and wounded fell—additional hazards with which the upright combatants had to cope. It would have been easy to trip over the bodies, scattered at random, of either friend or foe. Denis protected his space while struggling to maneuver closer to Patrice, when one such fallen German grabbed his ankle. He tripped. He fell to his stomach, landed hard on his elbows, and nearly impaled himself with his own sword.

Terribly startled and coursing with adrenaline, he rolled over and frantically kicked the injured boche in the face to break the grip around his lower leg. The grip was strong, and it wouldn't let go. Denis kicked and kicked at the man, who grunted and screamed with the first vicious strikes, but then fell silent. Denis only stopped kicking when the German's head had turned to mush and fell in on itself. His teeth were smashed in, blood poured from his every orifice, and his right eye had popped. It looked like a hatched turtle egg.

Death was death and killing was killing, but kicking a man's head in was a new and terrible first which, for a second or two, stopped the battle around Denis. He froze in brief, meditative thought, disgusted by what lay at his feet, and disgusted that he was the one who'd done it. *Is this what honor and fatherland requires of me?* Men were slaughtering one another, like animals, and suddenly he was afraid for the world. War was a sickness, yet century after century, man just kept on at it. Kept at it over lines, drawn on a map. Maybe man was the sickness, and war, just a symptom.

Bang! It was not the time or place for rumination. Shot number six went into the chin of a German who suddenly towered over him. Denis still lay on his back, trapped by his thoughts, and his assailant was inches from driving a gun butt into him. It was purely reflexive that he'd raised his revolver and pulled the trigger. He barely knew what was happening until the gun went off. *That could have been the end of you, Denis. Get up before it happens again!* He was out of bullets, and still in the thick of it.

"Denis! You're empty! Watch yourself!" yelled Patrice, who hurriedly ran toward him. His face and hands were spattered with fresh blood. His bayonet was dark red and dripping.

How did he know my gun was empty?

"We're all empty!" Denis hollered back. He rose to his feet and the two stayed close, protecting their circle.

Not *everyone* was empty. Far from it. There was still much shooting. It was an aspect of hand to hand fighting which boiled down purely to luck. There were Mausers with rounds in the chamber. There were Lebels with rounds in the chamber. Some officers had only recently drawn their pistols. In the grey, blue and red swirl, life and death quite often fell to chance. You either tangled with or entered the line of fire of someone who could still shoot, or you didn't. You either locked horns with someone who fought better than you, or you didn't. Your back was turned at the wrong time, or it wasn't. It was all chance. And odds. And eventually, odds always caught up.

Two Germans emerged from the crowd almost simultaneously, and confronted Denis and Patrice from opposite directions. Patrice jabbed his bayonet at the one in front of him, holding him at bay, while Denis bluffed at the other with his empty revolver, stopping him in his tracks. *He'll only fall for that once.* The two Germans circled around Denis and Patrice as the two friends stood back to back. The greater battle surrounded them. Patrice moved his upper body erratically from side to side, poking his meticulously sharpened and freshly painted *Rosalie* toward the German, who danced back and forth to avoid it. Both waited for a window to strike.

The boche facing Denis thrust his rifle and bayonet forth as well, probing for an opportunity. The man's craggy face was pitted and scarred, and he had to be well over forty years old. There was no humanity left in his eyes. Whoever he was before the war, it was likely little to none of him remained. Denis slapped each of the probing thrusts away with his sword, hacking small chunks from the Mauser's wooden fore grip with each strike. Neither man would commit to an attack. In fighting such as it was, fights lasted only seconds after one committed.

"Denis, we must do away with these fuckers before someone joins them!"

"I know, Pat! Maintain your guard!"

"I've got him..."

They spoke cautiously, while keeping eye contact with their respective marks. Denis could not see the friend at his back, but he could sense his movements.

"Yes...you Allemande cocksucker..." Patrice taunted the man circling him. "Boche fucker...We will leave you here!" He thrust his weapon again, then pulled back. "And then we'll march to Berlin and burn down your house, after I've raped your wife on your bed!"

The German screamed, committed to his attack and lunged at Patrice, who swung his rifle up at an angle into the man's Mauser, deflecting the blade. Patrice countered by swinging his rifle butt, and struck the boche in the mouth. The man fell to the ground and dropped his weapon. Patrice leapt onto him, pinning his arms to the ground with his knees as the man squirmed and tried to throw him off.

Denis's man committed as well, and he side-stepped and forcefully swatted the man's rifle again. In committing to the attack, the boche's full weight was behind his lunge, and he stumbled past. Denis twisted and slashed the off-balance German's lower back, beneath his pack. The blade did not cut all the way through his thick clothing, but he fell to his stomach and before he could recover, Denis was upon him.

With great force, he thrust the point of his sword downward and into the back of the German's neck. *Splat!* The blade passed through the man's neck and thudded into the ground underneath. Denis twisted the blade so it would be over quickly. The man gurgled and twitched, but that was it. He was done for. Victorious, Denis turned to Patrice—still kneeling on the other German's arms—and gasped.

"Patrice, stop!"

"You!" *thud* "Fucking!" *thud* "Bastard!" *thud*

Patrice was furiously hammering his fists into the German's face, ignoring completely the battle around him. Anyone could have stricken him dead. *My God, he's in hysterics.* He wept while he mercilessly concaved the German's face with his fists. The man was very much dead, yet Patrice kept punching and shouting obscenities. Denis ran to him and grabbed him by the shoulder straps. He dragged him from atop the dead man and yanked him to his feet.

"Patrice, goddammit!" he yelled, shaking the agitated soldier to gain his attention. "What's the matter with you?!"

"I told you, Denis!" Patrice screamed. "I fucking hate them!" He kicked at the corpse. His green eyes were crazed. Denis had never seen anything like the look in his eyes before. Maybe there *were* two people inside Patrice, but the other certainly wasn't a girl—it was a cold-blooded killer.

"Well you got this one! He's dead! You can kill him no more than you have!"

"Hey, you assholes!" Sergent Chouinard boomed from somewhere behind them. "If you're quite finished, would you shut up and give me a hand?"

In turning to face the sergent, they learned why he sounded so aggravated. He and a German were caught in a tussle. Chouinard, his nose heavily bloodied and dripping around the corners of his mouth, stood behind his foe, strangling the enemy with his own Mauser. Somehow, the sergent was able to maintain his grip around the rifle barrel even with his broken right hand. The German, for his part, was putting up a spirited struggle against the much larger sergent, and had managed to sneak his hands between his throat and the weapon, preventing Chouinard from fully cutting off his air supply. Kicking his legs and striking the larger man's shins with his boot heels, the beet-red German was not ready to give up.

When Denis and Patrice approached, the feisty German shouted to them with choked and teary pleas, "Kamerad! Kamerad!" He was scared, and rightly so.

His pleas could not have fallen on deafer ears than Patrice's. With a jerk of his hand and a leap forward, Patrice detached his *Rosalie* from his Lebel and—before Denis could stop him—grabbed the German by the hair. Chouinard continued holding the struggling man upright with the rifle. Patrice slowly pushed the tip of his needle-point bayonet into the soft flesh beneath the unfortunate young boche's jaw. He tried to scream, but blood filled his throat and sprayed from his mouth. Patrice pushed, and the point sank further into the man's skull. His eyes rolled back in his head and his body convulsed. Patrice's arms began to shake visibly as he applied more pressure to his bayonet, until finally he could push it no further.

"That's enough!" cried Denis.

Patrice yanked the blade from the dead man's jaw. A grotesque sucking sound accompanied its withdrawal. Chouinard released his grip on the rifle, and the bloody corpse collapsed at his feet.

"Kamerad means friend you fucking imbeciles!" Denis shouted. "He would have surrendered!" He was furious they had refused to take the man prisoner.

"I know what it means!" snapped Patrice. "Where would we have taken him in the midst of this?!" He threw up his arms and demonstratively looked around. "The first chance he saw to escape or kill one of us, he would have!"

"I sure hope if any of us are taken prisoner, they don't act as you have!" Denis countered, pointing forcefully at the corpse at Chouinard's feet.

"In a thousand years, I'll never be taken—"

The shrill toots of a bugle interrupted Patrice's blustering, and sounded 2nd Bataillon's retreat. To then, the two sides had battled to a draw. As many in blue remained as in grey. In the distance to the north, however, a grey swarm was on its way.

"Their reserves have arrived!" Denis shouted, having caught a quick glimpse of the approaching horde as soon as the bugles sounded. He scanned the immediate area to make sure they had a proper window in which to make an exit, and then tugged on Patrice and Chouinard's sleeves to get them moving. "We must leave!"

The weight of an entire army approached, troops fresh and replete with ammunition. Denis and Patrice had once again to run for their lives to avoid certain death. Chouinard, despite his mass, stayed close to them as what remained of the bataillon trampled over the fields and through the forest through which they'd passed earlier that day.

By nightfall on September 17, under the weight of the German counterattack, XVIII Corps had lost Craonne, having been pushed from the Chemin des Dames north of the town. They did, however, cling to their position atop the ridge half a mile west of the city, though just barely. The 144th Regiment's retreat brought them to low ground south of the ridge near Craonnelle. The last vestiges of momentum following the Entente victory at the Marne were lost. With their advance ground to a halt, French and British commanders ordered their men to dig in. The Battle of the Aisne ended in a bloody draw, with the Germans refusing to relinquish the hold on their far superior positions.

GORDON

Gordon opened the frosted glass door, and cautiously stuck his head inside. The French recruiter was sitting behind his desk. That desk—an oversized, intricately carved, reddish-brown mahogany monolith, sat near the far wall of a spacious, well-decorated and high-ceilinged office, confined within the walls of a magnificent three story limestone building. Two tall, round top windows faced the street outside, and the long, maroon curtains were wide open, flooding the room with sunlight. A giant map of Europe hung on the wall behind the Frenchman. Gordon took a breath, then stepped confidently into the room and approached the desk.

The recruiter smiled warmly, and then clasped his hands on the desk in front of him. "Bonjour," he said. "Senegal?"

What? Gordon froze, briefly confused by the one-word question. "I beg your pardon?"

"I asked if you hail from Senegal, but now I have my doubts."

"Oh. No I do not. I'm from the States. Good afternoon, sir. My name is Gordon Graham."

"My apologies, I jumped to a conclusion before hearing your words," the man said. "A number of Senegalese have come through my door this month."

"No apology is necessary, sir. I've been called much worse."

"Allow me to revise my greeting. Good afternoon to you. My name is Sergent Bellamy. What can I do for you, Monsieur Graham?"

Monsieur? Sometimes even the most basic social courtesies could come as a surprise—being greeted with dignity was one of them. Sergent Bellamy was fairly young, in his early thirties at the latest. He had chestnut hair, slicked back on his head, and a tightly maintained moustache, darker in color than the hair atop his head. Dressed in a dark blue tunic with a high red collar and shiny gold buttons, he looked as well put-together as any uniformed man could. On appearance, he did not belong behind a desk at all. *Why is he not serving at the front?*

Wishing to cut to the chase immediately, Gordon, projecting utmost confidence, let the sergent know exactly what it was the man could do for him. "I would like to volunteer for service and fly aeroplanes for France, sir."

Bellamy offered only a modest scowl before politely saying, "Monsieur, I fear this may not be possible."

Unsurprised by the response and undeterred, Gordon replied, "If I were to join the Foreign Legion I would be permitted to train and fight, yes?"

"Of course."

"And if I were permitted to fight, why should it matter whether I was in the air or on the ground?"

The Frenchman contemplated for a moment. His brown eyes stared directly into the bright, grey seriousness in Gordon's. Neither man blinked. Bellamy was sizing him up. *Is he trying to read my resolve, or searching the English dictionary in his mind for the most colorful way to tell me off?* Trying his utmost to stay poised, the tension and nervousness knotted Gordon's insides. *Please don't call me a nigger just yet. Give me a chance.*

Bellamy cleared his throat. "Monsieur, what makes you think that you are qualified to do such things? We already have pilots in training."

"I know, sir."

"Do the Americans not have flying machines for their army? If you wish to fly, then why not fly American machines?"

Gordon slipped his hand into the hip pocket of his grey suit. He didn't believe in bad luck and held no superstitions, so he wore the same suit and blue tie he'd worn to the recruiter in Dayton. With his four precious photographs in hand, Gordon reached across the broad desk and gave them to the Frenchman. "The Americans don't want a nigger like me flying their machines, sir," he said. "I've already been told as much. Coloreds serve with coloreds, and they get no access to aeroplanes. The machine in the pictures is mine. I built it with my own hands, from my own design."

Taking time to thoroughly examine each shot, Bellamy nodded approvingly at each one. "It looks quite similar to a Wright machine," he said.

Gordon was surprised, as well as proud, to hear him say that. He grinned.

Bellamy grinned too when he reached the fourth image. "And there you are, in mid-flight. That is quite the photograph."

"My sister captured it."

"She has an eye for photography."

"She very much enjoys it. She's twelve."

"Twelve?"

"Yes sir."

The sergent rubbed his chin. "Two talented siblings with very different skill sets, from what I suspect is quite the remarkable family. How old are you, Monsieur?"

"I'm twenty-one years old, sir."

The Frenchman raised his eyebrows and nodded his head, impressed. His curiosity was piqued. "That is an impressive feat for such a young man. But what makes you want to come here to fly aeroplanes if you've built one of your own?" Bellamy clearly still had reservations, but at least he'd yet to call him a name and send him on his way. At least he was listening.

"The machines here are more advanced, Sergent Bellamy, and I would love to fly the best that technology has to offer. My country refuses my service in that capacity, but if your country would just give me the chance, I'd be willing to lay my life on the line in gratitude."

"Were you ever to get in the air, you might have to do just that. They've begun to shoot at one another up there, you know."

That, I did not *know.* "Has anyone hit anything yet?"

Laughter. "No. Not yet. But as with all things, there will be a first."

Undaunted by the prospect, Gordon said, "Sir, if I was sitting in the cockpit, I wouldn't care if there were machine guns flying around up there."

"Brave words. Actions often prove different."

"Not mine."

The man sat at his desk deliberating silently, save for the index finger he repetitively tapped against the stack of documents beneath his right hand. He slid the photographs back to Gordon. "You must genuinely love flight, yes?"

"More than I can possibly describe, sir. I've loved everything about it since I was six years old. The science, the engineering, the act. You see, I'm from Dayton, Ohio, and when I was little I saw the

Wright Brothers performing experiments in a field that was mere miles from my family's house."

Bellamy smiled at Gordon's story. "And from that point forth you were…"

"Fascinated. Inspired. Obsessed, you might say. Maybe to a fault."

"Some obsessions, monsieur Graham, are worth such dedication. It sounds as though you've found one which, to you, is very much worth it, yes?"

"Absolutely."

"So in your obsession, have you kept abreast of the most recent advances?"

"I believe I have. I hadn't the resources to employ the latest engineering on my machine, but I've studied the journals and am fairly certain I've achieved a practical and functional understanding."

"What about engines? Are you adept at fixing machinery?"

The only way to truly learn engines was through a hands-on approach, no matter how smart the mechanic. *The Hawk*'s engine was a dinosaur, and though Gordon had learned it inside and out, the newest engines being placed in the latest machines were far more sophisticated, powerful and complex. He'd never seen one in person, let alone put his hands on one.

"Yes sir…" Gordon replied. His heart and belly fluttered. That the man behind the desk was even playing along without being dismissive had gotten his adrenaline flowing. His hands trembled and he fought to avoid stammering. "I…I'm a fast learner when it comes to such things." *I'd better be.*

Bellamy leaned forward and rested his elbows on the desk. He clasped his fingers together and placed his head against them. He closed his eyes. He waited. Then he drew in a deep breath through his nose, unclasped his hands and sat upright. He again looked Gordon in the eye. "Monsieur Graham, this is what I will do for you," he said. "I cannot make the promise that you will ever be permitted to fly aeroplanes, for that is not my decision to make. But what I shall do is write a recommendation, requesting you be accepted to study as a mechanic. I know a man at one of the training schools well, and I will ask this favor of him because I believe you to be a smart young gentleman in need of a chance. Your country failed to give that to you, but here you may be permitted to try."

Bellamy began writing on a sheet of paper. Gordon's heart thumped into his throat as he realized the window of opportunity he so desperately craved had just opened up a tiny crack.

"I have yet to encounter a situation such as this, and to be quite honest with you, Monsieur Graham, I am unsure of the legality," Bellamy said, still scribbling on the paper. "But I will allow you to sign your Foreign Legion documents and for the time being, forego the standard training. You will attend l'école Blériot de Pau, where you will study strictly as a mechanic, and only as such. If this proves too much for you, then you will be required to leave the school and join in training for the ground forces. Is this agreeable?"

Gordon did not hesitate. "Yes sir. Thank you, sir."

"Very well, Monsieur Graham. You will travel to Pau. There you will be required to pay a training fee. The standard is eight hundred francs, but that is for pilots, and yours should be less. I don't know how much. Is this a cost you can afford?"

"Yes, I believe I have just enough extra money saved up. Did you say Pau, sir?"

"I did."

I'll be damned.

Bellamy continued, "You will ask for a Monsieur Plamondon, and present him with this letter. He is a friend who owes me a favor, and that favor will be you."

"Thank you, sir," Gordon said, on the verge of becoming emotional.

A man he'd just met was handing him more of an opportunity than he ever would have been given back home. That fact did not escape him, and it placed him in a debt he could only repay through unwavering success at the Blériot School. If he never saw Bellamy again for the rest of his life, he would always remember the kindness the French sergeant had shown him.

Gordon signed each line of the necessary paperwork pushed to him from across the desk. His hands were so shaky his signatures were nearly illegible. When he finished signing the forms, the Frenchman gave him the documentation he'd need to bring with him to Pau, including the hand-written letter to Monsieur Plamondon.

"I believe you are set," Bellamy said. "Have you any further questions?"

"No sir," answered Gordon.

"Well then..."

The sergeant pushed against the desk, and his chair rolled back. Gordon figured he would stand up and salute, or perhaps walk around the desk to shake his hand. This was a man he absolutely wanted to shake hands with. Instead, Bellamy reached his arms down on either side of his chair, and began pushing its bicycle-like wheels forward.

I didn't even notice...

Bellamy was wheelchair-bound. When he rolled his chair around the desk, his affliction was no longer hidden from view. Both his legs were missing at the knee. His trouser legs were pinned, and dangled over the edge of his seat. Gordon tried not to stare.

"Monsieur Graham, I cannot assure that you will not meet hostility in your quest. The attitude toward men of color may not be quite so harsh here as it is in your country, but that does not mean you will be seen as anyone's equal. If you are to succeed, you will only do so with tremendous difficulty. I wish you the best of luck. Please do not make a fool of me for giving you this chance."

"I won't sir, I promise."

Gordon stepped forward to shake Bellamy's hand. The Frenchman had a stony grip, but so did Gordon. *I wonder what happened to him.* The war was not yet old enough to have taken his legs. There was no way he'd have been able to recuperate that quickly, even if he'd lost them on day one. Whatever had happened to the sergent, it happened before the Great War began.

"Thank you so very much, Sergent Bellamy. You will not regret this."

"I hope not. Farewell and good luck, Gordon Graham."

"Again, sir, from the bottom of my heart, thank you. Goodbye."

Gordon, trembling with relief and infused with vitality, left the office and walked onto the streets of Paris. He had come all the way to France to ask for an opportunity, and a small one had been granted. Now it was entirely on him to prove exactly what he was capable of. As he walked the streets smiling at everything and everyone, people must have thought him mad.

The city looked different than it had before his meeting with Sergent Bellamy. His focus had been so zeroed in he'd hardly bothered to take in the spectacle until that moment. Paris was a glorious city, one of the world's largest. He'd ignored New York for the eighteen hours or so he'd spent there, being so focused on his objective, but with the mood he was now in, he let Paris infiltrate his senses. It was a living, breathing, gigantic work of art, and beautiful to look upon. It even smelled different than before. That piss was one of the smells was trivial—after all, no one went to the Louvre to *smell* upon the Mona Lisa. There were so many more scents swirled together—auto exhaust, bakeries, restaurants, cafés, a hint of horse manure—that no emanation overpowered the other.

While a large number of Parisians had evacuated the city during the run-up to the Battle of the Marne, there still remained hundreds of thousands either unwilling to evacuate, or trusting the Germans would be held at bay. To that point, those citizens' trust in the Entente's resolve was well-founded. The German retreat from the Marne had alleviated much of the fear and tension which had built up in the city during the war's first month.

Life in Paris had returned to a state of relative normalcy. Hundreds of Parisians promenaded about. Black Renault taxicabs passed by on the street, with their open, boxy driver's cabins and closed, carriage-style passenger cabins, shuttling paying customers to and fro. Horse hooves clacked against the cobble street, pulling wagons stocked with supplies, passengers or munitions. Bicycled riders rolled leisurely past, living life as if the northeastern corner of their country was not bathed in fire and blood.

Just one presence betrayed the casual atmosphere. Uniformed French soldiers were everywhere, going about their soldierly business just as the civilians went about theirs. There may have been a war on, but the men wearing the kepis, greatcoats and red trousers were the only ones who gave it away.

As he made his way to the cheap and dingy hotel where he'd found a room, he gawked upward at the stone architecture of the buildings on either side of the street. He was a guest in a city that had been around for over a thousand years longer than his own country had ever existed, if he could even call the United States his own country. It belonged more to others than it did to him. While the buildings surrounding him weren't *that* old, many had stood for hundreds of years before his great-great-great-grandfather was captured and brought to the Americas aboard a slave ship.

There was more history laid out before his eyes than had ever been written back home. Paris had outlasted the Romans, survived the Black Death (more than once), had seen kings, emperors, conquerors and conquest, revolutions, siege and defeat spanning countless wars over nearly two thousand years, yet the city still stood, a testament to its resiliency and greatness. Gordon saw himself staying in a place like Paris, long after accomplishing what he hoped to accomplish. Maybe one day he might invite his little sister Liza to come visit. For her, that would have been a dream come true.

In the distance, close to the Seine, he spotted the Eiffel Tower, the tallest man-made structure in the world and a more modern addition to Paris's silhouette, it having been constructed just twenty-five years earlier. Gordon once read that many Parisians hated Gustave Eiffel's design, but from where he stood, the imposing, iron lattice tower was magnificent. He would have loved to go and see it up close, but the sooner he got to Pau, the better. The Eiffel Tower could wait.

Gordon retrieved his suitcase from the crummy hotel and made his way to the train station. He purchased a one-way ticket to Pau. He wasn't coming back to Paris on anything but a troop train carrying him and his fellow pilots to the front.

VOGEL

Vogel checked his Luger one last time, making sure the safety was on before tucking the pistol into his waist belt. Adler likewise checked and holstered his. They were ready to climb into the respective cockpits of their Rumpler B.I biplane, new from the factory in Berlin. True to his word, General von Kluck had ensured they were given one of the finest aircraft available.

While fastening the closure on his holster Adler said, "Vogel, if we see an enemy machine approach, do not show them we're armed until they've come in close. We'll surprise the hell out of them."

"Yes sir."

"And if they shoot at us..." the oberleutnant said, pausing while he stepped onto the lower port wing. "Well...don't get shot."

The Rumpler B.I was similar to their LVG in design, having a biplane and the same Mercedes D.I engine, which emerged well above the line of the fuselage, obscuring the occupants' forward view. The Rumpler had a slightly shorter upper wingspan of forty-seven feet (seven inches shorter than the LVG), and the lower planes were correspondingly shorter. At just under eleven feet from upper plane to ground, it was also not as tall. Its twenty-seven foot length made it stouter than the LVG by two and a half feet. The Rumpler's tailfin and rudder assembly were rounded, like an elongated teardrop lying on its side, and its horizontal stabilizers were triangular, with rounded tips.

Because of its smaller construction, coupled with a reduced weight of 1700 pounds when empty (nearly three hundred pounds lighter than the LVG), the Rumpler could reach a top speed of almost ninety miles per hour. Its cruising speed was approximately seventy-five miles per hour, significantly faster than the LVG in both regards.

It had the same basic paint scheme—plain, light-tan doped fabric, and a black Iron Cross within a white stripe on the side of the fuselage, behind the pilot's cockpit. Though not apparent with the craft sitting on the ground, a new mandate had been issued calling for a wide black stripe to be painted on the underside of the lower planes of all German reconnaissance machines. The stripes were intended to make the German observation craft more distinguishable to their countrymen on the ground, thus lowering, hopefully, the probability of being fired upon by their own ground troops.

Vogel and Adler had already taken practice flights in the Rumpler, and Leon had made all the necessary tweaks and adjustments. It was time for them to fly over the lines to observe the French and British, who were busy entrenching their positions north of the River Aisne. The mechanics finished their last minute checks of the machine and Leon stood at the propeller. He gave the airscrew a few methodical, counterclockwise hand-turns (clockwise from Vogel's cockpit perspective), to prime the pistons and prepare the engine to fire. Vogel kicked the rudder bar back and forth with his feet and manipulated the control stick between his legs, swaying the rudder and raising and lowering the elevator and ailerons. Everything was in working order.

"Prepared for contact!" Leon shouted.

Vogel pressed the magneto switch, completing the electrical circuit to the spark plugs, and opened the throttle slightly. The machine was ready to start. He shouted back to Leon, "Contact!"

Leon grasped the propeller, and gave it a hard shove downward before backing away. The engine chugged once, twice, then roared to life as Vogel opened the throttle further. Leon moved toward the machine, clear of the spinning propeller arc, and crouched behind the whirling blades to remove the wheel chocks holding the aeroplane in place. He then gave Vogel a thumbs-up, and stepped away from the Rumpler as it began to taxi from the sheds and toward the wide, grassy field of the aerodrome.

Vogel opened the throttle to full power. The hundred-horse Mercedes pulled the aircraft down the field. It didn't matter how many times he took off in an aeroplane, the feeling was still every bit as sensational as it had been on his very first solo flight. The machine rumbled across the aerodrome, vibrating from the growling engine and bouncing on the uneven grass surface. When it reached proper speed, Vogel eased back on the control stick, his backside pressed into the seat, his belly fluttered, and the vibration stopped.

He had taken his departed LVG to its maximum service ceiling of over a mile before, but just once. Machines grew sluggish when they reached their ceiling. So he'd know going forward, Vogel decided to see how high his Rumpler could go as they approached the Aisne. It took some time, as the machine could only climb a few hundred feet per minute, but eventually they reached a height where the aeroplane would go no higher.

Vogel examined his altimeter, the clock-faced gauge which used a barometer to measure atmospheric pressure, thus giving a fairly accurate estimate of his height. The gauge read 8,500 feet. *This is by far the highest I've been!* It astounded him that two men, sitting in a crate made of mostly wood and fabric, could soar so freely a mile and a half above Earth. It also astounded him how much colder it was up there. The weather was starting to change.

Following a descent to a height more conducive to observing, Adler peered over the sides of the machine, scanning the ground thousands of feet beneath. Vogel flew the machine up and down the French and British lines, with the serpentine Aisne and the northern heights past it serving as clear lines of delineation between German-held and French-held territory. When two hours had come and gone, Adler turned to him and pointed north, signaling he'd seen everything he needed to. Vogel gently eased the control stick forward and to the right with a touch of right rudder, banking the Rumpler toward the German lines and their aerodrome beyond.

Five minutes after their turn north, they'd descended to just over two thousand feet. Adler was first to catch a glimpse of a machine approaching from the north. He waved his arms to Vogel and pointed emphatically in the direction of the craft. He then reached beneath the lip of his cockpit.

He's cocking his pistol.

"I see him!" Vogel shouted excitedly. His stomach fluttered. He reached for the Luger in his belt with his right hand. He let go of the controls for only a second with his left in order to cock the pistol. The occupants in the other machine, another Blériot XI monoplane, most certainly saw the Rumpler, as Vogel watched the nose of the approaching machine tilt and head straight in his direction. The thrill tickled inside his belly as the distance between the two machines shrank. *I can't believe what I'm about to do. A gun fight in the clouds. This is unique in the history of mankind.*

At approximately five hundred feet distant, Vogel spotted the rifle jutting from the observer's cockpit. The distance would close in a flash. He raised his Luger, and rested his arm on the fairing around the right side of the cockpit, as the enemy would pass on the Rumpler's starboard side. Vogel closed his left eye, and trained the sights on the Blériot's observer, while maintaining the Rumpler's trajectory with his left hand on the control stick. He waited until the hostile machine was within a hundred feet before pulling the trigger twice.

Poom... Poom. He'd fired a few guns in his life, but the sound of the Luger over the rushing wind and roaring Mercedes made the normally loud *bang* of his gun sound muffled. Adler, unencumbered by flight controls, fired all eight shots from his magazine in rapid succession, to no apparent effect. Just feet away, his shots were even more muffled.

The enemy machine continued south when it passed the Rumpler. Each of the three shooters had missed their mark, which was to be expected. No training protocols existed for discharging a firearm at a target passing by at over a hundred miles per hour, while thousands of feet in the air. Vogel was exhilarated nonetheless. His heart pounded. *What if I'd been shot? What would Adler have done? What if we'd killed the other pilot?*

When they landed back at the aerodrome and climbed from their cockpits, Adler was energetic. It was a nice change of pace for Vogel, as usually his observer, for one reason or another, was an asshole upon landing.

"That was an experience! Wasn't it Vogel?!" Adler exclaimed, with uncharacteristic animation in his voice. The square-jawed Prussian slapped his cap enthusiastically onto his blonde head. Had he been imbued with even an ounce more energy, the young officer might well have leapt in the air and clicked his heels.

"Yes sir, it was," Vogel smiled, not sure how to respond.

"Do you think either of us hit his machine?"

"I don't think so, sir. You'd likely need a touch of luck to hit a target closing so quickly."

"Yes, you're probably right. Maybe next time we'll get lucky. I wonder who will be the first crazy bastards to take a machine gun up with them."

"I'm sure it's only a matter of time, Oberleutnant."

"Maybe we should try!"

"Um..." Vogel had no idea what he should say, though the thought of lugging a heavy MG 08 into the air sounded anything but enticing.

As they conversed, Leon approached from the sheds in his dirty grey coveralls. He kept his head pointed toward his feet when he reached them. "How did your new machine fly, sir?"

"Quite well, Leon," Vogel replied.

"That is good to hear."

"Leon," said Adler, "we just exchanged fire at two thousand feet."

"Sir?" Leon lifted his head and eyeballed the oberleutnant. He was clearly confused.

"We shot our pistols at an enemy machine, and he fired a rifle at us. What do you think about that?"

"Sounds frightening, sir."

"It was damn well exciting, Leon," Adler said. He slapped the bewildered mechanic on the shoulder, walked past him, and repeated himself. "Damn well exciting."

As Adler strode away, Vogel and Leon shared a perplexed glance. *Was Adler just being affable?* He smiled at his mechanic friend.

"What's gotten into him?" asked Leon.

"I don't know, but I think he quite enjoyed that. Just over a week ago he was furious the enemy had the gall to shoot at us. Now he's apparently overjoyed."

"Strange, sir."

"Leon, please. Johann. Or Vogel, if that feels more comfortable to you."

Once again, Leon ignored his request and the two inspected the machine in silence. Just as Vogel had expected, none of the enemy observer's shots had found their mark. The rigid fabric skin of his brand new Rumpler would need no patchwork yet.

That evening, while the men ate their dinner of mashed potatoes, corn and overcooked beef in the mess tent, Adler approached Vogel and Leon at their small table. When he plopped down in a chair next to them, the two men glanced up from their plates in perfect synchronization.

"Sorry, sir," Leon said, "I'll move right away."

"Sit down, Leon," Adler replied. "I came to speak to the both of you."

Vogel met eyes with Leon, and then winked at him. Leon gave a slight shrug, mostly with a raise of his eyebrows and a turn of his left wrist, which rested on the tabletop.

"I have a wife," Adler said. "Her name is Frieda."

What in the world? Is he trying to associate with us?

"Are you men married?"

"Um...No sir," said Vogel. "I had a girlfriend for quite some time. But not anymore."

"And you, Leon?"

"Uh...yes sir," the mechanic replied timidly. "I married Wilhelmine when we were both eighteen, sir."

"That's very nice, Leon. Do you miss her?"

"Yes sir, I do. Very much so. I miss my little ones, too."

"Ah, you have children. Tell me, what are their names?"

"Um...our first born was Ludwig. He's six. Franz is four, and little Berta, she's two."

"Frieda would like to have children..." Adler said, reflective. "Perhaps, when the war is won..."

Vogel watched the bizarre spectacle unfold. He was dumbstruck. Adler was downright cordial as he spoke to Leon, who looked like he might piss his pants out of fear and confusion.

"Vogel," Adler said, turning his attention away from Leon. "You say you had a girlfriend for some time. Why no longer?"

"Well sir, when I joined the Flying Corps, it frightened her. That's partly because I was dumb enough to tell her about the two boys who died after crashing their machines during training. I should not have told her, but I was only being honest."

"I remember them," Adler said. "Kohl and Wechsler. She left you because your duties frightened her?"

"Yes sir. She said that the stress of knowing I could die every time I sat in an aeroplane was too much for her. I told her I loved it, that I was a good pilot and she needn't worry, but..."

Adler actually seemed to listen, and take it in. "...But now that the war has started, would she rather you were an infantryman? More infantrymen will probably die tomorrow than have all the men who've ever taken to the air, combined."

"...You know..." Vogel answered hesitatingly, unable to conjure a rational retort. "I guess I've not thought of putting it to her that way. We ended things, the war began, and I haven't seen, spoken, or written to her since."

"What's her name?"

"Kunigunde."

"A good Prussian name," Adler said. "Well Vogel..." he gently slapped the table with both hands. "I think you should write to her. Write to Kunigunde and tell her you miss her. You do miss her, yes?"

"Well, yes sir. But I don't think—"

"Nonsense. How can a girl refuse a man who writes from a warzone, just to say he misses her?"

You know, he may actually be right.

"Consider it..." Adler said, then he pushed against the table, slid his chair back, and stood. "Yes...well...gentlemen, I'm spent. I'm off to get some rest."

Gentlemen?

Leon was nervously chewing on his bottom lip. He wanted to say something, but was too afraid to go through with it. Before Adler could walk away, Leon found the courage.

"Sir?"

Adler stopped. He peered over his shoulder and back at the table. "Yes, Leon?"

"Do you miss Frieda?"

"Of course I do. With all my heart. Good night, gentlemen."

"Good night, sir..." the two quietly replied.

Adler left the mess and the two men remained seated at the table, their dinners growing cold. The oberleutnant had never spoken to them in such an engaging way before. Vogel, ashamed for saying some of the things he'd said about the man in the past, went to bed that night questioning his harsh judgment of Heinrich Adler for the very first time.

HENTSCH

Hentsch crawled on his stomach, snaking through a stand of maple trees toward the lip of the ridge, his rifle in hand. The colors had started to turn, and thousands of desiccated yellow leaves, the earliest to fall, lay on the forest floor; they crunched and swooshed as he slid over them. To his ears, the crunching was more like a roar, announcing his presence to the enemy the same as would a klaxon horn. In reality, the French were far enough away that they'd never hear him coming.

A number of III Bataillon's best shooters had been selected by their respective commanders to place targeted, concealed, harassing fire upon the men of French Sixth Army, busily digging their trenches in the valley below. The French were currently in the process of fortifying their position between the Aisne's northern bank and the ridgeline. Upon finding a favorable spot with ample cover, Hentsch examined the activity and immediately realized the lack of virtue in his present task. *These men don't even hold weapons, let alone aim them in my direction.*

Orders were orders. His marksmanship had gained notice during the previous engagements, and on Strauss's recommendation, Hauptmann Fleischer suggested Hentsch try his hand at sniping, though it was less a suggestion and more a command. For several hundred yards in either direction, skilled shooters hid themselves along the edge of the ridge, spaced a hundred or more yards apart, to keep the Frenchmen below on constant alert. The heavy 21cm field howitzers had also been brought up behind the German positions, so every now and then Hentsch would hear the *FOOM* of a large shell whistle above his head as it fell from a high angle somewhere in the vicinity of the French lines.

The sound of a passing shell immediately preceded an eruption of earth, or if the shell fell too long and landed in the Aisne, of water. Upon explosion, the blast wave spread away from the epicenter and sometimes, especially if there was smoke or mist, he could actually see the wave itself zip at high speed across the landscape, expanding outward in a sort of ghostly half-orb, though that was difficult to capture even with the sharpest eye. The echoing explosion, out of synch with the visuals, would reach his ears a fraction of a second later, and roll through the river valley. Depending on the ambient noise, after the shell's passing and exploding, he'd occasionally hear the distant, echoing *foom* of the offending shell's gun, as the howitzers were far enough behind the lines that the sound from the launch took longer to travel to his position than did the shell.

The sounds occurring disjointedly were trivial—basic physics, nothing more—but Hentsch found them intriguing. He also found them troubling. Enemy shells were bound by the same physics. Were an enemy shell of a similar caliber traveling his way, all he'd ever hear was the short whistle of its approach as it rained down upon him. That didn't leave much time, if any at all, for escape.

In the first phases of the battle along the Aisne, the French had, for the first time, offered a truly heavy dose of their artillery, especially between Compiègne and Soissons. General von Quasts's IX Korps occupied the mid-point of that span of front, and until they'd reached the northern heights overlooking the valley, the French cannons gave Hentsch and the men around him quite the scare. The 75s were relentless. Ackerman was an almost completely broken man by then, and Hentsch figured it would only be a matter of time before the young man was withdrawn from service. He should have been already, but manpower shortages were rearing their ugly head, especially since the disastrous Battle of the Marne.

There. He offers a clean shot. The Frenchman must have grown tired of crouching to dig his small spade into the earth, and stood to stretch his back. It wasn't an easy shot. From his spot on the ridge, Hentsch was just over three hundred feet above the flat ground below, with the French positions more than four hundred yards away from the ridge. Firing downward at a target made it look further away than it actually was, so he quickly made the necessary mental calculations as to where he should aim. *No wind. Aim straight above him, at the ground about ten feet behind.*

Hentsch closed his eyes, slowed his breathing to steady himself, and then opened his right eye. He trained his sights above the Frenchman's head. *Do your duty, Augustus, unpleasant as it may be.* He couldn't tell for sure, but the trigger actually seemed to resist his finger's pull harder than it normally did. Maybe he just imagined it. *I could always miss...*

With an attacking enemy on the approach, toying with the notion of intentionally missing was complete nonsense. Toying with that same notion while aiming at a man distractedly digging a ditch, however, was far less irrational. Hentsch *could* miss. The Frenchman would endure a scare from the close call. The trigger would have been pulled, as ordered. One less man murdered. One less corpse to haunt his conscience. As with every choice in life, though, there was a flipside, and Hentsch was all too wary of it.

He *could* spare the Frenchman's life. Then, maybe a week, maybe a month, maybe even a year from the day he chose to spare a life, that same Frenchman might, without flinch or hesitation, kill him, a friend, or a hundred Germans. Was it possible each missed shot could mean a dead countryman? Hentsch had missed before; was he culpable if those misses ultimately led to dead Germans?

Pow! The Mauser kicked into his right shoulder. He opened his other eye. The Frenchman collapsed, struck, and vanished into the entrenchment. Hentsch was too far away to tell exactly where he'd hit him. He put his head down, as he knew the French would pick up their rifles and begin blindly firing at the ridge.

Rounds cracked into the trees in his vicinity. Most missed well over his head or many yards to his left or right. Hundreds of rifle pops from the gaggle who'd just given up digging for shooting echoed from the French line. *It must be stressful down there. I bet they would love to know my exact position.*

Hentsch stayed in his spot for more than three hours. It wasn't a safe place to be, but it was much safer than being on the other end. Each time one of the snipers took a shot, the French opened fire on the ridge. During one such instance, with the French fire directed toward a shooter further along the ridge, Hentsch took advantage. He hit a Frenchman who had positioned himself too far out of the entrenchment. The bullet hit the man somewhere in the upper torso. Hentsch assumed it killed him, because he'd slumped forward atop his rifle and lay there before finally being dragged back into the ditch by his fellow soldiers.

Over the course of his three hours on the ridge, Hentsch took six shots, not all of them successful. It was grim work, terrorizing men that way. It was predatory—lying motionless for an extended period, waiting for an "opportunity" to strike. As he crawled away with the sun trickling toward the horizon, Hentsch debated whether or not he should tell Simon he'd killed yet again, if it were to come up.

For protection against enemy artillery, the German entrenchments were dug a fair distance back from the ridgeline. After crawling far enough away that he could stand without worrying about catching an errant French bullet, Hentsch slung his rifle and coolly commenced his walk back. He strolled, biding his time. He looked forward to having something to eat.

When he'd gotten closer, he was surprised to hear Simon's high-pitched voice screeching from the trench. No longer moving casually, Hentsch dashed forth to see what was causing the commotion. Before he'd made it all the way there, some of the shouting became clearer.

"What the fuck did you do to him, Michael?!" Simon screamed.

"I didn't do anything!" Michael's voice boomed back. "He's completely lost it!"

Hentsch leapt over the earthen parapet and slid on one knee into the trench, not taking the time to ascertain whether anyone might be standing beneath him. Luckily, no one was. He landed gracefully on his feet in the middle of some sort of altercation. Kirsch and Nussbaum were holding a fanatic-eyed and purple-faced Ackerman by the arms, while Engel held his hand against Ackerman's chest, restraining him further. Ten feet away from them, Michael sat on his backside in the dirt, his hands trembling and covered in blood. Near him stood a frightened Simon, who turned his head back and forth from the injured Michael to the crazed Ackerman, who was apparently struggling to free himself in order to attack the already wounded man.

"What happened?!" cried Hentsch, as more men from 1 Korporalschaft crowded around the scene.

"He attacked me is what happened!" Michael answered. There was fear and panic in his voice. "He's fucking crazy!"

"You set him off!" shouted Engel.

"Yes, there it is! Blame everything on me you cocksucker!"

Ackerman continued to struggle, and all manner of strained grunts and growls poured from behind his gritted teeth as he fought against the men who were supposed to be his brothers.

"Can't somebody calm him down?" Hentsch asked. "Can someone please tell me what they saw?"

Engel, still pushing his hand against the broken man's chest, had seen something and said, "Ackerman was sitting by himself, with his back turned. Michael kept throwing pebbles at him every so often and snickering to himself. We told him to stop, but he wouldn't. And all of a sudden Ack just lost it. He pulled his bayonet and tried to stab him."

"It's true," Kirsch added, nodding toward the bloodied man. "That son of a bitch is lucky he grabbed the blade before Ack killed him...You hear that, Michael, you lucky bastard?! This is your fault!"

"Fuck you!"

"God dammit..." Hentsch mumbled to himself. "Ackerman, they're going to arrest you...they'll have to. Can you calm down for a minute and talk to me?"

Singularly focused on breaking free to finish what he'd started, the maniacal soldier gave no reply. The veins popped from his chubby neck. Tears poured from his eyes and he growled.

"Will somebody please get him out of here?" asked Hentsch, aiming an index finger at the bloodied instigator sitting in the dirt.

A few men from 1 Gruppe helped Michael to his feet and turned his palms over to check the severity of his wounds. Across both palms were two deep, dark-red gashes, the skin split so wide his hands looked like they'd nearly been amputated. His thumbs were also cut, almost to the bone. With such injuries, Michael would not be able to grip a weapon of any sort. He could not remain on the front lines. He'd need surgery, and weeks of recuperation. The 1 Gruppe men led him away to clean and bandage his injuries.

"Look Ack, he's gone," Hentsch said. "Can you talk to me now?"

As soon as Michael had gone, Ackerman stopped his struggling and lowered his head. "Yes...I guess so..." he answered softly. He sobbed.

Kirsch and Nussbaum waited for a go ahead from Hentsch before loosening their grip on the man's arms. Engel, looking toward the distraught Simon, was not paying attention as closely as he should have been. As soon as they let Ackerman go, he lunged for the bayonet dangling from Engel's belt. Kirsch tried to grab hold of his arm once again, but the determined man pulled free. Kirsch stumbled backward. The troubled soldier had made his choice.

"Ackerman, don't!" Hentsch shouted, to no avail. He lunged, but he too was not fast enough.

Unable to stop him, the three men who had held him back and thus prevented him from attacking Michael, failed to protect Ackerman from himself. He raised the blade to his throat and sliced deeply into the soft flesh. The first spurt of blood shot outward, spraying Engel in the face. Nussbaum tackled the suicidal man to the ground. It was too late. A fountain of blood gushed from Ackerman's neck and pooled in the brown soil on the trench floor. He was still alive, and a mortifying wheeze gurgled from the opening in his neck as he struggled to breathe.

"Jesus Christ!" Engel yelped, squeezing his eyes closed and spitting Ackerman's blood from his lips.

"Someone do something!" screamed Simon, red-faced and crying as he ran to the dying man's side. "We need to help him!"

No one else moved a muscle. They saw how deeply Ackerman had cut himself. No doctor in the world was going to save him. It didn't take long for the wheezing and gurgling to slow, and less than a minute after slicing his own throat, he was dead.

"Come on!" Simon cried. "Help me turn him over!"

"Simon..." Hentsch said, "...he's dead."

"What is happening to the world?!" Simon bawled, staring at each man standing idly by while the blood pooled at their feet. "Everyone's completely lost their fucking minds!"

Alerted by others from 1 Korporalschaft, Unteroffizier Strauss arrived far too long after it would have mattered. "What in God's name happened here?!" he snarled, albeit justifiably. Still wearing his damaged pickelhaube with the torn cover, the worn down officer eyed each man as he walked past them and toward Ackerman's body, lying face-down in a massive pool of blood.

Simon, kneeling next to the corpse, the blood soaking his pant leg, was the first to respond. "He killed himself, sir."

"Why did he do that?"

Hentsch cleared his throat to get the officer's attention. "Sir, Ack hadn't been the same these last two weeks. Whatever was wrong with him, Michael said or did something to him to put him over the edge. After that he wasn't coming back."

"Are you not responsible for the men beneath you?"

"Aren't you?!" Hentsch snapped. "I was lying on my fucking stomach shooting at Franzmenn all day, as ordered. I wasn't even here when it started."

"What about the rest of you?" asked Strauss. "What were the rest of you men doing while this took place?"

"It happened so quickly, sir," Simon replied. "No one expected Ack to lash out like he did. As soon as Michael left, he really seemed like he might calm down and cooperate."

"We only let go of him for a second," Kirsch said shamefully. "But he stole Engel's bayonet...and..." The gruff man's voice cracked as emotion overcame him. Hard as he was, witnessing the suicide of a soldier he'd fought alongside so closely had affected him.

Pondering mutely for a time, all the while resting his hands on his hips and staring down at the heartbreaking sight, Strauss had little else to say to the stunned men. "...I'll inform the Oberleutnant and the Hauptmann of what's transpired here," he muttered, "and I'll get a stretcher sent up to take Ackerman's body."

With that, Strauss calmly left. A group of onlookers silently parted, allowing him to pass. Hentsch, Simon, Engel, Kirsch and Nussbaum waited, unspeaking, for the stretcher bearers to arrive. The men of 1 Gruppe did not stick around. Death and gore were already second nature to most of the fighting men, but suicide was not. In that way, Ackerman's death by his own hand was somehow far more troubling to many of them than it would have been had an enemy shell or bullet killed him instead.

The stretcher bearers came, the sun went down, the moon rose up, and life had to move on. Happy or sad, content or discomfited, there was still a war to be fought. It would have been easy to dwell on it—the wild look on Ackerman's face when he opened his own throat was seared into Hentsch's brain—but as sickening to see as it had been, Hentsch hadn't eaten or drank in hours. Lying on his stomach for a protracted period had given him a headache, and the day's subsequent events had worsened it tenfold. Only the empty pit in his belly competed with the throbbing in his head, and a meal was the only cure for both.

They quietly prepared what little food they had, but the silence could only last for so long. While their dinner was still boiling over the small fire, Engel must have grown tired of the depressed atmosphere.

"Well?" he asked out of the blue.

"Well what?" Hentsch replied.

"Any kills?"

"Jesus..." Nussbaum whispered to himself, before standing up and walking away.

"Where are you going?" Kirsch said, pushing himself to his feet to follow. "Nice work, Engel," he grunted, "you could have waited to ask about such a thing."

"Hey, what else are we supposed to talk about?" Engel answered defensively.

"Do you really want to talk about it right now?" said Hentsch, trying with his eyes to tell Engel to let it go. "Hasn't this day been dreadful enough?"

"I was just curious."

Hentsch scanned Simon's pale face to gauge whether he should share the story or not. Simon's pale yellow eyebrows sagged over his pale blue eyes. The dark, puffy bags beneath them were the only color on his entire face. *Christ, Augustus, he looks like death. Of course he hates the thought of hearing about any more of it.*

"No, Engel," Hentsch lied, "I didn't get any clean looks."

"No? I thought you might have. It was hard to hear, but we could tell when one of our shooters fired. There'd be a solo report, and then a whole slew would ring out a few seconds later."

"I know. I was there. They'd just fire at random spots on the ridge," countered Hentsch. "They couldn't hit anything."

"When the French bring up their howitzers, you won't be able to stay on the ridge for long," Simon added glumly. "They'll call it in and blow those positions to pieces."

"Yes, you're right about that," Hentsch said.

In the light of the small fire tucked within the confines of the entrenchment, the three men sat on their packs to eat dinner together. Hentsch broke off a large piece of hard field biscuit, and stuffed it in his mouth with a bite of the potatoes they'd boiled. They split some salted meat with one another, and Hentsch jammed a bit of meat in his mouth along with the potato and biscuit. Combining the bland flavors made the monotonous eating a bit more tolerable. "It was a lot better eating when we were in Belgium," he grumbled.

"It was. Long supply lines can't help with the variety," Engel replied.

"They'll eventually straighten that out, won't they?" asked Simon.

"Eventually," said Hentsch. "We were supposed to have beaten the French by now. I have a hunch the coordination of our supply trains was almost certainly tied into that."

The corners of Simon's mouth drooped. "So for us, that means?"

"It means we'll be eating this same shit for a while," Engel laughed. "And probably not very much of it. Not unless we find a way to win soon."

"We're not going to win soon..." Hentsch stated morosely, only because it was what he genuinely believed. Based on the radical momentum shift after the Marne, he knew the allies still had much fight left in them, and probably more than any commanders were willing to admit.

"Is that what you really think?" asked Simon.

"It is. Look around. We're hurting. We haven't the resources to launch an attack, at least not one strong enough the push them back on Paris."

"Then what will happen here?"

"That, I don't know. But unless I'm missing something major, from where I sit it looks like we'll be in this a lot longer than we were originally supposed to be."

"Oh..." the pallid, sullen young man responded, hushed and unenthusiastically. He stood up momentarily, and then knelt down next to his haversack. Opening the flap, he began digging around inside. He found what he was looking for—a small package wrapped in decorative paper. Holding the little package in his hands, Simon stared at it as he returned to his seat atop his pack. Upon sitting, he smiled at Hentsch and Engel, but he couldn't mask the sadness and disappointment hiding beneath his façade. "I've been saving this for a while," he said, "but I'd like to eat it now. I want to share it with you."

He tore the paper, exposing a bar of chocolate. Simon broke it into five pieces, not even considering taking a larger piece, even though it was his to begin with. He handed one piece each to the two men seated with him by the fire, and held onto the other two for Kirsch and Nussbaum, whenever it was that they decided to return.

Hentsch was hesitant to eat it, delectable as it would no doubt be. "Simon...Why were you saving it?"

"I don't know," he replied solemnly, "I suppose for a special occasion. You know, when we had a reason to celebrate. But we have nothing to celebrate. Just more killing, dying, and apparently, waiting."

We could celebrate not having to deal with Michael anymore. The joke was too morbid to say aloud.

"We can still win," Hentsch reassured him, "it will just take more time."

"You don't need to feign optimism now, Augustus. I know exactly what time means for us. The longer this goes, the worse off we are."

"Maybe I'm wrong."

"Yes...maybe. But if we haven't been killed come Christmas and the war is still under way, then we'll know you were right."

"That's a gloomy way to verify a gloomy prediction," muttered Engel.

"These are gloomy times," Simon countered. "Engel, we've got a little left, why don't you boil up some coffee," he said, "and we can enjoy a proper dessert. After today, we could definitely use it."

Engel made the coffee and the three men slowly ate their chocolate, savoring each nibble, prolonging the flavor as long as possible. Typically, their coffee did not taste all that great, but that night they might as well have been sitting peacefully in a café in Paris, drinking the finest brew Europe had to offer. It was nice to have something, anything, to help them escape their reality. In the company of friends, sharing a warm drink and the sweet taste of German chocolate, the three were able, if only for a short while, to separate themselves from the war. Even Ackerman's sad demise took a backseat, and for those ten or fifteen minutes, nearly two months of constant marching, combat and stress drifted away. Ten minutes of peace while the world burned around them.

"Have either of you yet to write any letters home?" asked Simon.

"No," answered Hentsch, "not yet."

"I've tried, but we've been so damned busy I've had trouble," Engel replied. "And I don't know what I should say to my mother. I mean, does your mother want to know that you've killed a man? Hentsch is that something you'd share with your mother?"

"I don't know. Probably not. I suppose when I write I'll say I'm doing well, they treat us fine, generic things so as not to worry her. It wouldn't do my mother any good to know how horrible it is."

"You're right," Simon agreed. "I couldn't write that I'd shot someone either. No one in my family should have to know that."

Engel chuckled. "You couldn't write it because you don't want to lie! You haven't shot anyone!"

"Yes I have," Simon whispered. He looked down. "I shot a Franzmann during one of their final pushes toward the ridge. I shot him square in the chest, and he fell dead right where I hit him. Right there..." he said, pointing a finger to his chest. "Shooting men is just a part of our job, I know that. I didn't want anyone to look at me like a coward anymore."

Dammit, Simon. You weren't a coward. Hentsch could tell by the look in Simon's eyes that he spoke the truth. He would have preferred Simon never kill anyone, that he'd survive the war and come out clean on the other side, having never murdered, but that ideal was over and done with. Now Hentsch had to try and rationalize it for the gentle young man.

"Look, Simon," he began, "I know you must feel badly about killing, believe me I do as well, but you must tell yourself that you may have saved a comrade's life by pulling the trigger. You never know, that Franzmann could have killed a number of men had you not shot him first."

"Or maybe, later in life, he would have written the next great novel...a beautiful symphony...cured an incurable disease..." Simon muttered. "Maybe he would have saved thousands."

"You'll go mad, looking at our world through that prism. You mustn't."

"I had the shakes for an entire day when I killed my first," Engel said. "But that was back in Belgium. Now I try not to think about it. You can't think about it. You have to get used to it or this war business will eat your insides."

"I don't think there's any getting used to this," Simon mumbled. "I'm not sure that would be the best thing. Say we do make it out of here. What do you plan on saying to your families if you see them face to face? Then would you consider telling your mothers what you've done?"

That was something Hentsch hadn't considered. "If she asked, and truly wanted to know, then I might share some of my story with her. I'm sure Pauline would want to hear all about it."

"You really think your sister would want to hear such things?" Simon asked quizzically.

"I know she would. As would my father and brother."

"Of that," Simon grinned, "I have no doubt. Herr Hentsch probably waits every day for the postman to deliver the letter detailing his son's exploits."

Until Simon said it, Hentsch hadn't thought of it that way, not from his father's perspective. He didn't want his mother to know how awful it all had been, but his father, a student of history if there ever was one, must have been dying to learn how history was being written from his own son, caught smack-dab in the middle of it. Still, a letter to his father had a strong chance of finding its way into his mother's hands. She might want to know her son was okay, but her son absolutely did not want her to know his reality. A letter would have to wait.

"I know we've all shared stories about our families here and there," said Engel, "but just to fulfill a curiosity of mine, I wanted to ask, what subject is it that your father teaches? I don't recall you ever mentioning it."

"History," Hentsch and Simon replied simultaneously. They met eyes and grinned.

"Was he particularly interested in ancient Rome?"

"Yes he was..." Hentsch answered. Engel had just figured something out.

"I can't believe I didn't think of this earlier," Engel declared, shaking his head. "Your older brother's name is Julius, and your name is Augustus. Do I need to ask either of your middle names?"

"You do not..." (it was Caesar on both counts). Hentsch's older brother Julius was a university professor. He was stricken with polio as a boy, and was unfit for military service.

"Did you realize that, Simon?" asked Engel.

"I had my suspicions, you might say."

"The last dictator of the Roman Republic and his posthumously adopted son, the first Emperor of Rome. Tell me, why does your sister not have an ancient Roman name?"

"You know your history quite well, Engel," said Hentsch, surprised he knew as much as he did.

"I've been known to pick up a book from time to time."

"To answer your question, though, after two children, my mother refused to allow my father any part in naming their third child, boy or girl."

"That's a good thing," Engel grinned. "Yours and your brother's names are bad enough."

"That's funny coming from a man called Amadeus," Hentsch quipped.

Simon tittered. No one called Engel by his first name. Most of their fellow soldiers didn't even know it. There was nothing wrong with his name, as a matter of fact Hentsch liked it, but for whatever reason, Engel did not.

"Come on, Hentsch," Engel said, and he gently shoved him.

VERNON

Dearest Sal,

While I hold out hope for a hasty end to this war, I fear it may not happen. In the past two weeks we've pushed north of Paris and across the River Aisne, but Fritz has since resisted any further advance. We took heavy losses scaling a ridge where they have taken up the defence. Lew and I made it back fine, apart from a nasty tumble I had. Don't worry about that, I picked up a few scrapes is all.

Lew saved an officer's life during the fight. Lieutenant Hood was shot in the shoulder, and Lew dragged him to safety. You wouldn't believe it, but Bannister bawled him out afterward. Honest to God, Bannister may quite literally be out of his mind. He poses a danger to us all, through his flagrant disregard of our safety and morale. I spoke to Cortland, our company sergeant major, a day after it happened, and he said he would try and put Llewelyn up for a decoration. I haven't had many occasions to speak with Sergeant Cortland in the past, but he was very candid as to his personal opinion of Bannister. I think a commendation would be a topping thing for old Pritch, he could use the boost.

After our attack waned, we dug in. At first we dug just a shallow ditch, about three feet deep, to afford us protection from shrapnel and gunfire when crouching. Later we scoured the village and surrounding countryside for spades, pick-axes, buckets, and anything else we might use to deepen our entrenchments. Now we're able to stand inside our ditch without having to worry so much about catching one in the nob.

The battalion took on reinforcements and a new commanding officer, a Major Young. That was several days ago. He seems nice enough, though we only met him briefly. I'll bet top dollar Bannister is sour about not being awarded command of the battalion. At least I hope he is. Maybe Major Young will be the one who finally gets Bannister off Llewelyn's back. The platoon got some new lads in the deal, I believe eight in total, all of them green as can be. Two were sent to us in 3 Section, though their names elude me for the time being.

As it stands, command appears content with holding our positions. We are opposed by a formidable defence, but west of us the French have begun to move around his flank to try and gather momentum for a further attack. I do not know what can happen in the near future that will bring the fighting to a close, but I hope the Frenchies manage some success in their advance.

Fritz occasionally fires rather large cannon shells our way, but now that we've dug in the odds of our being hit have fallen some. If we leave the ditch, those odds change of course, as it's hard for Fritz to land a shell between the walls but it's quite easier to get that shell close on either side. A few have landed inside, but those were further down the line. Gruesome sight to see is all I'll say about it. I'm not sure how long we'll stay in place, but you may be able to write back if you so choose. I would most certainly appreciate a word from my dearest wife. All my love.

Vernon finished writing his letter and folded it up, placing it in his pocket. What he chose not to include on the page was just how deplorable their situation had been since the Battle of the Aisne stalled. Missy initially had to be evacuated because of heavy shelling, which Vernon had witnessed firsthand. The 5th Division's artillery remained south of the river, unable to cross and only able to respond to the German shellfire ineffectively at best. After the evacuation of the town, the troops eventually returned and established a trench line north of Missy, in between the village and the foot of the Chivres Spur.

"How many letters have you written to her thus far?" Pritchard asked, while munching on a biscuit. He took a sip from his water bottle, swished it around inside his mouth and swallowed. He cringed. "A lot of dirt in there," he noted, and then spat.

"Maybe six or seven, I haven't been counting," answered Vernon, "but I hope she answers this one."

"She's probably answered all of them. I'm sure you'll get a bundle all at once. And hopefully there'll be baked goods somewhere in there, too."

"That would be a welcome treat, indeed. I grow more tired of biscuits with each bi—"

BOOM! A distant, but heavy explosion made both Vernon and Pritchard jump. It came from the east, atop the heights, and a deep echo rolled through the valley, followed a second later by the *foom* of the shell's launch, which emanated from the Royal Artillery's positions somewhere south of the Aisne.

"Blimey! That came from one of our batteries!" shouted Vernon, pointing toward the German positions east of them. A billowing column of white smoke rose skyward above the top of the Chivres Spur. "See the smoke? Our HE smoke is white!"

"Well it's about bloody time!" Pritchard cried. "Maybe we can finally get some damned supply depots situated north of the river."

It had not been easy for 5th Division to supply its troops. Owing to the Germans' superior positioning, any attempts to place supply dumps on the northern bank were met with powerful shellfire, of the same type that had fallen upon Missy on September 15. Those high explosive shells, with their thick black smoke, were fired by 21 cm howitzers. They quickly came to be known by the men suffering their wrath by two nicknames: "Black Marias," and "Jack Johnsons," the latter referring to the champion American boxer of the time (because the smoke from the explosions was black and packed a punch).

Due to the ever-present threat of shelling, all resupplying had to be done piecemeal, with wagons crossing the river on pontoon bridges built by the Royal Engineers and carting their wares directly to the trenches. Those temporary bridges were all within range of the German guns, and depending on the weather, could potentially be swept down the river if a strong rain raised the water levels enough. It all combined to make the delivery of even the most basic supplies a colossal and dangerous undertaking.

"I wouldn't get excited about the supply situation just yet, Pritch," Vernon said, waiting intently for more British shells to sail across the river. "As much as I'd love for our guns to blow them to high heaven, it may take a while."

Pritchard shrugged and said, "So long as I'm able to wipe my arse with fresh paper in the next week, I'll be a happy man."

Vernon laughed heartily. Toilet paper was becoming a rare commodity, as was just about everything else. Such things were easy to take for granted, right up until the point they were no longer available.

BOOM! The sound was so gratifying when it wasn't directed at him.

The men had spent days cursing the artillery for offering such paltry support while it lingered to the south, but from the sound of it, they'd finally brought up guns heavy enough to make a difference. Losses had been harsh during the earlier fighting for the heights, and that was thanks in no small part to the disparity between the two sides' artillery. Though the 5th Division held their ground north of Missy, the Germans had made multiple pushes on their front. Defending against those pushes came at a cost, and timely artillery support could have curbed those losses.

BOOM! The frequency of explosions increased. Each blast echoed through the valley and raised half-sarcastic cheers from the men of 5th Division in the trenches below. The Royal Artillery was clearing a section of the high ground half a mile east of Missy, close to the town of Condé-sur-Aisne. The bombardment scattered the German defenders there and exacted a small revenge for the grief given to the 5th Division in the preceding days.

"They might be late, but it's a relief to hear them, isn't it?" said Corporal Spurling. He hadn't been sleeping much the past week, if at all; Vernon saw it plainly on his face. The corporal was skinny before the fighting began, but the Great War was nibbling away at him bit by bit, and that day he looked worse than usual.

Twenty-four years old should not look so aged.

"Hey Spurling," Vernon said, concerned. "Why don't you try and get a spot of rest, aye?"

"Rest..." The corporal turned to him, squinting through one eye as if making the decision whether or not to sleep was an earth-shattering choice requiring all the thinking power his brain could spare. "I don't think I'll be able to fall asleep, not with our guns blasting away."

"Still, maybe you ought to make an effort," Vernon said. "Come on, sit down here. Pritchard and I will keep an eye on things." He guided the groggy Spurling to a spot against the trench wall.

Sporadic rains had left pools in the trench's lowest points and the entire floor was muddy, but during their dig they unearthed an enormous boulder, still half embedded in the floor and wall. Far too big to move, the giant stone's potential as a chair was quickly recognized by the men of Fourth Platoon. A backrest had been dug into the soil above the rock, and it was there, seated atop the boulder, where each of them tried to steal a nap whenever they could. Smaller fellows could go two at a time. It was the only perk afforded Fourth Platoon in their segment of the trench and although it had initially caused squabbles, a reasonable usage schedule was eventually worked out.

Vernon opened Spurling's backpack and found his greatcoat. The corporal was so wobbly he nearly toppled face-first into the boulder.

"Whoa, Spurling! Don't fall asleep while you're still standing," Vernon warned, catching the corporal by a shoulder strap. "Let's just slide your pack off and sit you down, all right?"

"Sure…"

Vernon unbuckled the man's equipment belt and wrapped him in the greatcoat before sitting him down. "Now get your arse to sleep, yeah?"

"Hayes, why aren't you an NCO?" Spurling asked interestedly. "Everyone respects you, and dammit, you're old. You should be in charge of at least a platoon by now." His sunken eyes, red and rife with branching capillaries, gazed curiously upward at Vernon, six years his senior.

"I'm not that old," Vernon answered.

"Still…why?"

"It's not something I've sought, and truthfully, each promotion would bring me one step closer in the chain to Bannister. The thought of working in any closer concert with him is more than enough to dissuade me."

"So you'd let one man all but decide your future as a soldier?"

"If you put it that way…" Vernon paused, "…yes."

"But the only way to supplant men like him is to put better men, like you, in their place. Don't you agree?"

"I don't know. What if being like him is what it takes to get there?"

"I know you don't believe that. Plenty officers and NCOs are better men than he. Hell, they might all be. Look at Sergeant Major Cortland. I bet he's either blunted or completely ignored the captain on a hundred separate occasions when Bannister demanded he discipline some of our boys for whatever petty infractions he saw fit to bawl about. No doubt he's helped you without your knowing it."

Spurling had a point. Vernon wondered how many times Cortland had protected both him and Pritchard. Bannister could shout and intimidate, humiliate and belittle, but in most instances it was up to the highest ranking NCO in the company, the company sergeant major, to carry out disciplinary measures. While discipline among the ranks was essential, unnecessary and excessive discipline only bred dissent. Cortland couldn't close Bannister's obnoxious mouth, but he did serve as a buffer between the captain's sadistic whims and those men who might suffer them.

"You're right about Cortland," Vernon admitted. "Still, I can't shake the fact that somehow we managed to get the captain as a commander. How does a rotter like him ever get there? So long as he's in charge of E Company, I will not strive to be anything but a private."

"Suit yourself, Hayes," Spurling said, yawning, "but it's not only you who's missing out..."

SEBASTIAN

Lashed in position atop the conning tower and clad in a heavy black, rubberized, double-breasted greatcoat, rain boots and a sou'wester drawn tightly over his head, Sebastian scanned the choppy, grey water. For miles in every direction, horizon to horizon, U-20's only company was the rolling swells and whitecaps of the North Sea. As the boat sliced through the rough water, the wind spritzed him from head to toe with briny spray. He grew increasingly thirsty, though he and anyone else with any sense knew not to swallow the stuff splashing against his face in any significant amount, as that would do nothing but make it worse.

Watch duty was boring, but necessary, and all the lower ranks had to take their turn in the routine. When the weather was nicer, the watch officer and even the kapitänleutnant would spend time on deck, but when bad weather broke, they were the only men permitted to abandon routine. That's all life had been for the past three weeks—routine, routine and more routine. The only excitement had come in the form of report over the wireless telegraph not long after they'd left Heligoland, but since then, nothing of import had apparently taken place. The telegraph report, though, was significant.

There was a war at sea as well. While it unfolded much slower than the land war, on September 5 the Kaiserliche Marine's U-Boat fleet received its first good news since the opening of hostilities. On that day, the vessel U-21 attacked and sank the British cruiser HMS *Path-*

finder with a torpedo. The successful attack represented the first time in history a torpedo was used by a submarine to sink an enemy vessel. It was also the first successful submarine attack in fifty years, as the last time a submersible had been used to destroy an enemy vessel was during the American Civil War. On February 17, 1864, the Confederate vessel CSS *H.L. Hunley* used a long spar to attach a tethered explosive charge to the hull of the USS *Housatonic* then anchored in Charleston Harbor, South Carolina. The attack sank the *Housatonic*, making it the first successful submarine attack in history. The *Hunley*'s success was marred shortly after, however, when it sank of the coast of South Carolina, taking its entire crew with it.

Where the *Hunley* succeeded in its attack but failed to remain in service, U-21 was victorious, and lived to fight another day. The announcement by Kapitänleutnant (lieutenant commander) Otto Dröscher, U-20's commander, of their sister ship U-21's success, was met with cheers and whistles by the crew. But two weeks later, U-20 had still yet to spot, let alone engage, any British targets.

The British Grand Fleet, under the command of Admiral John Jellicoe, had made their base at Scapa Flow, a large harbor sheltered in the middle of Scotland's Orkney Islands, just north of the main island of the United Kingdom. Jellicoe had moved the Grand Fleet to Scapa Flow at the outbreak of war to control the entry points to the North Sea and deny the Germans access to those points.

Germany's High Seas Fleet, commanded by Admiral Alfred von Tirpitz, while formidable, did not possess the surface vessels to compete with the might of the British Navy. Their defeat at the Battle of Heligoland Bight had strongly reinforced that notion. However, the German unterseebooten (under sea boats), U-Boats for short, were another story. Germany had the best submersibles of the time, and they were viewed by some as a means of potentially leveling the playing field. In early August, Tirpitz had sent out the first U-Boat patrol in history, with modest hopes, though many high-ranking officials (Tirpitz included) in navies around the world viewed submersibles as nothing more than a novelty. While the first patrol hadn't panned out, the sinking of the *Pathfinder* silenced some of the doubt, and proved that if given an opportunity, Germany's U-boats might be utilized as an effective weapon of war.

Standing on the conning tower, bored and soaking, Sebastian found himself craving excitement. He hoped that at any minute he might see a British ship bob over the horizon. He didn't know how long he'd been outside, but when the conning tower hatch opened and

Jollenbeck's head poked out, he wasn't entirely convinced his shift had quite yet ended.

"Am I done already?" Sebastian asked, wiping a fresh splash of seawater from his face.

"For now," Jollenbeck answered. "Dröscher has an announcement to make and he wants the entire crew present."

"What is it about?"

"I don't know. He didn't say. Take one last look around and get down here."

Sebastian scanned the horizon for 360 degrees, and as before, saw nothing. Intrigued by what the kapitänleutnant had to say, he may not have given his last look the utmost attention, but he doubted it would matter. In the heavy waterproof gear, slickened considerably by the copious spray which accompanied watch duty in bad weather, the climb through the hatch and down the conning tower's ladder was slightly treacherous. One slip could have easily meant a broken leg, and a broken leg in the middle of the North Sea was not the best thing to have. He climbed cautiously, past the pipes and levers and wheels of the diving controls and into the control room.

When Sebastian stepped away from the ladder and onto the control room's steel floor, the wireless operator was still sitting at his post, headphones on, tapping away at his telegraph key. The rest of the crew was crowded into their quarters, forward of the control room and past the officer accommodations, waiting for Dröscher, who stood in their midst, to deliver his message. Whatever the commander had to say, it had obviously been a message delivered externally by wireless, hence the telegraph man's presence not being required. As the wireless operator, he would have been the first to receive and decode the Morse signal before delivering it to the kapitänleutnant.

Sebastian exited the control room prior to removing his wet attire, as the wireless man would have been displeased were his equipment splashed with saltwater. Freeing himself from the foul-weather gear left him wearing his standard battle dress, the clothing of choice for most of the men on the boat. It consisted of loose-fitting, greyish-green trousers, adjustable at the ankle cuff, and a blouse of the same color and material. The blouse had two large, flap-closure breast pockets and metal buttons, painted grey. At sea, most men removed their caps, especially those who were taller, like Sebastian. In the pressure hull's cramped conditions, caps were frequently bumped against hatches, doors, and all manner of low-hanging obstructions, knocked from heads often enough to make them a nuisance. Instead of their heavier service boots, most opted to wear lighter, reinforced canvas shoes. The extra agility the shoes provided came in handy in tight quarters.

Upon cramming his way into the crowded crew's quarters, the commander spotted Sebastian, as he represented the last man on whom they waited. With all but one of the crew stuffed into the single space, and having just come from the cool, fresh sea air outside, Sebastian was repulsed by the stink. Washing came secondary to just about everything else on board, but normally the crewmen were a little more spread out and their unwashed stink dispersed accordingly. Even in the narrow confines on the pressure hull, that dispersion made an appreciable difference in the air quality.

"Now that everyone is here..." Dröscher observed, craning his neck to ensure his head count was correct. He was thirty years old, a handsome man with a casual command style, not uptight and stuffy like some officers became when given a command posting. He wore comfortable battle dress similar to that of the crew, though he retained the shoulder boards from his service dress and wore a peaked cap with gold leaf embroidering around the national cockade.

"How does it look out there, Eberhardt?" the commander asked.

"Grey sky and sea in every direction, sir," Sebastian answered, "but no grey ships."

"That's only a matter of time," Dröscher said. He paused to look at the men surrounding him. He then raised his voice. "Which brings me to this. I know how excited you men were when informed of U-21's victory two weeks ago. Well, a message just arrived over the wireless informing me that yesterday, after an engagement lasting less than one hour, vessel U-9 attacked and sank three British ships."

Rather than whistling and cheering at the news, the crew stood in dumb silence, unable to fathom the significance of what the kapitänleutnant had just told them. Sebastian's heart fluttered at the thought, but he wasn't entirely sure Dröscher was telling the truth—it just sounded that unbelievable.

For his part, the commander must have realized that his news sounded outlandish. "Men, this is no ruse," he insisted. "I do not possess every detail, but U-9's victory has been confirmed. Six torpedoes fired, three British vessels sunk, all in under an hour."

Incredible, Sebastian thought. He rubbed his left hand over his stubbly chin. Shaving was not viewed as a necessity at sea, and every man who could grow facial hair was wont to leave it be so long as the ship was on patrol. Each crewmember exchanged looks with the men next to them, and as the information sunk in, excited smiles began to gradually infiltrate their faces. All at once, a cathartic cheer and heavy clapping, coupled with the banging of fists against the ceiling and walls of the pressure hull filled the vessel with the noise of thirty-three ecstatic and celebrating crewmen.

On September 22, U-9 attacked three British vessels, the HMS *Cressy*, HMS *Hogue*, and the HMS *Aboukir*. The three ships were patrolling together near the eastern entrance to the English Channel, in an area of the North Sea called the Broad Fourteens (the water there was a relatively consistent fourteen fathoms, or eighty-four feet deep). As Dröscher said, in less than an hour, U-9's commander, Kapitänleutnant Otto Weddigen, ordered his crew to fire all six of his ship's torpedoes, sinking the three enemy vessels in succession and killing 1,459 British sailors in the process.

The astonishing success of U-9 silenced any doubt as to the destructive power of the U-Boats. Perhaps the most impressive aspect of the successful attack was that as an early design, U-9 was already outdated and relatively obsolete. It utilized engines which ran on paraffin (kerosene) that, at cruising speeds, produced thick, billowing exhaust smoke. The engines lacked power, consumed large amounts of fuel, giving them a short operational range, and required large ventilator tubes that emerged from the vessel's deck, to provide the engines with enough air and to vent the heavy exhaust. The tubes had to be lowered before the ship could submerge, and they lengthened by no insignificant amount the time it took to get U-9 below the surface. Paraffin engines were also unable to run the propeller shafts in reverse, which meant that even while surfaced, the task fell to its electric motors.

The four U-19 Class vessels (of which U-20 belonged along with U-21 and U-22), were the first U-Boats to be powered by two Maschinenfabrik Augsburg Nürnburg (MAN) diesel engines. Although the new power plants had their share of problems, overall they promised better fuel efficiency, higher cruising speeds and greatly reduced exhaust plumes. They were also capable of running in reverse, eliminating the necessity of running the electric motors while surfaced and so conserving additional battery power. The electric power plants were two AEG (Allgemeine Elektricitäts-Gesellschaft or General Electric Company) Motordynamos, each capable of producing six hundred horsepower.

The combination of internal combustion engines for surface cruising, whether they be paraffin or diesel-powered, and battery-powered electric motors when submerged was an immutable necessity, as the combustion engines required air ventilation, an impossibility when the vessel was underwater. The electric motors were powered by giant rechargeable batteries, stored beneath the floor inside the pressure hull. Recharging was accomplished by running the combustion engines while surfaced.

Large, heavy and expensive, the batteries took up precious space within the hull, added huge amounts of weight to the ship's displacement, and constituted a high percentage of a U-Boat's overall cost. Due to limited battery capacity and air supply, an overwhelming majority of the U-Boats' time was spent cruising on the surface. Submerging was only for attack or escape. The batteries were volatile, and dangerous if exposed to enough seawater. Were a vessel to develop any major leaks, the infiltrating seawater could potentially react with the acid in the batteries and produce toxic chlorine gas, a caustic poison deadly if inhaled in high doses.

When the hooting and hollering died down, Dröscher ordered the crew to return to their posts, which meant Sebastian had to once again climb into the foul-weather gear and head outside. Before he'd put on the slicker, he was stopped by Jollenbeck.

"Which boat was your brother on again?" his friend asked.

"U-7."

"How do you suppose Uri will react when he hears the news? If he hasn't already."

"My guess is he'll be as excited as anyone else."

"Do you still worry about him?"

"What kind of a question is that?"

"Well do you worry about your other brother?"

Sebastian frowned at Jollenbeck as he stepped back into the rubberized trousers. The subject of his youngest brother had been broached numerous times in the past, but it always managed to get brought up again and again under a different subtext. He never understood why his friend cared so much about it. "Like I told you before, Jollenbeck," he said, "last I heard, he ran off somewhere in Mecklenburg Province and joined the infantry. That's all I know, and it's all I care to know."

"Why are you so bitter about him?"

"I'm not bitter at all. I'm indifferent, and that's not the same. He was always a disrespectful little shit, and even though my father tried and tried to make a better man of him, it never took. I bet my old man got him five different jobs on the docks and he quit showing up to each and every one of them. When he turned seventeen and left home one day and didn't come back, Uri and I didn't bother to look for him. I think the only person who was genuinely worried about him was my mother, and he couldn't even be troubled to send her a letter saying he was all right. She only found out where he'd gone after a distant cousin of ours spotted him in a tavern in Schwerin."

"That's sad. How did he end up so different from you and the rest of your siblings?"

Sebastian slung the heavy black greatcoat over his shoulders, pushing his arms through the sleeves. "I don't know," he answered, "I guess sometimes a person just comes out rotten."

"Maybe..." said Jollenbeck as he turned away.

The conversation made Sebastian reflect on the vastly different relationships he shared with his two brothers. He and Uri both loved the water, and had worked on the Königsberg docks together during the summers before they enlisted in the Imperial Navy. Uri was the only brother who inherited their father's Prussian features, but despite their contrasting appearances he and Sebastian shared a strong kinship. Their younger brother, on the other hand, shared none of their interests. He hated the water and inherited none of their father's work ethic. The only common ground tying him and Sebastian together was their blood relation and their physical resemblance, passed down from their Russian mother.

As boys, both Sebastian and Uri had hammered on their younger brother in vain attempts to adjust his attitude, but the beatings only served to make him worse. Eventually, their only course was to ignore him completely. When he left home unannounced and never came back, Sebastian secretly rejoiced. After it happened, the only sorrow he felt was for his mother, upon seeing the pain and disappointment on her face from her belief that she'd failed as a parent.

He thought of his family back in Königsberg every day, and worried constantly about Uri aboard U-7, but he could go weeks at a time without giving any thought at all to his youngest brother. For the pain he'd caused their mother and the embarrassment to their father, Sebastian didn't care whether the youngest Eberhardt boy survived the Great War or not.

Freshly invigorated by U-9's smashing success, Sebastian pulled on the rubber boots and yanked the sou'wester over his head. He entered the control room, scaled the ladder, and crawled through the conning tower hatch. Lashing himself back into place, he scanned the horizon with renewed focus, the image of crippled and floundering British warships dancing through his head.

ARTHUR & PERCY

The ships carrying the various units comprising the BEF's 6th Division, the overall command of which fell to Lieutenant General Sir John Keir, had arrived in Le Havre while the titanic clash at the Battle of the Marne still raged. From Le Havre, the division boarded the trains that carried them west of Paris and around the city, finally detraining them several miles behind the front. As the Germans retreated to the Aisne, 6th Division paced the allied advance, but in so doing remained well back of the front lines.

During the Battle of the Aisne proper, 6th Division crossed the Marne. At different points during the fighting, Field Marshal French had toyed with the notion of ordering them forward to reinforce I Corps, who would have then moved west to alleviate the pressure being placed upon II and III Corps. Later on, there was talk of sending them to assist in relieving the pressure on I Corps when the Germans ratcheted up the intensity of a push against their front. Ultimately, though, it was decided they should join III Corps as was originally intended. That happened on September 21, when the bulk of the division was ordered forward.

The 16th Brigade (of which the 2nd York and Lancaster was part) was sent to relieve the 7th Brigade in their trenches, while the 17th Brigade relieved the 5th. Though the 2nd York and Lancaster moved forward, Arthur, Percy, and the others they'd arrived with in France were kept in the reserves and remained behind the lines. Rumors had begun to circulate of the entirety of the BEF handing their trench line over to their French counterparts to then initiate a move further north, though if and when that was coming was entirely up to Général Joffre and Field Marshal French.

Arthur and Percy's commanders were hurriedly attempting to whip the remaining reserves into shape before sending them into combat, whether that be in the trenches along the Aisne or a reestablishing of the mobile warfare fought in August and the first half of September. The word that they would not be sent forward with the rest of the 2nd Battalion had not come as a surprise, and to the two nervous eighteen-year-olds it was hardly disappointing. They'd yet to see any actual fighting, but they'd heard the rumbling artillery, and any rumbling as loud as what they'd heard wasn't something a rational person would be itching to run toward. They'd also seen the hospital trains, and witnessed all manner of casualties in various states of maiming being transported to the clearing stations.

The two boys didn't talk much about their families after they sailed from England; they had other, more frightening and pressing topics to discuss. But Arthur had been withholding a question that lingered in the back of his head from the day they left port. When the troop ship had moved far enough from the dock to where Arthur no longer saw Elizabeth, he left the stern and went to the bow. When he found Percy, he told him Elizabeth had been there. Percy claimed he had no idea she was there and was wondering where Arthur had run off to. He'd also enquired as to the whereabouts of his cap.

When drills wound down for the day, Arthur planned to press Percy a little harder, to see if he'd had anything to do with her being there. All but certain he did, he nonetheless wanted to verify just to be sure, and to then thank him accordingly.

"GHAAAA!"

Arthur, Percy and a line of their fellow reserve troops shouted like wild men and charged toward a row of dummies standing in defenseless opposition straight ahead. Arthur drew his rifle back, plunging the bayonet into the chest of the dummy in front of him. Percy kept his rifle held tight to his hip, and crashed into the dummy first with the bayonet, then with his shoulder and the full force of his body. The wooden post which held the dummy upright split in two, sending the two dummies, one made of straw and one made of flesh, tumbling to the ground. The men roared with laughter as Percy picked himself up, raised his rifle and plunged his bayonet straight through the dummy's head.

"God dammit, Ward! Don't break the bloody dummies!" the sergeant shouted, but Arthur could tell the man was secretly amused. *If*

Percy can break a post in half, he can certainly knock a German off his feet.

While some emphasis was placed on bayonet charges and hand to hand fighting, their Lee-Enfields were expected to perform a far greater role than swinging and stabbing. From constant practice, Arthur could now consistently score fifteen hits in the mad minute, and his best performance was nineteen. He had surpassed Percy in marksmanship, as Percy was having trouble with his consistency, scoring fifteen only a few times, and reaching his best mark of sixteen but once. If it ever came down to a bayonet charge, though, Arthur was betting his money on Percy over just about anyone.

Following their assault on the straw dummies, the men paired off to practice parrying and deflecting bayonet thrusts with jousting sticks, crafted to be similar in shape and weight to the Lee-Enfield. The sticks had a small, L-shaped bend where the barrel would have ended, before extending further out to simulate the bayonet. For safety, the sticks had a small pad on their tips, lest an enlisted man lose an eye during an exercise.

Naturally, Arthur paired with Percy and the two stood opposed to one another, stances wide, mock rifles held out toward their mock enemy. Percy jabbed forward first, with Arthur side-stepping to the left. Arthur then did the same. Percy dodged to his right. They did so back and forth, clacking the sticks together in the space between them, looking for an opportunity to "kill" the other man.

"You're not fast enough," Arthur taunted. "I'll have gutted you so quickly you'll smell the shit before you've felt your guts falling out."

"Bull," laughed Percy. "I'll take your weapon and jam it so far up your arse you'll taste the wood before you realize there's a tree stuck up your bum!"

Percy lunged forward and Arthur speedily rapped him on the hands. Percy instinctively pulled back from the pain, thus raising his jousting stick. Arthur saw the opportunity to strike at his opponent's stomach, but miscalculated the angle of his attack and thrust the padded end of his weapon directly into Percy's groin.

"OOMPH!"

Percy grunted as the wind escaped from his lungs. He fell to his knees. The big, strong, tree of a man tipped forward, and thumped to the ground on his stomach. Nauseated and disabled, he lay on his face in the cool, damp dirt, worried the strike had caught him hard enough that he might vomit in front of everyone.

"Oh bloody hell Percy I'm sorry!" Arthur yelped. He didn't mean to hit him there, but the guffawing from those who'd witnessed the unfortunate strike were probably more than enough to convince Percy to the contrary.

Percy, coping with the aftereffects of what was, to his memory, the worst shot he'd ever taken to that part of his body, rolled on the ground, clutching his groin and moaning while the burning, nauseating feeling crept further up his abdomen. His smaller friend had certainly equalized the strength disparity. Unsportsmanlike as it was, it worked, and in a combat situation, Arthur would have come out the victor, Percy, the dead man.

"Arthur you knobhead!" groaned Percy, his voice more guttural than usual. "Just couldn't wait to go at my bollocks, could you?"

"No, I swear it was an accident!" Arthur began to giggle. "Your bollocks are the last thing on my mind!"

"Cheeky little twat!" Lying prone in the grass, the suffering Percy clasped a handful of dirt. "Wait until I take a shot at your nethers, there'll be nothing left I'll hit them so hard!" He threw the dirt.

Arthur hopped out of the way. *I hope he doesn't mean that.*

The exercises ended for the day, and Percy slowly began to recover from the vicious but unintentional attack. Following a good degree of convincing, he accepted the inadvertency of what had happened and vowed to exact no revenge, much to Arthur's relief. They got some hot stew from the field kitchen and sat down on their packs to eat. After they'd shoveled the meal into their mouths and wiped their mess tins clean with a slice of fresh bread, Arthur thought it time to get his question off his chest.

"Hey Percy," he asked, swallowing his last mouthful of bread, "you saw Ellie on the dock before we left, right?"

"No, Art, like I told you before. My mind must have wandered off somewhere," Percy smiled, his cheeks stuffed with food. "And all of a sudden you weren't standing next to me. Didn't see you for a few minutes then."

Arthur wagged his finger and said, "You're a liar, Percy. You were a head taller than everyone on that boat. You could have seen me no matter where I was. And no way you didn't hear me shout to her." He took a swig of water from his bottle and swished it around his mouth to wash the bread from his teeth.

"A lot of people were shouting, on the ship and off," Percy replied, gulping his last mouthful. "How should I know your voice when it's drowned out by hundreds of others?"

"Because I was standing right next to you."

"No you weren't."

"I was at first. Either way, in my letter I didn't mention to Ellie from where we'd depart. How could she have known where to be if she didn't learn it from you?"

"Considering that there were thousands there, clearly a lot of people knew. Maybe she just figured it out. She's a smart girl."

"Yes, she's smart, I'll gladly give her that, but I'll bet you nearly everyone there either lived near the harbor or had been informed directly by one of the boys who'd be on the ship."

"Maybe she read it in the newspaper."

On the surface, that might have sounded reasonable. But Arthur knew better and said, "They don't announce troop ship departures in the papers."

"Why not?"

"Don't you think it would give the Germans a pretty good chance at sinking one?"

"How should I know?"

"You're right, how should you know? You don't know much of anything."

"That hurts, Art," Percy joked, but he had a salient point to make. "I think a better question is, why didn't *you* tell my sister where we were leaving from? Didn't you want to see her?"

"Of course I did! I'd like to see her any time she was willing. I want to see her right now! But I didn't want her to think I expected her to come. I didn't want to inconvenience her."

The confidence thing, or more precisely the lack of it, was something Percy was all too familiar with, and he wasn't going to give Arthur any harder a time for it. "Maybe you're more aware of it now," he said, "but she would have loved more than anything to hear it directly from you. Just so you know that."

"...I should have told her. But how about you go ahead and answer me without sidestepping. Was it you?" Arthur punched Percy on the shoulder, trying to prod the truth out of him.

Again, soft blue fire burned behind the eyes looking at Percy. Arthur was clearly sick of screwing around. He wanted an answer. It was time for Percy to tell the truth. "Sure was, mate," he said. "Before we left Lancashire I found a telephone and called her from the train station while everyone else was messing about. I told her to get her arse to the harbor right quick and say goodbye to you, because I knew you were too lily-livered to do it yourself."

You're right about that. "Now that you've finally copped to it, I just want to say thank you. Even though..."

The image of the teary Elizabeth waving from the dock still made Arthur's heart ache. He had been so happy to see her, but knowing it hadn't gone exactly as she intended still made him feel terrible. If ever a memory of one person was so heartwarming, yet so heart-rending all at once, it was that of beautiful Elizabeth standing on that dock. Her tears, in Arthur's opinion, would have made even the coldest heart melt and the hardest man wilt. As long as he lived, he never wanted to see such tears in her beautiful eyes again. Still, knowing her tears were for him was what made it so special, and in that way, those tears made him happy.

"Even though what?" asked Percy.

"She got there late, as you know," Arthur said, still picturing it. "She was crying. She probably had to scramble just to make it in time. It broke my heart to see her cry."

"I know it did, Art," Percy said. He didn't like seeing his sisters cry either. "But she saw you, and you saw her, and that was the most important thing, right?" Percy reached over and clamped a beefy hand on Arthur's knee, giving it an affectionate squeeze. "By the way, I did watch you throw her your cap. That was a fine thing to do, and I'll bet it made up for her disappointment in being late. Thank you, Arthur, for doing that for my sister."

Drifting deeper into the memory and further from the conversation at hand, Arthur stared at the sky and distractedly replied, "I wish I could have done more, but..." he shrugged, then all at once snapped back to the present and fired a smirking glower at Percy. "Hey! You said you never saw her!"

"Well if I lied about calling her then it bloody well stands to reason I lied about not seeing you two shouting to one another!"

That day, Percy, standing, as Arthur said, a head taller than nearly every man on the boat, continued to move toward the bow while Arthur shoved his way to the stern. Able to see him every step of the way, Percy couldn't help but feel proud when he saw his best friend toss the cap overboard. He knew how honored Arthur was to wear the York and Lancaster badge, and to chance losing it in the water just to give it to Elizabeth was a powerful and meaningful gesture. Arthur had since been issued a replacement cap, but had yet to receive another badge.

"Maybe next time you can show some initiative of your own, and see her without my involvement," Percy ribbed, only partly joking. Initiative was something he couldn't always take responsibility for. At some point, the torch had to pass to Arthur in all matters pertaining to Elizabeth. It should have already.

"I will," Arthur answered, appreciating that his overly shy and cautious approach to her had fully run its course. It was time for him, when he got the chance, to tell her how much he cared. "Why did you resist answering truthfully for as long as you did?"

There wasn't a particularly good reason. "Just wanted to take the piss out of you a bit I suppose."

"Right. Of course. As noble a reason as any." Arthur rolled his eyes.

"If I've got to play matchmaker for you, with my own sister no less, don't be surprised if I obfuscate once in a while."

"Obfuscate?" Arthur pulled his head back in surprise. "Goodness, Percy! How did you manage to get that to stay inside your head with all the coal and rocks tumbling around in there?"

"Did I use it right?"

"Yes you did. Well done mate."

"Thank you."

"You know, I should probably write Ellie to tell her how happy I was to see her. Maybe she'd have time to reply before we're sent forward."

"If you plan to, best to do it soon. Any day now, and we may be in the thick of it."

BERTHOLD

September was drawing to a close. The Russians had retreated to their border fortresses, and the crew of Gun Number 6 sat around a small fire beneath a starlit sky, joking and conversing amongst themselves. In war, it was much easier to relax when your first two months of combat saw your forces annihilate one army and send another scurrying back home with its tail between its legs.

The horses stood calmly nearby, their only offering the occasional snort or shifting hoof. In the eerie, flickering orange glow of the fire, the animals with darker coats seemed to fade in and out of the shadows, like mythical beasts able to vanish whenever they pleased. Less mythic was the cannon, also sitting nearby, its carriage trail still attached to the artillery trailer. The polished barrel reflected the dancing fire. Even in inaction, the gun was menacing.

Had the two thousand pound gun not been sitting there, the crew could have been out on a simple camping trip in the wilderness. Instead, they sat around one of many small fires in a tent city which dotted the nearby landscape, with many hundreds of their fellow artillerymen circled around those fires. The thousands of infantry manned a defensive line further east. They sat and relaxed, a confident and victorious army, awaiting their opponent's next move.

When General von Hindenburg ordered the southernmost forces of German Eighth Army to advance on Russian First Army's rear flank at the Battle of Masurian Lakes, Rennenkampf managed to avoid the

348

envelopment by ordering his forces to retreat northeast, past Gumbinnen on September 12 and Stallupönen on the 13th. Because of his maneuvering, Pavel von Rennenkampf managed to save a sizeable portion of his army from annihilation. However, the precariousness of his situation led Rennenkampf to completely withdraw Russian First Army from East Prussia.

For the time being, German Eighth Army could resupply and receive reinforcements without having to concern themselves with harassment from any opponents. Because the entire army still sat on German soil, they enjoyed complete control of the rail lines and were able to supply the troops far more efficiently than what was taking place on the Western Front. To Eighth Army's southwest, a new German army had also formed. General August von Mackensen, promoted to command the newly constituted German Ninth Army, was in the process of shifting his forces even further to the south in order to assist the Austrians.

As it turned out, what Weber had heard just before the incident with the Cossacks was spot-on. The Austro-Hungarian Army had been getting shellacked by both the Russians and the much smaller Serbian Army. Austria had not expected Russia to mobilize as quickly as it did, with the Russians sending 1.2 million men to the Austrian frontier within twenty days of mobilization. In contrast, the Austrians only managed to send approximately one million men. The massive Russian Southern Army Group was led by Commander-in-chief Grand Duke Nikolai Nikolayevich, a second cousin of Tsar Nicholas II. Nikolayevich's forces consisted, from furthest north to furthest south, of Russian Ninth, Fourth, Fifth, Third and Eighth Armies.

Opposing the Russians were, from north to south, Austrian First, Fourth, Third and Second Armies. The Austrian forces fell under the overall command of Count Franz Conrad von Hötzendorf, Chief of the General Staff for the Austro-Hungarian Army. The bulk of the fighting between the opposing army groups took place in the northwestern Austro-Hungarian province of Galicia. From August 26 to September 11, the Russians managed to take more than 130,000 prisoners and inflicted over 300,000 casualties on von Hötzendorf's forces on the Galician Front. Russian losses were heavy as well, but much less so, and they were the clear victors.

Over four hundred miles south of the fighting in Galicia, on the Balkan Peninsula, the Austrian forces fighting on the Serbian Front did not fare much better. The relatively small Serbian Army, under the overall command of Chief of the Serbian General Staff Radomir Putnik, faced Austrian Fifth and Sixth Armies, commanded by General Oskar Potiorek. Fighting for their very homes, the Serbians pushed back several advances by Potiorek's forces, with both sides launching multiple attacks and counterattacks to capture/recapture lost ground. To prove themselves unable to crush the Serbian Army in one fell swoop came as quite an embarrassment, both politically and militarily, to the Austro-Hungarian Army.

"By the way, I told you half-wits the Russians were kicking the shit out of the Austrians!" Weber said, poking himself in the chest with his thumb, gloating. "Nobody wanted to hear me, though."

"You were just repeating what someone else told you!" laughed Berthold. "If you'd predicted it before it happened, then I'd say you were on to something. All you're onto right now is everyone's nerves."

"Yeah, yeah…" Weber said.

"Those fucking Austrians," Lang snarled, "Anxious to drag us into war yet can't even hold their own on the battlefield."

"Why else do you think they dragged us in?" Berthold said.

"Get us to do all the work…cocksuckers…" Lang said. "And they'll share in the credit when we win." He didn't think much of the Austrian's effort, which Berthold couldn't really blame him for. Their Austrian allies *had* pulled them into the conflict, and so far were unable to bear their share of the burden in the alliance. Germany's leaders weren't exactly innocent in the matters which led to mobilization— in fact they were far from it, but Berthold, Lang, and the rest of the crew were about as far away as anyone could be from the highest military circles, and didn't know any better.

"I agree with you, Lang," added Roth. "What will we do if the Russians push them back any further? What if the Austrians collapse and are forced to surrender?"

"Even if that were to happen," Ostermann interjected, "it's safe to say it's still a long time away. They have a large army and plenty more men to spare, regardless of how poorly things have gone thus far."

"So we don't have to worry about them now," Lang scoffed, "just later. Say, for instance, when Rennenkampf gets his affairs in order and re-crosses the border. Maybe the Austrians can raise the white flag then, and we can deal with a few hundred thousand Russians to the east and a few million more to the south."

Berthold didn't want to think about what might happen were the Austro-Hungarian Army to suffer total defeat. If such a scenario unfolded, depending of course on the timing, a million or more Russian soldiers might be free to advance either due north to attack German Eighth and Ninth Armies, or perhaps head northwest directly into the heart of the empire. In the former scenario, it would end up just as Lang envisioned: two German armies surrounded by five or more Russian ones. It would be a reversal of the envelopment at the Battle of Tannenberg, on an even grander scale.

The latter scenario might have been even worse. If Rennenkampf's forces to the east managed to regroup enough to hold Eighth and Ninth Army's attention by themselves, the thought of a million marauding Russians storming through the fatherland more or less unopposed was about the worst thing Berthold could imagine. That, of course, was the worst of worst-case-scenarios, but having witnessed the heartless savagery inflicted upon the two airmen by the Cossacks, he couldn't stand the thought of the disgusting and treacherous Ivans laying his fatherland to waste. What horrors would the women of Germany face were such a scourge to fall upon them? To keep the Slavs as far from the German citizenry (and by association his mother and sister) as possible, Berthold would scratch and claw to the death if that was what it came to.

"Let's change the subject," Lang said, dropping his frustration with the Austrians in the blink of an eye. "When do you think we'll be given our first leave? I would consider it a fitting reward, considering our stellar performance to date. This is the longest I've gone without getting laid since I was seventeen."

"It might be a while yet," Hertz said somberly, finally joining in the discussion. Up to then, he'd been staring directly into the fire, expressionless.

"What makes you say that?" Weber asked him.

"We don't have enough reserves to fill in for us, so we shouldn't expect to go home until one of two things happens. One, France falls, or two, more reserves are called up. From what we've been hearing so far, I think it's probable we'll be waiting longer for France to fall than we will for more reserves. So, when they come, then we can worry about leave."

Deep down each of them must have already known as much; Berthold certainly did. It was frustrating, though, as some crewmen were within a hundred miles of their hometowns, he included. Leave was simply a luxury that none of the belligerent armies could afford two months into the Great War. So many men had been wounded or killed that the replacement rate could not keep pace with the attrition. Even in victory, the reality for the Germans on the Eastern Front was simple and straightforward—they'd beaten the Russians thus far, but their comparatively small force was the only thing protecting the eastern half of the empire from enemy invasion.

"Hey Kastner, have you ever been laid?" asked Lang, abruptly changing the subject yet again. The gun commander was ostensibly the conversation commander as well.

Berthold knew the question would come sooner or later, and was not surprised in the slightest that Lang was the one who'd posed it. Because of the mobile nature of the war's early weeks, conversations about home, life and loved ones hadn't taken place with much of any frequency. When they had, Berthold mostly listened. Now that his name was being called, he didn't feel the need to be dishonest so he played along.

"Yes, Lang," he sighed, "I've been laid."

"Lies..." Lang teased from across the fire. "I bet Weber over here's been laid more times than you."

Weber, unwittingly setting himself up for ridicule quipped, "I'm still a virgin, Lang, so if he's been laid once he's been laid more than me."

The men exchanged looks and began laughing. Minus Weber, of course, who fell silent.

Hertz raised his voice over their chuckling, "So you and Kastner have both done equal damage, then?"

More laughter.

"Hertz, you asshole," Berthold said. He threw a small stone in his direction. "I haven't told you about my girlfriend because you and Lang were too busy talking about your piggish whores."

"Oh, you've got a girlfriend?" asked Lang, "Has he a name?"

"Go easy, will you?" Berthold didn't mind sharing, but there were lines he didn't want the brash man to cross. "I'll only speak of *her* if you take it easy. Don't try and compare her to the hookers you're so fond of. I don't hear you shitting all over Ostermann about his wife so please do the same for me, yeah?"

"Fine."

"Fine. Her name is Pauline. I met her in Schwerin, two years ago. That's where she's from."

"Who cares where she's from, Kastner!" Hertz said impatiently. "What does she look like?"

"Yeah, Kastner," the rest of the men said almost in unison, "tell us what she looks like!"

"She's beautiful. Blonde hair, blue eyes, long legs and you'll make fun of me for this, but she's an inch taller than I. Maybe even two."

"That's a big bitch!" Hertz exclaimed.

"I knew that was coming," Berthold chuckled. "Yes, she's tall. So what?"

"Name, height, who cares how tall she is?" Lang cried. "How big are her tits?"

"Christ, Lang, I said take it easy. But, to answer your question, she's got a marvelous pair. Not too big, not too small."

"Too big?!" Lang howled, "What the hell does that mean?!"

The six artillerymen cackled at Lang's boisterousness.

"I'm with you," Hertz agreed loudly. "I've never seen a tit that was too big. I remember this one girl, a year or two back, tits so big they had nowhere to go but to hang below her ribs."

"Yeah but I bet her belly hung down to her knees!" cried Weber. Everyone roared as Hertz tried his best to deny it, but his denials fell on deaf ears. Mocked for his inexperience earlier, Weber had gotten revenge.

"So you found a woman willing to slum beneath her standards, huh Kastner?" Lang asked, in a tone less boorish than his previous queries.

The men around the fire all chuckled again, including Berthold. The hypocrisy of a man who stuck exclusively to whores talking about standards did not escape anyone.

"If you must put it that way," Berthold said. "I lucked out when I met her."

"That or you paid her more."

"I told you to watch it, Lang!" There was a line about to be toed, unless something was said. "I have genuine feelings for Pauline! Just because the war has prevented us from moving things forward, it doesn't make me feel any less strongly for her. When this is done, I might even ask for her hand."

"On your knob?" said Hertz.

Again, laughter.

"Yeah, that first," Berthold replied, "but then in marriage."

That was the first time he'd voiced such an intention out loud to anyone, and the announcement was met with blank stares. It would have been news to Pauline as well. She and Berthold had never once discussed the matter. Lang sat in silence for a moment, rubbing his chin. Berthold hoped the crass man wouldn't say anything too appalling. Before Lang could speak, Ostermann got a word in first.

"Well I'm happy for you, Kastner," he said with a warm smile. "And don't you worry about us making it home. We'll keep sending the Ivans back across the border until they've no more Ivans to send!"

"Hear, hear," the crew said.

"Don't get me wrong, I'm glad you have someone too, Kastner," added Lang, "even though she's just one woman. See me, I have access to scores of them, and I don't have to take them out for dinner before or after! Don't even have to speak to them if I'd rather not, save for negotiating the price."

Ostermann and Berthold shared an incredulous look. So far as anyone could tell, Lang genuinely believed prostitutes were a practical alternative to ordinary women. Berthold wasn't sure whether that was comical, or whether he should feel bad that a friend of his could have such a sad outlook on such a major facet of life. "You really don't believe in romance, Lang?" he asked, not expecting a well-worded or thought out answer.

"What am I, a woman? Of course not!"

He didn't get one.

"What about my wife and me?" Ostermann prodded, offended by the notion, even if it was just the opinion of a carouser.

"Look…" began Lang, backpedaling a little. "I'm not saying that romance doesn't exist for others. You and your wife are probably very happy. I'm just saying it's got no place in any life that I want to live."

"That's really sad, you know," Berthold interjected.

"Maybe to you, but it isn't to me."

"You're hopeless," Ostermann said. "Hey Kastner…" he turned his attention away from the lost cause that was Lang, "You said she was from Schwerin. Why so far away?"

"I have cousins there. I met her one day, we enjoyed each other's company, and we stayed in touch after I'd left. I went back when I could, and she even came to Rastenburg once. Met my mother."

"Did they get along?"

"Sure they did."

"Does Pauline have a last name?"

"I thought I mentioned that already."

"Nope."

"Oh. It's Hentsch."

THE SHIFT NORTH

On September 14, as Entente forces pursued his troops across the River Aisne, Kaiser Wilhelm quietly removed Helmuth von Moltke as Chief of the Oberste Heeresleitung. The decision to replace von Moltke was made both because of the man's flagging mental and physical health, and his perceived failures in implementing the Schlieffen Plan. His replacement was Erich von Falkenhayn, the former Prussian Minister of War. A new phase of the Great War had then opened, as von Falkenhayn and Joffre began ordering their westernmost commanders to try and outflank their respective opponents' forces by maneuvering select armies further and further north, in an attempt to regain lost momentum.

French Fifth Army, the BEF, and much of German First Army largely stayed put for the last weeks of September. Though some forces were in the process of being shifted from eastern France, the lines there held firm and remained relatively unchanged. While men in the trenches still died every day from Alsace-Lorraine to Verdun and along the Aisne, the German and French armies which shifted to the north were clashing violently in open engagements reminiscent of the fighting in August.

After the Battle of the Aisne ground to a halt, the French and German forces immediately began trying to outmaneuver one another in order to attack the opposing army's exposed flank. The first of those attacks came on September 17, during the Battle of the Aisne proper, when Maunoury's French Sixth Army attacked the right flank of von Kluck's First Army north of Compiègne, along the banks of the River Oise. Maunoury's intention was to turn von Kluck's flank and get in behind the main body of German First Army, a move that would have all but inevitably compelled the Germans to retreat further east. Instead, von Kluck's right flank held.

Général Joffre had dissolved Edouard de Castelnau's French Second Army in eastern France, forming a new Second Army and deploying it north of Maunoury's forces near the city of Amiens, about seventy miles north of Paris. The new Second Army, still commanded by de Castelnau, crossed the River Avre on September 22. They advanced toward Crown Prince Rupprecht of Bavaria's Sixth Army, moved by von Falkenhayn from Alsace-Lorraine to the area around St. Quentin. At the same time, French Sixth Army made another attack on von Kluck's right flank on the River Oise.

By the 24th, the French and Germans were in a large-scale engagement along a north-south line from Albert to Noyon. That became known as the Battle of Picardy, and lasted for two more days. Picardy was the second northernmost region of France, much like a state or province. During the battle, the Germans attempted to drive a wedge between French Sixth and Second Armies, by attacking the weak point joining the two armies at Roye. Maunoury's forces were able to beat back the Germans and hold the line, forcing the Battle of Picardy to a stalemate.

On the 27th, the German II Kavallerie Korps advanced toward Albert, fifteen miles northeast of Amiens. The Battle of Albert had begun two days before, and the French continued to hold the line just east of the town, not yielding to the German onslaught. That same day, a detachment of infantry and cavalry from French Second Army moved north toward Arras. The detachment was commanded by Général Maud'huy, reassigned from his command of XVIII Corps.

On the 28th, Falkenhayn ordered Crown Prince Rupprecht to move his forces north once again to try and outflank the French. This brought the Germans near the city of Arras and into Artois, a former province now part of the Nord-Pas-de-Calais, the northernmost region in France and home to the vital port cities of Dunkirk, Calais and Boulogne. The early phases of the Battle of Artois actually commenced on the 27th, but the heavy fighting did not begin until Rupprecht's Sixth Army reached Arras on the 28th.

Also on the 28th, Falkenhayn ordered Duke Albrecht of Württemberg's Fourth Army, pulled from just west of Verdun, to launch an assault on the Belgian fortress city of Antwerp. That decision was made in response to the potential for the landing of British forces and supplies in the port cities of northern Belgium. Because the remaining six divisions of the Belgian Army had taken refuge in the city, Antwerp needed to be captured by the Germans in order to minimize the threat posed by an enemy force still capable of conducting operations behind the lines. The Belgian divisions within the city were still capable of disrupting any German advances toward the ports, through both direct battlefield action and sabotage. Reducing Antwerp would also allow the Germans to gain access to the Channel ports, and at the same time completely deny that access to Britain and Belgium.

To help protect Antwerp, the British had already landed their 7th Division in northern Belgium. However the Germans, as they had done at Liège in early August, brought their big siege guns, the Krupp 42cm and Škoda 30.5cm howitzers. The bombardment of Antwerp would begin on October 3. The city's fortresses didn't stand a chance.

GORDON

Gordon stepped off the train and onto the platform at the station in Pau in the mid-afternoon of October 1. As soon as he'd left the smell of smoke, oil and machinery at the train station behind, he quickly noted the absence of many of the big city smells he'd encountered in Paris, or at least at the intensity at which he'd smelled them there. The air at Pau was moister, and felt cleaner, and Gordon had a pretty good idea as to why. It was hard to miss.

The Pyrenees Mountains rose like a giant, craggy wall twenty-five miles south of the city. They were like nothing he'd ever seen before; there was certainly nothing resembling mountains like that in Ohio. The mountains were the ultimate air filter. Cool, clean air flowed down from the slopes and cleansed the countryside. The distant mountain peaks were shrouded in mist, reaching so high they touched the clouds. In spite of the warm weather where he stood, Gordon could see large snowcaps in the higher elevations. *Amy was right. What an incredible place,* he thought, *and Spain is on the other side.*

He had to walk a few miles through the city's streets to get to l'école Blériot de Pau, as it lay to the northwest of the city. The flat landscape there provided ample room for the collective aerodromes then in use. Six different training schools operated near Pau, including the one founded by the Wright Brothers and still run by associates of Orville Wright.

A good way into his walk, as he neared the city outskirts, Gordon gazed in awe at a Blériot XI flying low overhead, its engine buzzing. It was right there, right over his head. He'd never been so close to such a marvelous machine. He hoped against hope that one day he'd get the chance to fly one.

After reaching the Blériot School and asking several people—each of whom only gave him an odd look—as to the whereabouts of Monsieur Plamondon, Gordon eventually found the man he was looking for inside one of the training ground's large hangars. The hangar, a large, wooden barn painted bright white, had a broad set of doors which opened wide enough to accommodate an aeroplane's full wingspan. Because the large doors were closed, Gordon quietly entered through a side door. It was much darker inside the barn than it was outside. Plamondon, his back turned, was overseeing two mechanics sitting at a workbench as they tinkered with a huge, shiny new aircraft motor. The instructor leaned against a cane, attentively looking over the mechanics' shoulders. He failed to see or hear Gordon enter the building. Past the bench, in front of the hangar's double doors, was a large biplane.

"Excuse me, Monsieur Plamondon?"

The work stopped. The man turned around and met eyes with Gordon. He immediately scowled at the sight of the young black man standing near the door. Like Sergent Bellamy, Plamondon was fairly young—maybe even a year or two younger. The cane he leaned on had probably kept him away from the front, or perhaps he used a cane because he'd been there a short time. He had dark hair, smooth facial features and had likely just shaved that morning. He had a large, but not gigantic nose. The man cocked his head to the side, as if unable to comprehend what he was looking at.

"Yes, I'm Plamondon," he said, suspicious. "Who is asking?"

"My name is Gordon Graham, sir. I'm here to train as a mechanic. I've a letter from Sergent Bellamy and all the necessary papers."

"Bellamy?"

"Yes sir."

"A colored American boy, at a school in the south of France. I must say, I've heard many things, but this one is new. Had I not heard you speak before laying eyes on you, I would have guessed you hailed from Senegal."

"Apparently, my complexion has that effect on certain people."

"Let me see this letter from Bellamy."

Gordon stepped forward and handed the letter to Plamondon. It was written in French, so Gordon never got a chance to read what it said. Upon reading it, Plamondon appeared troubled, maybe even a little sad, which was strange. He folded the paper back up, and tucked it into his own front coat pocket.

"Foreign Legion, oui?" he said, clearing his throat. "Let me see the other papers."

Gordon handed them over.

"How was my friend Bellamy?" Plamondon said, straightening the papers in his hands as he looked at them.

"Seemed to be in fine health, sir."

"Fine health, aside from the wheelchair..."

"Uh..."

Plamondon looked up from the documents. "I've never heard of this being done before, M'sieur Graham, but then, without firsts, our world would never change. I will trust the contents of Sergent Bellamy's letter, no further questions asked. He is a dear friend, and to me his word is currency. So..." he said, shifting gears much faster than Gordon ever would have expected, "Do you know what type of engine this is?" He moved to the side, presenting the motor, which sat inclined on a mount.

The engine's seven gleaming cylinder cases, each one textured by parallel rows of small, ribbed cooling fins running horizontally around their exteriors, were arranged in an evenly spaced circle around a central crank case. The arrangement was shaped much like a chunky, oversized metal fan with seven blades. A propeller hub extended outward from the crank case in the center, but there were no blades bolted to it. At three feet wide, and with its accompanying oil pump, carburetor and oil and fuel lines running behind it, over three and a half feet long, the engine was immense compared to the pathetic motor which Gordon had purchased back home. Gordon had seen the same engine in one of the last aviation journals he'd read. In terms of engineering, it was on the leading edge, and completely blew away in every regard the weakling he'd used to propel *The Hawk*.

"Yes sir," Gordon replied. "That is an eighty horsepower Gnome Lambda rotary engine."

"Very good, M'sieur Graham. Why does it have an odd number of cylinders?"

It was an easy question, but Gordon mulled it over before he answered. "I believe an odd number of cylinders allows for proper ignition timing and balance, and so reduces engine vibration, making the motor run smoothly."

"Correct again, M'sieur. At least you know *something*. That in itself, however, does not impress me. Why don't you go and find a place to change out of that suit and come take a closer look, oui?"

"No need, sir," Gordon said. "I've a pair of coveralls in my suitcase." He dropped his lone piece of luggage on the floor and dug
around inside for his grubby, oil and dirt-stained grey coveralls.
When he found them, he clamped his suitcase shut, and stepped into
the feet of the coveralls, pulling the dirty outfit directly over his suit.
Plamondon raised an eyebrow, but Gordon's simply wanted to
demonstrate how anxious he was to get started.

"Have you worked on a Gnome engine before?" Plamondon asked.

"No sir. I've only read about them."

"Time to put your reading to use."

The two mechanics, who until that point had been staring slack-
jawed at Gordon, mumbled to one another in French, likely scoffing
at his inexperience, and indignant that Plamondon would even enter-
tain the notion of letting a black man study the engine along with
them. Gordon eyed each of the two men, and was thoroughly unimpressed. *Where in the hell are these two from? French peckerwoods. I
should have known they had them everywhere.*

The man closest to him was skinny, and had a pronounced under
bite and bad teeth. His hair was black and scraggly and so greasy it
looked as if he'd dipped his head in castor oil. The other man was
short and fat, but his barrel chest and thick hands made Gordon
think he might be a tough fellow to brawl with. He had a round face,
dotted with large pimples and a dense, black five o'clock shadow that
reached halfway up his cheeks. Gordon could not reconcile the way
the two looked at him, with the way they looked. *These two judge you
for your appearance? My, what a world you live in, Gordon Graham.*

"This is a good engine, M'sieur Graham," Plamondon began. "It is
reliable, and does not have as much complicated machinery as rota-
ries being produced by other manufacturers. May I ask whether you
understand the basic principles of how an engine such as this functions internally?"

"I do sir," Gordon replied coolly, "but only the basics." It would
have been far from worth it to pretend he knew more than that. Lying would not get him anywhere, and might only serve in making
him appear the fool.

A rotary aircraft engine was configured as such that its cylinders
were arranged in an evenly-spaced circle around the centralized
crankshaft. In most engines, the firing pistons spun the crankshaft,
which then imparted the pistons' linear motion into rotational motion for propulsion. In the rotary configuration, however, the crankshaft was fixed to the airframe of the craft and remained stationary.
Instead, the pistons spun the entire engine block around the crank-

shaft. The propeller, affixed to a hub at the center of the crank case, spun with the engine.

"Very well, M'sieur," Plamondon said, "The four of us will disassemble this motor, examine each of its parts in detail, and then reassemble it before the end of the day. How does that sound?"

"That sounds fantastic, sir," Gordon replied.

"Good. Let us get started then."

The two mechanics sighed and hung their heads.

"Tais-toi!" Plamondon snapped at them.

They might not have liked the idea, but Gordon didn't care. He had learning to do, and to him, learning was the spice of life. The four men got to work stripping the engine, with Plamondon taking a short time to explain each part and, if necessary, its function. Gordon absorbed every step, visualizing the task performed by each component and filing it away in his memory.

Piece by piece, the engine came apart. He learned that the Gnome Lambda, while innovative in its means of delivering fuel to the cylinders, was also difficult and inconvenient to service for that same reason. Rather than piping fuel into the cylinders from the exterior for combustion, the Gnome used two valves: one in the cylinder head, and one contained within the piston itself. Such a setup meant that each time the fuel valves needed adjustment or repair, the whole cylinder had to be disassembled, a time-consuming process as Gordon quickly ascertained.

They worked for hours. Plamondon did most of the talking, save for when Gordon asked questions. Unless spoken to directly by their instructor, the two mechanics didn't say a word. The men finally finished the disassembly, having spread out, in organized fashion, every part from the two hundred pound piece of machinery across the large wooden work bench. Everything on the table was still shiny, as the engine had yet to be mounted in an airframe. Even after working for hours without rest, Gordon was still excited. *I can't believe it. Day one and I'm working on one of the best aircraft engines available!*

He marveled at the precision-crafted equipment laid out before him. He ran his fingers along the cooling fins ribbing the exterior of one of the cylinder cases, and was awed by their exactness. The cylinder cases were ribbed because the rotary engine was air-cooled, and the fins greatly increased its surface area. Increasing the surface area meant more air contacted the cylinder, thus dissipating more heat. Using only air to cool the rotary engine worked well, because the firing cylinders were constantly spinning, meaning there was enough airflow over them to keep the motor from burning up during operation. Air-cooling eliminated the need for a heavy radiator, which gave the engine an excellent power-to-weight ratio.

With the parts spread out and the engine in as many pieces as it could be, Plamondon checked his watch and rose from the table. He picked up his cane. Under the hangar's dim lights and with his back to the door and windows, Gordon had failed to notice the sun had long since gone down.

"Well, gentlemen, I believe I shall call it a night," the instructor said. He rapped the cane against the floor.

Gordon and the two mechanics stood. They wiped their hands on their coveralls, but the teacher only glanced at them quizzically. "What do you think you're doing?" he inquired. "I said *I* was calling it a night." He pointed at the dismantled motor. "You three, put the Gnome back together, and don't leave this hangar until it's done. Good night."

Stunned, the two mechanics dropped back into their chairs, and Plamondon walked away. Gordon didn't mind nearly as much as they did. When Plamondon departed, Gordon noticed that the man's left leg did not bend properly when he walked, hence the cane. *I wonder what happened to him.* When the instructor had gone, Gordon refocused on the project. He was okay with continuing to work on the engine, but the two mechanics did not resume. Instead, they glowered.

Well, they clearly blame me. Before Gordon came up with something to say to alleviate the tension, the fat one mumbled something in French. Gordon didn't speak French; he planned to lean heavily on his proclivity for fast learning when it came to picking up the language. But he did hear one word that rang a bell. *Nègro.* The man with the under bite translated, in a thick accent, what had just been said.

"My friend says niggers should not work on aeroplane engines. Their brains are not big enough."

Gordon was taken aback. *Did he honestly just say that?*

"You do not belong here," the man continued, "Americans or niggers, and especially not American niggers. Now we must do extra work because of you."

"Hold on a minute," Gordon retorted, his face crinkled. "You can't blame me for that. He might have made you take the engine apart anyway, even if I weren't here."

The English-speaking mechanic laughed and said, "We just finish putting together when you walk in, nègro. We already been working four hours."

Gordon would not let himself overreact. They'd have to do much more than call him names to get him riled up. He viewed himself as being mere steps—long ones perhaps—away from sitting in the cockpit of a French aeroplane. He wouldn't do anything to screw that up. He tried to be reasonable.

"I didn't know that," he said, "and for that I apologize. But couldn't you help me out this one time? I will learn everything I need to know if we put this thing back together right now, the three of us. Apart once, together once, then I've got it."

"You will learn it," smiled the mechanic, "on your own." He bared his filthy teeth in a grotesque smirk, patted the fat one on the back, and whispered something in French. The pair rose to their feet, and the skinny one looked at Gordon once more. "You do not tell Plamondon of this," he said, pointing a bony finger. "We will go to bed, and you will finish yourself. When you give up, tomorrow we tell Plamondon that you keep make mistakes so we can't finish."

"Right..." Gordon said, gnawing angrily on his lower lip.

"Good night, nigger." The two men laughed and headed for the door.

"Yeah...Good night," Gordon said, his tongue literally in his cheek. "Try not to choke on each other's cocks when you get there ten minutes from now. Fucking French hillbillies."

They exited the hangar, leaving Gordon alone with just machinery and tools to accompany him. The lights overhead hummed, and insects clustered around them. When he started working, every sound he made seemed louder, and echoed throughout the shadowy hangar. A tool set down on the table. *Clunk!* A component affixed in place. *Clink!* Tired but determined, Gordon dove headlong into the complex task, more anxious than ever to prove someone wrong. He desperately wanted to make those two French hicks look even dumber than they already did. *Redneck assholes. But what do you expect, Gordon? This was what Bellamy warned you about and there will only be more of it.*

When he awoke the next morning to a cane poking him in the middle of the back, Gordon worried he might be in trouble. He had no idea what time it was when he'd finished rebuilding the Gnome, but when he did the night sky had just begun to brighten with scattered light from the sun, which still lay beyond the eastern horizon. He figured it was around 5:30 in the morning then, but with less than twenty-four hours spent in southern France, sunrise and sunset weren't something with which he was familiar. Too exhausted to try and find a proper place to sleep, he'd rested his head on his forearms atop the workbench and slept in his chair.

"Wake up, M'sieur Graham."

Gordon sprung to his feet. He wanted to rub his eyes to moisten them, but he refrained—his hands were a mess. "Yes sir, I'm awake," he said. He grunted to clear the phlegm from his throat. Staying up as late as he did and sleeping in such an awkward position had left him feeling miserable. He tilted his head back, felt a relieving crunch, and then drew his shoulder blades together, crunching his upper back as well. A mild headache, nagging thirst and rumbling belly complemented perfectly his sore hands, forearms, and stiff neck and back—his body was a cornucopia of aches and pains.

"Did Matthieu and Giles help you finish?" asked Plamondon.

Which one is which? Gordon, not wanting to point fingers, didn't answer. He might not have wanted to tattle on them directly, but he sure wasn't about to lie to cover for them, either. The instructor knew the answer anyway.

"I'm impressed you were able to finish by yourself. In fact, I'm more than just impressed, I'm astonished. You must be a bright young man indeed."

"Thank you, sir."

"You hear things all the time about those with colored skin, negative things, and sometimes you wonder if it might be true. For why else would it be said? But maybe people say the things they do because they know nothing themselves."

Gordon listened, mildly offended at first, until he realized that, in just one night of work, he may have shattered one man's backward and prejudiced opinion. Or at least dented it. "Have you known many colored people?" he asked, not wanting to sound disrespectful. It wasn't his intention.

"No," Plamondon replied, and he smiled. "Though we French do have colonies in Africa, and so there are a fair amount of Negroes who've made their way here. I myself have not had the occasion to make the acquaintance of any such Negroes. I must be honest with you, I always had my reservations."

"Most people do," Gordon assured him, "even if it's misplaced and absurd." He watched Plamondon's face to gauge whether his speaking freely was perceived as being out of line. Back home, telling a white man he was dead wrong might not be taken in stride, especially not after having known him for less than a day.

"Seeing what you've done with this engine after mere hours with it, I would be inclined to agree with you," Plamondon replied, with not a trace of offense or crossness. "There is not a mechanic here who I believe could have put it back together on their first day. That includes Giles and Matthieu."

"I don't think those two like me." *Though I also don't care.*

"No, I suppose they might not. I will speak with them today and inform them that they will keep it to themselves. Bellamy believed in the impression you made on him enough to send you here, and now I've seen something from you firsthand. I will ensure your ability to learn and progress just as I would any other student. There are others who will not give you that same courtesy, but I will do what I can, so long as you promise to put forth your very best effort."

"I promise. Would it be inappropriate for me to ask what was in that letter?"

"That is a discussion we might save for a later time. Let us see how you progress here, and perhaps then we will revisit the contents of Sergent Bellamy's letter."

Gordon didn't want to badger the man, but he had one more question. "If I had come here without Bellamy's letter, would your reservations about Negroes have remained in place?" *Don't push it!*

"Yes, I am sorry to say," Plamondon said, a twinge of shame in his voice. "I may have sent you on your way without allowing you to lay a finger on this engine. For that, I do apologize." He looked at his watch. "It's 7:30; perhaps you should get some rest."

"I don't know where I'm supposed to stay, sir."

"Ah," Plamondon said, and he slapped himself on the side of the head. "Again, I must apologize. I failed to think of that when I left you last night. Come then, I will show you to your quarters."

Gordon followed Plamondon to a small barracks on the edge of the training ground. They walked through the door and into a white room with dirty wood floors, two rows of small beds against either wall, a lavatory at the far end and not much else. Gordon's bed was next to the lavatory, and might have been just a little sequestered from the others. He didn't mind that—it was far less segregated than any accommodations would have been back in the States. He imagined there might be objections raised by some of the trainees as to his presence in the barracks, but such sentiments were an underlying theme in life since the day he was born and long before it. He was used to it.

"When you are rested, M'sieur Graham, we will get your fees and paperwork situated. If you are willing to work hard in this place, then you will learn all the skills necessary for you to succeed as a mechanic. Perhaps one day you may even be dispatched to service the machines flying over the front. That is, if the war lasts that long."

"I will do whatever it takes to get there, sir, but my ultimate goal is to be in the air."

"Yes…" Plamondon sighed, "Bellamy's letter said as much, but…"

"I know it won't be easy, sir."

"It most certainly will not."

"I'll do what it takes."

"It will take much. For you to have even a chance at this, you must first become the best mechanic, and by that I mean quite literally, you must be better than every mechanic in France, to prove your faculties beyond a shadow of doubt."

Gordon nodded.

"*If* you're successful in that, then your next step would require you become the best pilot trainee in France, that is, if you found a flight instructor willing to work with you. I cannot train pilots on account of my leg. To be certified, I believe you would need to demonstrate a capacity for learning and adapting, beyond anything that other trainees might show."

Gordon nodded again.

"If you were somehow able to manage those things, then your third and final step would be to become the best certified pilot in all of France. It would be hard, then, even for the most prejudiced of men, to justify not letting the best pilot fly, even if his skin was not the right color."

"Is that all?" Gordon replied sarcastically.

"Yes," Plamondon answered with a smile, "that is all."

"Then I'll be flying in no time."

"We shall see."

Gordon thanked Plamondon again, before peeling the dirty coveralls to his ankles and flopping onto the bed face-first, still dressed in his grey suit. He crashed into a deep sleep before the man had even left the barracks.

VOGEL

Vogel's fingers were cold. In fact, they were freezing. Flying at two or three thousand feet during the summer might have given the occasional chill, but on those hot days, a chill was refreshing. In October, flying at anything above a thousand feet was getting downright icy. The pilots of FFA 12 had been flying sorties over the French lines along the River Aisne for weeks. The real action was going on to the north. Since their encounter with the British machine in mid-September, Vogel and Adler hadn't come close to another enemy in flight.

The wind shear was fairly rough at half a mile up, and Adler glared back at Vogel more than once as the Rumpler swayed and dipped from strong gusts. A powerful enough gust could cause problems for their machine if it hit them at just the right angle, but Vogel was ready to respond to anything, and kept a firm but instinctive grip on the control stick. In the cold, his fingers throbbed as he held onto the controls. *This is the last time I come up without gloves.*

When Adler was ready, he gave Vogel a thumbs-up. Rather than turning north, Vogel kicked the left rudder bar and moved the control stick forward and left, putting the Rumpler into a wide, loose, downward spiral. He liked descending that way, a giant leaf, tumbling gently. Adler ducked into his cockpit and reemerged holding four hand grenades. The small bombs were made of black iron, with a grid-like pattern of fragmentation grooves machined into their exteriors. A brass igniter plug emerged from their tops. He planned to drop them into the French trenches from a low height, to add another dimension of stress to the already stressful lives of the Frenchmen below.

Vogel held the stick and rudder bar steady, keeping the machine in its wide, gradual spiral. His hands were so cold by then that flying lower would not warm them; he'd have to wait until they were on the ground at the aerodrome to get warm. When the Rumpler neared two hundred feet, he leveled out the aircraft. Adler, facing Vogel, leaned against the back of his cockpit fairing, over the starboard side. He held one of the grenades in his right hand.

Because the observer's cockpit was centered between the upper and lower planes, the oberleutnant had to lean quite far to see the ground beneath him. Vogel kept the aircraft flying in a straight line, directly above and parallel to the trench. He hoped there were no French deadeyes taking aim at the Rumpler's underbelly. Two hundred feet was not a miracle shot. Adler pulled the first grenade's arming wire and lobbed the device away, and one by one hastily loosed the other three. He then hung nearly his entire body out of his cockpit to see if the bombs found their mark.

After a few seconds, Adler pulled his body back into the cockpit sharply and slapped his hands together. Vogel assumed that meant he'd missed. A miss, however, would still serve its intended purpose of keeping the men below on constant, restless alert. In the minds of the men on the ground, each machine passing overhead now carried bomb-dropping potential. Vogel turned the machine north and headed toward the aerodrome, pulling back on the control stick to safely clear the ridge overlooking the Aisne. Because they had descended so low to drop their bombs, Vogel was nervous the Germans atop the plateau might ignore the black stripes on his wings and try to shoot at his machine, as he'd be presenting them with a tempting, low-flying target.

So far as he knew, they hadn't encountered friendly-fire for several weeks. Of course, the men on the ground could have been firing at them all along—he and Adler may have just failed to notice. He preferred to believe the ground troops exercised increasingly more discretion as they accustomed themselves to the sight of aeroplanes flying overhead.

When the grassy field of the aerodrome came into view, Vogel throttled back the engine, easing the Rumpler toward the Earth. Wind gusts swayed the machine. Any errors in his compensation for that wind while manipulating the controls would have been disastrous. There was no room for correcting mistakes when an aeroplane was that close to the ground. Vogel had seen more than one pilot killed by a crash during landing.

Two hundred feet. The machine swayed, dipping the starboard wings. He compensated.

One hundred feet. The wings had to be level now.

The wheels touched down heavily and the machine bounced against the ground, hopping several feet into the air. It jolted Vogel and Adler in their cockpits. *A little bit hard on the landing, Johann. Dammit.* A hard landing could severely damage the aeroplane's structure, but Vogel's touchdown was not so bad as to cause serious problems. He'd learned the hard lessons about rough landings during training. Out of Vogel's first twenty solo landings, he'd damaged the undercarriages of three separate machines. The embarrassment of putting a machine out of commission due to his own errors in judgment made him extremely conscientious of his landings thereafter. Since then, he criticized himself harshly each time he made an imperfect landing, and stayed mad for many hours later.

The aircraft came to a stop and Adler jumped from his cockpit excitedly. "I almost hit them!" he shouted, "this close!" He held his thumb and index finger an inch apart to indicate just how close his grenades had fallen. Vogel, blowing into clenched fists, did not acknowledge the oberleutnant. He climbed out and began to walk around the Rumpler, bending over at the waist to look for damage to the undercarriage.

"Bad weather, Vogel, that's all," Adler assured him. "It wasn't that bad a landing." Then he left.

"Son of a bitch!" Vogel shouted, as his attention was drawn beneath the fuselage, to a crack in the undercarriage's port wheel strut.

"Shouldn't take long to fix that, sir," Leon said. He'd snuck up on him.

"Had a hard landing," Vogel admitted.

"We've seen others do much worse, sir."

"I suppose we have."

Vogel helped Leon and four other mechanics pull the machine toward the sheds. It would probably take the mechanics at least a few hours to fix the cracked strut, so Vogel was obliged to assist. His hands were still freezing, and he continued to blow into his clasped fists.

"Sorry for the damage, gentlemen," he said, as the crew began their work.

"It's really no problem, sir," Leon said. "I know you're cold. You should head to the mess and have some coffee."

Normally Vogel would have stuck around a while longer to help, but he really wanted that coffee. His hands ached, and they'd lost all dexterity. He made his way to the mess, where Adler was already seated. A coffee cup, sheet of paper and a pencil were laid out on the table in front of him. He sat with his elbows on the table, clutching his hands together and resting his chin atop them. His eyes were closed.

I wonder what he's thinking about.

Since the night when Adler sat down and talked with Vogel and Leon, his behavior had begun to change. He didn't speak as harshly to the lesser ranks, and he would sometimes sit by himself, in total silence, aimlessly staring off in no particular direction. Vogel figured the conversation must have caused Adler to reflect on just how much he missed his wife, and maybe put in perspective the sacrifices all men were making, regardless of rank or social standing.

"Are you writing to Frau Adler, sir?" asked Vogel, as he approached the oberleutnant's table. Just a month earlier, Vogel never would have asked him such a question. He wouldn't have approached him at all.

"I'm trying, but find myself unsure what to say," Adler replied. He removed his elbows from the table, and picked up the pencil with his right hand.

"My guess would be she'd just love to hear from you." Vogel sat down opposite Adler, neglecting to grab a coffee for the time being.

"What about you, Vogel? Have you written your girl?"

"No sir."

"And why not? You've more than enough spare time."

Vogel had no excuse, but didn't want to admit the truth. He was afraid that Kunigunde no longer had any interest in him. Flying in service to Germany was something he would continue to do, regardless of how she felt about it, and it had hurt enough when she left him for that reason the first time. He didn't want to receive a letter from Kunigunde reiterating the same rejection he'd already endured once before. "I don't know, sir," he muttered, shaking his head.

"I've debated whether I should tell Frieda we've exchanged fire up there," Adler said. He pointed at the ceiling. "She may not be as excited about it as I."

Vogel smiled. "No sir, I doubt any wife would be. I don't think I'm as excited as you are, in point of fact."

"You will be if we ever manage to shoot one of them down! Wouldn't that be something?"

"It would," Vogel replied, "but not if one of them shoots us down instead."

"Well Vogel, that actually brings me to my next point, which I only just learned. Yesterday, a French aeroplane shot down one of our machines near Reims, an Aviatik B.II if I'm not mistaken. The French crew used a machine gun."

"Christ..."

"Don't let it shake you. If they can do it, so can we."

"We can what? Get shot down with a machine gun?"

"You know what I meant."

"I suppose your next step is gaining permission to lug up a gun of our own."

"That's the idea."

"I can't say I'd look forward to carrying the extra weight," Vogel said. "It'll slow the Rumpler and reduce its rate of climb." He'd never carried or fired a machine gun, but he didn't need to touch one to know they were heavy.

"Reduce it only to the equivalent of any French machines doing the same," Adler reminded him.

"Yes, of course. If you'll excuse me sir, I'll leave you to your writing and get myself a coffee."

"Good day Vogel," Adler said. He nodded, and brought the pencil to the paper.

Vogel got his coffee and walked outside the mess. He leaned against a stack of wooden boxes, cradling the ceramic cup in his palms while he drank. When he'd finished, he brought the cup back to the kitchen and began his short walk down the dirt road to the pilots' quarters, an abandoned cottage approximately a mile from the aerodrome. The six pilots of FFA 12 made the drafty cottage their temporary home, as its occupants must have fled during the French retreat in August. The officers' quarters were further from the aerodrome, in a house much larger and more accommodating than was the cottage. Vogel didn't mind sharing the small house with five other men. It was better than the shacks in which the poor mechanics stayed.

"Vogel, wait!" a stern voice called out behind him. It was Hauptmann von Detten, and in his hand he held a single sheet of yellow paper. The expression on his face spoke as loudly as any words would have—he was about to deliver bad news.

"What is it, sir?" Vogel asked, preparing for the worst. He already felt it in his stomach.

"It's...your brother."

"Fred?"

"I'm sorry," the hauptmann said. He held out the sheet of paper.

Vogel was dizzy as he gingerly reached for the telegram. His stomach nearly flipped upside-down. He swallowed hard to retain the nervous vomit bubbling into his esophagus. Just two lines long, the scribbled message was as cold and impersonal as could be.

Attn: FFA 12 Flieger Johann Vogel. Regret to inform that Flieger Frederick Vogel has been killed in action after crash in East Prussia.

One, feather-light piece of paper, two lines long, delivered a massive, crushing reality. How could it be? *Was he shot down?* Vogel blinked and read the message again, just to make sure it was real. The words remained unchanged. That the telegram was vague did not matter; the end result was the same. His little brother, whom he had inspired to take to the air in the first place, had died whilst performing that very duty. *Frederick Vogel has been killed in action.* Frederick's death in action may have been in service to the fatherland, and could possibly have even been at the hands of the enemy, but in Johann's mind, as the older brother, he was every bit as culpable.

"...I...I need some time..." Vogel said as he lowered the paper and glanced up at von Detten.

"Certainly," the hauptmann said softly, "as you were."

As soon as the commander turned his back, Vogel began to cry. He reached into his breast pocket for the picture of him standing with Fred. He was so proud on the day of Fred's certification, the whole family was, and now neither he nor they would ever see his brother in person again, not ever. *Vogel Brothers, April 1914.* That was the last photograph they'd taken together. A proud memory, frozen in time. One black and white image was all that remained of his twenty-year-old sibling, the only photograph capturing him at the age at which he'd forever remain.

The dizziness, nausea and tears did not dissipate as Vogel walked the remaining distance to the cottage. The news had sucked the strength from his legs and he lumbered sadly and sluggishly onward, dragging the toes of his shoes along the dirt road. Every third or fourth labored step saw him nearly fall flat on his face as he stubbed his toes against rocks, dragged them through puddles and carelessly stumbled in and out of wagon-wheel and tire ruts.

When he walked deliriously into the cottage, there was no one else inside. The other pilots were either still up in the air or performing assorted tasks on the aerodrome. Vogel plodded up the small flight of creaky stairs in the center of the cottage. The stairs led to the two bedrooms, one on either side of the second level. With just two bedrooms, each not much bigger than a closet, and just two beds in the entire household, four of FFA 12's pilots had to sleep in cots. One cot was placed in each bedroom, and the other two were downstairs, near the hearth. When the pilots drew straws to determine who would sleep where, Vogel had won a spot in the room to the left of the staircase, but didn't win the bed.

He shambled into his room and lay in his cot, and wept until he was no longer able. In training, Vogel had twice borne witness to the ultimate dangers of flying, but even in knowing the risks, the thought of either him or his brother dying in a crash, or dying at all for that matter, had always seemed so foreign. It wasn't long ago that Frederick was just a little boy. A smiling, loving, smart little boy, who worshipped his older brother. Frederick had wanted to be like Johann, and so strove to be. And now, because of that, because of the love shared between two brothers, Frederick was dead.

Life was fragile. And short. Vogel's mother and father had just lost one of their two sons to the war. Fred, who'd never married, who'd not gotten the chance, would never pass on the family name to any children. It was up to Johann to do that now, to survive the war and start a family, and there was only one woman he wanted to do that with. She might reject him again, but if he didn't try to reach out to her at the very least, his time on Earth might come to an end as well, having never known what might have been. So long as he was breathing, he had to try and get things right.

He wiped his eyes and rose from the cot to grab a pencil and sheet of paper from the canvas bag he'd left on the floor, and then he snatched a book from a small shelf on the wall. It had a French title, words he didn't know. Lying back in his cot, knees bent, he rested the sheet of paper atop the book. Struggling just as Adler had, unsure what he should and shouldn't say, he nonetheless put pencil to paper and began. His intention was not to mislead Kunigunde, but the omission of certain information, i.e. Frederick's death and gunfire a half-mile above the ground, was not, in itself, a lie. She'd learn of Frederick's fate at some point, just not in this letter.

Dearest Kunigunde,

I know our parting was not a pleasant one. While the possibility always exists that a man in a flying machine might come crashing back to Earth, I'm sure you must have read by now of the death occurring each and every day on the ground. No matter what duty I chose to perform in service to the fatherland, I would be placed in harm's way. In many ways, I might be considered far safer in the air. Alas, mortal danger is the reality we face as soldiers, and that our loved ones must face with us.

I must confess that I love and miss you dearly. The longer we're apart, the more it burns inside to know I've lost you. Perhaps now that it's clear how dangerous it is, to be a man at war, you will forgive me for the path I've chosen and instead accept that were I an infantryman, I may already be dead.

The fighting where we are has slowed considerably, if you care to know. The lines have stabilized, with all major movements happening further north and west of us. I and the other fliegers have taken up quarters in a small cottage. It is quaint but tiny, and unless a majority of the men are away, one has no privacy.

I do not wish to burden you with several pages, and so I shall leave you with just one request. I would love more than anything to hear from you. It would mean everything to me, and I will look forward to a response. I will also understand if you do not wish to contact me. Again, I love and miss you more than I can express.

Sincerely,
Johann

HENTSCH

After gaining permission from both Unteroffizier Strauss and Oberleutnant Richter, Hentsch, a day pass in his pocket, wandered a mile
or two back of the lines. The urge to eat something that was not a
field biscuit, potato, or cured meat had grown stronger with each
passing day, and he was out for something different.

Simon and Engel had pressured him into requesting he be allowed to seek fresh game, if only just once. It was an atypical request, one which would generally have met stern refusal, but because he'd gone back to the ridgeline several times, to snipe under
increasingly dangerous circumstances, Strauss and Richter agreed to
let him go on the condition that if he bagged anything larger than a
bird, he'd share some of the bounty with them. Much of the French
citizenry still remained in their homes, and he had strict orders not
to take any livestock were he to come in contact with any. It was an
odd restriction, considering the army was in the process of taking
those same people's very country away from them.

Because the activity surrounding an army, even a stationary one,
was so great, Hentsch had to venture quite far before finding an area
where wild animals might still be around. On the way, he passed
hundreds of marching troops, most likely heading to the heavier
fighting in the northwest, along with supply wagon convoys and
hundreds of horses. At a particularly rough section of road, he came
upon the crew of a motor lorry which had broken a wheel in a deep
rut. After he helped the men replace the wheel, they gave him a ride

further north, and dropped him off on the side of the road next to a dense wood.

Stomping around aimlessly in the woods would not have done anything for him, so when he'd walked deep enough into the trees and out of sight of the road, Hentsch found a spot to sit atop an old tree stump. For what must have been two hours, he sat on the stump in total silence, waiting for prey to come to him. But time was running out. Darkness would fall within the next forty-five minutes. Still, it was relaxing there, especially since he wasn't sitting between the walls of a ditch. Alone for the first time in months, his mind drifted.

So much had happened since he'd first crossed into Belgium, and while the forced marching had ended and the rapid advances had ceased, the killing continued. A week after Ackerman's suicide, a French shell killed Nussbaum and grievously wounded Kirsch, along with three fellows from 1 Gruppe. So far as anyone knew, Kirsch was still alive, but he'd be a deformed shell of himself if he ever managed to pull through. Hentsch saw how badly he'd been hurt, and was left with little hope that Kirsch would live a good life going forward. One by one, the Great War was picking them all apart, and it was only a matter of time, Hentsch thought, before it picked at him too. Would it take a leg? An arm? Or would he pay the ultimate price, like so many thousands already had?

If I were a lesser man, I'd stay in these woods until dark and make my exit from this awful war. They'd never find me if I didn't want them to. But no, I could never leave Simon and Engel. I'm no coward.

Something rustled in the leaves behind him and to his left. Stifling his excitement so as not to scare whatever it was away, he slowly turned his head to see what type of creature it might be. He turned his head a little more. Out of the corner of his eye, he spotted a pheasant strutting through the leaves on the forest floor about thirty yards away.

Having anticipated the likelihood that he might need to move quietly, before he'd sat on the stump Hentsch had cleared away all the dried leaves and twigs in a four foot radius surrounding the stump. Now, he cautiously lifted himself up with his hands, and turned around to kneel in the dirt. Using the stump to steady his hand, Hentsch took aim at the pheasant. Normally he'd hunt a bird with a shotgun, but his Mauser was all he had. *I can't shoot it in the body. It'll ruin the meat.*

The bird wasn't so far away that shooting it in the head or neck was impossible, but it was hard, and if he wanted to bring back any edible meat, that was where he had to hit it. A 7.92mm round traveling at 2,800 feet per second would devastate a pheasant's body—

maybe even explode it—ruining the meat and defeating the purpose of shooting the bird in the first place. *I'd rather miss my mark completely and scare it off than waste a perfectly good bird.*

Hentsch held his sights on the fowl, slowing his breathing, blocking out the world around him, centering himself, hoping nothing would spook it in the interim. He had as good a shot as he was going to get. He slowly exerted pressure on the trigger, and a thought crept its way into his mind. *Do you really need to kill something else? Haven't you had enough of it? Or is this all you're good for now?* Hentsch shook his head once and rolled his eyes. *Oh, shut up, Augustus. A man has to eat.*

POW! The pheasant's head vanished and the body flipped into the air from the bullet's momentum. The gunshot echoed through the woods, a roar, which lasted much longer than he expected. *A rifle is even louder when you're alone.* Hentsch looked around nervously, worried the shot might attract unnecessary attention.

It was a clean kill. He and his two friends could now enjoy a brief change of pace in their eating. Strauss and Richter weren't getting any. They might be pissed, but five men could not make a meal of one small bird. It would be hard enough to satiate three. It took him more than an hour, walking briskly, to get back to the lines. When he got there, it was dark.

"How far did you go?" asked Engel. "We'd begun to think you deserted."

"I almost did, but thought better of it when I realized you two pansies would be lost without me. I had to walk miles before I found a good spot."

"All that time, and *that's* what you brought back?" Engel teased.

"Next time you go then, ingrate. Here, Simon," Hentsch said, tossing him the headless bird. "Show us what you can do."

Simon plucked the bird and placed it above the small fire, on a makeshift spit he'd fashioned while Hentsch was away. The hot nights of late summer had turned, overnight it seemed, into the chilly nights of early fall, and the small fire beckoned as they waited for the food to cook. Hentsch caught a chill and edged closer to the fire.

"It's small, but it still smells incredible," commented Engel.

"Any change will be nice..." Simon replied, turning the spit with hypnotized focus.

When the bird finished cooking, the three friends began picking it apart. Hentsch took a chunk from the breast and a leg and ate ferociously, crunching the roasted skin and savoring the juices of a freshly cooked meal. Though he'd grown tired of boiled potatoes, a dietary staple and the troops' main source of energy, having the potatoes with fresh meat made them taste much better. They were so hungry that by the time they'd finished, there was nothing left of the pheasant but bones. They went to sleep that night, satiated for the first time since sharing Simon's chocolate bar two weeks earlier.

Hentsch awoke early the next morning with a deep pain in his stomach. The pain had jolted him from his slumber. He rolled over, pushed himself to his knees and began to feel dizzy. Attempting to stand despite the dizziness, he centered his weight above his feet and prepared to get up. As he rose from the crouch, a searing hot pain tore through his insides and he was unable to stand tall. He fell to his knees, clutching his belly, and the contents of his stomach suddenly and violently gushed upward, pouring from his mouth and onto the ground with a messy *splash*. The world spun. Abdominal pain gripped him. Something was seriously wrong, he just didn't know what. In a panic, his first thought was, *my God I've been poisoned!*

On his hands and knees, Hentsch continued to gag even after evacuating most of whatever was left in his stomach. His esophagus burned and his throat stung. He hadn't thought to check on Simon and Engel, but when he did he saw both men lying on their sides, clutching their abdomens as well. Large pools of frothy white and yellow vomit were spread over the ground by their heads. Only then did Hentsch know exactly what was wrong.

Between powerful gags, he managed to growl out, "It was the...*hurk*...bird!"

His two friends did not respond to the revelation. They may have been unconscious. Convulsing so uncontrollably that the veins in his neck and head swelled and the blood vessels burst under his eyes, the world around him swirled ever faster. Was he panicking and making it worse? Or was the illness actually doing something to his head? The swirling became too much. His arms gave and he flopped to the ground. He rolled onto his back and dug his fingers into the dirt. It was as if someone had grabbed him by the ankles and was twirling him around at high speed. His last thought before he passed out was *I hope I don't choke to death on my vomit...*

The next hours went by in flashes. He vaguely remembered Strauss finding the three of them lying on the ground and ordering stretchers brought up. He also recalled being thrown in the back of a flatbed motor lorry. Emerging from the blackness a time later, he saw Simon deliriously swinging his arms back and forth at two medics holding him down. He remembered pain, searing hot pain, throughout his entire body, but centered in his abdomen. Hentsch faded in and out again and again, once awakening just long enough to hear Engel ask, "Am I dying?"

When he next opened his eyes, he was in a dark room of some sort, but his vision was so blurred he had difficulty discerning anything beyond that. Still in great pain, he had just emerged from what he thought was a nonsensical dream, in which a childhood friend, laughing, doused him with a bucket of cold water. In reality, he *was* wet and cold, but for another reason entirely. Head to toe, he was drenched in sweat. A strained, focused glance upward revealed a white ceiling, gently illuminated by a ray of moonlight streaming through an uncovered window. *Am I in a hospital?*

Unable to remember how he got there or how long it'd been since he arrived, Hentsch keyed on something else—he was lying in a bed. To wake in an actual bed, regardless of circumstance, was incredibly luxurious and shockingly unfamiliar. He may have been cold, soaking wet and wracked by body aches and stomach pain, but he hadn't *seen* a bed for two months, let alone slept in one. Sick in a bed beat the hell out of sick in a dirty trench or a drafty medical tent.

He was still delirious when a nurse approached him and placed her hand on his forehead. Hentsch reached up to grab her wrist, but his strength was so pathetic he could hardly squeeze. The nurse took her other hand and rested it on top of his. In contrast to his cold, clammy hand, hers was soft and warm.

"It's hard to imagine how one with such fever could have such icy hands," she said sympathetically. She had an unmistakable French accent, and for a moment Hentsch feared he may have somehow been taken prisoner. At that point he really didn't care, he was just thankful to still be alive. Her voice would have been soothing regardless, but with his having not heard a woman speak in so long, hers was downright angelic.

"Where am I?" he asked.

"You are in a hospital at Guise."

"Guise?"

"Yes."

But Guise is forty miles behind the lines! Hentsch tried to sit up, but the nurse rested her hand upon his chest and gently held him down. He was in no condition to move, and he knew it. He wasn't going to fight her. With blurred vision, he glanced up at her face. In his lingering delirium, her features were hard to make out, but her voice and the soft warmth of her hands led Hentsch to assume his caretaker to be the rarest of beauties.

"How long have I been here?"

"You arrived two days ago, in the evening. You've spent much of that time unconscious, and while awake you shouted all manner of nonsense. That is, while you weren't vomiting of course. Two men arrived with you and shared your symptoms. Are they your friends?"

"Yes. Are they all right?"

"They, like you, are not out of the woods yet. You were each very, very sick and have lost significant weight. We've just recently been able to give you water without you promptly returning it. A day or two more of rejecting water and you would have died."

To think, all the fighting and dying I've seen and I'm nearly killed by a pheasant. The short conversation was exhausting his energy. He kept trying to lift his head to get a better look at her face, but his neck was too weak, his vision too out-of-focus. His entire body ached. Though he had many questions, he found it more and more difficult to keep his eyes open. The nurse rested her hand against his forehead once again as he tried to speak. Though he was fading, the warmth of her soft touch radiated through her fingertips and into his skin, comforting his pain and lifting his spirit.

"When...do you...think..." he dozed off before he could finish.

When he awoke again, the room was still dark. Darker, in fact, than it had been before. His stomach felt slightly better but it still ached, and since he hadn't eaten anything in days, he was utterly famished. A throbbing headache pulsed in his head. Merely sitting up was a Herculean task, and when he finally managed it, that made the headache even worse. *At least now I can sit up.* For the first time in days, Hentsch's head was lifted out of horizontal alignment with his heart. He clenched his eyes shut, to prevent himself from fainting. His heart thumped erratically for thirty seconds before re-acclimating itself to the vertical.

A deep grumble in his belly demanded he take immediate action. *I must find something to eat.* His abdominal pain had not subsided by any means, but the empty chasm in his gut was the one ill he knew how to alleviate. When he thought himself able, Hentsch swung his legs from beneath the blankets and over the edge of the bed. The sheets were soaked in his sweat, as was the white hospital gown he'd been dressed in. The air was cold against his moist skin, and he shivered. Goose bumps covered his entire body. *When did they put me in this gown? Oh no, did the nurse see me naked?*

Something was crinkling and bunching up where his underwear should have been. Hentsch lifted his robe to ascertain why his underpants felt different, and was tremendously embarrassed and disappointed by what he saw. Someone had put a large cloth diaper on him. He sighed, deeply and shamefully. *I shat myself in my sleep. That poor nurse probably hates me.* He buried his face in his hands for a minute, cursing himself in disgust.

After he'd dealt with the reality of having soiled himself and that at least one nurse knew about it, Hentsch decided to leave the bed. So far as he knew, he hadn't left it in days. Resting his bare feet on the chilly floor, he slowly stood. The stabbing tightness in the middle of his stomach was still there, but was not nearly as crippling as before. An acute weakness in his legs caught him off guard and he wobbled, nearly falling before catching himself by resting his hands on the bed.

"Simon!" he whispered loudly, "Engel!"

Hentsch checked the two beds on either side of his. Neither held his friends. In both beds were combat casualties. One man had bandages wrapped around his entire head, save for his mouth. Fresh blood and yellow ooze had dotted through the outer layer of white gauze. *He was probably hit by shrapnel.* The man on the other side was an amputee. His right arm was gone from about halfway between his shoulder and where his elbow would have been. *These poor fellows are here because of grievous wounds. Why in the world are you here because of an upset stomach?*

Laboring his weakened body from bed to bed looking for his friends, he came to the door at the end of the long room. Simon and Engel weren't there. Hentsch opened the door and stepped into a brightly lit hallway. On a quest for food, he made his way around a corner and found a short flight of stairs. His joints ached as he moved slowly down the steps, and his very bones creaked each time he bent his knees. He had no idea where he was going, but good fortune brought him to a small cafeteria. The smell of fresh coffee lingered in the air. His mouth watered.

There were a handful of men seated throughout the room, scattered randomly among the square tables. Most were in various states of bandage or amputation, except for two. Simon and Engel were seated at a table on the opposite side of the cafeteria, near a window. Both gradually sipped the contents of small, white ceramic mugs they held in their hands. When Hentsch approached them, he was taken aback by how sickly the two looked. Their skin was pale, and sucked against their face bones. Their eyes were retracted deep into the sockets and were shadowed by black circles. Their lips were split, and the hands gripping the white mugs were skeletal and delicate, with pathetic, tiny blue veins visible through their translucent skin.

"You men look like shit."

"Find a mirror, cocksucker," Engel mumbled. "You look the same."

Hentsch examined his hands. They were whiter and bonier than he remembered. "What are you drinking?" he asked.

"Broth," Simon answered. His voice was raspy. "It's all they think we should have right now. Don't ask for the coffee. We already did and they won't let us have any."

Hentsch shuffled over to the kitchen and asked for a cup of broth. He was given the same type of white ceramic mug that his friends had. He raised the cup to his nose to take in the aroma. The simple, warm, briny liquid smelled superb. He sipped it sparingly, praying that it would stay down. He was tired of throwing up. Grabbing a chair, Hentsch meekly dragged it to his friends' table and sat down with them.

"They put a diaper on me," he whispered.

"Same here," Simon smiled sheepishly. "Engel, too. They said we almost died."

"Maybe we should have," Hentsch joked, still embarrassed. He pictured the poor nurse having to clean his ass for him. He still didn't know what she looked like, but knowing what she'd had to put up with from him over the last forty-eight plus hours, he wasn't sure if he wanted to.

The three men shook their heads. They didn't need to say anything else. They sat at the little table, quietly sipping their broth, taking the first steps toward recovering their strength.

VERNON

Kaiser Bill is feeling ill,
The Crown Prince, he's gone barmy.
We don't give a fuck for old von Kluck
And all his bleedin' army!

The men aboard the troop train erupted into the spontaneous song, and chose the rather poetic number which had become quite popular of late, for obvious reasons. No longer anywhere near a full-strength unit, it was that much easier to fit the four battalions of the 15th Brigade onto one train. The 1st Cheshire Battalion only required a few cars.

Whether it was because they were simply glad to have left the Aisne, or for another reason altogether, the mood aboard the train, despite all that had happened, was a spirited one. Men chatted loudly, broke into song, and just generally behaved as if the war, hard as it tried, could not break them.

"I can't believe after all that bloody retreating," Pritchard complained, "we're on a train headed back to the same damned spot."

"It's not the *exact* same spot," Vernon corrected him. "We're further west. Besides, this move north just means we're taking back some of Papa Joffre's territory. I'd rather he have it than Fritz, wouldn't you?"

"I don't give one shit or another about Papa Joffre, Fritz or Kaiser Bill. I'd rather be back in England."

"We're *closer* to England."

"Ever the optimist."

"I'd hardly consider myself an optimist."

In order to ease the strain on the BEF's supply situation, Field Marshal French and First Lord of the Admiralty Winston Churchill had lobbied Général Joffre to permit the BEF to withdraw from the Aisne and move north. The move greatly shortened the British supply lines, and relieved some of the pressure being placed on the French railway system. Because the Belgians were in the process of losing Antwerp, the Germans would soon control the ports of the Belgian coast. In light of that fact, British defense of the ports of northern France was paramount, as most of their supplies were moved via Calais and Boulogne, which were separated from the English coast by the Strait of Dover, the English Channel's narrowest point. Ships crossing the strait had to travel less than twenty-five miles to reach the two ports.

To facilitate the shifting of three army corps occupying miles of trench line, the British positions were evacuated sequentially. Beginning on October 2, under the cover of darkness, II Corps withdrew first. From there, they marched south for five days, and then boarded the trains on which they presently traveled. I Corps and lastly III Corps would follow in the ensuing days, with the French forces on their left and right shifting correspondingly to close the void the left by the BEF.

"Hey Vernon, do you think we're heading toward an end to this business?" Pritchard asked. He wasn't sullen, but he didn't fully share in the lively atmosphere.

Vernon didn't either, and wasn't about to bullshit him. It was nice that the men were spirited and all, better than downtrodden for sure, but reality flew in the face of their spiritedness. "You know it won't," he said. "The Belgians have lost nearly every square inch of their country, save for the western corner." He exhaled against the window beside him to make a patch of fog, and began to roughly diagram the war's recent movements, as he'd come to understand them. "On top of that, Fritz hasn't given back much of what they captured here. Almost everything they've taken, they still hold. This movement north..." he drew a sequence of short arches up the window, stacking one over the other, "...It's just both sides rushing to outflank one another, because no one can think of anything better. It won't work. Eventually, they'll reach the coast and have to try something else."

Pritchard shrugged. "Racing to the sea."

"Drawn on a map, that's exactly what it will look like."

385

"I wish they'd just chase each other right into the Channel."

"If only. But now we'll be in the chase, too."

"I can swim."

"If it meant getting out of this nightmare, I might give swimming to Dover a try."

The train, one of several which were required to transport an army corps—even one as battered as II Corps—had begun slowing. It came to a stop at the depot at Abbeville, twenty-five miles northwest of Amiens and just ten miles from the Baie de la Somme, where the River Somme entered the English Channel. They were still more than fifty miles southwest from their planned objective of La Bassée.

The train's doors opened, and the soldiers immediately transferred to a waiting convoy of motor lorries and omnibuses, which were provided by Général Ferdinand Foch, commander of the French armies operating in the north. The waiting vehicles were to carry the brigade northeast, to II Corps' staging area, just past Béthune and within marching distance of their target.

Fourth Platoon managed to cram its surviving members into one omnibus, which looked much like an oversized French taxicab. The platoon's new commander, a Second Lieutenant Fordham, had arrived just before the evacuation of the Aisne. He sat quietly at the front of the bus. He was even younger than Hood, just twenty-two, and had yet to see a day of combat. Seated, along with Pritchard, directly behind Fordham, Vernon could not help but notice just how nervous the young officer was.

"Are you all right, Lieutenant?"

The officer turned in his seat to face rearward. He was of average height and build, with an unremarkable but smooth face, and his peaked cap was a half size too small for his head, riding higher than it should have. His blue doe-eyes, full of fear, twitched ever so slightly as he apparently fought to keep his cool. He didn't need to answer Vernon's question, his countenance told the truth, but he lied anyway. "Yes sir, I'll be fine."

Sir? "Uh...Good," Vernon said. "Keep calm, trust your training and your men, and you'll stay that way."

"Thank you..." Fordham said.

Vernon nodded.

The motorcade rumbled down the uneven dirt road. Compared with the train, the ride was extremely rough. Half an hour of silent jostling passed, and then Pritchard gently elbowed Vernon in the ribs. "I hope Fritz doesn't catch us while we're riding in these buses," he whispered. "We'd never get out in time."

"I don't think they'll take us that close to the lines," Vernon replied.

"A Fritz cavalry patrol could be raiding behind the lines somewhere, though. There's no way the French and Belgians have every inch of the front covered."

The thought of taking fire while stuck inside the bus was an unsettling one, but Vernon pushed it from his mind. Running into German cavalry that far beyond the lines was unlikely, and the certainty of the approaching battle far outweighed any fears he may have had of an ambush. The Germans would be in front of them at some point, and the fighting would be bitter.

"Do you suppose God is on our side?" asked Pritchard, completely out of the blue.

The question caught Vernon unexpectedly. He and Pritchard had attended services together in the past, but neither of them was pious, and he firmly believed that the battlefield was no place for God.

"I doubt God takes sides in war, Lew," he answered. "And I wouldn't presume to speak to the whims of a deity."

"A lot of boys believe we'll pull through because we're fighting for God."

"If we win, then those boys will say they were right."

"And if we lose?"

"Then they'll say the Lord works in mysterious ways."

"Did you hear the story of what happened at Mons?"

Vernon scowled. "Nothing happened at Mons, save for a whole slew of good English and German boys dying. You and I saw that with our own eyes," he tapped his finger against the side of his face, next to his right eye. "Remember?"

"Of course I remember. Do you believe there were angels there?"

"What? What sort of hogwash question is that?" Vernon said, his scowl deepening. "Angels? At Mons? What were they doing there, Lew? What were they doing while thousands died? Were they cutting men down themselves? Because they certainly weren't protecting anyone."

"I've heard men say there were angels watching over us as we retreated," Pritchard replied. It was almost as if he believed it. "Someone said there was a story written about it in the papers back home."

"What are you talking about?"

"That's just what I heard."

"It's nonsense either way."

"The Bowmen" was a fictional short story written by Arthur Machen, and first ran in the September 29 issue of London's *The Even-*

ing News. In the story, a soldier fighting at Mons calls upon Saint George to save the British from crushing defeat at the hands of the Germans. Saint George answers his prayers, and the bowmen from the Battle of Agincourt (an important English victory over the French in 1415, during the Hundred Years' War) ascend from the heavens to shower the Germans with arrows, holding them at bay and allowing the British to escape.

Apparently, some members of the battalion, most or all of whom were probably the reinforcements who came in mid-September and had nothing to do with Mons, had caught wind of the story in the last few days and ran with it. Vernon however, knew better.

"Llewelyn, don't listen to that rot for one second," he said, pointing a stern finger. "I'll guarantee you there were British boys shot right in the head along that canal *as* they prayed for God's help. Angels? Please."

"So you believe God doesn't care who wins?"

Vernon sighed and he said, "I think God weeps at what we do to one another. Evoking his name to justify killing our fellow man is the worst form of blasphemy I can imagine."

"Where do you suppose the stories about angels have come from?"

"From men who weren't there. Men with fertile minds. Maybe even sick minds."

Pritchard appeared perplexed. "And the Germans probably think they fight for God as well?"

"No doubt they do. The Germans, the Austrians, the French, the Russians, it doesn't matter who, they'll all claim divinity in their cause. How could the populace oppose a war effort if it's convinced God has thrown his hat into the ring? You and I, we've seen a few dead Germans, haven't we?"

"I'd say."

"Have you noticed what's printed on their belt buckles?"

"No."

"They say, *GOTT MIT UNS.*"

"Yeah? Well I've got mittens, too. So what?"

"It means 'God is with us.'"

"I know what it means, damn you. You've made your point."

"Angels at Mons..." Vernon scoffed. "Bloody hell..."

"All right, all right..."

After another hour of riding, the motorcade stopped. The troops were still a few miles west of Béthune. From there, they would march the rest of the way to La Bassée, approximately seven miles further east. Their intended destination was only about fifty miles west of Mons, Belgium, the sight of their first clash with von Kluck's First Army nearly two months before. When the bus doors opened and the men of Fourth Platoon began filing out, Vernon and Pritchard took a deep breath before slapping one another on the shoulder.

"Are you ready for another go?" Vernon said.

"Quite ready. Let's go and show Fritz who really wears the mittens," Pritchard joked.

After 1st Battalion debussed and organized to commence their march toward Béthune, their column joined up with the other battalions of the 15th Brigade. The BEF may have been stationary on the Aisne for more than three miserable weeks, but that did not make another march toward an engagement with the Germans any easier. The battle was still a day or more away, but it loomed nevertheless, and not far off. Vernon had not slept well for the past week owing to the almost constant movement, and he'd spent more and more time thinking about his wife. He reached to his hip, and wrapped the red handkerchief around his hand as they marched.

"You'll help Sal out if I'm killed, won't you Pritch?" Vernon said. A sudden onrush of fear had struck him, and he was compelled to ask.

"What makes you think I'll get out if you don't," answered Pritchard matter-of-factly. "I'll be a goner. Bannister will see to that." His fear of the captain, while understandable, might have begun shifting nearer to irrationality.

"Llewelyn..." Vernon said, giving him a look.

"Llewelyn what?" Pritchard replied.

"He's a despicable arsehole, which goes without saying. But unless you disobey direct orders, desert, or worse, he'll never take it so far as that. What would his justification be? Sergeant Major Cortland would never stand by and let that happen. So I ask again, will you be there for Sal if I don't make it?"

"Yes, Vernon, I will. But you'll make it."

"Don't get me wrong, I plan to. But it's not entirely up to me. Unfortunately, the Huns get a say."

"Aye, but who's asking those sausage-eating cunts anyway?"

Vernon chuckled. There was no denying that Pritchard had been doing better as of late, his fear of Bannister of course being the exception. In the trenches on the Aisne, every man in Fourth Platoon had made sure to congratulate him for saving Hood's life on the Chivres Spur. Hood himself had sent an entire carton of cigarettes and two big chocolate bars from his hospital bed, along with a letter expressing not only his gratitude, but his wife's as well. Pritchard let Vernon read the letter, which, in sloppy handwriting, said that Hood had lost the use of his right arm. He was still in the process of learning to write with his off hand. That, however, was much better than the alternative. Llewelyn Pritchard was extremely proud of what he'd done, even if Bannister had sought to diminish him for it.

"What made you bring up Sally like that?" Pritchard asked.

"Why just then? I don't know. You and I haven't discussed it, even though we probably should. I've had brushes if you need reminding, and if it weren't for you...One of these days, that might catch up with me. I need to make sure she has a friend she can count on if I'm gone."

"The odds could just as easily catch up with me, old boy."

"They'll catch up with most of us after long enough. But chance will save some. So if one of those it saves is you, just promise me you'll be there for her."

"All right, I promise."

"So we're clear though, Llewelyn Pritchard. If I die, you do not have my blessing to marry Sally. I'll come back and haunt you for the rest of your days if you do."

"Jesus Christ, Vernon, you're getting a bit ahead of yourself."

A loud and familiar voice made the two friends cringe. They hadn't seen or heard much from him in more than a week.

"Listen closely you whores!" shouted Bannister from the back of his trotting horse. His mount, a sturdy Andalusian with a splotchy grey and white coat and a long, black mane, was not the same horse he'd ridden on occasion during August. He'd shot the first animal in full view of E Company's men one day, and gave no indication as to why. "I've just learned the Belgians have formally surrendered Antwerp, the cowards!" he cried. "Their forces have marched west, along with our 7th Division, and are taking up positions behind the River Yser."

Every man but himself is a coward. Vernon stared at the captain spitefully, and wondered just what in the hell it was that compelled Bannister to be such an unflinchingly terrible man. It certainly didn't help company morale, and it endeared him to no one.

"Funny," he said to Pritchard under his breath, "when the Belgians retreat they're cowards, but when Bannister himself calls one without any orders from HQ he pretends it's something entirely different. He's the only true coward amongst us."

"Shut up, Vernon," Pritchard hissed through clenched teeth. The captain's back was turned and his horse had carried him more than thirty yards ahead, but his mere presence totally changed Pritchard's demeanor.

What had to then been a lively and spirited march by E Company, their clunking footsteps drowned out by laughing, singing and lewd banter, withered into yet another dreary slog of the type reminiscent of late August—minus the roasting heat. With Bannister around, only three things registered above a whisper: his obnoxious squawking, the heavy footsteps of his freshly dispirited soldiers, and the singing and laughing emanating from the other companies who didn't hate their commanders.

DENIS

Cli-cli-cli-click! Denis sat on the firing step, aiming his empty revolver at the trench's back wall. He held the trigger, and fanned the hammer to see how quickly he could cycle through the six chambers.

"That cannot be good for its firing components," Patrice said, looking on.

"I don't do it often," Denis replied.

"You probably shouldn't do it at all. What if it breaks? Or worse, it wears out and breaks when you most need it?"

"You're right," Denis said. He reloaded the pistol and buttoned it back in its holster.

"Denis, can I show you something?" Patrice asked, like he suspected Denis might for some reason say no.

"Sure, Pat. What is it?"

At first, Patrice gave the impression that whatever it was he wanted to share, he planned to share it right away. Instead, he waffled. His mouth scrunched to the side, and his eyes shifted down and away from Denis. He was the picture of diffidence.

What is it you're hiding, Pat?

The BEF had finished their evacuation of the trenches in the Aisne sector the day before, and French Fifth Army's corresponding shift had brought the 144th Regiment to a new locale on the map. New was a relative term. It was no less unfavorable, and every bit as much another dirty trench overlooked by a ridgeline. Denis, Patrice and the rest of 2 Section were just getting situated in their new "home," which was so much like their old one they wouldn't have been able to tell the difference had they not been present for the shift. The better part of their previous month was spent in what was, save for a select few defensive improvements, a glorified ditch.

A trench. Parapet. Front wall. Firing step. Floor. Rear wall. Parados. Those were the accommodations, all crafted in dirt. The parapet, or breastwork, was a raised mound of earth just past the trench's front wall (the front being the side which faced the enemy). It offered additional protection from shrapnel and bullets. The firing step was just that—a step cut into the front wall, which served as a place to sit, but more importantly, as a place to stand in order to fire over the parapet. The parados was another breastwork, built past the back wall of the trench, also for protection from shrapnel.

Sporadic rain had passed through the region almost every day that week. Everything was damp. An inch of standing water sat on the trench floor, and a further inch of sloppy muck sat beneath that. The rain had stopped for the time being, but the air remained moist and chilly. The sky overhead was grey, making the world around them all the more ugly.

The new locale promised little or no respite from the same conditions they'd dealt with since being forced from the Chemin des Dames and losing Craonne during the Battle of the Aisne. Snipers, shells, and the occasional localized attack became the standard, and every so often a man nearby fell victim to one thing or the other. The Germans, for their part, were every bit as battered and depleted as the French, and could not muster sufficient strength to launch any large-scale offensives. Both armies' resources were being funneled to the northwest. Even in stalemate, however, death found myriad ways to take what it sought.

"Will you show me whatever it was, or should I wait until you're more comfortable?" Denis couldn't help but be intrigued at that point. "Or must I shuffle through your things when you're asleep?"

"Maybe it should wait," Patrice said.

"You were the one who brought it up. I think you should go through with it."

"Well, all right. But you must assure me you will not laugh."

"We have had very little to laugh about lately. I doubt I have it in me today."

Patrice sighed and reached into the front of his greatcoat. He left his hand inside, waffling again, but eventually pulled his arm free. Extracted from what must have been the breast pocket of his tunic, was a solitary photograph. "Cécile insisted we have a portrait done before I left," he said. "I stare at it when you're not around." He gazed longingly at the picture as he spoke. "I really miss her, you know. I may laugh about not having her address and joke of not seeing her again, but I truly wish I knew where to send the letters I've written."

Denis was surprised. "Why wouldn't you look at it when I'm around?" he asked. "And wait, letters?" He hadn't once seen Patrice gaze at a picture or write a letter. *When did he have time for writing? We're around one another constantly.*

"I don't know why I didn't want you to see. Maybe I thought you would deem me distracted. Like my head was not in the fight."

How could I accuse anyone of not having their head in the fight? I'm an aspirant who is unfit to lead. "Distracted for writing to someone you miss? What sort of monster would I be?"

"I almost told you about the letters once."

"Why didn't you?"

"It wasn't the time."

Patrice appeared ashamed, and Denis felt guilty his friend would ever assume he'd have reacted in such a way. He reached out and gently took the photograph from Patrice to have a look. Cécile stood in front and to Patrice's left. She wore a nice, light-colored dress that clung tightly to her bosom. *Probably wore that so he'd get a decent look at her chest while he was away. Thoughtful.* Patrice posed in his parade uniform, and his hands were rested on her hips. It was easy to tell by their expressions that the two were happy to be together. Denis still found it funny that they were the same height, and smiled about it as he handed the photograph back to his friend.

"She is very pretty," said Denis. "I understand why you miss her."

"Thank you. Could I ask a favor?" Patrice gently ran his thumb across the surface of his precious memento.

"Of course you can."

"One of these days, a boche shell or bullet will catch me, or one of those bastards will run me through with a bayonet. It's coming I tell you."

"Come now, Patrice you cannot think that way."

"I know it sounds defeatist, but that is not my intention. I hate the boche as much as ever, and I'll fight them to my last breath, but that means nothing if a shell lands on my head. A lucky shot, an attack while my back is turned, you and I must both acknowledge how easy it is to die here."

It was a morbid assessment, but true at its core. The Germans had been consistently lobbing shells over the ridge, day after day. Like clockwork, shells fell at dawn and dusk, and sometimes in between, shaking the ground beneath the Frenchmen's feet and showering them with ejecta. German snipers likewise caused much consternation, though that had diminished some since the trenches were deepened. The sniper threat still remained, however, and they would fire at just about anything peeking above the top of the trench. It had long since become close to impossible to relax one's nerves, for even one moment, as the threat from one thing or another was constant.

Rest came at a premium, with men often attempting to rush into a nap immediately at the detonation of a nearby shell, assuming another would not arrive for at least a short while later. For men like Denis and Patrice, taking a nap on command wasn't so easy. The lack of sleep showed in Patrice's eyes, as the handsome green was surrounded by a veiny pink. His eyes had sunk deeper into his skull over the past month, and the bags underneath them were purple. Denis hoped he didn't look as sullen as his friend.

"What is this favor you wish to ask of me?"

Patrice stood and went for his pack, which he'd rested against the trench's back wall. Because of the limited space offered between the walls, and the stationary nature of their present situation, the wearing of haversacks had all but ceased. Ease of movement in the confined space was greatly hampered by the heavy and cumbersome packs.

Paper crinkled while Patrice dug inside his haversack. After about twenty seconds, he held in his hand a veritable stack of pages. Denis was surprised how many there were. *He must have written thirty letters!*

Patrice plopped down next to him on the firing step. He began sorting through the papers. "I've written the dates on them," he said, "in case they fell out of order, which they clearly have. Would you help me to organize them?"

"Sure."

Patrice began handing him the pages one by one. He offered a running commentary on each, starting with the first note he'd scribbled to her while still on the train from Bordeaux. It had apparently been written while Denis napped. The pages were handed to Denis face-down, to prevent him from reading them. When they'd finished, he said, "Was that the favor?"

"No..."

"Pat, come out and ask, already."

"Fine. If I don't make it, and you do, would you find your way back to Bordeaux and get these to Cécile?" Patrice patted the stack of papers and nodded toward them. "It would mean a lot to me."

Denis raised an eyebrow, but of course he was not going to say no. "Yes, I can do that. But such a promise, it's moot. You'll give them to her yourself when we've beaten the boche."

"I hope so."

"I'll tell you what," Denis said, "I don't have anything useful with me, but someone around here will. I will go and find you a paperclip or an envelope so you may more easily keep track of your letters. Sit tight and I'll come back with something."

Denis affectionately slapped Patrice on the back. The slap rocked him forward. Denis stood and began to walk away.

"Do you want me to come with you?" Patrice asked.

"No, you stay put," Denis replied. "Try and get some rest." He turned to leave.

"Wait!"

"Yes, Pat, what is it?"

"This has been a shitty two months," said Patrice, "and we've been through and seen so many terrible things." He looked at his boots, sighed, and then looked Denis in the eye. "Going through it with you has been the one aspect of the whole affair that I'd never take back, and that can keep me going for as long as I need it to. You're a good man and a great friend, Denis, and I love you for that."

"I love you too, Patrice," Denis said with a tender smile. They nodded at one another, and Denis wandered east through the muddy trench. After about thirty feet, the trench gradually bent southward, putting him out of Patrice's view. He first came across a group of poilus from 1 Section who were sitting on their haversacks, smoking cigarettes and playing a card game. Their table was a small board, centered atop a rusty bucket which had been overturned and pushed into the mud.

"Sorry to interrupt, gentlemen," Denis said, "but might anyone have an envelope to spare? Maybe a paper clip? A folder? Anything?"

The men looked up from their game and each answered no. Just as they returned their attention to their cards, a strong, crisp gust of wind swirled through the trench, scattering their cards about and tossing nearly half a deck into the mire at their feet. The men shouted and cursed, blaming Denis for distracting them and ruining their game. Denis apologized, sniggering at the same time, then snuck between them and moved on.

He continued walking down the line, asking man after man if they had something, anything he could use to organize a stack of papers. Finally Denis came across a young soldier who had just received what must have been a care package from his mother. The soldier was in the process of writing to someone, probably a thank you letter, and was scribbling his words in a handsome, leather-bound journal. He looked like the organized type. If anyone had extra supplies, it was him.

"Excuse me, might I have a word?" said Denis, unnoticed to that point.

"Of course sir," the startled young man replied, resting the journal beside him and springing to his feet. "My apologies for being distracted sir." A marked lack of grime, wear and bloodstains on his greatcoat made it clear he was a recently arrived reinforcement. His suddenly nervous demeanor suggested he was anxious to make an impression on any officers with whom he might have cause to interact.

"At ease," Denis assured him. "I only need to ask a favor."

"By all means, sir."

"Might you have an envelope or a paperclip to spare? I've some documents which need organizing, but nothing with which to do so."

"I have just the thing," answered the young man. He reached a hand into his greatcoat pocket and withdrew a veritable handful of wire paperclips, plucked one from the tangled mass, and handed it to Denis. "Hope this helps," he said.

"It will. Thank you. I've been looking for nearly half an hour. My friend will wonder where I've gone off to."

"You're welcome, sir. Good day."

Denis made his way back, passing by the men he'd spoken with in the preceding minutes. A few asked if he'd had any luck, and he stopped to chat for a short while. He interrupted the card game once more, having to walk through the middle to move past. Both the makeshift table and the playing cards were significantly wetter and dirtier than before. A couple men jokingly shoved him as he moved by, and chided him for his relentless intrusions into their entertainment. Leaving the game behind, Denis stepped around the corner to show Patrice what he'd found.

Patrice was standing on the tips of his toes on the firing step, leaning his stomach against the wall with his torso toward the parapet. Because of the angle at which he stood, Denis was unable to see him from the shoulders up. *He must have seen movement on the ridge. He'll probably take his shot within a few seconds.* It was comical that Patrice could barely stand up high enough to get in a proper firing position.

He didn't want to distract Patrice's attention from the shot, so he quietly moved toward his friend without saying a word. Next to Patrice's feet sat his stack of letters. His canteen rested atop them. Something wasn't quite right. The letters beneath the canteen were disorganized and dirty, and some were soaking wet. A cursory glance around the immediate area revealed to Denis both his and his friend's rifles still leaning against the trench's back wall, right alongside their haversacks. *If his rifle is down here...*

"Patrice, what are you doing up there?"

No response.

What are you so focused on?

"Patrice, if you're not firing at a boche, then get your ass down from there!"

His friend remained against the parapet, ignoring him. Denis jumped atop the firing step to see what was so interesting. Patrice lay face down. His right arm was fully extended in front of him and lay flat on the ground, his outstretched fingertips clutching the picture of him and Cécile.

He's been hit.

Denis grabbed the back of his friend's tunic to pull him into the trench and ascertain where and how badly he'd been wounded. Patrice slid away from the parapet. The full weight of his lifeless body collapsed into Denis and knocked him backward. The two men fell from the firing step and thudded hard against the floor, splashing into the slimy mud and brown water. The way Patrice landed, half on top of Denis, made his body roll slightly to the side. Denis could not see his face.

"Patrice!" he cried. "Are you all right?!"

Denis reached an arm around his friend, and pulled himself from beneath Patrice's body so he could sit up to help him. The movement caused the weight of Patrice's head to shift. His head rolled limply on his neck, swiveling in Denis's direction.

"OH MY GOD, NO!"

Denis recoiled and he pushed himself backward. His hands and boots slipped in the muck, and he pushed until he'd pressed his back against the wall. A firm, strangling knot formed in his throat and his eyes welled with tears. There would be no help for his friend.

The sniper's bullet struck Patrice two inches above his hairline. His dark brown hair was slick and stained almost black from the blood which had erupted from underneath. His forehead was covered with dirt and blood, which pasted the dirt to his skin. His green eyes were bloodied, and rolled back in his head—only the very bottoms of his emerald irises showed from under his eyelids. Blood had gushed from both his nose and mouth, staining his teeth, which were clenched and bared. It was as if he'd been straining or concentrating on something the moment he'd been shot.

He had been. It wasn't hard to piece together. The same gust of wind that ruined the card game around the corner had scattered Patrice's letters, which he'd then picked up and placed under his canteen. A cruel twist of fate had seen to it that the wind carried his beloved portrait up and out of the trench, and dropped it barely within arm's reach. Patrice had probably just gotten his hand to the photo when the German sniper atop the ridge pulled the trigger. He died just as his fingertips grasped the picture, having never heard the shot that killed him.

Denis sat on the cold, slimy trench floor, his back against the wall, forcefully squeezing his hands behind his neck. Rage, sorrow, fear and frantic incomprehension swirled inside him as he attempted to rationalize the finality of it, and of the awful way in which his friend had just died. Patrice, unarmed, had reached out of the trench to grab the only photograph he possessed of the girl he'd left back home. If the German who shot him had known what he was doing, would he still have fired? *One gust of wind, and Patrice is gone.* Patrice was right. It was easy to die there.

Could he have just let the picture be? Chocked it up as a loss? Of course. But how many sad and lonely soldiers would let their best and only reminder of home just blow away and disappear? Denis took his hands from behind his neck and grabbed hold of the shoulder of Patrice's uniform, and he squeezed until his fingers hurt. He wanted to hug the body, to somehow squeeze life back into it, but that was a fool's notion. He couldn't bear to look at the horrid expression on his friend's face.

He asked to come with me. This is my fault.

Every man who'd answered the call of duty in the early days of August had since lost friends. Some lost brothers, fathers, uncles, respected commanders, but not every man lost every single close friend with whom he traveled into battle. Denis had considered each of his squad mates a true friend, and in just two months of fighting they were all gone. Yes, two of them (Emery and Gustav) were not dead, maybe even three if Maurice was still alive somewhere, but they likely weren't coming back. It was little consolation.

Sitting there in the muck, resting his hand on the shoulder of his dead best friend, Denis wept, unable to mask his despair. Nearby soldiers were finally catching on to what had happened, and they made their concerned presence known, but their questions, sorrowful condolences and angry cursing at the boche fell on numb ears. To Denis, the movements and voices around him were a meaningless blur. He'd left Patrice half an hour earlier in order to find something, the smallest gesture, that might lift his friend's spirit, and now Denis had absolutely no one to lift his.

That could have been it for him. So much loss, so much disappointment, so much death, it could have broken what remained of his willingness to fight. He'd already backed away from the leadership role for which he'd spent two years of study and training at Saint-Cyr. He'd already failed in his responsibilities to his men, and to his best friend. He still did not know his family's fate, only that if they remained in Cambrai during the Germans' initial invasion, the northward shift now placed their home well behind enemy lines.

Denis might have failed in many regards, but an underlying truth did not escape him. All the killing, dying, fighting, and destruction, everything that had brought him, *pushed* him toward his failures— there was only one entity truly responsible for it all. The Germans. The God damned Germans. Were it not for them, his world would still be in one piece.

With tears streaming down his cheeks and his hand still clutching Patrice's shoulder, a fire sparked deep within Denis. The fire did not burn for honor, or fatherland, for family nor true love. It was a different kind of fire, the embers of which lay in the darkest reaches of every single human being who ever lived, or would ever live. In some, the fire was easy to start. In others, it took much stoking. Denis had struggled with it for weeks, not wanting it to take hold of him as it had Patrice after the Marne. The boche sniper on the ridge might just have been doing his duty—every German boot on French soil might have been doing the same—but that didn't matter anymore. The fire had been lit, and it burned within Denis, a blistering inferno. It was the fire of hatred.

Denis Roux *hated* the boche.

HENTSCH

He'd never seen the French and British operate in such close concert with one another. In fact, he'd never faced them simultaneously at all. Their units were intermingled such that blue and red blended together with khaki. The thunderclouds overhead were so dark that the afternoon sun could not penetrate them. Dusk was brighter on most days. The rain, cold and heavy, pelted his skin and turned the entire battlefield into a quagmire. It fell so hard that its dull roar drowned the shouting and shooting, yet still, the Anglo-Franco force advanced closer, stomping through the puddles and bogs that grew deeper with each passing second.

How do they coordinate this attack? There had to be some semblance of command structure with their units mixing together like they were. It was a curiosity, but it didn't matter. Hentsch had to kill as many of them as he could, regardless of their uniform color, or they'd kill him and his friends. His friends. He'd just been standing with them. *Where are they?*

"Simon!" he shouted, "Engel! Where have you gone?!"

He couldn't see the two of them, not anywhere. He could have sworn they'd been there just seconds earlier. Swarms of French and Englishmen outnumbered the German troops so greatly that Hentsch was certain his position would soon be overrun. He had to find his two pals before that happened. Scanning the battlefield for signs of them, he had difficulty seeing more than a few yards around him due to the drenching torrent pouring down from above.

Pow! Hentsch raised his rifle and shot at a Frenchman, to no apparent effect. *But I had my sights dead on his chest...* The battle was not going to end in Germany's favor. If Hentsch was going to miss shots as easy as the one he'd just lined up, it would end for him sooner than later. Fire from his countrymen was producing results, of that there was no question. French and British bodies began piling up, but it was as if every time an enemy fell, two more rushed forth to replace him. In contrast, the number of German rifles holding the line was rapidly dwindling.

CRACK! A bolt of lightning illuminated the field ahead of him and an earsplitting thunderclap shook him to his foundation. In the lightning flash, he saw Simon crouched behind the rim of a shell hole fifty yards ahead. The enemy had advanced so close that soon they'd be right on top of him. Hentsch had to get Simon out of there before then. He stood and tried to run. Normally he was fast, but for some reason his knees insisted on pulling together, as if there were a rubber cord binding them to one another and tugging them inward. Unable to take full strides, he was forced to drag his feet. He almost had to waddle.

"Simon!" he called, waving his arm to draw his friend's attention. His labored, staccato paces grew increasingly difficult. Never in his life had he felt a sensation so bizarre as the one drawing his knees together and inhibiting his movement.

Come on, just ten more yards! He fought against himself, against his failing legs, refusing to succumb to incapacitation. Then his foot got stuck. He heard the mud suck against his boot as it caught hold of him. Hentsch pulled with every ounce of his strength to free himself. He lost his balance and toppled forward into the slop. Already sopping and chilled from the rain, the sludge was even colder. Coated by clingy, icy filth, his skin ached.

Dragging himself through the muck for the final ten yards, Hentsch made it to Simon just in time. A bevy of Frenchmen were approaching, but one man had outpaced the rest of them. The black-haired soldier, in a blue tunic and red pants, wore no cap. He moved quickly, with purpose and malicious intent. He also moved in a straight line, making him an easy target. Hentsch raised his Mauser, setting his sights right in the middle of the Frenchman's forehead. The man was close, but for some reason his face was obscured. Was it mud? A trick of the eye? *Why do I feel like I somehow recognize this man?*

Pow! Hentsch's aim was true, he was sure of it, but the Frenchman's head did not split open and he did not fall. He cocked the bolt and aimed again. *Pow!* Again, he missed.

"Come on Augustus!" he screamed, admonishing himself. His sights were right over the man's heart when he pulled the trigger for the third time. *Pow!* The bullet hit the mud behind the charging man.

"Just aim, dammit!" Hentsch yelled furiously. He tried to aim again, but his hands trembled so violently he could barely hold onto his rifle. Panic rushed through him, a tingle, a numbness, which made him weak. His rifle grew heavier, and he could no longer keep it raised in front of him.

"*AHHH!*" Simon cried out suddenly. Hentsch was so focused on the Frenchman that he and Simon had not acknowledged one another. He turned to see why the young man screamed, and was met with a horrific sight. An Englishman had appeared from nowhere and shoved his bayonet directly through Simon's heart. The Englishman's back was turned to Hentsch, but he bore a familiar distinction—a red streamer dangling from the pack on his hip. In all the fighting with the Belgians, the British and the French, Hentsch had only ever seen one soldier with a streamer like that. The man who had just killed his friend was the same man at whom Hentsch had shot and missed at the Battle of Mons.

"You son of a bitch!" he shouted, but the Briton ignored him. Just as he was about to lunge forward to attack and exact revenge, a colossal force crashed into the side of his body, knocking him off his feet. He sprawled into the freezing mud for a second time. It was the Frenchman, and now Hentsch knew exactly who that Frenchman was. He still could not see his face, but he didn't need to. Somehow he just knew. It was the Frenchman who'd nearly killed him with the machine gun during the Battle of the Marne, another enemy soldier at whom he'd fired and missed.

"I've got you now, Augustus," the man snarled in a sinister voice.

"How do you know my name?"

"There are many who know your name," the Frenchman answered. "Some have learned it the hard way." He pointed to deep a puddle next to Hentsch. As soon as he pointed, a corpse floated to the surface of the murky water. It was the Belgian gunner, the first man Hentsch had ever killed, with the same lifeless expression and dead eyes that had since troubled him so greatly.

What is going on?

"Where is Engel?" Hentsch asked, trying unsuccessfully to pull himself from the sucking mud. "What have you bastards done to him?"

"The same thing we'll do to you I'm afraid," said the Frenchman. He stepped toward Hentsch, who struggled and writhed to try and escape but could not. Hands clutched at his wrists and ankles beneath the muddy water's surface. The man who was about to kill him took a knee in the mud beside him and leaned in close. Even then, his face was indistinct and featureless.

"You're all right," the Frenchman said kindly, his voice suddenly much softer than before. He placed his hands on Hentsch's shoulders, clutching his uniform. A curious warmth radiated from the hands, but Hentsch still fought to free himself. The Frenchman leaned in closer. Hentsch shut his eyes, waiting for the killing strike to come.

"Augustus!"

Hentsch opened his eyes to see a face within mere inches of his own. Instinctively, he recoiled backward, and bashed his head on the wall behind his bed. The face was not the featureless one of the Frenchman, but that of a beautiful young French woman, with a white nurse's cap situated atop her head of shiny black hair. Hentsch was not stuck in the quagmire of a battlefield, beneath a dark and stormy sky. He was still in the hospital at Guise.

"You were having a nightmare, Augustus," she whispered, "but you are all right now."

Still startled and confused, Hentsch tugged against her warm grip on his hospital gown one last time before finally accepting that he was not about to be killed in the heat of battle. His heart continued to thump, but he breathed a sigh of relief. He buried his face in his hands in exasperation. For another consecutive night he'd soaked his gown, bed sheets and pillow in sweat. Cold and shivering, he tried to rub warmth back into his arms. He stared at the nurse, but did not say anything.

"Do I repulse you so that you will not speak to me, even as I stand beside you?"

She sounded offended, and Hentsch knew why. He'd avoided her whenever possible over the preceding days, too embarrassed to face the lovely French nurse who'd been forced to change his diaper while he lay unconscious and on the brink of death.

"No, that's not it at all," he answered, "I just expected *you* to be repulsed by *me*."

"In what way?" she asked.

"Where do I start? Number one, I'm German and you're French."

"Shhh! Don't tell the other twenty French nurses who are here helping German boys. They may brand me a traitor," she replied sarcastically. "Yes, I am French. Most of the girls working this hospital are. But I am a person, and you are a person, and helping sick and injured persons is why I am here. I see no reason to distinguish which colors a person wears before I help them."

"That is kind of you. If I must be honest, my real reason for avoiding you is because I am embarrassed."

"Why?" she asked with a puzzled frown.

"The diaper..." he answered, averting his eyes. "I am so sorry you had to deal with such a thing. You must understand my shame in knowing I've been such a burden."

"Were that the greatest burden I faced day to day..." she trailed off, looking at some of the wounded men in the other beds. "Four boys have died here in the last two days, and ten so far this week." She turned back to him, and rested a warm hand on his arm. She looked him directly in the eye. With hair as dark as hers, Hentsch would have expected her to have brown eyes, but even in the dark of the unlit infirmary he saw that hers were bright blue. "Sick men, dying men, they sometimes soil themselves," she assured him, "I've seen it many times. It is nothing to be embarrassed about."

"Still, I feel the need to apologize."

"If you must, then I accept your apology. May I sit?"

"Please do."

She sat on the bed next to him, resting one leg on the floor. It was an odd sensation, having a beautiful girl sit next to him on a bed, especially in a context such as the present one.

"Forgive me for prying, but might I ask what your nightmare was about?"

"I'll tell you, but first I wish to formally make your acquaintance."

"You do not know my name?"

"No, but I'd like to."

"Well then, Augustus, my name is Louise," she said, reaching out her hand.

"It's very nice to meet you, Louise," Hentsch replied. He wrapped his much larger and clammier hand around her soft, radiating palm. It might still have been delusion, but being touched by her seemed to send a healing energy through his veins.

"And you," she countered.

They smiled at one another. It came as no surprise that she'd have a lovely and tender smile, and it further warmed the sweaty chill which had taken hold of him during his sleep.

"Now about that nightmare..." Louise gently directed the conversation back to where she wanted, waiting only briefly before speaking again. "What is it that's got you so spooked at night?"

Unsure of how much he should share, Hentsch gave pause, weighing the words he'd use before he used them. Was it already implied that he was a killer? If so, would she be mortified to know how many men he killed? Was it appropriate to tell her he was afraid that men he *didn't* kill might go on to kill other Germans later?

"You needn't worry about sparing me the details," she said frankly, interrupting his train of thought. "I've seen enough blood to fill this hospital from floor to ceiling. Whatever horrible things you are seeing or reliving at night, I've seen wounds and death here to match it."

Hentsch presumed most girls, especially one as stunning as her, would have been more squeamish about the terrifying nature of armed conflict, but she was clearly different in that respect. Whatever questions she had, he would answer them honestly.

"I dreamt that a man, whom I specifically remember shooting at and missing, found his way back to me and killed Simon. And another man, whom I also missed, was about to kill me just before you woke me."

"You remember the times you missed? I would think you'd remember the ones that found their mark. Is it such a rare thing to miss?"

"Not necessarily, but I am a good shot."

"Yes? How good a shot are you? How many men have you killed?"

Hentsch sighed at how quickly she'd cut to the chase. "Nineteen. Maybe more."

"I see," she said softly. She looked away. "And are you proud of this?"

"No," he replied sternly. "I'm duty-bound, and I do what is asked of me. Am I proud to serve my fatherland? Yes, I would say that I am. But proud to serve in *this* capacity?" He leaned closer to her to speak in a more hushed tone, and she turned a curious ear to him. "I hardly believe laying Belgium to waste and invading France without provocation was a noble cause of which one should be proud to have been a part."

"So you do not hate the French soldiers, even though you shoot and kill them?"

"Why should I *hate* them? Until our army invaded, no Franzmann ever bade me any ill will, at least not to my face, nor did I ever feel a nationalistic obligation in the reverse."

Louise rested her hand atop Hentsch's and locked eyes with him. "You and I, we share a similar view of the state of things."

"I never would have expected to hear a French girl say that to me. Not now."

"I told you, Augustus, I'm a person before all else. As are you. If we are to call ourselves civilized, *truly* civilized, then our humanity should trump our nationality. Just because your Kaiser, or my president, or this king or that emperor declares you an enemy does not mean I should not help you when you're sick or hurt. I am duty-bound by nothing but my humanity. I would hope that were the tables turned and the French army stood on German soil, a German woman might do the same for my brother."

"Your brother?" Hentsch gasped.

"Yes, my brother. We did not want him to serve in a fighting role, my mother, father and I, but he went to a military academy anyway. I came to Guise, along with others, pacing the advance of his army. We were caught here during the retreat. It happened so quickly, and we couldn't leave those who were already here, so many of us chose to stay, even as your army took control of the hospital. In some ways, I feel obligated to work in a hospital on this side of the lines to compensate for any pain and suffering my brother might cause. To balance the scales, as it were. Then again, he may already be dead. I've heard nothing from him."

What a horrible coincidence it would be were I the one who killed him.

"I...I'm not sure what to say," Hentsch murmured, still taken aback. That a French nurse would have blood ties to the French army should have come as no surprise. It was a fact with which he swiftly came to grips. The size of the armed forces in a conflagration as massive as was the Great War meant that most every citizen in France had blood ties to at least one soldier. "Do you fear for his safety?" he asked.

"I do," she replied, nodding her head once. "How could I not? But he made a choice, and it may come with a dire consequence. I might not like it, but I *do* accept it. If he's still alive today, which I pray every day he is, he might just as easily be killed tomorrow. Such is the way of a thing as terrible as this war. When you've fully recovered, it might even be you who takes his life from him. Who can say?"

"I will pray that it never comes to that, Louise."

"And I will pray that he does not do the same to you. It would be a sad thing to meet a man as decent as you, only to have him killed by my own flesh and blood."

"You consider me a decent man?"

"Yes. Many Germans, men and boys, have come through these doors since I arrived here. And French too. Some were nice, some were not. You are a nice one, as are your friends."

"Even hearing what I've done, you still feel comfortable saying that?"

"If you had said you were proud of killing those men, that you *liked* it, then I would doubt the kind of man you were. But that is not what you said, and that is not, I believe, who you are."

"I could be lying…"

"Are you?"

"No."

"I already knew that anyway."

"But how?"

"Men don't lie in their sleep. I learned things about you, tending to you in your unconscious state."

"What sort of things?"

"Things that are for me to know, and you to be left wondering about," Louise said, creating a mystery where before there was none. She shifted her position on the bed and pressed the back of her hand against Hentsch's forehead. Her touch was so uniquely soothing he couldn't help but ever so subtly lean into her hand. "You're still feverish," she observed, "you should go back to sleep." She stood, but before she could leave he took hold of her hand with his. She was startled, but only a little, and did not yank her hand away.

"Thank you for helping me," he said. "And my friends. You are truly kind."

"You are very welcome," she said, and she smiled her lovely warm smile again.

"It was nice talking to you," Hentsch said.

"And to you. Good night, Augustus."

"Good night, Louise."

GORDON

"Gordon, can you tell me why it is that many of an aeroplane's major structural components are given French names?" Plamondon asked, as the two of them slowly paced around a machine flown by the pilots-in-training.

The machine was a pusher-configured Farman MF.11 biplane, manufactured by Farman Aviation Works, a company founded by brothers Maurice, Henry and Richard Farman. The MF.11 (MF stood for Maurice Farman, the designer) was colloquially known as a *Shorthorn*. The nickname stemmed from a modified design feature which separated it from its predecessor, the Farman MF.7 *Longhorn*. In the latter craft, the elevator was mounted above a long set of landing skids which extended from the landing wheels to out in front of the machine like a pair of horns. In the former, the elevator was moved to the tail section and the size of the skids greatly reduced, hence the craft's "horns" were shortened.

Gordon was well aware that Europe had become the epicenter of powered flight, it was why he was there, and so replied, "I know that while the Wrights were pioneers, and led the way for five years, much of the progress made in the years after their initial successes has happened here, across the Atlantic. Especially after 1910."

"That is correct. And many of those progressions are thanks to we French. Take these ailerons, for instance."

The two men stood near the trailing edge of the starboard wings. Plamondon reached up with his cane to push up a flap hanging loosely at an angle from the upper wing. The lower wing had a similar flap, as did both port wings. Each aileron was joystick-controlled by wire and built into the wing, so as to be flush with the edge when held level during flight.

"The aileron concept was invented by an Englishman more than forty years ago, but it was the Farmans and Louis Blériot who have implemented them to great effect on their aeroplanes. Do you know what aileron means?"

"Little wing?"

"Correct. And what of its function?"

"Rolling, or banking."

"Yes. Mark my words, the aileron will soon replace wing warping altogether when it comes to controlling roll."

"It's a much more efficient set up, sir, I agree."

"When you built your aeroplane, did you attempt to use the aileron?"

"No sir, I used warping. It did not go as smoothly as I'd hoped."

"You made it into the air, which says a great deal," Plamondon assured him. "Even smart men have mishaps. Mishaps are how many of them got to being smart men."

Gordon nodded, appreciating the complement. He'd been at the Blériot School for more than a week, but Plamondon was still the only person, instructor or student, who'd give him the time of day. Everyone else either ignored him or mocked him when his back was turned. For most of the first week Gordon spent his time with engines, and only when his lone supporter, the only one affected by Sergent Bellamy's letter, had the time to work with him. Even their present conversation was taking place after sundown, when the other students were free to relax or head into Pau for entertainment.

So far, in their after-hour instruction sessions, apart from the Gnome Lambda which Gordon had already familiarized himself with, they'd worked on a Le Rhône seven-cylinder, which was another type of rotary engine. They'd also spent time with the Renault eight-cylinder, the engine which powered the Farman they were standing next to. The Renault was much more akin to a traditional automobile engine.

"How about the tail assembly?" the instructor asked, turning his back to the wings and moving aft. He leaned against his cane as he headed toward the rear of the aeroplane.

Because of the Farman's pusher configuration, the machine's rear had no plywood and fabric covering, which exposed its framework. The tail consisted of a large rectangular horizontal stabilizer and elevator, attached to the superstructure by four large wooden structural spars. The spars, two on each side, were set wide enough apart to allow the single propeller to spin between them. They formed a triangular frame on either side, braced by vertical struts and wires, which tapered toward the tail. The Farman had two tailfins/rudders, mounted above the horizontal stabilizer and attached to the ends of the two upper structural spars.

"What is the word for this section of the machine?"

"The empennage."

"Indeed. And it means?"

"Arrow feathers or something along that line, right?"

"Yes, a sensible description considering the features, oui?"

"Agreed."

"Now this," Plamondon moved on, hobbling around the tail and heading toward the front of the machine. "Where does the pilot sit?" He aimed his cane at the section of the machine which housed the occupants and flight controls.

"The cockpit."

"Yes yes, the English get some credit, but what is the name of the greater structure in which this particular cockpit is situated?"

"The nacelle."

"Very good, and what does that mean?"

"It's a type of small boat."

"And what if this were a tractor-configured machine?"

"Then we'd be talking about the fuselage rather than the nacelle. It means tube, or spindle-shaped."

On the Farman, the nacelle was a bathtub-shaped pod suspended between the planes by struts above and below the pod. In pusher planes of that type, the nacelle served the same function that the fuselage would have in a tractor-configured machine. The engine, a one hundred horsepower, eight-cylinder inline Renault, was mounted behind the pilot's cockpit. Since the engine was air-cooled it was not housed within the nacelle, but instead exposed to the open air.

"I'm sorry to have to walk you through something so elementary as this," Plamondon said. "I was sure before we started you'd know everything."

"It's quite all right, sir. A refresher never hurts."

"Have you had any success in making anyone's acquaintance here?"

"You mean besides Matthieu and Giles?" Gordon answered sardonically. "No, not yet sir. Half the instructors don't speak a word of English, and I think the ones who can just pretend they don't. As for the trainees, it's clear that my presence here insults them."

"It's a question of empathy, Gordon. None of these men under-stand where you come from because they have not lived it, so they cannot relate. There exists no analogue for comparison in their lives. Bear in mind, I might have done the same were it not for the letter from our mutual friend. These things are what they are, and the best you can do is to continue showing your capabilities and hope that they speak loudly enough."

"I will."

"I know you will. I must retire for the night, but perhaps tomor-row we will examine the cockpit and have a closer look at the control wires and their rigging."

"I look forward to it sir."

Plamondon's mouth upturned slightly and he began to walk away from the Farman. He stopped just before he reached the hangar door. "Gordon," he said, "Have you considered going into town to be around people, perhaps having a drink at a pub?"

"I think I might be given a hard time if I tried."

"Maybe. Or you might just make a positive impression on some-one besides me. You're an intelligent, polite and charming young man. But those things are intangibles, and must be shared before they can be recognized. You need to make them apparent to more people than just me."

Gordon had confidence in himself, but his lack of faith in the kindness and understanding of others hadn't been dispelled simply because of Bellamy and Plamondon. He wasn't aware of any overt segregation in France, but he also wasn't entirely sure he wanted to find out the hard way by stepping into the wrong pub or restaurant.

"I'll think about it, sir," he replied. "But not tonight."

"All right. We'll speak tomorrow then. Good night."

"Good night sir."

Gordon waited for Plamondon to leave before returning to the barracks. He never would have admitted it out loud, but he was starting to feel lonely. *Maybe I should try and find Amy in town one of these days.* The only problem with seeking out the girl he met on the boat was that he had no idea where she might be staying. Pau wasn't exactly small.

It being a Saturday night, the barracks were empty. Not even the first stragglers had begun to drift in. Gordon walked through the deathly silent room, toward his bed at the far end. With no ambient noise, the creaking floor was so loud it sounded as though the floor-boards might shatter under his feet. When he reached his bed he knelt down and slid his suitcase from beneath it.

Most of what he'd brought with him to France fell into the category of the barest of essentials. Socks, trousers, underpants, a few shirts and his coveralls took up most of the space, barely leaving room for anything else. He spared just enough room for one nonessential, his only slice of home. It was actually two items paired together, and one meant little without the other. They were his leather baseball mitt and accompanying baseball, both heavily used and well-worn.

The Wright Brothers may have been his idols, and the embodiment of his intellectual inspiration, but Gordon had interests all over the map. He found athletic inspiration in the players of the colored baseball leagues, and especially from John Henry "Pop" Lloyd, a superbly talented shortstop who'd played for and managed the all-colored Lincoln Giants for the 1912 and 1913 seasons, seasons which Gordon had followed in the papers. He'd watched Lloyd play once, in an exhibition, and thought him far better than any of the white players on Cincinnati's pro team, the Reds. In his early teens, much of the time Gordon spent away from studying was spent playing baseball with the boys in his neighborhood, at least until he began working on his aeroplane and for his father. Baseball had taken a backseat in his later teens, but he never lost his appreciation of the game.

Gordon picked up the mitt and slid it onto his left hand. He sat on the bed. He bobbed the dirty baseball in his right hand and spun it with his fingers. *It'd be nice to have a catch with somebody.* He doubted there was a single person in Pau who owned a mitt—baseball was a decidedly American sport. He wasn't even sure the French knew what baseball was. Since no one had come back from the town yet, he pushed himself up from the bed and walked outside. With nobody asleep inside the barracks, there was nobody to disturb. With clear, starry skies and a large half-moon overhead, there was just enough light to still see the ball.

Setting up about sixty feet from the lavatory wall, the only one without windows, Gordon leaned forward, bent at the waist, his mitted left hand resting on his left knee. He looked menacingly toward the building and the imaginary home plate and backstop it represented.

"Bottom of the ninth inning, the Chicago American Giants at the bat and down to their last out," he said in his best announcer's voice, building up the atmosphere. He pictured himself, on a summer afternoon, seated in the stands and listening to the play-by-play echoing from the loudspeakers. He didn't have many opportunities to go and watch games, but when he did, the memory of those days stayed with him. "Pop Lloyd and his Lincoln Giants cling to a one-run lead. One more out, and the Lincolns are the undisputed champions of colored baseball."

Gordon swiveled his neck to survey the imaginary field, and to make sure he hadn't attracted the attention of any actual people.

"Cyclone Joe Williams checks the runner, now eyes the batter at home plate." He hunched over, swinging his arms loosely on either side of his body, gripping the baseball in his right hand.

"Cyclone winds up..." he said, standing upright and raising his left knee to chest height while cocking his arm back. "Delivers the pitch!" Gordon lunged forward and tossed the baseball forcefully against the wall.

SMACK! The ball ricocheted off the wood with a sharp report, much louder than he'd anticipated. The noise echoed off the walls of the surrounding buildings.

"A hard-hit ground ball up the middle! Cyclone can't get to it!"

He took a few steps back and to the right, in order to give himself extra room to run and field the ball.

"Pop Lloyd has a play on it!"

He dashed forth, to cut off the rolling ball's path. He scooped the ball into his mitt, and turned toward the barracks. Flipping the ball into his right hand, he brought his arm back and threw it again.

"Lloyd fields it! He makes the throw!"

SMACK! The ball pounded against the building, rebounding and rolling in his direction. "And he gets him out by a nose! The inning is over! The Lincoln Giants have won the championship! Pop Lloyd has saved the day!"

He stopped the tumbling ball beneath his foot, and then crouched to pick it up. On one knee, he surveyed the area around him for a second time to make sure nobody had been watching.

"Dammit, Gordon," he muttered, "you need to find a friend."

VERNON

Festubert sat at roughly the halfway point between Béthune and La Bassée, just north of a line drawn between the two cities. The 1st Cheshire Battalion arrived there early in the morning of October 12, after departing Béthune on foot under the cover of darkness. Tasked with holding an outpost line from Festubert to Givenchy more than a mile further southeast, it was a large swath of ground for one depleted battalion to cover, and it stretched them thin.

The weather, while colder than it had been the night they'd first crossed the Aisne in mid-September, shrouded them in a similarly thick and misty fog bank. An attack was planned for dawn on the 13th, but little was known about the area and any enemy concentrations that might be lurking further east, so two small patrols moved forward the night before to ascertain more information.

No one from E Company was chosen for those patrols, which were to move east toward the small farming village of Rue d'Ouvert, a mile from Festubert. The intervening terrain was mostly flat, and utilized extensively for crops ranging from corn and soybeans, to canola and sugar beets. Owing to its lack of anything more than rolling hillocks as high ground, Artois reminded Vernon of Cheshire County, the exception being Artois's abundance, as a low-land, of small streams and earthen dykes. However, the Artois countryside would soon be soaked in blood, and that was the last thing he wanted to associate with his birthplace.

Both Major Young, the battalion's temporary commander at the Aisne, and his replacement Major Vandeleur, formerly of the Cameronians (Scottish Rifles), who joined the battalion on October 6, went forward together on one of the patrols, with the strength of half a company. Their first objective was a large farm called Chapelle St. Roch, where, under the supervision of Vandeleur, the patrol was to establish a foothold. To augment the attack planned for the next day, they'd seize what buildings and strategically significant points they could, hold them, and wait for the larger attack to begin.

Sitting in darkness, damp and chilled, with the under-strength battalion drawn wire-thin for hundreds of yards on either side of them, Vernon and Pritchard waited. They were entrenched, but preparations had been hasty and the trenches dug shallow. Strictly by the numbers, 1st Battalion had, on average, only one man for every four or five yards of frontage. They were not dispersed so accordingly, instead small groups or pairings set themselves up every ten yards or more. Visual contact was maintained along the line, but barely, with each neighboring pair or group on the outpost line appearing as little more than a hazy silhouette. If any appreciable number of Germans had decided to launch an offensive there in the next few hours, they'd have had no problem breaking through—a fact of which Vernon was painfully aware.

"Remind me again," Pritchard said quietly, "why in God's name did *both* Young and Vandeleur go on the same patrol? We've lost enough officers. I don't see why we'd risk losing two COs at once."

"I don't know Lew," Vernon whispered back, "but if our officers keep getting the short end, it's only a matter of time before the whole battalion gets the short end, if you know what I'm getting at."

"I do. Captain Bannister, CO of the 1st Cheshire Battalion."

"More like Major Bannister."

"Major...Has quite the ring to it, aye?"

"A ring, all right. The same sort your ears get when a shell blows next to your head. A worse bane could not fall upon us, save for of course maiming or death."

Most of the moonlight was gobbled up by cloud cover, but even in the fog the two men were seated close enough to one another that Vernon saw Pritchard's lips curl into a grin.

"Don't write off maiming as worse just yet," Pritchard said, stifling a chuckle. "I think I might volunteer for a bullet in the arse cheek before I'd take the captain as CO."

Vernon was about to respond with a wise-crack when a muffled *poom* in the distance to the east froze him stiff and likewise wiped the smile from Pritchard's face.

"Gunfire..." the two whispered together.

"Maybe one of the boys got squirrely," Vernon stated, hopeful but pessimistic.

Poom...

Poom...

One shot could have been chalked up to nerves, but three? Something more serious was going on. When indiscernible, far-off shouting worked its way through the fog it became abundantly clear that the patrol had made contact with the enemy. Judging by how distant the upstart battle sounded, Vernon estimated that Young and Vandeleur's patrol had at least reached the Chapelle St. Roch farm.

"Will we help them?" asked Pritchard. If anyone wanted the patrol and its officers to come back safely, it was him.

"Not without orders, we won't."

Approaching footsteps thumping into the damp soil startled the two for the second time, but the crouched shape coming toward them moved with a familiar, slinking gait. Vernon had instinctively brought his hands to his rifle, but quickly relaxed his grip on the weapon as soon as he heard the voice.

"Hayes, Pritchard, you two sit tight for now," Corporal Spurling urged, "but be ready to move at a moment's notice. I'm going to check in with everyone else and have a chat with Lieutenant Fordham."

It was odd to sit idly by while men from his battalion were shouting and shooting only a mile away, but if the attack wasn't ready to commence, it wasn't ready to commence. Until word was given for the remainder of the battalion to do otherwise, the patrol was on its own.

They remained in place for much longer than Vernon would have liked, hours in fact, and he grew edgier with each passing minute. Spurling made his rounds and gave what few updates he had, but even as dawn broke and the cloud-dimmed sun rose higher, no orders were issued. The fighting to the east ebbed and flowed and sometimes nary a shot emanated from that direction for minutes at a time, but no conclusion was reached. After every lull, a series of shots would invariably erupt and the battle began anew. With the volume of fire, there had to be casualties, yet command did nothing. Whether the patrol was holding firm or not, the moment had to inevitably come when they needed relief.

As frustrations mounted from their inaction, 3 Section's men clustered together, chomping at the bit to move east and provide assistance. In a tight circle Vernon, Pritchard, Milburn, Granville, Lockwood, and the two replacements, Chilcott and Saunders, discussed what they thought should be done. The five battle-hardened warriors did most of the talking, while the two newer arrivals just listened. Chilcott and Saunders hadn't experienced Mons, Audregnies, the grueling retreat, the Marne, or the initial attack across the Aisne, so they had little to offer in the way of meaningful opinions.

"If we don't get over there and help them, who's to say Fritz won't roll right over them and into us?" asked Milburn.

"What'll it say about us if they're all killed or taken prisoner?" Granville added.

"And where in the devil is Spurling?" Lockwood said inquisitively. He swiveled his head to and fro while the others continued complaining. Vernon, focused on the conversation, paid no mind to Lockwood until the man distractedly patted him on the upper arm.

"What is it, Lockwood?"

"Better keep it down, chaps," he replied, his voice trance-like.

The group turned their heads in the direction of whatever it was that had caught Lockwood's attention. They promptly shut their mouths. Captain Bannister and Sergeant Major Cortland were nearby, speaking with Second Lieutenant Fordham and the four corporals of Fourth Platoon.

"Well, there's Spurling," said Chilcott, stating the obvious.

Vernon tried to read the body language of the officers and NCOs, but more often than not, a conversation with the captain usually ended up looking just like the present one—hanging heads and solemn nods. Bannister wasn't animatedly berating anyone, not yet anyway, but whatever was being said didn't appear to be encouraging, which probably meant that they would remain in place. Vernon couldn't stand for that; not while part of his battalion was pitched in battle. He broke away from 3 Section and moved, with purpose, toward the captain.

"Vernon, no!" Pritchard whispered loudly. He attempted to grab Vernon's arm, but Vernon's mind was made up. He tugged his arm away and ignored the similar pleas from the rest of his section mates. They were too afraid to chase him.

As he approached, Spurling saw him first and went wide-eyed. The corporal tightly shook his head and tried in vain to signal with his eyes for Vernon to back off.

"Captain Bannister, sir," Vernon said, without even waiting for an opportune moment to interject. "We're going east to help them, correct?"

"Jesus Christ, Hayes," Spurling said under his breath, bringing a hand to his forehead and rubbing his eyebrows. It was just loud enough for Vernon to hear.

"What in the fuck do you think you're doing, Hayes?" an angry Bannister asked. His bushy moustache covered his mouth, but the snarl beneath it was more than evident.

"I've asked a question, Captain. We're going to help the major's patrol, are we not?"

Bannister flinched, but not in a conventional sense, more as if a jolt of electric rage had torn through him head to foot. He spun like a tornado, putting him and Vernon face to face. The captain's breath was sour and repulsive, but Vernon held his ground, subtly inflating his lungs to push out his chest.

Cortland, in an effort to intervene, tried to mollify the captain and said, "Sir, I think Hayes is just—"

"No Sergeant Cortland," Bannister said, cutting him off, "I'm curious what Hayes, the brilliant tactician, has got to add to this discussion. Go on, Hayes," he said, thrusting his index finger hard into Vernon's chest, "what does a thirty-year-old private have to say that's worth listening to?"

Um, first and foremost, fuck you. Vernon took a breath. He'd screwed up already, and he knew it, but now he had to follow through. "Sir, we'll accomplish nothing by our sitting in wait in these shallow trenches. If we stay any longer, that patrol won't come back."

"We have no orders to proceed, Private. Until brigade says otherwise, we stay put."

"And how much contact have you had with brigade, sir?"

"Enough."

"Enough for them to know that our CO is in trouble and needs help?"

"Enough!" Bannister said, repeating his answer fiercely.

"Yes, Captain. Enough to get those men killed or taken prisoner so you'll be given command of the battalion!" Vernon snuck a glance at the other five men, each of whom were obviously mortified, and no two more than Spurling and Fordham. Even Cortland, normally the coolest of customers, was tensely gnawing on his lower lip.

"Watch your tongue, Hayes," Bannister growled, but Vernon wasn't done.

"You've got no qualms issuing an order to retreat without approval from HQ," he said accusingly, "but a chance comes to save our men and secure an objective and you tuck your tail between your legs and chalk your dithering up to a lack of say so from brigade!"

The captain had clearly had enough. He raised both hands, smacked them forcefully against Vernon's chest, and grabbed two fistfuls of his greatcoat. Bannister was an inch taller and had a heavier build, but the strength with which the captain grabbed him still caught Vernon by surprise. Had there not been two heavy hands clutching the front of his coat, he would have reeled backward and fallen into the ever-dampening mud at the bottom of the shallow entrenchment. Bannister pulled him close, so close that their noses touched. The enraged officer's putrid and reeking breath curdled the contents of Vernon's stomach.

If another man, one without pips or bars, had grabbed him in such a way, Vernon would have already thrown the first punch in the inevitable fight which would have then ensued. But Bannister was an officer, and there existed no reasonable defense for a private striking an officer. Fighting the urge to physically retaliate, Vernon glared into the captain's soulless eyes. He might already be facing a court-martial, but physically lashing out would get him shot on the spot. Needless to say, that was not worth it. What he'd already done was not worth it, even though he'd already done it.

"Hayes, this matter is decided, but your fate is still up in the air. If you drop the subject right this instant, and I mean right this fucking second, I will not reach for the Webley on my belt. But one more word, one more squeak or movement of any kind other than you turning around and getting your stupid arse away from me, and I'll draw my pistol and shoot you in the head. Am I clear?"

Cognizant from the get-go that he'd not just toed the line but rather stomped over it, Vernon obeyed the captain's ultimatum. He nodded. With angry tears clouding his vision, he scowled to prevent them from running down his cheeks. Bannister released his grip on the greatcoat, and Vernon took two steps back, before turning to walk away. There wasn't a single German, save for maybe the cavalry major who shot Willoughby after Mons, that he hated as much as the captain. But that cavalry major had already gotten what he deserved.

"Vernon, have you gone absolutely barmy?" Pritchard asked accusingly when Vernon made it back to 3 Section's huddle. He punched Vernon in the chest, and not playfully. The others were so shocked and appalled by his foolishness that they simply stared at him slack-jawed.

"We'll sit here until every last one of them is killed or captured..." Vernon muttered, wiping his eyes clean.

"It's a bloody shame," Pritchard said, "but we're under Bannister's thumb. You nearly got yourself shot, you damned bloody fool. It's a wonder you weren't!"

"I don't want those men to feel abandoned..."

"There's nothing we can do," Pritchard said, and then he lowered his voice. "None of us want to get shot in the back as we run toward the fight, and we all know the captain will do it. He'll make our own boys do it."

For the rest of the day the men remained hunkered along their outpost line. The fighting for the Chapelle St. Roch farm continued for hours. When the fog dissipated and thick columns of smoke began rising up around the area encompassing the farm, it became clear that the Germans had set fire to the haystacks and outbuildings, to flush the defenders out. Day turned to night, and the fires glowed orange, all the while the gunfire slowing until it eventually stopped at or about midnight. A small handful of men, all of them wounded, managed to escape the farm. Among them, wounded himself, was Major Vandeleur. He'd gotten away, but his wounds were serious, and he could not remain in command of the battalion.

Vernon was dismayed at having not gone to the patrol's rescue. Fifty-five NCOs and privates were killed, wounded or taken prisoner, and an additional four officers captured, Major Young included. Day by day, the men of the 1st Cheshire Battalion who'd landed at Le Havre in August were slowly being bled away. Attrition was grinding them to nothing. The original officers were all but gone, Captain Bannister being one of just a few who still remained.

The patrol may have lost their battle at Chapelle St. Roch, but Rue d'Ouvert still remained the battalion's objective. At some point in the coming days, they would have to make an attempt to seize it.

SEBASTIAN

The men were laughing in the crew's quarters. Sebastian awoke with a start to the sound of their uproarious howling. Rather than trying to steal a nap in the usual quarters, Sebastian had fallen asleep on the floor, nuzzled up to the engine room's bulkhead.

The engine room was further astern, past the control room and the petty officer's quarters, with only the aft torpedo room beyond it. Each such room was separated from those next to it by a watertight bulkhead, and access through those bulkheads was provided by hatches which opened and sealed by the turning of a hand wheel. Most of the time, the hatches in the sleeping accommodations remained open, while the fore and aft torpedo rooms and the engine room stayed closed.

Sleeping there was uncommon and not as soft as a bunk, but the engines generated considerable heat and, though they were loud, a steady, unchanging drone, which masked other, less consistent noises. A spot prone to the occasional kick from an inattentive foot, he only laid there when the commander and officers were above deck. Lying close to the engine room might have been warmer, but Sebastian still awoke feeling much the same as he always did when waking up aboard U-20. His head pounded, his nose was clogged with mucus, and his hair and skin were greasy.

He pushed his hands against the metal floor to prop himself up. The floor was warm to the touch, as opposed to the damp iciness of the pressure hull's outer walls. He sat, arms wrapped around his knees, and yawned deeply, then smacked his lips to try and rid his mouth of the foul, oily and metallic taste which always found its way into his maw during a nap. When he'd sufficiently wakened, he stood and quietly approached the crew's quarters, listening intently to learn why everyone was laughing. Crewmembers were shouting back, forth and over one another. They were so loud and boisterous, it was hard to hear them, but from what he could make out, they were saying some pretty outrageous stuff.

He ducked through the hatch of the empty petty officers' accommodations and passed into the control room. The wireless operator, headphones on, seated at his usual station, ignored Sebastian as he moved through and into the officer's quarters. A barricade of men was clustered near the next hatch. Their backs were turned to him and they obstructed his view into the crew's quarters, but by then he was close enough to hear every word.

"My great grandfather fucked Queen Victoria! You might say I'm royalty by association!"

Laughter.

"My father got pissed drunk and beat the Kaiser in an arm wrestling match! Walloped him in fact!"

"Yeah but with which arm?!"

The men roared again. Kaiser Wilhelm suffered from Erb's palsy, a deadening of the nerves of the upper arm that arose from complications during his birth. The disease permanently crippled his left arm, leaving it six inches shorter than his right and much weaker. He spent his entire life masking his ailment from the public, and in nearly all official photographs could be seen employing a number of tricks to hide his withered arm.

While mocking a man for his lifelong ailment may not have been particularly kind, Kaiser Wilhelm did firmly believe that his family was of divine blood and thus superior to the common man. That, coupled with his boorish personality, a likely overcompensation for his physical deformity, and his tendency to frequently dress in the most garish of military uniforms, not to mention the fact that he'd since led his nation into a war that had already killed hundreds of thousands of men, made him quite the ripe target for ridicule. Just not to his face, or to anyone who might take offense.

Sebastian chuckled to himself while remaining unnoticed. He crept closer, and peered over the shoulders of the crewmen blocking the entry.

"My father took a trip to Siberia about six years back," Jollenbeck stated exuberantly. "He ate an entire plate of sausages one night and BOOM! Leveled a whole forest with one blast from his ass cheeks the next day!" The young seaman clapped his hands together then spread his arms outward to simulate an explosion. The men doubled over, cackling at the absurdity.

Someone shouted between guffaws, "I think I read about that in the papers!"

Sebastian pieced together what all the laughing was about. The men were playing a game, trying to see who could come up with the best lie. From the sound of it, though, *best* must have at some point morphed into *ludicrous.* They still didn't know he was there, and it was then that he hatched a clever idea to announce his presence. He stepped forward, pushing his way into the room, his best grim and serious expression plastered across his face.

"Everyone, listen up," he said gloomily. "I've just overheard a conversation between Kapitänleutnant Dröscher and the officers above deck. He says we're to make a raid on Scapa Flow."

The giggling and conversing stopped. Every jaw in the room dropped simultaneously. They'd gone from having a grand old time to having a harsh and sobering reality shoved in their faces. No one spoke. Only the humming engines and buzzing lights had anything to say as the crew blankly stared at Sebastian. A few shifted nervously in their seats or on their feet.

Sebastian let them stew, let them marinate in their concerns, before he smiled and shouted, "I think I just won!"

The men groaned and began and throwing every loose object they could find in his direction. Many shouted at him, smiling with relief but aggravated by his ruse nonetheless.

"I almost had a heart attack!"

"You asshole!"

"Son of a bitch!"

"You piece of shit, Eberhardt!"

To actively search for and attack British ships on the open sea was one thing, but attacking the hulking giants where they slept was something entirely different. For a U-Boat to enter the harbor and attack the anchored ships of the British Grand Fleet was near suicide. No commander in his right mind would actually want to try and infiltrate Scapa Flow. At least that was how the crew viewed it.

What they didn't know at that point, what not even the wireless operator had heard yet, was that the day before, on October 13, U-9 and her commander Otto Weddigen had scored another victory. They attacked and sunk their fourth British ship, the HMS *Hawke.* Two days prior to that, U-26, commanded by Kapitänleutnant von Berckheim, attacked and sank the Russian vessel *Palluda.* Those successes were significant on their own, but they also led to a marked shift in the British Navy's mindset. Disturbed by the successes won by Germany's submersibles to that point in the war, Britain's Admiral John Jellicoe was thrust into a state of panic.

The thought which had frightened the crew of U-20 at its mere mention, and which likely intimidated every other U-Boat crew at sea, was the very same which Jellicoe viewed as a potentially serious threat to his own fleet. As such, at that very moment, the anchorage at Scapa Flow was in the process of being fully evacuated. The harbor represented a mind game of sorts, not one which the two nations played against one another, but rather one which each nation played against itself, and through intimidation, lost. Britain's Grand Fleet would return to the Orkneys, but only after they had installed exceedingly sufficient defenses against the submarine threat.

Taken on the whole, U-20's war so far was boring. Their first patrol came and went with no success, and they'd unceremoniously returned to Heligoland to resupply before leaving for their second. Because boredom had long since begun to set in, the men often sang songs or played games or discussed home to try and pass the time. The thirty-five men living in the boat's cramped conditions were not provided much freedom, if any, and so keeping their minds occupied was the best way to prevent the strange, otherworldly environment from getting to them.

Bland became the norm, and bland could be frustrating. Bland food, mostly from cans after the fresh stuff spoiled, bland colors, and mostly bland, treeless and landless scenery took a psychological toll. Sunrises and sunsets on non-cloudy days were two of the very few things the eyes had to look forward to. Even for a seafaring man as seasoned as Sebastian, going day after day on such a cramped boat without seeing, let alone touching land was difficult to reconcile.

After he interrupted the laughing and shouting from the game, the men calmed down and began quieter, more reserved conversations amongst themselves. Some sat on the bunks, but most stood or sat on the floor. Because of the limited space, there were only a small number of two-man bunks, not nearly enough for everyone, so the crew slept in shifts. Each bunk, even those of the higher ranks, was truncated far short of affording its occupant the luxury of outstretched legs. As well as each bed being hardly bigger than a sardine can, weeks of unwashed men sharing a small number of thin mattresses turned each bunk into a disgusting, cramped and soiled box, which reeked of stale sweat and oil. The stink lingered throughout the air, but it worsened nearer the source. Sleeping in it was sometimes nauseating.

The change in atmosphere from rowdiness to comparative tranquility led to some crewmen slinking into those smelly bunks and curling up in the fetal position behind their shipmates still sitting on the edges. Sebastian, about as refreshed as he could have been from his nap, took a seat on the floor next to Jollenbeck. They rested their backs against the bulkhead between theirs and the officers' accommodations.

"That was a pretty good one," Jollenbeck complemented him.

"Thanks."

"Although it wasn't really in keeping with the spirit of how we were playing."

"Yeah, I got that much," Sebastian replied mordantly, rolling his eyes as he recalled some of what was said. "Yours was funny."

"I was hoping you'd heard it," Jollenbeck said, smiling proudly. "Do you remember reading about that in the papers when we were younger?"

"You mean that thing in Tunguska?"

"Yes."

"Of course I do. My mother is Russian. She was very curious about it. She had my grandparents send her Russian newspapers and she read them to me, since I don't read Cyrillic."

"What do you think it was?"

"You mean it wasn't your father's ass?"

"I think he was home that week."

"Then it was probably beings from space." They'd both read a translation of H.G. Wells' *War of the Worlds* as boys, but Sebastian wasn't much for literature. The premise had interested him, but he didn't buy it as a viable possibility. Jollenbeck, apparently, did—the book had given him nightmares back then.

"Really?" he asked excitedly, "Do you think so? Because I was—"

"No," Sebastian replied.

"Oh. Honestly then, what do you think it was?"

"I don't know."

"I think it might have been a weapon," Jollenbeck stated, a hint of enthusiasm in his voice, "like a bomb or something." Curiosity glimmered in his eyes, and with his deeply discolored left one he looked far more sinister than he probably intended. It was obvious, though, that the thought intrigued him.

"I'll tell you this, I hope it wasn't a weapon," retorted Sebastian. "From what I remember about it, it was destructive enough that it could have flattened an entire city. A large city."

"Then it's a good thing it went off in such a remote place."

"But what if it hadn't? Just imagine if one of our enemies had a weapon so powerful. What if Russia somehow managed to use it against Königsberg?" He seriously doubted that whatever caused the explosion in Siberia in 1908 was actually a weapon, but the idea wasn't so far-fetched as to be written off as ludicrous. The greater and more realistic danger to his home city was an ordinary land invasion, which the Russians had nearly succeeded in before being pushed back across the frontier. Still, the imagination could run wild if given proper material, especially while at sea.

"No civilized nation would use such a weapon against a city with so many innocent civilians," Jollenbeck said, waving his hand and dismissing the hypothetical scenario outright. "War is and always will be barbaric, but wouldn't such deliberate targeting of civilians cross into a whole new realm of barbarism?"

"I think so," Sebastian agreed. "I certainly don't want any civilian blood on my hands and I hope our leaders feel the same. It should be up to us servicemen to decide the outcome, not women and children. We're trained for it, and we're signed up for it."

"I agree."

ARTHUR & PERCY

On the Aisne, the BEF's three corps were arranged in numerical order from east to west. The shift north changed that alignment, and placed Haig's I Corps furthest north, Smith-Dorrien's II Corps furthest south, and Pulteney's III Corps in between. The last to leave the Aisne and the last to arrive in Artois, III Corps reached the rail junction at Saint-Omer on October 10. Their first fighting in Artois began on the 13th, after receiving orders the day before to move southeast from Saint-Omer, past Hazebrouck and toward the River Lys.

Also on the 13th, command learned that the city of Lille had been occupied by elements of Crown Prince Rupprecht of Bavaria's Sixth Army. Lille was important to the British plans, so measures to wrest it from German control were ordered. On the 15th, III Corps received the order to advance against Armentières, a city less than ten miles northwest of Lille. Tasked with taking the city, repairing the bridges across the Lys, which flowed through the northern part of Armentières, and then preparing for the attack on Lille, the 4th Division assumed the bulk of the job. On October 17, they succeeded in taking the city, and from there III Corps continued its advance south and east toward Lille.

As the corps deployed and assumed its share of the front, the 6th Division moved further south of the 4th Division. Positioned six miles due west of Lille, the division was about to commence its advance toward the city.

Arthur and Percy had remained in the reserves while the BEF held along the Aisne, but the change in locale brought a corresponding demand for additional personnel. The area to be contested was wider than that which the British had previously held, and so the two boys, along with their fellow reserves, were called into action.

Now marching with what was a front-line unit, the excitement the two boys had felt in July and August had long since evaporated. Only nerves and fear remained. They were assigned to 1 Section of First Platoon, in Captain Otis's G Company. In command of First Platoon was Second Lieutenant Fuller, and 1 Section was led by Corporal Abbey. Introductions had been decidedly brief.

As two of the youngest members in the entire battalion, Arthur and Percy had already accepted what would likely be their being labeled as pants-pissing newcomers, until such time as they might demonstrate themselves otherwise. Both also recognized that Percy would have an easier go of proving his mettle for no other reason than that his considerable size and propensity for growing facial hair veiled his youth.

"So where are you two lads from then?" asked one of their section mates as the battalion marched.

"Lymington," they answered.

"Sounds like a shithole," the man said dismissively.

"Do you even know where—"

"No worries, though," the man said, cutting Arthur off. "I grew up in a shithole myself. There must be eating aplenty where you boys are from, building a bloke as big as this one." He slapped Percy on the back. "My name's Baker. And you two?"

"Ellis."

"Ward."

"Are those your first or last names? Because Baker's my first name. Last name's Dussin. Baker S. Dussin at your service." He tipped his cap to them.

Arthur and Percy looked at one another curiously. Both wondered if the man's parents had actually given him such a silly name. Percy snorted, stifling a laugh.

"Those were our last names," Arthur answered.

"Mine too," Baker grinned.

Private Baker was about twenty-five, and an inch or so taller than Arthur. Mustachioed, the hair lining his upper lip matched the light brown hair on his head not covered by his cap. Like a large number of men who'd ended up in the trenches along the Aisne, he'd removed the wire stiffeners from his peaked cap, thus making it flatter and floppier. Aesthetically, it was far less dignified and presentable, but that was a fair tradeoff when it came to reducing the cap's visibility to snipers. The alteration was generally gaining acceptance with the higher ranks.

"What'd you lads do before this mess started?"

"I worked at a colliery," Percy said.

"I was at University College," said Arthur.

"Ah, a university man," Baker said. "Impressive. I'm an Oxford man myself."

"You went to Oxford?" asked Arthur.

"*Dominus Illuminatio Mea*," Baker said, holding a hand to his chest. "What, you don't believe me?"

"No, it's not that," Arthur said, "I just expected…"

"Expected what?" Baker said. "An Oxford man to be a foppish cunt is that it?"

"No, I uh…"

"Do I not strike you as bright enough? Shall I say something brilliant?"

"I…"

"Relax, Ellis," Baker said with a grin. "I'm only taking the piss out of you. So why have you left university? You're a young lad, certainly not old enough to have graduated."

"I guess I just wanted to try something different."

"The search for self…" Baker said, reflective. "Mayhap the battlefield is not such a good place for that." He paused, and then said, "Or, mayhap, it's the best place."

Arthur had nothing to say.

"Where's your badge?" Baker asked, pointing to Arthur's cap.

"He threw it to my sister," Percy answered first. Arthur had planned on lying about it, until his cover was prematurely blown. *You duffer, Percy.*

"Threw it to her, or *at* her?" Baker said.

"*To* her," Arthur said.

"I see, so she's a lady friend and *not* a wife," Baker said. "And they've yet to give you another one?"

"No," Arthur replied. "I got an arse chewing for losing it, and the quartermaster had no badges, just caps."

"Well I suppose that's fitting then," Baker said, "a cap badge should be earned. Ward, you might consider handing yours over as well."

"What have you done to earn yours?" Arthur asked. "We landed at Le Havre nearly the same time as you."

"I've been in the 2nd York and Lancs for three years," Baker replied, "not to mention those of us what's been here spent time under fire on the Aisne. Already lost one man as a matter of fact, name was Vance. I knew him for two years. He earned his badge, paid in full."

"I'm sorry," Arthur said.

"Not your fault," Baker answered. "Credit goes to the lone shrapnel ball what caught him above the ear. That's all it took was one. I haven't decided whether it's good or bad luck they've sent you two in his place."

"Why would it be bad luck?" Percy asked.

"Because one man gone and two to replace him means our section's got thirteen. That is, unless you count Corporal Abbey to make it fourteen. So maybe the additional man actually makes us luckier than others."

"Are you really that superstitious?"

"Ask me again in a day or two."

It was hard for Arthur, being new to the experience, to gauge how far away the fighting north and south of him actually was. No matter the distance, the rumbling disquieted him. During the previous nights on the march from Saint-Omer, distant artillery flashes occasionally lit up the sky, like the lightning of a far-off storm. He tried to count the seconds from flash to rumble, to estimate the distance, but there were so many he was unable to match them. In watching the pulsing lights and feeling the reverberations in the soles of his feet, the thought of being caught beneath a man-made storm had made him sweat, even in mid-October's evening chill. Percy felt the same, but neither spoke on it. They did not want their new cohorts, or their best friend, to know just how afraid they were.

On the morning of October 18, the 2nd York and Lancaster Battalion found themselves five miles south of Armentières, near the small village of Radinghem-en-Weppes. The assumption was that the Germans had already evacuated the town and that any resistance offered would be light. The battalion moved quickly. Advancing along with the York and Lancs were the 1st Battalion of the Royal East Kent Regiment, or "The Buffs", a nickname inherited from the regiment's maritime past, when its members were issued soft leather buff coats.

The Buffs would approach Radinghem from the south, while the York and Lancs moved against the center and north. Arthur and Percy in G Company moved toward the village center. The move separated G Company from the battalion, and Captain Otis subsequently ordered the company to split in two, with First and Second Platoons moving along either side of one of the small village's streets, and

Third and Fourth Platoons paralleling them on the next street over. Otis went with the second group. He led from the front rather than lagging behind.

As First Platoon moved along the left side of their assigned street, Arthur cautiously scanned each small house as he walked past. In peace, Radinghem would have been a quaint little village. Instead, it was creepy. Most of its windows were shuttered, and every curtain drawn. More than once, he spotted a curtain flutter or a nervous head peek through—there were still civilians hiding in their homes, cowering in fear. In one yard, a flock of chickens clucked and ambled, oblivious to the hundred-odd armed and uniformed men passing through the neighborhood.

It was impossible to let down one's guard. Radinghem might have been quiet so far, but the sound from the battles elsewhere guaranteed that even if the Germans weren't there, they were still close. When the company neared the village center, Percy spotted Captain Otis running, by himself, through an unfenced yard. He'd left Third and Fourth Platoon, to speak with the lieutenants of First and Second Platoon. The three officers conversed for close to a minute, and then Otis dashed back through the same yard and rejoined the other party.

Fuller gestured for First Platoon to continue moving ahead, and Second Platoon's Lieutenant Collins did the same for his men. After another fifty yards, they reached the main street which ran north to south through Radinghem. From an off-white two story house across that street, a solitary man, uniformed in grey and holding a tan helmet in one hand and a rifle in the other, darted from the front door and made for the house's back corner.

"Halt!" shouted Fuller. To no one's surprise, the German failed to comply.

At the front of each platoon's column, the faster to react got off a shot at him, but he disappeared behind the house.

"Where there's one, there's more," Fuller called back to his men, "be ready."

The moment had passed so quickly, but it represented a first, however mundane, for Arthur and Percy. It was the first time anyone in their remote presence had shot at an enemy soldier. They'd missed, but that might have been the best thing, to receive such firsts in small doses. A death would come, that was guaranteed. It needn't be right away.

Percy squeezed his Lee-Enfield with his enormous hands, trying to slow his breathing and his heart rate. It didn't work. His shooting, while not terrible, faltered on some days more than others, and that was while aiming at a stationary target. A man, armed and moving and able to shoot back, represented a vastly more difficult mark. On his worst day at the colliery, Percy had never been remotely close to as nervous as he was in that instant.

"What the fuck have you gotten me into, Arthur?" he whispered.

Arthur gulped before softly saying, "Nothing you weren't jumping to go along with. You could have told me to shove off if you really wanted to."

"Too late now."

"Far too late."

With the rest of First Platoon, they scampered across the street trailing Fuller, who, upon reaching the house from which the German had exited, drew his pistol, opened the door and charged inside without hesitation. Two men, one his red-headed sergeant and the other a private, joined him, while everyone else gathered around the house, covering its windows and the windows of the surrounding homes with aimed rifles.

"Is he loony?" Arthur asked. He was certain the platoon was about to lose its sergeant and officer. With more than fifty rifles trained on and around the house, though, any Germans still inside would have been better off surrendering. While the three men were inside, Captain Otis headed up the street to join the Tommies gathered in waiting in front of the house. Ultimately, no shots rang out, not from within the house or outside. Upon clearing the building, Fuller and the two men emerged unharmed. The lone German had been its only occupant, or at least its last one.

"Looks like they've packed up and headed east," the lieutenant said. He tucked his revolver back into its holster.

"I doubt they've gone far," Otis commented. "We'll have to check the remaining houses on this street. Split up your platoon, a section per house. Four men go inside, the rest surround the exterior and keep a watchful eye to the east. When we've cleared the town, we can link up with battalion and The Buffs and begin fortifying the eastern end against attack."

"Yes sir," replied Fuller. "All right First Platoon, you heard the Captain, let's get moving. 1 and 2 Sections, you take the next two houses," he pointed to the home on the left of the one he'd just checked, "3 and 4, you take the two after that."

Fuller took no more than ten paces toward the next house, and many of First Platoon's men had yet to move to follow him, when a heart-stopping chatter broke out from the east, somewhere in the farmlands beyond the village's last houses. It was the most terrifying sound Arthur had ever heard in his young life, worse than the distant artillery blasts.

TAC-TAC-TAC! A hail of bullets cracked into the house's wooden siding, and three men standing in the open to the right of the front steps suddenly dropped to the ground.

"Get behind the houses!" the lieutenant cried, ducking just as rounds snapped over his head. An alert private from 2 Section grabbed Captain Otis and shoved him out of the line of fire.

Caught in the open space between the houses, Arthur and Percy dashed toward the second house—a one story cottage sided with grey shingles. Wherever the German machine gunner was positioned, he spotted them and turned his fire in their direction. The well-aimed burst just missed them, and hit the corner of the house as the two boys dove behind it. The burst caught one of their trailing section mates in the upper thigh and he yelped and fell to the ground, dragging himself to safety before another bullet found him.

Baker had also joined them behind the house, and he hauled the wounded man further behind cover. Arthur stared in horror at the gruesome leg wound; it only took seconds for the fountain of blood spurting from it to stain the entire upper leg of the man's trousers a dark red. It was another first, and an unwelcome one.

"Oh fuck, oh shit, oh fuck!" the wounded soldier said, groaning his words in agony. He grabbed the wound with both hands, covering them in blood, and stared at his leg, eyes wild with fear.

"All right, Green," Baker said calmly, fishing a roll of bandage from his coat pocket. "I'll have to tie off your leg to slow the bleeding, understand? Ellis and Ward, you two hold him down."

"What?" Arthur squeaked.

"Don't be squeamish, Ellis, for fuck's sake! Green's life depends on it! Now get your arses over here and grab his arms!"

Arthur and Percy knelt down on either side of Green. Each boy clutched one of his hands in theirs, and used their other hand to take firm hold of his upper arm. His skin had already turned a ghostly white, and the blood continued to drain from the hole in his leg. He didn't have much time.

Baker removed a roll of cloth from his greatcoat pocket and placed it around Green's thigh, just above the wound. He pulled it as tight as he could without tearing it. The wounded man struggled and whimpered from the pain, enough that Percy let go of his arm to press down on his chest instead. At the same time, he placed a knee atop Green's uninjured thigh to further restrict his movement.

"We need a stretcher to get him out of here!" Baker shouted as the machine gun continued to chatter away.

434

But it was too late. The bullet had likely severed Green's femoral artery, and before any further action could be taken his eyes rolled back in his head and his mouth drooped open. A slow gasp escaped from his mouth as he exhaled for the last time. Percy felt the body go limp. He couldn't believe how quickly a leg wound had just killed a person. One shot to the thigh, and no more than two minutes later Green was a corpse. Arthur too was appalled, and incredibly afraid. He gasped for air.

"Bugger..." Baker muttered after searching Green's neck for a pulse for longer than he needed to. He patted him on the chest. "I guess you chaps aren't good luck, not for Green at least."

There was more than one machine gun east of Radinghem, of that they'd become acutely aware. Unable to advance any further, the entirety of G Company was pinned along a hundred yard length of street, ducked behind a row of houses as machine gun bullets slowly shredded the structures to pieces. The soldiers shouted back and forth to one another, but with the gun chatter and the wailing of those who'd been wounded, little of it was discernible. In spite of the chaos and the fear for his own safety, Arthur sincerely hoped there were no civilians inside the homes on that street. No one had emerged from them yet so if people were inside, there stood a good chance they were already dead.

Watching the first house to see what Otis and Fuller would decide to do, Arthur saw a man from 2 Section, who'd been crouched next to the two officers, spring to his feet. Fuller grabbed the soldier by the arm and tugged it hard so that the man stooped over. The lieutenant shouted something in his ear, then they nodded at one another and he shoved the private by the backside as the man took off running across the street. *What in the heck is he doing? A runner?*

He didn't get far. Before the runner reached the safety of the next row of houses, he flung his arms in the air and fell hard, losing his rifle and flopping face-first onto the street. Arthur couldn't tell where he'd been hit, but the runner didn't move an inch after he fell. Over the course of the next hour, the men of G Company remained pinned, unable to retreat nor advance. A further two runners made attempts to get away, but neither managed to make it to the other side of the street. Each time anyone tried to peek around the edge of a house, he was met with hostility of the highest order before he could ascertain the position of any enemy machine guns.

"How many goddamned bullets do they have over there?" Percy asked with anger in his voice. He had no idea how long being under fire was supposed to last.

"Wait until they bring up the Black Marias!" Baker replied. "If they call up the artillery, we're in for it. Best we could hope for is the whole company makes a mad dash west, and the lucky ones will get away before the gunners have a chance to hit everyone."

Arthur, nonplussed but half-listening, continued to stare toward Fuller and Otis, who suddenly beckoned to him. He held a hand to his chest as if to say "who, me?" and they both nodded and beckoned again. He stood, and crept closer to the edge of the house. At the two officers' behest, he was about to risk a bullet to see what they needed him for. He had to. He couldn't say no.

"Art, what do you think you're doing?" Percy inquired.

"I'm supposed to go over there," Arthur answered. He sounded much braver than he felt. If he hesitated at all, he might psych himself out so he gave himself no option but to act. He grasped the corner of the house with his left hand, leaned back, and launched himself forward. Even as an undersized little boy he was a runner, and that hadn't changed as he grew up. Five or six long strides were what he needed to get there. His legs churned, propelling him across the dangerous gap. One bullet zipped by his head and a few thumped into the ground close to his feet, but he made it. He slid on his knees and came to a stop, breathing heavily. That was the stupidest, most dangerous thing he'd ever done. And he'd signed up for it.

"Private Ellis is it?" asked Otis. He looked to be in his mid-thirties, and had a sandy-blonde moustache, groomed so well it could have served as a barber's template. His stony grey eyes reflected a calm that did not mesh with the intensity of the situation. Arthur and the captain had yet to meet one another, and he'd only briefly met Fuller, exchanging little more than a handshake and a hello.

"Yes sir, Captain Otis. Arthur Ellis."

"We need a runner," Fuller said, cutting to the chase. "And you're a smaller target than many of the lads here." A lanky six-footer with dark hair and pale skin, Fuller was in his late twenties. He was surprisingly calm, too, but his voice conveyed more urgency than did the captain's. "Word has it you're fast, Ellis."

Arthur's heart dropped into his belly when he realized what they were about to ask him to do. *Word has it?* "I guess I run all right, sir," he answered. *But I doubt you knew that. Probably just trying to shore up my courage. It's not helping.*

"We need you to get to battalion HQ," Otis said sternly. "It's only a matter of time before these Huns begin to advance, and I will not order my company to make a run for it only to see them shot in the back. If we can get another unit to outflank them, they just might delay or withdraw."

"Where's HQ?" Arthur asked. It was hard to focus on the task at hand while simultaneously concentrating on not throwing up on the two officers.

"They should be about a half mile northwest of here," Otis replied. "You might want to consider moving up this side of the street first, close to the houses, before you try and cross. In case you missed it, our other runners have not fared well in crossing first."

"Yes sir." *I'd say they haven't.*

"You'll want to leave your equipment. And your Enfield."

"What?"

"They'll only slow you down," Otis said. He grabbed Arthur's shoulder straps. "You've got one job, and that is to move with haste. I'll give you my Webley, but I'll be wanting it back, so you'd better make it to HQ alive." Otis drew the revolver from his holster. He opened the cylinder to ensure each chamber was loaded, snapped it back into place and then handed the weapon to Arthur, who'd just finished removing his cap, equipment and greatcoat.

It was chilly outside, but a chill was the least of his worries. He'd soon be running for his life and the lives of his entire company. If that couldn't keep him warm, nothing would.

"Are you ready, Ellis?" Fuller asked.

Of course not.

Arthur took in a deep gulp of air and let it out. His lungs and diaphragm quivered as he exhaled. "Yes sir."

"Then good luck and Godspeed to you."

Percy, who'd watched the scene unfold, didn't understand why Arthur set his rifle down and removed his gear. He didn't understand why Captain Otis had drawn, then handed over his pistol. He didn't understand it when his best friend took off running toward him but didn't slow down. Instead, Arthur kept running, past him and toward the next house.

"Where are you going?" Percy cried, but Arthur didn't answer. "Where the hell is he going?!"

"They've sent him for HQ," Baker said. "For help."

Percy tried to stand. "I've got to go with him!"

Baker grabbed him and yanked him back down. "Stay here you big bloody oaf."

Bullets chased Arthur as he dashed across the open yards between each home. The German machine gunners raked each structure as he sprinted past them. One, two, three, four, the gaps went by in a blur, and he uselessly held his right hand by the side of his face as if to shield his head from the supersonic metal hail decimating the world around him.

When he made it a quarter mile up the street and the guns had a less favorable angle with which to fire, he stopped running north. He pressed his back against the front door of the house at which he'd stopped, pausing to catch a breath.

"All right, Arthur," he gasped, "time to head east." He sucked wind from his lengthy sprint. His legs were weak and his whole body trembled from the mental and physical strain he'd just pushed himself through. No drill or exercise could have possibly prepared him for the events of that day, he just wasn't ready for it, and yet there he was, a key player in a do or die situation. He surveyed the homes on the opposite side of the street, to find the yard he thought offered the most cover.

Settling on an unpainted, ramshackle cottage with a line of shrubs in the yard, he placed the sole of his left boot against the door behind him, and then did the same with his palms. As he was about to push off, movement in the corner of his right eye paralyzed him. He slowly turned his head to see a group of German infantrymen emerge from behind a house no more than fifty yards away. He didn't stick around to count them, but there were at least twenty, maybe more.

In a split second, he launched his body away from the door and charged toward the middle of the street. He fired the Webley at the soldiers twice, without aiming. One German shouted something that sounded like *stop*. Fear clouded Arthur's judgment, and before he'd reached the shrubs the enemy infantrymen opened fire. His first instinct, however warped, drew him to the cottage's front door, and as bullets snapped by him he again covered the side of his face with his right hand. His body involuntarily flinched with every stride, in anticipation of being hit.

The run wasn't a long one, but it took an eternity for him to reach the door. He barreled into it shoulder-first, crashing through and falling onto the bare wooden floor. *What do I do?!* He scrambled on all fours while the German soldiers poured rifle fire into the house, shattering the windows and puncturing the thin walls. Arthur was discombobulated. He searched for solutions, but came up with none.

A small staircase led to a tiny loft; when Arthur reached it he stood from his crawl and dashed up the stairs, stumbling and bouncing off the railings on either side as he climbed. When he reached the loft, it finally registered in his mind how poor a decision he'd made on entering the house in the first place.

"Fucking hell Arthur, think!" he shouted, frantically trying to get his thoughts in order. "COME ON!"

With the numbers heavily in their favor, the Germans would not just hang back and pour rifle fire into the cottage from one side. It wouldn't be long before they surrounded him, and that'd be the end of Arthur's war, and perhaps even his life.

There were two small windows on either side of the loft. One faced the Germans, but the other faced the opposite direction. With the enemy soldiers still firing into the house, they failed to hear Arthur smash that window with a child-sized wooden stool. Barely able to squeeze through, he wormed his way out and fell about twelve feet to the hard grass on the south side of the cottage. The fall hurt, but he'd not been injured. He sprung to his feet and broke for the back yard, and unexpectedly crashed headlong into a grey monolith of a German who'd stepped around the house's back corner.

The Webley fell from Arthur's hands and as he fell, he spun his body away from the heavier man, who'd also dropped his Mauser when they collided. Arthur landed on his right side. He grabbed handfuls of grass to swing his body around and grab the revolver, just as the German regained his balance and hurriedly stooped over for his rifle. Their actions took place just milliseconds apart from one another, but Arthur made it to his weapon first. He fumbled with the Webley for just a moment before firing twice at short range into the German's chest and belly. The man dropped his gun again, and fell alongside it. He stared at Arthur accusingly.

Another soldier jumped from around the front corner of the house. Arthur fired his last two shots, hitting the cottage, but spooking the German enough to make him dive back behind cover. Arthur stuffed the Webley into his tunic's hip pocket and ran. Chugging his legs hard and grunting frenziedly, a tingling sensation in the middle of his spine was Arthur's subconscious telling him to brace himself for a bullet in the back. The Germans behind him shouted and their rifles popped, but he'd gained enough of a head start that if their next few shots missed their mark, no one would catch him, not on foot. Some of the bullets came close, but his furious zigging, ducking and zagging was enough to throw off their aim. They did not follow, lest they risk being cut off from the main body of their own forces for the sake of one Englishman.

In ordinary circumstances, a sprint of such length was patently unsustainable, but he made it to battalion headquarters without resting or slowing. Singularly centered on escaping and thus fulfilling his objective, he did not focus on the fact that he, as an eighteen year old boy, had just killed a man at point blank range. After he'd stumbled into the CO's tent and relayed his message in between deep, desperate gasps, he nearly fainted from the ordeal. Runners were immediately sent to the other companies, while Arthur was ordered to remain at headquarters until he'd rested and eaten.

His heart rate finally slowed and he realized that, for the time being, he was safe. He sat down on an ammunition crate and tried to come to grips with the day's events. Yes, he'd been in a warzone for more than a month by then. He'd seen, mostly from afar, the wounded men on their way to the hospitals many miles behind the lines. He knew that in combat, men died at one another's hands. But seeing Green die up close and personal from a solitary leg wound, then running, literally, for his life, *and* killing his first man, was just too much at once.

Dwelling on the life he'd taken, the intensity of what he'd done began to build inside of him. His heart raced again, he grew dizzy, his vision blurred and he doubled over, throwing up on the grass between his feet. Had he fumbled with Captain Otis's Webley for one more second, a *second*, or if the gun had fallen from his hands and landed just inches out of his reach, the dead German would be alive instead, and thinking about the young English boy he'd killed. If war was like that every day, surviving only by teetering on the razor's edge, Arthur doubted he could hold up.

Percy and the men of G Company, meanwhile, clung ferociously to the line they'd established, even as the Germans encroached. From the eastern *and* northern ends of the town, the enemy closed in. The same patrol which Arthur had narrowly escaped threatened those caught behind the houses and commanded attention away from the east, but they did not succeed in overwhelming First Platoon, which represented G Company's left flank.

A few more of the platoon's men were hit, but none fatally, and with each minute that passed, Percy feared more and more for Arthur's safety. He saw what happened to the first runners. Why Otis and Fuller had chosen his friend out of all the men in the platoon was completely befuddling. Was it because he was new, and they did not value him as much? Could that really be the mindset?

The company held, and around mid-afternoon the fire from the east slowed considerably, relieving much of the pressure G Company had been under. Arthur had successfully delivered his message, and another company moved northeast and managed to turn the left flank of the German force. The enemy's assault on Radinghem halted, allowing both the 2nd York and Lancaster and The Buffs to fortify their positions.

VOGEL

Flying had not come as easily nor been as enjoyable for Vogel since learning of Frederick's death. On top of that, Kunigunde should have received the letter he sent within a week of his mailing it, yet he'd still not heard from her. He and Adler flew their sorties, did not miss any that were assigned, and occasionally ended their flights by trying, and, generally, failing, to drop more grenades on the French lines. Neither they, nor any enemy machines they spotted in the distance took any action toward one another. Adler had, for the time being, given up on the idea of mounting a machine gun on the Rumpler, probably wishing to cause Vogel no further stress.

Condolences on the aerodrome were accepted graciously, though each time a new person offered theirs it only salted Vogel's wound. Wracked by guilt, his only motivation was one of vengeance, and even that was largely aimless—pointless even. Whatever had happened to Fred, it hadn't come at the hands of a Frenchman. To his knowledge, it might not even have come at the hands of a Russian, since crashes were all too common. If it had, though, then exacting revenge on the aviators or ground troops of a different nation wouldn't fulfill much of any vengeful sentiment beyond his ordinary call of duty.

Much of the weather in October had been rotten for flying—misty, rainy, cold, and miserable. Even at lower altitudes, a heavier coat, scarf, leather flying cap and gloves were now essentials. When the wet weather wasn't so bad as to prohibit flying altogether, Vogel debated donning flying goggles to shield his eyes, but goggles were prone to fogging and he didn't like how they restricted his peripheral vision. A water droplet in the eye at seventy miles per hour did hurt, however, so goggles were worth consideration at least.

In many ways, the relative tranquility of the battlefront ahead of Kluck's First Army further contributed to Vogel's downtrodden mood. Sure, it was important to watch for troop concentrations and movements as well as that of the supplies and artillery, but the French in front of First Army just didn't seem to be headed any-where. The fliegers attached to the northern units must have been engaged in much more important observational duties, and thus had more stimulating work keeping them occupied. When the BEF left the Aisne, their aviators went with them and to that point in the war, British airmen had, taken as a whole, proven to be a much pluckier and more aggressive lot than their French counterparts. That might not have been the best thing to look for in an opponent, but at least it helped keep things interesting.

They'd already flown one sortie that morning, and Vogel sat in the mess, slowly eating a warm bowl of stew. Meat, onions, carrots, pota-toes, he pondered how it was that Germany managed to feed its mil-lions of soldiers such a hearty meal each day. The truth of it was that if the majority of infantrymen knew what the airmen were served on a daily basis, they might actively seek opportunities to shoot German machines out of the sky purely out of jealousy. Blissfully unaware of that, Vogel enjoyed his meal.

"Vogel, might we talk for a moment?" asked Adler, who'd snuck up behind him.

"Yes sir," Vogel answered, "would you care to sit?"

"I would." The oberleutnant sat on the opposite side of the table. He took off his cap and set it aside. He ran his hand through his short hair, and then took a deep breath. "I know you've struggled since your brother was killed. For that I am truly sorry. But I, along with the hauptmann and some of the other officers, have been discussing ideas as to how we might make ourselves increasingly useful."

Vogel was intrigued. "Such as?"

"We've already tried dropping grenades on the French, and that might give them a scare every now and then, but what if we were to take up something larger? Perhaps travel further beyond their lines?"

"To do what?"

Adler's blue eyes smiled. "Drop bombs on targets of opportunity," he said. "The British have done it to our zeppelin sheds; I see no rea-son why we can't do something similar to the French. And I don't mean dropping them on Paris, as you'll recall one of our countrymen doing in September. I find that...distasteful."

Vogel was no dummy, and he quickly saw the potential. "I agree about Paris. But we could hit supply columns, rail stations, even artillery emplacements if we felt bold enough."

"Exactly," Adler said. "So are you interested?"

"I am."

"Good. Because we were going to do it anyway. Finish your stew and we'll head to the machine to discuss our strategy."

Vogel shoveled the last of his meal into his mouth and in ten minutes they'd put on their coats and were standing next to the Rumpler. They, along with Leon, stood with hands on their hips, staring at what would be their new cargo. Resting atop a blanket laid over the grass were four bombs, each one shaped like a thin, elongated teardrop with fins on the narrower tail end. The bombs, about two feet long, weighed just over twenty-seven pounds each.

"Do you think she can handle all four?" asked Vogel. "An extra hundred and eight pounds is a lot to lug up."

"To be honest, sir, I'd be more comfortable if you started with two," Leon replied.

"I'm inclined to agree," Adler said. "I'm the one who has to sit with them."

"Two sounds reasonable to me," Vogel declared. "When do you want to go up next?"

"Now."

"What?" He didn't expect the oberleutnant to implement their new tactic so soon. He thought they were there to discuss it, not put it in motion. He'd hoped the answer might be "tomorrow" or at least "later today." "Is she even ready?"

"Checked and fueled, sir," Leon replied.

Shit.

"So what are we waiting for?" Adler said excitedly. "Do you have your gear?" he asked, turning to Vogel.

Should I lie?

"Yes."

Nope.

When it had become clear the chilly weather was there to stay, Vogel made sure to always carry his gloves and scarf in his coat pockets. He left his flying cap on his seat in the Rumpler. He tugged the articles from his pocket, wrapped his neck in the scarf, buttoned his coat and put on the gloves. On the ground, the gloves were warm, but after a certain amount of time in the air they hardly served their function at all.

"When we find a target, you'll need to descend to a low altitude," Adler said. "We won't be able to hit anything if we're a half-mile up."

"How low should I take us?"

"As low as you're comfortable with."

"Four hundred feet?" They dropped grenades from lower, but that was because of their fuses. He didn't like being so low over the enemy.

"It depends on the size of the target," Adler said, "but I'd prefer you go lower."

Pilot and observer climbed into their cockpits and when Adler was ready, Leon gingerly handed him two bombs, one at a time. Jostling and turbulence were certainties both in takeoff and flight, and Vogel couldn't help but feel apprehensive about two unsecured bombs sitting in the cockpit ahead of him. It wasn't far-fetched to imagine a hard enough bump causing the bombs to either clang together or bounce off the cockpit floor and detonate. *What a lousy way to go that would be.*

Vogel checked his controls, and Leon worked the propeller through a few rotations.

"Prepared for contact!" the mechanic shouted.

"Contact!"

Chug...Chug...VROOM! The engine came alive, Leon pulled the wheel chocks, and the aspiring bombers were on their way across the aerodrome. Tensing his body far more than he normally would have during a bumpy takeoff, Vogel stared at the back of Adler's head, waiting for it to explode. Each bob and shift made him tense even further, until he pulled back on the joystick and the machine left the ground. The usual tingle he got in his belly in the first seconds of takeoff was greatly magnified by his concern for their dangerous payload. He had forgotten to breath, and he sucked in a huge lungful of chilly, rushing air when he realized how out of breath he'd become.

Since their present objective was not to observe large movements and concentrations but rather to choose specific targets, Vogel did not attempt to gain significant altitude as they approached and then crossed the lines. They crossed about five miles west of Soissons, at an altitude of just over two thousand feet. Realistically, just about any road they'd chosen between Soissons and Compiègne would have had some sort of enemy activity on it, but Vogel wanted to make a splash. Without question, Adler did too.

The only problem with venturing behind the French lines at low altitude was the threat of engine failure. Were their engine to fail at such a height, they'd have no chance whatsoever to turn the Rumpler around and glide back to safety in German territory. Risks had to be weighed, and trusting the Mercedes engine to get them home was a calculated one.

Villers-Cotterêts was the largest town with the most in and out roads south of, in-between, and closest to Soissons and Compiègne. It lay approximately ten miles behind the French lines. Surmising that a fair amount of the supplies being brought to the French forces opposing First Army traveled through or near there, Vogel pointed the nose of the Rumpler toward the town. The countryside over which they flew bore the scars of the earlier fighting of September. Some areas were far more pocked by shell holes than others.

When he gained sight of the town, Vogel nosed down the Rumpler slightly so Adler could pick a good target. Adler, leaning out the front of his cockpit to gaze at the ground beneath, signaled with his hand that he wanted to turn further west. Vogel wasn't sure what the oberleutnant had his eye on, but he complied, and banked the machine to starboard. When he did, he saw exactly the same thing Adler did.

Just outside of Villers-Cotterêts, on the main road heading north, was a fairly large convoy of horse-drawn wagons and motor lorries. His heart skipped a beat when he realized that as long as Adler managed to drop the two bombs remotely close to the convoy, it would cause a significant amount of consternation. If they scored a hit, they might even delay the convoy for most of the afternoon. He aligned the machine so they'd pass over the column lengthwise, from north to south.

Before they took off, he'd offered a height of four hundred feet as the lowest he might be comfortable going. In the heat of the moment, he decided to go much lower. Because the convoy was coming up fast, he pulled back on the throttle to reduce airspeed and nosed the Rumpler down even further. It was enough that Adler briefly looked back over his shoulder to make sure everything was all right.

The machine fell further and further and their target grew bigger and bigger. The oberleutnant, holding the first bomb with both hands and leaning half his body over the cockpit fairing, waited for the supply line to pass beneath. Aside from controlling the machine, all Vogel could think about was his hope that Adler wouldn't hit the lower starboard wing with the bomb. If that were to happen and the bomb detonated, either the explosion or the subsequent crash would kill them. And if those didn't, the Frenchmen they'd tried to bomb probably would.

Adler tossed the first bomb, clearing the wing's trailing edge. Vogel yanked back on the control stick and opened the throttle, pulling the Rumpler out of its descent only a hundred feet about the ground. He didn't hear or see the explosive detonate, but a tiny shockwave did hit the aeroplane. The oberleutnant all but jumped from his cockpit in celebration. *He must have hit something.*

Not fully satisfied, though, Adler frantically waved his arms signaling Vogel to circle around and try again. Vogel put the machine into a tight bank, and approached the convoy for a second time, but from the rear rather than head-on. During the bank, he was able to observe the damage caused by the first bomb. A third of the way from the column's lead, a motor lorry was missing its right front wheel, and a small shell hole was punched into the road directly where the wheel should have been. Either Adler's bomb hit the road and the truck drove into it, or the bomb hit the wheel itself. Wherever it hit, its effect remained the same. Behind the broken truck, the convoy had ground to a stop. The drivers of the remaining vehicles and wagons were abandoning their transports and taking cover on the road's shoulder.

They'll be shooting this time, Vogel thought. And they did. Approaching the column in the same diving fashion as before save for the change in direction, Vogel saw the rifles aiming skyward from the men lying or kneeling in the roadside ditches. Adler loosed his second bomb and Vogel pulled up. Something strange happened that hadn't happened the first time.

KABOOM! Rather than feeling the small punch of a shockwave bumping the aircraft, a tremendous blast shook Vogel's guts and lifted the Rumpler unevenly upward. The machine skidded diagonally in the air and the tail section, lifted by the blast, rose higher than the nose.

"Holy shit!" Vogel screamed. In the split second aftermath, the controls went slack in his hands. At first he thought the wires had been severed. Reacting with pure instinct, he tugged back on the control stick and kicked the rudder bar hard to try and level the machine out before it crashed to the ground. The Rumpler swayed violently and dipped; a weightless feeling tickled so deeply in Vogel's belly he thought he might piss himself. If they lost any more airspeed, the craft would fall into a spin and they'd crash.

Fifty feet above the ground and still not in complete control, he fought to fully straighten the wobbly machine. The road was just inches away when he straightened out the tail, leveled the nose and opened wide the throttle. The engine roared at full RPM and the Rumpler's undercarriage bounced lightly off the ground, bounding the machine skyward as it regained airspeed. Adler pumped both fists in the air and shouted back at Vogel. Even over the roaring machinery and wind, he heard the ecstatic oberleutnant howling in triumph. When they'd risen to a few hundred feet, Vogel looked back over his shoulder at the road and the convoy. His eyes went wide as an owl's.

Near the column's rear, fifty yards behind the damaged motor lorry, was a gigantic, smoldering crater. Chunks of burning canvas, wood, and horse were scattered around it. Fires, small and large, burned in a hundred spots over a wide radius surrounding the crater. The French supply troops scrambled, corralling escaped horses and helping those men who weren't vaporized by the explosion.

"We hit a munitions wagon..." Vogel said to himself, not sure if he should be proud of just how much destruction the two of them had caused.

Adler was. During their flight back to the aerodrome, he looked back at Vogel time and again, to take turns applauding, saluting, or giving him the thumbs-up. It was a comical sight, to see a man who'd once spoken to him so harshly acting giddily about notching a triumph.

When Vogel brought the machine in for a smooth landing and they'd taxied to a stop near the sheds, Adler leapt from his cockpit and onto the lower port wing. He ducked through and stepped around the bracing wires, positioning himself right outside Vogel's cockpit. He got within inches of his face.

"That was the best flying I've ever seen!" Adler cried, smiling from ear to ear.

"Thank you, sir."

"No, that was no bullshit! Thank you, Vogel! Did you see that fucking explosion?!"

"I might have been a touch preoccupied."

"You saw it afterward though, right?!"

"Yes I did."

"Wasn't it something?!"

"I suppose so." Vogel had to grin. Adler's excitement was rubbing off on him, but only a little.

Leon, who'd jogged from the sheds to meet them, ran to the Rumpler's tail end first. He touched the fabric for a moment, then approached Vogel's cockpit.

"Why is the lower half of her skin discolored?" he asked.

"What do you mean?" Vogel replied curiously.

"The fabric on the lower half of your machine has changed color. It's at least a few shades darker. It almost looks singed."

447

"Jesus Christ..." Vogel said, trailing off briefly. "...It's because we almost caught fire."

"How did you manage that?"

"How did we manage that?" Adler asked loudly. He jumped from the wing. "I'll tell you how we managed that!" He put his arm around Leon and began to proudly regale him with the story of their latest exploit.

Vogel tuned the oberleutnant out, and dwelled on the aspect of their narrow escape of which he'd been unaware. Nitrocellulose fabric dope was extremely flammable, and once it caught fire, there stood a good chance it wasn't going out. Had the Rumpler caught fire from the flash of intense heat from the explosion, his mid-air recovery would not have mattered. Once lit, the machine's skin would have burned, then the superstructure would have caught fire, and unless they put down and jumped the hell out, they'd have crashed and burned alive. He felt sick.

"I need to file a report with the hauptmann," Adler declared, having finished telling Leon their incredible story. "We might receive a commendation for this!" He spirited away at full-steam.

"I don't think he knows how lucky we were..." Vogel said quietly.

"I don't think he cares..." Leon replied.

BERTHOLD

It almost felt like a waste of time. After Eighth Army's smashing victories at the Battle of Tannenberg and the Masurian Lakes, to Berthold's mind they'd been relegated to little more than sentry duty, holding vigil along East Prussia's frontier.

Eighth Army had largely been dismantled, and General von Hindenburg was promoted to overall command of all German forces operating on the Eastern Front. Only two corps remained in East Prussia. Most of Eighth Army's strength was absorbed into General August von Mackensen's Ninth Army, which had moved southeast into Poland to assist the Austrians. For a man itching to show the Russians what he thought of them, especially after witnessing the gruesome deaths of the two German airmen, for Berthold the lack of combat was maddening.

Because of Austria-Hungary's disastrous performance on the Galician Front, seeing a window there, the Russians had more or less abandoned East Prussia. Pavel von Rennenkampf's First Army had moved south to bolster Grand Duke Nikolai's push toward the Carpathian Mountains and the Austro-Hungarian frontier they represented. In Russian First Army's place was the newly arrived Tenth Army, which held along its home frontier the same as were the Germans defending East Prussia.

On October 4, Mackensen's army and the Austrian First Army initiated their joint offensive, moving on Warsaw, Poland. Having anticipated the offensive, the Grand Duke shifted two of his armies to the north, in order to assist Rennenkampf's forces. General Pavel Plehve's Fifth Army and the reconstituted Second Army under General Scheidemann, both moved around and north of Warsaw.

The plan was for the larger Russian force to collapse upon German Ninth Army, forcing them into a southerly retreat which would push their backs against the Carpathian Mountains. Russian Fourth and Ninth Armies would keep the Austro-Hungarian portion of the Central Powers' offensive occupied. If that were achieved, the Russians could then launch a largely unopposed attack into Prussian Silesia, a resource-rich province of the German Empire. Meanwhile, Russian Third and Eighth Armies would remain in the south, pressing their advance into the Carpathians.

On October 20 the Russian counterattack was launched, and the German advance on Warsaw fell short. Mackensen ordered his forces to retreat westward, avoiding the enemy's flanking maneuver and the southward retreat it was intended to provoke. With the Russians in pursuit, Ninth Army was currently in the process of moving north by rail toward Thorn, in West Prussia.

Berthold and his fellow artillerymen waited daily in anticipation for updates concerning the fighting to their southeast. Generally, news reached them within a day or two of its happening. While guarding the frontier was boring when taken as a whole, the lack of any immediate threat from the enemy afforded time for the artillery crews to practice without facing the threat of counterbattery fire.

At the Battle of Tannenberg, where the German artillery decimated Russian Second Army, the 7th Batterie's positioning atop an area of high ground allowed them to place direct fire onto the Russian lines. While direct artillery fire had been the standard in warfare over the preceding centuries, advances made in both weapons engineering and propellant strength meant that increasingly, the target at which an artillery piece fired was not within visual range. Under normal firing conditions, Gun Number 6's FK 96 n.a. had an effective range of well over three miles. Some of the larger guns could fire much, much farther.

Unless they were fighting on flat plains, the general likelihood was that in most combat situations, the enemy *would* be out of view. Because of the rapidity of I Korps' movement in the first two months of the war, the 7th Batterie had not received many opportunities in the way of shoring up their indirect fire skills. They'd trained for it extensively before the war, of course, but all skills required maintenance, and gunnery was definitely no exception.

For every artillery piece in every army then engaged in the Great War, initial projections as to the number of shells needed for each gun had fallen far short of actual requirements. Nearly all artillery ammunition reserves had been used up, and production was not keeping pace with demand. Such shortages posed serious problems during combat, but they also greatly hampered the ability for crews to practice and train. The artillery units of Eighth Army were in that boat too, and each practice round fired was only done so with great caution and focus. Conservation presently outweighed other considerations.

Though both direct and indirect fire ultimately relied on calculated trial and error when it came to striking a target, direct fire was, for obvious reasons, a much easier system in which to make corrections. Any crew able to observe firsthand where its round landed could then make immediate adjustments. With an obstructed target, other methods were needed. The simplest way to properly range indirect fire was to position a forward observer either on higher ground or, if possible, ahead of the obstructing feature, and to maintain contact with said observer via field telephone. The observer could then verbally relay the location in which the shell landed, and recommend the necessary changes.

Observation balloons were also an effective platform with which to observe shelling accuracy. Made of fabric and filled with hydrogen gas, the large, sausage-like dirigibles were tethered to a flatbed truck by a steel cable, and could be winched down for transport or during poor weather. The balloon's observers, typically two men, were suspended in a basket beneath the gasbag. Since the balloons were connected to the ground by a wire, their crews were also able to verbally relay their information to the designated battery using a field telephone. The drawbacks for balloons were their immobility while in the air, their limited maximum altitude, and their susceptibility to even modestly high winds. A third method, by which a two-seater aeroplane, fitted with a wireless telegraph transmitter, would relay targeting information to a receiver on the ground through Morse code, was still in its infancy and not yet ready for wide implementation.

7th Batterie was conducting a practice indirect shoot on an area of remote and unused land, utilizing a ground-based forward observer with a telephone. Situated more than two miles away from the guns, was a series of white targeting posts, spread in lines to simulate enemy formations. The landscape wasn't radically varied, but the terrain rolled enough that a number of hillocks and trees completely obscured the target posts from the battery's view.

Berthold sat in his seat behind the splinter shield, his neck turned toward Wachtmeister Trommler who was kneeling in the grass about fifty yards away. The commander, holding a field telephone receiver to his ear, was obtaining targeting information from the forward observer. The battery waited silently while Trommler took his instructions. When he placed the phone back into its wooden box and stood, it was time for the battery to get to work. He consulted his gun's range table and relayed instructions to the gun layer. With the exception of Gun Number 1, each cannon was only permitted five shells during the exercise, but some practice was better than none.

Gun Number 1 would, as always, serve as the pivot, meaning it would find the target first and the remaining guns would align themselves to match it. In a combat situation, the pressure would have been on to range the targets as quickly as possible. With the ammunition restrictions, it was more important to move deliberately. Here, hitting the target was paramount; time was not.

BOOM! No matter the scenario, cannon fire was loud and jarring. The first shot made Berthold's ears ring. He watched Trommler walk back to the telephone, pick it up, nod his head a few times, place it back in the box and rejoin the pivot gun's crew. *BOOM!* Again, to the telephone, back to the gun, and after going through the same process a third time, the commander loudly addressed the entire battery.

"Elevation, two-seven eighty!" Trommler yelled, "Azimuth, eight-seven degrees! One round gunfire, thirty seconds!"

With Lang looking over his shoulder, Berthold adjusted the elevation and traverse hand wheels and manipulated the dial sight to Trommler's specifications. The elevation of 2,780 was the range, in yards, at which Gun Number 1 had found its target. Its azimuth, measured in degrees from due north on the horizontal plane of the Earth's surface, specified the direction in which the barrel aimed. Using due north as the reference point, azimuth traveled the full 360 degrees to cover every orientation on the compass. Due east was ninety degrees, due south 180, and due west 270. North was referenced as either zero, or 360 degrees. The battery aiming their guns at an azimuth of eighty-seven degrees meant they aimed east-northeast, just three degrees shy of due east.

Trommler's third order of one round gunfire, thirty seconds, meant that each gun was to fire just one shell, in numerical sequence, with each round spaced thirty seconds apart. The timing allowed the forward observer to differentiate between each shell and log where they'd fallen.

"Fire!" cried Trommler, and Gun Number 2 let loose.

Lang, holding a pocket watch, stared at the timepiece in his palm, counting the seconds. When the echo of the first shot dissipated, Berthold heard the watch *tick-ticking* behind him until Gun Number 3's commander shouted the order to fire. Each *BOOM* grew incrementally louder, and Berthold gazed toward the area in which the shells landed. Each far-off detonation sounded like a heavy *thud*. Over the rise which obscured the distant targets, columns of smoke and dust slowly climbed into the air.

He wasn't necessarily tuning out the next two gun blasts, but the ringing in his ears and his focus on the rising smoke put him into a daze. In a way, they almost didn't register with him, even though the ringing ears intensified each time.

"Fire!" Lang shouted, two minutes to the second after Gun Number 2 launched its projectile. When Weber pulled the firing mechanism, the round blasted away and the barrel recoiled, snapping Berthold out of his trance.

The shoot went on that way, Trommler communicating with the observer to range the first gun and relaying any corrections to the other five, until each of the five allocated rounds per gun was used up. From what the wachtmeister told them afterward, they had performed well. Berthold, however, was not particularly confident. When they arrived back at their camp and were preparing supper, he said as much.

"I know we're skilled at what we do, but is anyone worried that out of all the artillery units in the war, only those of us in East Prussia are not accumulating further experience?"

"So what?" countered Roth, "we've produced the strongest results thus far."

"True…" Berthold agreed, "But while we conduct small, leisurely and infrequent shoots against wooden posts, Ivan's got a whole slew of artillery units engaged in real combat as we speak."

"What are you trying to say?" asked Weber.

"What I'm saying is that it doesn't matter if we were better when the war started. As long as we remain short of ammunition and sit on our asses, the Ivans will improve."

"Their troops just over the frontier are in the same situation as us, aren't they?" Weber said.

"Yes. But I'm not talking about the shell of an army on guard duty across from us. I'm talking about the millions of Ivans to the south, hammering the Austrians and forcing Ninth Army into retreat. At some point, we'll have to deal with the fact that Russia just has more men to throw at us. If our shooting isn't fast and accurate, we'll lose."

"I don't think you give us enough credit," Ostermann said. "Trommler said we performed well today."

"And I'm sure we did, when it didn't matter whether or not the pivot's first shots were on target. But what will happen the next time we're engaged and under pressure, and can't quite find the proper range? What if we end up in front of an opponent with more experience? What if they find our range faster than we find theirs?"

"Jesus, Kastner, what's gotten into you?" Lang asked, taking a sip from his liquor ration.

Berthold sighed. His worries weren't entirely misplaced, but vocalizing them to his crewmates was pointless. Whether or not the others shared in his opinion or vehemently disagreed was irrelevant. They weren't decision makers. They couldn't acquire more practice shells with the wave of a hand, nor could they influence anyone else to.

"If we're just going to be sitting here guarding the frontier, they should use this lull to grant us leave, even without reserves," Berthold said, changing the subject. "Even if it's just a few days. I'd like to see my mother and sister. They're so close, yet I've not seen them for months."

"What about your girl?" Weber asked.

"That would be great, but I'd need more time to get to Mecklenburg if that were the case." He'd begun keeping up a correspondence with Pauline when the fighting eased, but the first of their letters were brief. The same went for the letters to and from his mother. The tone of her replies left suspicion that she might be withholding something from Berthold, though he had no idea what that might be. It was just another reason why he wished to go home and see her.

"I wouldn't mind finding a whorehouse," Lang professed, "it's been more than a while since I patronized such an establishment."

"Again with that," Ostermann chided. "Surprising that's the first thing you mention. Don't you have parents you could visit?"

"Yes," Lang replied, "but they're not as interesting as pints and pussies."

"Lang, if I didn't already know you better, I'd find you repulsive," Ostermann said. "If you lost your cock in the war you might end up being the smartest damned artilleryman in all of East Prussia. Imagine how much space you could free up in your head if it wasn't crammed full of pussy."

Lang took stock, looked up at his own eyebrows, smiled and said, "Imagine how much space pussies could free up if they weren't crammed full of me."

"Ugh..." Weber said, appalled.

"How's he going to lose his dick?" Roth asked. "There isn't a man alive who can shoot that well."

"Hey…" Lang replied, hurt.

"A shell could get him," offered Hertz.

"If a shell blew Lang to bits, his syphilitic little pecker would be the only thing left behind!" Berthold laughed.

"You fuckers," Lang said angrily, standing up and taking hold of his belt buckle. "Do you want to see it?"

"No!" the crew shouted and guffawed, shielding their eyes.

"Ask any whore in Königsberg and they'll tell you!" Lang declared.

"Don't be so sensitive, Lang," said Hertz.

"Yeah, it's not our fault you pay them to pretend it's not tiny!" cried Weber. Everyone howled at the youngster sticking it to the most senior crewmember.

"You're all assholes," Lang said quietly, sitting back down. "Every one of you."

HENTSCH

"Would you like to know something I just realized?" Louise asked. She'd just entered the cafeteria, where Hentsch and his two pals were eating their breakfast of oatmeal, hard-boiled eggs and coffee. The meal might have been a simple one, but it was warm and filling, and far more than what most men at the front could say for the vast majority of their meals.

"What is it?" Hentsch asked, smiling warmly after swallowing a mouthful of oats.

Simon and Engel looked up from their bowls at the pretty nurse. There were a number of attractive young girls who worked in the hospital, but with her jet black hair, button nose and sapphire eyes, petite Louise was far and away the prettiest. Even in what might be considered her unflattering hospital attire—a baggy, ankle-length cornflower blue dress and matching long-sleeved blouse with white cuffs and a high white collar, along with a white apron with a red cross on the bib—she was still a vision.

Her hospital duties kept her busy, but following her and Hentsch's late-night discussion, she'd made a point to visit with the three friends on those occasions when time permitted. They began to look forward to seeing her more and more, no one more so than Hentsch. She was an interesting person, with interesting things to say.

Louise pulled out the empty fourth chair at the table and sat down. "We have another man from your company staying at the hospital," she replied. "At first I didn't realize it because, like you, he'd been issued a gown upon his arrival. But I just saw him on the grounds outside and sure enough, his uniform bore the same insignia as was on yours when you arrived."

"How long has he been here?" Engel asked, his mouth full of egg. A mushy white chunk flew from his mouth. "Excuse me," he said sheepishly, and picked up the bit of egg to place it back in his mouth.

"It's quite all right, Amadeus," Louise assured him. "I've seen much worse come from your mouth."

Hentsch and Simon glanced at one another and snorted in amusement.

"Please, just call me Engel."

"If you insist," she said, rolling her eyes. "To answer your question, he arrived here more than a week's time before you. You'll have to excuse me for not remembering precisely which day. So many have come through our doors. I do remember his injury quite well, though. A deep gash, across both palms."

Simon, who'd still been scooping oatmeal into his mouth, dropped his spoon loudly into the bowl. He stopped chewing. The three men exchanged looks and disgusted expressions.

"I must be honest..." Louise continued, scowling suspiciously at their sudden and highly apparent change in mood, "from my brief interactions with him, I did not gain a favorable impression. He was rude, temperamental, and ungrateful, especially to the nurses. I'm sure I remember his name..." She stared contemplatively out the cafeteria window. "But it eludes me at the moment. It was Eb-something...Eben...Eber..."

"Eberhardt," Hentsch said dejectedly, finishing her thought for her. "His name is Michael Eberhardt. He's not just in our company; he's one of my men. He's here because another tried to kill him."

"My God, why?" she asked. She placed her palm over her mouth.

"I'd rather not get into specifics," Hentsch said, "other than to say that if anyone deserved such an awful thing, it might have been him. He has been a thorn in my eye since August. How can he have been here this entire time yet we haven't seen him once?"

"It's because of his wounds," she replied. "They were serious, of course, but not life-threatening. After the surgeon sutured and bandaged his hands, he stayed in the infirmary for only a few days before they moved him to the barracks across the grounds for recuperation." She pointed out the window and across the grassy courtyard, to a set of white buildings two hundred yards away. "He obviously couldn't serve with his hands in such a state, but he also did not suffer any serious structural or nerve damage. Those in charge must have deemed it unnecessary to send him home while he healed, let alone invalid him."

"Probably because if they sent him home, they knew he wouldn't come back," Engel quipped.

"They'll move us from the infirmary any day now, am I correct?" asked Hentsch.

"Yes," Louise answered, "but even though you're no longer symptomatic, they will still have to keep you away from the front until you've regained more of the weight you've lost. If you were to get sick again, in the physical condition you're in now, you might not have the strength to fend off an illness."

Their recovery, while progressing, had been going slowly. The illness with which they'd been stricken had passed, but it had taken an alarming portion of their respective body weights along with it. Hentsch lost more than twenty pounds from his already lean frame. Consuming proper meals had also started out with difficulty, as their digestive systems had trouble re-acclimating to normal eating.

"So we'll be reunited with our beloved compatriot in the barracks until we're discharged?" asked Simon.

"You will."

"God dammit," Engel grumbled. "Forgive my language, Louise, but you must understand that the negative impression he made upon you is the very same impression he's made upon everyone else. The only difference is that we've been around him longer."

"It's all right. Why does he act that way?" Louise inquired.

"No one knows," Hentsch replied.

"Have you boys singled him out?"

"Absolutely not."

"Are you able to ignore him?"

"Sometimes, but you see I was directly responsible for him. In battle it doesn't work that way. You can't ignore one another. We survive by entrusting the men on either side of us with our lives. Imagine being in our shoes, and having to trust a selfish bastard with your survival, in the midst of the largest war in the history of mankind. To make it through this, we must trust and communicate."

Simon and Engel both nodded their heads in agreement, but Louise apparently was not satisfied. She wanted to explore the issue further.

"Do you think he feels the same way about you?" she asked.

"You mean does he trust us?"

"That, but also, does he dislike you as much as you dislike him?"

Hentsch thought back to the first days of mobilization, from the very first time he saw Michael and learned his name. He could not think of one instance, not one, where the young gemeine had shown himself to be polite, respectful or friendly. Louise expected an answer. He offered the only opinion he could, based on his collective observations.

"From what I, and I'm sure Simon and Engel would attest they've seen, I don't think Michael trusts or likes anyone."

"That must be difficult and lonely for him," Louise said. She showed a sympathy in which the men around her did not share.

"No one forced him to act how he acts," Engel insisted. Then, reflecting for a moment, he admitted, "Although I did almost scrap with him one time. But he started it."

Louise set her eyes on Engel, admonishing him with her gaze. She sighed and said, "Your army crossed borders to wage war against others, yet even that can't keep you and your countrymen away from one another's throats." She laughed, but she was not amused. Her laugh was one of derision. "It may well be that our governments, the great powers of the world, set out to conquer the peoples of far-flung lands whom they consider unruly savages, but even the most decent and intelligent of the lot of you, and I speak for men on both sides of the conflict, you're all every bit as savage."

"So you'll compare us to say, African tribesmen, or jungle-dwelling Orientals?" Engel asked. "You see no difference between them and us?"

"I see superficial ones."

"Such as?"

Louise stared, unblinking, directly into his eyes and said, "Well, your skin is paler, and you have finer weapons to more efficiently kill one another. And your words are different. Other than that, no, I see no difference."

"What about the fact that we live in modern cities?" Simon interjected. "That we're better educated? What about the fact that a large majority of us are literate? Think of all the books and knowledge we have that they do not."

"I'm sorry," Louise said, with a hint of attitude, "do you argue for my point, or against it?"

"Well I..."

The beautiful young nurse's voice grew a measure louder. "Because it sounds to me, Simon, that if having access to those wonderful things you mentioned, namely education and knowledge, are what determine one's level of savagery, it is entirely counterintuitive that the most civilized and *least* savage nations should presently be engaged in sending millions of young men to shoot and kill one another. Do you disagree?"

"Not in principle..." the still skeletal wisp of a man said meekly, looking down at the table.

She turned her attention to Hentsch and Engel. "How about you two? Do you disagree? Do you honestly believe you fight the good fight? That your leaders have made the proper decision in sending you here?"

Engel opened his mouth to defend himself, but Hentsch placed a hand on the man's forearm and spoke first to interrupt him.

"You know how I feel about what's happening," Hentsch said, having sensed that Louise's frustration with the war was bubbling to the surface. He appreciated and respected her passion and inwardly, he agreed with her. "But you also know from what you and I have discussed before, that we fighting men no longer have a choice in the matter. We're in this, and we're in it until a conclusion is reached. One way or another." Peering directly into her bright blue eyes, through them even, Hentsch's heart sank when he saw that they'd grown glossy.

Softly, she said, "And what if it only concludes when the world is reduced to rubble?"

"You must finish what you start," Hentsch replied.

She snorted derisively again and said, sadder this time, "It's not akin to reading a book or starting a jigsaw puzzle, Augustus. You're talking about lives."

He didn't know what to say, but he knew without a hint of doubt that after seeing her sad reaction, and the way it made him feel inside, his regard for her had begun to change. She'd gone from being just the kind, gentle and friendly French nurse, albeit a very attractive one, to a person for whom he held an increasing and genuine affection, even admiration. Hentsch stared at her, searching his brain for something to say, but he came up with nothing.

"I'm sorry..." Louise said. "I've worried much more about my brother of late. A number of wounded French prisoners have needed treatment here, and it has got me thinking negatively."

"Louise..." Hentsch said.

"I've tried so hard to be pragmatic about his being a soldier in a time of war, but that's just it—being pragmatic is the very thing that causes me the most worry. Soldiers fight, and many die." Her voice wavered and she shook her head, disappointed that she'd shown emotion in front of them. "Please excuse me but I must get back to work." She pushed her chair away from the table and stood. She looked away.

"Louise, wait," Hentsch said, "I didn't mean to upset you." He was upset with himself, a German man speaking to a French girl about seeing his country's war with hers through to its conclusion. It was insensitive.

"I know you didn't, Augustus, but it's like you said. Men and boys on every side are caught in this horrible thing until it's over. Someone has to lose, and in the process, everyone will lose. Your Kaiser will sit in his palace, eating and drinking the finest and toasting to victory, and his minions will send more and more to replace those thousands killed or crippled in the name of God only knows. King George, President Poincaré, the whole lot of *civilized* savages, they'll talk of patriotism and condemn their enemies, and sell their savagery to a cheering populace. They'll send more to die, and they'll do it while never truly taking stock of the pain their actions and greed have caused."

Hentsch couldn't see her face, but could tell she fought back tears. "I wish there was something I might say to ease your mind," he said.

"But there's not," she replied. "This war will take and take, and when it finally ends, the victors will take even more from the vanquished."

"I know, Louise, it's difficult to rationalize."

"It's *impossible* to rationalize," she corrected him, "and it takes a confidence man to justify. That's all our leadership is, really, yours and mine. Greedy, selfish, wretched confidence men."

"You're right," Hentsch agreed. "And we must suffer the consequence. Our world is backward and unjust, but it's still our world and we've only got the one."

She nodded, and turned back to the table. She'd collected herself, not allowing one tear to trickle down her cheeks. "Promise me that when they do send you to the front, you'll protect one another and make it out alive."

The three men's faces were uncertain. Hentsch would do what he could to protect his friends and knew that they would too, but that alone just wasn't enough. They'd need luck on their side on top of it.

"I promise," he lied.

"Me too," said Simon.

"I do too," Engel said.

"Thank you boys," Louise said. "Good day to you."

She left the cafeteria and they finished their cold, thickened oatmeal and lukewarm coffee. They could have discussed their impending reunion with Michael, but Hentsch had no desire to broach the subject. Judging by their glum faces, Simon and Engel didn't either.

DENIS

After Patrice's death, Denis struggled to hold himself together. The rage which welled up inside him was far too intense to allow anyone around him, especially his superiors, to become aware of. In a sense it was fortunate for him, then, that on the day his best friend was killed, Lieutenant Armistead was close by, and on his way through that same section of trench. The lieutenant waded through the crowd surrounding the sobbing Denis, convinced him to relinquish his grip on Patrice's coat, and picked him up out of the mud.

He didn't know what sort of strings Armistead pulled after that, but without being given any say in the matter Denis was removed from front line service—temporarily, he was assured—and granted one week's leave on top of it. It could have been that the lieutenant recognized the potential for certain irrational, even reactionary behaviors in the aftermath of such a painful loss, but he never offered Denis any explanation as to why the decision was made. If that was the reason, though, the rationale behind it was sound. Denis had since envisioned himself, numerous times in fact, leaping from the trench to make a run on the boche positions, to bayonet Germans in unbridled bloodlust. As much as he wanted to, he'd only have ended up dead. Had Armistead and Bex kept him at the front, he might have tried it anyway.

Leave was something nearly every man at the front longed for, but Denis could not have gotten it in a more undesirable way. He wanted his revenge. He wanted to kill ten boche for every man of his they'd killed, and twenty for Patrice. A hundred. A thousand. He'd made a promise to his friend, however, and with a weeklong pass, he intended to follow through.

There was no way to tell when another week's leave might come around, or even if he'd live long enough to get another, so as soon as his time began, he found his way to the first passenger train bound for Bordeaux. Before Cécile had a chance to read it in the newspaper's casualty lists, he'd get to her first and let her know in person what had happened. His family was still high on his mind, too, but travel to Cambrai was not an option, and if they'd left their hometown, he had no idea where to start looking. To find them, it might take a month of leave. Cécile would be much easier to find.

So many thoughts swirled through his mind as he sat in his seat aboard the train. The anger and hatred had not subsided, but getting away from the front alleviated some of the tension he'd been living with, from even before Patrice died. Conditions since the first day of the Battle of Charleroi in August had been miserable, with hardly a minute of respite. Clean clothes, clean shaves, and clean quarters were nonexistent on the front lines. The elements, no matter what they were, were only ever separated from a fighting man by his clothing and at best, a tent cloth.

And so, even with all the disappointment, the rage and the sadness, Denis had to appreciate, if only a little, the fact that he was sitting in an actual padded seat rather than on a cold boulder or a damp lump of earth. His cheeks were clean-shaven, his moustache trimmed, and his officer's tunic, pants, boots and kepi freshly washed. Not a single article on his person was soiled in any way. It was alien to not smell the stink of dirty men, and to not stink himself. No shells, bullets or bombs would fall on the train as it chugged further and further away from the front. He wasn't healed emotionally, not at all, but safe for the first time in months, he dozed off with his head rested against the window.

"Excuse me, son?" asked a man's shaky voice behind him. It stirred Denis, but he did not wake.

"Hello there, young fellow?" the voice said again, accompanied by a finger tapping him on the shoulder.

Dammit, just let me sleep.

"Hello?"

"Yes?" Denis answered impatiently. He bolted upright in his seat and turned to face his disturber. "Can I help—"

When he saw the person, he paused, and was instantly ashamed at his own tetchiness. "...you?"

Seated behind him was an old man, gentle in appearance, dressed in shabby clothes and a worn-out, dusty, brown bowler hat. His face was thin, deeply wrinkled, and unshaven. A layer of white stubble clung to the wrinkles of his cheeks and neck, following the contours. The old timer smiled at Denis with a closed mouth. Beneath his bushy white eyebrows, his dark eyes twinkled. "Have you come from the front?" he asked.

"Yes sir, I have," Denis answered.

"How goes it there?"

"Hard to say. We were entrenched north of the Aisne and holding firm, but so were the boche."

"Why have you left?"

"I was not given a choice."

"Have you committed some offense?"

"No. Nothing like that. I was a squad leader, and my men have been lost, most of them killed."

"So you were withdrawn to grieve them?"

"I suppose that must be part of my commander's intention, but I could just as well grieve them with a rifle in my hand."

"That's not always true. Are you an officer?"

"An aspirant, so not quite yet. But I strive to become one when I go back."

"I was an officer once," the old man said, reflective. "I fought the Prussians."

"So did my grandfather," Denis replied, "He was a capitaine."

The man nodded contemplatively. "Did he survive the war?"

"No."

"Pity. I lost family and friends to the Prussians as well. Loss is hard swallow," he said, "take it from me. I've seen my share, but know this." He looked Denis square in the eye and said, "A lost friend is a painful burden, but defeat on the field of battle resonates through the ages. Defeat at the hands of another race turns generations of enthusiastic young boys into bitter old men. Mourn your friends, remember them to the end of your days, but do not lose sight of what they died for. The fatherland is more important than the individual."

"What about millions of individuals?"

"If it came to that."

"It could," Denis said somberly, "We do not fight the same war you fought forty years ago."

The old man laughed. "War is always the same. You may have bigger cannons, finer rifles and those horrid machine guns, but no matter what weapon a man holds in his hand, the end result remains unchanged. Someone will die. To the dead individual, it matters little how he was killed, nor how many others are killed after him. He's already dead."

Denis was unable to separate the generalized comment from the very personal mental image of his dead friend. "So you believe it matters not how many men are killed in this war, so long as we win?"

"I am saying it doesn't matter whether our army is a million strong or a thousand strong. If the fighting men lose the fight, the fatherland suffers their defeat as well, and *that*, young man, is the ultimate humiliation. To be bested by another country, another race, to surrender to them because you could not defeat them, it will haunt you to the end of your days. I'd rather have died than see my country defeated, but I was not spared the humiliation. I have lived with the shame for forty years. I pray the boys who survive this war do not have to feel a similar agony." He reached out and grabbed Denis by the arm, squeezing harder than a withered old man should have been able. "I pray that you win."

"Thank you, sir."

Denis disagreed with the first part—a million dead would always be worse than anything with less zeroes, but he understood exactly what the old man meant about defeat. The boche had already taken so much from he and his countrymen. Losing the war was something France just could not do. Capitulation was not an option, no matter the cost. He *would* rather die than see his country surrender. If it meant defeating Germany and saving France, he'd gladly pay the final price. Their conversation ended then, and Denis rested his head against the window, closing his still heavy eyes.

"Next stop, Bordeaux station!" the conductor announced, waking Denis from a deep sleep. He hadn't realized they were so close to their destination, though he was clueless as to how long he'd slept. A sudden wave of panic ran through him as he realized that he'd soon be giving the worst possible news to someone who had no idea it was coming. He'd never broken such bad news to a person before, and he dreaded seeing Cécile's reaction. Having to witness what would invariably be her sadness would only serve to reinforce his own. But first, he had to find her.

The train passed across the railway bridge spanning the River Garonne and headed toward the Gare de Bordeaux Saint-Jean, the train station located close to the river, in the southern half of the city. As the train moved over the river, Denis thought back to the days before the mobilization began, and he smiled to himself. He and Patrice had, on more than one occasion, gotten stumbling drunk and pissed off of that same bridge and into the Garonne. One particularly quiet night, the two had fallen into hysterics at the sound of their twenty-foot urine streams splashing into the water below. They laughed so hard that Patrice nearly fell from the bridge. The memory was a happy one, but even it caused him pain and his smile quickly vanished.

Slowing to a crawl, the train finally chugged to a stop at the platform. Denis retrieved his haversack and joined the other passengers filing out of the car. Bordeaux was one of the larger and more historic cities in France, with a population of well over 250,000. Much of its architecture had stood for centuries, including ancient ruins which dated back more than a thousand years.

Bordeaux's size was problematic, considering Denis did not have Cécile's address. He did, however, remember Patrice's indecisive mentioning of the cemetery, which was near the center of the city, a fair distance northwest of the train station. He hailed a taxicab, and had the driver take him to the northern side of the Cimetière de la Chartreuse, and drop him off there. He planned to perform a door to door search, the prospect of which was daunting, but he had no other option. Eventually, he'd have to come across someone who knew her, and he didn't plan on looking for accommodations until he'd found her.

Like most of the larger cities in France, houses in Bordeaux were packed tightly together along narrow streets, and they shared a relatively homogenized aesthetic. The streets were crowded, and he hoped he might encounter Cécile by chance while roaming them, but luck had not been kind to him to that point, and he doubted it would turn for him then. On his way, he rehearsed over and over what he'd say to her, but none of it sounded good. He knew he'd stumble over his words anyway, no matter what speech he pieced together beforehand.

At the first door on which he knocked, he received no answer. The second and third doors opened to reveal elderly people who, though friendly, were of no help. Door after door, right to the end of that first street, a variety of people, mostly women or old folks, had no information to offer. The same went for the second street, except behind one of those doors was a mother whose son was at the front. When she opened the door and saw Denis, she immediately burst into tears believing he was there to deliver bad news of her son. After taking time to assure her that was not the case and that he knew nothing of her son, he moved on.

For the better part of three hours he searched up one street and down the other. His uniform frightened more than one mother and he began to feel guilty for his presence causing undue stress to undeserving people. The search had started to feel like a fruitless endeavor after only an hour, but he refused to give it up, even as the afternoon sun of late October threatened to drop beyond the horizon. His searching had to produce a result eventually. It finally did when he knocked on the door of a house near the end of the sixth street. A lanky, not entirely unattractive girl answered the door. She was about Denis's age.

"May I help you?" she asked. Her voice was soft and timid.

"Possibly," he answered. "I'm looking for a girl, roundabout your age, named Cécile Lejeune. Do you know her?"

"Yes," the girl replied, "we attended school together. But why are you looking for her here?"

"I've been checking street by street."

"Well you'd have been checking for much longer had you not found me. She lives east of here, not far from the Pont de Pierre."

"Ah," Denis said. He was angry with himself, but he didn't show it. He'd glanced at the bridge on his cab ride from the train station, and gone right past it. He had chosen the wrong neighborhood. "Would I be imposing if I asked you to take me there?"

"No, I suppose not," she replied. "Why are you looking for Cécile?"

"I've bad news to deliver."

"Oh dear, what is it?"

"A mutual friend of ours was killed recently."

She raised a hand to her mouth. "Was it her boyfriend?"

"Yes. He was my best friend."

"I'm sorry for your loss. You know, I met him once. He had beautiful green eyes."

Denis couldn't stop his memory from flashing back to the day Patrice was killed. The grotesque look on his bloody face, those green eyes, smeared with crimson and rolled back into his head, had given Denis sleepless nights. "Yes," he said solemnly, "that he did."

They stood there for a moment, staring at one another's feet, until Denis cleared his throat.

"Right," she said, "I'm sure you're exhausted from your search. Shall we be going then?"

"If you wouldn't mind."

"I'll get my coat."

They walked silently for a distance. She was shy, which Denis didn't mind. He'd done enough talking to members of household after random household. He hoped she wasn't offended by his silence. She was kind enough to do him a favor, and he'd have been completely lost were it not for her volunteering to help.

"You know..." she said, waiting longer than necessary to spit it out, "...you never told me your name. My name is Océane."

"Please forgive my rudeness," Denis replied, embarrassed by his lack of courtesy. "My name is Denis."

"Nice to meet you, Denis."

"And you, Océane. I must say that is a lovely name."

"Thank you."

They made small talk the rest of the way, but she never asked how Patrice was killed. That came as a relief to Denis; he wanted to relive the moment as little as possible. It already plagued him so deeply. During their walk, he realized just how poorly he'd estimated the location of Cécile's neighborhood. Had Océane not opened her door, Denis would have searched all day and not found a thing. As it stood, it was almost dark outside.

"There it is," she said, stopping in her tracks. She pointed to a row of taupe, two story houses. "It's the middle one, with the flower pot on the front step."

"Will you come with?" Denis asked, wishing she'd say yes.

"No, I cannot see her receive such news. I have a brother at the front."

Denis took a longer look at Océane's face. "What's your last name?" he asked curiously, tilting his head to the side to stare.

"Girard," she answered, and her face suddenly became more familiar. She was Caporal Girard's sister.

"Your brother and I serve in the same section!" he declared with enthusiasm. "I don't know him particularly well, but I've fought near him in battle and we've spoken on occasion."

"He's written us..." she said, "but not as much as my mother wishes he would. Is he well?"

"Last I saw him."

"Well that's great news!" she said, and she gave Denis a wiry hug. "I'll be sure to tell my mother what you said. Goodbye, Denis. Break the news to Cécile gently."

"I will. And I'll be sure to tell your brother we met."

Océane smiled and nodded, then turned and more or less fled. Within seconds, she'd rounded a corner and was gone. Denis was at his destination; all he had to do was knock on the door. He'd lived through savage battles, tugged on death's tail, but for some reason he was every bit as nervous to speak to Cécile as he was before the shooting started.

He stood at the Lejeune household's doorstep, staring at the clay pot full of dried, dead flowers. He raised his hand two times to knock on the door, but each time he lowered it back down without contacting the door. *Come on, Denis, you promised him.*

"Fuck it," he said, and he rapped the door with his knuckles. Within seconds, he heard floorboards creaking inside the house as a hurried pair of feet scampered toward the front entrance. When an excited Cécile flung open the door to see Denis and his somber face, her excitement turned to confusion.

"Where's Patrice?" she asked, craning her neck and looking down the street in both directions. When he didn't answer, her confusion shifted to concern, which visibly deepened on her face second by second.

"I have to tell you something," Denis said, his eyes already welling with tears. He couldn't look at her.

"What is it?" she replied, a catch in her voice. She knew what it was he was about to say.

"It's Patrice..." he said, tensing up his body so he wouldn't cry. "He's dead."

Without warning, Cécile turned away and slammed the door in Denis's face. He flinched, caught by surprise, and he listened to her retreating footsteps across the creaking floor. She'd begun wailing, and he did not know what to do then. As it would any man with a heart, the sound of her cries pained him. He could fight his tears no longer. He blinked hard to wash the sting from his watery eyes, and then wiped his cheeks clean with his tunic sleeve. The wool scratched against his skin, leaving some moisture behind. He wiped the remaining tears away with his hand.

He still had the letters in his knapsack. He couldn't leave without delivering them. He stood there, debating whether or not he should knock on the door again. *Maybe I should find a place to stay. I can always come back tomorrow.* Deciding that might be his best course of action, he stepped away from the door and back onto the street.

When the Lejeune's door reopened, he'd already begun his walk.

"Young man, wait!" a woman's voice called to him. It was Cécile's mother. Denis stopped walking and turned around. Mrs. Lejeune was an older, slightly heavier and even bustier version of her daughter, with the same, attractive round face, long blonde hair and hazel eyes. She must have been in her late forties, but she was surprisingly youthful, and a very comely woman. She wore a flowery yellow apron over a short-sleeve tan housedress.

"Yes, Madame?" Denis said.

"I assume from Cécile's tears that Patrice has been killed?"

"Yes, he has."

"You came all this way to tell her?"

"I promised him I would." Denis reached into his knapsack and removed the stack of letters. "He wrote these to her. It was important to him that she got them. Would you mind giving them to her for me?"

"I would mind, actually," she said, and she folded her arms across her bosom. "You promised your friend that you'd deliver the letters to her, so do not betray him by coming all this way just to hand them to me."

"I don't think Cécile wants to see me right now."

"She wants to see no one right now. But she'll finish crying, and when she does, you can show her the letters. Besides, have you a place to stay?"

"Not yet. I was about to go and find one."

"Nonsense. Tonight, you'll stay with us. You've come all this way, and you must be tired. I'll bet you're hungry, too." She beckoned him to follow her and said, "Why don't you come inside and have something to eat?"

She wasn't wrong about his being hungry. His belly had been grumbling well before he knocked on Océane's door. "If you insist," he said.

"I do."

He followed her into the house. Through what must have been a thin wall, he could hear Cécile crying in her bedroom. It made him uneasy, but if her mother wasn't going to deliver the letters for him, he had no choice but to wait it out and do it himself. He followed Ms. Lejeune into the kitchen and sat at the table.

"I was about to bake some bread," she said. "Maybe by the time it's done that poor girl will be finished with the first bout of sadness and she'll come out and join us."

"What do you mean by that?" Denis asked, "Might she not just stay in there the whole night?"

"She could, I suppose. But sadness and tears, they come in waves, much like the tides. When first you get bad news, it's like high tide. There's water everywhere. But you cannot cry ad infinitum, just as the tides must also recede. She'll cry herself out, calm for a time, and then sometime tomorrow, probably while reading those letters you've brought, the tears will begin anew."

It made sense to him. He took Patrice's death just as hard as Cécile was, and his sorrow and rage had ebbed and flowed just as Ms. Lejeune described. He didn't have enough experience with women to know if they responded to sorrow any differently, but from the sound of it, they didn't. He did not want to bring it up, but he knew that Mr. Lejeune had died a few years back, so if any woman had an opinion on coping with losing a loved one, it was the woman standing before him.

Denis had spent much of his day outside, and while the weather wasn't dreadful, there was a chill in the air and his nose had grown stuffy and numb. Now that he was inside, his nostrils were clearing and he began to smell the meal that Ms. Lejeune was working on. He didn't know what was in the large pot on her stove, but the unmistakable smell of simmering meat, onions and potatoes tickled his nostrils and made his mouth water. She must have noticed him sniffing the air.

"Have you ever tried Garbure?" she asked, sliding a bread pan into the oven.

"I think our cooks may have taken a stab at it while we were garrisoned here, but I doubt they got it right," Denis replied. "It's soup, right?"

"Was it watery?"

"Everything the cooks make is watery."

"Oh no no, it should not be runny at all," she said, shaking her head. "Wait until you've tried my recipe. I've been working on it for most of the day. Cécile was helping me, so hopefully when those first tears run dry the smell of Garbure and fresh bread will lure her out."

"Well it smells great," Denis said, and she smiled at him. She worked quietly by the stove for a time, occasionally turning to ask basic questions about family and the like. It surprised her to know that he had no clue as to the whereabouts of his parents or his sister, but when Denis explained how the fighting had shaped up south and west of Cambrai, it made more sense to her. He could tell she wanted to ask more in-depth questions about his combat experiences, but she restrained herself. She didn't ask how Patrice died either.

When the bread was done, Ms. Lejeune removed the pan from the oven to allow it to cool. Denis helped her set the table. Just before she served the Garbure, she excused herself and left the kitchen. Denis heard her knock on Cécile's bedroom door, and after a minute or so of cajoling, the door opened. Red-eyed and disheveled, the sniffling Cécile sat down at the table, clutching a damp handkerchief. Her mother ran a hand through her hair and kissed her on top of her head, and a few more tears trickled down the poor girl's cheeks. When Denis looked at her, his eyes welled. It was so hard to see a girl cry.

Dinner was served, and it nearly knocked Denis from his chair. Garbure, when it wasn't prepared by fumbling cooks for hundreds of men, was absolutely delicious. Ms. Lejeune sliced up the bread and poured the Garbure over the slices. The "soup" was so thick that the ladle stood straight up in the middle of the pot, and never touched the sides. It was a heavenly blend with a long list of ingredients, from salt pork and smoked ham, to white beans, celery, garlic, leeks, onion, turnip and cabbage. It was, hands down, the best meal he'd eaten in months, and he restrained himself from shoveling it down his gullet in front of the two ladies.

Cécile ate slowly, but she did eat, with her head hung low and her eyes aimed at the table. Ms. Lejeune served Denis a second helping, and he finished it at about the same time his hosts finished their first.

"I think it's time I let the two of you talk," Ms. Lejeune said, and she rose from the table to collect their plates. "You're welcome to more if you'd like, but I'll be adjourning to my bedroom to allow you some privacy. Cécile, you'll sleep in my bed tonight so Denis can stay in yours."

"Yes, mother," Cécile said, hardly above a whisper.

"Good night, Denis,"

"Good night, Madame Lejeune. Thank you for your hospitality, and for the lovely meal."

"You're quite welcome."

When her mother's bedroom door closed, Cécile looked up at Denis. Her watery, hazel doe-eyes nearly triggered his waterworks again.

"I'm so sorry," he said, gulping down a knot in his throat.

"How did he die?" she asked.

That was not the first question he wanted to answer. *Reaching for your picture.* The unadulterated truth was not something she ever needed to know. Such knowledge would only bring pain and unwarranted guilt. "We were entrenched below a ridge held by the Germans," Denis said, "Pat, he was leaning out of the trench, looking for a sniper, but...the sniper found him first."

"Where was he shot?"

"Cécile..."

"Tell me."

"The head."

"Did he suffer?"

"No, it came quickly."

"Were you with him?"

"No, I was looking for..." his mind froze for half a second before he conjured another white lie. "...an officer."

"Did he speak of me often?"

"He did. That's why I'm here, you see." Denis's knapsack was resting on the floor beside his chair. He reached inside and produced the letters for a second time. He set them on the table, and then slid them to Cécile.

"What are these?" she asked. "What do they say?"

"They're the letters he wrote to you," replied Denis. "I don't know what they say; I haven't read them. They're not mine to read."

"Why did he not send each one after he'd written it?"

Again, glazing over the truth would do her no harm. "I think he wanted to bind them together, you know, to make them more presentable. He just never got the chance. He asked me to get them to you if the worst happened. I promised him I would."

She gently leafed through the pages. "Why are some of them so dirty?"

"We've done much of our fighting in a very dirty environment. It's a wonder any paper makes it out of the trenches at all."

She sniffled and ran her hand beneath her reddened nose. "Did he do a good job?" she asked. "Was he a good soldier?"

"He was. He fought hard, and he was brave, and through it all he never forgot about you. I think that says a lot about him. And you."

Her eyes welled up again, and tears trickled down her cheeks. Denis's instinct was to leave his chair and hug her, but instead he reached across the table and gently pressed his palm against her cheek, wiping the tears away with his thumb. She clutched his forearm with both of her hands and pressed her cheek harder into his palm.

"Thank you, Denis, for telling me in person," she said between sobs.

"It was the least I could do for him," Denis replied, "for the both of you."

She gathered herself again, and lifted his hand from her cheek to hold it between her own hands. "Have many boys you know been killed?"

"I lost my entire squad," Denis admitted, hanging his head. He gritted his teeth in an attempt to stifle the tears. He'd been battling them ever since Cécile's mother left the table, but he could fend them off no longer. His eyes stung and his sinuses burned, and his shoulders heaved as one sob overtook him. He couldn't stop the tears, but he fought off any further sobs. It didn't matter, his façade had already cracked.

"Ohh," Cécile said sympathetically, and she dragged her chair next to his. She wrapped her arms tightly around Denis's neck and hugged him close. The two grieving young adults held one another, and they both wept. For Denis, it was incredibly cathartic to be able to cry on a shoulder that would not judge him for his sadness. That she was an attractive girl was secondary.

They shared their hug, he didn't know for how long, talked for a short while further, and then, both of them tired, said their good-nights. Cécile joined her mother, and Denis, exhausted both emotionally and physically, collapsed in Cécile's bed, still dressed in full uniform.

The next morning, Ms. Lejeune served a simple but delicious breakfast of buttered toast and jam, bacon and coffee. The mood in the house was a quiet one, and little was said whilst they ate. Denis had a train to catch at noon.

When he announced his intention to take his leave, the two women each gave him a hug and a kiss on the cheek, pressing their large breasts into his chest, which he didn't mind at all. Ms. Lejeune sent him off with a hefty slice of bread wrapped in a clean handkerchief, and Cécile, still red-eyed and disheveled, thanked him one last time for delivering the letters in person. She hadn't read them yet, and was probably anxious to.

The Lejeune women requested that Denis be careful in his future exploits, and that he occasionally take the time to write them and let them know he was doing all right. He swore he would, and when they said their final goodbyes he made sure to not make the same mistake Patrice had. As soon as the door closed behind them, he made a mental note of the address.

VERNON

Vernon plunged the spade of his entrenching tool deep into the wet ground in front of him. As he dug, he kept a wary eye trained toward the east, but he could barely see over the lip of the deepening trench.

Following Major Young and the majority of the patrol's capture at the farm, it took the 1st Battalion an additional three days to successfully advance beyond Chapelle St. Roch and take control of Rue d'Ouvert. A day later, they were infused with a much needed dose of new life, when three officers and close to 250 NCOs and men arrived as reinforcements. Since then the battalion had moved an additional mile, seizing the town of Violaines after a difficult struggle. The town was less than half a mile northwest of La Bassée.

On October 19, they attempted to strike out from Violaines and attack the German positions at La Bassée, but were met with heavy and focused resistance. The attack bogged down after covering only five hundred yards. On the 20th, the Germans there received reinforcements of their own, which coincided with the launching of a larger German offensive extending from Arras further south, all the way to the Belgian coast in the north. That offensive forced the battalion to fall back to their positions at Violaines. Against long odds, they'd managed to repulse the Germans to that point, and were in the process of strengthening their defenses in the fields on the town's southeastern outskirts. It was now October 22.

Vernon's eyes were not the only ones nervously glancing eastward. Though they couldn't see far, each time any man lifted a spade full of earth and hoisted it onto the growing pile in front of the trench line, that man glanced east, scanning for movement. With an entrenching tool in hand, it was even more nerve-wracking to anticipate a German attack than it would have been while holding an Enfield. Their rifles were piled behind them in pyramids of four, butts in the mud, muzzles in the air, to prevent their firing components from becoming clogged with dirt. Piling arms helped stave off some dirt, but the men's hands, clothes, and just about everything else was dirty anyway. Digging a trench and living in it was just dirty business.

"They haven't sent a shell our way in a bit," Pritchard commented, grunting as he lifted a lump of soil.

"Well dammit, Pritchard, they will now!" Milburn said, thrusting his spade into the ground.

FOOM! On cue, the German artillery positioned east of La Bassée sent their first shell sailing overhead. It detonated more than a hundred yards behind the toiling Brits. Only the men who'd arrived as recent reinforcements flinched at the sound. Some new arrivals flopped into the dirt, prompting mocking glances from the more seasoned members of Fourth Platoon. Even Chilcott and Saunders, 3 Section's two greenest youngsters, snorted at the newest arrivals' jumpiness.

Pretending that Pritchard's comment had actually led to the firing of the German shell, Milburn picked up a handful of mud and threw it in his direction. It splattered against Pritchard's pant leg. "Nice work," he said.

"You prick, Milburn, that was the one spot I had hoped to keep clean," Pritchard said, with no small amount of sarcasm. He bent over at the waist and picked up a handful of mud, which Vernon expected he would launch back at Milburn. Instead, Pritchard smeared the mud on his own leg, on the same spot he'd just been stricken. "Just let me wash this off," he said, bending down to pick up another handful. "Oops, looks like I've missed a spot." He spread more onto the front of his trousers. "I'd hate to look unpresentable for our next inspection."

Vernon and the other 3 Section men chuckled. Even with his intentionally wiping added grime on his trousers, Pritchard wasn't much dirtier than anyone else. Unless he'd bathed in a mud puddle, his lack of cleanliness just wouldn't stand out in comparison. Not one to miss a chance at a punch line, Vernon played along with Milburn's superstitions and said, "Hey Pritch, maybe you should mention your surprise at Fritz having not landed a missile on the captain's tent."

"Shh!" Pritchard snapped, timidly glancing over both shoulders to make sure Bannister hadn't heard. The captain was hundreds of yards away, though. He'd set up a command tent well behind E Company.

"Oh hell, Lew," Vernon replied, "Bannister might have ears like a bat and be batty to boot, but unless I shout it into a speaking trumpet, he's not going to hear a damn thing."

"Cortland is back there with him..." Pritchard said.

"It was just a joke, Llewelyn."

"Keep digging, gentlemen," Second Lieutenant Fordham said, softly but sternly. He'd not been as nervous of late as he was on the bus from Abbeville; then again it wasn't so hard to tell men to dig when all was quiet. He paced up and down the line behind his charges, supervising their toil.

In the rush to entrench, the battalion had deployed companies C, D, E and B, in that order, on a diagonal from northeast to southwest. A Company remained further back and north. Each entrenching company deployed a covering party ahead of their positions, tasked with spotting any threats and thusly informing in due time the large numbers of men holding shovels instead of rifles. In E Company's case, the men of Second Platoon were designated the covering party.

"It might go without saying, but you boys be ready to snap up your rifles at a moment's notice," said Corporal Spurling. "I'm not sure our covering parties have gone far enough ahead."

Two more shells had fallen within earshot, which prompted the corporal to climb out and have a better look east.

"Far enough ahead for what?" Chilcott asked.

"What do you mean for what you dolt?" Spurling chided, "To warn us an attack is coming is what!"

"What should we do?" asked Saunders.

"Keep digging," Spurling said, "just don't fumble your rifle when it's time to trade shoveling for shooting."

That Spurling thought the covering parties were poorly positioned made Vernon even more uneasy. Were a large enough German force to move west against them and Second Platoon fail to act quickly, E Company might easily be overwhelmed. The same was true for the other three companies on the line.

When the first *crack* of a rifle shot rang out somewhere ahead of D Company, Vernon didn't waste any time. He detached the head of his entrenching tool from the helve and stuffed them both into his haversack. His section mates joined him, and the platoon joined soon thereafter when Second Lieutenant Fordham ordered them, with a shaky voice, to grab their weapons. More shots echoed from the fields ahead of D Company.

From inside the trench, the gentle roll of the landscape obscured the covering parties from view, but when Vernon stepped out of the shallow trench and onto what was to become the parapet, he gasped. The Germans had struck out from La Bassée, and they'd struck rapidly. Charging closely on the heels of D Company's retreating covering party, the furthest advanced of those Germans had caught by surprise the very screen tasked with preventing those digging the trenches from being caught by surprise. There was absolutely no way those men had given the rest of their company an ample warning, and now, in their haste to flee, some were being shot in the back.

"My God!" Vernon exclaimed. He jumped back into the trench. "D Company is going to be overrun!"

His declaration was met with startled and confused faces all wondering the same thing—where was the warning? If the Germans stormed the line there, it would drive a wedge between C Company and E and B Companies. Any number of flanking attacks by the German force would then be on the table. The 1st Battalion was one of II Corps' easternmost units, so their grip on the ground they'd taken was tenuous at best. A break in their line would make falling back urgent, since no reinforcements could readily be called upon.

By the time D Company started shooting with any appreciable volume, the Germans had already successfully rushed them. The men in E Company temporarily turned their backs to the east to watch a number of men from what was now the retreating D Company shot in the back by their pursuers. Stragglers fell victim to bullet or bayonet, and Vernon watched his battalion's tactical situation deteriorate in a flash of grey. The line was already breached.

"Fourth Platoon, hold positions!" Fordham called out over the shooting, an audible quiver prevalent even in his raised voice, "Fix bayonets!" His voice cracked.

Vernon was close enough to the lieutenant to see the young officer gulp, and then nervously exhale after issuing his order, before drawing his pistol with a trembling hand. He didn't mind the young gentleman being afraid—he was too. He just hoped the officer's nerves would hold up enough that he'd remain functional. He complied with Fordham's order, drawing and snapping his bayonet onto the end of his rifle. There was something undeniably chilling about fixing a blade to the end of a long-range weapon. When a gun, deadly at a range of eight hundred or more yards was forced to become a spear, deadly at a range of four feet, the man holding the spear had best hope there wasn't a round in his opponent's chamber. Vernon had one in the chamber and nine more in the magazine. He shuddered at the sound of the rest of the platoon snapping their bayonets in place.

In the confusion and alarm of watching one quarter of their line dissolve away, most of E Company's men failed to notice their own covering party beating a hasty retreat toward the trench. Second Platoon's men, scattered haphazardly for fifty yards in either direction, leapt into the trench shouting their worthlessly belated warnings of the approaching Germans. Vernon and Pritchard were two of the first to fall against the partly finished parapet and aim their Enfields toward the enemy. As soon as the last of the covering party's men had cleared the line of fire, E Company began shooting, and Germans began dropping. They had more to spare than did the Cheshires.

His thumping heart filled his entire torso, and punched against the dirt he lay in. Vernon frantically fired his first ten shots in fewer than that many seconds. *Snap-pow! Snap-pow!* Cocking and shooting became one, unbroken chain. He and his fellow riflemen, well-trained in the art of massed fire, did what a depleted company could to effectively spray and slow the oncoming Germans. It was plain that the Englishmen holding the trench were outnumbered, and though their fire took its toll on the enemy, each second that passed brought the attackers closer.

Vernon saw a looming potential for an opportunity to right one of Bannister's wrongs. *Maybe it's time for us to pay our penance for abandoning the battalion at Audregnies.* If the company could delay the Germans long enough, the other companies might have a better chance at escaping.

The gap between defender and attacker narrowed, and defenders started falling. It was getting harder to put down the attackers at the lead of the charge. Medics and stretcher bearers ducked and scurried through the ditch to help the wounded, but they were just as likely to catch a bullet as anyone else, especially when they tried to carry a casualty out of the trench and to the west. With bullets smacking into the dirt ahead of him and cracking past his ears, Vernon was amazed none of his section mates had yet to be hit.

Despite the withering fire produced by the Cheshire contingent still holding the trench line, the first Germans made it into the trench in the midst of the men from First and Third Platoons. Those first brave arrivals were quickly dispatched with the bayonet.

Vernon downed man after man with his Enfield, but after emptying his magazine for the third time, a hard-charging Hun reached the line and jumped right over his head, landing on his feet in the trench. Vernon rolled onto his back to take action. Saunders sprung from his prone position first, just ahead of Vernon, and the young private screamed, leaping at the German with his bayonet extended. The German, a decent sized fellow, deflected Saunders's attack and struck him with a gun butt, knocking him to the ground. By then, Vernon was up and lunging, and he drove his bayonet into the enemy soldier's abdomen, pushing him against the trench wall, before sticking him two more times in the chest, to the tune of his blood-curdling screams. Saunders groggily stood, and hardly seemed like he knew what had happened to him.

More German boots were landing on the trench floor, enough that they were now able to kill before being killed. There was hand to hand fighting up and down the line. C Company, cut off from E and B, had retreated back to align itself with A Company. Their withdrawal allowed the Germans to divert all attention on the remaining and now foremost two companies. Facing an enfilading attack from the north and a frontal assault from the east, E Company could do no more. The time had come for both E and B Company to evacuate their positions or be destroyed. First Platoon was the first to scramble from the trench, being the most threatened by the attack from the left flank. When the other lieutenants saw First Platoon bolt, they immediately called for their men to retreat as well.

"FOURTH PLATOON!" Fordham cried loudly, fumbling with his whistle before blowing into it hard. "WE'RE OVERRUN!" He blew his whistle again, leapt out the back of the trench and shot a German who'd just leapt in. "FALL BACK!" He whistled a third time. "FALL BACK!"

"You heard the lieutenant! Up and out let's go!" Spurling shouted to the seven members of 3 Section. Those who were still shooting rolled onto their backs, clutching their rifles against their chests, and sprang to their feet to run. It wasn't easy turning one's back to armed men, and Vernon took three fast breaths through his nose to steel himself.

After barely getting off his back, Lockwood fell to his knees, dropping his rifle. "Agh! Shit!" he croaked, and he brought a hand to his neck. Vernon turned to him and saw blood trickling between Lockwood's fingers. *Dammit he's got a bad one.*

"Can you run?!" Vernon shouted.

"Bet your arse I can run!" Lockwood yelled back. The look in his eyes said otherwise, but they hadn't the time to argue.

"We'll stay close to you, all right?" Pritchard said, pulling Lockwood to his feet.

Still clutching his neck, the wounded man nodded in agreement. "Yeah..." he replied, wincing. There was already blood on his teeth.

The three of them ran together. At first, they kept up with the others from 3 Section and most of Fourth Platoon. But Lockwood was hurt worse than he let on. Beneath the grime on his face, his skin grew whiter. The further they ran, the more red ooze spurted from beneath his hands and onto his greatcoat collar. His strides slowed and he started to stumble, but Vernon and Pritchard grabbed him on either side and propped him up. When his legs gave out, he threw his arms around their necks, removing his bloody hand from the wound. Blood pumped from the hole in his neck, soaked the shoulder of his coat and poured down the lapel. When his head sagged and he became a dead weight, Vernon knew that he and his best friend were putting their lives on the line for a corpse.

"We've got to drop him!" he shouted, breathless.

"No, Vernon! We can get him to the aid post!"

"He's already dead!"

"You don't know that! He may have fainted!"

"Do you want to bet your life on it?!"

"Would you bet yours he's dead?!"

"I'd bet it because I'm right!" Vernon shrugged Lockwood's lifeless arm off of his back and released his grip on the man's greatcoat. The corpse fell to the ground, and Pritchard fell with it. "We can't save a dead man!" yelled Vernon.

"For Chrissake Vernon, help me pick him up!" Pritchard screamed.

"No!"

"Then fuck you!" He bear hugged Lockwood's corpse and dragged it upright, groaning as he slung the limp body over his shoulder. In so doing, he was soaked in Lockwood's blood. "You go ahead," he said.

Vernon wasn't about to do that. *He's saved you once, but now he's going to get you killed.* "You stubborn bloody arsehole, Lew, you'd better move as fast as your boots will carry you!" He unslung the rifle from his shoulder, snapped in two charger clips and faced the approaching Germans. "I'll be right behind you."

Pritchard lugged the body step by heavy step, the weight bouncing on his shoulder. Vernon kept pace, alternating between shuffling sideways and jogging backward, watching for the nearest German heads to pop out of the trench the battalion had just wasted hours in digging. Each time a spiked helmet emerged, he tried to make an accurate shot, not a simple task when striding backward. His feeble attempt to cover Pritchard might have accomplished little, as any number of the random bullets cracking by could have clipped them both, but if he was going to move slower and remain by his friend's side, he felt better doing it with a rifle trained on the men chasing him.

"If there were ever a time when you and I needed guardian angels, it's now!" Vernon yelled, harkening back to their discussion about Mons. But Pritchard was busy pushing his body beyond its limits, grunting and groaning with each step and he didn't answer. They were nearing the withdrawal point. Vernon emptied his magazine and fumbled with two charger clips in his ammo pouch, dropping one in the grass as he pulled them from the pouch. "Piss," he said, snapping the lone clip in and firing another round eastward.

When they made it to within fifty yards of E Company's new position near a small farm, Spurling and Granville charged out from behind their cover, offering to help Pritchard carry Lockwood to safety. Vernon could tell every inch of his friend's body was burning and on the cusp of total failure. So when Pritchard cried out, refusing their help and, roaring like a lion, carried the corpse the rest of the way, Vernon could not deny the astounding and inspiring lengths that Pritchard's determination could take him.

He'd loved and respected his best friend since they first met years before, but Llewellyn Pritchard's latest display, reckless as it might have been, was the most incredible thing Vernon had ever seen. It didn't fully settle in until he'd made it behind cover and aimed his rifle eastward again. That was when he gauged the distance. Pritchard had, with impressive speed and without stopping, hauled the full weight of another man, both dressed in full gear, for close to half a mile, bullets and death all around him.

"My heart would have exploded..." Vernon whispered to himself.

Pritchard, meanwhile, though he'd burned every ounce of energy he had left, knelt, gasping and wheezing, next to Lockwood as Spurling and Granville checked the body for a pulse. The retreat brought them to the same place where Captain Bannister had set up his command tent, and now he and his small staff were dispersed amongst the newly arrived and disorganized line of infantrymen. Vernon split his attention between watching and firing at the enemy to the east, and observing how Pritchard would take the news when he learned Lockwood had died. It wasn't more than thirty seconds before Spurling hung his head and looked Pritchard in the eye. The corporal somberly shook his head, and Pritchard, still out of breath, rose quickly to his feet, turned his back to his section mates, tore his cap from his head, and flung it into the dirt at his feet.

"FUCK!" he roared, kicking his cap away. He grabbed fistfuls of his hair and held his head tightly. Vernon was just about to lower his rifle and stand up to console him, when Bannister emerged from behind an outbuilding, not far from Lockwood's corpse and the two men still kneeling next to it. Vernon stayed put, but coyly observed over his shoulder.

"What's the matter, Pritchard?" Bannister smirked, taunting. "Did our hero nurse let someone die on his watch?" He nudged Lockwood's corpse with his boot. Both Granville and Spurling's jaws dropped.

"Why, His Majesty is sure to award you the Victoria Cross for such a dashing exploit! You've saved a dead man!"

Pritchard, his eyes bloodshot and teary, turned to face the captain. Lockwood's death was hard enough to take, but Bannister's awful jeering crushed him. His mouth hung agape in profound bewilderment. Nothing he could ever do would positively alter the way the captain treated him.

A hundred thoughts swirled through Vernon's mind, every one of them inspired by the fact that all he saw was red. For a fraction of a fraction of a second, he reached for the end of his rifle and the bloody bayonet clipped to it. Bannister's cruelty was completely out of hand, and it would have been the sweetest of pleasures for Vernon to take hold of that bayonet and plunge it deep into the captain's belly. Amidst the clatter and confusion of the retreat and the increasing volume of rifle fire, he might have been able to pull it off, to convince his mates to help him cover it up.

He resisted the urge, but he had to do something to defend Pritchard. He made a motion to stand, but when he did, he met eyes with Spurling. The corporal was not a physically intimidating man. He may have led like a true blue officer and fought like a gladiator, but the wiry twenty-five-year-old did not cut an imposing figure. In that moment, however, when he gritted his teeth and glowered at Vernon, the message was clear and did not require words. With just an expression, Spurling demanded that Vernon stay right where he was. Vernon obliged.

"Captain Bannister, sir," Spurling said, still eyeing Vernon while slowly rising to his feet. The captain, who'd been focused on Pritchard, turned to the corporal. Appallingly, as he turned his head, Vernon caught a glimpse of the vile sneer which had been spread across Bannister's face, just before it evaporated.

"Yes, Corporal?" the captain growled. He sounded irritated.

"Sir, Lockwood was wounded while we were still on the line, I saw it. I don't know when it was that he collapsed, but however far Private Pritchard carried him, it was a long way. He did his best to save him."

"And he failed. That's the end of it and you'll say nothing more. Now leave that fucking body alone and pick up your rifles."

"Yes sir," Spurling answered.

Bannister turned back to Pritchard. "You too, *hero*," he said with biting sarcasm. "Pick up your bloody cap and get your sorry arse on the line."

"Yes sir..." Pritchard muttered. His shoulders couldn't have slumped any further as he stumbled, spirit defeated, to the spot where his cap hand landed. He picked it up, flopped it onto his head and walked past the captain, who glared at him all the way.

Pritchard dropped like a stone into a prone position on Vernon's right side. He aimed his rifle to the east and fired a shot without a peep. Vernon waited until Bannister had left before tapping his friend on the shoulder.

"Llewellyn, are you all right?"

Not averting his eyes from his rifle sights, Pritchard answered, "I should have just fucking left him lying in the grass out there like you said."

After witnessing what he'd done to try and rescue a fallen brother, Vernon wouldn't agree with that, not in a million years, even if it had been his initial instinct. "He might have been dead either way, but you did more to save him than I've seen any man do for another. That run would have killed most of us, and now, because of you, Lockwood should get a proper burial. He didn't make it, but you're a hero to his family, I can promise you that." He patted his friend hard on the back. "Just as you're a hero for saving Hood and I. These things you've done, Pritch," he said, pressing his hand firmly against Pritchard's back and jostling him a few times to let him know he meant what he was saying, "they can't be taken away from you. If I had King George's ear, even for a moment, I'd make bloody well sure he personally pinned you with the VC."

Granville, lying on Vernon's right side, had been listening. "Hayes is right, Pritchard," he declared loudly. "The captain might say otherwise, but it's no lie. You're a hero."

Pritchard fired another shot, and four hundred yards away a German fell dead in the grass. "Not to Fritz, I'm not," he said.

The following day, it became clear just how much of a debacle the previous day's fighting had been. The battalion had suffered more than 220 casualties, lost several officers, and surrendered hard-won ground to the Germans, who retained their hold on La Bassée. In the wake of yet another close call, the decimated and fatigued battalion, who in one day of fighting had lost nearly the same number of men as had been sent just days earlier to reinforce them, was briefly taken out of action.

Because of glaring shortages in men, however, they were soon back on the line, forced to assist in digging trenches. Pulverized to the point that an officer from another battalion had taken command, Vernon and the men of 1st Battalion labored, with little food and no energy left to speak of, in the muddy ditches that had become their home. With the late October weather growing ever colder and wetter, the trench digging process grew more difficult and exhausting by the day.

GORDON

Fitting in hadn't gotten any easier. That wasn't to say Gordon had not been learning—he'd just been doing so mostly on his own. It was only through his keen intellect and deductive prowess that his knowledge arc was able to pace or even surpass the other mechanics-in-training at the Blériot School. With Plamondon's willingness to assist and to allow him to perform repairs and the like outside of normal instruction hours, Gordon had already accomplished a feat which no one else at the school, not even the instructors, had done. Forgoing sleep on several nights, with no outside help or guidance, he'd successfully dismantled and fully reassembled one of each type of aeroplane engine then in use at the school. It wasn't something the instructors *couldn't* do; it was just that they hadn't.

Giles and Matthieu, the "gentlemanly" pair he'd met on day one, had recently received their certifications and been quickly dispatched to service the aeroplanes at the front. As the days and weeks passed, more and more machines were entering service, facilitating the need for further numbers of trained pilots and mechanics. Aside from their salty words and their rude exit on day one, the two men never tormented Gordon, per say, in fact, no one at the school had. It was just that no one acknowledged him. Not as a person, and not for his abilities.

He wrote his first letter home while on the train to Pau, to let his family know that he was all right and that an opportunity had been presented to him. He wrote a second letter a week after arriving at the school, but he'd yet to hear anything back. A word from his family was something he looked forward to, whenever it might arrive, but in the meantime, and in the absence of any additional socialization, Gordon's relationship with Plamondon was all he had. They'd grown closer and shared a trust with one another that Gordon had never had with a white person before.

"Did you finish checking the wire tension on the port wings?" Plamondon asked. He was lying on his back next to the machine's undercarriage, making the last few turns of a wrench.

"Yes, they're all set," Gordon replied. "Flight controls are good, and we both know her engine is ready. Now all we need is for the kids not to crash her during their tests."

"They will be fine. Demarais has learned his lesson since the last time, and I am confident that Yount will do well."

It was early in the morning, before the other instructors and students had risen. Plamondon and Gordon got up before sunrise to prep the Farman Shorthorn for flight. Two students were to take their certification tests later that morning, and it was a good chance for Gordon to show the others that a machine he worked on would perform every bit as solidly as any other, if not better.

A perfectionist, Gordon circled the machine looking for the slightest inconsistencies in the fabric while waiting for Plamondon to finish with the undercarriage.

"Gordon, I know you want to see her fly," the instructor said, still lying on his back and shaded by the machine's lower plane, "but why don't you go and get a few hours of rest? You were in the sheds late again last night and we were up early yet again today."

"No, I'd really like to see the machine up in the air. It's gratifying to see my work get airborne."

"I know. But the tests won't begin until noon or later and we've done all we need to. I'm about to head to my quarters, and I think you should head to yours for a short nap at least."

"Maybe you're right," Gordon agreed, "just promise me that if I do fall asleep, you won't let me miss the tests."

"I'll be sure you're there," Plamondon said, smiling. He tugged the wrench one last time and sat up. "You go ahead, I'll finish cleaning up."

"All right, I'll see you in a couple hours."

He really was tired; his eyes had been heavy all morning, so it felt good to lie down knowing he'd already accomplished something for the day. It hardly seemed like he'd fallen asleep before he woke to his arm being shaken.

"We'd best get out there, Gordon," Plamondon said, continuing to shake him. "They will be starting soon. I've got something to give you when the tests are done." He grinned.

"What is it?"

"You must wait."

Gordon rolled out of bed, still dressed in his coveralls. Being so tired as to render their removal tedious was fast becoming his trademark. He put on his shoes and joined the instructor in marching across the training ground. At first, they walked at a brisk pace toward the machines, which had already been rolled out of the sheds and onto the field. A small crowd of students and instructors were gathered around the aeroplanes.

When a Blériot XI fired its engine and began creeping forward, Gordon and Plamondon turned to one another with surprised faces and started to run. Gordon would probably have been faster than Plamondon anyway, but with his gimp leg, the hobbling instructor quickly fell behind. The plan was, all along, to have the certification flights take place in the Farman Shorthorn. The first student was about to take off in a machine which no one had checked.

"Wait!" Gordon screamed, waving his arms.

"Ne le laissez pas prendre son envol!" yelled Plamondon from even further back.

Over the growl of the rotary engine and with their attention focused on the machine rolling down the field, no one heard or saw the two men frantically trying to signal them to stop the flight from getting airborne. Gordon ran at an angle down the field, trying to place himself in the pilot's peripheral vision, but the Blériot had already picked up too much speed. Its wheels lifted off the ground and the machine rose skyward. Gordon slowed to a jog and stopped, placing his hands on his knees, and watched the unchecked monoplane creep higher. The engine, though it had received no maintenance or adjustments, sounded good. *Maybe it won't be a big deal.* It wasn't as if the Blériot was in a state of disrepair, there was just a difference between an inspected machine and an uninspected one.

Keeping his eye on the aeroplane while it made its first circuit around the training ground, Gordon saw that Plamondon had finally caned his way over to the group that'd seen the Blériot off. He couldn't hear the verbal exchange but it must have been heated, as Plamondon waved his arms, used forceful hand gestures, and even pointed his cane toward the machine circling above. When the argument came to an end, the instructor joined Gordon and they stood together watching the flight.

"Who is it up there?" asked Gordon.

"It's Demarais," Plamondon answered. Gordon knew most of the students' names, even if they all avoided him. Demarais was a bit of a cocky shit, overconfident in his abilities and his capacities. Weeks before, he'd managed to convince the instructors he was ready for a solo flight, and quickly smashed up the undercarriage of one of the Farmans. His piloting and landing skills had since improved, hence his taking the certification test, but Gordon was wracked by a gripping tension as he watched Demarais performing the requisite maneuvers overhead.

The maneuvering portion of the test went well, but the end was the difficult part. The trainee had to perform five good landings in succession, taking off immediately after making the first in order to perform each subsequent one.

"Will they signal him to stop on his first landing?" asked Gordon. Even though the machine looked and sounded all right, he didn't want the test to continue.

"No," Plamondon answered, "they will allow him to finish."

"How can that be?"

"They said the machine looks and sounds fine."

Gordon sighed and rubbed his face with both hands. Demarais made his first landing, a good one, and then took to the air again, opening the engine to full throttle on his takeoff. There was no denying it, the roaring Gnome Lambda sounded healthy. Landings two and three likewise went off without a hitch. *Come on, Demarais, just two more.* Gordon didn't particularly like the cocky young Frenchman, but rooting against a man trying to do a dangerous thing, and the very thing Gordon loved most, was out of the question.

The Blériot touched down for the fourth time, the engine revved again, but instead of making a tight circuit and repositioning for the final landing, Demarais flew straight, and the machine climbed higher.

"What is he doing?" Plamondon said quietly, more to himself than to Gordon.

Yeah, what the hell are you doing Demarais?

They watched the machine climb, and then Gordon knew exactly what the cocky son of a bitch was going to do. It was just the thing for an overconfident showboat. Before his final landing, Demarais was going to loop the loop. Simple in principal but difficult in execution, looping the loop was a dangerous stunt, even for a skilled pilot. It entailed nosing the machine downward to gain airspeed, then yanking the control stick straight back to put the machine into a climb, nosing the machine right over the top to then close the loop and return to level flight. In 1913 the French pilot Adolphe Pégoud was the second man ever to perform such a maneuver, and he'd likely inspired many of the young men who now strived to become pilots themselves. Gordon hoped Pégoud's inspiration wasn't about to get one of those young men killed.

Vrooooom! The machine's engine roared at full throttle as it rapidly descended, gaining speed all the while. For all his cockiness, at least Demarais had been smart enough to take the machine to an elevation where he stood little danger of crashing to the ground at the end of the loop. He just had to execute the move. Gordon glanced at Plamondon for a second; the instructor was furious, but also afraid. The other instructors likely shared in his furor.

Turning his head back to the sky just as Demarais pulled up, Gordon held his breath. Up, up climbed the machine, until it was on its back and its pilot was hanging upside down in his cockpit. *So far, so good.* The Blériot had lost a significant airspeed, but as long as the pilot finished nosing it over to close the loop, he could regain the necessary speed and come in for his final landing and a likely ass-chewing.

It was too hard to tell exactly where Demarais screwed up, or at the precise moment when his port wing failed, but when the aeroplane entered into the second half of its loop, the entire port wing sheared clean off.

"My God, no!" Plamondon cried.

Gordon froze, his mouth agape and his eyes bulging. The wing gently fluttered away from the crippled machine—a feather, caught on a light breeze. The machine fell faster, spinning like the seed from a maple tree. Gordon had watched such seeds fall to the ground many times in his life, nature at work, but watching a disintegrating machine with a man inside it falling in such a manner was utterly horrific. To make it worse, when the Blériot was about halfway to its inevitable crash, Demarais jumped from his cockpit.

From a rational standpoint, the young man was dead either way. As panicked and afraid as he must have been, he had to know that. When the Blériot's second wing sheared off shortly after Demarais jumped, both man and machine fell at roughly the same speed. Gordon barely heard a tiny *thump* when the flailing pilot slammed into the ground more than two hundred yards from him. The aeroplane's crash was considerably louder. It fell not far from Demarais with a loud *CRUNCH*, and then burst into flames.

Gordon didn't know why he ran toward the site, but he did. He was the first to arrive at Demarais's mangled body. It wasn't necessary to check his pulse. He'd landed face-down, and his limbs, shattered on impact, had flopped into strangely contorted positions. His neck was visibly kinked to one side, and bent like a drainpipe. Gordon expected to see more blood, but the only crimson visible to him was a trickle coming from the dead man's left ear. *This is what grandstanding in an aeroplane gets you.*

He might have survived a low altitude crash in his flimsy aeroplane back home, but the brutal death he'd just seen made it abundantly clear—the better, faster and higher-flying the machine, the less likely surviving its crash became. The other students and instructors soon arrived around Demarais. Some of those who'd known him better were crying, while other trainees exchanged terrified expressions. Yount, who was supposed to go next, appeared ready to have a heart attack.

Plamondon, slowed by his leg, arrived last. "Gordon, go back to your bunk and I'll speak with you shortly," he said quietly, taking hold of Gordon's arm and gently pushing him away. "You don't want to be around for what is next."

"Yes sir," Gordon replied. He hadn't gone far when the shouting began. It was in French, but he heard plenty of curses, which were generally the first thing any young man learned in the course of picking up a new language. He also heard the words *Farman, Demarais and loop*, and figured Plamondon was making the point that if they'd rolled out the correct machine—the much clunkier Shorthorn—to begin with, then the dead pilot would never have tried to fly a loop in the first place. The argument continued until Gordon walked out of range.

He was still tired, but he didn't bother trying to lie down. Instead Gordon sat on the edge of his bed, waiting for Plamondon to arrive. In the back of his mind, he worried that the very reason the wrong machine had been rolled out was because he'd worked on the intended machine. *Will that really be the reaction to my hard work?* It was just speculation, but life experience dictated that his having such thoughts wasn't entirely misguided.

The door opened slowly, and sounded about as sad and somber as an opening door could. Plamondon shuffled into the barracks, his cane clacking against the floor as he hobbled toward Gordon's bunk in the far corner.

"Are you all right?" Plamondon asked.

"I'd feel a lot worse if he'd taken the Shorthorn instead, and that had come apart on him."

"Yes, nothing which happened was your fault. The other instructors said it was through simple miscommunication that Demarais took the Blériot. It wouldn't have mattered either way, had he not been such a damned fool."

"My dad taught me to be confident in your abilities, but modest when exhibiting them," Gordon said.

"It seems poor Demarais learned no such wisdom from his father. Instead he sowed the wind, and reaped the whirlwind. Now Monsieur Demarais will be forced to hear the same news many French fathers have heard of late." Plamondon stopped and thoughtfully stared at the floor. "Was his the first dead body you've ever seen?"

"I've been to funerals before," Gordon replied. "Then again I didn't watch any of those people die. He's definitely the first person I've seen killed right in front of me. I guess I am a bit shaken."

"Does this alter your opinion of flying?"

"Not in the slightest."

"I knew you'd say as much. I felt the same way after my crash."

"Your crash?"

"Yes. The fear could not have kept me out of the air, not the guilt either, but this..." he reached down and lifted his left pant leg, revealing a polished, wooden prosthesis from the knee down. "This clumsy thing has taken flying from me." He rapped against the prosthetic shin with his cane.

"Sir," Gordon said, staring at Plamondon's wooden leg while his mind turned elsewhere, to a different crippled man altogether. "Does your crash have anything to do with Sergent Bellamy?"

"You are very sharp, Gordon," Plamondon replied. "It does." He shuffled toward the next bunk and lowered himself to sit across from Gordon. "You see, he and I were friends when aviation started to catch on here in France. It was something for which we both developed a keen interest, so, with our both being in the military, and the concept of air reconnaissance gaining shape, we surmised it was what we should be doing. We trained together, as pilot and observer, and since we both wanted to fly the machines, we'd switch, performing each job equally."

He smiled after a pause and said, "We obtained our certifications on the same day. We'd both become fairly skilled pilots, Bellamy perhaps a bit more so than I, though I took to the mechanical side much better than he. One day, maybe two weeks after we read in the newspaper that Pégoud had looped the loop, I decided I was good enough to try stunt flying. After all, I'm five years older than Pégoud, and older *must* mean better and wiser. And so, in a Shorthorn of all things, and with my unsuspecting friend in tow, I tried. Not a loop of course, not in a Farman. Just a steep dive and zoom."

He stopped and frowned, rolling his eyes and shaking his head at the same time.

"The top planes buckled almost as soon as I pulled back the stick. Lucky for us, if you could call it luck, the lower planes did not completely fracture, and offered partial lift as the machine fell. When it crashed, I don't remember exactly our orientation, but something, probably the engine, tore both his and my left leg clean off, mine below the knee and his just above, and his right leg was shattered and mangled so badly it had to be removed as well. It was months before we left the hospital. So you see, Bellamy and I are cripples, because I was stupid and arrogant. The worst punishment of all is that he ended up even worse than I, yet he still found it inside himself to forgive me."

"So the letter..." Gordon said softly.

"I don't know where he came up with the idea that I owed him one solitary favor. So far as I see it, I owe him my life, and all the favors he might ever conceive to ask of me. Allowing you to train here was hardly a favor to Bellamy; his sending you here was more a favor to me than anything."

"I'm sorry you went through that, sir," Gordon said. To think that the man sitting across from him could have acted so carelessly was a surprise. The crash had only taken place around a year earlier. Disaster did have a way of profoundly changing a person, though.

"Be sorry for Bellamy," Plamondon said sadly, "not me. I was the fool, yet here I am, still able to walk, and to at least be around machines. My poor friend still wished to serve, but a desk is the only place he can be."

"So was it doubly hard for you to see Demarais crash?"

"In that I know firsthand how naivety and cockiness can lead to catastrophe? Yes. But with so many pupils watching, his death from sheer foolishness will serve as a supreme example of the discipline and self-control it takes to pilot an aeroplane. No one here will soon forget seeing the Blériot come apart as it fell."

"I certainly won't."

"That's good." Plamondon reached into his coat pocket and took out a small piece of paper, folded in two. "Today's events might not have gone as planned, but as I said earlier, I have something to give to you. This would have done you some good anyway, but after today's shock, it will undoubtedly do you better. Here." He reached out his hand, holding the paper between two fingers. "I think this may be of interest to you."

Gordon leaned forward and cautiously plucked the paper from his instructor's hand. When he unfolded it, all it said, in effeminate handwriting, was *Pau Castle, 8:00 p.m. Don't be late!*

"Do you know how to find the Château de Pau?" asked Plamondon.

"No, but, who..."

"Just minutes after you left the sheds this morning, a friendly American girl stopped me. She asked if I knew anything about a handsome colored boy training to be a pilot."

Amy!

"How did she know I'd been sent to Pau?" Gordon asked, overlooking the fact that Plamondon had no idea who Amy was. "When I met her, I didn't even know this was where I'd end up."

"So you *do* know her?"

"Yes."

Plamondon smiled. "She told me she made the rounds at the other flying schools, on the outside chance you might be at one of them. You should have seen her excitement when I told her you were here."

"Why didn't you come find me?"

"I told her I would, but she asked me to deliver the message to you instead. She then ran off in quite the rush. For her sake and mine, you had better be at the Château tonight. Do I need to force you, or will you go of your own volition?"

"She was very kind to me one night on the boat trip over here. I wouldn't dare insult her by not showing up."

"Very good. It is about time you left the grounds and socialized. The Château is more than a two mile walk from here. Would you prefer to go on foot?"

"I would."

Plamondon took a few minutes to explain to Gordon exactly the location of the Pau Castle. The directions were simple enough. It wasn't far from the train station, and if he managed to get lost, all he had to do was walk south until he reached the Gave de Pau, the river which flowed through the southern part of the city. Since the castle was visible from the riverbank he could, if necessary, simply travel along the river's northern bank until his destination came into view.

"Is there anything I might be able to do for you, Gordon?" Plamondon asked. It warmed Gordon to know that the man, who'd already done so much to help his cause, was even willing to offer help when it came to personal matters.

"No sir, but I sincerely appreciate the offer."

"Then my role here is finished. Enjoy yourself tonight, Gordon. We'll speak tomorrow."

"Yes sir. Thank you."

"Of course."

Gordon lingered at or near his bunk for the remainder of the afternoon. He alternated between pacing, sitting, or lying down, while contemplating what he might say to the girl he met only once and hadn't seen in close to a month. For a full hour, he lay on his back, mindlessly tossing his baseball toward the ceiling and catching it right before it hit him in the face. At about six o'clock, just after sunset, he put on the only decent article of clothing he brought with him to France—his grey suit. It was either that or any of the number of unwashed undershirts he rotated wearing beneath his coveralls.

As it ended up, he didn't need to walk to the river. Plamondon's directions were clear enough that Gordon made it to a location from which the castle served as its own beacon. Now that he knew what and where it was, he remembered seeing it from the train station on the day he arrived in the city. The castle rose considerably higher than most of the structures in Pau, and its mostly white stone construction reflected light from the streetlamps around it, highlighting its stone walls even at night. When he'd spotted it, it was almost impossible to get lost no matter what streets he followed to get there.

Drawing nearer, he grew just a little nervous. Amy had thought enough of him from their initial meeting that she actively sought him out, and that without even knowing he was in Pau to begin with. For her to go from training ground to training ground asking about him meant she wasn't just being nice on the ship, she was genuinely interested in him. If her interest was a romantic one, that made Gordon even more nervous. In America, such a relationship was all but unthinkable. In France, he wasn't sure.

Pau Castle was another of the many magnificent and historical structures in France. Because of its imposing beauty, when Gordon rounded the corner of the last street and the castle came into full view, he had to stop and stare, just to take it in. Translated to English, it was called Pau Castle, but normally when Gordon thought of castles he pictured drab, grey stone walls, crenelated towers with slits for windows, a heavy iron portcullis, a drawbridge, a moat—an utilitarian structure above anything else. What he saw in front of him, however, was not a castle, but a *palace*, a much more fitting translation of *Château*. The mostly white or off-white Château had towers with black, pyramid roofs, and large windows on every floor and every facade. The only justification for calling it a castle was its one crenelated rectangular defensive tower, constructed of reddish-brown brick and looking quite out of place, and the fact that the entire Château sat atop a small, steep hill, another defensive measure from a bygone era.

When he'd finished marveling in place, he continued to marvel while walking slowly toward the Château. So enraptured by the building was he, that he literally bumped square into Amy, who was also staring up at the incredible gothic architecture. Nearly bowling her over, and not realizing it was her that he'd run into, he apologized profusely, while her back was still turned.

"I am so sorry madam, please forgive me I—"

"Gordon?" She said, straightening upright. She turned to him, a smile across her lips. Amy was dressed in a knee-length violet coat, with a matching hat and a black scarf wrapped around her neck. Her red hair hung straight from beneath her hat. The bottom of the checkered dress she wore under the coat reached to her lower calf. Owing to cooler weather, her clothing was much heavier than what she'd worn the last time he saw her, but she looked quite handsome. She still had her little white parasol, which she rested against her shoulder.

"Amy! I'm sorry I bumped into you I was just—"

Without giving him a chance to finish, she leapt toward him and gave him a firm hug. It surprised him, but he hugged her back.

"I'm so happy to see you!" she said, squeezing her arms around him harder.

"It's nice to see you too. I see you've got your trusty parasol with you."

"You never know when it might rain," she said, releasing him from her clutches and stepping back. She raised the small umbrella to her shoulder and twirled it demonstratively.

"I can't believe you came looking for me," he said.

"Well when I found out there were so many flying schools here, I just had to check. So it looks like you didn't come all the way to France for nothin', right? Have you been in any of those aeroplanes I've seen buzzing around over the fields?"

"No…"

"And why not?"

"I'm not training to be a pilot. At least not yet."

Naturally, she continued to ask questions, so he filled her in on what took place since they parted. She expressed no small amount of anger at the notion that the students and but one of the instructors at the school were of no help.

"So you depart America in the hopes of leaving the bigotry behind, only to learn it's alive and well here? I applaud your resilience, Gordon. The miserable curs who mistreated you along the way would have long since given up were they in your shoes."

"Maybe. But I'll get my chance at piloting. I just need patience."

"That's the spirit," she said, taking hold of his arm.

They strolled around the Château together, arm in arm, discussing what they'd read of the war, what they thought of France itself and what they'd been doing to pass the time. Gordon's tales mostly involved aircraft engines and solitude, though his most recent experience, that of witnessing the death of Demarais, was an interesting but grim addendum to his month. Amy mostly talked of exploring the city—its sights, its restaurants, its people. She clearly had a much easier time getting along than he had.

"Have you been picking up the language at all?" she asked.

"Not as much as I thought I would. Plamondon speaks English very well, and I spend so much time working in the sheds that I'm just not around conversations enough to pick anything up. How about you?"

"I'm trying, but I fear I'm just no good at it. Which makes finding you all the more special. I've met a number of people who speak English, some well, but when I meet someone who can't speak a word of it, it makes me feel silly."

"Don't say that," Gordon said, resting his free hand on her forearm. "Another language isn't always easy to learn."

"Especially for an uncultured American girl like me."

"You don't give yourself enough credit."

"Maybe you give me too much."

"Possibly."

She gently elbowed him in the ribs and said, "You're supposed to keep complementing me, regardless of how many times I brush it off."

"There's no need to brush it off. When I complement you, I'm being sincere."

"Sincerity," Amy said, patting his arm. "A girl can appreciate that. I bet the girls back in Dayton sure did. Would it be forward of me to ask if you had someone special back home? That is to say, when your head wasn't buried in a book or an aeroplane engine."

Gordon made a mildly dismissive face, shrugged and said, "Not really."

"Did you ever make time for girls?"

"Once in a while. If I thought someone was worth it."

"Would you consider me worth it?"

"I was here by eight, wasn't I?"

Amy turned her head to look at him and smiled, then leaned her head against his shoulder for just a second. "Thank you, Gordon. Say, I know you're often busy," she said, "but we should do this again when next you have the free time. Is that something you're able to know ahead of schedule?"

"Things usually slow down during the weekend," Gordon replied.

"Well how about this," she said, stopping to talk. "Saturday night, you meet me here at seven o'clock. Maybe we can branch out and I'll show you more of Pau. How about it? Would you be interested in accompanying me?"

"As a matter of fact I would."

"Good, then it's settled. I'll see you Saturday night." She kissed him on the cheek and turned, striding gracefully away while twirling the parasol on her shoulder.

"Wait," Gordon said, "would you like me to walk you home?"

"That's very gentlemanly of you," she replied, still walking. "But I'll be fine. Good night, Gordon."

"Good night, Amy." He raised his hand to wave, but she'd already turned her back to him.

ARTHUR & PERCY

THWACK-THWACK-THWACK!

"1 Section listen up!" Corporal Abbey shouted over the machine gun chatter. "I know that bastard is pouring it on, but we must try and return fire!"

He and the men of 1 Section were hunkered in the trench, backs pressed against the front wall. They'd all quickly thrown on their full gear in anticipation of what might be coming. A German machine gun peppered the ground above them and decimated what remained of a house beyond the parados. Just ten days removed from the 2nd Battalion's taking of Radinghem, most of the village's houses, especially those on the eastern end, had been blown to bits by artillery and or shot so full of holes as to resemble giant wooden cheese graters. The trench line was established just beyond the last houses.

Arthur and Percy were pressed to the wall right beside the corporal. Both fought to remain calm. An icy, pelting rain had fallen since early that morning, and they were shivering cold. The sky was an even darker grey than usual. A grey storm of a different sort was blowing in from the east, one of grey bullets and shells fired by grey men. Percy flinched each time a bullet managed to find the angle and smack into the upper half of the trench's back wall. Arthur pulled his cap so hard against his head he stood a chance of popping right through its top.

The battalion, indeed the entire 6th Division, had repulsed attacks of varying size and endured daily artillery bombardments since establishing themselves on their present line. The York and Lancs and The Buffs held at Radinghem, and the division's line extended from there to Prémesques three miles to the northeast. The enemy's current push was of a particular severity, more intense than what the battalion had repulsed over the previous days.

CRUMP! A large shell landed just outside the trench, near the men of Second Platoon. Arthur's eyes were fixed in that direction when the shell hit, and he saw a tremendous fountain of brown earth surge upward and then collapse onto the men beneath it. So much dirt was ejected by the blast that it buried some men completely. Their mates leapt quickly into action, digging into the loose soil bare-handed in order to free them before they suffocated.

BOOM! The artillery blasts grew in frequency. The German attack intensified by the minute.

"Could someone please get a bloody rifle on that machine gun?!" Abbey yelled.

"You first!" Baker replied.

No one wanted to stick their head into the line of fire. The corporal clutched his rifle to his chest and stood on the firing step. Cautiously, he peeked out of the trench, just enough to see over the parapet. Within seconds of his doing so, the machine gunner spotted him and a burst spattered into the ground. The corporal yelped and ducked out of the way just in time. Two rounds smacked into the back wall on a line right through where his head had been.

"Are you hurt, sir?!" Percy yelled.

"They're close!" replied Abbey, ignoring him. "Maybe a hundred yards distant. They've concealment in a small hedgerow, but not much. When I count to three I need everyone to get your arses up, train your rifles on those bushes and open fire!"

The corporal was only nineteen, perhaps twenty, but his battlefield maturity was that of an older and more experienced soldier. He had a smooth, babyish but handsome face, darker hair, and though his jaw, when closed, sat straight, when he talked, it was through the left corner of his mouth. Officer-like in demeanor and appearance, he was one of but a few NCOs in G Company who refused to remove the wire stiffeners from his peaked cap. As Abbey stood just over five foot six, Arthur assumed the corporal kept his cap stiffened to retain a taller aesthetic.

"Is everyone ready?" asked the corporal.

Arthur clicked his safety catch off and took a breath. Some men nervously gestured the Sign of the Cross. He closed his eyes and thought of Elizabeth.

"One!"

Percy wrung his hands around the stock and fore grip of his weapon.

"Two!"

The two friends looked at one another, fear spread across their grimy faces.

"Three!"

The men of 1 Section swallowed their fear and leapt atop the firing step. In a life and death game where fractions of a second made all the difference, Arthur rapidly scanned the terrain ahead for the bushes. Lag or distractedness was deadly. He spotted the concealing feature immediately and, following Corporal Abbey, was the first rifleman to squeeze off a shot. The rest followed milliseconds later.

Arthur racked the bolt to shoot again as the German gunner returned fire. Private Lee, shot in the head by one of the first retaliatory bullets, fell backward and flopped onto the trench floor, splattering into the mud. He was the first 1 Section man to die since Private Green. Arthur and Baker briefly turned to see if they might help Lee, but the bullet hole in his forehead meant their attention belonged with the German gun.

Perpetually damp from near constant wet weather, the loosened soil flung into faces and eyes as German rounds smacked into it. The first time Arthur had faced machine gun fire was the scariest moment in his life. Chattering, zipping and cracking past him so close he could hardly fathom how he'd not been hit, his fear of the machine gun had not subsided. Only his fear of being labeled a coward kept his head, shoulders, hands and rifle out in the open and engaged.

The enemy gun ceased firing, either to reload or, Percy hoped, its gunner had been killed. Seconds later, though, the firing resumed, even as 1 Section's men stepped up their rate of fire to try and take advantage of the brief lull.

"*AHH!*" screamed Private Wilson. He fell in controlled fashion back into the trench. His rifle landed in the mud and he knelt down, clutching his right hand. "Fucking hell!" he groaned.

Percy, needing a reload, crouched to put two charger clips in his magazine and saw why Wilson dropped his rifle. A bullet had torn three fingers from his firing hand clean away, leaving just his thumb and little finger. Percy cringed.

"You got a Blighty one, there, Wilson!" Baker shouted, laughing amid the chaos.

Blighty was slang for England, adopted by British soldiers as a bastardization of the Hindustani word for *foreign*. Catching a Blighty one meant receiving a wound serious enough to warrant being invalided and sent home. The assigned meaning had little or nothing to do with the word from which it was derived, but it became widely popular amongst Tommies nonetheless.

"It's only a Blighty one if we don't die here first, you damned silly cunt!" Wilson yelped, stuffing his mangled hand beneath his left armpit. "I can't shoot!"

"Go find yourself some help!" Abbey yelled at him. "Ward! Get your arse back up here!"

Percy snapped his bolt back into place and stood. A bullet cracked past him so closely he thought it had taken his ear off, and he brought his hand up to check if it was still there. He'd nearly pissed his pants. Inches decided everything. Three to the left and he was dead. Two to the left, and Wilson wasn't running through the trench looking for a medic to bandage his hand—he was lying dead in the mud with a bullet through the eye. Two to the right, and Wilson was still shooting. Percy hoped the inches were on his and Arthur's side as the battle raged on.

KABOOM! A big shell landed within the confines of the house behind 1 Section's trench. When the shell detonated, the entire structure disintegrated in a cloud of black. The men dropped to their knees on the firing step, covering their heads and tightening their bodies to protect themselves from the exploded debris. Jagged board, shattered brick, tiny shards of glass and nails fell from the sky. A large, heavy chunk of something struck Arthur in the ribs. From the force, he assumed it was a brick. He grunted and nearly fell over, the wind knocked out of him. A kick to the ribs would have been pleasant in comparison.

The heavy stuff fell quickly; when only particulates remained in the air, Percy turned to Arthur. "Art, you all right?!" he yelled.

Clutching his side and groaning as he tried to breathe, Arthur croaked, "I'm okay."

CRUMP! The German guns were on the mark, and another heavy shell landed further down the trench line, a direct hit. Men, body parts and tattered gear hurtled into the air in a fountain of mud.

"Holy Christ!" Corporal Abbey exclaimed. His voice squeaked. "It's not looking good here, chaps! The infantry will be on us before long!"

The shell impact was the most destructive blast Arthur had yet seen. It dazed him. *That must have killed fifteen men at once.* Mortified by the devastation left in its wake, he almost forgot about his throbbing ribs and shortness of breath.

"Should we keep at the machine gun?" asked Private Lowsley.

"Who cares about the bloody machine gun?!" Baker cried, "These shells are going to blow us sky-high! If command doesn't call for an evacuation we're fucked!"

"We must hold until we hear otherwise, so let's get back up and do our duty!" Abbey shouted. To the last man, the section listened, and exchanged fire once again with the contemptible machine gun.

The volume of small arms fire increased as the German infantry prepared to launch a full assault. The Germans were laying Radinghem to waste, but the Tommies holding the village clung to it, holding the enemy advance at bay. Time, so easy a thing to measure during the normalcy of everyday life, was impossible to gauge in combat. It might have been as short as half an hour, or long as half a day, but at one point, while reloading, Arthur spotted Captain Otis and his adjutant crouched low and running through the trench toward his position. They stopped for a short time to speak to Second Lieutenant Fuller, who at that moment was standing near the men of 2 Section. After a short exchange, the captain and his adjutant ran past 1 Section toward the other platoons.

Fuller then moved from section to section, delivering whatever order had just been passed to him. When he reached 1 Section, his words caused panic.

"The whole division has been pushed back! The enemy has already taken—"

"*AH!*" Private Lowsley yelped, a strange, frightened and guttural staccato yelp, interrupting the lieutenant. He'd been standing between Lance-Corporal Herbertson and Private Deadman. Lowsley's yelp was so loud and abrupt that it startled Fuller. Like everyone else, Lowsley had stopped shooting to listen to what his platoon leader had to say. Unfortunately he didn't crouch low enough to do it safely. He fell from the firing step face-first and landed near Fuller's boots.

A bullet had caught the back of Lowsley's head at an odd angle, knocking his cap away and tearing a chunk from atop his skull. Arthur gawked; he couldn't quite see the man's brain, but he could see the wound plain as day. Where the scalp had ripped from the bone there were pinkish, blood-stained edges around the dark hole in Lowsley's cranium.

Fuller fell to his knees beside the gravely wounded man. Shockingly, Lowsley was still alive. The fingers of his right hand squeezed in and out of the mud. His right leg twitched.

"MEDIC!" the lieutenant roared. Because Lowsley's face was buried in the muck and turning him over might spill the brains out the back of his head, Fuller knelt beside him and lifted his head just a few inches. He then scooped the water and mud from beneath Lowsley's face to keep him from drowning.

A lone stretcher bearer made his way through the chaotic trench, dragging the back of his stretcher along the floor, leaving tracks in the mud behind him. "I can take him, sir!" the man yelled.

"Where's your other man?!" cried Fuller.

"Dead, sir! I'll need to borrow one of yours to get him out of here!"

"Private Hughes!" Fuller shouted, pointing to the fellow on Percy's left. "Help this man carry Lowsley!"

Hughes did not protest. He helped Fuller and the stretcher bearer slide the injured man onto the stretcher. The stretcher bearer then hurriedly placed a bandage over the hole in Lowsley's head. Hughes took hold of the handles at Lowsley's feet. The other man took the lead, and they picked up their charge and proceeded down the trench. Lowsley's arms dangled limply over the sides of the stretcher, and flopped with each step they took. The rest of 1 Section watched them move away. Arthur couldn't shake the image of exposed and broken skull.

FOOM! KARUMP! It was as if the most sinisterly-intentioned German artilleryman had aimed specifically at Hughes, Lowsley and the stretcher bearer. A big shell exploded; its epicenter—right where they stood. The whole trench shook. The *Earth* shook. Fuller and 1 Section's men flopped to their stomachs, and the three men, the stretcher, and the 3 Section boys near them vanished, vaporized, as the round cratered the floor and collapsed the walls around it.

"DAMMIT!" Fuller screamed at the top of his lungs. His shout was so loud his voice cracked and went raspy. He pushed himself out of the mud and onto his knees before standing. "Listen up!" He sounded as though there were sand in his throat. "We've held this shithole long enough! Captain Otis says the battalion is to fall back to positions west of the town! The RE have already begun preparations, now let's move!"

The 2nd York and Lancs and The Buffs evacuated Radinghem after defending it steadfastly, even as most of the 6th Division had already retreated. While essentially the entirety of Artois was low-lying country, even slight elevations in terrain were highly sought and fiercely contested. When the division ceded the Prémesques-Radinghem line to the Germans, they ceded precious elevation as well. Their retreat brought them to lower ground, and forced them to entrench positions even nearer to the water table. On an increasingly wet and cold battlefield, the situation was anything but ideal.

HENTSCH

"Good afternoon, Michael," Hentsch said as politely as he could bear to the young man, seated by himself at a mess hall table. The man had his back turned, but his head lifted and his ears perked up. Hentsch had his attention.

"Come to drag me back to the front before I'm ready?" snapped Michael, not bothering to look over his shoulder.

"No. We're patients here, same as you."

"We?" Michael turned to face the three men of 2 Gruppe, who stood shoulder to shoulder behind him. "You're not wounded," he remarked. "Did you three turn yellow and conjure something clever?"

Engel snarled and replied, "Listen here, you son of—"

"Engel," Hentsch said, stopping his friend. "We took ill. Nearly died."

Michael scanned them from head to toe. "You look it. Uniforms are baggier than last I saw you."

"It took its toll, to be sure," Hentsch admitted. He was surprised himself by how loose his uniform was when he put it on earlier that morning. There was no way he'd be able to gain back all the weight he lost before they sent him forward again.

"How are your hands?" asked Simon.

"Sutures should come out within the next week," Michael replied. He looked at his bandaged palms. "What did they end up doing with

505

that fuckhead Ackerman? Straight from court-martial to the mad-house?"

"Is that some sort of cruel joke?" Hentsch asked, appalled.

"No," Michael answered, raising an eyebrow and shrugging his shoulders. "You don't think he belongs in an asylum after what he did to me?"

"He's in the ground, you fucking lunatic," Engel snarled. "He killed himself."

"Bullshit..." Michael scoffed.

"You mean to tell us you honestly didn't hear?" Hentsch said. "Christ, it happened only minutes after they took you away. He cut his own throat."

"You're serious?" asked Michael.

"It wouldn't be a very funny joke, would it?"

"Depends on the audience."

"Jesus..." Simon mumbled, bringing his hand to his face and rubbing his eyes.

"All right, so he killed himself," Michael said, throwing his hands in the air. "You think that's my fault?"

"You were the only one who fucked with him!" Engel declared loudly. "Why couldn't you have just left him alone?"

"He didn't belong at the front anymore! You know it as well as I do!"

"So treating him like shit was your answer?" Hentsch asked.

Michael looked away. He shook his head. "Ackerman whispered to himself at night," he said, "really weird stuff. I heard him. He was dangerous. I thought if I could get him to break down, maybe get him crying in front of an officer, they might send his ass home."

"Even if that really is what you thought, Eberhardt, I can't imagine a worse, more roundabout and cruel way to go about it," Engel said. "You're every bit as cracked up in the head as Ackerman was."

"Is that so?"

"Yeah. It is."

"Which one of us cut his own throat?" Michael said. He stuck his tongue out the side of his mouth and ran his thumb across his neck. "Let me ask you this, Engel. Who would you rather have fighting alongside you? A chubby, whimpering pansy like Ackerman? Or someone who enjoys shooting Franzmenn and Brits as much as I do?"

"You're not supposed to enjoy it," Engel said. "I'd rather fight alongside men who serve the fatherland with pride, not men who relish doing the cruelest thing the fatherland asks of them."

Michael shrugged. "I don't care what you think anyway, but Ackerman would have lost it at one point or another. Be thankful it wasn't with an enemy offensive underway."

"I won't be thankful for any of it! You speak to the hypothetical while Ackerman rots in the ground, because you pushed him over the edge."

"You wouldn't bother to sympathize with me even if I was right," Michael said, and he eyeballed his hands again. "Even though I'm the one who the crazy bastard nearly killed." He held out his bandaged palms for them to see.

"Can we stop talking about Ackerman?" asked Simon. "What's done is done, regardless."

"Imagine that, something we can agree on," Michael smirked. "I've got something else we can discuss. How about these French bitches, walking around like they're saving the world, pretending they care about us?"

"You can't mean that..." Hentsch said glumly.

"Of course I can, and I do."

"Jesus, Eberhardt, they're here trying to help sick and hurt men," Engel said. "They helped us if you hadn't noticed." He sounded deflated by Michael's apparently unflinching cynicism.

"Yes...They're here to help," Michael jeered, looking toward a young nurse walking nearby. He followed her with his eyes while she moved away. "Help poison our food, pass along secrets and send more men to the grave."

"What secrets are kept here, you imbecile?" asked Simon.

Michael shrugged.

"They're volunteer nurses, not soldiers," Hentsch said, exasperated. "They treat men equally, irrespective of nationality."

"So they say."

"Do you truly believe these women are here with ill intentions?"

"They're French, aren't they?"

"That doesn't matter."

"What, have you grown sweet on one of them?"

"...No," Hentsch said, keeping a stern face, though he pictured Louise's smile. "But we've no reason to treat them with anything but respect and courtesy."

"I'll respect them as soon as one drops her skirt and sits down on my face. Then I'll believe they have my best interests at heart."

"God you're a fucking asshole," Simon muttered.

"Are you going to do something about it, Simon?" Michael asked. He sat taller and puffed out his chest.

"No, Eberhardt, I'm not," Simon replied, rolling his eyes. "You're so tough and courageous. I'd never dream of standing toe to toe with a statesman and warrior such as yourself. You're the pride of the fucking fatherland."

"Yeah, well, why don't the three of you just go to Hell and leave me alone?" Michael said. "I'd rather not have to deal with you until we're sent to the front and have no choice." He turned away from them and placed his elbows on the table.

"Suit yourself, Michael," Hentsch said, "if that's how you want it to be." He gestured to his two friends. "Let's go."

"Wait," Michael said as they walked away. He'd turned around again. "Are Kirsch and Nussbaum still alive?"

"They were hit by a French shell," Hentsch told him, trying not to picture it. "Killed Nussbaum and blew the hell out of Kirsch, but he was alive when they took him away."

"You think he came through here?"

"I didn't think of that until just now," Hentsch replied, wondering if perhaps Louise might know. He could use it as a convenient excuse to go and find her. "I suppose he could have, if he didn't die on the way."

"Oh well," Michael shrugged. "Had to happen one way or another, right?"

"Good thing you look at it so casually," Hentsch remarked, with angry sarcasm. "You only fought side by side with them for two months. Who knows how many of the bullets those two fired were ones that saved your ungrateful ass."

"What about the shots I took that saved theirs?"

"My guess is they would've had no problem thanking you if that were the case," Simon interjected, stealing the words from Hentsch's mouth.

"Too bad they can't," Michael said.

"Yes, too bad," Engel replied. "I'm sure you're devastated."

"Nussbaum was all right," Michael declared, matter-of-factly. "Never gave me any shit. Kirsch was a cocksucker, like you."

Engel laughed, probably to keep himself from going berserk. "You bark and bark, Michael, but barking dogs don't bite."

"Kirsch only ever gave you shit when you deserved it," Hentsch said.

"That's just your opinion," Michael replied. "Means nothing to me." He turned around and put his elbows back on the table. "This was nice," he said, copping serious attitude. "Let's chat again soon."

Engel snorted and clenched his fists.

Before anyone could say anything else, Hentsch put one hand on Engel's shoulder and the other on Simon's, and nudged them away. He had to find something, anything, to bandage the widening rift between Michael and his friends. He just didn't know how.

GORDON

He beat Amy to the Château the second time around. He paced back and forth on the street, anticipating her arrival. Over the days leading up to his looming dalliance with Amy, Gordon had grown increasingly self-conscious about his glaring lack of appropriate clothing, not to mention his empty wallet. Were it not for the meals served in the Blériot School's mess, he would have either starved or been forced to find a job in town, which would have drastically cut into his time in the sheds. He already was debatably the best mechanic at the school, but he took Plamondon's early words to heart—in order for him to progress toward the cockpit, he needed to be so far beyond his peers in knowledge and skill as to render them all but amateurs in comparison. To do that, he needed the proverbial wrench time. No side jobs.

Socializing was not a side job. At least *some* time allocated to it was permissible. Certain things were different now that Amy had inserted herself into the picture. Before, Gordon's lack of money and socially appropriate clothing hardly mattered. Now that he was hitting the town with a woman, one suit and no cash would not cut it. What if she wanted to go to a restaurant? How degrading would it be to have the other patrons' eyes on him as the pretty white girl paid for the colored boy's dinner?

Lucky for Gordon, Plamondon was on his side. During an earlier discussion in the hangar while they worked on a machine's rigging, Gordon let slip his concerns, not for sympathy, he was simply speaking his mind. Plamondon didn't say much about it then, but in the early afternoon of that Saturday, just a few hours before Gordon was to leave for the Château, the instructor stopped by the barracks to see him. To Gordon's astonishment, Plamondon arrived with one of his own suits draped over his arm.

Not only did the man hand over the brown suit and tell Gordon to keep it, he also slipped him thirty francs. If that wasn't already enough, Plamondon removed the hat from atop his head and dropped it onto Gordon's. The hat, a Homburg (a type of fedora), was a darker brown than the suit, and essentially brand new. It was stylish, and not a cheap thing for anyone to just be giving away. Gordon, so touched he could hardly muster a word, fought to prevent his emotions from overwhelming him.

"It looks good on you," was the only thing Plamondon said, grinning all the while. In a fatherly gesture, he reached forward and adjusted the hat on Gordon's head, and then slapped him on the shoulder.

His throat knotted, Gordon wanted to say thank you but knew if he did, the burning in his nose would have made the tears fall from his eyes. Instead, he did the only thing he could think of and gave Plamondon a hug. For his part, in what was obviously the first time a black man had ever wrapped a set of arms around him, Plamondon didn't recoil an inch. He patted Gordon on the back, the hug ran its course, and after wishing Gordon luck on his date, he departed the barracks as quickly as he'd entered. As Gordon watched the man leave, hobbling on his cane, an idea sparked in his head, an idea of different pieces and components coming together, an idea that would at least partially repay Plamondon for his kindness. At the conclusion of his date with Amy that night, Gordon planned to get to work on his idea right away.

"Nice hat," Amy said as she approached, "very handsome." She was dressed in a dark green tunic with a matching calf-length skirt, and her red hair was styled atop her head and pinned with a flower. The ever-present parasol twirled habitually on her shoulder.

"Thank you," Gordon replied, bringing a hand to the brim and tilting it downward. "You look very nice, too."

"I should hope so," she said, "it took my aunt close to two hours to style my hair this way. Doesn't seem worth it taking so long to look pretty."

"Well the end result is lovely."

"That's sweet of you to say." She crooked her arm and held it out, waiting for Gordon to take hold. Once he did, they put their backs to the Château and headed into the city.

"Where are we going?" Gordon asked.

"There's a small restaurant, a couple blocks from here."

"How do you know they serve—"

"Don't you worry about that."

They walked the rest of the way without speaking, their arm-in-arm stroll garnering only the occasional uncomfortable stare. When they reached the restaurant's front entrance, Gordon stopped just short of the front step. The restaurant's name, *Amitié*, was printed in gold and black on the front window, in attractive scroll. Gordon wondered what it meant, but he didn't ask.

"Are you sure I'll be able to eat here without causing a stir?"

"Just trust me," she said, and she pulled him toward the door. He opened it for her and stood to the side as she walked in. As he followed behind her into the entryway, he breathed a sigh of relief. The maître d' was a black man, dressed in a very nice suit. Both black and white patrons sat at the tables, and of the two members of the wait staff Gordon first glimpsed upon entering, one waiter was white and one was black.

The atmosphere inside was romantic. The décor was simple and mostly dark in color, the lighting dim, and the mood hushed and tranquil. Each table had a small candle for a centerpiece, which cast soft and gentle flickering light and shadows across the diners' relaxed faces.

"See?" Amy said gleefully. "Some restaurateurs are far more socially progressive than others. They're the ones who deserve our business. Plus, the food here is as good if not better than any of Pau's snootiest restaurants. What do you think?"

Gordon smiled. "I think it's great," he said, then in a softer voice he asked, "Do they speak English?"

"They do their best," she said, turning to the maître d' and smiling. "Deux, s'il vous plaît," she said, and she winked at Gordon. "If they have to."

The man nodded and guided them to a small table, one of only two that were not already occupied. No one gave Gordon and Amy an evil eye as they sat down. No one cared that they were there at all.

"What should I order?" Gordon asked her. "I don't know anything about French cuisine."

"Nothing?"

"I eat what they serve in the mess. I don't read about it."

"Too bad there wasn't a culinary aspect to flying machines, right Gordon?" Amy mocked. "You'd be a connoisseur."

"Could you recommend something?"

"How about I just order you the same thing that I get? It's nothing too exotic and I think you'll like it."

"I trust you."

"Good."

A waiter sidled up to their table and in a friendly tone asked, "Est-ce que vous voulez quelque chose à boire pour commencer?"

Gordon had no idea what had just been said. It was verbal scribbles. He turned to Amy, hoping she'd take the reins.

"Oui," she answered, nodding at the waiter. She turned to Gordon. "Would you like some wine?"

He shrugged.

"Deux pinot noir, s'il vous plaît," she said, holding up two fingers.

The waiter nodded. "Est-ce que vous voulez commander?"

"Cassoulet," she answered, holding up two fingers again.

"Très bon," the waiter said, taking a step back from the table. He turned on his heels and disappeared through the kitchen door.

"So…" Gordon said, embarrassed, after waiting for close to a minute. "Is cass-oo-lay the dish we'll be eating? Or have we yet to order?" While the ability to navigate a conversation in a foreign language might not have been the single strongest metric for measuring one's intelligence, he certainly felt like the dumbest person in the room at that moment.

"You've never even *heard* of cassoulet?" Amy asked, grinning. Gordon could tell she was eating up the fact that she knew more than he did.

"I can't say I have."

"It's delicious. They slow cook it for hours, so it's only available around dinner time. It shouldn't take long for the waiter to bring it out." She watched the kitchen door, as if she knew the precise second the meal would emerge. Timed almost perfectly, the waiter backed through the door, large tray in hand. He placed the wine glasses down on their table and then presented the cassoulet.

"Bon appétit," he said.

"Merci," Amy replied.

"Mercy," Gordon said, sounding very American. He didn't feel comfortable accentuating the limited selection of French words he knew. It felt disingenuous.

The waiter departed, and Gordon turned his attention to the glazed, truncated-conical earthenware bowl in front of him. Its contents smelled quite good, but he couldn't tell exactly what they were, since they were jumbled together in a stew-like mixture. "What am I about to eat?" he asked.

"Well there's duck, pork sausage and pork skin, white beans, some spices..." Amy replied, ticking them off on her fingers. "If you'd eat it instead of asking questions, you'll find all the answers you need inside the bowl."

He wasn't fickle. He picked up his spoon, dug it into the largest chunk of duck meat to cut it in half, and then scooped it, some broth, and some white beans into his mouth. The slow-cooked meat was so tender and juicy he barely had to chew. The beans had soaked in the flavor of both the duck and the spicier pork sausage. The aromatic broth was so tasty it could have been served on its own. Gordon let out a satisfied sigh through his nose and nodded his approval to Amy.

"I knew you'd like it!" she said happily. Her smile was so genuine and cute, and Gordon stared at her for a moment, astonished he'd had such good fortune in coming across someone like her.

They ate quietly, sipping from their wine glasses and shooting one another the occasional smile. Gordon didn't say it out loud, but as he glanced at the pretty redhead sitting across the table, the positive change in his fortunes since his arrival in France boggled his mind. Things might not have been perfect at the school, but most things rarely were. With Plamondon's unflinching help, the lack of recognition he'd been suffering was little more than a hiccup in the grand scheme of things.

"Gordon, what are you thinking about right now?"

"What?" He realized he'd wandered off. "Oh, I'm sorry. I was just thinking about a side project I'm going to begin working on soon."

"What is it?"

"I think it will make a friend of mine very happy."

"Is that all you're going to share?"

"It's for Plamondon. I've only just come up with a picture of it in my head," Gordon said, tapping himself on the temple with his finger. "I'd rather not discuss it aloud until I've actually begun putting it together."

"I suppose that's fair," Amy replied, "but I expect you to fill me in on the details later."

"I will."

They finished eating, and when the waiter presented the bill, Amy reached for it first. Gordon couldn't allow her to pay, so he reached for it as well, taking hold of her hand and gently guiding her fingers away. "Please, allow me," he said.

"Such a gentleman," she said, turning her palm over to wrap her fingers around his hand.

After paying and exiting the restaurant, the two went for a short walk, arm-in-arm. The temperature was crisp, and Amy nuzzled into Gordon while he escorted her through the streets. It had been a very fine night, but it was winding to a close. Gordon had to head north, to get back to the school, while Amy's relatives were somewhere on the city's eastern side. The two stopped walking at an intersection, not far from the Church of Saint-Jacques, a large and elaborate stone building no more than a third of a mile from Pau Castle.

"It's late," Gordon said, putting the church to his back so he could speak to Amy face-to-face. "I should be getting back to the barracks."

"You mean the sheds?" Amy corrected, seeing right through him. Bathed in the soft light of the streetlamp above her, with Pau Castle in the backdrop just over her shoulder, she was a vision, and Gordon was mesmerized. He barely heard what she said.

"Uh..."

"Yes, yes, I know you're anxious to start your next project. Don't stay up all night working on it."

She'd gotten to him just then, and not about working in the sheds—that was a given. No, she'd gotten to him another way. Judging from the gleefully sly look on her face, she knew it too.

"I'll try not to..." Gordon said dreamily. "Um...Would you like me to walk you home this time?"

"No, that's not necessary," Amy replied.

"All right, then I guess—"

"But I would like you to kiss me."

Gordon felt palpitations in his chest. "What?"

"You heard what I said," Amy stated in a stern but flirty voice. She stepped closer to him. "We've just had a delightful evening, the third such evening we've shared, and I think it's time you showed me you're as interested in me as I am in you. You are interested, right?"

"Yes, of course I am."

"Then show me."

His heart racing, Gordon looked around. A number of pedestrians were ambling about on either side of the street. Whether or not those pedestrians were paying attention mattered less to him than the simple fact that they were there.

"Gordon?"

"But all these people..." he said quietly. Where he came from, you just didn't do what she was asking him to do. Not in public. You didn't do it where she came from either.

515

"Oh, Gordon, again with the peanut gallery. Never mind…" Amy said, visibly frustrated by his hesitance. She softly poked him in the belly with her parasol. "It's not the same if I have to goad you into it. And here I could have sworn you came to France to do things you couldn't do back home. Good night."

"Good night…" he muttered, feeling the fool as she walked away.

VERNON

His hands and arms trembled as he plunged his entrenching tool into the mud with pathetic force. The cold, bland meal he'd just eaten had hardly served to energize his mind or his muscles. Vernon and the men of his ravaged battalion were dead men walking, with no end to their exhaustion in sight. Each time he strained to scoop the cold muck and heave it from the ditch, more slid in and took its place—a weak and feeble anti-Hercules, battling a muddy hydra.

Even when freezing cold rain wasn't falling from above, which it had with great frequency, the water seeped up from beneath the men's boots anyway, soaking and chilling their feet to the bone. The end of October had been cold, but the nighttime temperatures of early November were dipping below freezing, and the days weren't much better. Foggy, misty, chilly, everything stayed perpetually wet, even the air.

The day before the 1st Battalion's savaging at Violaines, developments further north during the Battle of the Yser were putting in motion events that would reshape and come to define the northern battlefront. In northern Flanders, the lowland region encompassing northwest Belgium and northern France, the tiny Belgian army held the front along the River Yser, from Nieuport on the coast, to Bixschoote just over ten miles inland. On October 21, in the face of a push from Duke Albrecht of Württemberg's German Fourth Army aiming to seize the last of the ports on the Belgian coast, the Belgians made a crucial decision. Heavily outnumbered, outgunned, and with their backs to the wall, it was decided that to prevent Albrecht's Fourth Army from capturing any more territory, a most drastic action should be taken.

And so, with limited other options, the Belgians chose to open the sluice gates and flood barriers which protected the low country of Flanders from being inundated by ocean water. Over the next few days, that action eventually flooded hundreds of square miles of land—from Nieuport to Dixmude—with saltwater, rendering further military operations impossible. German Fourth Army was forced to shift its attack to the south, ensuring that Nieuport stayed in allied hands. Although flooding their own countryside allowed the Belgians to stave off the German offensive, it brought dire consequences for the BEF and French units holding the line south of the flooded areas. It also served to protect the Germans' right flank.

Already pitched in fierce combat east of the Belgian city of Ypres, General Haig's I Corps was further east than any other allied force in Belgium. When Albrecht's Fourth Army shifted south, the French and Belgian troops south of Dixmude were forced back, creating a dangerous salient north, east and south of Ypres. Haig's troops fought tooth and nail to remain in control of the Ypres Salient, repulsing attack after attack even as the Germans threw more troops into the fray. Army Group Fabeck, commanded by General Max von Fabeck, and Army Group Linsingen, commanded by General Alexander von Linsingen, joined the German line in between Albrecht's Fourth Army and Rupprecht's Sixth Army. The arrival of those groups placed additional and considerable strain on the BEF.

After Violaines, Vernon and the 1st Battalion were briefly sent to Neuve-Chapelle, a small city three miles north of La Bassée, to strengthen the 14th Brigade, however little, in its defense against a German attack during the Battle of Armentières. On November 7, the 1st Battalion moved again, this time to the Ypres Salient and their current locale, south of the Menin Road. The Menin Road was the main road east out of Ypres, and thus was a crucial thoroughfare for supplying the front line troops holding the salient.

A November roll call of those members of the 1st Cheshire Battalion who landed in France in August would have broken the hearts of even the stoutest of Britons. Sadly for the BEF, 1st Battalion's story was all too common. Originally a thousand strong, they'd been bled away to just a few hundred, even after two infusions of reinforcements. Nearly every original officer had been lost, Captain Bannister being among the tiny sliver of exceptions.

Only whispers had circulated as to why, but no one in E Company could explain how the captain, with such a dearth of experienced officers, was continuously overlooked for promotion to battalion CO. Vernon had his suspicions that the wounded Lieutenant Hood must have somehow gotten the ear of some higher-ranking decision maker. If that were the case, Bannister might remain where he was no matter how many officers the battalion lost.

In their weakened state, the battalion was tasked with defending just 350 yards of front, and even that was a tall order. Even so, they held firm. Since arriving in the salient, they'd repulsed small, localized attacks, but despite the pressure the Germans exerted against the Ypres Salient on the whole, 1st Battalion's portion of the front remained comparatively quiet for the first few days. That was little consolation. The food was sparse and always served cold, and the environmental conditions were worse. Cold water and mud stayed pooled on the trench floors in perpetuity. Because of the constant wetness, Vernon had developed a throbbing in his toes that, at times, felt crippling.

Early in the morning of November 11, having endured a frosty night when his toes were particularly achy, Vernon unfolded his arms and gave up on the prospect of sleep. He looked at Pritchard, seated next to him. His friend was out cold, snoring lightly. Here and there, a few men sat awake, unable to rest even in their state of exhaustion. Corporal Spurling was up, smoking a cigarette and blowing the smoke into his clenched fists to warm them. His bony face was reflective, like he was deep in thought, or maybe that was just how men looked when they were worn thin. When he noticed Vernon looking at him, he silently raised the hand with the cigarette in it and solemnly nodded his head as if to say, "Who needs sleep anyway?"

Vernon nodded back. His senses were fuzzy, so he didn't register it as quickly as he should have, but a faint whistling noise was fast approaching, and exponentially growing in volume.

FOOM! A surge of adrenaline energized his exhausted body the instant his weary brain realized what was coming. *CRUMP!* The shell burst nearby, shaking the ground, launching mud, and jolting Pritchard and the other sleepers awake. Even in the relative quiet of the previous days, near ritualistic shelling by the Germans was commonplace. It had been ever since the BEF first entrenched along the River Aisne. Typically, the shells arrived heaviest at dawn and dusk, though the threat was constant. Due to severe shortages, the Royal Artillery was unable to respond to the German shelling in kind.

British artillery fire was reserved only for those moments when it was needed the most.

It wasn't something Vernon could truly get used to, no man could, but because of the consistency, of the knowledge and certainty that German shells would arrive, it became possible for most men to make the psychological adjustments which allowed them to remain functional under shellfire. No matter one's ability to cope, however, shelling strained the mind. Oftentimes, Vernon's strain manifested itself as anger. He'd curse the German gunners, grind his teeth, and clench his fists.

Everyone took shelling differently. Pritchard would clasp his hands behind his head and stare at the ground, flinching at every explosion. Spurling tried his best to stay completely calm, smoking a cigarette or cleaning his weapon as destruction sailed overhead. Saunders trembled, teeth chattering, while his equally frightened and wide-eyed friend Chilcott wrapped an arm around his shoulder and hugged him close. Granville and Milburn reacted much like Vernon. Swearing helped them blow off steam. It prevented the fear and anxiety from bottling up inside.

The first thing anyone did in the seconds trailing a shell burst was pick up his rifle, if he wasn't holding it already. Falling shells always left the prospect that an infantry attack might follow. Everyone had already grabbed their rifles, and the men of 3 Section checked to make sure those around them were okay.

"They starting in on us early this morning?" Pritchard asked Vernon, while he simultaneously checked his rifle's breech to make sure no mud had splashed onto it.

FOOM! CRUMP!

"Looks like it," Vernon replied, pulling his weapon to his chest.

FOOM! FOOM! FOOM!

Three rapid explosions quaked the terrain, sloughing layers of mud off of the trench walls and making the goopy floor even goopier. Up and down the line, a volume of shells much heavier than the typical dawn bombardment began to fall. Spurling, who'd played it cool at first, grabbed the cigarette dangling from his mouth and flung it into the mud. He leaned into the front wall, hunching his shoulders and crouching to make himself smaller.

"Keep your heads down, chaps!" the corporal shouted. He was only ten feet away, but Vernon barely heard him over the brain-rattling explosions. Every man in the trench hunkered down in a position similar to Spurling's, cowering helplessly as the shells continued to increase in volume.

"They're going to make a push on us today!" Spurling cried. "When this fire breaks, we'd better be ready for it!"

Vernon was both astounded and terrified by the strength of the German bombardment. The thundering explosions overlapped one another, a linked chain of deep, bellowing explosions. The most powerful thunderstorms paled in comparison. It was as if a long line of giants stood above the trench line, pounding furiously on enormous war drums. *BOOM-BOOM-BOOM-BOOM-BOOM!*

The trench hadn't collapsed around them yet, but with shells raining down as far as Vernon could see and hear in either direction, there was no doubt a lot of British men were dying. He and Pritchard were huddled close, and he kept an eye on his section mates too. Chilcott and Saunders had their arms wrapped around each other. Saunders was crying. Vernon didn't hold it against him.

There was nothing they could do but endure. Outlast the bombardment, and then defend against the German push. Just one question continuously ran through Vernon's mind as the shells fell. *How bloody long will this last?*

The bombardment's length was not measured in minutes, but hours. Somewhere behind the thick layer of cloud overhead, the sun had come up. The pale white light struggling to find its way through the overcast sky and rolling, stinking powder smoke was the only way Vernon could gauge that a significant amount of time had passed. Mists and fog drifted over the top of the trench and across the fields, serving to obscure much of the goings on in every direction.

CRUMP! A shell landed short of the trench, in front of the men of 1 Section about twenty yards away. No one was hurt by the explosion, but following the shell burst, almost twenty feet of the trench's front wall fractured and slid into the men cowering behind it. It didn't bury anyone alive; instead it knocked them against the back wall, partially burying many from the waist down, trapping them. So much earth had slid away that the men there were completely exposed. To compound the situation, the shellfire stopped almost immediately thereafter. The attack was coming.

"We've got to help them, Vernon!" Pritchard said, grabbing the back of Vernon's greatcoat. They'd been crouched for so long that Vernon's legs were numb. It was hard to move. When Pritchard tugged on his coat, Vernon stumbled, stubbing the toe of his boot and sending a searing pain through his foot and up his leg. It hurt him so much that he let out an uncharacteristic yelp. His face contorted. He held his breath. The throbbing persisted. *You can worry about how much this hurts later!*

He snatched his entrenching tool and limped toward the missing segment of trench wall. The collapse pinned every man from 1 Section and a few from 2, including platoon leader Second Lieutenant Fordham, who'd been standing behind them. Some managed to free themselves right away, but others needed help. The first rifle shots rang out from the British trenches, signaling that the German infantry was on the move.

"Hurry up over there!" Spurling screamed. He was already firing his weapon.

Vernon scraped the sodden earth away from the legs of a trapped man. Each man freed then scrambled to help the next. Fordham was buried deeper than most of the others, and Pritchard dug frantically to free the officer's legs from the heavy soil. Minus those affected by the collapse, the entirety of 1st Battalion's line was now popping away at the approaching Germans.

"We need everyone up here!" Spurling yelled.

The other men had all been freed. Only Fordham remained. Vernon and Pritchard shooed the others away, and then took hold of the young officer's arms to drag him from the muddy tomb. They groaned as they pulled, and Fordham groaned as he pulled against them.

"Get the lieutenant behind cover!" Spurling screamed, even louder than before. "NOW!"

Battling the throbbing in his foot, Vernon dug his boot into the ground and slung Fordham's arm over his shoulder. The lieutenant's legs emerged from the mud and he rose to his feet. The three of them wasted no time. As soon as Fordham was free, they turned to make for the intact trench.

Thwack-thwack! Two bullets struck Fordham when he turned. One hit him in the ribs, the other in the head. He grunted and fell. Reflexively, his hand shot forward and grabbed hold of Vernon's greatcoat, near the collar. Fordham's weight tugging downward and backward so close to his neck took Vernon's feet out from beneath him. He fell on his back.

Pritchard, on Fordham's heels when he was hit, tripped over the lieutenant's body and fell into the mud, sprawling onto his hands and knees. Vernon rolled over to assist Fordham, and got a good look at the officer's face before Pritchard had a chance to. The side of Fordham's skull above his left eye was torn up and collapsed. Stringy pink and grey bits of bloody brain dangled out. His eyes, opened wide but filled with mud, blinked rapidly and his tongue hung out. Blood poured from his nose and mouth as his heart beat its last beats.

Pritchard pushed himself up. "Come on, Lieutenant!" he said, before laying eyes on the grizzly sight.

"Leave him!" Vernon yelled, right before Pritchard turned.

"Oh, fuck!" Pritchard shouted angrily, "FUCK!" he screamed, at the top of his lungs. "I can't stand this shit anymore!" He snarled and reached into the hip pocket of his greatcoat while springing to his feet. From his pocket he tugged the Luger pistol he'd liberated from the German cavalryman after Mons. He ran up the slope of the collapsed trench wall, rapidly emptying the magazine at the oncoming enemy. *Bang-Bang-Bang-Bang!*

Christ Llewelyn what are you doing?!

"LEW! STOP!"

"You bloody fucking sons of bitches!" Pritchard yelled. He slid the empty magazine from the pistol and hurled it eastward.

Vernon scurried up the muddy slope on all fours to subdue his incensed friend, reaching him just as Pritchard snapped in a fresh magazine. German bullets cracked all around them. It was a miracle they both hadn't been shot by then. Vernon didn't lollygag and try to reason with Pritchard. Instead, remaining on his knees, he wrapped both arms around Pritchard's waist and tugged him back forcefully, twisting the trunk of his body at the same time. He overpowered Pritchard, tossing him backward at an angle, which sent him sprawling down the slope and closer to cover behind the undamaged trench wall.

Not about to let his friend get back up and try anything stupid, Vernon leapt like a frog, tackling Pritchard again before he had a chance to stand. He took hold of the thick lapels of Pritchard's greatcoat and shoved downward, pushing his back against the ground.

"Let me go, Vernon, goddamn you!"

"Llewelyn! They need our rifles on the line right now!"

"We had him! We just had to get him behind the wall!"

"We're both lucky we're not lying there with him! Now stop wasting your pistol rounds and save them for a time you might actually need them!"

"AHHH!" Pritchard screamed, slapping his hands into the mud in frustration. Vernon let him go, and they scrambled to rejoin 3 Section in defending the trench. Pritchard tucked his Luger back into his coat and they took up their rifles.

"Fordham's dead," Vernon informed Spurling as he leapt onto the firing step.

"I saw," the corporal replied, squeezing off a round. "Not a safe job, being an officer in this war."

Pow! Vernon fired his first shot. "It's no safer for a private!"

Corporal Mondy of 2 Section tumbled away from his firing position, shot in the upper chest. Without missing a beat, Spurling coolly retorted, "Nor a corporal!"

Accurate rifle fire from the Tommies holding the trench line drained any momentum the German attack had built up. In spite of the structural breach in Fourth Platoon's trench, the enemy troops were unable to reach and exploit it.

In the larger battle, the Royal Artillery made a strong, morale-boosting contribution by opening up deadly accurate fire on a group of Germans concentrating their numbers in a wooded area south and east of 1st Battalion's line. The British shells scattered the enemy and prevented the force from furthering any assault.

Elsewhere on the line, the Germans managed to capture portions of the British trenches, but those actions represented the last throes of the enemy's offensive momentum, and the British artillery was able to force the Germans to evacuate those areas a short time later.

Though the larger battle for the salient which had raged for the last week of October and the first eleven days of November was collectively called the Battle of Ypres, the actions on the 11th came to be known as the Battle of Nonne Bosschen. The battle earned the name because the last major action, which put an end to the German offensive, occurred when a German regiment, forced to retreat, took up positions in the Nonne Bosschen woods. The 2nd Oxfordshire Light Infantry pursued the Germans, forcing them from the wood and ending the battle.

With both sides sapped of momentum and strength, the only available option was stalemate along the entire Western Front.

VOGEL

There was no way around it; Vogel and Adler's first smashing success in bombing French supply lines was some sort of fluke. In the days and weeks since, they'd tried five more times to duplicate the results, failing in each instance. The weather had undoubtedly been bad, hampering or downright preventing flying more days out of the week than it allowed. Even on days when they could take the machine up, the brutal cold froze them solid and made snap timing and judgment close to impossible.

Their last bombing attempt was the worst of all. Vogel swooped the machine low over a supply convoy just south of Soissons, only to realize that one of the French wagons was equipped with a machine gun on a swivel mount. The French gunner peppered Vogel's Rumpler, severing a set of bracing wires on the port wing, tearing holes in the fuselage's fabric, and nearly snapping a wing strut in two. Adler later swore up and down that a bullet passed so close to his face that it scraped hair from his upper lip.

It was hard for Vogel to say whether or not fate intervened in such close calls, but of all the holes put in his aeroplane by that machine gun, it was a wonder not a single round impacted and disabled his engine, or worse, hit him or his observer. As it was, the machine was out of commission for a few days while Leon and the other mechanics patched the fabric and replaced the damaged bracing wires and wing strut.

In addition to the repairs, Leon had also added two accessories to the Rumpler. One was makeshift, which he designed and machined himself, and the other would become standard on many reconnaissance machines by the beginning of the next year. The makeshift accessory was a steel bomb rack, which Leon fitted to the Rumpler's underbelly, directly behind the undercarriage mounting. A maximum of four bombs could fit into the rack, released with the pull of a lever installed in Adler's cockpit.

The second accessory was a Görz photo plate camera, mounted low on the outside of Adler's cockpit, aft of the port wing. The first ever aerial reconnaissance photographs were taken three years before the onset of the Great War, but command was just beginning to understand the importance of piecing together a photographic mosaic of the enemy trenches. The technique had yet to be perfected, but Vogel and Adler were airborne anyway, Vogel trying to keep the machine perfectly straight and level, and Adler struggling to take proper exposures of the trenches below. He fumbled with each plate as he swapped them out. They were on their first such photographing sortie, and Vogel did not envy his observer's task. Adler had only learned to use the Görz camera the day before.

Vogel stared ahead, the biting cold of seven thousand feet elevation nipping at his cheeks. In front of him he watched Adler, hanging out of his cockpit to work the camera, suddenly lunge forward and nearly tumble from the aeroplane. An object fell from Adler's reach, vanishing into the air beneath the machine. He'd dropped one of the photo plates. Vogel stopped himself from chuckling when he saw Adler shout an emphatic obscenity and irately reach into his cockpit for another plate. Keeping the Rumpler steady in the wind shear was simple compared to what poor Adler was going through.

When the oberleutnant had gone through the last of the plates, Vogel turned the Rumpler north and began the gradual descent to the aerodrome. It didn't matter what type of clothing he wore up there, by the end of a flight lasting any appreciable amount of time, the cold in his fingers and toes was painful. Flying in harsh weather was an exercise in physical endurance as much as in piloting skills.

When the aerodrome came into view, Vogel was happy to see that no fog banks had rolled in to obscure it. The week before, another pilot was low on fuel and made a forced landing in heavy fog. He pancaked his machine, crushing the undercarriage, snapping the propeller and folding up the wings. The machine was a total loss. Though the pilot and his observer walked away physically unscathed, no doubt they were left with bruised egos. Fog was the bane of any pilot's existence, a hazard regardless of skill level.

Descended lower, Vogel spotted a gathering of personnel loitering on the edge of the field. They didn't appear to be up to much, just standing around. He brought the Rumpler in, landing smoothly, and taxied his machine past the group of loiterers. When he cut the engine and climbed from the cockpit, Adler started in on the complaining right away.

"Lousy damned camera," the oberleutnant snarled, "it would be so much easier to use film rather than swapping out these damned plates."

"I know sir," Vogel replied, "but like they told us, the plates have better resolution than film. From that far up, resolution is the most important thing."

"It's a pain in the ass," Adler mumbled.

"Yes sir."

Vogel hopped from the lower starboard wing to the ground, wincing when his frozen feet impacted, driving imaginary nails into his toes. He'd have to make it back to the cottage and hang his feet next to the fireplace before they warmed. Both he and Adler failed to see that the group of personnel had followed their machine and were now standing close by. When Vogel finally noticed them, he saw Hauptmann von Detten at the group's forefront. Adler stepped from the wing, cradling the photo plates under his arm.

"Vogel, Adler, I need to speak with you," Detten said.

"Yes sir," they replied, shuffling forward and standing at attention.

"The plates, sir," Adler said, holding them out, "I lost one."

"Fine, fine," Detten said. He took the plates from Adler and handed them to his adjutant, who then handed the hauptmann a sheet of paper. Vogel braced himself. He prayed internally that Detten holding a sheet of paper would not become established as a precedent for bad news. The commander held the sheet in front of him, eyeing Vogel and Adler one more time before beginning to read.

"For their actions dated fifteen October, in which they severely damaged an enemy supply convoy a half mile north of Villers-Cotterêts, Oberleutnant Heinrich Adler and Flieger Johann Vogel are hereby awarded the Iron Cross, 2nd Class." Detten glanced up, and smiled at their surprised faces. "Congratulations, gentlemen," he said.

"Thank you, sir," they said incredulously, chins raised.

The group of pilots, observers, mechanics and assorted ground personnel clapped enthusiastically. The EKIIs (Eisernes Kreuz 2. Klasse) were the first decorations of any kind awarded to their unit. Detten fished a yellow envelope from his coat pocket. He opened the flap and dropped the envelope's contents into his palm. It was their EKII medals. The hauptmann gave the empty envelope to his adjutant, and placed a medal in each of their hands.

The Iron Cross medal was the same shape as the symbol. It was made of iron, painted black, and edged with silver. Measuring one and three-quarters of an inch wide and tall, it had a crown embossed on its upper arm, a *W* (for Wilhelm) in its center, and *1914* on its lower arm. Attached to the top of the medal with a silver loop was the ribbon, black, with two thin white stripes near the outer edges. It was a very handsome little medal, weighty for its size, and Vogel was extremely proud when von Detten placed the object in his hand.

When Adler had first brought up the notion of winning a commendation, right after they'd landed that day, Vogel had dismissed it offhand. It made it that much sweeter, then, to arrive at the aerodrome and have an unexpected award presented before every man in the detachment. The hauptmann gave Vogel and Adler a firm handshake, they exchanged salutes, and he departed. The crowd clapped again.

Adler, beaming, nudged Vogel in the ribs with a light elbow. He dipped his chin in a proud nod of acknowledgement when they made eye contact. The crowd began to disperse, but Leon, revealed by the scattering personnel, stayed put. He was waiting to check the Rumpler.

"Congratulations, sirs," he said.

"Thank you, Leon," Vogel replied.

"Yes, thank you," Adler said.

"Did the repairs and modifications hold up?" Leon asked. "Did it throw her off balance or anything?"

"She flew just fine," Vogel assured him. "You wouldn't believe the cold up there, though."

"I can only imagine. It's cold enough down here."

"It's difficult to work the camera with frozen fingers," Adler complained.

A contemplative look spread across Leon's face. "There's a chance that Görz might redesign or modify the cameras if it becomes a widespread problem," he said, "but I don't know enough about cameras to tinker with it myself. I'd hate to break it while trying to learn more."

"Don't trouble yourself, Leon," Adler assured him. "I'll get used to it. I get the feeling we'll be doing photo reconnaissance more than just about anything else. Although I'm much more interested in trying out your bomb rack."

Leon had obvious concerns about that. "If you don't mind my saying, sir, I would very much appreciate if you were to perform a practice run with dummy bombs before you attempt to carry any live bombs over the lines."

"Do you not trust your own work?" asked Adler.

"I do, sir, and the releasing mechanism worked flawlessly while on the ground. I tested it over and over to make sure..." Leon paused, running a grimy hand across the back of his neck. "It's just that it hasn't been tested at altitude. It might seize up in even colder temperatures."

"Will it?" Vogel inquired.

"I don't think so, but that's exactly my point. I can't say for sure, and I don't want to make any guarantees at the expense of your safety."

"We'll test it, Leon, all right?" Adler assured him. "But not today. I'm going to head back to my quarters and write to my wife. You should do the same for your parents, Vogel. Write to Kunigunde as well. You're a decorated soldier now, a woman could not ask for anything more."

"That's not a bad idea," Vogel admitted.

"Of course it isn't." Adler then turned to Leon. "You know, the accolades might not have gone to you directly, but it's your work on our aeroplane that brings us home safely." He held out his medal and dropped it into Leon's hand. "I'm sure your wife and kids would appreciate knowing that."

"Yes sir," Leon said, admiring the medal for a moment before handing it back. "Perhaps I'll write home when I've finished inspecting the machine."

"Ever-diligent," Adler said, walking past him, bobbing the medal in his palm. "Good afternoon, gentlemen."

"Sir."

DENIS

"I fail to understand your refusing to let Sergent Chouinard volunteer," Denis argued, walking through the trench alongside Lieutenant Armistead. Their boots squished and slid on the sludgy floor, occasionally making them wobble to keep their balance while they weaved around the soldiers who remained in place.

"I refused him, because he is not right for the task," Armistead replied. "And the capitaine agrees with me."

"But he's a good soldier, and he's already voiced his willingness to participate."

"He's a fat ass," Armistead insisted. "Slow. Lumbering. He'd get your entire party killed or captured before you had a chance to accomplish anything."

"He's a large fellow, yes. It's not fair to call him slow."

"Fine. He is all of the things I said, apart from slow. He's still not going."

"But I barely know Sergent Veilleux, sir. Chouinard and I have fought in the same section since Charleroi."

"I know that, Roux, so have I, if you need reminding. But Chouinard has other responsibilities more suited to him. Besides, you and Sergent Veilleux share a commonality of which you may be unaware."

"What is it?"

"While you were on leave, a German shell landed atop one of his squads, killing every one of them along with his lieutenant, a good friend. Veilleux saw it happen from fifty feet away. Additionally, his brother-in-law was killed at Rossignol in August, leaving his sister a widow. His motivations in volunteering for a mission of this type run deep, just as yours do."

"That being the case, will he be able to keep himself under control?"

"Will you?"

Denis stopped walking and replied sternly, "I will, sir. I'm ready."

"I hope so," the lieutenant said.

"What of the others? What are their motivations?"

"Each has his own. You might consider discussing it with them rather than me, so as to learn more about one other."

"Yes sir."

"There's Veilleux." Armistead pointed to a man seated alone on the firing step a short distance away. "Better go and acquaint yourself with him. He is your second in command, after all."

"Sir," Denis answered, nodding in the affirmative. He approached the sergent cautiously, as the man was deeply absorbed in sliding a whetstone along the blade of a particularly nasty looking dagger.

"Good day, Sergent," Denis said.

Veilleux stopped sharpening his blade and slowly lifted his eyes. "Sir," he said quietly. He was older than Denis by at least ten years, and had grey hair in his bushy moustache and in the stubble on his face. His eyes, grey and distant, didn't look much different than those of the grizzled boche whom Denis killed in close quarters during the fighting on the Chemin des Dames. The hair on his head was also flecked with grey, and thin enough to see his greasy, dirt-smudged scalp beneath. It was another cold, gloomy day, but the sergent's greatcoat sat bundled atop the haversack next to him. Greatcoats were not to be worn on that night's mission, as they would only hamper movement and slow the wearer down. Speed and stealth were of the essence.

"That's quite the blade, Sergent," Denis said. "Is it standard issue?" His question was a sarcastic one. It only took a cursory glimpse to ascertain the dagger's custom design.

"No. Made it," the sergent confirmed. He picked the weapon up by the blade and held it out for Denis to examine. Taking hold of the handle, the grip of which was wrapped tightly in cord, Denis took stock of the dagger's features. The blade was about eight inches long, double-edged and razor-sharp. Built into the grip and serving two functions—one offensive and the other defensive—the finger guard resembled a set of brass knuckles, with a loop for each finger and a small knob above each knuckle. Even the dagger's pommel had been ground and polished to a conical point. Thrust downward, the pommel could puncture a skull and render the man on the receiving end dead or at the very least unconscious.

"Have you used this on anyone yet?" Denis asked.

"Yeah."

"Care to elaborate?"

"No."

"Have you met the rest of our party?"

"No."

"Nor have I," Denis said. "Why don't you join myself and Lieutenant Armistead and we'll go and acquaint ourselves?" He handed the dagger back to the sergent.

"Sir," Veilleux replied. He slid the dagger into a leather sheath on his waist belt and stood. They joined the lieutenant, and the three sought out the six additional men who would accompany Denis and the sergent on their mission.

The six weren't hard to spot. Whereas the trench's other occupants moved about with or remained close to their rifles, the six were busy familiarizing themselves with the assortment of hand-to-hand weapons they'd be working with later that night.

One man had cut and re-sharpened his *Rosalie*, making his bayonet less sword-like and more knife-like. Two were armed with black police batons, and were alternating between swinging the batons at invisible targets and slapping the blunt force weapons against their open palms. Another man had a set of brass knuckles on each hand, and was tapping his fists together, creating an ominous clinking sound. He stared at his fists and smirked, as if he was excited to hear the sound his fists might make against a boche's skull. That or he already knew what it sounded like, and was reminiscing about how much he liked it. Of the last two, one held a hunting knife, and the other grasped the handle of an entrenching tool. Swung like a club, the entrenching tool could easily cleave the soft flesh of the neck, or even split the skull. The weapons were deadly, but more importantly, they were quiet—at least as weapons went.

When the first man spotted Denis, Veilleux and Armistead approaching, he immediately jumped to attention and saluted. The other five followed suit.

"As you were, gentlemen," Armistead said, and the men relaxed. "I'd like you to meet Aspirant Roux and Sergent Veilleux. Roux, Veilleux, this is Hennequin," he pointed to the man with the modified *Rosalie* first.

Hennequin, like the other five, was under six feet tall. Unlike most common soldiers, he and the others had been issued dark blue cloth covers for their trousers, to match their tunics and help camouflage their movement in the dark. Rather than a kepi, he had a knit stocking cap pulled over his ears. The others did as well. Not all soldiers were lucky enough to have winter caps; in fact most didn't, not unless they'd been sent one by a friend or family member. Denis had been issued one as well, but he'd yet to put it on.

Hennequin was fairly young, but under the dirt smudges masking much of his face, it was hard to tell how young. The dirt made it clear he hadn't had a wash or shave for some time; a lack of facial hair beneath that dirt meant he rarely needed a shave anyway. His bright brown, lively eyes seemed to indicate the war had yet to affect Hennequin the way it had many other soldiers afflicted with the long stare.

"This is Barbot," the lieutenant said, pointing to one of the baton-wielders. Barbot raised the hand with the baton and lightly tapped his stocking-capped forehead with it. He was a bit older, maybe in his early thirties, and had a pencil-thin black moustache beneath his small, pointy nose. He had the long stare, like Sergent Veilleux, only Barbot's eyes were light blue.

"Delamare." He had the brass knuckles and a devilish gleam in his dark brown eyes. He was wiry, almost sickly so, with high cheekbones and creased cheeks, but he'd been selected for the mission so his look must have been deceiving.

"Guitton." His weapon of choice was the entrenching tool, and he looked strong enough to use it effectively. He had a thin moustache like Barbot's, a thick neck, and the broadest shoulders of any of the six. Guitton stared at Denis through dark, perpetually squinted eyes that didn't give anything about him away. With pursed lips, he nodded hello.

"Rose." The other baton-wielder. He was the tallest, but couldn't have stood more than a fraction over five foot ten. Long-faced both physically and in expression, his sunken cheeks and eyes, brown with heavy, corpse-like rings around them, epitomized the depression that was infiltrating the minds of more and more soldiers as the Great War dragged on. Denis hoped the sad-looking man moved faster and, if it came to it, fought more ferociously than the vibe he gave off. Again, he'd been selected, so he must have.

"Schwartz," the lieutenant said, pointing to the final man, the one with the hunting knife. He could stab and slash with it, of course, but his basic weapon had one distinct advantage over those brandished by the others. His was the only weapon truly suitable for throwing. Whether or not he knew how remained to be seen. Schwartz was a youngster, nineteen or twenty at the most. There was a sort of calm about him, and it shone through his hazel eyes and the neutral expression on his face.

"Good day to you gentlemen," Denis said, stepping forward. The six greeted him back, and then he shook hands with each. Veilleux did not move.

Armistead waited for the meet and greet to end, and then gestured for Denis and Veilleux to join the six. "If you two would join them," he said, "I'll outline your parameters while I've got you together."

The sergent took longer to join the group than did Denis.

The lieutenant cleared his throat. "Based on aerial reports obtained in the past week, there is a segment of enemy trench about half a mile east of here which is far closer to the ridgeline than much of the enemy's defensive works. Furthermore, the slope there is gradual, and not quite as high as elsewhere. That is where you will strike. Your orders are basic. Kill the sentries, capture or cripple any machine guns, take any and all documents or maps you may come across, and if you happen upon an officer, quietly subdue him if possible, and bring him back with you for questioning. Speed and silence will be your most effective weapons. No packs, no rifles, no heavy coats. Only Aspirant Roux will carry a sidearm, and will use it only in the most pressing of emergencies. The first shot you hear, you are to retire post-haste. Keep communication to a minimum. Use hand signals whenever possible. You've all volunteered for this duty, but you were selected because you can run, you're agile, and you're motivated. Remain focused, move quickly, protect the man beside you, and you'll come back fine."

"Sir?" Rose said, raising his hand.

"Yes?"

"If we're moving to another unit's trench, should we be worried about crossing back to our lines? Will the sentries there know we're coming?"

"Capitaine Bex has been in communication with the officers there. The sentries will be notified of your mission for hundreds of yards in either direction of your departure point. Furthermore, the sentries and other troops will be issued a password. If unsure of your identity, they will call out one-half of the password, and you must respond with the second half."

"What's the password?" Rose asked curiously.

"Crème Brûlée."

Denis and his six subordinates chuckled. Veilleux remained stony.

534

Armistead grinned as well. "Laugh if you must, gentlemen," he said, "just don't forget it. That password could save your life tonight. I suggest you try and get some rest before then. Best of luck to you."

The eight men saluted the lieutenant, and he turned on his heels and departed.

Though their mission would not begin until two o'clock in the morning, Denis could not find the calm inside himself to take a nap or eat his rations. Patrice's death had never left him, and he'd waited weeks to repay the Germans for taking his friend. He replayed that emotional October day over and over in his head. As far as Denis was concerned, every boche from that point forth was the one who pulled the trigger and killed Patrice. Their penance would be paid in blood until, through death, defeat or victory, Denis's war was over.

He spent most of the remainder of the day perfecting his chosen weapon. His sword was not suited for fighting within the confines of trench walls, so he found a replacement that was simple, yet incredibly brutal in its simplicity. A number of tools and implements had seen heavy use during the entrenching process, and some were bound to break. Denis obtained a pickaxe handle, the head of which had seen too much wear and tear and finally given way. The handle on its own was heavy enough to use as an effective club, but motivated by hatred, Denis sought to increase its brutality. To both add weight to the end and increase its killing power, he wrapped the top six inches of the handle with a length of barbed wire.

The temperature dropped well below freezing after sundown. When midnight came and went, it grew even colder. Every man minus Sergent Veilleux remained bundled in his greatcoat while waiting for zero-hour to arrive. Each breath they took rose into the air like a puff of cigarette smoke. Denis surveyed the faces around him. Their expressions were unreadable. A clever last-minute suggestion from Delamare that each man should blacken his face with ash had homogenized their look and rendered each man little more than a white-eyed shadow. The time had come. Their first trench raid was about to begin.

"Stifle your breathing as best you can, by exhaling into your collar or the crook of your elbow," Denis said, as each raider shook off his heavy coat and took hold of his weapon. They huddled around him. "We need to look for their sentries' breath," he continued, "so take care to prevent them from seeing yours. Keep an eye open for the lit ends of cigarettes. Some of our sentries smoke on duty, I'm sure theirs do too. If you're the one who comes across an enemy, strike at his head, mouth and neck to prevent your man from warning others nearby."

"And remember, Schwartz," Hennequin said, a glint of white from his smirking mouth emerging from underneath the black, "just because they're your cousins doesn't mean they're not the enemy."

The others snorted nervously. They weren't ready for jokes.

"Up yours, Hennequin," Schwartz snapped, "my family has lived in France for a hundred years. If I've got any boche relatives, I've never heard of them." He wasn't as calm as earlier, but why should he have been?

"All right, you two," Denis said, turning his attention back to the group. "Remember what the lieutenant said. Speed and silence. We've got two minutes at the most, and then we're out of there, understood?"

"Yes sir," the men responded.

"Then let's go."

Denis stood first, and slinked out of the trench on his belly. He crawled over the parapet and through a narrow path in the barbed wire barrier that had been cleared for him and his men after dusk. When he crossed that point, he'd entered into no man's land, the unoccupied gap between the opposing trenches. The term had been around for a long time, and described any contested area of land, meaning it belonged to no one. In the Great War, it had already begun to take on a second meaning. In that increasingly shell-pocked area of limbo, between the friendly and enemy trenches, any man caught out there in the open would not survive for long. Owned by cannons, machine guns and rifles, it was no man's land indeed.

The eight shadowy figures scurried on a generally northerly but meandrous course, going where concealment was best, Denis in front the entire way. The circular mounds of ejecta surrounding the largest shell holes provided good cover. Smaller shell holes could be climbed into if needed, though climbing in and out of them was noisier. With each transition toward the German trenches, Denis paused to survey the ground ahead for threats. Tension grew as the distance between the raiders and the protection of their friendly trenches lengthened. If they were spotted, it was a long run across mostly open ground, with what would likely be their squirrely countrymen waiting, with fingers on triggers, for their return. If just one man was unaware that the raiding party had been sent out, a mad dash return on the raiders' part could easily lead to friendly fire. It was one of the many scenarios which Denis played out in his mind.

There were less shell holes on the hill leading up to the enemy trench, making navigating the hill with stealth a dicey proposition. A thirty yard gap of almost undisturbed ground lay between the raiding party's last remaining cover and their next one—a large crater left by a shell from one of the big French guns. Denis beckoned his men to come so close to him that their faces were nearly pressed together.

"I'll get to the crater first," he whispered almost inaudibly, his voice quivering from both nerves and his being out of breath. "Once I get there and decide it's safe, I'll signal you to join me one at a time. Is that clear?"

Seven nods.

Crouched low to make himself small, he moved as silently as his boots allowed. Each footstep thudding against the frozen ground sounded to him much louder it actually was. *Clump-clump-clump-clump*, he might as well have been wearing full gear, he thought, with his canteen, mess tin and pack straps rattling and his greatcoat slowing him down. *Now I see why the lieutenant wouldn't let Chouinard volunteer.*

He made it to the crater, and lay against the dirt rim on his stomach to try and spot the enemy. He still could not see their line, nor could he spot any telltale signs of sentries. Rolling over on his back to signal the first man to join him, he did so one by one until all seven were with him again.

"I still can't see them," he whispered, "but I think it would be best if we belly-crawled from here. Watch me. If my hand comes up, you put your heads down and don't move."

A dark blue snake, with Denis as its head, slithered quietly up the hill and onto flat terrain. When the ground leveled out, the first fence posts which held up the enemy's barbed wire emerged from the darkness. The wire was a few rows deep, and would need to be cut.

Denis slowly rolled onto his back and lifted his head up high enough to see the men behind him. He held his right hand over his chest and held out his index and middle finger, opening and closing them together to mimic a pair of scissors. He was signaling to Barbot, who had a set of wire cutters tucked beneath his tunic. Barbot, third in line behind Denis and Sergent Veilleux, rolled onto his back, removed the cutters from his tunic, and slid his baton into his sleeve. He turned back onto his stomach and the snake began to slither again, even slower and more cautious than before.

When they reached the barbed wire, Barbot sidled up alongside Denis. The other six joined on either side of them, lying flat and still while Barbot got to work. Denis selected the first wire to be cut, grasping it with his hands a few inches apart. Barbot, lying on his side for extra leverage, placed the cutter's blades between Denis's hands. He flinched as he pressed the handles down, snipping the wire with a soft *click*. They all waited to see if the noise had alerted anyone to their presence. The first snip, at least, had not.

The cutting process went on for minutes. Each careful snip was accompanied by a flinch, then tensed nerves and increasingly heightened senses. Bit by bit, nail-biting cut by nail-biting cut, Barbot and Denis inched their way into a tiny channel in the boche wire. With only a few cuts remaining, a familiar sound and sight revved Denis's already sky-high heart rate up to hummingbird speed. A match strike. A flash. A boche sentry stood no more than twenty feet away. He'd just lit a cigarette.

The final cuts would have to be made right under the sentry's nose. If he didn't spot Denis and the other raiders, the unsuspecting boche would have to be taken out quickly and quietly. Denis didn't need to signal his men as to the German's presence, they'd all spotted the man and turned to stone as soon as his match lit up.

With his axe handle lying in the dirt next to him, Denis took hold of the barbed wire again. *Snip.* Flinch. Wait. The boche didn't move. Again, *snip*, flinch, wait. Nothing. One last cut remained, and though his pistol was a last resort, Denis could not refrain from rehearsing the rapid sequence—hand, holster, pistol, trigger, aim, shoot—in his mind. If the sentry heard them and raised his rifle, Denis would have had no choice but to draw his revolver to protect himself and his men.

Snip. The final wire was severed, and the enemy soldier, distractedly puffing his cigarette, failed to notice.

Hennequin was the first man to crawl through the gap behind Denis and Barbot. He had the modified bayonet, which made his weapon the quietest of the three. If he could reach the sentry undetected, he could slit the man's throat, preventing him from making a peep. Denis ground his teeth apprehensively as Hennequin inched toward the unsuspecting man. The adrenaline surged through his veins. *Come on; kill that son of a bitch.*

The strike happened in a flash. Hennequin sprung from his prone position and wrapped an arm around the German's head, driving his bayonet through the thickest part of the man's neck. He then twisted the blade and wrenched the man's head to the side, tearing the flesh so deeply that he cut the sentry's neck halfway through. From twenty feet away, Denis heard the fountain of blood splash to the ground. He turned to the rest of his men, and pointed his finger emphatically toward the trench line, signaling them to crawl through the cut wire, jump in the trench and commence their raid. Hennequin lowered the soon to be dead boche to the ground and slinked into the trench before everyone else.

Denis leapt in at the same time as Sergent Veilleux. Expecting to use his axe handle right away, he was surprised to find no enemies in his immediate vicinity. He took a few seconds to turn right and left in order to look for a target, and as he brought his attention back in the sergent's direction, he caught sight of a figure emerging from a small dugout in the trench's back wall. They didn't have dugouts in the French trenches, and so that was a surprise. Before Denis could react, Veilleux lunged at the German, pushing a forearm into his neck and pinning him against the wall. Brass-knuckle dagger in hand, he rapidly plunged it in and out of the man's belly.

Veilleux was a human sewing machine, stitching up the unfortunate boche's guts at industrial speed. What must have been fifteen or more blade thrusts later, he yanked his forearm away from the German's neck, swung the dagger at his throat, slicing it deep and, repeating the movement in the opposite direction, slugged the man right between the eyes with the heavy brass finger guard. Denis heard the *crunch* of fracturing skull, as bone shattered against brass fist. Killed three times over, the dead boche flopped to the ground.

Past the sergent, Rose had caught the only other boche outside the dugouts with a vicious baton strike. He was in the process of beating the unconscious man to death, while the others hastily sifted through the packs and other equipment that had been left outside. With no lamps or light sources, it was unwise for the raiders to venture into the unlit shelters. There was no way to tell how many sleeping Germans dwelled inside, even though the dugouts were where they might find any officers or important documents.

The clock was ticking, and they had to leave soon. It didn't appear they would find anything useful, but the three dead bodies would certainly be a mysterious surprise when their comrades found them in the morning or when the next sentry reported for duty. *The next sentry...when do they change shifts?*

"ACHTUNG! ACH—" *Aghh!* Another German, armed with a rifle and about to raise it to his shoulder, had come out of nowhere, and while a fast-acting Schwartz had successfully thrown his hunting knife into the soft flesh between the man's ear and jawbone, an alert had already escaped into the cold, calm darkness. Schwartz dashed toward the gagging German, who fell to his knees and flailed his arm in an uncoordinated fashion in an attempt to remove the blade from behind his jaw. Schwartz kicked him in the face to knock him down, stepped on the side of his head, and yanked the hunting knife free, before stomping his head to finish him off.

Denis drew his pistol. Their secret was out. "Go! Go! Go!" he whispered loudly to his men, waving for them to make an exit. In seconds, they were climbing over the parapet and dashing single-file through the gap in the barbed wire. Denis climbed out last. Looking back over his shoulder, he spotted the first of the alerted Germans emerge from a dugout holding a rifle. Firing twice, Denis shot the man dead and then dashed after his seven men. They sprinted toward the French trenches at breakneck speed, ignoring the hazards of crossing the pocked ground in the dark, in the hopes of gaining enough separation from the boche riflemen and machine gunners who would soon be firing at their backs.

Leaping over small holes and zigzagging around the larger ones, each obstacle materialized out of the darkness mere steps before requiring negotiation. The shooting gained considerable volume when Denis's party had covered almost half the distance across no man's land. Bullets, fired blindly in the moonless dark, zipped all around them as they neared the French trenches. Firing arms were at the raiders' backs, and drawn arms, alerted by the firing ones, were certainly waiting in front of them.

"Crème Brûlée! Crème Brûlée!" Rose shouted wildly as they neared the French lines. His voice bounced in concert with his strides. He wasn't messing around with exchanging password for password. "Crème fucking Brûlée don't shoot!" he screamed.

Grouped close together, Denis and his seven trench raiders leapt headlong over the row of tangled barbed wire in front of the French line. They weren't wasting time to stand in the open looking for the small path through which they'd departed. Crashing to the ground beyond the wire, they scrambled over the parapet and rolled over the front wall and onto the trench floor. A few of the soldiers in the trench checked to see if they were all right, which they were.

When they'd caught their breath and calmed down, they began exchanging looks. Slowly, a grin spread across each of their faces. Even the quiet and reserved Veilleux cracked a half-smile. Hennequin playfully shoved Rose, and in a mocking tone held up his hands and said, "Crème Brûlée! Crème Brûlée!"

The entire group laughed, and Schwartz let out an enthusiastic and cathartic whoop. They shook hands, slapped one another on the back, and eagerly discussed what had just taken place. Denis voiced his disappointment in not being able to use his axe handle, as did the others who'd not utilized their weapons.

Their first trench raid was not a resounding success, but one thing was certain. They were going to do it again.

ARTHUR & PERCY

Dearest Artie,

Thank you so very much for the letters. I've taken my time in writing back to prepare the gifts I've sent in the accompanying package. I hope you like them. I put much thought into the best possible way to keep you comfortable and functional. Christmas may still be a month away, but there was no good reason to make you wait. I was very proud when I read in one of your letters that your actions helped to save your company from attack. You're incredibly brave. I just hope you and Percy stay safe.

I'm sorry to hear the conditions there are so poor. Were I there with you, or more preferably, were you here with me, I would hold you so close that we'd forget the cold altogether. Alas, I must wait for my brave Artie to help win the war, so my knight may return home to me. Until then, I'll wait for more letters, and pray every day for your safe return.

Love, Elizabeth
p.s. I'm taking good care of your cap!

Conditions *were* bad on the line. They were deplorable. But as Arthur read Elizabeth's letter, the cold food, wet and frozen feet, the localized attacks and the daily shelling faded away—briefly. He read her words four times over before turning his attention to the package. It was wrapped in brown paper, and bundled tight with string. Rather than tearing into it, he carefully untied the knots in the string and placed the twine in his greatcoat pocket. He then unfolded the brown paper, exposing a cardboard box. When he opened the flaps on the box and removed the first item, his stomach fluttered with excitement and relief. Never in his life had he been more excited to receive an article of clothing as a gift.

He took the khaki serge wool sweater from the box and held it up to get a look at it. Pinned to the collar was a short note, which he plucked and read. *I did my best to match the yarn to the color of your cap. The sleeves are tapered at the wrist to keep out the cold.* Arthur folded the sweater and placed it in his lap. He'd put it on shortly; it would go a long way to shielding him from the perpetual cold.

A second layer of khaki serge wool was next in the box. It was a scarf, with another note. *Just in case your coat collar is not enough.* Beneath the scarf, a stocking cap of the same color and a third note. *I made the top from much finer yarn so it would fit beneath your service cap. The thicker ear band should sit just below.*

Arthur examined the stocking cap and was impressed by Elizabeth's attention to detail. He removed his floppy peaked cap and pulled the stocking cap onto his head. It was comfortable, but most importantly, for the first time since the winter weather began, his ears were covered without his having to clamp his hands over them. He placed his peaked cap atop his head, and the band slipped right over the winter hat, barely riding any higher than it normally did. It fit snugly against the thicker wool band around his ears. Elizabeth had painstakingly knitted the hat in such a way that it was perfectly tailor-suited to his head. She'd also reinforced the band with a layer of stitching so it wouldn't unfurl and cover his eyes in a combat situation. *She must have worked incredibly hard*, he thought, and he wished there was some near-term way to repay her.

The gifts he'd already taken from the box were incredible, and more than enough, but there was one last article at the bottom, and one last note. *I obviously didn't make these, but I did alter them a touch. Check the button loops on your sweater sleeves.* The final item in the box was a pair of fur-lined leather gloves, a costly and luxurious item. Elizabeth had sewn a button onto the top and bottom of the wrist of each glove. Arthur did as the note said. Sure enough, there were corresponding button slits on each sleeve, reinforced with thread. She'd also cut halfway through the gloves' fingertips, and then reinforced the cut edges, enabling them to convert to fingerless gloves in case he needed added dexterity. Each finger fastened closed with a small loop that fit snugly around a tiny button sewn into the underside of each finger.

Arthur slipped the absurdly comfortable gloves onto his hands, and was awed by Elizabeth's alterations. The miniature buttons on the fingers were barely noticeable, and her simple fastening loops were easy to secure. She hadn't overlooked a single detail.

Percy received a similar package from his mother, and was just about finished unpacking his. He'd gotten a comparable khaki serge sweater, stocking cap and scarf, but no gloves. "Where in the bloody hell are my gloves?" he asked, holding his box upside down and symbolically shaking it.

"I think Ellie must have saved her money to buy them for me," Arthur said. "Your mother must not have had enough to spare. These aren't cheap by any means."

"I don't see why you get them," Percy griped, "I'm her brother."

"I guess I'm just a smidge more special," Arthur teased, though he secretly felt a little bad. He opened his greatcoat and unbuttoned his tunic, shrugging them off his shoulders. The cold air nipped at him through his undershirt, and he hurriedly pulled his new sweater on over his head. It was soft and fit him well, and the sleeves were the perfect length, just short of where his tunic cuffs fell. When he'd thrown his tunic and greatcoat back on, he wrapped his neck in the scarf and shivered, as additional warmth began to radiate through his body.

Baker had been absorbed in a nearby card game with Deadman, Sutton, Wood and Corporal Abbey. When he saw Percy follow Arthur's lead and put on his sweater, he left the game and approached the two friends. "Better watch a Hun doesn't kill you chaps for your new accessories. Especially you, Crash. Those gloves are a prize."

The men of G Company had taken to calling Arthur "Crash" after hearing his story of jumping from the window to escape the German patrol. It wasn't the cleverest of nicknames, but they had gotten a pretty good laugh when he described to them the ungraceful way in which he'd landed upon squirming through the window. It wasn't funny to him, he'd nearly been shot, but at one point or another, so had everyone else.

"No Hun is taking these from me," Arthur said. He folded his arms to conceal the gloves and further bundle himself against the cold.

"Watch out a Tommy doesn't kill you for them, then," Baker joked.

"If I have to worry about that, then I seriously doubt our chances of winning the war," Arthur replied.

"I was kidding, of course," Baker said, suddenly turning serious. "But take my word. Keep 'em hidden when you're not wearing them, or I assure you some wily passerby will gladly liberate them. That goes for your scarves and stocking caps, too. Morality as it relates to personal property doesn't mean as much when we're out here killing one another. Stealing is barely a sin in comparison."

"I'll be careful with them," Arthur assured him.

"Me too," Percy said, "thanks, Baker."

Baker shrugged nonchalantly and returned to the card game.

"Would you take something from a dead body?" Percy asked when Baker had gone.

"I don't know. I guess if I really needed it. Better it not go to waste."

"Seems so callous…"

"More callous than killing him in the first place?"

"No I guess not," Percy said. "You know, we haven't talked much about that day, when you shot that Hun. What went through your head when you pulled the trigger?" The York and Lancs had seen their share of action, but Percy was unsure whether any bullets he'd fired had actually killed any Germans. Arthur, however, saw the man he killed for certain up close. He saw his face. Percy wanted a perspective on that feeling, and no one's perspective meant more to him than his best friend's.

"I…ah…" Arthur fumbled for words, unwilling to share how haunting that moment had been to him. An extra instant of hesitation and the dead German would have fired first. It woke him up almost every night since. "It's hard to say just—"

FOOM! Arthur and Percy flinched and covered their heads at the same time, as a solitary shell landed just yards beyond the parados and showered them with cold mud.

GOD DAMMIT! Arthur's subconscious screamed, and a familiar panicky chill ran up his spine, and tingled in the middle of his back. His heart rate skyrocketed. His hands trembled. To try and alleviate the tension welling within himself he forcefully pounded the side of his fist against the trench wall. It was a compulsion he could not stifle. "Shit! Shit! Shit!" he grunted, trying but failing to stay quiet. Pain radiated through his hand with each punch. He closed his eyes, concentrating on slowing his rapid breathing. *Come on, Arthur, keep it together!*

"Art, what's the matter?" Percy asked.

"Oh, nothing, I'm A-1," Arthur muttered, squeezing his fists to try and stop the trembling. The tingle in the middle of his back would not go away. "This is a ripping good time," he said, faking a pathetic smile. Hard as he tried to mask them, he knew Percy could still hear his quivery breaths.

"You'd tell me if you weren't, right?"

"Yeah," Arthur answered, letting out a long exhale. His diaphragm rattled beneath his lungs.

Percy gave him a concerned look, but didn't ask any more questions.

"Deadman, either stop sitting so close to me, or change your fucking name," Baker said, inching away from the private.

"What's that supposed to mean?" Deadman asked.

"What I mean is, that name of yours has got to be bad luck."

"I'm still here, aren't I?"

"Lowsley's not, and you were right by him when he was hit."

"Coincidence. Nothing more. Besides, 'what's in a name?'"

"I'll tell you exactly what's in your name, you knob. Dead. Man."

"Just bugger off and deal the bloody cards."

The men involved in the card game had already resumed their play, but Arthur couldn't calm down. He was sickened at how quickly they could collect themselves, and ashamed at how poorly he coped with shelling. He couldn't help it. His reaction was automatic.

It was a secret he'd kept since the division retreated from Radinghem—shelling scared the living shit out of him. It scared anyone with a pulse, but for Arthur it ran far deeper. Shelling had surpassed machine gun fire in the realm of living nightmares. Shells indiscriminately blew everything all to hell, and that was terrifying. Every time a bombardment started, no matter the intensity, he panicked. Near misses did him much worse. But he had to internalize the panic, swallow it down, and bury it before it revealed to his peers what he feared was his true nature. Under fire, he'd begun to lose his nerve. Only cowards lost their nerve under fire. No one could know. Not even Percy.

Arthur wiped away the flecks of mud which had landed on the paper, and held the letter from Elizabeth in his hands once again. He tried to imagine the added warmth from her gifts as representing her embrace. Nuzzling his back against the trench wall and bundling himself up, he read her words yet again, gradually calming himself to a manageable level. *I'll get used to the shelling,* he thought over and over. *I have to.*

HENTSCH

The ranking medical officer at the hospital had summoned Hentsch, Simon, Engel and Michael before him all at once. They knew why. Michael's sutures were out, and the three friends had gained back enough weight that their skinniness was no longer a danger, at least no more than it was to every other hungry serviceman wallowing at the front. The men of 2 Gruppe did not belong at the hospital for a second longer.

The last three days had been especially disconcerting for Hentsch. He worried they'd overstayed their welcome, even though their discharge was not up to them. The guilt of looking across the grounds at the main building, knowing that men were losing limbs, suffering, and dying made him fearful he might face disciplinary action for milking his illness. The thought ate at him, made him sweat. He did not need to look over his shoulder, but he felt like he had to.

Because of the guilt, he could not permit himself to cross the grounds to see Louise. Not in the context of his situation. Indulging in a personal relationship with a French civilian—a volunteer whose time was spent helping those who actually needed help—was beyond the pale. Maybe if he returned to the front and subsequently lost a limb, or by some magic the war ended sooner than later, or he was granted what had, due to his illness, become an unlikely leave pass, then he'd have less qualms in seeking her out and interacting with her socially.

There was, however, a reverse side to his quandary. What if Louise—sweet, kind, intelligent and beautiful Louise—was slighted by the fact that he'd not crossed the grounds to see her? She'd come and said hello here and there, but her time was precious. When they were finished speaking to the medical officer, Hentsch had to find her and say goodbye.

They stood shoulder to shoulder in front of the desk in the whitewashed office, waiting for the man seated behind it to address them. There were framed photographs on the walls—a mountain, a river, trees—generic images probably put there by the Frenchman whose office it once was. The decor stayed when he left. So did his framed medical degree, which hung on the wall behind the German officer. The French doctor must have left in a hurry. Hentsch didn't know if the degree was kept there ironically, or whether it remained out of respect for the man who might one day return.

"Four men, from not just the same kompagnie, but the same gruppe..." the officer said, leafing through a stack of pages. "Is this indicative of your leadership, Gefreiter Hentsch, or is it simply profound coincidence?"

"I know how it must look, sir, but the three of us did not choose to get sick, and we didn't ask to be brought here," Hentsch asserted. "As for Eberhardt, his wounds were the result of bizarre circumstance and very poor timing. Nothing more. If, however, disciplinary action should be necessary, I take full responsibility." He lifted his chin and straightened his posture, flattening his arms at his side. "Sir."

"No offense has been committed, Hentsch, so no cause for discipline exists," the officer said. "But as I'm sure you men already knew, you are being returned to duty forthwith."

"Yes sir. I've anticipated our heading south for several days now," Hentsch said.

"You will not be going south."

Hentsch looked at his two friends, concerned. They shared the same concern and it showed. Michael stared at the floor. He probably didn't care in the slightest where he ended up.

"Sir?" Hentsch said, confused.

"You have been reassigned to a new unit," the officer replied. "You'll be going north. To Belgium."

"Belgium?! Sir we're Mecklenburg Fusiliers! We've been within forty miles of Paris! How can we be sent all the way back to Belgium?"

"The fighting there has been heavy. Significant casualties. Turns out those damned British won't cede an inch without making a ruckus. A number of raw recruits have already been brought forward to replenish our northern forces. We need experienced men like you to fight with them. Hentsch, I'm sure you'll be a gruppe leader straight away." He then pointed a finger at the other men in the room. "You three may be expected to accept elevation to gruppe leader as well." He looked at Simon cockeyed. "Maybe not you. But that will all be sorted out upon your arrival."

"Sir, is there any way to override this order? To get us back to our regiment?" Hentsch asked. Like they had to that point in the conversation, the trio behind him stayed dumb and let him do the talking.

"I'm afraid not," the officer replied, shaking his head. "You'll go where your orders state." He stared at the papers in front of him for a moment. "XIX Korps is manning the line about halfway between Armentières and Ypres. You've been assigned to Infanterie-Regiment 139. They're with 47th Brigade, 24th Division."

"A Saxon regiment?"

"Correct."

"Will we be issued new insignia?"

"There is enough trouble getting necessary supplies to the lines," the officer said dismissively. "You can worry about pins and patches at a later time. Transportation by motor lorry has already been arranged for you. Gather your gear and report for departure. That is all."

"Yes sir," Hentsch said, hiding his disappointment. Arguing would have been useless.

On the way to the barracks, Hentsch stared at the windows of the main hospital building, namely those of the infirmary, to try and spot Louise. He had a narrow timeframe in which to find her and say his farewell, but it was too hard to see inside through the glare. He had a nagging tickle inside him; the kind where he wasn't sure time would permit him to do what he wanted to do. Regretting being unable to say goodbye was not something he wanted to bring with him to the trenches.

They reached the barracks and gathered their gear, strapping on their haversacks for the first time in a long time. Gear was always heavy, but Hentsch felt as though he'd just slung a full-grown man onto his back. *I hope I don't have to run for my life anytime soon.* He geared up faster than the others, in a hurry to make his way across the grounds to the infirmary. Jogging with the heavy pack was taxing, and his boot heels clunked and dragged on the barracks' wooden floor as he made his way to the door. He worried he might stumble if he pushed his pace when he got outside.

He didn't have to worry about stumbling. When he opened the door and stepped out, a smiling Louise was waiting for him. She still had her nurse's cap and outfit on, but it being cold and overcast she had a long, maroon coat on over her uniform. Her pretty little nose and cheeks were rosy from the November air's bite.

"I saw you staring at the infirmary windows," she said, "you looked like you had something to say to someone."

"I did," Hentsch admitted, "I do. We're leaving. Right now."

"I know," Louise said somberly, "a friend of mine removed Michael's sutures, and I figured your time would arrive any day now."

"Was he polite to her?"

"Of course not."

Hentsch sighed through his nose. "I was just about to come and say goodbye to you."

"I beat you to it."

"I'm glad. I was worried I might not be able to find you in time. You look very pretty."

Louise smiled. She might have blushed, but her cheeks were already pink. "That's nice of—"

Simon, Engel and Michael emerged from the barracks. When the door opened, Louise stopped speaking. The three men slowly and quietly positioned themselves behind Hentsch.

"I just wanted to thank you once more," Hentsch said, "for taking care of us. For taking care of all our wounded countrymen who've come through here. Your heart is the sort of which this world sorely lacks."

"Yes, thank you," Engel said.

"Thank you, Louise," Simon parroted.

Unsurprisingly, Michael stayed mum.

"You're all very welcome," Louise said, "I hope you can stay safe and go home to your families when this is over."

"We'll be going to an area contested by the British," Hentsch told her, "so it looks like your brother won't be killing me after all."

Louise scowled. "I don't want to hear anything about killing in your parting words, Augustus," she scolded. Even her scowl was lovely. She reached for his hand and wrapped both of hers around it. Even in the cold, warmth radiated from her grasp. "I don't want any of you to think about killing until you absolutely have to."

A loud voice in the distance shouted something, directed at the four men. It was the motor lorry driver, and he was growing impatient. Michael began to walk away and he mumbled, "I knew you were sweet on one of them, Hentsch, fucking prick."

"Stay safe, Michael," Louise said, and she watched him leave. She grinned when she saw the look of disgust on Hentsch's face after Michael did not acknowledge her.

"We have to go," Hentsch mumbled.

"Once more unto the breach..." said Louise. She patted his hand.

"You know that line is delivered by an Englishman, right?"

"They're just words, Augustus." She stood on the tips of her toes and kissed him softly on the cheek. He didn't expect that. She then quickly kissed Simon and Engel on their cheeks as well. "Promise me, all of you, that you'll be careful."

"We'll certainly try," Hentsch assured her. "Goodbye, Louise."

"Goodbye," she said.

The men began to walk away, but after a few steps Hentsch turned around and strode back to her. "Before I go," he said, "I must ask. If at some point in the future I'm given leave, or if this conflict somehow comes to a timely end, would you mind if I were to come back here to see you?"

Louise smiled, blue eyes sparkling, and reached into her coat pocket. "I wouldn't mind," she said, and she handed Hentsch a slip of paper. "This is the address of a nearby house where I and some of the nurses are staying. You can write to keep me updated, and that way I can let you know if my situation here changes."

Hentsch squeezed the paper and triumphantly held it up in front of him. "Hopefully we'll meet again then."

"Yes, hopefully," Louise said. "Maybe even in a time of peace."

He said goodbye for a second time, then trotted to catch up with Simon and Engel, who'd kept walking toward the motor lorry. It felt good to hear Louise call out a final goodbye to him as he traipsed away, even if he was moving toward a wholly uncertain future, one in which he stood a good chance of never seeing her again.

VERNON

In my days I've met a number of wicked men,
Who've made foul impressions on me.
But I've never met one more sinister,
Than Bannister of Company E.

He's cruel and he's loud and he's evil,
No doubt he's a miserable cunt.
We'd trade out our captain for anyone,
Including any Hun at the front.

When Bannister shouts, our bums pucker,
Even hard men, they straighten up quick.
You can't blame us for hating that fucker,
'Cos Bannister's one ornery prick.

I won't tell you the captain's the devil himself,
If he is, he's not confessed it to me,
But if Lucifer's switched with any son of a bitch,
It was Bannister of Company E.

Vernon put the final touches on his poem and tore the page from his journal. He tried to hand the page to Pritchard, who was unabashedly squatted over a tin pail, relieving himself.

"Wait 'til I've finished, yeah?" Pritchard said, straining. His face developed a reddish hue and he let out a grunt.

"Can't you find a dark corner somewhere to shit behind, Lew?"

"What difference does it make?" Pritchard replied crossly. "We've been living in shit, eating shit, and putting up with Fritz's shit every day since we got here. And no matter where I choose to drop my loaf into the bucket, I'll fling it out the trench and into no man's land regardless. And then, maybe a day from now, maybe two, when it rains knives and forks for the hundredth time, that shit and piss will trickle its way back in here so you and I can get a fresh layer on our boots. In fact, you're probably standing in the crap you took two or three days ago."

"Thank you for painting such an eloquent picture."

"The truth is rarely eloquent," Pritchard replied. "And ours most certainly is not." He dropped a small wad of toilet paper into the bucket and stood, fastening his trousers. Just as he said he would, he took hold of the waste bucket and flung its contents out of the trench and into no man's land. "Dinner's served, Fritz!" he hollered with an exaggerated German accent. Then something else grabbed his attention. "Hey look, tea time," he said, seamlessly shifting gears. The service troops were on their way through the trench, carrying the steaming pots of brew.

The battalion's quartermaster had managed to send forward hot or warm tea every day since the fighting stopped, behooving morale as greatly as any beverage could. Apart from sizzling hot bullets and shrapnel, the much more desirable tea was the only heat anyone had the distinct pleasure of experiencing. In the constant, biting cold, something like that helped a lot.

Vernon and Pritchard dug in their packs for their cups and accepted the precious tea when the quartermaster's men came to them. They cradled the warm chalices with both hands to warm their fingers, slowly and silently sipping the brew, enjoying every bitter gulp. Each time Vernon drank the quartermaster's tea, he imagined Sally drinking a cup of her own back in London. He chose to believe that somehow he and his wife were sharing a drink together over the distance which separated them.

"All right," Pritchard said. He took his last sip and set his empty cup next to him. "Let me see what it is you've been working on all morning."

Vernon handed him the poem and waited for his reaction. Pritchard read what couldn't have been more than a few lines, then cautiously looked down the trench in both directions before he continued reading. When he finished, he smiled and passed the paper back to Vernon. "Funny," he said, "just make sure it never finds its way into Bannister's hands. He'll blame me for writing it."

"I'll keep it tucked away."

The larger Battle of Ypres fizzled out over the days following the Battle of Nonne Bosschen, owing to dropping temperatures, snowfall, bitter frost, and pure troop fatigue. The engagements which collectively made up the month-long battle had resulted in somewhere between 125,000 and 162,000 total allied casualties, and almost 135,000 German casualties, including nearly 20,000 confirmed dead and more than 31,000 missing in action. The BEF, severely depleted even before the battle began, suffered 7,960 killed, 29,562 wounded and a further 17,873 missing in action, and possibly only avoided complete collapse when the Germans halted their offensive under Falkenhayn's orders. It was said afterward that the professional BEF died at Ypres, because from the start of the war in August to the end of First Ypres, close to 90 percent of the original Expeditionary Force became casualties, with 30 percent or more of those men being killed.

The fighting had slowed, but that didn't make life on the front lines any easier, safer or more comfortable. Food remained sparse, and all meals were delivered cold. Rain fell almost daily. When the ubiquitous water and mud weren't frozen stiff and jagged by frigid temperatures, they pooled ankle deep or higher on the trench floor and made staying dry impossible. The daily tea, and a three times per week rum ration were all Vernon or anyone else had to look forward to.

The rum, delivered from the quartermaster to the trench in gallon stoneware jugs, was doled out by the sergeants of each platoon and poured straight into the cups of the men, to be drank on the spot in order to prevent hoarding and drunkenness. For the men eagerly awaiting the next arrival of the glossy white jugs with a brown top marked SRD, the acronym SRD changed meanings from day to day and from company to company. The assigned acronym was generally humorous or vulgar, and very few knew what it really stood for, but it actually stood for Supply Reserve Depot, the supply base in England where it originated.

The Germans had recently brought forward a new type of artillery piece and were beginning to use it with some frequency, much to the chagrin of the Tommies manning the trenches. The *Minenwerfer* (mine thrower), was a low-velocity, short-range mortar capable of lobbing a 110 pound shell into the British trenches. Each round fired by a "Minnie," as the British came to call it, carried a larger explosive payload than a comparably sized shell fired by the longer range cannons and mortars. The larger payload was due to the mine thrower's low muzzle velocity, which allowed for thinner shell walls and thus more space for ordnance inside the casing. The infantry assaults may have largely ended, but the exhausted men still faced the constant threat of sniping, and of mauling or death at the hands of artillery salvos and the dastardly "Minnie".

"Hey did you two hear the news?" Corporal Spurling asked Vernon and Pritchard. He knelt into the mud in front of them. Whatever news he was about to present, it brought a smile to his gaunt and bony face.

"Nope, what is it?" Vernon inquired.

"We're being relieved," Spurling said. "Tonight."

"What?"

"Yep. Worcesters will take our place after sundown."

"Where did you hear that?"

"Word's been spreading all morning."

"Well I won't get my hopes up until we're on the road and moving west," Vernon said. "Gossip is for those with nothing better on their minds."

"I won't believe it until we're actually billeted," added Pritchard.

"Fine if you don't want your hopes *up*," Spurling said, "just keep your bloody heads *down* in the meantime. It'd be a shame to catch one in the bonce only hours before being relieved."

"Will do," Vernon replied.

At eight o'clock that night, under cover of darkness and blowing snow, 1st Battalion was indeed replaced by men from the Worcester Regiment. It was November 19. Following a cold and labored march, the battalion holed up for the next day in reserve dugouts prepared by the Royal Engineers. The Germans sent some shells their way, but as bombardments went, the intensity was unremarkable.

At one o'clock in the morning on the 21st, the battalion was on the march again. The temperature had remained below freezing for the entire day before, turning the roads into a transportation nightmare. Muddy wheel ruts turned into cement channels, breaking wagon wheels and tripping battered and weary feet. Instead of sinking into mud, ankles rolled on jagged, unmoving lumps of the frozen solid mess. The poor horses towing the wagons suffered as much as the battered troops, and the entire column progressed slowly in the miserable conditions.

Clunk! "AH! You damned dirty bugger," Vernon growled, stubbing his foot on a frozen outcropping. He nearly lost his balance. His feet had not stopped bothering him, not for a day, and the last time he'd removed his boots to have a look at them made him not want to do it again. He couldn't believe how bad they'd looked—pasty, wrinkled, even a bit blue—but worse than that was the sensitivity. It took what must have been close to half an hour just to get his boots off the last time, and his skin hurt so badly that when he tried to massage his feet and return some circulation to them, it pained him enough that his eyes welled over.

"You all right?" Pritchard asked.

"I'd give anything to rest my feet close to an open fire," Vernon replied in frustration.

"Just hold out for a few more hours. And watch your step from now on."

"I'm trying. One more misstep and I'm worried my toes just might come off."

"I think you can manage a bit longer."

At seven o'clock in the morning, the worn troops arrived at their billets in the tiny village of Locre, four miles back of the front lines and less than a mile from the French border. For the first time in months, they were given a chance to rest, and to do it while not under the threat of fire, or while struggling to find comfort in a muddy, watery ditch. Vernon and many others received treatment for the rheumatism which had plagued their feet in the trenches. Some had it worse than he did, far worse, and they endured excruciating and prolonged pain just to get their boots off.

One poor fellow from 4 Section, whom Vernon was seated close enough to see firsthand, screamed as a medic assisted him in removing his boots. When his feet were eventually freed, some of his skin sloughed clean off, exposing the reddish and bloody infected flesh beneath. The skin that remained resembled a raw fish filet—clammy, greyish-white, and dead. Vernon knew right away that it would have been a matter of weeks, if not months, before the man's feet properly healed. Conditions had given the 4 Section man a Blighty one, but it wasn't a very good one to get.

Vernon dealt with his share of discomfort, especially that first day, but the relief of dryness and warmth vastly outweighed the pain. Just to get out of the wet, cold, muddy trench, even for a day or two, was enough of a break for his feet to return to normal.

GORDON

Securing the adjustable leather straps around his upper shin and ankle, Gordon pushed down and locked into place the spring-loaded quick release handle on the outside of his left leg, just below his knee. The two-pronged, talon-like clamp on the outer side of his foot closed shut, securing itself around the rudder bar and holding it firmly against the sole of his shoe. It was an ingenious design—simple, elegant, and most importantly, it worked. He went to bed that night, very proud of his little invention, and even more excited to give it to Plamondon.

He kept the device wrapped in cloth on his way to the hangar so no one would see it. His plan was to hide the item until a time presented itself when he could deliver the gift to his friend. It was still early, so Gordon didn't expect to see anyone working inside the hangar just yet.

It surprised him then, when he walked into the building and a short, scrawny, well-dressed young man emerged from behind the Farman Shorthorn. The petite, almost boyishly small fellow seemed enraptured by the aeroplane, and didn't notice Gordon enter.

"Bonjour," Gordon said softly, not wanting to startle him.

"Oh, hello," the dark-haired young man answered. He turned around.

"Are you new here?" Gordon asked, slowly approaching.

"Yes."

"But you are a student?"

"Yes, my name is Georges Guynemer," he said, and he reached out his hand. "And you are?"

Gordon took hold of Georges Guynemer's hand. It was dainty and delicate, but as he told Guynemer his name and looked into the young man's dark eyes, a powerful confidence radiated from them, as if his undersized body was just a vessel that could barely contain the formidable soul it held within. The Frenchman had a nose that was a size too large for his face, and a scattering of dark hair above his upper lip that hardly qualified as a moustache. The dark hair atop his head was curly, much like a girl's.

"Where are you from, Georges?"

"Compiègne. You are an American, no?"

"Yes, I am."

"From New York City?"

"No, I'm from Dayton, Ohio."

"Oh-Hi-Oh," Guynemer smiled. "Is that an Injun word?"

"It is."

"Have you ever met an Injun?"

"No."

"Pity. Did you ever know any slaves?"

What?

"That was a bit before my time," Gordon laughed uneasily. "But there are some old-timers I know who lived through it. My great grandfather was born a slave and died free, though I never met him." He was more curious about Guynemer's present than his past and asked, "Will you be training as a pilot?"

"A mechanic..." Guynemer answered. "...for now. And you?"

"A mechanic is all they'll let me be," Gordon said. "For now."

"Yes..." Guynemer replied, looking away. He sounded disappointed, and looked it too. "Are you a skilled mechanic?"

"More than just about anyone here. Even some of the instructors."

"Interesting..." Guynemer squinted. He stared at Gordon. "Then perhaps later you would take time to teach me things. That is to say, in addition to what they teach during instruction."

"I'd be glad to, so long as you don't mind being associated with a Negro."

"Why should I be?" Guynemer said snappily. "If you know more than I, what would be the merit in ignoring the things I might learn from you?"

"Not everyone here would agree with your take on it."

"I don't make it a point to go along with what others say. Do you?"

"If I did," Gordon said, "I wouldn't be here."

"Nor would I. I must be going, but I look forward to speaking more with you soon. It was a pleasure to meet you, Gordon Graham."

"And you, Georges Guynemer."

The delicate young man with the commanding eyes nodded to Gordon, a sort of gentlemanly and sophisticated bow, not in line with the working-class mannerisms of the other mechanics. He strolled out of the building and vanished, leaving Gordon to ponder just who in the heck the guy was, so quick to ask a black man to teach him with no hesitation or pretense.

"I see you've met Monsieur Guynemer," Plamondon remarked upon entering the hangar a minute later.

"Yes, who is he exactly?"

"He comes from a wealthy family. The poor little fellow, in spite of his willingness to serve, was deemed unfit for military service on account of his frailty. His father had to pull strings just to get him here, in point of fact. He's been denied more than once, told he'd never make it as a soldier."

"But he just wanted a chance..."

"Yes, such a foreign concept, is it not?"

With a smirk, Gordon replied, "I can't imagine how *that* must feel."

"Indeed. What is that you've got under your arm there?" Plamondon asked. He pointed a finger at the bundle which Gordon had not gotten the chance to hide.

It was as good a time as any to present it. "This is a gift," Gordon said, "for all that you've done for me." He held out the cloth-wrapped device, which the instructor took with curious suspicion.

"I do not help you to get something in return."

"Of course, sir. But I had an idea, which I then had to make a reality. And this was what I came up with."

Plamondon unfurled the cloth, revealing the metal and leather brace. "And what, exactly, is it?" he asked.

"I used mostly scrap parts and machined the others," Gordon informed him excitedly, not really answering the question. "It's adjustable, too."

"But what does it do?"

"What? Oh, yes sorry I skipped that," Gordon said. He stepped forward to point out the features. "See, it will allow you to affix your prosthetic leg securely to the rudder bar and stay attached, so it can't slip from the bar during flight." He pointed to the clamp, the brace's most important feature. "The grasping claws open wide enough that they'll ride alongside your shoe while in the open position. You can walk around wearing it without them digging into the ground. And this locking handle," he tapped his finger on the upside-down, L-shaped lever at the top. It was connected to the clamp by a metal tube, through the center of which ran the clamp's mechanism. "This has a spring inside, which both closes and releases the claw simply by pushing the handle down and twisting, so you can quickly and easily detach your leg from the rudder bar if need be."

Plamondon's expression changed from one of confusion, to one seized by emotion. His forehead wrinkled, his eyebrows rose, and he pursed his lips as his eyes began to glisten. "Gordon, this is..." he paused a moment and pursed his lips further, obviously battling tears. "I cannot believe you took the time to design this."

"Do you like it?"

"It's beautiful."

"So you'll try and use it I hope?"

"I will have to build up to that, but I believe I will. Thank you, Gordon, from the bottom of my heart."

"You're welcome, sir."

Plamondon sniffled and cleared his throat, folding his arms over his present. "How have things been with your *petite amie*?"

"My what?"

"Your girlfriend."

"Well, I would certainly hesitate to call her my girlfriend. But since you asked, I haven't heard from her since our last date. I guess I sort of bungled the goodbye."

"How so?"

"She asked me to kiss her, and I kind of..." Gordon closed one eye and scratched the side of his head. "...shillyshallied."

"What in heaven's name does that mean?"

"I hesitated."

"As confident a young man as you are? Why?"

"There were people around us!"

"So what?"

"I guess some things from home just stay with you. I didn't want her to have to deal with any sort of ridicule or harassment."

"You presume there would have been. Do you know where she stays?"

Gordon shrugged. "No."

"Well then you had best hope she gets past your... shilly... shallying... and comes back here to forgive you."

"I know."

That evening, Gordon was working by himself in the machine shop, attempting to repair the salvaged, but severely damaged rotary engine from the crashed Blériot XI. The engine was written off as a total loss, but he viewed working on it as another skill building opportunity. With spare parts, patience, and time, he thought he might be able to get it back into proper working order. It would save the school money and maybe even impress some people. While struggling to remove a crushed cylinder case, and cursing to himself as he did, he heard a giggle behind him. It wasn't a man's giggle, and he glanced over his shoulder to see who exactly it was that found his struggles so amusing.

As he'd hoped, it was Amy. She had on the violet coat she wore that first night at the château, but no scarf or hat. Her parasol was folded closed, and she held it in her left hand.

"Well good evening, stranger," she said. "How long has it been?"

"Eleven days," Gordon replied, turning away from the engine and standing to stretch his sore back.

"And whose fault is that?" she said accusingly, crossing her arms.

"I didn't know how to find you..."

"I'm just teasing. I thought I'd make you sweat it out for a while since you rebuffed my request for a simple kiss."

"About that..." Gordon said. "It's not that I didn't want to..."

"Oh, don't worry about it," Amy said, waving her hand. "I didn't come here to pout or dissect that one moment; I came here to ask if you planned on celebrating Thanksgiving tomorrow."

"Now that you mention it, I hadn't."

"And why not?"

"I figured since we're in France, there was no point."

"No point for the French, maybe, but that doesn't mean you and I can't. So would you like to?"

"I can't think of any reason not to," Gordon said.

"Would you want think of one if there was?" she asked, giving him the eye, taking a step toward him.

"Of course not."

"Then just say yes." Another step closer.

"Yes," Gordon said softly. His heart fluttered. He thought about kissing her. It seemed like that might have been what she wanted.

"Good," she said, stepping to within inches. "Meet me at the same restaurant tomorrow at eight." She leaned forward, kissed him on the cheek, then pulled away and gently slapped the same cheek she'd just kissed. "And don't be late."

"I won't," Gordon said, admiring her decidedly unorthodox and straightforward manner. She really had the habit of not only making an exit, but also getting in the last word beforehand.

BERTHOLD

It was much more difficult, but far more entertaining to play fussball (soccer) in winter weather. It was still autumn, but in name only. Enough snow had fallen and enough ice had formed that the ground was slippery, and with the competitors bundled up in extra layers of clothing, playing with coordination was greatly hampered. The teams spent as much time laughing at one another as they did attempting to defend or score.

The men of 7th Batterie had taken to playing the game in their downtime after a crewman from Gun Number 4 received a ball in a package from home. They had a six team league, of sorts, though pride, and around payday, a few wagered marks, were the only prizes for the victors. The current game pitted Berthold and the crew of Gun Number 6 against the men from Gun 3.

Apart from having a proper ball with which to play, everything else pertaining to the game was glaringly makeshift. The field was uneven and small, the boundary lines drawn by boots dragged along the ground, and the goals, saplings that were chopped down and crudely nailed together—no nets. It didn't take regulation facilities to make the competition enjoyable.

Berthold received a pass from Lang after Roth, the goalkeeper, deflected a kick from the other team. Berthold dashed down the left sideline, fighting to maintain his balance as his boots slid over ice patches concealed by snow. He faked the ball left and sprung right, fooling a defender in front of him. All the while, his eyes remained focused on the rickety goal with the opposing keeper waiting between the posts.

Another fake. A spin. A minor slip. Past a second defender. Just one more to beat. A goal would give Gun Number 6 the win, and on top of that fifteen marks, split six ways. Eyes on the goal, feet controlling the ball, he brought back his leg for the winning kick.

OOMPH! A perfect blindside tackle knocked Berthold off his feet and the wind from his lungs. He'd focused too much on the goal, and too little on his periphery. He and his assailant fell to the ground, tackler on top, tackled on the bottom. Unable to muster anything more than a pained groan, Berthold meekly pushed away the man who'd just leveled him. As both teams surrounded the two downed players, hysterical laughter broke out when the men got a chance to hear the long, drawn out groans of agony as Berthold struggled to catch his breath.

"It's not funneeee," he moaned, involuntarily stretching out the last syllable to comedic length. It only made everyone laugh harder.

The addition of pushing, tripping and tackling to their game might have diminished its integrity, but for bored young men, itching for a fight they weren't getting, it was a good way to let out some of their pent-up aggression.

Mostly good news had been arriving from the south. Mackensen's Ninth Army made a push out of West Prussia on November 11, hitting the Russian army's right flank and forcing them back to Lodz, in Poland. Rennenkampf's Russian First Army was caught in a bad position near the River Vistula, which allowed Mackensen's army to nearly surround the newly constituted Russian Second Army at Lodz. In pushing for encirclement, the German XXV Reserve Korps and Manfred von Richthofen's Kavallerie Korps moved east and south of Lodz, placing them further into Russian-held territory than the rest of Mackensen's army.

The Russians were only able to survive the encirclement when, through a five-day forced march from November 17-22, Pavel Plehve's Russian Fifth Army moved north to assist in the defense of Lodz. An additional Russian force was also scrambled together near the city of Lovich, northeast of Lodz, and sent south to assist Second Army. The Russian maneuvers placed XXV Korps and Richthofen's Kavallerie in grave danger, facing them with encirclement of their own. Only after three days of savage fighting in frigid temperatures, lasting from November 22-25, were the two German forces able to battle their way northwest to escape defeat. Though the initial advance on Lodz ended with the retreat of two German korps, German Ninth

Army had firmly established itself on Polish soil, and was favorably poised for future operations.

Berthold recovered from the punishing tackle and the game went on for a short time, with the crew of Gun 3 scoring the final goal to take the match. His crew might have been out a few marks each, but he was just grateful none of his ribs were broken.

At dinnertime that night, his ribs were still tender. He rubbed them gently, while waiting for the service troops to bring around the food. The fare was standard but good—a small portion of meat, some boiled carrots and potatoes, and a slice of bread. More importantly than what the meal entailed, though, was that it was delivered warm. With their roles resembling that of a reserve army, but not being billeted like reserve troops, comforts remained at a minimum. They manned what was technically a front, just an inactive one, though the guns were further back than the infantry. Hot meals made the humdrum job easier.

Berthold finished eating, and rested his mess tin at his feet to rub his ribs again. Not one to miss an opportunity, Lang sidled up beside him, jabbing an elbow into his sore flank to ask, "Hey Kastner, how do you feel?"

Grunting and wincing, Berthold shoved Lang's arm away from him and answered, "I'm fine. Thanks for caring, you shithead."

"Say, have you gotten any letters lately from that girl of yours? Paula?"

"Pauline."

"Who cares?"

"Just one..." Berthold paused. "...and not a particularly enthusiastic one, either."

"Tough break."

"I'm more worried about the exchanges I've had with my mother. I know she's keeping something from me."

"Have you asked her about it straightaway?"

"I have. I've asked in letters to my sister, too."

"And?"

"Nothing. My sister hasn't written to me at all in fact, not in my mother's letters, let alone one of her own. I don't think I'll find out what's going on...unless..." Berthold trailed off, as he noticed Wachtmeister Trommler and his batman (a servant, more or less) approaching.

"Attention, gentlemen, I have an announcement to make," Trommler declared. The chattering of the crewmen halted; utensils clinked against mess tins as everyone stopped eating in order to listen. "As you all know, Eighth Army's numbers were reduced significantly to strengthen our forces in the south. As such, though we remain at a standstill, to this point command has considered it unwise to offer leave passes, another fact of which I am sure you men are painfully aware. However..." He surveyed all the attentive faces, and one corner of his mouth turned up. Berthold was close enough to see it; good news was coming.

"Starting tomorrow, and continuing for roughly the next three weeks, we will grant each crewman a three-day pass, to be used one man at a time, in a pre-decided order." Trommler paused again briefly, to let the news sink in.

The men traded excited glances, pats on the back, and copious other friendly celebrations. Lang, of course, elbowed Berthold's ribs again. It hurt, but it couldn't diminish the excitement.

"I guess you can ask your mother in person, now, yeah?" Lang said.

"All right, all right, quiet down," the wachtmeister said, waving his hands like a conductor. "Now, to make this as fair as possible, the leave periods will end before Christmas. This way, you will all be back before then, and neither I nor any other commanders will have to deal with any gripes." He held out his hand, and signaled for his batman to hand him a sheet of paper, which the man then did.

"These are the first six men who will be granted a pass," Trommler said. "If your name is called, I urge you to prepare for departure tonight, in order to be ready first thing tomorrow morning." He cleared his throat before announcing the first name. "Dietrich, please come and get your pass."

The crew of Gun 1 hurrahed for their breech man as he jumped to his feet and accepted the telegram-sized pass from Trommler.

Dietrich sat back down, and the wachtmeister read the second name. "Schubert."

It was Gun 2's turn to celebrate.

Berthold's stomach rose as his commander read two more names. Everyone would get a pass eventually, but he wanted his first. He needed to get home.

"Jung."

More hurrahs.

Only Gun Number 6 remained. Would he be on his way to Rastenburg tomorrow, or would anticipation continue to jumble his guts for as little as a few more days or possibly as long as two-plus weeks?

"Kastner."

"Yeah!" Berthold yelped, throwing a celebratory and retaliatory elbow into Lang's ribs. He sprung to his feet, shoving Lang hard to boost himself from his seated position. Prancing gaily in front of Trommler to accept his pass, Berthold incurred the laughter of all those present. He barely heard them; his mind was already fixated on packing his things.

Managing only two or three hours of sleep that night from anxiety, he nevertheless woke up the next morning energized. He gathered his equipment, which he'd left in a neat pile, and said a short good-bye to his crewmates while they ate their breakfasts.

To get to Rastenburg, he hitched a ride on a motor lorry bound for Gumbinnen, the main supply junction for Eighth Army. Even in stagnation, an army's rear areas were a constant flurry of activity, especially the roads and rail lines. The trains had to deliver ton after ton of food, supplies, and equipment to the supply depots, which then had to deliver those items by cart, wagon and lorry to the front. From Gumbinnen, Berthold took a train west to Insterburg, and then boarded another train that took him the forty miles southwest to Rastenburg. He caught up on his sleep on the longer train ride, which went by without a hitch.

He thought about telephoning his mother from the train station to let her know he was coming home. Ultimately, he decided against it, his thought being that her opening the door to find him standing there might be a better surprise. The city had seen its share of activity during the Battle of the Masurian Lakes, and some signs of that activity still remained two months after the fact, mostly in the form of light damage to buildings on the city outskirts. With the Russians pushed out of East Prussia, though, Rastenburg had returned to normal.

It might have been intuition, or he may have just remembered it that way afterward, but as he walked down the street toward the Kastner home, he could have sworn a pall hung over the house, as if the structure itself conveyed the mood of whoever lived inside. To get such a feeling from his childhood home was decidedly strange— the Kastners were a strong, loving family. As a career military man, and an officer at that, his father Mathias provided them with a comfortable lifestyle. He had an affectionate demeanor, if only a little on the stern side, and oversaw what was a mostly happy family, in a mostly happy home. Whatever it was that now loomed over the two story half-timber and white plaster house, it wasn't happy.

Berthold knocked on the front door, anxious to see his mother's reaction. When the door opened inward and a tired, unkempt mess of a woman peered out from behind, he almost couldn't believe she was his mother. Frieda Kastner was only thirty-nine, but she looked like she'd aged fifteen years since he'd last seen her. Her long, blonde hair, which she had brushed straight and smooth every single day since Berthold could remember, was frizzy, tangled, and even grey in spots. Her eyes, once strong, blue-green and stern, just like her husband's, were weary, bloodshot and baggy. She looked like she hadn't eaten in days, and bathed in many more.

"Mother?" Berthold said, a catch in his throat. He spoke in an interrogative manner, almost subconsciously, unable to reconcile his many memories of her with the form standing in the doorway.

"My dear boy..." she said quietly. Then she fainted.

"Ma!" he cried, lunging forward to try and catch her. She collapsed before he got to her, and thudded against the wooden floor, banging her head. Berthold flung off his equipment, left it next to the door, picked her up by the armpits and dragged her to the living room. He lay her down on the sofa.

"Yvonne!" he shouted, calling out to his sister. "Yvonne get down here! Mother needs help! Yvonne!"

The house was eerily quiet; his voice sounded much louder than he expected. His sister wasn't there. A thin blanket of snow lay on the ground outside, so Berthold hastily found a cloth towel in the kitchen and took it to the front yard, bundled up a handful of snow and placed it on his mother's forehead. He sat beside her, resting the cold cloth on her head, urging her to wake up every few minutes.

When she came to, groggy and confused, it took her a moment to realize that it was her son sitting there with her.

"Good afternoon, mother. You bumped your head."

"Berthold..." she said, reaching up to touch his face. Her hand was bony. "How is it that you're here?" she asked.

"They gave me three days' leave. Where is Yvonne?"

His mother's face crinkled and she began to weep.

"What is the matter?"

"Your sister..."

"Yes?"

"She was killed."

"What?!" Berthold yelped, horrorstruck. His voice echoed through the house. "When?!"

"September," she whimpered. "During the fighting."

During the fighting?! That was ludicrous. "How? How could she be killed during the fighting?"

"I don't know," Frieda sobbed, covering her face with her bony hands. "She was out, on the eastern side of the city, doing what I don't know, and a bullet hit her in the belly. She wasn't even caught between sides; the fighting was more than a mile further east. It was as if that one errant bullet just sought her out. To tear our family apart."

"My God..." Berthold said. He rubbed his face. A lump balled up in his throat. His sister was a good person, as harmless as anyone could be. She never acted snobbish, or petty, or uncompassionate, not in her entire life. Siblings fought, sure, but he couldn't recall any fights they had which he hadn't started. War had no business taking non-combatants like Yvonne. The news was going to be hard enough for Berthold to take back to the lines with him, but for his father, who adored his daughter more than anything, it would be a difficult burden to bear for an officer in charge of hundreds of men.

"Does father know?"

Frieda wailed, loud and long, a haunting, mournful cry the likes of which Berthold had never heard before. It chilled him to his core, but more than that, it primed him for more horrible news to come.

"Ma?" Berthold said. The burning in his nostrils pushed the first tears from his eyes.

"Your father died in August..." his mother said, doing her best to collect herself. "He was killed during the British retreat from Mons."

"NO!" he shouted, springing to his feet. Major Mathias Kastner was always so imposing, so strong in his cavalry uniform, that Berthold just never imagined him dying in it. It wasn't possible. "How can I have gone three months without knowing this?!" he yelled, tears streaming down his face. "Why didn't you tell me?!"

He realized then that he was shouting at his own mother. She'd lost her husband and her only daughter, and had been left alone to grieve for two months. His father never would have stood for it.

"Mother, I'm sorry..." he said more calmly. Tears rolled down his cheeks and into his mouth "...but you could have told me. You should have told me. I might have been able to come home sooner."

"I just..." she sobbed, "I couldn't bear the thought of my sweet boy having to deal with such pain on the battlefield. You're all I have left."

Berthold fell to his knees beside the sofa and wrapped his arms around his mother, hugging her close.

"My dear, sweet boy," she said, squeezing him firmly as they both wept. "I just didn't want to cause you any pain."

After a long hug, Berthold pulled away, his face red and glossed with tears. "Were there funerals?"

His mother placed her hand on his cheek and wiped the moisture away with her thumb. "Your sister was buried two days after she died. Many people were there. She had many friends. They buried your father in Belgium."

"He won't even rest in his homeland..." Berthold said. His sorrow quickly shifted toward bitterness. "I hate the Russians, I hate the British, and I hate the French. I hope they all burn!"

"Berthold, please don't speak that way."

"Why shouldn't I?" he snapped.

"Because I'm your mother," she said calmly, "and I've asked you not to. It frightens me."

"Yes mother."

"Now, I know this has been much to take in at once, and I'm sure you're exhausted, so why don't you go upstairs to your old bedroom and get some rest? I know how dreadful I must look, so while you rest I'll straighten myself up and make us something for dinner."

"Would you like me to help with the cooking?"

"No. You rest. I need to find some semblance of normalcy, and with you here, working in the kitchen might help me get there. I'll wake you when it's done, all right?"

"Yes mother," Berthold said. He leaned in to kiss her on the forehead before he headed upstairs.

She was right. It was a lot of sadness to take in. He lay in bed weeping, noiselessly as he could, until his eyes dried and sleep overtook him. It was dark when he awoke. The warm, inviting smell of roasted duck coaxed him from his slumber.

He rubbed his eyes while walking down the stairs, wiping away the crust. He wasn't going to cry anymore, but the fact that neither his sister nor his father would ever walk down those stairs, not ever again, was difficult to abide. He had no illusions about death itself—he manned a weapon which had likely killed many fathers and brothers. Schoolmates of his who'd gone into the infantry had died, he heard about some of them firsthand, but family was different. It wasn't fair that Yvonne had been killed. She didn't sign up for it, didn't put on a uniform, and certainly didn't take up arms. She just happened to be standing in exactly the wrong spot, at exactly the wrong time. Why would fate betray an innocent twenty-year-old girl in such a cruel way?

"The butcher charged me a fortune for this duck," Frieda said.

"What?" Berthold answered. He'd gotten so lost in thought he was moving down the stairs at a snail's pace.

"I said the duck was expensive. The butcher said something about rationing, and requisitioning. Prices have gone up."

"Oh. Well you know you didn't have to buy a duck."

His mother sighed. "It was good for me to get out of the house. I haven't been eating well, and I figured, what better a time to make a good meal than the day my dear boy came home to me? Now sit."

It didn't surprise him that the dinner was the best he'd eaten since the start of the war, even if it was tainted by the loss of half his family. Berthold and his mother didn't talk much while they ate. She didn't want to know about the war, and he didn't want to tell her.

They didn't talk much the next day, either. They visited Yvonne's grave early that morning. It was somber, going to the cemetery, especially in the cold. The ground was hard, and blanketed in snow, and the trees were bare. And Yvonne was buried beneath it all. Berthold cried one last time when he rested his hand on her cold headstone and said his goodbye.

When they got back to the house, he took it upon himself to assist his mother in finding the normalcy she desperately needed. He helped her clean and organize, performed a few heavier tasks she couldn't handle herself, and before he realized it, it was morning on the third and final day of his leave. He woke up early in order to catch the first train out of Rastenburg. His mother was awake too. She stood by the front door, in the same spot where Berthold had dropped his equipment. His equipment. Where was his equipment?

"Good morning, mother," he said, sensing something was off. She didn't seem as calm or level as she had while they did chores together.

"Good morning, dear."

"Did you move my equipment?"

"I put it away."

"What for? I have to leave. I told you that."

"No, you can't go back there," she said, shaking her head. "I can't surrender my entire family to this meaningless cause."

"Meaningless?" Berthold replied. He was offended. "How can you say that? How can you say that my father, your husband, died for nothing? It's terrible what happened to Yvonne, I know, and I swear to you I'll wreak my revenge on the Russians, but..."

"It was a German bullet that killed your sister," Frieda said.

"What?"

"The doctor said so. Accident, errant bullet or not, she died at the hands of a German."

"Christ..."

"So who do you plan to wreak your vengeance against now?"

"The Russians still invaded our homeland. Forced us to defend it. If we hadn't pushed them back—"

"I'll hear no more about the war. You need to separate yourself from it, for the sake of our family."

"You cannot be serious. If I'm not back there tomorrow, I'll be in real trouble. Any longer than that, and they'll consider me a deserter. Do you know what the penalty is for desertion?"

"They won't find you, we'll—"

"I can't even believe we're discussing this! I will not desert! I shall fulfill my duty like every good Prussian should, like father would have done. Like he would have expected me to do."

"No! You can't go back! If you go back you'll never come home!"

"If I stay here, I'll die. But I'll die a coward. A second Kastner killed for no good reason. At least if I die in combat, I die fighting our enemy. I'd die nobly, as father did."

"We'll go away, move to another city! We'll find your girlfriend and you can start a family of your own. I'd love to be a grandmother."

"I'm not thinking about Pauline right now!" he snapped, surprising himself in that the revelation was true. "But even if I were, Pauline's brother is an infantryman! What sort of girl would ever want to marry a deserter, especially when she has a sibling in the fight?"

"A girl who wants her husband to stay alive."

"Pauline and I aren't married. And you've lost your mind. Where are my things?" He gave the first floor a cursory scan. His equipment was nowhere in sight.

"I've hidden them." His mother folded her arms.

"Where are they?"

"You don't have to go..."

"Please. Mother. I need to leave."

"You can't."

"GIVE ME MY THINGS!" he roared, unable to modulate the tension bubbling inside him. "I WILL NOT DIE A COWARD, THAT YOU MAY HAVE YOUR WAY!"

"Please!" she shrieked.

Berthold spun away from her and stomped toward the closet beneath the staircase. He rattled the doorknob; it was locked. Far too furious, his patience already long gone, he took a step back, raised his knee to his chest, and kicked the wooden door near the knob, splintering the frame and breaking the lock. He flung the door open, snatched his poorly hidden pack, flung his knapsack around his neck and made for the front door. His mother remained firmly planted in his way.

"Let me past," he said calmly, trying his best to empathize with her emotional state. The feat was proving itself challenging.

"The army will understand," she pleaded, her voice shaking. "I promise they will."

"No," Berthold corrected her, "they certainly won't. And I will not place them in the position to. Move."

He reached for the doorknob, and she smacked his hand away. She clutched the doorframe on either side.

They'd squabbled enough. He had a train to catch. "I'm sorry, mother," he said, "I truly am." He grabbed her by the shoulders, forcefully wrenching her from the door. She struggled and sobbed as he dragged her away, but he was much stronger. When he reached the sofa, Berthold shoved her down. He didn't wanting to risk injuring her by tossing her on the floor.

"How can you do this to your own mother?!" she cried at his back when he opened the front door.

"I wouldn't have," he said, looking over his shoulder, "had my mother not asked me to commit suicide."

He slammed the door behind him, his heart breaking from his mother's despondent wailing. He heard it even as he walked down the street. It stayed with him well beyond that, echoing inside his head as he rode the train back east.

VERNON

Getting pulled from the front lines for recuperation did not entail days of lying in a cot relaxing, or catching up on extra hours of lost sleep. After three days at Locre, 1st Battalion marched across the French border to the larger town of Bailleul, four miles further southwest. They spent their first two days there being refitted and inspected, and then the whirlwind began.

On November 26, they acted as honor guard for Edward VIII, Prince of Wales and son of King George V. The next day, the battalion stood before Field Marshal Sir John French, who congratulated and thanked them for their service. Vernon and no doubt most of his comrades were touched by the field marshal's remarks, but the fact was inescapable that hundreds of 1st Cheshire men who deserved French's thanks weren't alive to hear them.

The 28th was Vernon's proudest day yet. On that day, General Sir Horace Smith-Dorrien, former commander of II Corps, inspected the battalion. When the battered II Corps, which suffered 14,000 casualties in October, was effectively dismantled to reinforce I Corps during the Battle of Ypres, the general relinquished his command and departed France for England on November 10. He was relieved by General Sir James Willcocks, whose Lahore Division of the Indian Corps had begun arriving in late October. The Indian troops were gradually brought forward to the trenches, to relieve some of the BEF's ravaged front line units.

Smith-Dorrien returned to France two weeks after his departure. Vernon had never seen his hero up close before, and beamed with pride when the general acknowledged and thanked the battalion for their actions, emphasizing his appreciation for their stand at Audregnies during the retreat from Mons.

The four days following the meeting with Smith-Dorrien were a retraining period of sorts, with a strong focus on musketry, the skill that saved the BEF's skin many a time in just over three months of war. Along with musketry came parades and drills. Those exercises grew increasingly more scrutinized by the battalion's handful of officers with each passing day, until December 2, when the apparent tension the officers were under could no longer be brushed off as simply moods gone afoul. When the men returned to their billets on the evening of the 2nd, they all knew something was up.

Upon their arrival at Bailleul, 3 Section had taken up quarters in a drafty, cramped, thatch-roofed hut, but anything with a roof was better than an open trench. The hut had a small fireplace, and the seven men crowded around the soothing, flickering orange glow to keep warm.

"You boys happen to notice how red Bannister's face was today?" Granville asked no one in particular. The men around the fireplace looked at one another, none of them expressing any outward agreement or disagreement.

"His face is always red," Vernon commented. "It's a hallmark side effect of being a well and true arsehole."

Some of them snorted or chuckled.

"I'll give you that," Granville replied, "but I tell you, something had him wound up. As if he were nervous. What do you think, Spurling?"

The corporal had been looking away from the fireplace, out the one tiny window in the kitchen. He wasn't paying attention.

"Spurling?"

"Yeah, what?" the corporal said, coming to.

"I asked if you thought Bannister might be acting a smidge different today. Like maybe he was under some sort of additional stress?"

"You mean beyond being a crackpot, commanding a company in a decimated battalion, in what's shaping up to be the most destructive war in the history of mankind?"

"I guess, yeah."

"Well, let me think. We've already had visits from the Prince of Wales, the commander of the Expeditionary Force and the commander of II Corps," Spurling said, counting off the names on his fingers. "And Bannister was damned well uppity then. Which visitor, do

573

you suppose, might make the captain, and maybe the men he answers to, a bit jittery about having their troops tip-top?"

"The King!" blurted Saunders.

"Very good," Spurling complemented.

"Bull..." Granville said. "The best we'll get is Kitchener or Asquith."

"The king is in country, right now," the corporal declared, "glad-handing with Poincaré, Joffre and French. Kitchener and Asquith are likely otherwise disposed back in Blighty."

"How do you know?"

"Because I just told you."

The men began to argue about which visitors, if any, they might expect to see next, or whether or not there was even any merit to the debate. Vernon and Pritchard stayed out of it, Vernon because he was simply too tired, and Pritchard because he'd checked out of the discussion early, having taken to avoiding any conversations involving Bannister in any regard.

"Vernon, do you think we'll be inspected by the King?" Pritchard asked, beneath the spirited drone of the louder discussion.

"I don't know, Lew. Maybe we'll find out tomorrow." *Who cares anyway?*

When the argument went stale and the conversation died down, Vernon fell asleep quickly.

Breakfast the next morning only served to heighten everyone's suspicions. Each man received a large bowl of oatmeal, a hefty (and decidedly atypical) serving of bacon, a biscuit and a cup of tea, and after the tea, a pinch of rum. It was a much more substantial meal than normal, downright generous even. Vernon crunched into his first bacon slice, savoring the smoky flavor. He shoveled huge scoops of oats into his mouth. He finished his biscuit in three bites. It was nice to be able to eat fast, knowing he'd be full at meal's end. When he finished eating, he washed it all down with the last snort from his rum ration, rubbed his stomach, and let out a contented belch. It was the first breakfast that actually filled his belly in weeks.

Quiet conversations permeated the chilly air, until Corporal Spurling alerted the well-fed men to the imminent arrival of unpleasant company. "Bannister's on the way, chaps," he warned, "finish your grub and be ready to straighten up."

Those who hadn't finished eating shoveled the remainder of their meals into their mouths. The frantic scraping of spoons against mess tins replaced the talking. The captain, in full parade dress, accompanied by Sergeant Major Cortland, also in dress, arrived not more than two minutes later.

"I hope you enjoyed that meal, lads," Bannister said, "because believe me when I tell you, I expect something in return."

The scattered men of Fourth Platoon were silent, hanging their heads while Bannister addressed them.

"Today, His Majesty, King George the Fifth will honor the battalion with his presence," the captain declared.

Spurling gave Vernon and the rest of 3 Section an I-told-you-so smirk.

Bannister continued, "Having provided you with full bellies, I expect you men to be clean, crisp in your movements, and entirely mindful of your manners. You're not plodding around in the mud anymore, so don't act like it. Do away post-haste with any and all poor habits which you've likely picked up along the way. I don't care whether you're in front of His Majesty for ten seconds or ten hours, you will not, in any way, so much as sneeze to the detriment of your regiment's honor and prestige. Am I understood?"

The platoon grumbled a collective but somewhat disjointed yes sir.

"Hayes, I don't want to see that dirty fucking rag fluttering about your waist, you hear?"

"Sir," Vernon replied, fumbling at the knotted and stained red handkerchief before untying it from his knapsack. He placed Sally's talisman in his coat pocket for the time being.

"And Pritchard," the captain predictably snarled, "it goes without saying that I expect little from the likes of you, but you'd best be the crispest of all. If you stand out in any way I deem unsatisfying, it's Field Punishment Number One for you I swear it." The old walrus held up a thick index finger, wagging it back and forth in taunting fashion.

Vernon cast a furtive glance to his best friend. Pritchard wasn't looking up at the captain as Bannister addressed him. His chin against his chest, a pained, but angry scowl, a hateful scowl, spread over his face while the officer needlessly belittled him. Vernon shared in his friend's bitterness.

"I think they've gotten the message, sir," Cortland declared softly. "Perhaps we should leave them to clean up and prepare."

Bannister snorted. He waved his hand as if swatting a fly and walked away.

"Carry on, men," Cortland said politely. "Spurling, may I have a word?"

Spurling joined the sergeant major. The two conversed as they slowly followed the captain.

"You know..." Milburn said, breaking everyone's silence. He leaned forward, his eyes shifting slyly to each man in 3 Section. "I happen to know something about ole' Bannister that all of you might not."

"And how's that?" Granville asked, with a touch of derision.

"I've been writing to my wife, asking her to look into some things for me."

"Such as?" Vernon inquired.

"Well, you know Bannister fought the Boers, right?"

Granville scoffed and rolled his eyes.

"Yeah," said Vernon, "we all know that."

"But did you know he had two sons what fought as well?"

Pritchard picked his head up. He was curious.

"Bollocks," Granville dismissed. "You're talking through your hat."

"I am not!" Milburn insisted. "Two sons, I swear it."

"How could it possibly be that none of us has ever heard that?" Vernon asked.

"Because the old codger keeps it to himself, obviously."

"What do you mean he *had* two sons?" said Pritchard. With his curiosity piqued, he was suddenly willing to discuss the captain.

"I mean they're both dead is what," Milburn shrugged. "The eldest was a corporal. He died during the fighting in Africa in '01."

Vernon sighed. He did not necessarily feel sympathy for the captain, but it was at least something close to it. "And the other?" He almost dreaded the answer.

Milburn glanced solemnly at Pritchard. "Made it through the war, all right. He was beaten to death by some Welsh chaps outside a pub in '05. Two days after receiving his officer's commission."

"Bloody hell..." Pritchard muttered.

"How could you know this?" Vernon pressed.

"I already told you," Milburn replied, exasperated. "My wife has been doing some digging for me. Checking old census data, newspaper archives, service records, that sort of thing. It took her some time, but it turns out she's a right proper sleuth. His murder made the papers. Chaps what killed him are locked up in Shepton Mallet."

Chilcott then stated what had suddenly become an obvious point. "So Bannister harasses Pritch the way he does because some drunken blokes from Wales killed one of his boys? That's madness."

"No one's saying the captain's not completely barmy," Milburn said, turning to face Chilcott. "I've got my suspicions the captain was short of a full deck even before Africa."

"Does he hate the Dutch equally?" asked Saunders.

"Probably. Why don't you ask him?"

"To hell with that."

Spurling's conversation with Cortland ended not long after he left. He rejoined the group, a ponderous and distant expression on his face. Vernon noticed it first.

"What's with the look?" he asked. "What'd Cortland say to you?"

Spurling held out a clenched fist. He turned his wrist over and opened his hand. A small piece of off-white cloth, a chevron, sat on his palm. "I'm the platoon's sergeant," he said, sounding as though he might be on the fence about the promotion.

Vernon understood why. Fourth Platoon had lost two officers, which was bad enough. But their sergeants fared even worse—a revolving door of casualties, every one of them fatal. Spurling would represent the platoon's fifth sergeant since August. Two had died so quickly that no one remembered their names.

"Milburn," Spurling said, "obviously this means you'll be elevated to full screw. And Hayes, you'll be his second in command. You're a lance-jack now, congratulations."

"I didn't ask for that," Vernon protested.

"I know you didn't," replied Spurling. "But you don't have a choice in the matter anymore. It's time you start climbing the chain, old boy." He stepped around the clutter of packs and seated men to get closer to the newly promoted corporal and lance-corporal. "Cortland gave me your stripes as well," Spurling said, handing two chevrons each—one for each sleeve—to Vernon and Milburn. "Be sure you get them put on straight away," he said, deepening his voice to perform his best Bannister impression. "I won't have my men looking like a bunch of shabby fucking sods when they stand before His Majesty."

Whether it was through default or not, Vernon secretly felt the tiniest amount of pride as he sewed the stripes on his tunic sleeves. Yes, a thirty year old lance-corporal wasn't much in the way of an accomplishment, but in his years spent as a professional soldier, avoiding any opportunities for advancement, a number of men no better than he had far surpassed him. Maybe Spurling had been right all along, that moving up in the world was something he should strive for. Lance-corporal and even corporal wouldn't take him any further away from Pritchard, after all.

The men were abuzz, waiting for the call to march. Most had never seen the king before, and tradition was a powerful thing. Dressed in clean clothes, polished boots, a re-stiffened cap, a freshly shaven face and a stripe on each shoulder, Vernon was off, with the rest of the 1st Cheshire Battalion, to stand before King George V.

VOGEL

Someone was knocking on the pilots' cottage door. Although persistent, it was a patient knock, not a frantic one. Vogel, curled up tightly in his cot to combat the cold, opened his eyes to see only a sliver of sunlight coming through the window. It was early.

"Fire must have gone out," he grumbled to himself, throwing his blanket away and shuddering from the chill. He slid his feet into his boots, which were so cold they might as well have been left outside overnight.

At the door, another knock.

"Why don't they just come in?" Vogel grumbled again. One of the pilots mumbled something angry, but it was indiscernible. He lumbered down the creaky steps, and trudged to the door. He opened it before the caller had a chance to knock one last, annoying time.

It was Adler. "Come on Vogel," he said, "they want us on the aerodrome. Right away."

"What for?"

"Some general wants a better look at one spot or another on the French lines. Since our photographs have been coming out cleaner than anyone else's, the hauptmann wants us in the air bright and early."

Vogel's belly snarled—an empty chasm. "Have we time for breakfast?"

"If you've got a spare biscuit or something in this shack, grab that and eat it on the way. I'm going to run ahead and get the camera ready. Leon will be fitting us with a pair of bombs as well."

"We're *bombing* something, too?" Vogel asked, surprised.

"I don't see why not. We'll get the plates, drop our bombs, the general will get his photos, and we'll have a bit of fun harassing the Franzmenn."

"While they curse our mothers and take potshots."

"Naturally."

"Excellent. You know, we'd better hope we never crash behind their lines. I get the sense we would not be received kindly."

"I trust my pilot," Adler grinned, his square Prussian jaw jutting confidently outward. "That reminds me. You haven't yet given up on Kunigunde, have you?"

"No. Though her failure to write back has got me thinking I should."

"Give her a bit longer. When you send her a Christmas card or letter, as I'm sure you will, include this along with it." Adler pulled an envelope from his coat pocket and passed it to Vogel.

"What's in it?" Vogel asked.

"Never you mind. Just send it to her, and as a courtesy to me, give me your assurance you won't read it yourself. Do I have your word?"

"Yes sir."

"Good. Now go get ready. I'll see you there."

Vogel stared at the envelope in his hand as the oberleutnant walked away. *Should I open it?* He lifted it up to hold it in front of his face, debating. *No, I gave him my word.* He closed the door and climbed the stairs to grab his heaviest, warmest clothes. He wasn't looking forward to flying at altitude. Temperatures at more than a mile up would be near or even below zero. It more or less didn't matter how thick was his coat, nor the quality of his socks, boots or gloves. After just a few minutes in the air in December, the chill would needle first into his toes and fingers, and gradually spread, reducing his reaction time and dexterity from there. Vogel tucked Adler's letter into the notebook he kept in the pack by his cot. He got dressed for the mission while his fellow pilots slept.

On the aerodrome, the few ground personnel roused for the early sortie were gathered near the sheds, smoking cigarettes. A thin layer of snow was dusted over the ground. The Rumpler had already been checked and rolled onto the field. When Vogel arrived, bundled comfortably in his heavy coat, boots, knit cap and scarf, he smiled when he saw Leon and Adler standing next to the machine. Both men were chuckling and carrying on like they'd been friends for years.

"Ah, Vogel, there you are," Adler called out. "I've just been sharing with Leon a secret I heard in the officer's quarters last night."

"What sort of secret?" Vogel asked curiously.

"The sort to which you and I should have been privy."

Vogel scrunched his nose, as if trying to solve a complex riddle. Adler let him stew on it briefly then asked, "Have you heard of B.A.O?"

"No," Vogel shrugged. "What does it stand for?"

"Brieftauben Abteilung Ostende."

"The Ostende Carrier Pigeon Detachment?"

"That's what it's called," Adler confirmed. "Do you know what it is?"

"I don't know, a training ground for pigeons?" Vogel replied sarcastically.

Leon snickered.

"The name is just a cover," Adler said. "It's a bombing group, comprised of all volunteers, which will operate, as I'm sure you might have guessed, from the Ostende area. They've already put the whole thing together and in case you hadn't noticed, no one bothered to ask if we wanted to be a part of it."

"Maybe the hauptmann or someone higher up has placed more value in our reconnaissance duties," Vogel replied.

"We won our EKIIs based on what we did with bombs!" Adler stated incredulously. "I think we should have at least been given a choice, don't you?"

"Are you truly that upset, sir?"

"No, I suppose not. Well, maybe I am. But I am a bit surprised at how little it bothers you."

"I feel that as long as I'm performing my duty, whatever that may be, then I'm all right with it."

"Indeed," Adler conceded. "Shall we have a look at the map so you know where it is we need to be photographing?"

Vogel nodded. The oberleutnant unfolded a map of the Aisne river valley and pointed to a spot on the map east of Soissons. "The general wants the plates to cover from the bend in the river here," he pointed to a small kink in the Aisne, "to this small town here," he pointed again to a spot half an inch further east.

"Seems simple enough," Vogel said. They'd been flying the area for some time, and he had the landscape pretty well memorized.

"And then we drop our bombs wherever we want," Adler reminded him.

They climbed into their cockpits. Vogel retrieved his flying cap and goggles from the seat. His reservations about goggles were long gone. He yanked the leather head cover over the top of his stocking cap. It fit snugly, if not a bit too tight. When he plopped into his seat and looked behind him, he noticed for the first time how beautiful that early morning was.

Most days for the past month had been cold, dull and grey. That day was just as cold as any other, only it wasn't grey. The sun was still low, and hidden behind a large bank of pillowy cumulus clouds. Golden rays glowed behind the clouds, illuminating their edges and turning the eastern sky into smooth brush strokes of orange and pink, on a faded blue canvas. It didn't make sense that in going up there, getting closer to that majesty, the conditions could be so hostile.

Leon went through his steps, shoving the propeller through its rotations, priming the cylinders. Vogel swung the rudder, checked his controls and gauges, and after getting the go-ahead, pressed the magneto switch.

"Contact!"

Leon rocked the propeller up and hurled it downward. The ice-cold engine chugged, gasped, and failed to fire. They went through the steps again, priming the cylinders, checking the gauges, pressing the magneto, and again, a few chugs, but no ignition.

"Are you losing your touch, Leon?!" Vogel called out from the cockpit.

"No sir!" Leon called back. "She's just caught a chill, that's all. She'll go this time."

And she did. With one perhaps slightly more enthusiastic shove of the propeller, Leon got the Rumpler's engine to turn over and fire. Vogel gave the machine an extra couple seconds to get warm, and then signaled his mechanic friend to remove the wheel chocks.

The run up to takeoff was extra bumpy with the ground being frozen like uneven cement. The stiff, unforgiving terrain jostled the machine hard, sapping its speed. Vogel debated backing off the throttle. He had faith in Leon's mechanical inclinations, but with two bombs in the rack and the machine shaking like it was, there was no guarantee they wouldn't wiggle loose. What was guaranteed, though, was that Adler would insist on bringing the bombs along, no matter how many attempts it took the Rumpler to get off the ground. Rather than squabble over it, Vogel opened the throttle wide as it would go, and finally coaxed the machine into the air with little room to spare between its nose and the withered hedgerow at the aerodrome's border.

It didn't take long for the cold to bite. His exposed nose and cheeks, not covered by cap or scarf, incurred its wrath first. With every uptick of the altimeter, the rushing air bit harder. Vogel banked the machine to port, putting the glowing cumulus clouds on his left and the still dark western horizon on his right. By the time the Rumpler reached altitude fifteen minutes after taking off, the gleaming sun climbed out from behind the clouds. In spite of its emergence, its rays did nothing to warm the air.

The landscape below was much like the majority of the weather. Drab. The leaves on the trees were gone, turning the windblown forests grey, empty and lifeless. The crops, all harvested, no longer formed a colorful patch quilt, but rather an ugly, faded blanket, splotched with white. Nearer the trenches the land was a desert, populated by warring ants. Artillery had churned up much of the ground between and immediately beyond the trench lines, leaving the terrain a largely greyish-brown, cratered moonscape. With Heaven floating in the sky just miles away to Vogel's left, he couldn't imagine the fires of Hell being any worse than the dirty, icy hell on the ground beneath him.

Half an hour after leaving the ground, Vogel's hands began to stiffen and ache. His toes ached by the time they reached the kink in the Aisne and Adler, probably frozen himself, began working the Görz. He toughed it out, and when he'd finished shooting the exposures, signaled to Vogel that it was time to turn around. Vogel doubted the oberleutnant was as excited about dropping their bombs as he was before they'd taken flight, but he had no designs in landing the Rumpler with bombs on her underbelly. They had to go.

Taking a wide, banking turn to get the nose aimed west and with the French front line directly below him, Vogel dipped the craft's nose to descend. The bitterly cold wind whooshed through the wings' bracing wires, singing loud enough to compete even with the Mercedes. The bite chewed through his heavy coat, chilling him to his furthest depths. If they spent much longer in the air, they might actually freeze to death. Rather than spend time venturing any distance behind the lines to search the supply roads for a target, they would make their delivery directly to the French trenches...

DENIS

Dear Cécile,

Forgive my hesitation in writing this first letter. I thought it appropriate to allow you time to grieve, without my serving as a further reminder. As this letter's arrival indicates, I've made it to the front safely, and in better spirits than when I left. Since my return, I volunteered for and was selected to lead a new type of mission, though I will spare you the details of what that entails. Suffice to say it appeals to me, and I believe I've found a calling, as it were.

As much as I write to let you know I'm well, and that I'd like to hear from you, I must also ask a favor. It would have been inappropriate to ask when we spoke in person, but now that you've had time, I must. I haven't the slightest inclination of what's happened to my family. I doubt they would have stayed in Cambrai as the Germans approached, and regardless of whether or not they did, I have no way of knowing. All letters I've sent have been returned to me unopened. Could you, if you've any time to spare, try to locate them for me? I know I ask much, and worse, I don't know where you could even start, but if you—

Denis stopped writing and cocked his head to the side, tilting an ear to the sky. Boche and French aeroplanes flew overhead just about every single day that weather permitted, but every now and again, a German one would do something obnoxious. The sound which grabbed his attention away from his writing was that of an engine, increasing in pitch and volume. An aeroplane was descending rapidly.

"Hey, hey!" he said to Rose, the man napping closest to him. Denis slapped him on the chest to rouse him.

"What, dammit?" Rose said. His long, sleepy face was particularly mopey.

"Grab your rifle," Denis told him, at the same time reaching for his own Lebel. The others still hadn't heard the diving aeroplane. "Everyone, pick up your rifles, quickly!"

In seconds, the diving boche machine was loud enough that all could hear it. There were so many ways to die in war, but something about airmen dropping bombs on their heads infuriated the men in the trenches. Worse than that, though, was that in each of the few instances where bombs were dropped near him, Denis swore up and down that he had his rifle's sights squared up for a kill shot. Many others swore the same, yet the boche bird always managed to drop its eggs and flutter away unscathed. It was maddening to aim dead on and miss.

I'll hit him this time, Denis assured himself. He held his rifle steady, angled upward. He didn't know much about aeroplanes, but the one diving toward him had a distinctive look—its bombs were attached to some sort of rack on the machine's underbelly. He hadn't seen that on any other machines. He resolved to try and shoot the bombs before the airmen released them. What a reward that would have been, to see the enemy aeroplane explode in midair. His fellow trench raiders and the hundreds of men manning that stretch of trench had the same designs for the boche. They soon sent a storm of bullets in the aeroplane's direction, like hail gone in reverse.

There weren't but a few seconds before the boche airmen would release their payload. Denis, ignoring the cold in his hands and the earsplitting chatter of hundreds of angry French rifles, zeroed his sights on the bombs. *Pow!* The butt kicked into his shoulder. The aeroplane failed to explode.

"Dammit!" he yelled, and as the bombs released, he gave up on aiming carefully. He snapped another round into the chamber. He fired again. If his shot hit the machine anywhere, it didn't count for much. The boche machine pulled out of its dive, its engine roared and the aeroplane rose higher. Not only did no one succeed in bringing the attacking machine down, the bastards had actually managed to land their bombs in the trench. A direct hit. The "eggs" exploded fifty yards east of where Denis and his men stood. They heard the explosion and saw the smoke and dirt billow upward. Undoubtedly, someone had just died.

"I swear on my life if I ever meet a boche pilot face to face, I'll kill him as slowly and painfully as is humanly possible," Denis mused aloud, while he watched the aeroplane shrinking north. His cohorts nodded in agreement. Everything the boche did was simply infuriating. "As it stands, we'll just have to exact our revenge tonight."

The trench raiders laughed, a menacing and foreboding laugh, one that would have chilled a rational person in a normal situation. They had another raid lined up, their fourth, and were planning on adding in a new wrinkle to their assault.

"Schwartz, have you gotten your presents ready yet?" Denis asked. He was still watching the aeroplane fly away, its engine noise fading to a whisper. He set his rifle down and approached the young man.

"Yes. I think they'll work well, too," the youngster replied calmly, his hazel eyes gleaming proudly. He rested his rifle next to a small wooden crate covered by a dirty cloth. He pulled the cloth away to reveal six mason jars, each filled with clear liquid. A length of fuse emerged from the lid of each jar.

"They look good," Denis complemented him. "Do you think you can get them there without breaking them?"

"I'll have to wrap each one in cloth so they don't crash against one another. That will help deaden the noise, too."

"Do you want to take all six?"

"I don't see why not."

"How will you carry them?"

"I took a breadbag from a dead boche some time ago," Schwartz replied. "I'll shorten the shoulder strap enough that it rides tightly against the middle of my back." He swung his hand over his shoulder to slap himself where he planned on carrying the jars.

"If you think you can get them out and light them fast enough, then I'm all for it."

"I can."

Theirs wasn't the only crew performing trench raids. Quite the contrary. The Germans were doing it as well, oftentimes with more men. Other French units did it too, some also with greater numbers. The problem with raiding with a larger number of men was simple odds—the more men involved, the greater the chance the party would give itself away, turning the one-sided nighttime raid into a two-sided nighttime engagement. Regardless of the number of men, the purpose remained the same—make the enemy ever-wary of the next raid. Disrupt his sleep. Get inside his head.

The philosophy was simple, but the execution of that philosophy varied. Denis envisioned his crew as operating like ghosts. Silent on the way in, silent on the kill, take what was useful and hopefully, silent on the way out. Their first raid had *almost* panned out that way, and the second and third actually had. The only problem was, apart from killing some sentries and a few boche NCOs, and dismantling one machine gun, they hadn't scored any maps, documents, or captured any officers. The risk/reward ratio to that point was skewed in the wrong direction. They were risking a lot, but gaining little. To increase not only the damage they inflicted, but to also amplify the lingering fear their raids instilled, their specialized unit needed to do something extra. That was where Schwartz's mason jars came in.

In the blackness of the very early morning, in vicious, low-teen temperatures that easily pierced through their tunics, Denis and his stealthy raiders found themselves across no man's land, lying face-down next to the enemy's barbed wire. They were hitting a different spot on the German line, one from which boche snipers were inflicting a particularly nasty toll. The ridgeline was higher there, and it gave the raiding party much greater difficulty in navigating it, but that was exactly where a small, nimble band could prove itself most effective. They'd made it up and over without incident.

Snip.

Denis wrung his hands around his axe handle. He still had yet to bludgeon anyone with it. He wanted to. His only kill as a raider was the first one, with his pistol.

Snip.

Just a couple more wires to go.

Snip...Snip...

He nodded to his men and they snuck through the space, slinked to the parapet and peeked into the trench. Denis couldn't believe what he saw when he looked down. Beneath him, a sentry had nodded off. Seated on the firing step with his back against the front wall, the boche was a sitting duck. Denis wriggled forward so that his torso hung over the edge. Axe handle in hand, he raised his right arm over his head, and swung the weapon into the trench like a pendulum.

Thwock!

He'd never heard a more sickening, yet satisfying sound. Some of the wire barbs on the end of the handle must have stuck into the German's skull, because when he fell over, he took the handle with him, yanking it from Denis's unsuspecting grasp. The dead or unconscious man slumped onto his side and lay still. The axe handle remained affixed to his head. Denis and his raiders slipped into the trench. He plucked his weapon from the boche's head. In case the first hit wasn't enough, he raised his club again, holding it high above his head with both hands. Ghosts weren't supposed to make noise, but he forgot himself in that moment, and unleashed his anger with a savage swing.

THWOCK!

It should not have made him feel so good to create such a loud noise. It likewise shouldn't have made him feel good to know that his second strike had crushed bone, concaved it—a certain deathblow. Breathing heavily, not bothering to conceal the large puffs of mist rolling off his lips, he watched with a demonic scowl as blood oozed from the dead man's crushed head. Denis didn't dare question the rewarding feeling that came with brutalizing another man. Instead, he embraced it.

His heart thumping in exhilaration, Denis snapped out of his barbaric trance. He turned away from the dead body, observing the actions of his men and keeping a watchful eye on the trench span in either direction. A boche might emerge from the black at any second.

While everyone quickly and quietly searched, Schwartz sheathed his knife and tugged the strap of the breadbag slung around his neck, sliding it from his back to his chest. He unfastened the flap and began unwrapping the mason jars from their cloth shrouds. Distracted by Schwartz for no more than a second or two, Denis had no time to object when Sergent Veilleux suddenly struck a match and crept into a dugout. The faint, flickering glow of the match briefly cast a shadow before going out.

The sergent's rash and decidedly unexpected action nearly sucked all the wind from Denis's lungs. With frantic eyes, he tiptoed over to Schwartz, grabbing him by the arm.

"Light the fuses!" he whispered, hissing like a serpent.

As Schwartz stuffed a hand into his hip pocket to grab his lighter, Denis hurriedly beckoned to the other men to join them. The sounds of a small scuffle emanated from the dugout. Boots scraped against the cold dirt floor. Someone grunted. More sounds, nondescript ones, perhaps hands wildly slapping and grabbing at their captor, then footsteps, kicking and dragging boots. Denis drew and aimed his pistol at the entryway. Sergent Veilleux emerged from the darkness, his left arm wrapped around the neck of a boche lieutenant, his right arm soaked in blood and holding his bloody dagger. As it was nearly every minute of each day, Veilleux's face remained expressionless. The other occupants in the dugout were either dead or fully incapacitated—put out of commission while they slept.

Schwartz was down on one knee, holding the lighter to the fuses. One by one, each fuse lit. Barbot grabbed the first jar, Hennequin the second. Denis grabbed the last one. Astounded that no one had followed Veilleux out of the dugout, or that any of the other trench occupants had yet to discover them, Denis stood, along with Rose, outside one such dugout. The four others holding lit mason jars paired up outside two more shelters. Schwartz, in the meantime, assisted Sergent Veilleux by bopping the German officer on the head to render him unconscious. The two picked the man up, hoisted him out of the trench, and prepared to lug their prisoner the long way back to the French trenches.

The fuses were burning down, and time was up. Denis silently counted to three, holding his fingers in the air. When he reached three, all six men hurled their jars into the silent dugouts. The jars shattered, igniting the kerosene contained within, spreading it throughout the shelters.

The screams started while the raiders left the trench and filed through the cut barbed wire. Only Veilleux knew how large the dugouts actually were, but to Denis's fleeing ears, it sure sounded like there were a lot of men screaming. He, Schwartz and Veilleux quickly fell behind the others, the latter two because they lugged an unconscious man with them, and the former, because the latter two needed cover. Denis strode sideways a few steps behind them, his pistol at the ready, keeping his eye on the orange glow rising from the boche trenches.

Because the fires burned inside the dugouts, there wasn't enough light escaping from the trench to betray the fleeing Frenchmen's locations. From Denis's vantage point, though, he was able to tell the precise moment the boche soldiers emerged to give chase. Enough distance separated them that it should not have posed a problem. The ridgeline was no more than a hundred yards, maybe two, away. They were almost there. Until the boche lieutenant woke up.

The officer's sudden wakening and spirited writhing caused Schwartz to drop him and stumble. The German broke free, punched Veilleux in the mouth and ran away, throwing a shoulder into Denis as he passed him. Denis shouted for Schwartz and Veilleux to stay put, ignoring their shouts calling for him to just shoot the bastard, and he gave chase after the fleeing boche.

He could not chase him for long. The distance between Denis and his own pursuers was now shrinking doubly fast. He'd been selected as a trench raider partly because of his agility and speed, but that damned boche, even with what was likely a pounding headache and a large knot on his head, sure could run. Denis chugged his arms and churned his legs, digging deep to try and recapture his men's prize, but the chase was fruitless. The man was more athletic than he.

"Nicht schiessen! Nicht schiessen!" the German officer yelled to his comrades through the darkness as he neared them.

Denis had run out of room. He skidded to a stop and raised his pistol. He'd sacrificed his head start and then some in his pursuit of the escaping boche. He had but one option to gain that lead back in order to make his getaway. It was something he'd practiced from time to time, mostly by dry firing his revolver or simply practicing the hand motion. Tucking his axe handle beneath his shooting arm, he placed his left hand atop the revolver and squeezed the trigger.

Bang! The first shot left the barrel and he fanned the hammer, rapidly firing five more times, *ba-ba-ba-ba-bang!* The odds were low that he hit anyone, but his last-ditch bluff worked. The Germans chasing him hit the deck, likely believing they were up against a bit more firepower than they truly were, though the escaped officer undoubtedly informed them otherwise.

In tandem with his last shot, Denis turned on his heels and made like hell for the ridgeline. The Germans behind him fired their rifles for a time, but did not pursue him with any vigor. He didn't catch up to Schwartz and Veilleux until after sliding down the slope, sometimes on his feet but frequently on his backside. It was a painful descent, the ground being frozen, but on the heels of another harrowing escape from a German viper pit, he and his raiders eventually found one another in the trenches. No one was hurt. They were all disappointed by the loss of their prisoner, but titillated by the havoc Schwartz's mason jars had wreaked.

When hearts had slowed and breath regained, Denis realized that his revolver was rattling. He harkened back to what Patrice had told him, on the day he died, about breaking his pistol. He sat down to inspect his weapon. The hammer was loose. So was the trigger. His pistol's firing components were broken.

"You were right..." he whispered, and he put the broken revolver back in its holster.

SEBASTIAN

It was his turn for watch duty again. In December, being lashed atop the conning tower was akin to torture. The spray was painfully cold, the air, piercing. The swells were nothing to thumb his nose at either, but he'd gained his seafaring legs years ago, and swells didn't bother him. U-20 was nearing the end of another unsuccessful weeks-long patrol in the Heligoland Bight. Spirits were low, boredom high.

The fleet saw two more successes in October, one on the 18th, when U-27 sank the British submersible E-3. It was the first time in history a submarine sank another submarine. As good news typically did, the sinking of the E-3 provided the crew's morale a temporary boost. On the 20th, U-27's crew boarded and then scuttled a British merchant vessel, the SS *Glitra*, after ordering her crew to evacuate. It was another first, in that a submarine crew had never before destroyed an enemy merchant ship.

Kapitänleutnant Dröscher and the crew of U-20 had ventured a great distance in October, successfully navigating the minefields in the Strait of Dover and entering the English Channel. Unbeknownst to them at the time, they were spotted off the Isle of Wight, mere hours before a convoy of Canadian troop transports was to arrive at Southampton. In a panic at receiving reports of a German sub in the vicinity, the British admiralty ordered the transports to land more than a hundred miles further west, at Plymouth. Neither Dröscher nor the crew realized the alarm they'd caused or how close they'd come to striking a serious blow.

Rather than running the risky gauntlet of minefields and patrols by British destroyers in the Channel on the way back to base, Dröscher chose to travel up the coast of western Britain. On the lengthy, roundabout trip, U-20 was briefly within visual range of some of the British Grand Fleet's ships, but was unable to close the distance owing to weather conditions.

November was a less-than-inspiring month for the Kaiser's U-Boat Fleet. No enemy vessels were destroyed, and U-18 was rammed and sunk after it surfaced while entangled in anti-submarine nets off the coast of Scotland's Shetland Islands. Sebastian turned twenty-two on the fifth of the month, but being where he was in the circumstances he and his countrymen were under, the day came and went unacknowledged.

December, not yet halfway over, had already been worse. On the 9th, U-11, patrolling the Strait of Dover, struck a mine and sank. Kapitänleutnant Dröscher had been hesitant to share the news then, five days after reporting U-11's sinking to his crew, that U-5 had also been destroyed by a mine in the English Channel. The crew was still sullen a day later, and so Sebastian, out on the conning tower, faced misery either way. On deck it was the miserable seas. Below deck, miserable men.

Bored, cold and shivering, he half-heartedly scanned the horizon at the peak of each swell. Only grey skies and seas greeted him north, south, east and west. His mind slowly, almost involuntarily wandered away from his duty, drifting years back, to the first time his father tried to bring his youngest brother aboard a ship in Königsberg harbor. Michael had kicked and screamed as soon as his feet left the dock. Sebastian and Uri laughed at their brother's bawling then, and they harassed him for it long later. The Eberhardt men were seafaring men. What sort of an Eberhardt cried on the water?

It wasn't just that Michael cried the first time; it was that he cried every time. He was such an annoying little shit. Their father continued to force him onboard ships, from fishing trawlers to passenger vessels, to stand next to him on the railing, arms wrapped tightly around his shoulders, holding him in place while the vessel moved over the water. Michael always cried, and after only a brief time at sea, would throw up, seasick.

Try as he might, Viktor Eberhardt, in all his patience, just could not get his youngest boy to take to sailing. He put forth much effort, and to both Sebastian and Uri, their brother's patent rejection of their father's guidance was sickening. It remained a heated point of contention until the day Michael outright refused to set foot on a ship ever again. The biggest insult, in Sebastian's mind, came in knowing his father's deep disappointment. That Michael just could not, or more accurately, would not push past his fears to make their old man proud was outrageous. Michael's rejection of their father was therefore a reasonable justification for Sebastian and Uri's rejecting their little brother. At least that was the way they saw it.

"Prick is probably dead by now," Sebastian muttered. He lowered his head and shook it ashamedly. Even after years of not seeing one another, Michael still annoyed him.

"Why couldn't he have just been norm—"

What is that?

Something on the northwestern horizon. A cloud? No, not a cloud. It was smoke. At the top of another swell, Sebastian spotted a ship's silhouette in profile. It was big. Was it a dreadnought? He couldn't tell at that distance. What a way to end a long and uneventful patrol it would be, to sink a British battleship on the last day. He stared at the ship, building destructive scenarios in his imagination.

"Oh! I've got to tell Dröscher!"

Sebastian flung open the hatch and climbed onto the ladder, closing and locking the hatch behind him.

"Sir! Sir!" he shouted, sliding excitedly to the bottom. "There's a large vessel off our port quarter, near the horizon!"

"Have you sealed the hatch?" Dröscher asked calmly. He positioned himself in front of the navigating periscope, grasped the handles on either side of the vertical, tube-shaped device, and peered into the eyepiece.

"Hatch is sealed, sir," Sebastian assured his commander.

"I see her," Dröscher said calmly, his eyes affixed to the periscope. "Matching our heading. We'll try to intercept." He backed away from the periscope and boomed, "MEN TO YOUR STATIONS!"

A flurry of activity began as crewmen scrambled through the boat, ducking through hatches and scooting around one another. The watch officers joined the kapitänleutnant and helmsman in the cramped control room. The diving officer took his position next to the wheels, gauges, levers, and pipes that comprised the ship's diving controls, which some of the men referred to as the "diving piano". The "piano" was the large bank of levers which controlled the ballast and air tanks. Sebastian hurried to remove his rubberized gear while everyone got in position. So excited his frozen hands trembled violently, he struggled to free himself from the heavy, sodden clothing.

"TURN OFF MAINS!" the kapitänleutnant shouted into the voice pipe that led to the engine room. Speaking tubes led from the control room to each compartment, allowing easier communication between commander and crew.

Seconds after the order, a brief but eerie silence enveloped the ship, as the engine crew shut down the noisy diesel engines. Sebastian wriggled out of the rain gear and slipped into his canvas shoes. He hustled toward the bow and joined Jollenbeck and several others in the forward torpedo room. Creaks and groans echoed through the pressure hull as the outer hull flexed in the cold, choppy water. So often, the diesels provided a vast, dominating majority of the ambient noise aboard ship. Without them running, everything sounded completely different. Unmasked by the engine silence, regular oceangoing noises were distinctly irregular.

In the engine room, the crew switched to battery power. The low hum of the motordynamos signified the switch. The comparative quiet of running on electric power was a much more soothing sound to Sebastian's ears. It was too bad they couldn't spend more time running the electric motors under normal conditions.

"Close main intake!" Dröscher ordered, speaking softer now that he wasn't competing with the diesel engines. Separated from the commander by two compartments, Sebastian barely made out the kapitänleutnant's faint instruction. The main intake valve fed air to the diesel engines. Without closing it before a dive, the engine room would flood, sinking the vessel. As the diving procedures commenced, hissing noises echoed through the ship, as air pressure was vented and seawater rushed into the ballast tanks. U-20's bow leaned forward as the tanks flooded. The diving officer spun the diving wheels and carefully played his "piano" levers in their rehearsed sequence. Soon, the lurching of waves ceased, and the submerged ship glided beneath the water's surface.

Sebastian and Jollenbeck glanced nervously at one another, and then at the ceiling above them, like two mice alert to the lurking owl's presence. It was one thing to spend years *on* the sea. To be *beneath* it was different, and still just a little unsettling. After all, they had just sunk their vessel. On purpose. The creaking which emanated from the outer hull at that point was due to pressure, not waves. It was hard not to imagine a weld or rivet giving way, and that icy water above them pouring in.

"Engines, full power," Dröscher called into the speaking tube. He said something else that Sebastian couldn't quite make out, but when the vessel listed slightly to starboard and the floor shifted beneath his feet, he knew that the commander had ordered the helmsman to steer the vessel to port, probably between twenty and thirty degrees. In the control room, the kapitänleutnant was watching the enemy vessel through the optics of the attack periscope, the only portion of the ship which remained above the waterline, roughly fifty feet above their heads.

Tense minutes followed. The atmosphere was unnerving. U-20 might have been stalking prey, but it wasn't akin to a man hunting a deer. It was more like a man hunting another, larger man who could run faster and happened to be equipped with a bigger and better gun. If the submarine managed to intercept the British ship but missed with a torpedo attack, the enemy vessel's massive guns and superior speed would put U-20 at a serious disadvantage. Their only leg up was stealth.

Alas, the attack was not to happen. After ten anxious minutes, the enemy ship turned north and began to outdistance the much slower submersible, long before any attack could materialize. Kapitänleutnant Dröscher instructed the helmsman to steer the ship southeast to the submarine base at Wilhelmshaven, a port city in Lower Saxony on Germany's North Sea coast. Another patrol was coming to its unsuccessful conclusion.

"Maybe next patrol will be better," said a disappointed Jollenbeck, after the commander ordered the crew to stand down.

"It could always be worse," Sebastian reminded him.

Wilhelmshaven was a busy port. Its harbor was much larger and better equipped to handle traffic than was Heligoland. Uniformed and ununiformed men were everywhere, stocking, fixing, parading, and a number of dockhands soon got to work on U-20. There was hardly time to get a wash and a meal. The next patrol was to begin just a day later. Before dismissing the crew upon their arrival, Kapitänleutnant Dröscher had them assemble on the dock, next to their vessel.

"I would like to thank each of you for service," Dröscher said, eyeing the group from end to end. "It has been my distinct pleasure serving as your commander. As of this moment, I will be transferring to another vessel in the fleet. Your new commander will join you on the morrow. Dismissed."

And just like that, U-20's commander was gone. He saluted the crew, the crew saluted him, and the officer who'd been with them for the entire war was off to command another crew, on another ship. Sebastian liked Dröscher, and was sorry to see him go.

The remainder of that day passed uneventfully. He got something to eat, shaved, got a decent night's sleep, and early the next day was at the dock again, loading the last of the ship's provisions aboard.

Sebastian hovered over a foredeck hatch, joking with a matrose below.

"ATTENTION! COMMANDER ON DECK!" an officer shouted. It startled Sebastian enough that the man looking up at him through the hatch laughed. The crew, scattered along the dock and the deck, stood at attention.

A clean-cut, handsome young officer in full dress was walking along the planks, his subordinate officers in tow. He appeared almost boyishly young, and wore no moustache. He looked young enough, in fact, that Sebastian wasn't sure if he could even grow one. His shoes were so polished, they glinted. Without so much as a word, the new commander stepped off the dock and onto the deck, nodding to each man who saluted him as he walked past. He and the officers climbed the conning tower and disappeared into the hatch. He must have wanted to acclimate himself to the ship before he formally met her crew.

A short time later, the crew was ordered to assemble at the bow. The new kapitänleutnant stood atop the conning tower to address them.

"Good afternoon, gentlemen," he said. His voice was far less boyish than his face. "I am Kapitänleutnant Walther Schwieger. I've heard kind words spoken of this crew from your former commander. I expect good things going forward. In fact, with this crew, and this vessel, I expect big things to come." He brought a hand to his white officer's cap in a crisp salute, and the crew saluted him back.

Sebastian couldn't quite put a finger on why, but when he gazed upon his dashing new commander, he expected big things too.

VERNON

"Hoy there chaps! Didn't your quartermaster tell you? Puttees go on your legs, not your heads!" Granville shouted enthusiastically, to the battered and dirty Lahore troops marching in the opposite direction.

The dark-skinned Indian soldiers, who wore turban head wraps rather than the peaked caps of their British counterparts, appeared out of place as they trudged past the pallid but moderately refreshed men of 1st Battalion. In truth, the Indians were only different from the neck up. Apart from their headwear and darker skin, their equipment and khaki serge uniforms were decidedly similar to those worn by the rest of the British army.

"Take it easy, Granny," Spurling scolded him from nearby. "Those boys are the main reason any of us got off the front line in the first place."

"Sorry Corp...I mean Sergeant," Granville replied.

The small column of Lahore Division troops ambled quietly past. They spoke English, so they'd heard Granville's unwarranted taunt. They just looked far too tired to acknowledge it in any way. Pritchard didn't appreciate the jab any more than the Indians would have. He was among the few in the platoon who heard it that didn't at least snicker. Instead, Vernon watched his friend nod in thankful acknowledgement to the Indians, waving to any of those men who glanced his way. Only a few nodded back. Most just marched on, blankly staring straight ahead. Sent halfway around the Earth from the jewel in the British crown, it wasn't their war, not really, yet there they were.

Following more than two weeks in reserve, 1st Battalion was healthy enough to be sent back to the trenches. They'd all known it was coming; it was just that the miserable conditions on the front line had not yet become a distant enough memory. The frequent parading, drilling and musketry (all in cold weather) of their time in the reserves only abetted in keeping that memory fresher.

Apart from Granville's discourteous outburst and the minor chuckles that followed, the overall mood of the marching battalion was not a festive one. To Vernon, the initial honor of standing before His Majesty the King had worn off quickly, if he could even consider it an honor in the first place. When they stood before King George V, in the pomp and ceremony, he was thoroughly unimpressed. The king was just a man, and nothing more. Figurehead, symbol, or what have you, he was still just a man. Flesh and blood. Fourteen days after the fact, marching back toward cannon shells and snipers *in his name*, but really, in his stead, the meeting no longer registered in any way as significant.

Given time to ruminate while not facing constant stress, sleep deprivation and prospective death, he'd changed his tune so far as His Majesty was concerned. They weren't really marching to battle *for* the king. At least Vernon wasn't. Not anymore. The king wasn't suffering with them. He might say he was, he might weep over dead soldiers, but win or lose, Georgie would still be rich, still be royalty. He'd still count for more than those that died, as foolish a notion as that was. No, rather the troops were marching for each other, *because* of the king. King George, Asquith, Kitchener, Poincaré, the Kaiser, the Tsar, those damned Austrians, they all could have worked to prevent what happened, but they'd failed, and good men had paid dearly for those immense failings. They were still paying dearly.

The machinations of George V, his royal cousins turned nemeses, and the throngs of sleazy politicians holding office across Europe had *caused* Vernon and his brothers to march, but Vernon's *cause* was no longer entirely in line with that of the king. Vernon's cause was Pritchard, and Granville, Milburn and Spurling, the chaps of Fourth Platoon, of E Company and 1st Battalion. The true cause was all the British boys, putting their lives on the line. His fight was in protecting his countrymen, his fellow soldiers. His fight was doing whatever he could to ensure they'd survive the Great War, which not one of them had a hand in starting.

"It's not bloody fair," Vernon mumbled, not realizing he'd verbalized what he was thinking. Night had fallen, and after crossing the border back into Belgium during the day, they'd moved into their home in the trenches near Wulverghem after sundown. Wulverghem was a blip of a village, five and a half miles east of Bailleul and six miles south of Ypres.

"What isn't fair?" asked Pritchard.

"Huh?" Vernon said, finally grasping he'd spoken aloud. "Oh, nothing." He nestled his back against the trench wall, and pulled his boots from the cold muck, tucking his knees against his chest for warmth.

It was cold, as usual, and a light snow was falling. The gallon jugs of rum had come around a short time earlier, a homecoming gift from the quartermaster. Spurling, in his new role as sergeant and therefore rum administrator, had allocated maybe just a drop or two more than the usual share into the cups of 3 Section's men. To the men in Fourth Platoon, SRD now stood for Spurling's Rum Delivery.

Vernon picked up his cup, which was pushed in the dirt next to him and took a swig. The rum was as cold as the air, but warm at the same time. It was like drinking sunshine at the North Pole. The warmth trickled into his belly, ran through his veins, it even warmed his fingers and toes. In a pub during peacetime, the delicious nectar would have been pure swill. Sometimes quality entirely depended upon locality.

"No, come now, Vernon," Pritchard said, not letting him off the hook. "What's not fair?"

"A lot of things, I suppose," Vernon generalized. "It's just that we're going to be sitting in this damned frozen ditch on Christmas. Can you think of a worse day out of the entire year to be holed up in a place like this?"

"I've had worse ones..." Pritchard said. "At least this one, I'm here with you."

Vernon's father might have died in Burma before he ever knew him or had a Christmas with him, but even that was better than the son of a bitch Pritchard had gotten stuck with. At least Vernon had been left with a kind and decent mother. Pritchard's mother was hardly any better than his father. As little as Vernon's mother had for him on Christmas when he was young, their days together were happy, and far more than Llewelyn ever got. That Pritchard, on top of his rotten childhood, had had less than ten Christmases with Daisy was a travesty. He deserved more. So had she.

"Still..." Vernon said, "Trenches on Christmas?"

"You can be assured there are a million German chaps saying the same thing as you," Pritchard said. "Huns or not, Fritz is praying to the same God as our boys, and will celebrate his birthday on the same day."

"In a way, that's my point. What in the hell are we all still doing out here? What's the endgame?"

"I think we're well beyond asking that," Pritchard admitted. Then, kidding, he said, "You should've asked King George when you had the chance."

"As good a question as any to receive Bannister's death sentence for asking, I suppose," Vernon mused. "Do you remember some time ago, what we talked about on the bus to Béthune?"

"You mean about Fritz's mittens, and whether we've got them too?"

"Yes, right," Vernon grinned. "So if Fritz has his mittens, and we've got mittens, and our French allies will surely say they've got mittens too, where in any of our bibles does it say it's all well and good we're murdering one another?"

"I doubt it does," Pritchard said. "I'm aware of no exceptions to the commandment. Then again, I've never lived in a monastery. I've never read that whole bloody book. Have you?"

"Start to finish? God no."

"But I have had plenty of time to think about the things you said before, and I must say I've come to agree with you. And I have no illusions about what this war means for me when I die. It's unlikely I'm going to meet Daisy when my time comes, if you know what I mean, not after what I've done. I've seen the faces of some of the German boys I've shot. Sanctioned by my king and government or not, it surely was murder."

"So what about King George and Kaiser Bill? Since they're not pulling the trigger, are they absolved of the bloodshed?"

"They're bloody well not," Pritchard said crossly. "No more than you or I. And on top of that, what would you say the good Lord thinks about kings and Kaisers presenting themselves as false idols? How does God feel about them claiming they've got his backing?"

"Haven't asked him," Vernon admitted.

Pritchard wasn't finished. "What's more, whoever wins this fight, whatever that means, does anyone here actually still believe that when the time comes for them to meet their maker, that he'll greet them at the gates and say, 'Jolly good show, chaps, well done. I was pulling for you'?"

"I can't speak for anyone but me, but I'll wager a lot of chaps believe exactly that."

"Then I pity them. They bought a cat in a sack. They're in for a sore disappointment when their number's up."

Vernon nodded contemplatively. He thought about his experiences from August to then. "Do you think there's a chance it's all bollocks?" he asked. "The book, the prayers, Heaven, Hell, the whole thing?"

"I don't know," Pritchard replied. "I can't say whether that would be better for we murderers or not. I guess in a way it might be, no fiery damnation and all. One day we'll find out, later than sooner I hope."

"Aye. Later than sooner."

"I will say this, though. If the devil isn't real, and he *doesn't* have a hand in all this..." Pritchard paused, to look at their surroundings. He raised his hands in the air to present as evidence the trench, battlefield and the war itself. "...Then humanity has to be one of the most wretched monstrosities on the face of the Earth."

"I'll drink to that," Vernon said, holding his cup in the air. He waited for Pritchard to reciprocate. "To wretchedness."

"To wretchedness."

GORDON

Guynemer was catching on quickly. The dainty, unassuming young Frenchman, born into money, approached the mechanical side of aviation with every bit the same tenacity as Gordon. In fact, some nights over the past two weeks, Georges Guynemer seemed perpetually energized, pushing Gordon to stay up longer, to teach him everything he could in the shortest time possible.

Gordon had lost track of the hour several hours before, but a glance out the machine shop window affirmed what he already suspected. Somewhere during their after-hours shop work marathon, the time had transitioned from late to early. Still, hunched over the decommissioned rotary engine, both men covered in grease, eyes bloodshot, he and Guynemer were nevertheless going strong. Each night, the broken Gnome approached nearer and nearer to functioning once again.

"Georges, we've been getting to know each other more every day, right?" Gordon asked, removing his hands from the engine. He stood up to stretch his back.

"Yes," Guynemer answered, grunting as he gave a wrench one final twist. He didn't look up from his work.

"If you don't mind me asking, why do you push yourself so hard?"

The Frenchman sighed, still facing the engine. "Look at me," he said, before turning to face Gordon. His eyes burned with intensity, a dark fire. "Since I was a young boy, I've been sick almost as much as I've been healthy. Physically, I am weak. I've always been treated as so. It's why I'm here. They would not even consider me as an infantryman. It is incumbent upon me to show that I am more than what I appear to be. So I push, harder than others. In school I took on the biggest fellows. In sport, I challenged the best. If I lost, so be it, but if I won, I defied expectation. I proved that I could."

Gordon was impressed, but in some strange way, what Guynemer said also worried him. He didn't know why, but there was something ominous in his words, his tone. "There is such a thing as pushing *too* hard, you know."

Without pause Guynemer replied, "Said the colored American fellow who crossed the Atlantic in the hopes to fly for France. Are you not pushing farther than others might be willing?"

"I've got no retort, Georges."

"I would think not."

Their conversation ended when the door creaked open behind them. A bright sliver of morning sunshine beamed into the dim shop, blinding Gordon temporarily. He rubbed his eyes with the back of his hand, trying to refocus. Guynemer did the same.

"My word have you two been up all night?" a dark silhouette asked from within the sunbeam. It was Plamondon.

Gordon held his hand up to shield the light. "Yes sir. Lost track of time."

"In impressive fashion," the instructor commented. He closed the door behind him, and the room seemed much darker. "How is the Gnome coming along?"

"He's doing all right," Gordon smirked, "And this broken engine is improving day by day, too." He nudged Guynemer playfully with his forearm.

"*Con...*" muttered Guynemer.

Plamondon smiled with one corner of his mouth. "I went to the barracks to wake you. I was going to ask you to ready the Shorthorn for a flight at noon."

"We can still do it," Gordon said, ignoring the heaviness in his eyelids. "Right Georges?"

"Yes, of course," the ambitious Frenchman replied.

"I will take you both on your word," Plamondon said. "You can finish up here; just make sure the machine is ready."

When their instructor left, the two of them, neither one willing to admit he was exhausted, made their way to the large white barn in which the Farman Shorthorn was housed. They began the process of inspecting the machine up and down, looking for structural cracks, checking wire tension, controls, control surfaces, the works. The pair climbed onto and crawled underneath, making sure everything was as it should have been. Then it was on to the engine.

"When was the last time you saw your friend Amy?" Guynemer asked when they'd begun the engine work. He'd seen her on the grounds the day she'd visited Gordon while he worked on the engine, and they'd talked of her since.

"Thanksgiving," Gordon replied. He'd already explained to Georges, after some initial confusion, what the holiday was and what it meant to Americans.

"Why has it been so long?"

"Her relatives were taking her on quite the trip, actually. First to the coast, then skiing in the Pyrenees. I'm not sure if she's back yet."

His Thanksgiving date with Amy went well, as their get-togethers generally did. They had a nice turkey dinner, which Amy had specially requested the restaurant serve beforehand (and apparently paid no small amount for). She did manage to confound Gordon afterward, when he, in what he thought was a spontaneous gesture, tried to kiss her after they left the restaurant. She turned away from him, deflecting his kiss to her cheek, then snickered, said goodnight, and he hadn't seen her since. What he told Guynemer about her trip was true, she shared that over desert that last night. It was just that she was supposed to have returned already.

"I think that some of the other fellows here, they are jealous that you spend time with a girl as pretty as her," Guynemer informed Gordon. He was nowhere near as much an outcast, the sin of being born sickly and wealthy not nearly as grave as being born of color, and so he was able to more easily intermingle with the other students.

"Really?" Gordon asked, surprised.

"Yes I think so."

"Good. Fuck them."

Guynemer laughed heartily. So did Gordon.

When he was certain they'd gotten everything on the Shorthorn in order, Gordon was so tired he stood on the verge of passing out. He and Guynemer dragged the Farman out into the slightly chilly late morning sun. The weather was much different in Pau, compared to that of northern France. Temperatures stayed significantly milder, due to not only the further southern latitude, but also the Pyrenees and a closer proximity to the Atlantic. As a result, temperatures generally only fell as low as the thirties, but could still, even in December, climb as high as the sixties.

"Are you confident she's ready?" Plamondon shouted. He was hobbling toward them with some haste. He was excited.

"Wouldn't have rolled her out if I wasn't," Gordon answered self-assuredly.

"That's good," Plamondon grinned. He reached into his coat and removed a leather flying cap. "It'd be a shame to die by your own hand." He tossed the cap to Gordon.

My God.

A jolt shot through Gordon's body. His legs weakened. He thought he would vomit. At first, all he could muster was a single, short gasp, just one shallow inhalation to express his disbelief. When Plamondon smiled and raised his eyebrows, Gordon finally managed to croak, "...What?"

"I will fly this crate today," the instructor said happily, "and you will come up with me. I've been practicing on the penguin when you're not around, and I'm ready to go up thanks to your little invention."

The "penguin," or Blériot roller, had truncated wings, making it flightless. It was a way for students to practice in a functioning cockpit, in a powered machine, without the associated risks of an accidental takeoff. For Plamondon, it was obviously a good way to test the function of his rudder bar claw. Apparently, the testing had gone well.

"Well, Gordon, are you interested?"

Finally coming to grips with the fact that the moment was real, Gordon proclaimed, "Hell yes I'm interested, sir!"

"Good. Then just take a moment to say hello to your lady friend, and we'll get started." Plamondon nodded, directing attention to something or someone over Gordon's shoulder. Amy, in a brown plaid dress, was jogging across the training ground toward them.

What a day this is shaping up to be!

Gordon excused himself to his two associates. He ran to meet Amy, who smiled at him affectionately as they drew nearer. Her red hair flowed behind her from beneath the brown derby hat which she held in place with her free hand. She had her parasol with her but it was closed, clenched in her hand like a baton. It took seeing her in person for Gordon to realize just how much he'd missed her in the two weeks they'd not seen one another. When they met, they embraced each other strongly. Amy kissed Gordon on the cheek.

"I was wondering how long it would be," Gordon said.

"Truth be told, I started counting the days right after I left," Amy replied. "So what are the three of you up to this morning?"

"Do you remember the idea I mentioned, our first night at the restaurant?"

"Your big secret."

"Yes, that one. Well, Plamondon is wearing it on his prosthetic leg right now, and he's about to sit at the controls of that machine! He's going to take me up!" Gordon exclaimed, taking her by the shoulders. "Today!"

"That's great!" Amy said. "Still not so specific about the actual idea, but...close enough. Are you afraid?"

"Why would I be afraid?"

"Well, you've only ever been in the air once, and you crashed. That's all."

The image of Demarais leaping from the tumbling Blériot flashed before Gordon's eyes. A pit formed in his stomach. Suddenly, he *was* just a little afraid. He looked back toward the Farman, Plamondon and Guynemer. Plamondon waved an arm, signaling Gordon to return.

"It looks like you're needed straight away," Amy said, a sweet concern etched onto her face. "Please don't get hurt."

"I trust Plamondon," Gordon assured her. "Just as he trusts my work."

"Well, all the same..." Amy said, and she stepped forward. She reached her hands to Gordon's cheeks, gently drawing his face toward hers. Her hands were soft, warm, and comforting. Their eyes closed and their lips met, and hers was the softest kiss he'd ever felt. Her lips tasted like she'd just eaten something sweet, or maybe that was just his imagination. She held him close, kissed him deeper, and then it was over.

"I...uh..." Gordon said, his heart thumping. He'd never been so flustered in such a good way. "I thought I was supposed to..."

"And you would have," Amy smiled. "Eventually. But I'd be remiss if I let you go up in that aeroplane without kissing you at least once beforehand." She reached for his hand, ignoring that it was filthy with grease. "I'm sure you'll come back fine," she said, stroking his palm. "But a good luck first kiss can't hurt."

"Do you want to stay and watch?" asked Gordon.

"What sort of a question is that?" she chided, slapping his hand. "Of course I'm staying!"

They walked together, joining the two men next to the Farman. They greeted Amy, and she them, and then it was time. Guynemer led Amy to a safe distance from which she could watch. She was a lot taller than him. Plamondon climbed into the pilot's seat in the nacelle, went through the steps of checking the controls, attaching his foot to the rudder and so on, while Gordon positioned himself inside the tail boom, next to the propeller. His petite mechanic friend wasn't quite strong enough to perform the push start, so Gordon had to start the engine himself before climbing aboard.

"Prepared for contact!" he shouted to Plamondon.

"Contact!"

Gordon shoved the prop. The engine started smoothly. Using the port wing's bracing wires for support, he leapt up between the planes and climbed into the front of the nacelle. He turned to his instructor, who had beads of sweat running down the sides of his face. Gordon didn't blame him. The man's last flight had nearly killed not only him, but his good friend as well. As much as it should have been unnerving to see the pilot sweating bullets, Gordon truly did trust him. Additionally, he just plain flat out wanted to be in the air. He gave Plamondon a thumbs-up, and Plamondon did the same. He then waved to Guynemer, signaling him to remove the wheel chocks, which he then did.

The Farman crept forward. Gordon had so much excitement coursing through him his spine tingled. His hands and feet trembled. He ground his teeth. He'd been around the higher powered engines for some time by then, but when Plamondon opened up the throttle, the Renault eight-cylinder's roar surprised him. The roar was different when it was just five feet away.

The machine picked up speed. A breeze began to whoosh past Gordon's face as the craft propelled him faster over the ground. He felt every bump, listened to every creak and rattle, and when their speed was sufficient, his backside pushed deeper into the seat as the Farman lifted away from the Earth.

For just the second time in his life, Gordon was airborne. Everything he'd gone through, the bricklaying, designing and building his project, the crash, the rejection at the recruiter's office, the long hours of studying, the staying up late, it was all worth it. Every second of it. Plamondon flew straight while they ascended, before banking the machine to circle the field. They were already much higher than *The Hawk* had ever flown.

Gordon, in sensory overload, hung over the lip of the nacelle, frantically trying to absorb all the scenery he could before the experience was over. The training ground, the clouds, Pau, the Pyrenees beyond, the world was so goddamned beautiful from up there. Below him, Amy and Guynemer were barely more than ants, waving at the magnificent man-made bird flying above them. Gordon, a huge smile, excitedly waved back at them.

His journey had taken him across the Atlantic on a desperate whim, in search of an opportunity. He'd gotten a slim one, and thus far he'd made good on the promises he gave along the way. To Sergent Bellamy, the first person to open a door to him. To Plamondon, who took it upon himself to open the door even wider. For those men, for what they'd done for him, he'd strived to do his best. And now, because of one idea, one simple invention, one of those two men had gotten back something he'd lost. That, in itself, would have been enough for Gordon. It had both helped Plamondon, his friend, and also gotten him back in the air. But it had also done something else that would have a profound effect on Gordon's future.

Until then, none of the other instructors at the school would give him the time. None of the flight instructors were at all willing to train him. With Plamondon's disability formerly holding him back, he could not have properly trained new pilots. But now, a thousand feet above the Earth, because of Gordon's simple invention, that notion was completely obliterated.

Gordon Graham had an instructor who could teach him to fly.

ARTHUR & PERCY

Thump-thump.
  "Art, is everything okay?"
  Thump-thump.
  "Art, can you even hear me?"
  Please don't bloody let them come across today...
  "Art?"
  Arthur's heart was thumping into his throat as he stood on the firing step, waiting for the order to stand-down. He was cold and afraid, and had gotten very little sleep that night. The low eastern sun was a hazy, whitish-yellow dot obscured by another overcast sky. It was the standard practice that, at both dawn and dusk, nearly all front line troops, rifles ready, stood in the trench on high alert. Dawn and dusk were the commonest times for the commencement of enemy attacks. Occasionally, those attacks came. More often though, the Germans across no man's land were also standing on high alert, waiting for a British attack.
  "Arthur!" Percy hissed. Arthur was breathing heavy. His eyes were closed. Percy was worried. He slapped his friend on the shoulder to snap him out of his trance
  "What?!" Arthur whispered jumpily. "You startled me."
  "How? I've been standing next to you the entire time." Percy could tell his friend was doing his best to breathe normally. Try as he might, though, Arthur exhaled shakily.

"At ease, men," Second Lieutenant Fuller said quietly. He repeated himself every few yards to inform the long line of men on the firing step. To shout the order loud and clear would potentially notify the enemy that the British trench was no longer on high alert. Upon receiving the order, Arthur took a long, deep breath and turned his back to the trench's front wall.

"I'm scared too, you know," Percy assured him as they sat down. "At home I was nervous working in the pit, I hated it, but this is a thousand times worse. A thousand times more dangerous. It's all right to be afraid."

Arthur shuddered. His eyes burned. He wanted to cry, but there was no way in hell he'd let himself do that. "I'm practically pissing in my britches, Percy. What an arsehole I was, pushing you to sign up for this when I'm the one who can barely hold it together."

"Oh, bugger that," Percy scoffed. He wrapped an arm around his friend's shoulder and hugged him close. "You saw all those boys who signed up when we were still back in England. We would've gotten caught up in all this anyway, just like your father said a lot of boys eventually would. It's just that we got here ahead of the curve."

With Percy, Arthur could share that he was afraid. However, he refused to share just how deep the fear ran. How gripping it was. Nearly every night he was having horrifying dreams, of shadows dropping into the trench in the wee hours, of a Jack Johnson landing beside him, shredding him to nothing, of cowering in an open field as machine guns chattered all around him, of never seeing Elizabeth ever again. He wrapped her scarf around his mouth every night just to muffle his whimpers, which he was certain he made during his dreams. He slept poorly, in short intervals, never making it through an entire night. If a dream didn't rouse him, an odd noise would. Every day was a struggle. The rum ration helped, not in that it got him drunk, it was little more than a snort, it just helped in that it was one of but a few luxuries. It was a taste of normal.

That morning's rum ration was on the way. Immediately after the morning stand-down was the easiest time to get the men their ration. Sergeant MacCallum, a fiery, red-headed Scottish transplant, was in charge of distribution. He, and strangely, Captain Otis, stood with the boys of 4 Section, pouring the contents of his SRD jug into their waiting cups.

"Looks like Scotland's Redheadedest Drunk is willing to split his hoard with us today," Percy kidded, nudging Arthur's ribs. It was the standing joke that the sergeant consistently snuck more than his allocation from the jugs, though the joke had little veracity. MacCallum had voiced his lack of appreciation for the humor in a profanity-laced torrent of Gaelic and English a week earlier, so now the alternate meaning of SRD was only whispered among the men of First Platoon.

Normally, MacCallum distributed the elixir by himself. Sometimes, Fuller would make the rounds with him. But that morning was the first time Arthur had ever seen Captain Otis assisting with the rum. It wasn't that Otis was not a man of the people, he was, it was just that the rum wasn't at all his responsibility.

Arthur liked the captain. Everyone did. Otis was the congenial sort; he took the time to speak with his men, to truly associate with them. He led from the front, and that earned him unflinching respect. Following Arthur's run through Radinghem, the captain took an interest in him. With responsibility for close to two hundred men, it wasn't as if Otis spent an inordinate amount of time speaking with Arthur—their conversations were brief and infrequent—but Arthur got the sense that the captain could tell everything wasn't all right in his mind.

Otis didn't coddle him, not in any sense of the word, but he did ask Arthur, or had Fuller ask him, to perform a number of menial tasks over the weeks. It was something that a bitter soldier might view as grunt work. To Arthur, though, tasks kept his mind occupied—a good thing for a nervous brain. Whether the task was delivering a simple message to the captain of another company, or a piece of equipment to another platoon, or fixing something that was broken, Otis did what he could to ensure Arthur kept it together. The two never spoke about it outright, but Arthur was sure the captain knew.

"Good morning, Ward. Ellis," Otis greeted them. He'd outpaced McCallum, who was still serving the men of 2 Section.

"Morning sir," the pair greeted back.

"Ellis, I've got something for you," the captain grinned. He held a rolled newspaper in his hand.

"Sir?"

Otis unrolled the paper. It was a week-old edition of *The London Gazette.* He opened to a particular page and pointed to a list of names. "Look about halfway down, Ellis, and tell me what you see."

Arthur scanned the middle column. It jumped out at him almost right away. He gasped when he read it.

Private Arthur Ellis, 2nd York and Lancaster Battalion

He'd been mentioned in the despatches! No doubt it was on Captain Otis's recommendation. That was something to be proud of, an acknowledgement to the people back home that his soldiering had proven noteworthy. *Maybe my parents saw it,* he thought, *maybe Ellie saw it!*

"Do you see there, Ward?" Otis said, placing his finger next to Arthur's name.

"How about that!" Percy exclaimed. "My best pal in a London paper. That is topping news!"

"Congratulations, Ellis," the captain said.

"Thank you sir," Arthur replied calmly. "I'm honored, truly."

"Modest..." Otis said. "An admirable trait. Say, Ellis," he continued, "I've got a communique here for the captain over in D Company. After Sergeant McCallum passes through and you've drank your share, why don't you run over and deliver it for me?"

"Will do sir," answered Arthur. There had been some light shooting over near D Company during the night. He wondered if they'd been shooting at the enemy, or if it might have just been nerves.

"That's a good chap," Otis said. He took the folded yellow communique from his breast pocket, handing it over. Then he took something else from his pocket. "For your troubles," he said, and he threw the item to Arthur.

It was a York and Lancaster cap badge.

"Better late than never, Ellis," the captain said. "Now you and Miss Ward both have one." He winked.

Arthur's eyes teared. He'd been waiting to get his badge, and he'd not expected to wait as long as he had. It meant a lot to him, to get it from Captain Otis. "Thank you, sir."

"Just returning what belongs to you," the captain said. "Well, carry on you two. Do try and be somewhat prompt with that message, Ellis."

"Yes sir."

The captain walked away, greeting each man or group of men as he passed them. Arthur quickly and proudly pinned the badge to his cap. McCallum finished serving the boys in 2 Section, and just seconds later, Arthur, Percy and the rest of 1 Section were crowded around the sergeant, thrusting their cups in his direction.

"Christ almighty, wait your turn, boyos," the fire-bearded McCallum said in his thick Scottish accent. "Ellis drinks first today." He grabbed Arthur by the wrist of his outstretched, cup-bearing hand, and poured far more than an allotted share, filling the cup to its very brim.

"And why does Crash get so much?" asked Baker.

"'Cos the boyo's been mentioned in the despatches," the sergeant said, "and that gets a boyo an extra dose of spirits!"

"If he gets a full cup for getting his name in the papers," Baker scoffed, "then what will you give me when I'm awarded the Victoria Cross? The whole damned jug?!"

The group laughed.

"I wager your prize will be a hefty dose of smelling salts and a pinch on the arse," McCallum declared over the laughter, "because you've taken a hard bloody knock to the head and it's got you unconscious and dreaming loads of bullshite!"

They laughed again, minus Baker, who shot angry scowls. When the sergeant finished pouring, the men raised a toast to Arthur. He showed them where his name was in the paper, a few of them huddled around to read some of the articles, and then he excused himself to deliver Otis's communique.

Snow had fallen intermittently during the previous few days, so the trench floor was particularly muddy. He tried to choose a path where he'd trudge through the least amount of melt water and mire, but missteps were inevitable. The mud coating his boots gradually crept up his puttees, climbing his shins toward his knees. He reached one spot where a large standing pool of brown water separated two groups of the trench's occupants. Some of the men warned Arthur about that spot as he moved through, even claiming that one poor Tommy had already drown there after falling in and becoming stuck while on sentry duty. At first, he didn't buy the story.

He hugged the back wall in an attempt to shimmy around the pool, but his boots slipped and he slid belly first into the icy water. A thick layer of mud sucked at his legs, nearly dragging him beneath the water's surface. With some effort, he managed to claw his gloved fingers into the mud and drag himself out of the deadly pool. Upon escaping the quagmire, he had no problem believing it had killed a man. The soldiers on the far side of the mud pit helped him to his feet, that is to say, subsequent to getting their enjoyment out of watching his struggle. He wondered how much trouble he would have had to get in for them to help when he actually needed it.

Arthur was covered in mud. Drenched to the bone. Since receiving his beloved winter cap, scarf, gloves and sweater from Elizabeth, he'd tried his damnedest to keep them clean. Now they were absolutely filthy. The water had soaked through every layer of his clothing. He knew how cold he'd be in a matter of minutes, but at that point, he was much too furious to feel it.

"BOLLOCKS!" he yelled. He flicked his hands toward the ground, flinging some of the mud from his fingers.

"Those were awfully nice accessories to be sloshing around in, making mud pies," a corporal taunted. "Since you've soiled them, I'll offer you five quid for the whole lot."

"Bugger that," said another man, "I'll give you ten!"

"Piss off," Arthur told them. He wiped all the mud he was able to from his trousers and the front skirts of his coat. The men on both sides of the puddle had a raucous laugh at his back. He didn't blame them for laughing, he just hated that he'd made a fool of himself.

Arthur wasn't looking up when he found the first boys from D Company. Not at first. They were seated on some scavenged wooden chairs, quietly chatting and smoking cigarettes. Passing off his drenched, stained uniform as a matter of course, he politely asked them, "Would any of you chaps know where I might find your captain?" He tried to sound as official as possible, despite his appearance.

"Haven't seen him," was the general reply.

"Might you point me in the direction of—"

It was then that Arthur happened to look directly above them, along the top of the front wall. That was when it caught his attention.

"What the?!" he cried, stumbling on his heels against the wall behind him. Above the group of men was a dead German soldier, white-faced and blue-lipped, sprawled over the parapet, his chin resting right on the wall's edge. His left leg rose in the air behind him, suspended by a run of barbed wire, drawn taut. His eyes were open, but rolled back in his head.

"Oh, I see you've met our Hun friend!" one of the men said happily. "I was wondering why you had yet to say hullo."

"Why is he lying there?!" Arthur asked, aghast.

"Check his foot, mate," an old-hand said. "He's caught up in the wire."

"Why don't you cut him down, then?"

"You want one of us to climb up there in broad daylight?" the older soldier replied indignantly. "I'm not taking a bullet from a Hun sniper just to cut a dead Hun free. Would you like to cut him down, young lad?"

"I...I just think something should be done for him, that's all," Arthur said. He backed away from the unfazed group and stumbled off, nauseated.

He eventually found a lieutenant, who informed him that D Company's captain was back at HQ. The lieutenant offered to deliver the communique himself, and sent Arthur on his way.

He didn't want to walk past the dead German again, but he had to. The group of Tommies saw Arthur coming. They greeted him from afar. He was moving quickly, head down, but he couldn't completely ignore them. He had to move through them to get back.

"Hey young chap, we took your advice," one of them said, pointing to the corpse above. "We did something for him!"

Arthur didn't want to look. But he did. His jaw dropped. The German now had a lit cigarette protruding from his blue lips.

"He looked like he could use a coffin nail!" a younger private guffawed. His laugh probably only sounded devilish and sinister to Arthur's ears, because the rest of his mates howled.

Arthur grew dizzy. How could his own countrymen act so insensitive toward the dead? His heart began to race, the same way it did when an artillery round whistled overhead, the same way it did at dawn and dusk stand-to. It wasn't just the Germans that scared him—it was the whole damned war.

Why did I sign up for this? Is this what will happen to me? The trench swirled around him. The laughter of the Tommies standing before him echoed loudly in Arthur's head. He blinked hard, wishing it was his imagination when he saw the old-hand reach up and pluck the cigarette from the dead man's mouth. He wished it wasn't real when the man placed the cigarette in his own mouth and took a long, drawn-out puff, before blowing a mouthful of smoke back into the dead German's face.

Three months of experience in modern warfare bubbled up from deep inside Arthur's soul. The fear, the squalor, the death, it wasn't what he read about as a boy. They were calling it the Great War. H.G. Wells had even called it 'the war to end war,' but from where Arthur stood, from what he'd seen already, it seemed more like the war that ended humanity.

He tried to stifle the vomit, to not show how disturbed he was by the scene, but he couldn't swallow it down. Three months of the Great War bubbled up and out of his body, through his mouth and onto the muddy trench floor.

Then Arthur collapsed.

DENIS

The snowfall had turned stealthy trench raiding into a near impossibility. While it didn't completely blanket no man's land, it came close. More fell every couple of days. When it wasn't cloudy, snow reflected the light from the moon, making it much easier for enemy sentries to see into the distance. Since neither Denis nor any of his men had anything resembling white clothing, if they risked a raid, their dark blue attire would stand out against a largely white backdrop. Worse, when nighttime temperatures fell, the snow became crunchy. No matter how lightly one treaded, boots on snow made noise. Because of that, they had not conducted a raid since their experiment with Schwartz's kerosene bombs.

December 22 had been a quiet day to then. No shells, no shooting, no activity. Just a cold, grey-skied morning. Denis was seated on an ammunition box, contemplatively smoking a cigarette. His men were seated too, some smoking, or chatting, or writing home. Except Sergent Veilleux. He was on his feet, facing the front wall, brass knuckle dagger in hand, shadowboxing, or something to that effect (shadow stabbing and slashing, maybe). Denis watched him with a sense of amusement, and a twinge of concern.

"You know..." Rose whispered, looking up from the letter he'd been working on. He elbowed Denis to get his attention. "I think Veilleux has lost his mind."

"What makes you say that?" asked Denis, only half serious.

"You're kidding, right?"

Denis shrugged.

"Hey Sergent..." Rose said. He cleared his throat. "What are you going to give me for Christmas? You've only got three days left, in case you've forgotten."

Veilleux ignored him. He continued to knife fight his invisible opponent. Rose looked back to Denis, apparently seeking an affirmation of his assertion about the sergent's state of mind. Denis shrugged again.

"The Kaiser's testicles..." Veilleux said suddenly, almost under his breath. "Still in the purse. I'll even leave the handle on." He tucked his blade into his waist belt. "I'm sure you like that sort of thing," he said, turning away from the wall to face the rest of the group. It was the most he'd said to any of them since their group had been formed.

Everyone stopped what they were doing the instant the sergent spoke. Denis's cigarette dangled from his slightly agape mouth. To his right, he watched as Rose's mouth, also agape, slowly curled into a smile. He laughed first. Then everyone else followed. Veilleux didn't smile, though; he just sat down on the firing step and stared blankly at the back wall.

I'm glad this queer fellow is on my side, Denis thought. The sergent was literally staring off into nothing.

"Good morning, gentlemen," a voice said to Denis's right. It was Lieutenant Armistead.

The raiders stood at attention when they turned around and realized that it wasn't just Armistead behind them, but also Capitaine Bex.

"Roux, may we have a word?" said the lieutenant. He beckoned for Denis to follow.

Denis handed his cigarette to Rose, who gladly took it. When he joined the lieutenant and the capitaine, whom he hadn't seen much of recently, he worried he might be in trouble for something. They didn't walk far, just enough so that the others wouldn't hear their conversation.

"Capitaine Bex and I have an early Christmas present of sorts to give you," Armistead declared. "Although I'm not entirely sure you will have wanted it."

"What is it sir?" asked Denis. Bex's face was expressionless, hidden as usual behind his large moustache and low-riding kepi.

"We've heard whisperings," Bex said, "that an Allemande colonel has placed a bounty on the heads of a group of men that the front line troops are calling *die Schattenmänner*."

Denis smirked for a split second. *The shit men?* He didn't speak German. "What does that word mean?" he inquired, forcing himself to stifle a laugh.

"The Shadowmen," Armistead replied. "Rumor has it that these Shadowmen sneak right under the noses of sentries, slash men's throats without so much as a whisper, even set fire to men in their sleep."

Bex had more to add, and smiled beneath his moustache. "Machine gunners take to their posts in the morning to find their weapons dismantled, broken. Sometimes, they say, the Shadowmen don't even leave footprints."

For the second time that morning, Denis's mouth fell agape.

"Yes," Bex said, "the Shadowmen have caused no small amount of consternation amongst our opponent's ranks."

"That's...incredible," Denis said. Incredible, because almost all of it was bullshit. They'd only dismantled one machine gun, threw kerosene bombs once, and two of their raids had ended in their fleeing for their lives from gunfire. War nerves and imaginations run wild had turned his party's moderately successful actions into full-fledged boche mythologies, and in a short time span at that.

"It *is* incredible," Armistead replied, "but you must also understand that it may be a double-edged sword. You've got their men scared at night, rife with anticipation, but as dangerous as your undertakings were before, they will be that much more so going forward."

"With a price on your heads," Bex cleared his throat, "you can be assured more of their men will be lying in wait. Is that something you and your men are prepared to face?"

Denis didn't need to mull it over. His men hated the boche every bit as much as he did. "Absolutely, sir," he assured. "It is invigorating to know that we're having a psychological impact."

"Outstanding," Bex said. "Now as for the request you made last week, pertaining to the allocation of white trousers, tunics and caps for your squad, I'm afraid that may take some time. Because, as you know, there are no standard-issue white garments, anything of that sort must be made custom, and will likely come in the form of a cloth outer cover rather than full garments fashioned in white."

"I understand, sir," Denis replied.

"As such," Bex continued, "and taking into account the recent developments, I and the lieutenant will persist in withholding our sending you on any further missions. That is, until said attire can be procured. I will maintain my ongoing correspondence in regards to obtaining the necessary materials."

"Yes sir. Thank you sir."

"Oh, I almost forgot," said Armistead. He extracted a small bundle from his coat pocket. "Here."

The bundle was heavy. Like a pistol.

"I had the gunsmith make a modification I believe you'll appreciate," the lieutenant said.

Denis unfolded the cloth bundle to find his refurbished revolver. The metal was polished black and shiny. There was a strange metal tube attached to the end of the barrel. "Is this a Maxim Silencer?" he asked.

"It is," replied Armistead.

"I thought they didn't work on pistols."

"The smith is skilled in what he does."

"Thank you, sir. Very much." Denis saluted the two officers and rejoined his men. He unscrewed the suppressor from his pistol's barrel and put them in his holster. When the time came, he'd be able to shoot sentries rather than his men risking being spotted taking them out by hand.

"What'd they say, Roux?" Hennequin asked curiously. He didn't waste a second.

"Yeah, come now," Barbot said.

"Have you men ever heard of *die Schattenmänner?*" asked Denis. He tried to hide his smile, but couldn't.

"The...shadow...men?" Schwartz said uncertainly. He spoke what might be considered a functional amount of German.

The raiders traded confused expressions, shrugging and shaking their heads.

"It's us," Denis announced, to more confused looks. "We're the Shadowmen."

"So you went ahead and picked a name for us," said Rose, "and you went with a boche one? For the irony?"

"No, you dolt," Denis laughed. "It's the name the boche have given to us! We've got them shitting in their trousers at night!"

"You're full of it..." accused Barbot.

"I assure you I'm not. That was what the lieutenant and the capitaine wanted to speak about. There's some pissed off boche colonel over there who has placed a price on our heads. We've got his men thinking we're evil spirits or some nonsense like that."

"Holy shit..." Rose said pensively. Then the revelation hit him in an apparently different way. "Holy shit!" he exclaimed, jumping to his feet. "They think we're fucking ghosts!" he laughed, and the other raiders began to laugh and celebrate with him.

Denis watched his men celebrate, with the exception of Veilleux, who remained seated and still, like a gargoyle that'd fallen from atop a medieval building and landed in a drainage ditch. Rather than holding vigil high above a cityscape, he stared at the brown wall directly ahead of him.

As the raiders laughed, congratulated one another and ridiculed the boche paranoia, Denis reflected upon his time since the mobilization in August. So much had transpired since then, and there was no way of telling how much longer it all would last. No way of telling how long *he* would last. No way to know whether or not his streak of vengeance would be cut short—before penance for Patrice's death was paid. Denis had already walked away almost entirely unscathed (physically, at least) from four major battles, including hand to hand engagements on more than one occasion. Countless bullets, numerous shells, and even a few blades had all failed to put an end to his war. As far as odds went, he was basically already living on borrowed time.

Patrice was dead. He would always and forever be dead. Denis wished every day that he wasn't, but war wasn't a business in which many wishes were granted. So the only thing to do, the only way to ensure Patrice died for *something* was to fight on. To win.

Fixated on vengeance or not, his anger toward the boche could never fully crowd out of his mind and heart the love for his mother, father and Louise. Nothing could do that. There were things he didn't know about them, things he had to know. He reached into his hip pocket for the brief letter he'd received from Cécile the day before. He must have read it fifty times already, but he unfolded and pored over it once again.

Dear Denis,

Words cannot express how much it meant that you traveled all the way to Bordeaux to see me. It was noble, and respectful, and I will never forget it. I am glad to know that you are doing well, and I appreciate your concern in allowing me time to grieve. I'm doing much better myself now as well. I can't imagine how awful it must be, to not know the whereabouts of your family.

Denis stopped reading to take a breath. He sniffled. His eyes were starting to sting. He rubbed his hand over his mouth and chin. Cécile was someone with whom, through loss, he shared an emotional bond, but beyond that bond, they really did not know each other that well. Yet in his hand was a letter from her, stating her intention to do something for him that transcended a mere favor done for an acquaintance. She was about to go well out of her way. He skipped over the rest of the words, to the letter's last line. The last line filled him with tremendous excitement, but also with fear as to what might ultimately be revealed.

I will board the train to Paris tomorrow. I shall start my search for your family there.

VERNON

"Good afternoon, Hayes," Sergeant Spurling greeted him.

"Sergeant," Vernon greeted back with a nod. He'd been staring at his last letter from Sally. Along with the letter came a package containing tobacco, chocolate bars, a small pound cake and some chewing gum. The gifts were nice, but her words mattered more, and he read them again and again, wishing there was some way he could see her.

"Quite a way to spend Christmas Eve, aye?" said Spurling.

"Huh?" Vernon said distractedly. He heard what the sergeant said; it was just that he was simultaneously reading the *Love, Sally* at the bottom of the letter for the hundredth time. "Oh, yes," he replied, "well at least Fritz is being quiet."

"They've been rather quiet the whole week, wouldn't you say?"

"I would. It's an odd thing really."

"What is?"

"We leave the front in one spot, where we scrap with one group of German chaps, and return to a different spot, so we're across the way from a whole new lot of them. They aren't shooting at us, and we're not shooting at them."

Spurling appeared to take stock of the comment before saying, "I think the Huns around Wulverghem are just as nasty as the ones further north."

"Yet you said it yourself," Vernon observed. "They've been quiet since we arrived."

"Maybe they're lulling us into complacency," retorted the sergeant.

"Maybe they think we're doing the same. Regardless. It's Christmas Eve, and the last thing I want to do is point and fire my weapon. With any luck, those Huns over there feel the same way."

"I hope your right," Spurling said. "Anyhow, I'm not here to discuss them. Where is Llewelyn?"

"He left about a minute before you got here," Vernon said, pointing down the trench in the opposite direction from which Spurling had arrived. "Should be back soon."

"I've got something for him," the sergeant declared softly, looking over both shoulders. Apparently, whatever it was, it was a secret. The others in 3 Section weren't paying attention anyway. Those close by chatted, or napped, or ritualistically cleaned their Enfields. In the dirt and mud of trench life, rifle cleaning was a daily essential, more valuable and practical than saying one's prayers.

"What have you got for him?" Vernon asked.

"Since you're his best mate, I suppose I've got no qualms in letting you in on it straight away. I was told by Sergeant Major Cortland to do this quietly. He was afraid the captain might go off half-cocked and spoil the moment."

"Why don't you stop going roundabout it and just bloody tell me what you've got to tell me?"

Spurling reached into the satchel on his hip and handed Vernon a telegram. It was from divisional HQ. "Don't read it aloud," he said, "Not yet at least."

Vernon held the telegram in front of his face, and read it with growing suspicion.

For marked bravery in his actions dated September 15, 1914, Pvt. Llewelyn Pritchard 7181, is hereby awarded the Distinguished Conduct Medal. On said date, under intense fire near Missy-sur-Aisne, he showed unabashed selflessness in carrying his badly wounded lieutenant over treacherous terrain, to safety more than a mile away. His actions saved the officer's life, and his consistent good conduct is a testament to His Majesty's armed forces.

"Hood..." Vernon said reflectively.

"Hood indeed," Spurling agreed. "No man deserves the award more than Llewelyn, and no doubt Lieutenant Hood made damned sure the proper ears heard it so."

"Do you have the medal as well?"

"I do."

"Would you mind if I was the one who gave it to him?"

Spurling only pondered the request for a second. "Wouldn't bother me at all," he said. He reached into his satchel again for a manila envelope. It jingled a little when he handed it over.

Vernon covertly opened it and slid the medal into his half-clenched palm to have a look. The silver medal was circular, like a large coin, just under an inch and a half in diameter, and bore a profile image of King George V on the front. There was an inscription in Latin above the king's effigy, though apart from the king's name, Vernon had no idea what it said. The award was attached to its ribbon—two crimson outer stripes and a dark blue stripe down the center—by an ornate metal clasp. He turned the medal over. On the back was the inscription, *FOR DISTINGUISHED CONDUCT IN THE FIELD*. He beamed with intense pride in knowing that his best friend was now a decorated soldier.

"When will you give it to him?" Spurling asked.

"I'll find a good time."

"I was hoping to be around when you did, but I have other matters to attend to. Merry Christmas, Hayes."

"A Merry Christmas to you, Sergeant. And thank you."

"I was just the delivery man. Good day."

It wasn't more than five minutes after Spurling left that Pritchard came back.

"Where'd you go?" Vernon asked him.

"Ah I was just carrying on with some chaps over in Third Platoon. They're all pissed up and jolly."

"Where'd they get the extra drink?" Vernon inquired. Without imbibing a copious amount of spirits, it was impossible to be jolly in their situation. Certainly no one nearby was jolly.

"They wouldn't say." Pritchard suddenly stepped up onto the firing step and gazed across no man's land. "Or share."

"What are you doing, Lew?" Vernon said snappily. "Keep your bloody head down!"

"Relax, Vernon. No one's shooting anyone today." Pritchard gazed across the hundred and fifty yard expanse separating the British and German trenches. After ten seconds or so, he sighed. "I never knew the world could be this grey. Grey sky, grey earth, grey sentiments. And chaps dressed in bloody grey across the way. They've got to hate this as much as us, right?"

"Who knows?" Vernon dismissed. "I've got something that will perk you up for certain, though. Why don't you sit down and—"

"Do you ever wonder what it would be like to just have a chat with one of those blokes over there?" Pritchard interrupted. "To see what they think of all this? What they think of us?"

HENTSCH

There was a Tommy across no man's land carelessly sticking his head out in the open. The sun, masked by the grey sky for the entire day, would stealthily slip beyond the horizon within the hour. Hentsch, his rifle in hand, steadied his breathing. He rested his sights on the British man's head, and then tapped the outer edge of the trigger guard with his index finger. He didn't fire.

"Merry Christmas, Tommy..." he said softly. There was no way he would shoot a man just minding his business—albeit foolishly—on Christmas Eve. Another day, maybe. After all, the British weren't shooting either.

It was mostly unspoken, but amongst the lower ranks a sort of live and let live attitude toward the men in the opposing trench had begun to take hold. Since his arrival with his new unit, Hentsch had fired very few shots. Artillery fire was light, offensives nonexistent. Why kill men who didn't seem hell bent on killing him?

The transition into a new regiment, in a new army, had gone smoothly. There was no reason for it not to. There had been no fighting to speak of. Upon arriving with the 139th Regiment, Hentsch, Simon, Engel and Michael were placed together in the same gruppe, Hentsch in charge. Leadership was not so desperately needed as they had been told at Guise.

"Augustus why don't you sit down?" urged Simon.

"There's a fellow over there staring across," Hentsch replied. "He does not move."

"You want me to shoot him?" Michael asked dryly.

Hentsch slid away from the parapet and slinked to a seat on the firing step. "No, I don't want you to shoot him."

"Maybe I will anyway," the defiant young man quipped. He started to stand.

"Sit your ass down, Eberhardt," Hentsch growled. Michael listened.

"We're still here," Simon said. His voice was quiet. "You were right."

"What are you talking about?" asked Hentsch.

"You said this would go on longer than was originally thought. Now here we are, just a few hours from Christmas, with no end in sight."

That fact had become obvious to everyone well before then. It didn't matter at all that Hentsch knew it a little earlier. He shrugged the comment off.

"At least we made it this far..." Engel interjected. "Dead in a ditch on Christmas Eve is far worse than merely living in one."

"You're right," Simon admitted. "Technically."

They hadn't been talking much that day, and the conversation died down again. Hentsch knew everyone was just as saddened by their circumstance as him. Upon settling back into trench life, he'd written two letters home, the cursory dishonest sort, leaving out the gruesome details just like he told his friends he would. He wept in secret when the reply letters arrived. His mother made sure to let him know how much he was missed. Pauline did, too. His father's usual tone, as expected, was one of curiosity. But Hentsch refused to oblige him.

He'd also sent a letter to Louise, the pretty French nurse. It was brief, outwardly unrevealing in regards to his adoration of her, and he waited for more than a week before sending it. The wait was a difficult one. In a way, he missed her dearly, though their acquaintanceship lasted but a few weeks. He wanted to hear from her, because that meant that she at least cared enough (or was nice enough) to take time from her day to write back. The reply had yet to come, but he remained hopeful.

He thought about her often. Occasionally, he even dreamt of her. It was such an odd and noble thing that those lovely French nurses were doing at the hospital. Their kindness was transcendent, their bravery in the face of modern war's horrors, awe-inspiring. Hentsch cursed himself for not asking Louse in his letter to both thank her fellow nurses for him and also to voice his praise and admiration for their selflessness.

He'd become lost in thought. He snapped out of it when Simon cleared his throat and stood.

"Excuse me, gentlemen," Simon proclaimed, his high voice sounding about as serious as it could. "Now, with night soon upon us, is as good a time as any to wish you all a Merry Christmas. So, Merry Christmas, everyone."

Some men, like Hentsch and Engel, said it back sincerely. Others, like Michael, barely troubled themselves to grumble their unenthusiastic reply. It was sad to spend Christmas in a trench, there was no way around that, and men could be forgiven for not reveling in Christmas cheer. Simon cleared his throat again and then, surprisingly, began to sing.

Stille Nacht, Heilige Nacht!
Alles schlaft; einsam wacht.

Hentsch knew the song after the first word; everyone did. What he didn't know, was just how beautiful Simon's voice would be. It was strong, voluminous, yet sugary sweet. It was angelic, and it stabbed Hentsch in the heart almost immediately. He placed a hand over his mouth to hide his woeful expression as the tears filled his eyes.

It was Christmas Eve, and millions of Europe's young men were away from their loved ones, stuck in the cold and wet trenches. Hundreds of thousands more were dead. And there they all were, on the eve of Europe's—indeed much of the world's—most unifying holiday, at war with their fellow man. With his hand, Hentsch masked the lower half of his saddened face, but he couldn't hide the tears welling in his eyes while the pallid young soldier with the cherubic voice continued to sing.

Nur das traute hochheilige Paar.
Holder Knabe im lockigen Haar,
Schlaf in himmlischer Ruh!
Schlaf in himmlischer Ruh!

By the time Simon had finished the first verse, tears were streaming down Hentsch's cheeks. He need not have been ashamed. Engel, his battle-hardened friend, was weeping every bit the same. Even Michael, clearly trying his best to act unfazed, surreptitiously ran his sleeve across his face while looking away from Simon. Every German within earshot had tears in his eyes.

When Simon began the second verse, he beckoned for his comrades to join in. To the man, after very few confirming glances around to one another, they did.

Stille Nacht, heilige Nacht!
Hirten erst, kundgemacht...

VERNON

Pritchard finally gave up looking at the German trenches and plopped down next to Vernon. "So what is it you've got for me?" he asked.

"What I'm about to give you is not a gift," Vernon said, "it's not been given out of kindness, or sympathy, or in the spirit of the holiday, this is something you've *earned*," he emphasized the word strongly, "by being the soldier you are." He took Pritchard by the wrist, turned his friend's hand palm-up, and rested his other hand atop Pritchard's palm, placing the Distinguished Conduct Medal in the hand of its rightful recipient.

When Vernon pulled his hand away, Pritchard gently, almost skeptically, picked the decoration up by its ribbon. He held it in front of his face with a mystified expression.

"The Distinguished Conduct Medal..." he said finally. His bewilderment was obvious, his tone—unbelieving. "What is it for?"

Vernon gave him the telegram. As he read it, the left corner of his mouth curled ever so slightly. "Let me guess," he mused, "Bannister had nothing to do with this whatsoever."

"You never know..." Vernon said.

"Yes," Pritchard replied surely, "this is something you *can* know. Hood, Cortland, and whoever else had a hand in this, worked around the captain to make it so."

"Which goes to show you, the right people believed strongly that you deserved it. You deserve it and more, my friend. Much more. Should we tell the others?"

"Maybe later," Pritchard said, "I don't want to make a scene. What if the captain happens to come through and—"

"The captain is off getting zig zagged, either by himself or with the rest of the officers," Vernon interrupted. "He won't—"

"SHH!" Pritchard held his hand up. "Listen," he whispered.

Vernon did. Sure enough, there was noise coming from the direction of the German trench. At first the noise was faint, nondescript. His first instinct was to reach for his gun. "Those bastards better not be readying up for an attack," he snarled.

"Shut up, Vernon!" Pritchard hissed. "They're singing!" He jumped onto the firing step once again, and this time Vernon joined him. The Germans really were singing.

Durch der Engel Halleluja,

The singing grew louder. More men on the German side were joining in.

Tönt es laut von fern und nah:
Christ, der Retter ist da!
Christ, der Retter ist da!

Soon a long line of Tommies stood on the firing step, staring toward the German trench. The English had their own version of the same song. It had been around for more than fifty years. Rather than question the strangeness of the moment, a few good-spirited fellows began to sing, quietly at first, more to themselves than anyone else. It was as if they were simply affirming to themselves that it was indeed Christmas, regardless of their circumstance. Pritchard was one of the first, and Vernon wasn't about to let his friend sing alone. The British boys started their version from the beginning, but sang their verses in unison with the later verses of the German song already in progress.

Stille Nacht, heilige Nacht!
"Silent Night, holy Night!"
Gottes Sohn, o wie lacht.
"All is calm, all is bright."
Lieb' aus deinem göttlichen Mund,
"'Round yon virgin Mother and Child."

Da uns schlägt die rettende Stund'
"Holy infant so tender and mild."
Christ, in deiner Geburt!
"Sleep in heavenly peace!"
Christ in deiner Geburt!
"Sleep in heavenly peace!"

The British men continued singing after the Germans had finished. As the song traveled down the line, it grew in volume, reaching a crescendo during the final verse. It was a touching moment, shared between the men of two nations at war, and when the song finished, the British men staring across no man's land saw the heads of their enemies slowly rising up from the trenches a hundred and fifty yards away.

"Would you look at that..." Vernon mumbled.

Pritchard smiled at him. His big brown eyes glistened. "Merry Christmas, Fritz!" he shouted. He waved his arms over his head.

"Merry Christmas, Tommy!" a solitary voice echoed back. One of the Germans waved his arms, too.

Just as suddenly, Pritchard backed away from the firing step and knelt down in the mud. He began digging inside his haversack.

"Lew, what are you doing?" Vernon asked.

"I'm going to go out there," Pritchard replied, "to see if they'd like to trade." He found his cigarettes and one of the chocolate bars Vernon's wife had sent him.

"Christ almighty, you'll be shot for certain," Vernon said. "By one side or the other." He stepped down to try and talk some sense.

"No I won't, Vernon, not today." He sounded so sure of himself that Vernon struggled to find the words to make an argument.

"At least keep a round chambered in your Luger," the dumbfounded Vernon managed to spit out.

"I almost forgot about that!" Pritchard said. He dug his hand into the hip pocket of his greatcoat for the pistol. Rather than chambering a round, he knelt back down and stuffed the gun into his haversack. "Bringing a gun does not show good faith," he said. With that, he sprung to his feet and clamored out of the trench, raising his hands above his head. "I'm unarmed!" he yelled, "I just want to talk!"

A number of men were urging Pritchard to get back in the trench, but he waved them off and stepped over the parapet. Arms up, he slowly weaved his way through the narrow protective barrier of barbed wire.

Vernon weighed his options while his friend crept through the wire. *Bugger it,* he thought, *it's Christmas.* He grabbed his kit by the

631

webbing and slung it onto his shoulder. There were plenty of things in his pack to trade; he just didn't want to spend potentially precious seconds sorting through them. In keeping with Pritchard's pledge to go unarmed, Vernon slid his bayonet from its sheath and plunged it into the mud. What he was doing went against every single soldierly instinct he had. He simply could not let his friend do what he was doing alone.

"You too, Hayes?!" Corporal Milburn whispered shrilly as Vernon climbed past him.

"Just sit tight for now and stay sharp," Vernon said over his shoulder. He raised his hands above his head just as Pritchard did, his heart thudding in anticipation of the first *pop* from a Mauser.

"Wait, Pritch," he called out gently, worried his tone might make the Germans skittish. "I'm coming with you."

HENTSCH

"Should we go out and meet them?" asked Simon. The way he said it sounded more rhetorical than inquisitive. It was obvious he'd already made up his mind. That was exactly what he wanted to do. He stared at Hentsch, waiting for an answer.

Hentsch didn't ponder it for long. "Well, those two are coming either way," he said, and then he turned to address the men around him. "I say that Simon and I go out and speak with them. Maybe we can set up some sort of truce. Get out of the trench for a while. Do you all agree?"

The general consensus was relayed by a number of uneasy nods in the affirmative. If there was anyone who disagreed, it wasn't voiced loudly.

"Then I guess Simon and I will be on our way."

"Augustus..." Engel said softly, taking a light hold of Hentsch's arm. "If it's just the two of you going out there, I think it would be wise if, at the very least, you hid a bayonet underneath your coat. That second Tommy has his packs with him, and there's no telling what he might have hidden in there."

"All right," Hentsch nodded. He crouched out of view to retrieve his bayonet. He opened his greatcoat and slid the weapon into the waistband of his trousers. The metal was ice cold against his skin. *I've got no real reason to trust them,* he assured himself, attempting to assuage the guilt spurred by his own treachery. *But it's only treachery if I reveal the weapon and use it.* He stood. The Englishmen were almost halfway across no man's land. They moved cautiously.

"All right, Simon, let's go," Hentsch said, inhaling deeply. "You stay behind me, understand?"

"Yes," Simon nodded. He sounded much more sure of what he was about to do.

Hentsch crawled out and onto the parapet, then reached his hand back to hoist Simon out as well. They inched through the barbed wire. As he gently pushed the curls and loops out of the way, he was surprised by how badly his hands were shaking. It wasn't just that he was afraid or nervous; he was also, in some strange way, excited. The two sets of men kept a watchful eye on one another as the distance between them closed. The lead Englishman had his hands raised, a neutral, innocent look on his face. On appearances alone, he certainly seemed not to have any hostile intentions.

The Englishman behind him, though, the one with the packs, he was the one who needed extra attention. Hentsch stared past the first man to that second man, examining him from head to toe. He was at least a few years older, maybe in his early to mid-thirties. The way his packs were haphazardly slung over just one shoulder, it would have taken him valuable time to remove any weapon from them, time in which Hentsch thought he might be able to get to him first with the bayonet.

The meeting happened about fifty yards from the German trenches. The first Englishman stood in front of Hentsch when they met, momentarily obscuring the second man from full view.

"Merry Christmas," the first Tommy said. He had big brown eyes, and a curious bend in the bridge of his nose.

"Yes, Merry Christmas to you," Hentsch replied. Subtly, he tried to keep an eye on the second man over the first man's shoulder. He couldn't keep his eyes off the packs. When the second man had closed to within a few steps, he readjusted the straps on his shoulder, and the haversack swung into view. Dangling from the pack's webbing was a short, dirty red streamer.

My God it's him! Grab the bayonet!

It took every ounce of Hentsch's restraint to not fling open his greatcoat and take the bayonet in his hand. His arm even twitched reflexively in an almost instinctive move to do just that. His heart roared inside his chest as he fought the urge to strike preemptively.

"My name is Llewelyn," the first man said. "I assume you're out here because you speak English?"

Hentsch's breath and hands trembled as he fought to stay calm. "Um, yes, I do. My name is Augustus. This is Simon."

"Nice to meet you two chaps," the Englishman said. "This is my friend, Vernon."

The second Englishman joined the first man, and they stood side by side.

"Merry Christmas, Augustus. Simon," the second man said, nodding to each of them.

"And Merry Christmas to you," Simon declared excitedly.

"Yes...yes and to you," Hentsch replied. "Might I ask you a question...Vernon?"

The rugged-looking Englishman nodded.

"What is the meaning of that ribbon there on your haversack?"

"It's not a ribbon," Vernon said. "It's a handkerchief. From my wife." He smiled, a longing sort of smile, then snorted, as if amused. "She said it was for good luck."

For good luck. Son of a bitch... Hentsch was mortified. There was no way he'd tell the man just how close he'd come to killing him at Mons. He'd targeted the poor fellow simply for displaying a talisman from his wife. He couldn't imagine a worse thing to kill a man over. Maybe it *was* good luck. He had missed, in point of fact.

"Well," Llewelyn said, breaking a short silence, "We've made our way out here, and that's a start. It being the Lord's birthday, we have no aspiration toward firing our weapons. If we gave our word that our boys would put their guns down for a day, could you and yours do the same?"

"We certainly would," Hentsch replied.

"Then let's go back to our men and arrange it," Llewelyn said happily. "We'll meet out here in the middle and have our Christmas together."

"Very well," Hentsch said. Before he could turn around to leave, though, Vernon said, "Wait!" and dug a hand into his haversack.

Here comes the English treachery... Hentsch readied himself for a fight. His right hand slowly crept toward the front flap of his coat. When the Englishman's hand came out of his bag, though, he held only a bar of chocolate, still in its wrapper. "Here," the man said, tossing the bar to Hentsch. Both surprised and relieved, he nearly dropped it.

"You would give this to me?"

"I would," replied Vernon. "Perhaps there are other items we might trade. But the chocolate is yours."

"Thank you..." Hentsch said, touched deeply by the man's kind gesture. Dumbstruck, he parted from them without saying another word.

In some ways, he wanted those two British men to be foppish, to be arrogant, for them to have nothing to offer but implied superiority and vitriol. He wanted them to be like Michael. It would have made it so much easier to dislike them going forward. He stared at the gift while he and Simon approached their trench and the many sets of curious German eyes who watched them, waiting for an appraisal of the encounter. Simon waited outside the barbed wire barrier while Hentsch wormed his way back through, kneeling atop the parapet to address the men beneath.

"They want a temporary truce," he informed them, "so we can all celebrate Christmas together. If you've got things to trade, bring them with. But no weapons." He reached into his coat and pulled out the bayonet. He stuck the blade in the frozen dirt. "I mean it. None."

One by one, men began to gather small things to trade with the Englishmen. Some scurried into their dugouts, scouring their belongings for trinkets, food and tobacco. With little hesitation, they climbed out of the trench and walked into the kill zone of no man's land. In the place of murderous intent, they moved forward with the purest of intentions. Whichever of society's cruel justifications had pushed them into the fight, induced them into doing the awful things they'd since been asked to do, it was their humanity which pushed them over the top and into no man's land that day.

Michael was the only man who stayed put.

"Are you coming?" Hentsch asked him.

"Not without a rifle," Michael replied, folding his arms in front of his chest. "And not to trade anything but bullets."

Hentsch rolled his eyes and walked away. He joined the line of Germans heading toward a line of Englishmen, the two groups armed not with an arsenal of spear-tipped rifles, but an arsenal of tradable goods, of battlefield currency.

VERNON

It wasn't hard to find that Augustus fellow again. He stood a head taller than just about everyone else in no man's land. As should rationally have been expected, the two groups were initially shy toward one another, hanging back, hesitant to intermingle. Having brokered the truce, however, Vernon and Pritchard hesitated less, seeking out and then exchanging smiles with the two Germans they'd already met.

To break the ice between the greater groups, the two pairs of men stepped forward and shook hands. Augustus had formidable hands; his firm grip surprised Vernon, although he didn't get the sense that the German's strong handshake was exaggerated for purposes of intimidation. Simon tried to shake firmly as well, but his hands were much smaller and not nearly as strong. A third man, a funny looking bloke with big ears, lingered close behind Augustus and Simon.

"Vernon, Llewelyn, this is another good friend of mine," Augustus said, twisting to present the third man. "His name is Amad—"

The big-eared fellow cleared his throat loudly.

"Excuse me," Augustus said. "His name is Engel. He speaks very little English."

Engel stood next to Hentsch, offering both Vernon and Pritchard a friendly handshake and nod.

Vernon turned to the men behind him and said, "Well come on then, it *is* Christmas!"

Slowly, two groups of men, members of the armed forces of two nations locked in a ghastly war with one another, cast the last of their reservations aside and began to shake hands. To introduce themselves to one another. In just a matter of minutes the impromptu (and very much unsanctioned) truce dissolved the differences between the men at war. Not every German spoke English, and not every Brit spoke German, they didn't need to. It was the spirit of the holiday, and the shared experience of miserable war in miserable conditions that spoke louder, clearer, than any words could. The enemies turned momentary friends exchanged Christmas greetings. They shared food with one another. They proudly displayed photographs of wives, or parents, or children.

Up and down the British and German lines, impromptu truces materialized in no man's land. Weary of what they'd already been put through, of the delusion they'd fallen victim to of winning the war by Christmas, pockets of men cast aside their bitterness and contempt, and embraced their deep desire to simply feel human again. That truces broke out independent of one another in numerous places along the line was a shining testimony to the power of goodness that dwelled within the human spirit.

Vernon stood, with his beloved friend Pritchard, conversing with Augustus, Simon and Engel. The two English-speaking Germans translated for their friend. They talked of home, of family, they smoked cigarettes, Vernon even shared the pound cake Sally sent him, without even bothering to ask for a trade. They discussed many things, just not the war.

He watched the beautiful, yet heartbreaking display unfold all around him. He saw Chilcott and Saunders embrace a weeping German, he saw Milburn having a laugh with another. Granville was enthusiastically bartering a handful of cigarettes for something or other with two confused Germans. Sergeant Spurling was enjoying himself; he had a small metal flask with him, and shared a nip of its contents with a German NCO with whom he was having a quiet conversation. A large number of men cried, hardened men, simply overcome by the emotional gravity.

During a brief lull in their conversation, Vernon decided it might be okay to heap a small amount of praise on his best friend. He doubted the German boys would blabber about it to Captain Bannister. "You know," he said, "Llewelyn here was awarded a decoration earlier today." He paused, in case they didn't understand. "He was given The Distinguished Conduct Medal."

Pritchard frowned at him, but the cat was already out of the bag.

"For what reason was it awarded?" asked Augustus.

Oh bollocks, he probably thinks it was for killing Germans, Vernon thought. "He saved the life of our lieutenant," he quickly clarified. "The man was shot and would have bled to death."

"Congratulations to you," Augustus said, nodding.

"Yes, congratulations," echoed Simon. He turned to Engel and assumingly relayed the same story to him in German.

"Would you like to see it?" Pritchard asked. He smiled proudly. He had no reason not to. His medal did not come at the expense of any Germans. If anything, it came at Lieutenant Hood's expense.

"If you are willing to show it to us, then yes of course," Augustus replied.

Pritchard reached through the front flap of his greatcoat, digging his hand in the area of his tunic's breast pocket. He held the decoration by its ribbon, and without a second's hesitation, dropped the medal into Augustus's outstretched hand. The three Germans examined the award, read the inscriptions, and seemed impressed.

"It is a very nice medal indeed," Augustus smiled. "One that should be worn on one's breast, not tucked away in his breast pocket." He handed the medal back to Pritchard, who smiled humbly in return.

The soldiers stayed together, intermingled, and the grey skied afternoon soon turned to black night. The temperature dropped, but with unexpected new friends and warm hearts, no one noticed. Solitary flakes of white fell from the starless sky, and as the minutes passed the flakes grew in number. Millions of snowflakes fell gently, peacefully, onto the heads of the grey and khaki jumble of men while they joyfully sang (in their respective languages), "O Tannenbaum", "Lo, How a Rose E'er Blooming", and "Good Christian Men Rejoice".

Like many around him, Vernon fought back tears as enemy caroled alongside enemy. Simon, the pale, friendly young German, had the loveliest voice Vernon had ever heard. That such sweet, soulful sounds were coming from the enemy was a painful, almost soul-crushing revelation. *If he and his friends weren't wearing grey and I khaki, I couldn't possibly imagine them as enemies.* In his subconscious, he again cursed Europe's leadership for letting their respective societies come to such a sad state. The men wearing grey were not barbaric Huns; they were good Christians, the same as the men in khaki. He almost wished they *were* as bad as the propaganda said.

He knew there wasn't a man out there who wanted the night to end. He didn't want it to end either. But in the midst of war something like that, no matter how good, how pure, *had* to end. And so, with the snow continuing to fall, the hour growing late, tired men began to trickle away, saying their goodbyes and returning to their home trenches.

With the group thinned out, his eyes heavy, Vernon decided to call it a night. He and Pritchard were two of but a handful of Fourth Platoon's men still out in the open. Similarly, Augustus and his comrades were some of the last to remain.

"It would appear to be that time," Vernon declared, counting the heads around him then looking back to the trench. "I must say, tonight has been a pleasant surprise."

"I agree," replied Augustus. "It was good to meet you, Vernon."

"And you, Augustus."

Vernon bade farewell to his German friends, then waited for Pritchard to finish doing the same. When they parted, he felt as if something had gone unsaid. Augustus had already stopped and turned around when Vernon looked back at him.

"We would not be opposed to doing this again tomorrow," the big German said.

"Nor would we," Vernon replied. He slung his arm over Pritchard's shoulder and they walked back to the cold, muddy confines of their home. That night, sleeping in a ditch didn't seem quite as bad.

The next morning, Christmas morning, Vernon woke to a deep chill. The light snow must have fallen all night; it left a layer of white on top of his blanket. *It's a wonder more men don't freeze to death in their sleep.* He shivered, then stood to shake the snow from his blanket. *Christmas morning,* he thought, and then for the first time he looked around him. No one was there!

"What in God's name..." he said quietly. Just as he was about to call out, he heard a shout from somewhere out in no man's land. Was the unofficial truce broken? He leapt onto the firing step to see. He had no idea what to expect.

They were playing football! Germans and Englishmen scurried and laughed, stumbling, tossing snowballs. On the outskirts of the game, onlookers from both sides stood elbow to elbow, smoking cigarettes, pointing, chuckling, simply being men and boys. Pritchard trotted in the midst of the ramshackle game, his greatcoat unbuttoned and flowing behind him. His DCM was pinned to the breast of his tunic. Whatever qualms he'd had about displaying his award were apparently gone. Spurling had probably already told everyone about it.

"It's an odd sight, isn't it?" said Spurling. He'd snuck up on Vernon, and was suddenly standing next to him on the firing step.

"Yes, but a welcome one," Vernon replied.

"It makes you wonder how we step back from this."

"I know. There's good chaps on the other side."

"I met one fellow who's got six children," Spurling said, shaking his head. He held up six fingers. "Six. All of them girls. He showed me a picture of them standing with his wife. They were beautiful, and so was she..." He stared mindlessly ahead, looking less *at* the football game and more *through* it. "And yet it's my duty, if it comes to it, to shoot him. To leave his six girls fatherless."

Vernon sighed. He understood exactly. "That Simon, you saw him I'm sure, the little blonde chap, I've never heard a voice like his. Misses his mother and father, and his bloody dog." He scoffed loudly at the absurdity of it all. "And that Augustus, big strapping bloke, as friendly as anyone I've met. This is madness." He stopped speaking to wave to Pritchard, who was beckoning him to get out there and join in.

"You're lucky to have a friend like Llewelyn," Spurling said, nodding toward the smiling man fifty yards away. "And he's lucky to have a friend like you. The platoon is lucky."

"Thank you, Spurling."

"Truths need no thanks. Merry Christmas, Hayes."

"Merry Christmas."

Much of the rest of the day was spent just as the morning. Different men rotated in and out of the football game, with no goals, no score, and no established teams. Vernon went in once or twice, mostly to get his blood flowing in order to warm his feet. He played on the same team as Augustus, who in spite of his height was impressively agile and fast. There was no aggression in the game, no hostility; the game embodied the very spirit of the Christmas truce.

At dinnertime, the two sides returned to their trenches to eat. The plan was to meet back in no man's land, to sing carols and continue the "festivities." While Fourth Platoon's meal was standard fare, Spurling came through with two jugs of rum, enough so that each man would have just enough drink to get his lips numb and his head a bit lighter. Most days, the platoon would have stayed spread out in case of trouble, but for Christmas dinner, a large number of men crowded together to make the best of the day's meal.

"I'd like to propose a toast," Granville said, raising his cup, "to Private Llewelyn Pritchard, not only for his decoration, but for being batty enough to go and say 'hullo' to our newfound Hun friends."

The crowd voiced their collective hear, hear, and everyone raised their cups. Vernon smiled when he saw Pritchard's sheepish grin. His shiny medal glinted from inside his open greatcoat. Pritchard had struggled through much of his life, but somehow, in the midst of the Great War, he'd managed to rediscover some of himself, some of what he'd lost when Daisy was taken from him. Vernon met Pritchard's big, glistening brown eyes with his own, and they smiled at one another, each nodding in deep respect and appreciation for the other. Vernon loved his friend. His friend loved him.

"WHERE'S THE HERO?" an awful voice inquired over the cheery din.

Pritchard stopped smiling. The platoon stopped celebrating.

Several men were shoved aside and the voice asked, "Where is our Welsh..."

Bannister, his walrus-face redder than usual, shoved one last man aside, and was suddenly right next to Pritchard. "...hero...?" he said, finishing his question in an ominous tone.

Pritchard hung his head as the captain reached for the medal on his chest. Bannister flicked the medal several times with his index finger. "I'll bet you're proud of this," he said with a sneer, "I'll bet everyone is proud for you. Proud of their little Welsh hooligan."

Vernon snarled. *On Christmas?* It was an outrage.

For the last twenty-four hours, their lives had all been different, been better. But what happened next could not have come at a worse time. Vernon's ears picked it up easily, it having made such an impact on him the night before.

Stille Nacht, Heilege Nacht!

It was Simon, and he was singing the German version of "Silent Night". Whether sung by a hundred men or by an angel-voiced soloist, it truly was a beautiful song. His voice projected strongly across no man's land, which meant he was likely not inside the German trench.

Please Simon, Vernon closed his eyes to listen, *please, be quiet until Bannister is gone. Please, God, if ever there was a time you might intervene...*

When he heard it too, Bannister froze. He turned away from Pritchard, and shoved another man out of the way to climb onto the firing step. Behind his back, the men of Fourth Platoon made nervous eyes at one another.

"What the fuck is that?" Bannister said angrily. His head snapped around and he glared at his frightened men. "Why in fucking hell is he singing? Why does he think he can get away with that? Why hasn't anyone grabbed their rifle and shot him?"

No one moved to grab their weapon.

Lieb' aus deinem göttlichen Mund,

It all might have gone differently had Bannister not seen Pritchard's eyes. Wide and terrified, they were aimed at Vernon, imploring him to find a way to get the captain to ignore Simon.

"Private Pritchard..." Bannister said, his angry voice morphed into a mean, scary calm. He grinned. "Shoot that man."

Llewelyn Pritchard's face fell a ghostly white. Simon's angelic voice was crystal clear over Fourth Platoon's silence.

"Sir, it's Christmas..." Sergeant Spurling muttered timidly.

"It's war," Bannister growled, "first and foremost. Now shoot him. Hero."

"Sir, you're drunk," Spurling said, "let's go and find Sergeant Major Cortland and we'll—"

"Back off Spurling or I'll have you demoted to private!" the captain warned, "Pritchard has been given an order!"

Pritchard didn't budge. Bannister drew his pistol. He clicked back the hammer.

"Shoot him, Private, or I swear I'll shoot you."

"God dammit sir, I'll shoot him!" Granville said, stepping forward.

Bannister turned the pistol on him. "You will not!" he snapped. "Pritchard will do it or be shot for disobeying a direct order! PRITCHARD!"

Still, Pritchard did not move. Bannister jumped from the firing step and stomped toward him. He grabbed Pritchard so forcefully by the back of his neck that it made the younger man, who'd once carried Lockwood's body on his back for hundreds of yards, flail like a poorly stitched ragdoll. Bannister dragged him, with one hand, toward the front wall, throwing Pritchard forcefully against the firing step. The captain snatched up a nearby rifle and shoved it into Pritchard's hands, then clutched him around the throat, forcing him to step into a firing position.

"You fucking shoot him right now or I'll see to it your decoration is revoked after I've rid the world of your toxicity."

Vernon didn't want Simon to die. He especially didn't want Simon's death on Pritchard's conscience. "SIMON, GET DOWN!" he screamed. If there was no one to shoot, the situation would have to diffuse. Bannister bared his teeth and looked back. He pressed his gun into Pritchard's side.

"SIMON! GET YOUR ARSE DOWN!"

The others joined in shouting their warnings, but the singing German either ignored them or just could not understand the fuss.

Pritchard trained the rifle in Simon's direction. His shoulders bounced up and down. He was sobbing.

"Fire, goddamn you!" Bannister cried. "And don't fucking miss!"

But Pritchard didn't fire. He never would have been able to. He set the rifle down and sobbed harder. "I didn't kill your son..." he muttered.

"What did you just say?" the captain growled.

For a moment, silence fell over Fourth Platoon again, while they waited in horror for Bannister to pull the trigger. Instead, the captain jerked Pritchard down from the firing step, grabbing him by the throat once again. He turned the pistol upside-down in his free hand, and slammed the butt of the weapon into the weeping man's face.

Vernon had heard the sickening, fleshy thud of a man being punched in the face many times in his life. He'd punched some of those faces himself. But the sound of Bannister's pistol butt striking Pritchard's face was utterly horrendous. He heard the bones break. The men gasped. Vernon was so shocked he simply failed to react. Simon's sweet voice was a haunting backdrop as that formerly cheerful Christmas night fell to pieces.

When Bannister brought his hand back a second time, grabbing the barely conscious and gurgling Pritchard by a fistful of hair to prop him up, Vernon's boots felt nailed in place. He wanted to act, but couldn't. As fast and vicious as the captain's first strike had been, his second was even fiercer. His arm swung in a wide arc, like a prize fighter throwing a gargantuan hook. He struck Pritchard in the side of the neck, metal against flesh, a butcher striking a tough cut with a heavy tenderizer. Pritchard crumpled to the ground, leaving the captain holding a fistful of hair.

"You son of a bitch!" Vernon cried, finally breaking free of whatever invisible force had held him still. His mates grabbed him. They didn't know how to handle such a scary, unprecedented situation, but they weren't going to let him get shot by the captain.

Bannister kicked Pritchard, who lay face down in the mud. "Looks like our hero won't be doing the shooting." He aimed the pistol at the unconscious man's head. "But his friend will." He nodded toward Vernon, who tugged at the arms holding him back. They let him go.

"I will not dawdle this time around Hayes. You've got ten seconds to shoot. Do not miss, that is an order."

What am I supposed to do?

"TEN!"

Will he really shoot Llewelyn with all these men around?

"NINE!"

Will Llewelyn be able to forgive me?

"EIGHT!"

What happens if Simon decides to hop back into his trench?

"SEVEN!"

Vernon had no choice. Pritchard's life was just more valuable to him. He hastily picked up a rifle and hopped onto the firing step. He racked a bullet into the chamber. Clicked off the safety. Simon, seated on the German parapet, was still singing, oblivious and cheerful.

Christ, der Retter ist da-a!

"THREE!"

He had to shoot Simon. There was no other way, save for his and Pritchard's deaths. It was one sweet, German boy for two decent British men. Maybe another man would have chosen differently. Maybe either choice was the wrong one. He lined up the Enfield's sights on Simon's torso.

Christ, der Retter ist da!

Years of training and months of intense war had conditioned his hands to remain steady while holding a rifle, regardless of the stress. For Pritchard's sake, Vernon could not miss.

I'm sorry, Simon. He squeezed the trigger.

POW! The solitary shot echoed for miles. It was the loudest gunshot Vernon's ears had ever heard. He didn't even look to see if he'd hit Simon. He knew. The shot was dead center. He could not see what went on in the German trench after that. He never would have wanted to.

Across no man's land, just as Vernon was pulling the trigger, Augustus Hentsch was reaching to grab Simon's leg, to pull him back into the trench. Over the singing, he'd thought he heard some sort of commotion coming from the British trench. Blood spattered into Hentsch's face a fraction of a second before he heard the shot. He pulled a gasping Simon, shot through the heart, back into the trench. The sweet young man was dead in seconds. There would be no more caroling that night. No more truce.

Vernon left the spent cartridge in the chamber, and threw the rifle in the mud. He ran to Pritchard's side, falling to his knees and placing himself within inches of Bannister's muddy butcher's boots. The captain reeked of alcohol. Vernon wrapped his arms around his beloved friend, picking his limp body out of the mud to hug him. Pritchard's breathing was shallow, labored. His face was covered in mud and blood. His eyes were closed.

"Llewelyn!" Vernon cried, "Llewelyn!"

"Someone get a stretcher and carry this lump of shit out of here," Bannister said, nary a shred of concern in his tone. "Enjoy the rest of your fucking Christmas." He holstered his pistol and reached a hand down to shove Vernon by the shoulder before walking away.

When the medics arrived minutes later, they knelt with Vernon, urging him to loosen his arms from around Pritchard's shoulders and chest. When he did and they lay the unconscious soldier on the stretcher, it took one of the medics but a minute to tell Vernon what he already knew. He'd known it as soon as he took Pritchard into his arms. Bannister had broken his neck. The medics had to get him to a base hospital as quickly as possible.

"I have to go with him," Vernon said, as the two men picked up the stretcher.

"You know you can't do that, Hayes," Spurling said. He took a gentle hold of Vernon's arm. "We've been stirred up enough, and there's nothing you're going to be able to do for him. Bannister would have a field day if you went absent now."

Vernon stared into Pritchard's dirtied, bloodied, unconscious face. The medics were starting to walk away. "Wait!" he exclaimed. "His eyes just opened!"

"Vern..." Pritchard wheezed, his voice slow and faint.

"Yeah, Lew, I'm right next to you," Vernon replied, going in close. He took hold of Pritchard's limp hand, squeezing it. There was no squeeze whatsoever in response.

"What...happened?" His breathing was very much labored.

"You...ah..." Vernon gritted his teeth to fight back tears. "You were hurt. They're taking you to the hospital..." His voice wavered, because he was about to lie. "They're going to fix you up."

"Can't...see..."

There was so much mud and blood in his eyes, he was blind. There was nothing clean with which to wipe it away. Vernon tried to use his hand, but he was too dirty, and he only made smears in the mud and blood on his broken friend's face.

"Just stay calm, and you'll be able to see soon."

"Can...you...go with..." Pritchard said. He seemed to lose consciousness again.

"Pritch...I can't..." Vernon sobbed, but his friend didn't hear him.

And then, the medics were on their way. Pritchard was gone. Vernon watched them carry his best friend off. It dizzied him how quickly his world had just changed. His mind, his thoughts, even his senses were so numb as he stared at the trailing medic's back vanishing into the darkness, that he couldn't find any more tears. He just stared, confused, blank, and stupid. He felt distant pats on the back, sympathetic squeezes on the arm, there may have been comforting words spoken, but he processed almost none of it.

He could have stood there for hours. He would have, until a brief metallic glint from the trench floor flashed in the corner of his eye. Whatever it was, it pulled him back into stark reality. The object lay in the mud directly where Pritchard had fallen. It was almost entirely buried. Vernon moved slowly, cautiously, toward the spot. He knelt. The item had a round edge. Was it a coin? He took it into his hand. There was a ribbon attached to it, its crimson and blue stripes wet and stained brown. He ran his finger over the circular metal piece, revealing the profile image of King George V.

God damn it...

There were commitments men made. Vows they took. Promises they kept. Pledges to others, or to themselves. Things like that, pledges and promises, commitments and vows; those were the things that tested a man's mettle. Vernon Hayes had made pledges. He swore a vow of marriage to Sally, his dear wife. Swore an oath of allegiance to the British crown. He was a man of his word. He followed through on his commitments. That Christmas night, sitting alone, running his thumb repeatedly across Llewelyn Pritchard's Distinguished Conduct Medal, polishing it obsessively, angrily, Vernon made another commitment.

There was a chance the Germans might get him first. For shooting Simon, he may well have deserved it. And he couldn't simply follow through with his commitment with the conspicuousness of a drunken belligerent. He needed to bide his time, to find the perfect opportunity—to get away with it. That was the thing with commitments; they didn't always come with deadlines. Some simply required patience. A thousand variables might prevent his seeing it through to the end, but if the opportunity *did* present itself, he was going to take it. He'd already made up his mind.

Vernon was going to kill Captain Bannister.

I would sincerely like to thank you for taking the time to read this, my first novel. If a readership permits me, it would be my honor to continue telling this tale.

Writing an historical fiction such as this would be impossible without leaning heavily on the works of researchers, for whom I hold a deep and profound respect. Furthermore, the world owes a great debt to the warrior-poets who lived through such a horrific conflict, to then tell of their experiences in their own words. Their works and the diligence of researchers serve to keep ever-increasingly distant memories alive and well, so that the present may not lose sight of the past.

The works listed here are limited to those I opened specifically when researching for this book. In no particular order, they are: *The First World War*, Martin Gilbert; *A World Undone: The Story of the Great War 1914 to 1918*, G.J. Meyer; *1914*, John French, Viscount of Ypres; *The Historical Atlas of World War I*, Anthony Livesey; *West Point Atlas for the Great War: Strategies & Tactics of the First World War*, Thomas E. Griess; *The Routledge Atlas of the First World War, third edition*, Martin Gilbert; *An Illustrated Encyclopedia of Uniforms of World War I*, Jonathan North; *The Illustrated History of the Weapons of World War I*, Ian Westwell; *The Sleepwalkers: How Europe Went to War in 1914*, Christopher Clark (a book whose title I could not help but to borrow as a chapter name. No one word better described the mindsets of the time.); *Aircraft of World War I: 1914-1918*, Jack Herris and Bob Pearson; *Jane's Fighting Aircraft of World War I*, W. E. De. B. Whitaker; *The Arms of Krupp: 1587-1968*, William Manchester; *The Marne 1914*, Holger H. Herwig; *The History of the Cheshire Regiment in the Great War*, Col. Arthur Crookenden; *The U-Boat War: 1914-1918*, Edwyn A. Gray; *U-Boats of the Kaiser's Navy*, Gordon Williamson, Ian Palmer; *U-Boat Crews: 1914-45*, Gordon Williamson, Darko Pavlovic; *Guynemer: Chevalier of the Air*, Henry Bordeaux

I encourage the curious reader to delve deeper into the Great War as a subject, through these fine works or through the great many thousands more written over the past century.

Made in the USA
Charleston, SC
09 July 2014